CONQUEROR

Arise 6

Jez Cajiao

Arise: Conqueror

CONTENTS

<u>DEDICATION</u>

This story is dedicated to a very special little man, called Gunnar. I'd written the last dedication before I knew of Gunnars situation, but due to the vagaries of the publishing world, by the time the story released, it was months after. I decided even then, that I wanted to dedicate this book, the completion of the Arise Saga, to him.

Gunnar is an incredibly brave boy, one who has dealt with his diagnosis of Leukemia with stoic determination, patience—and I'm sure as his parents will agree—more than a touch of sass. He's endured tests and chemo, emergency helicopter flights and living out of a suitcase, not to mention being parted from his best friend Disa Svanhill the dinosaur hunter, all with an attitude that is inspiring.

He and his parent's faith, bravery and good cheer is a lesson to us all, and I'll forever have the greatest of respect for him, and his family, who I'm fortunate enough to call friends.

If you're a believer or not, I know his family would appreciate a kind thought sent in his direction.

To Gunnar; you're a legend already little man, keep climbing the mountain.

Jez Cajiao

<u>**ARISE ALPHA SYNOPSIS**</u>

Steve, a one-time thief and enforcer, is hiding on the Greek party island of Crete. He was involved in a botched bank robbery, and rather than the hundred grand plus each of the team were promised, there was a hundred grand in total.

Seeing this, and having already decided that he would run as soon as he had "his" money, Steve chose to skip the splitting of the cash, and moved straight to hiding out. With all the money.

He flew via Toronto, taking multiple flights, until he finally wound up in Crete, paying a corrupt Greek policeman for a recently deceased tourist's ID.

The next few months passed as a dream: drinking, partying, and working the bars of Crete; a new friend moved into Steve's apartment and life was good.

Right up until he decided to throw it all away, risking his life to save a pair of drowning women he'd met earlier in the day. He rode his bike off the cliffs, diving out over the treacherous rocks below, and swam down, rescuing first Marie, and then later Amanda.

Other tourists nearby had captured the whole thing on camera, and the footage went viral, helped in part when word spread that not only was he a "hero" for saving them, but that he'd been fired in turn because he was late for work.

The footage was shared, and quickly made its way to an enforcer named Kevin Sinclair, one of the organizers of the original robbery. He, in turn, hired a local ex-army, Russian enforcer named Mikhail to punish Steve, and his friends when they got in the way.

Steve, however, had already vanished.

His bike, abandoned in the sea, had begun to leak gas, and in turn the local police took his ID—including the fake—as well as his money, forcing Steve to recover his bike before he could flee the island.

In the process of attempting to raise the bike, Steve was pinned beneath it, underwater, when a hidden section of an old ship collapsed. His bike took him with it into the depths, and as he blacked out from asphyxiation, his last sight was a tentacled metallic-looking monstrosity attaching itself to his face.

Steve woke sometime later, alone, wet, and shaking with the cold. Once Steve realized where he probably was—buried deep in the bowels of an ancient shipwreck—he started to try to escape, putting the tentacled monstrosity down to asphyxia and a passing sea creature.

The superstructure was old, he realized, later finding it to be millennia more ancient than he'd first guessed. Over the course of the next several hours, Steve would find out just how old the ship—an actual long-abandoned spacecraft—would be.

The human race, he discovered, were biological weapons, ones long since discarded by our uncaring creators. In the process of escaping the ship, Steve was wounded, dying from blood loss and hypothermia; he begged for help, and his plea passed a level that a damaged, failing medical AI deemed appropriate to enable it to respond.

He was given a choice, and with no time to examine the options, agrees to a "Support package." Unfortunately for him, the ship's supplies of anesthetic were long depleted, and the first stage of the Support package integration involved a full skeletal "strip," with everything from muscles to eyes being replaced.

When he awakened, over a day later, he was massively changed, rebuilt as a prime Biological Weapon Variant, and ready for war, with his own nanites, in addition to a nanite harvesting tool integrated into his right forearm—something that all humans, or BWVs as the system designates them, have—now unlocked.

Through the wonders of the nanotech, he was able to defeat the incoming basic security systems designed to terminate the trespasser, as the security AI attempted to kill him.

By the time Steve had escaped what he had thought was a sunken and forgotten container ship—and he now knew to be Facility 6B—he had managed to unlock both his War and Hack trees, investing points to make himself more versatile and dangerous.

Steve went back to the shore, finding the bike he'd borrowed to return to the beach was still there, and used it to return—naked—to his apartment.

On arrival, Steve climbed up onto the rear balcony and looked inside the apartment, finding his friend and houseguest, Dave, being beaten for information by the local enforcer. Torn between stepping in and saving his friend, and maintaining secrecy, he hesitated, only for Marie, the girl he'd first saved, to knock on the front door, and be captured by Mikhail.

Steve decided that he couldn't leave them to Mikhail's tender mercies and attacks, being soundly beaten, as the ex-soldier demonstrated that the training afforded to Russian special forces was significantly higher than Steve's own ex-army training was.

In a last-ditch attempt to escape and defeat Mikhail, he triggered the Assault specialization tree under War. Instantly, the tables were turned, as the inbuilt system guided him to a vicious and resounding victory. Steve ordered Marie and Dave out, and warned Sinclair, the enforcer back in England, to stay away or he'll suffer the same fate; then he killed Mikhail.

Using the Harvest function of the system embedded in his forearm, Steve stripped Mikhail of his nanites, gaining a number of attuned and usable nanites, as well as a larger number of corrupted ones, that his own systems began the process of purifying.

Dave helped Steve to burn down the apartment, concealing the damage done to the body of Mikhail, and his identity, and the two friends escaped with Marie.

Marie left them in a bar, before returning shortly with her friend Amanda, and as Steve told a much abridged and sanitized story of his adventure—keeping the nanites and ship out of it entirely—they are joined by the rest of Amanda and Marie's group.

Jonas, who led the team, recruited Steve and Dave on the promise of high wages and adventure, including the opportunity to kill criminals and murderers. Steve took the position, planning to use it as a cover to harvest more nanites and upgrade himself, while Dave took it on the grounds of a lot of money.

As a trial, Jonas sent Steve to recover his ID from the police station, and to insert a device into their network, opening it to the team, while Dave was sent to seduce a reporter who had been investigating a spate of recent murders.

Steve left the group, upgraded his Hack abilities, invested nanites recovered from Mikhail and gained access to the police systems, before he bluffed his way in, recovering the ID and money, and planting the data spike, and escaping.

Jonas and the team were surprised, but pleased at his success, and they went to observe Dave's trial. They arrived, just as Dave and the reporter were kidnapped, the group she had been tracking deciding to remove the threat.

Jonas, Steve, and Amanda followed the group into the old catacombs outside of Heraklion, splitting up when the tracks led in different directions.

Steve rushed ahead, finding a father and daughter being systematically slaughtered in a pit by *werewolves*. Steve's system identified them as an alternate "viable line" of Biological Weapon Variants.

Steve attacked the werewolves, harvesting them as he fought, and using the corrupted nanites to form tentacles of weaponized nanites, slaughtered the werewolves, as Amanda—not knowing Steve's true capabilities—ran to get backup.

By the time Jonas and Amanda returned—having rescued Dave and killed several other werewolves—Steve claimed to have killed the werewolves with the silver-edged knife Jonas had given him on arrival.

The father agreed, backing Steve, and the daughter had already lost consciousness, leaving Jonas and Amanda suspicious of Steve, but without any evidence.

Jonas suspected that Steve was a fresh "Arisen," and took him deeper into the catacombs, testing him and his abilities, and in the process, disturbed several ghouls; then he frantically escaped, his suspicions met.

Once they had joined the group outside, Jonas arranged for them to be retrieved by their shadowy employers, before having an argument with Steve and abandoning him by the side of the road, warning him that the vampires and their servants have his scent and that anywhere he ran to would only ensure more locals died.

Jonas left him, believing that it would force Steve to either admit to what he was, and they would have discovered a newly rising immortal—gaining much in their employer's eyes—or that he was a "plant" from an enemy faction.

Steve invested in his stealth abilities, hiding as the vampire and its master, Hans, arrived by the side of the road, and Hans ordered the vampire ahead. Hans then spoke to Steve, unable to locate him, but able to sense his presence.

Hans offered to teach Steve, to induct him into his new world and to answer any questions, before ostensibly leaving. Steve killed the ghouls still there, before finding Hans hadn't really left; he'd simply moved off to observe.

Again, Hans made the offer, before leaving Steve to go and rescue his former teammates and Dave.

Arise: Conqueror

When Steve reached the others at the retrieval site, he found one of their number—Dan, their tech specialist—dead, and the others captured, wounded, and at the vampire's mercy.

Steve killed the remaining ghouls and the vampire, before being captured as Jonas's master—Shamal, a member of the Blessed faction—arrived.

Taking advantage of a distraction, Steve escaped, Dave helping him, and the friends parted ways, with Dave being forced to help the Blessed faction as part of Jonas's team in truth, and Steve hiding in a nearby gully overnight.

The next morning, Steve recovered the team's abandoned drone, hijacking it, and used it to guide himself around people until he reached an old friend and borrowed a motorbike, setting off for the meeting with Hans, needing more information.

Hans was as good as his word, filling Steve in on the ostensible history of the two groups. The Blessed are essentially believers in "guiding" mankind to their future, while keeping them firmly underfoot as the cattle they are.

The Awakened and Accursed, on the other hand, the faction that Hans belonged to—or paid lip service to, at least—believed that they had been cursed with immortality. Some, like Hans, simply viewed it as their right to party and enjoy life; most believed that they had been cheated of their meeting with the gods, and they will do anything to "fix" that, up to and including starting a nuclear war and killing all life.

Steve chose not to join Hans, but agreed to reach out when he had more questions. Hans, in turn, was glad to have an unaffiliated and apparently skilled new Arisen to talk to, having been pushed to the outside of his own faction by his unwillingness to aid in the genocides planned.

Hans left Steve to his own devices, while maintaining an unobtrusive watch over the younger man, and Steve returned to the nearby area of Malia, moving into a cheap apartment while he planned his next step. Before he settled, a local fight broke out, and he intervened to help two new holiday workers from being blackmailed, before leaving them to stammer their thanks.

Over the next day or so, he crafted prototype armor, designing it despite being too low in nanites to actually deploy it, then returned to the catacombs, hunting more werewolves and other creatures, before encountering two huge figures on ornate thrones guarding an entrance to a further section.

He was warned by the system that they were "Beta Level Threats" and were far beyond him, and escaped, looting several ancient artifacts as he went.

On his return to the apartment, he hid again until the sunrise, when he strolled out onto the roof terrace, half asleep to relax in the sunlight.

Realizing he's not alone, Steve silently berated himself for the stupidity, as the workers he rescued previously had been joined by several others, including an old acquaintance of his and Dave's. He also met two girls who were with the group; one realized he's the eponymous hero who saved people only days ago and vanished, and attempted to film him.

Steve remotely hacked and erased her phone, before making his excuses and leaving them to it. Once inside his room, he moved quickly, gathering up all evidence of himself, before sneaking out, believing that the group had moved on.

Unfortunately, outside he bumped into the second woman, Ingrid, a Danish archeologist. She recognized the dragon staff he carried—looted from the catacombs—and forced herself on him, demanding answers to where it was looted from.

Rather than cause a fuss where others might see, he allowed her to come with him, then gifted her the staff, asking her to leave him be. She kissed him, and for a brief moment he let himself just be a man with a beautiful woman on a sun-drenched island, rather than an immature immortal, hunted on all sides.

When Ingrid insisted on coming with him, wanting more details on the artifacts and unwilling to accept his refusal, he gave in, knowing it was a mistake, but desperate to hold onto the last vestiges of his humanity.

He took her farther across the island, helping her to arrange shipping for the dragon staff to her own museum, before taking her to dinner and arranging a room for the pair, one with twin beds.

The pair danced around each other as he attempted to use her to translate the writing on the artifacts, searching for clues as to the truth of history and "his kind." She, in turn, tried to force him to take her to the original site he'd looted the artifacts from, unaware of the infestation of lycanthropes and other creatures that still survived there.

Ingrid called in a friend, Lars, a well-respected archaeologist, to help her, and he set off, flying in.

The pair eventually gave in to mutual attraction and slept together, moving to a larger room, and made friends with the hotelier, Val. Val directed them to a second "palace" on the south side of the island that he believed Ingrid would find interesting, and where Steve would be able to find more evidence of what he was seeking.

Although the ruins were interesting, and Steve deployed his newly upgraded drone to show them the site from the air, the taverna that Steve expected to get information from—a "rescue" center for dogs injured in dog-fighting rings—instead turned out to be a cover for another group of werewolves, connected to the first.

When they attacked, and Steve revealed himself to Ingrid, she left, heartbroken and confused. Steve, hurt, decided to finish the fight, harvesting the dead and then hunting the pack leader who fled into a nearby cave.

The cave turned out to be a much larger catacomb, with a trapped creature that the ancient people of Thera and the Minoans had captured. The Reta Variant was eventually defeated, but Steve was gravely injured in the process, collapsing as soon as it was constrained again.

Ingrid, who had control of the drone, and had unknowingly taken Steve's phone in her bag, had seen the fight and the injuries he suffered. She returned, and after apologizing to him, recovered several of the bodies from the taverna. Steve, in turn, uses an unlocked ability called System Replenishment—essentially an advanced and technological version of cannibalism—to strip the dead of their genetics and biological matter to repair himself.

Arise: Conqueror

Over the next few hours, Ingrid explored the site; then the pair got replacement clothing—Ingrid's was ruined by the bodies she recovered and dragged to Steve—and new phones, tablets, etc.

Eventually the pair hired a car and went to meet Lars at the airport. Ingrid, who now had a friend to help her, eventually convinced Steve to come fully clean about who and what he was, back at the hotel.

The trio returned to the site, finding the owners had returned, searching for unpaid rent, and bodies have been found. Lars started the process to buy the site and its surrounding lands, to "find" the archaeological site later and have a viable way of bringing the artifacts to the light again.

Upon return to the hotel that night, Lars and Ingrid spent the entire night arguing over translations and more, deciding that Atlantis was most likely real, and all the issues that would cause for archeologists.

Steve left the pair to sleep, and on the way to visit a local potential hidden site, came across a family who had fallen victim to people smugglers. Steve rescued the mother—who'd been taken due to her looks, when the father and two children were discarded—and he killed the majority of the smugglers.

Although the rest of the smugglers were killed, the "boss" escaped, and Steve returned the mother to her family, paying for them to stay in the hotel that he, Ingrid, and Lars were staying in.

Leaving them to recover and feeling he'd finally done something worthwhile, he went to the site he planned to visit first, and found a hidden cave system. Inside it was a woman, eons old, encased in crystal that was slowly growing and converting what was left of her body into itself.

He also discovered that the crystal was actively lethal to nanites, and that the long-dead Minoans and Therians were harvesting it, using it in creating weapons that were in turn used to fight the monsters of the ancient world.

Upon his return to the hotel, though, Steve found Hans and other Arisen waiting for him. Hans convinced him to go peacefully, as the alternative was the utter destruction of the area by another Arisen, the sadistic Athena.

Steve explained the truth of the situation, and the discovery he made, to Ingrid, Lars, and Val, injecting a laptop he recovered earlier from the people smugglers with nanites and upgrading it to help them.

Then he left, and was taken to an Arisen sub, hidden offshore. Steve was examined by the Arisen scientists and doctors, and although he managed to hide the majority of what he was—they had no clue about the ship or their technological beginnings—they did know that he was special, and they set out to find out all they can.

They chose to do so by spending the next three years torturing him over and over to death, reasoning that they were expanding their species' knowledge, and that as he can't really die, there's no long-term loss.

By the end, they found out all they could through destructive methods, and had moved to drug-induced programming as methods of control, attempting to learn ways that Steve was able to sense—albeit in a limited fashion—certain metals.

The end goal of this research was ostensibly to enable them to find and recover long-lost Arisen who were bound in metal coffins and hidden at sea. The Arisen were not above cruelty for cruelty's sake, however, and were amusing themselves with the torture.

Hans, while this was going on, had been protecting Ingrid, Val, and Lars, as well as forcing their council to intervene on Steve's behalf.

The end result was that Ingrid was permitted access to Steve, while Steve, drugged and compelled, had no clue who she was, as his "wife"—an Arisen by the name of Vitoria—amused herself by making him beg her for sex and more in front of Ingrid.

The drugs used to keep Steve pliable and confused were by necessity extremely powerful, and when a kink in the feedline stopped the drug, his mind began to clear.

Confused and faking sleep, Steve managed to force the line free, and quickly regained his wits, finding, to his dismay, that the reason he's incessantly vomiting—the only constant in his life currently—was because the Arisen had been testing the effect of force-feeding liquified humans to him.

They were unaware that it was the nanites that were responsible for his, and their, abilities, but one of the strongest of their oldest members was a cannibal, and they sought to find any connection between Steve's meteoric rise in power and that ancient.

The end result was that for months they'd been essentially feeding him on a diet of nanites, one that his own systems were frantically attempting to hold onto and assimilate.

When Vitoria and her companion brought Ingrid in to clean the room, and Steve saw her, all his memories rushed back. Knowing who she was, and who she was to him, triggered a chain reaction that unlocked his nanites.

Seeing the way that the Arisen beat Ingrid and had clearly been doing so for a while, Steve went nuclear and killed Vitoria, before being trapped in his room. The hardened walls held him for a short while, but with the nanites in his system now purified and in vast quantities, he purged his body of all contamination, before activating his armor, and creating a gravitational cannon.

Steve escaped his prison, slaughtering the guards on the way out, and all who stood between him and Ingrid, rescuing her, and declaring "open season" on all the Arisen who stand against him, before deploying wings and destroying the roof of Athena's medical wing, escaping with Ingrid in his arms.

<u>ARISE DARK CRUSADER SYNOPSIS</u>

Steve and Ingrid landed on the abandoned island of Skantzoura, Ingrid suffering from the cold of flight, as Steve began to learn to control his new armor. The distributed neurons of the armor's management system prevented him from removing it for several hours, and the pair explored, catching each other up on the last few years from their point of view.

Ingrid explained how she came to be at Athena's island as a servant and that Hans had been fighting to free Steve for three years, while Steve explained his new abilities, and they made a plan.

In the short-term, they needed money, clothing, and safety, and the decision was made to plunder a moored yacht for clothes and to enable them to clean up, before hitting a cash machine and finding a cheap hotel.

The first yacht was badly damaged by Steve's inexperience in flight, and they were forced to land on a second one. Ingrid made the most of the shower, before Steve unlocked the ability to "repair" others, as the system designates healing.

Upon using the skill on Ingrid, returning her—despite horrific pain—to perfect health, Steve was issued a quest, unlocking a new "tree" dedicated to the Support classes. Before the pair could fully explore the new situation, they were forced to escape as the owners' children came to check on the yacht.

Steve and Ingrid flew to a quiet nearby town on the mainland and used an old train—after raiding an ATM—to travel to Athens. Steve unlocked more of his Support tree and researched the new quest—to heal multiple people—before scaring Ingrid witless as the data download rendered him unconscious.

On arrival, Steve talked Ingrid into staying at a luxury boutique hotel, under the false identity of the "Athertons," hacking the system and ensuring that they were classed as returning guests, who have received a free upgrade to the highest levels, due to unexplained issues in the past. Issues that Steve has inserted into the hotel's systems.

The pair bluffed their way in, and were accepted, meeting James, the suite's butler, the next morning. After they spun a tale of being the victims of a robbery to him, James set about to "replace" everything they need, from clothing to toiletries and more, including electronics and underwear.

Steve and Ingrid set off the next night to begin their new plan to raise funds and get themselves out of reach of the majority of the Arisen, as Ingrid explained her plans, ones she'd spent the last three years working on.

The couple decided to convert a trawler, if they could find one, into a luxury vessel, to provide both stability and safety, as well as plenty of room. They agreed that they'd need to hire and develop staff, recruiting engineers, soldiers, researchers, and more, eventually using the team to bring some of the more desperately needed alien tech to the world.

Steve realized that in order to gain access to more "points" to spend in his upgrade trees, he needed to complete quests, and the first of those was the multiple-tier healing one recently granted to him.

That night, while Ingrid slept, Steve traveled to a local hospital, raiding several morgues on the way and stealing any viable nanites. Once there, he encountered a doctor, just before he would have stepped off the roof to his death. Steve saved him and forced the doctor to explain, discovering that a child lies dying beneath them, due to a mixture of honest mistakes and happenchance, with her best prospect of a replacement heart now lost.

Steve realized the opportunity that the situation granted, and to prevent questions, deployed his armor, now switched to a more impressive and imposing model with glowing eyes, declaring that he "will heal the child."

The night passed in a blur as he healed as many as he could, before returning to Ingrid, exhausted but ecstatic. The pair agreed that this situation gave them an opportunity to unlock trees and abilities that would be beneficial and help to make sure that they'd be safe in the future.

The first phase, however, was to get money, and both the local criminal and gambling elements would provide that easily, if not willingly.

On the way to the casino—having decided that as most casinos were rigged to ensure the "house" wins, then hacking them and flipping the tables so that they won instead was fair play—they found that the limo had additional hidden cameras, and Steve hacked them, shutting them down.

On arrival, Ingrid played on the machines, ostensibly losing money, while Steve worked on the Hack tree, moving from device to device, completing minor quests and gaining more experience with his abilities, as well as earning extra points, before the pair start to cheat.

The casino quickly banned the pair as they revel in their "luck," winning over four hundred thousand euros, and in the limo on the way back, Steve found the cameras had been reset.

Steve explained the situation to Ingrid, hacking them and shutting them down again, but in the process, found a much more paranoid security setup on the attached storage device, failing to hack it and instead triggering a program that wipes the data.

On return to the hotel, they were soon visited, at the open-air restaurant, by Yanni, a representative of one of the local mobs, an Albanian gangster who threatened Steve and Ingrid and demanded restitution…"or else."

Steve, being the gracious and subtle man that he was, hacked his phone and pointed out that Yanni's family were just as accessible to him, as he and Ingrid were to the mobster.

Yanni left, furious, and the hotel apologized for the situation, with James arranging guards for Ingrid while Steve returned to the children's wing of the hospital and resumed his healing.

Several hours later, he was interrupted by a call from Ingrid, panicked. Yanni and several of his men had broken in, killing both the guards and James the butler, and kidnapped her.

He tore his way through the nearest wall, launching himself into the air, and returned to the hotel, but too late. In a rage, he threw himself into the problem of the nanites, and found a way both to unlock the basic "healing" process of the nanites in James, and then forced his own to "fix" him, restarting the older man's heart and bringing him back to life.

Using the pattern he had seen for the encryption on the storage device the limo had been using, he retreated to a high point over the city. When he quickly identified another of the gang's vehicles, he struck, tearing the roof off and questioning the driver.

When he gets limited cooperation, he instead used the driver's body to smash the skylight on the second location he identified the encryption being used, before raiding it and slaughtering all but one of the people he found there.

The last person hid in an emergency secure vault, and Steve flipped the situation, having used local computers, and found the location Ingrid was being held. He then locked the vault from the outside, and sent the location, as well as the unlocking codes, to the local branch of Interpol.

Ingrid, meanwhile, was being taken to the gang's headquarters. She met Yanni's mother, the gang kingpin, and she distracted them all, until Steve could arrive, shielding her with his wings as they fired on the pair.

Then she asked Steve, very nicely, to "hurt these people, please."

The pair escaped a few minutes later, this time with the gang's hard drives and the boss's laptop, including her bank access to over a hundred and forty million euros.

Ingrid and Steve decided that they couldn't risk returning to the hotel, not now, and instead went to a cheap "no-tell motel" and spent the night, breaking into a store on the way to dress Ingrid.

The next morning, the pair made their way to a local marina and purchased a yacht of their own, getting the seller blind drunk and getting a few lessons on how to sail as they went.

Steve bought some new clothes, realizing he's far too distinctive in the tailored suit he'd been wearing from the visit to the casino, and abandoned the suit in the bin at a marina shop.

The following morning, Steve and Ingrid made their way to a local shop, buying all the basics they think they'll need, introducing themselves to the couple who own the next yacht over, before being invited over for dinner later, along with their "uncle," who waited inside their yacht for them to return.

On entering, the pair were overjoyed to find it was James, the butler, who has tracked them down, then calmly requested an explanation, before joining them as the first member of the team.

James joined the team both for a flat fee of two million dollars a year, and, far more important to him, the healing of his son, Michael, who had a replication issue related to his nanites, mis-diagnosed as an autoimmune disorder.

James then assisted the pair in recruiting Zac and Casey, a married couple for the crew. Zac was a world-class engineer, with a somewhat murky background, and Casey, his wife, was a highly experienced and skilled steward and qualified marine geologist.

Next recruited was Jay Beraz, a highly qualified American chef, and finally Jack Cameron, recruited to the position of deckhand and general dogsbody, as well as tech support.

While James and Ingrid attempted to make contact with the doctor at the hospital, aware that he is now likely being watched by the Arisen, Steve acted as a decoy, reaching out to Hans to make contact, and carried a large boulder into the air, unbeknownst to Athena and her people, who were in a yacht below him.

When Athena interrupted the call and threatened Steve, he attacked, using the boulder as an almost orbital attack weapon, devastating her yacht and killing over half the crew aboard as it impacted.

Steve followed the boulder into the yacht, dispatching the majority of the security contingent, before fighting—and killing—Athena in single combat.

Steve stripped her of her nanites, as Hans killed the last of her security contingent, with the surviving Oracan and staff swearing allegiance to Steve.

Hans took over, agreeing to loot and raise the yacht, with it being repaired and given to Steve as a conquest, and Hans covering the costs, in exchange for half of the loot.

Steve escaped and Hans claimed to the rest of the Arisen that he was playing along with Steve to keep him close and maintain contact, while Hans instead had thrown his lot in with Steve, joining his fledgling faction.

Steve looted a safe from the sunken yacht on the way out, and returned to his own yacht, stripping the safe with the help of Ingrid and James, looting papers—both normal documents and rolled-up ones encased in wax, jewelry, bags of coins and gemstones, as well as…a desiccated body, hermetically sealed in glass.

The body was discovered to be that of Scylla, the second of Athena's daughters, kept imprisoned for centuries, according to Hans, for crossing her mother.

Steve appealed to Hans to help him set up a détente with the Arisen, basically offering to leave them alone, provided they leave him alone. Hans advised against it, pointing out that as the only one who can comprehensively and permanently kill the other Arisen, Steve was a massive threat, one that may be "resolved" with the use of nuclear weapons.

Some of the other Arisen might not want to use them, but if need be? The loss of a city to a "terrorist attack" that resulted in Steve's death would be an acceptable cost for many.

Steve agreed to keep hidden for now, and Hans filled Steve, Ingrid, and James in on more of the Arisen's ancient history, before recommending the group go off and essentially train, keeping a low profile.

Over the next few days, the remaining crew arrive, and Steve upgraded his abilities to include creation of separate artifacts, allowing him to upgrade the engines, as well as convert random matter into "null blocks," blocks of compressed high-density matter that can be used as the building blocks for almost anything.

With that done, Steve and the crew set sail for the Ambracian Gulf, a location Ingrid had identified as a potential monster nest. En route, Steve and Ingrid called her parents, having arranged a secure communication line. Steve was grilled on their relationship and condition by Ingrid's family, and over the next few days, they made several calls, getting to know one another.

Arise: Conqueror

By the time the yacht landed at the Ambracian Gulf, the crew knew that there was more going on than they'd been told, but trusting James, they agreed to wait until the end of the trip for answers. Jack was left aboard ship, and the others accompanied Steve and Ingrid to the suspected infestation, finding that the local rangers were very welcoming.

At first, Steve and the others put this down to the donation they made, but as the mission went on, it became clear this was not the case.

The fens were the home to two species—beyond humanity and the "known" species—the fen nymphs were more or less friendly, although they did attack the party, both for trespassing and due to being forced to capture others for their masters, the mavka.

The second species—the mavka—were far more aggressive, a snake-like naga species with a short-range hydro-warp capability. The mavka attacked Steve, and when that went badly for them, they attempted to escape using this ability, and accidentally dragged Steve along with them to the main nest.

Steve fought and slaughtered the rest of the nest, including the queen, a massive BWV. Upon killing the remaining mavka, Steve completed his most recent quest to protect the Support class, gaining three points in the War and one in the Espionage trees. The three War points were spent, unfortunately, in surviving the injuries the mavka queen had inflicted due to her terrible acidic bite and jaws.

The three points were spent on the Armor sub-tree specifically with Biological Weapons—to understand the acidic compound better—then Atmospheric Integration and Biological Cleansing, to both provide oxygen regardless of the location, and to remove the harmful buildups of toxins.

While Steve fought and recovered, Ingrid spent time with the fen nymphs, convincing them of her potential as an ally, and when Steve returned, depositing the head—almost as big as he was—of their most feared predator, the mavka queen, the nymphs swore fealty.

One of their number, Par'a'nuit, joined the crew, bonding to three trees planted in the hot tub, and began to evolve after escorting the crew down into the underground ruins.

The locals, no longer being drugged and forced unknowingly into accepting the mavka's orders, slowly awakened and were distressed over the years of events they'd been living through. Steve and the others left, filling Jack in on the realities of life, and scaring him half to death in the process.

Upon contacting Hans, they found he was under watch by the other factions, and he recommended Steve go to Russia, specifically to the wild forested lands where other monster species still lived, hidden. Then he destroyed the phone and cut off communication for their safety.

Steve agreed, and although the others weren't happy about it, they eventually accepted that with Steve headed north and leaving enough traces along the way, that freed them up to take action to the south.

The group planned to buy an abandoned recycling plant in the Sudanese desert, one filled with radioactive and biological waste, using the converters to reduce the waste to usable null blocks, which simultaneously gave them a legal and easily verified income.

Eventually Ingrid agreed to the plan, but on the condition that Steve met her parents, properly.

James arranged for Ingrid's father, Anders, to "win" a prize: an exclusive dining experience at the most expensive and prestigious restaurant in Denmark for the entire family. Although Anders knew the truth, the rest of the family didn't, and were surprised when Steve and Ingrid arrived.

Steve admitted more to Anders than he should have, and the older man, due to his navy background and current "titan of industry" experience, signed on with them as a general manager and front man for the company.

Steve and Anders agreed that the criminal element that were prevalent in the city had no need of the wealth they'd been making, and Anders sent Steve after some of the local criminals, notably an Albanian gang focused on both people and drug smuggling.

Steve's approach, and his subsequent loss of control, both horrified and impressed Anders and the crew, as Steve slaughtered his way through the lower echelons to the top of the chain. In the process, he captured the leadership, stealing their bank accounts and draining them into the one the group was using.

Unfortunately, an innocent was killed during the mission, and Steve lost control, his rage let loose as he slaughtered the remaining gang members, before being caught on camera by a news channel's helicopter.

Steve, in a fit of rage, nearly attacked the helicopter, being stopped by Ingrid calling him and demanding he back down. Steve realized the situation he'd created, and the only available solution.

He escaped, delivering the money and laptops taken from the gang, then left, heading to Russia ahead of schedule. Ingrid was furious, and her father, who had gone to the yacht, intervened, learning the truth of Steve and his situation.

Steve allowed himself to be tracked leaving the city, and Ingrid and the others left quickly, heading back to the Med, and toward Sudan.

The next several weeks flew by, as Steve vanished into the wilds of Russia, reaching and passing Tunguska, before he encountered a wild tribe of Oracan, led by Eto, spending time with them after fighting one of their number to earn a place.

He learned the language, more or less, and traveled with a small group, thinking they were guiding him, when in reality they were taking him—as ordered—to the Erlking.

The Erlking was revealed to be one of the ancients that artificially uplifted the human race, and, when annoyed by Steve, slaughtered him in several horrific ways, after the Oracan left, returning to their tribe.

The Erlking agreed to give Steve limited help and advice, on the condition that he both heal the world, and, to prevent him taking the opportunity to gain power, he must leave it.

When Steve agreed, the location of two more of the buried facilities were shared with him: one buried on Yuzhny Island and the other sunken in Lake Tengiz, with suspected ones off the coast of Jakarta and another near Algeria south of Monaco and west of Sardinia. An additional potential site was due west of the

Pillars of Hercules in the Atlantic. Lastly, he was given a quest to help the Oracan, both saving them, and power-leveling Steve.

While leaving the details open-ended, the Erlking was also horrifically powerful enough, and unwilling enough to allow a new faction to rise and control the planet, that Steve agreed, regardless, knowing that at the least he would be able to save Ingrid and the others and leave them in a position of strength before he had to depart.

He was joined by Maribellya—or Belle, as she was more colloquially known—an elder dryad, and one of only four left in the world with her sisters: Barishka, hidden in a valley far to the south; in the middle of Africa, Annai lives hidden on an island paradise; and Jamya, the youngest, buried long ages ago in a landslide.

Steve agreed to help Belle, due to her potential to rewild the Sahara and other places, her natural growth abilities being powerful additional tools, and took her with him to search for the Oracan.

On arrival, he found that many of the clan's warriors had been killed, and fought off the werewolves, before allowing Eto and some of the other warriors to join him, tracking the werewolves back to their village.

En route, they encountered a unicorn, one of the last of its species, and Steve, attempting to tame it, was killed.

When he recovered, they continued to track the lycans, and Steve, traumatized by the ongoing deaths, had a minor breakdown. Belle helped him through it, and the lycans attacked, giving him the opportunity to take out his issues on them. After the battle, Steve admitted that although he has great advantages in battle, he was untrained in edged weapons and more, and needed help.

He traded his portion of the loot from the lycan village they destroyed for training by the Oracan, and found that, as the trainee, he was now the lowest of the low, forced to carry the litter that Belle, who had overreached in the fight, rested on.

The next of the lycan villages was more of a trial, with a much larger population, led by an alpha, with ghouls and a vampire, as well as a pair of Minotaurs. The Minotaur, Oxus, and his "calf" Xous, agreed to join Steve when Belle made him aware that Oxus was being forced to fight, under threat of Xous being eaten by the vamp.

By the end of the fight, Steve had gained the rights to the lycan camp, a formerly Oracan major village, and Eto and the rest of the clan left him, to reclaim the village.

Ronai, one of the warriors of the tribe, as well as Leo, Agnin, and Tenit, joined Steve in payment of the debt of honor owed, as well as the next morning being joined by seven more Oracan: the new ex-chief of the tribe—Kim—and his immediate family, including a daughter named Oba, and two nieces.

Steve's gift of the village to Eto had been taken to mean directly to Eto, and he had claimed the chief's role, before understanding that as chief, he'd have far more work to do.

The old chief was overjoyed, and followed Steve along instead, refusing as Eto tried to recruit him or change his mind about the chief's position.

Over the next few days, trapped in a cave by an unseasonably heavy storm, Belle spent time using her abilities to help more of the group learn English in preparation for their inevitable return to civilization.

The final village of the three was in the midst of an internal "debate" when the group found it, with the losers being noticeably dead already, and the group waited until the fight was almost over, before wading in and dealing with the survivors of the little civil war.

When the group finally reached the nearby human village—with Steve fortunately finding some pants at the last lycan village—he introduced himself and tried to make friendly contact, immediately coming under fire, as one of the small number of villagers recognized his pants as belonging to a recently vanished family member.

Once things were calmed down, the villagers turned out to not only be English, but a back-to-nature commune group of hippies and Gaia worshippers, led to the wilds and summarily abandoned by a shady figure named Oberon and his brother.

The pair had stayed long enough to avail themselves of the ladies of the group, basing their community on a "free love" model, and then moving on when they grew bored, taking all the villagers' wealth with them as they ostensibly went to "get supplies" to save the failing village.

Steve explained the realities of life to the group, including that the damage to their boat, that had necessitated the pair returning to society, was done from the inside of the boat. It also looked to have been done with a survival knife, not, as Oberon had claimed, by razor-sharp rocks in the water.

The group, now realizing the facts of their situation, agreed to help Steve, and he used the remaining points he'd gained in the Support trees to improve his construction abilities. As part of unlocking so much data, however, the download damaged Steve's brain, and he went into shock.

Over a period of several hours, Steve lost control, thrashing around and breaking much of the quarters he'd been given, before burning himself on a log kicked loose from the fire.

Steve automatically pulled up his armor to defend himself, and in doing so, activated the distributed network of neurons stored in the suit to help him deal with complex tasks. In a moment of lucidity, he upgraded the communications device at the base of his brain to store future downloads, limiting the damage done by massive amounts of data being dumped into his brain unprepared.

That helped him to survive the experience, although he was left unbalanced and confused for several days as he recovered. Belle helped him to deal with the situation, reducing his emotions to manageable levels to enable him to concentrate on the boat he needed to build to equip them to travel to a distant airport.

Once the situation had time to settle in, rather than, as Steve had hoped, the Oracan and Minotaurs settling with the hippies and staying there, the hippies joined Steve's group.

He led them all, while being considerably frustrated by their lack of common sense, to the airport, before sinking the boat to prevent questions, and hacking the local airport systems.

They found an appropriate plane being refueled, ready to be flown to Nepal and sold, and stole aboard, hiding while the pilot, a Greek named Dimi, flew them out of Russia.

Once they were clear, Steve introduced himself and eventually convinced Dimi to help them all, partly by converting some of the farm machinery in the transport section into gold bars and bribing him.

The plane was registered as having issues and the original buyers were in turn bought out by Steve, with Dimi flying them all to the Sudanese airport closest to the recycling plant, stopping several times to refuel.

Over the course of the flight, it was discovered that Dimi, a smuggler, had lost his license to fly in Europe and America due to a joke played on a stewardess when he was a commercial pilot. Steve recruited him, granting him permission to use the plane as he wants—provided Dimi pays for the fuel and stays within a certain radius—and sorted out his license with Interpol, reinstating him.

Dimi flew off to pick up his girlfriend from Germany, and Steve and the rest of the group were collected by Jay and Jack from the airport on a coach and were driven out to the now partially operational recycling plant.

Ingrid, her father Anders, and her mother Freja had taken more and more of a lead in things with the plant, and had it minimally operational. People who could be trusted had been hired, including a large number of Anders's ex-navy contacts, as well as a small cadre of engineers from Zac's past.

The German pair of tourists who Steve had rescued from the lycan fighting pit so long ago had also been recruited, Isolde and Lukas, and were traveling to join the group, as they were both under watch as a possible threat to the Arisen and themselves, and as they were gifted machinists.

Locals had been hired to do low-skilled, but massively important repair and uncovering work. Once the groups were reunited, the discovery was made that the plant, home as it was to a huge amount of biological and nuclear contaminated waste, was being monitored by a great many people.

Defunct spying devices were discovered scattered across the site, detected when Steve demonstrated who and what he truly was to a small number of the more trusted individuals.

Steve and Ingrid were reassured that the monitoring devices were "dead" but they continued to track them down, with Steve using them to level his abilities.

It was determined that Scylla's prison was cracked, and Steve, when checking for any potential issues, found new, and highly sophisticated, monitoring devices hidden in his and Ingrid's room. A trap was laid, and while waiting for the spy to retrieve their device, Scylla was allowed to regenerate, after much discussion.

She was provided food, water, and null blocks to assist, and left to regenerate, as the spy finally appears…and it was Anders.

An Anders, in addition to the one by Steve's side as they watched over the recovering Scylla. Belle confirmed that this was the real Anders with Steve, and Steve set off to chase the imposter, watching them through several cameras as they shifted, becoming Ingrid and fleeing, naked, from the building.

The creature masquerading as Ingrid ran to the local tribesmen, begging for protection as Steve launched himself from the nearby main structure, and the locals, having never seen Steve before like this, but knowing Ingrid, attacked him.

He forced his way through them, saving one of their number when she was injured by the changeling, and eventually fought and defeated it. He was then attacked by two more, this time wearing the forms of Oxus, one wielding his hammer, and they used a high explosive combined with a sensory overload device to stun Steve, before fleeing.

Steve and the others discovered that the trio had arrived recently, pretending to be washerwomen, and when Annabeth, the leader of the hippies, annoyed Ingrid, Ingrid asked for her help, for a "really important job."

Annabeth agreed, and was given the job of chief washerwoman, much to Steve's amusement. The site was searched and when it was declared as "clean," Steve decided that they could no longer wait.

The creatures admitted to working for Shamal and the Blessed faction and Steve was forced to accept that the risk was too large to continue as they were. He remembered that the most effective weapon against the Arisen was the crystal spears and blades, weapons that he'd ordered the Oracan who swore to him, and were now under Hans's protection, to gather and keep safe.

Ingrid explained the truth to the entire group, locals included, and then Steve called Dimi, ordering him to Athens, as it was faster than Dimi flying to the site's airstrip that was still being repaired and then continuing on from there.

Steve set off in search of the escaped changelings, checking the area as best he could, before he turned and headed to Athens, desperate to reach the Oracan and bring them and their weapons back to defend the recycling plant.

On arrival at Athens, Steve stole a bike to get to the yachts, not wanting to expose himself too much, and spotted Dave, his old friend, observing them. Realizing Dave was being watched, presumably by his old companions, Steve left a few gifts for him in Dave's toilet, one of the few places not covered by cameras and observation devices, then left.

Steve stole into the water and crept along the bottom to the yachts, finding a network of spy devices had been deployed. Rather than attacking, he instead invested all three of his available Hack points, upgrading his capabilities through synergistic alignment until he unlocked a new ability: Contagion.

The Contagion ability was a mixture of a Plague upgrade, spreading out across connected systems, and a Control one, giving Steve ultimate control over the technological systems he accessed. It was limited in the most basic form to a single "jump" once the indicated system was infected, "jumping" to another connected system and spreading the infection there, before settling into quiescence.

Steve attacked the detection net, taking control, before attempting to slip aboard the now refloated and undergoing repairs superyacht, one that had once belonged to Athena, and had now become Steve's by right of conquest.

The sensor net in the water, however, wasn't the only one, and as he breached the surface, an additional one, separate from the first and floating, detected him, setting off alarms that were connected to a second group of observers.

Arise: Conqueror

On entry into the superyacht, Steve met and freed Athelas, the Oracan "First Warrior" and their local group leader, who admitted that they'd been captured by Shamal and Cristobel, a second Arisen who had arrived to claim the yacht.

They had managed to hide several of the crystal weapons, but the majority were stolen by the new interlopers. Steve recruited the group again, then fought and killed the guards on the pier nearby, before facing Cristobel.

In the ensuing conversation and threats, Dave managed to make contact with Steve, drawing his attention to two more yachts incoming, both in an extended firefight with each other.

Dave pointed out that the more damaged of the two was the one Jonas and the others were aboard, and begged Steve for help.

Steve attacked Cristobel, and in the course of the fight, she managed to stab him with a crystal-tipped dagger, damaging the harvest tool.

Steve was forced to use his time compression and distortion device to give himself time to react, and the vorpal blade to carve his own right arm off at the elbow, before killing Cristobel.

The infection caused by the crystal destroyed the harvest tool, and due to the nature of the lockouts the ancients set into humanity, once Steve lost it entirely—he'd been forced to strip his own nanites from the surrounding area, essentially relinquishing control over the harvest device accidentally—it could no longer be recreated.

Steve realized that to regain the harvest tool and his primary means of securing nanites, he needed to return to the facility under the ocean and recover a second one. But for the short-term, he rebuilt his lower right arm and included a nanite creation tool instead.

Steve rescued Jonas, Marie, and Amanda, and Dave rejoined him, as Steve healed Jonas, eradicating his long-term cancer in the process, and the old team—Jonas, Amanda, Marie, Dave, Paul and his wife Courtney—joined Steve.

Steve was helped by Laia, the leader of the yacht team, to contact the local mayor and warned him to draw his people back, both the navy and local forces. The mayor agreed.

Steve was contacted by Dimi, who admitted that there was a problem with the plane—an engine had failed—and Steve in turn contacted Freja, who arranged to purchase a replacement VTOL that had been embroiled in a local legal battle.

Steve ordered Dimi to change planes as fast as possible and get to the rendezvous.

The much larger group, now including the Oracan and survivors from the yachts who had sworn to follow Steve, headed for the foot of the pier, before realizing that the incoming vehicles were not, as expected, transports. Instead, they were troop transports and tanks, sent, it turned out, by Beowulf, another Arisen.

Beowulf stabbed Steve, using an advanced stealth ability to sneak up, and declared himself, making a call to Shamal and ordering his ally to lead the attack on the recycling plant.

It was Beowulf and Shamal's plan to be "forced" to come out of hiding by the situation, before swearing to the Old Ones that they'd be guided by them, keeping the other Arisen hidden, while the pair took control of the world publicly.

Beowulf admitted to Steve that he had several artifacts of his own, and in the ensuing fight, Steve killed him, contacting Dimi and rerouting him to the foot of the pier, then gathering up the team as Dimi landed nearby with their new VTOL airplane.

Steve got hold of Ingrid, explained what had happened, and found that the three changelings who had escaped him were now outside the facility, trapping the others inside and waiting for Shamal.

Steve and the others set off for the recycling facility, six hours' travel away, and en route, Steve used the nanite-filled bodies of Beowulf and Cristobel as building materials, beginning repairs and upgrades on the old VTOL, enabling them to massively decrease the time required to reach Ingrid.

Shortly after they took off, the Hellenic Air Force surrounded them, and Steve reached out to their squad leader, Flight Lieutenant Papadopoulos, taking control of his plane and giving him a demonstration of how easily he could divert or remove them, then promised to be in touch with their leaders soon, to discuss how he could help.

Between the carrot and the stick, implying that he could just as easily take over missile silos on the ground and retarget them, the Hellenic Air Force and any others nearby backed off, leaving Steve to upgrade his new plane, installing replacement engines—one at a time so that they could continue to fly while the upgrade was done—a new stealth reflective coating and a power core, as well as a rail gun.

Dimi was unsure whether he could bring himself to fire it, but his fiancée happily took it over, after they were fired upon, discovering that she actually loved heavy weaponry, and she'd just never known until then.

Steve stormed the upper floors of the recycling plant, crashing through a damaged section and killing several soldiers, as well as one of Shamal's pet Arisen, before taking their weapons and attacking the soldiers.

In the ensuing fight, Steve was seriously injured, and had his armor integrity reduced to a bare handful of percentage points, forcing him to recover additional null blocks and repair his armor into a far less secure version, essentially coating himself in solid metal.

In the assault on the next floor, fighting his way toward Scylla's cell, having realized that was where everyone had retreated to, he managed to kill two more of Shamal's Arisen. The last of them, Festus, killed Steve with his hammer as he completed the Emergency Wipe of the nanites in the dead bodies.

Steve was brought to the cell, stripped and nailed to the wall, being used as a threat to force Ingrid to open the door and let Shamal in.

Shamal tore Steve's jaw free, torturing him, before turning back to threaten Ingrid, while Steve reached out, gathering the attuned and ready nanites farther down the corridor that he'd left when he was killed, and routed them through air ducts to reach Scylla, before getting Shamal's attention and making noises.

Shamal replaced Steve's jaw, curious to find out what Steve was trying to say, only to be told: "the enemy of my enemy is my friend."

Arise: Conqueror

Shamal dismissed it as bravado, only to hear it spoken again, as Scylla stepped through the previously sealed door, fully armored, and standing as Steve's ally.

Steve and Scylla fought together, Steve controlling the nanites as a weapon for Scylla, and her centuries of fighting experience along with the unpredictable nature of the nanites enabled them to win. Steve then converted Shamal into more blank nanites, using them to heal and rebuild himself over the next few days, splitting the cost between null blocks and the nanites themselves.

Several local leaders, including representatives from Europe, the UK, and North America reached out, coming to meet Steve, ostensibly to investigate the dark crusader, and at least in part to make sure that the facilities they were shipping their most hazardous waste to was actually doing something with it.

As Steve met them, half in and half out of his armor, glistening black bones on show as bubbling nanites rebuilt him before their eyes, the questions were fairly simple to field.

Mainly being around was he, and his organization, a threat, and what could they get from him.

Lastly, Dave had proposed in the midst of the battle to Amanda, fully expecting that he'd die in the fight, and wanting to go out on a high.

Unfortunately for him, he survived, and she was holding him to it.

ARISE RECLAIMER SYNOPSIS

On recovering and after the fight for the recycling facility, Steve and the team spent the next few weeks on essential repairs, as well as integrating their new recruits into the family.

Some, such as the Oracan, were perfectly able to fit in, simply joining the existing security details and beginning to train with their new teams, used to the fluid nature of life under an Arisen.

Others, however, had more of an issue.

Scylla agreed to be bound by Steve and Ingrid's rule—"for now"—as she quickly learned that the world she had awoken in was nothing like the one she lost.

She did, however, have numerous quirks that caused issues, including being well aware that she was "born to rule" and was significantly stronger than the average breed of humanity. Local diplomats, deciding to manufacture offense at her clothing choices as a negotiating tactic, found this out…to their dismay.

When the blood was cleaned off the walls, floor, and ceiling, unsurprisingly, the surviving diplomats were considerably more willing to deal in good faith.

The surrounding countries of the Sudan—Libya and Chad—were very happy when Steve revealed his plans for the area, but Egypt refused to allow him and his team access. They went so far as to threaten the group that they would "take action" if they trespass. So, in the course of discussions, the group agreed to simply ignore the Egyptian negotiators and rules.

They were, after all, only human.

Steve and the group moved forward with their plans for the local area, including their intention to rewild the Sahara, starting with establishing a new lake nearby.

Plans were drawn up to dig down and create converters to transform the dead sand into usable materials, as well as to form a stone basin to act as the base for the new lake, with an access river running through Libya to its northern coast.

A second river would extend due west to Chad, and a smaller lake would be situated there. Water, now found to be long buried deep below the surface, would be pumped up and used to fill these huge lakes, while converters would be used to chew up the local sandy ground.

These mobile converters would leave behind massive tracks of usable land through a mixture of mass conversion and intermixing the lower levels of sand with even deeper sections of less damaged soil.

Steve and the team knew that this would be no easy feat, but if they could manage it? The potential gain for the planet would be massive.

Zac and the team of engineers worked with Steve to develop a miniature factory complex—only a handful of small systems to begin with—but they took in the null blocks gained from breaking down the waste brought to the recycling plant.

That was then fed to the converters and factory units, producing significantly upgraded solar cells, and the engineers rejoiced that they now had a method of upgrading the base overall, with the walls slowly being converted to a diamond-hard coating that would be impervious to most attacks.

Hans arrived with news from the Old Ones, and when confronted with a seemingly brainwashed Hans, Steve explained the truth of their origins.

Hans left the camp and marched into the desert, seemingly unable to accept the truth, while Scylla, already dealing with a seismic upheaval of her world from the technology of her era, accepted it easier.

When Hans didn't return, the group made plans without him, and decided that waiting to see what he would choose to do was just too dangerous.

Steve revealed the location of the crashed ship to the wider leadership group, and plans were made to reclaim it, eliminating the security AI's presence and making use of the ship itself, as well as most importantly to Steve, replacing the harvest blade and upgrading more of the group.

Secondarily and of equal importance, was that Steve suffered from mental breakdowns brought on by the massive influx of knowledge into his brain from the various classes he'd managed to unlock, and he continued to suspect that all was not right with this capability.

Steve flew ahead while Ingrid, James, Scylla, Jonas, Zac, Casey, Paul, and Courtney sailed the yacht from its berth on the Sudan. While the others would take several days to reach the ship, Steve covered most of the distance aboard the reconfigured VTOL plane, jumping out over the Med and flying the remainder of the distance on his own power.

After several hours of searching and examination, Steve hit upon the idea of using the grainy "radar" that he could generate from his tentacles to map the entire structure beneath him. Then, using a combination of this and the design and modeling facilities that he had unlocked from the various upgrades, he stripped the sand, silt, and accumulated debris of ages from the ship's image.

Using this, he found several entrances to the ship that had clearly been repaired after the crash, and more sections that were slowly being repaired, or that were in progress and were seemingly abandoned due to lack of materials.

Steve attempted a hack to gain access to the ship, only to find that the security AI was ready for him, having detected him scanning the ship.

Although Steve had easily overcome the original security systems, he quickly found that this was due to two things. First, the security AI had weathered thousands of years of inactivity and was woefully unprepared for his intrusion.

Secondly, through being able to physically breech the systems using the harvest tool and active nanites the first time around, he'd had a significant advantage.

With the loss of the harvest tool, and his subsequent wiping of the majority of his nanites to weaponized status, Steve had none of these advantages now, and the fight was much more difficult.

Steve was forced to employ both time compression capabilities, distraction in the form of the half-complete authority bequeathed to him by the Erlking, and spinning up nine sub-minds to assist.

He still barely succeeded, and upon entry into the ship, found that most of these previously unexplored sections were devastated by the long-ago crash and the march of time.

Steve received a quest to reclaim the ship. To do so, he must claim the local security stations, as well as secure those sections he had recovered against intrusion.

Over several days, the AI resurrected and repaired more and more heavily armed sentinels, as Steve fought his way across the ship.

Sections were reclaimed, and he began the process of stripping and recovering sentinels and custodians of his own. Next came converters and factory units, and the first defensive turrets were made.

As more and more sections and rooms were claimed, the security AI grew desperate and, unbeknownst to Steve, reached out to the original creators, requesting aid and authority.

A solution for the pain of data downloading was found, almost accidentally, when Steve forced one of the sub-minds he still had access to, now buried in his armor, to maintain a watch for him as he upgraded himself.

He was awoken by the sub-mind as more sentinels attacked, and the sub-mind took control of a tentacle, saving his life. After some careful consideration, Steve set this sub-mind up with more storage, and then filtered the downloading information for the Hack upgrade through that mind, creating a sub-mind with a Hack and Espionage specialty skill set.

He began setting it automated jobs, including maintaining and programming the factory units, and running the defenses.

Steve set up a remote link from the ship he was aboard to the yacht, which had now arrived overhead, and the group aboard the yacht disagreed with his intentions to secure the entire ship before they gained access.

They used the custodian Steve had sent them to upgrade their weapons and provide basic body armor.

The AI launched a counterattack, and in the process, Steve was badly injured. The combination of acids, poisons, and gamma radiation stripped the vast majority of his armor and nanites from him, and in a panic, he ordered the sub-mind to help him and to protect Ingrid.

His last thoughts before he died were of Ingrid.

The sub-mind accepted these orders, and using the remote link, continued to fight the AI to a standstill, holding the currently claimed ground, while Steve was evacuated to the ship overhead.

Steve recovered over several days, and then agreed that his time as a lone wolf was over. He returned to the ship below, now with Ingrid by his side, and with most of the crew already aboard the alien vessel.

Arise: Conqueror

Where Paul, Jonas, and Courtney worked hard to fight the sentinels, using their upgraded weapons and training, Zac essentially caused more problems than he solved, trying to get control of the factory systems.

When Steve arrived on site, he quickly took over and set up a second sub-mind, one housed in a factory unit that Zac could control, and at last the gifted engineer could do what he was best at.

With the sub-mind no longer hamstrung by the limited data access it could manage remotely, the tide of battle turned and the group consolidated the area.

Steve and Scylla agreed that they would loop around and secure the medical suite, while Jonas et al. would draw its attention.

The flanking attack was a dismal failure, as Scylla was killed immediately upon reentry to the ship, and the medical suite was being destroyed when Steve reached it. He died shortly after. Again.

When Steve was reawakened by his nanites, he was considerably weaker, and was being carried by a robot to be reduced to his constituent atoms in a furnace.

His body was unresponsive, and a control collar of some kind had been used on him, rendering him paralyzed. He used the small number of nanites he had access to, to form a small tentacle and damage the collar, before discovering that its construction also lent itself to a form of high-speed data access.

The tentacle carved the collar apart, and he used it to hack the robot, quickly counterattacking mere moments before he and Scylla—whose body had been recovered as well—would have been rendered down.

The security AI, realizing that it had lost control of the local area as Steve captured nearby sentinels being produced, abandoned it and fled, shutting the systems down in an attempt to prevent Steve from using them, as there was no localized power generation once that had been shut off.

Steve found that the energy generated from the conversion of higher density materials to null blocks could be siphoned away, providing power if he accepted the loss of some of the end product, and used this to kick-start the factory units around him and to repair the medical suite that had also been cut out and brought here for destruction.

When Scylla reawakened, she and Steve argued, and she struck him, before storming off. Unfortunately for Steve, by this point he was almost entirely out of nanites. Although he was more powerful than a regular human due to the changes that had been made, without the nanites to actively support him, to repair and heal him?

He was badly injured.

His last action before losing consciousness was to order the medical suite to repair him and the sentinels to protect him. As injured and desperate as the order was, it was transmitted to *all* the sentinels under his command.

Unbeknownst to him, when Scylla realized that she had caused significant damage to him, she relented and gave him a small number of her nanites through a blood transfusion.

When he reawakened, it was to the sight of Ingrid and the others, who followed the sentinels; Ingrid was berating Scylla, who fortunately refrained from stabbing her.

Steve accepted the medical suite's requests and gave it directions, regaining the harvest tool, before being stripped and repaired.

The process was horrific, as he once again was rebuilt, his upgraded skeleton and some parts being retained. But significant sections were removed and although they were reattached later, granting him his improvements again, he was reduced to a small number of nanites.

When he was finally released, he explained the process to the others, and forgave Scylla, before explaining that as Scylla had nanites still, but in far lower levels than a normal Arisen of her age, she had a choice.

She could take up residence in the medical suite, and she would have her nanites gradually unlocked, whereupon she would be upgraded and released, but the process would literally take decades. Or…

She could give up her nanites, being reduced somewhat in strength to that of a very low-level Arisen, as hardly any of them were unlocked, and the recovered nanites would be used to unlock some of the others' abilities.

Before any decision was made, the final push was made and the security AI fled into a secure fallback location, cut off from the rest of the ship. Steve and the team captured the last holdouts, but weren't granted the quest complete bonus.

Scylla suspected she was being punished for striking Steve, but accepted the removal of her nanites as it provided opportunities to upgrade Zac, Jonas, and Ingrid, who chose the paths of Support, War, and for Ingrid, the Commander class.

Where the others were determined by the design of the person, Ingrid had originally been a Support class, and would have had problems with another class being simply slapped atop her own. Due to Steve's command level access, though, and the capabilities of the Commander class, Ingrid was able to upgrade to it, unlocking group Support options.

She became the heart of the team even more, granting the abilities of silent communications, a shared command net, and being able to link to the others and highlight or project details as she unlocked more and more capabilities.

Steve, Ingrid, Jonas, and Scylla returned to the yacht with James, and headed for a nearby location that Marie, Amanda, and Dave identified as a people and drug smuggling center. Courtney, Paul, and Zac stayed below, and Casey swam down from the ship to join her husband on the alien vessel.

Steve and the small team presented themselves to the people smugglers as a target too good to let slip, and they were attacked. It didn't end well for the smugglers, and they were harvested.

Steve realized that, unfortunately, he'd been spoiled by the long years of being force-fed nanites and pureed people, as well as the constant fights against other Arisen and their attendants, as the small—in comparison—numbers of nanites harvested and then split between the team were too little.

He begrudgingly accepted that he would need to take the team to richer harvesting locations, and they attacked a nearby main base of the smugglers, freeing their victims and letting the others get more experience.

Once the enemy had been drained and the nanites shared, Steve regained access to his harvest blade, and he contacted Interpol, sharing the locations of the criminal network with one of its vice presidents, as the president of that organization was found to be corrupt.

The decision was made to spend a significant portion of the recovered nanites to have Belle flown out and then to upgrade her, and she was given, through Steve's command access, the Harvest class.

Once the team was ready, they set off to the wilds of Russia, and Steve shared as much of the quest to eliminate the Stelek as he could.

The team were threatened and attacked when they reached the Oracan village, with Steve being forced to kill Eto, before realizing that Eto set this up deliberately.

He was unable to manage as a leader of the tribe, and due to the Oracan societal norms, couldn't step down. He'd made recent poor decisions, in sending the majority of the tribe's remaining warriors to clear out the Stelek in their ancestral home nearby, and the village was failing.

By provoking a fight with Steve, he gained the chance to do the one thing he was excellent at—fighting—and remind the tribe of who he was. Also, if he lost? He would die with honor.

When Steve killed him, he got his wish, but Steve was also left with the Oracan village, who were unable to accept him as direct leader, and yet that he couldn't simply abandon. The solution was to send Dimi back to the recycling facility, collecting the old leader of the tribe, Kim, and several others, with orders to come back, retake control over the village, and get them ready to move to the Sahara and set up a new village there.

While Dimi was doing that, one of the tribe who remembered Steve from the fighting with the lycans led the group to the nearby Stelek hive.

The Stelek were driven up from the deeper places long ago, and had in turn displaced the Oracan from their hidden city, slaughtering the majority and driving out the survivors.

Steve and his small group explored the caverns and found a preserved and ancient city that Ingrid recognized as similar to other underground locations she had studied in Turkey.

Scylla, unfortunately, recognized it as something far worse. In the course of the fighting, the group realized there were frequent sections wider than others, but beyond that, the entire supposed city was a single corridor, literally miles long.

Scylla, however, had seen this before, and she and Ingrid explained to the others what had happened, with Steve using a tentacle to verify.

The defenders of the city had been driven out, but the majority of the inhabitants hadn't. Instead, they'd closed off their living areas with great slabs of stone—emergency measures that had then turned their private quarters into tombs.

When the defenders were unable to retake the city, their families died, suffocated, starved, and dehydrated, while the insectile Stelek roamed the empty corridors, uncaring.

The group, troubled, moved on, fighting their way through successive defenders, until Steve accidentally linked his System Replenishment ability to his armor and active nanites.

The result was an abomination, as the system informed the rest of the group, ordering them to kill him and promising significant rewards if they did.

The Devourer, as Steve was identified, was named as one of the "most feared of all the legions of the ancient enemy," leading Steve down a new path of concerns as he wondered what was accurate in the information the creators had shared, and what was seemingly propaganda.

He'd been told, over and over through system messages, data leaks, and from the literal mouth of the Erlking, that humanity was an experiment that had rebelled against its creators.

That made a certain level of sense, and that once the first generation had rebelled, that the second generation was abandoned here? Well, it was short-sighted. Steve would have simply eliminated the threat personally, rather than leave it to eventually rise again, but it was understandable.

Now, though, knowing that there had once been legions of Devourers? And that whoever had interfered with the system to send that message—as it'd been different from the regular messages received from the system—viewed humanity as an ancient enemy?

It didn't fit. Either humanity was an experiment abandoned, the first generation of which had launched a full-scale war against all the galaxy seemingly, or…

Or it was once a far greater group. One that wasn't restricted to a single group of first-generation warriors, but entire legions. Ones that had been around long enough to be identified as "the ancient enemy."

Steve was left troubled, both by the revelations and by the new abilities he'd unlocked. He discovered the ability to simply burrow his way through his enemies, the coating over his still-regenerating armor literally devouring any living thing it touched and feeding him its constituent parts.

Steve and the others gained a significant number of nanites, and Steve spent more of his points, believing that even after he'd lost access to the sub-mind he'd set up before—when he'd lost access to his armor, it'd compressed down into him—he should be able to use the War tree at least.

The first of his upgrades worked well, but, buoyed up by the knowledge of his success, he invested in unlocking another ability: a nanite Tsunami conversion wave that was linked to far more than he expected at first, rendering himself catatonic. He spent most of the nanites he'd gained in the fights until now on recreating the basic version of his helmet and decompressing the Hack sub-mind into it, followed by a more basic version of a sub-mind for the Support tree as well.

Ingrid and the rest of the team, recognizing that there was nothing they could do for him, agreed to leave him behind, protected by a defensive creation of Belle's own design. Two sentinels they'd brought with them to protect the group, when and if they needed to sleep, were set up to watch over him.

When Steve regained consciousness, it was to nearby fighting and distant screams. Realizing the stupidity of his actions and the risk he had put his friends in, he joined them as they fought the Stelek queen and her guardians.

The next several hours passed quickly as Steve entered the fight as Ingrid and the others were pinned down. He used the gravity inverter to give him the gift of flight, and dropped off the sentinels to snipe at the enemy, before taking the airborne versions of the Stelek down.

The queen was killed, as were most of the hive. But at the end of the fight, they were warned by the system messages they received, and the new quest tag, that when the old queen had sensed the threat roaming the halls, she released her daughter.

With the Stelek, only a single queen could rule, and although old and weary, the queen was driven by biological demands to drive her daughter from the hive, a small number of guardians dutifully left with her.

Steve and the group harvested the dead, planning to advance and chase down the infant queen, when they received word that the sunken ship was under attack.

Returning as quickly as they could to the surface, they found that Dimi was on his way back to meet them. Already on the ragged edge from so many hours of flying, unsupported, he was barely able to keep on course, and the group made the decision to spend their nanites and points on developing their armor for flight.

A short time was spent learning to fly, aided heavily by very low-level RI—restricted intelligences—implanted into the power cores that Steve created for each of the group.

They extended their wings, and with Ingrid supporting Steve, he reached out and formed gravity bubbles around the others, helping them to fly. They were practically carried by him for great distances, before Dimi reached them, looping around and lowering the rear hatch.

The group landed aboard the plane, being practically thrown in by Steve, and they rested for a short time, with Jonas sent to assist Dimi as a second pilot.

The ship had been attacked from both ends, close to the shore, by a mixed group of lycans, werecats, and vampires, and at the other end, much deeper in the ocean, by a pair of the horrific Xi-Ma.

Two of the Xi-Ma, huge creatures that were the inspiration for the legends of giants and once the protectors of the ancient pharaohs of Egypt, had boarded the ship, aided by the security AI.

As they continued through the deeper sections of the ship, being led on a chase by sentinels that Zac had created and sent off, a small handful of enemy sentinels and custodians followed behind them, claiming sections of the ship that hadn't been fully secured.

Steve boarded the ship at the deeper point close to the Xi-Ma, but the others, not having their diving gear, nor any ability to breathe underwater, nor protection from the crushing depth, instead boarded the ship from closer to the land, reinforcing Ingrid's father Anders and the small security contingent that he'd gathered and flown in.

They took the boarding team of lycans and more from behind; the advanced weaponry and loyal sentinels that Zac had been producing made the difference in the fight.

Paul and Courtney, on the other hand, had been using their weapons and years of teamwork to slow the Xi-Ma as much as possible.

The Xi-Ma, though, were so saturated with nanites, that their wounds, including direct hits to an eyeball, simply healed over in seconds.

By the time Steve reached the fight, at around the halfway mark of the ship, Paul and Courtney had been forced back again and again, and the ship had been badly mauled by both their tridents and a high-powered energy scream attack that the Xi-Ma could unleash.

Steve, discovering that the pair were almost invulnerable due to their sheer mass of nanites, set about to steadily drain them, hacking and slashing, tearing hundreds free with each blow, but being beaten and battered in the process.

The tide of battle turned when Scylla and the team reached the fight, and heavier and specialist weapons were brought in. Ingrid's battle net ability helped to grant the combatants additional awareness of one another and the spaces around them.

Scylla managed to drive her spear through an unprotected underarm, one of the few unarmored sections of the Xi-Ma, and pierced its heart, killing one of them and sending the second into a furious counterattack.

Steve's Tsunami nanites surprise, injected earlier into one of the Xi-Ma's throats, enabled him to take control of the local muscle groups, as more and more of the nanites in the creature converted to attuned to Steve and Steve alone.

As the Xi-Ma attempted to use its energy shriek attack, Steve triggered the muscles and slammed its jaw shut, locking the lips closed, and the attack instead detonated its skull.

The death of the Xi-Ma ended the majority of the fight. The last of the secondary group, a vampire who had been hiding, attacked, thinking to use Paul as a combination of human shield and snack.

He was, however, unaware that Paul wielded both upgraded, cutting-edge weapons, and was an ex-Marine. It ended badly for the vamp.

When the battle had entirely settled down, Steve and the group took the time to dig the security AI out. Steve, now able to use his Hack ability again without fear, and having nanites to spare to form a physical bridge, directly hacked the security AI, forcing it to shift its loyalty to him, and discovered that things weren't as simple as they'd believed.

The AI had received a response when it requested help, and that was why it'd changed from the previous path of careful management of the resources it had access to, to rebuilding the factories and stripping the rest of the ship to create new sentinels.

The response came from one of the creators—not the Erlking, but one of the other two, and they'd been the one to name Steve "Devourer."

They had ordered the AI to strip the ship and make an army of sentinels, to destroy its playthings that even now ran amok.

The second of the creators was awakening, aware, and filled with hatred…hatred for the entire human race, and every single one of its offshoots.

Steve might not have gone looking for a war, but he knew instinctively he'd found one.

ARISE DEVOURER SYNOPSIS

Steve and the team have won the fight, but he's now started to realize just how many enemies he has—and that they're not only legion, they're also more powerful than he and his allies.

His greatest strength, however, was also his greatest weakness—the animal within.

Steve had felt it coming out many times over the last few years, and mostly it's been to his great advantage, enabling him to win despite the odds. But now, as the stakes grow higher, he's realized that he'll need that fury more than ever.

Steve admitted his fear to Anders, that he will give in to the rage that fills him, and that he may not regain control before he's made a fatal mistake, only to be stunned as Anders conceded to knowing it as well.

Anders explained his own past, and that he, too, let the beast within loose on more than one occasion. In Anders's situation, rather than a furious rage and willingness to die to win, it was a willingness to risk the lives and property of others to enable himself to climb the ranks higher.

The pair recognized that the rage and the desire they both felt were sides of the same coin: the beast within that all carry. Anders proving that mastery was possible gave Steve hope, though, and he thanked him, summoning his council together to discuss and plan their next step.

The next of the group to be "ascended" from the base stock of humanity to the next level were decided to be Corey and Joseph, the engineers, Paul and Courtney from Jonas's old team, and Oxus, the Minotaur.

Laia, formerly Athena's megayacht chief steward, was pointed out to still be suffering from issues related to her recovery, and due to the tremendous pain that engendered, there was a minor but growing concern over an addiction to medication. She was selected for ascension, as was Ronai the Oracan, his argument that he'd fight for or against Steve happily any day of the week being a valid one.

Lastly, James and Lars were selected—James so that he could essentially work even harder, and along with Lars, would be visiting extremely dangerous locations.

That the ascended could literally come back from the dead changed everything when it came to taking them to places that were dangerous, in Steve's mind.

Facility #6B and its now exposed location was dealt with next. The attack on it had been led by the Xi-Ma, with the attendant vamps, etc., supplementing it. Although it'd been carried out at the orders of another of the creators, it'd been overt enough that human witnesses had seen that something was going on.

Social media was flooded with shaky stills and camera feeds showing both them using the entrance to the ship, and Anders and his reinforcements streaming into the sea to access the ship behind them.

The decision was made that the cover story—a movie being shot in the area—wouldn't last long, and so, due to the condition of the facility, Steve decided, and convinced the others to go along with it, to destroy the ship.

The only actually intact systems, he pointed out, were those that were already under their control and were best off being moved to a secure location, or were in serious need of upgrades and repairs.

As that involved replacing them entirely with new versions, all that was left was the outer hull of the ship.

Rather than allow anyone else access to such technology, even broken as it was, Steve made the argument that converting it all to null blocks was a faster and entirely reasonable way to deal with it. They agreed to leave the shell of the ship there, and to build a supposed rocky outcropping around the small sections that Zac wanted to keep.

The resultant image was simply that another section of the ship was destroyed on impact, leaving part of the rocky seabed exposed.

Everything else was to be stripped out by massive constructors, ones that would then transport the null blocks, etc., to a heavily damaged oil tanker that Freja will have sailed into position over the ship.

That oil tanker—the *Pacific Princess*—was badly damaged by eco-terrorists earlier in the year, and had been languishing at anchor nearby as the parent company tried to offload it. Laia was picked to take over its management—and along with Joseph aboard it, and Zac and the others helping remotely—to convert the oil tanker into a floating dockyard.

The megayacht, formerly owned by Athena, was to be sailed to meet up with the oil tanker, and Zac had been given a week to oversee—with Joseph and Laia's help—its conversion into a heavily armed and armored new form.

While they're doing that, Steve and his team—Ingrid, Jonas, Scylla, and Belle—planned to assault the Xi-Ma's home, intending to try to take down the creator before it recovered from its hibernation fully.

Before that, though, the team spend their accrued nanites and points, mainly investing in new armor for them all. And as part of the process, Steve and Ingrid discovered that it was possible to "cheat" the system.

Essentially, if two people were linked together, one of those people could spend double the points and unlock an additional section of their skill tree.

If it would cost an engineer a single point to unlock the basic construction systems, then they could instead spend two and unlock it for another as well. Although that was a waste for one engineer, the other would get an artificial boost to unlock higher tech, as they only needed to spend their points on unlocking data further down the line.

Steve unlocked upgrades to his biological weapons facility and RIs, regretting that because it required an enormous amount of programming before it'd be viable. War tree upgrades were unlocked as well, first in Unarmed and then in Force, increasing the force he could deliver on impact. Finally, two more were invested in unlocking the mk4 gravity gradient cannon, or GGC as he christened it.

That left two more points to save, knowing that he needed a minimum of four points to unlock the ability to join the biological weapons systems with the GGC.

Arise: Conqueror

When that was done? He'd become an unholy terror to his enemies. More so than he already was. For now, though, those points were kept as a reserve, in case he desperately needed something further down the line.

When that was done, Steve headed to Heraklion—arranging to meet Hans to discuss the Elder situation after this—and searched for the local governmental officials. Most of the local Greek infrastructure, unfortunately, was so byzantine and complicated that he eventually gave up, storming out of the local offices to find a coffee shop, calling Ingrid and getting her to help remotely as he searched the area, tracking down the local leadership.

While doing so, he became aware of a team shadowing him; he judged them to be local security, essentially tracking him for the Greek government. He decided to ignore them until he'd completed his current mission: warning the Greeks to stay well clear of the sunken ship until he was done with it, and getting the oil tanker moving.

He eventually found that, despite the posted details, the local secretary general, the de facto ruler of Crete, was not currently away at an all-important conference.

He was instead busily railing his secretary in the very building where Steve had first gone looking for him. Steve kicked the door in and threatened the man, making it clear that if he did as he was told, he'd live, and even cured his lung cancer in the process. He ordered that everyone be kept clear of the sunken ship's location until he was done, on pain of death, and that "one of his servants" would be in touch to sort out the oil tanker.

That was as far as he got before being attacked by an unknown Arisen.

This one, rather than the local security, who were almost laughably ineffectual thanks to his nanites' armor, used first a regular assault rifle to get his attention, and then switched to a much more powerful and advanced weapon.

Steve was shot and injured, and the figure held up a tube, making sure he saw it, before vanishing. Before he could recover the tube and chase them, he was attacked by three more Arisen, although of lesser power.

Steve killed two of the team of three, draining them and making it clear to the dying third member that they would never rise again. The third, terrified, explained that they were sent as a warning by the Elders.

Steve had asked for a month, and they had agreed, but Steve never specified the calendar in use. The Elders and their group, being many thousands of years old, used a base twenty-nine-day month, and Steve had expected them to understand he meant a thirty-one-day month.

A common, and understandable mistake to make, perhaps, but in agreeing to the timescale, and then not attending, he was marked as an Oathbreaker, and this, an assault that would have killed any other Arisen outright, was the first warning.

Steve stripped the nanites from the two dead, and most of the nanites from the third member as an example, then dumped the body, taking the message cylinder and leaving to meet up with Hans.

Steve received a new quest to learn to split his focus, enabling a more efficient control over his Hack or Support systems, and chose the Support path, before losing the connection, leaving him in a foul mood when he reached Hans.

On arrival, Hans was furious over what he saw as Steve's failures, but over the course of the discussion, he returned to Steve's side, and agreed to go to the recycling plant, to protect the rest of the group while Steve completed one last mission, before heading to the Elders.

Steve led his team to the location he'd last seen the Xi-Ma, and after a long trek through the underground caverns and catacombs, he found that the area had been sealed off.

The blocks used were too large for him and his team to break through or move, and he was forced to accept what that meant.

Steve and the team arranged for converters to be set up in the passage, chewing through the blocks, to create a weapons emplacement, planning for whatever could be on the far aside, before reaching out to the recycling plant. Unfortunately, the first thing they found out was that Hans, in an attempt to be helpful, had invited his own sponsor, Petros, to the recycling plant to assist.

Petros admitted on the call to Steve that he had ulterior motives, mainly that he wanted help to find and recover his own sponsor, whose body had been "locked" away and disposed of in the ocean long ago.

Steve and the team, not sure they could rely on Hans, let alone this unknown Petros, were forced to separate, with Ingrid and the rest of the team going to the plant, while Jonas and Steve—flown by Dimi—instead headed off to the Elders' base in the mountains of Tibet.

On arrival, Steve and Jonas were separated from Dimi, who was escorted to a special accommodation area for humans. Their guide, Matthias, took them to the valley, passing through miles-long hangars and airfields, demonstrating that without the permission they had granted Steve and the others to land, there would be no chance they could have survived to assault the sheltered location.

More heavily armed fighters and drones were seen, ready for flight, many times more than either Steve or Jonas had ever seen before. Hints were dropped that this was only one such facility, and that the valley was nigh on impregnable.

Shortly after arrival, Steve found that not only did he have no signal—having planned to share the view from the apartment he and Jonas were assigned with Ingrid—but after a few tests, he figured out that the signals were being actively suppressed.

Spending the last two points he'd been planning to save, Steve unlocked Escape and Illusion, enabling him to create a life-size simulacrum of himself, positioning it on the couch and, with Jonas's help, making it look like he was simply being grumpy and not talking, when instead he used his Conceal ability to sneak out and explore.

Finding a local human's home after a short while, Steve hacked a baby monitor, quietly pleased that the community here didn't make everything "in house" and instead brought in supplies, including that device, which gave him unfettered access to the local network, after a little work.

Returning to Jonas, he contacted Ingrid, being reassured that the recycling center and their people were safe, for the time being, before resting.

The next day, Matthias offered to show them around the valley, enabling them to meet the local people and to study in the "lesser" libraries. After a confrontation, Steve forced the guide's hand, and when he made to leave the valley, Matthias agreed to contact his superiors.

Instead of spending several more days being forced to wait, as the Elders made their position as the more powerful of the two groups clear, Steve and Jonas were fast-tracked through to the Great Refuge, and on the way, were told more of the true history of the world, as seen by the Elders and their servants.

After Matthias realized he wouldn't be permitted to learn any of Steve's secrets, he stormed off in a mood, leaving Steve and Jonas in the car with the driver of their car, who in turn subjected Steve to one of the most vicious auditory assaults known to man…J-Pop.

Steve and Jonas were greeted at the entrance to the Great Refuge by Timurlan, a much higher-placed guide. He explained that the Elders—those the outside world simply call the Old Ones—were working on something and would summon Steve and Jonas later.

It was explained that no slight was intended, it was simply that they were busy. Instead, the pair were led to the lower-grade artifacts, the guide expecting to overawe them with the ancient and unidentifiable artifacts of the deep past.

The first of the intact artifacts was identified as a gravitational construction device, and when Steve—after agreeing to share the information he had—explained the information he had on it, it changed the dynamic.

Steve and Jonas, after explaining the grim reality of the world to their guide, continued to explore, examining the grade-five to grade-two artifacts, being diverted and prevented from access to the grade-one level.

They were told that the grading system was based partly on use and response, and that something that was still usable, or had been in recent history, was classed as a higher grade than something that was not.

Eventually, Steve and Jonas were brought before the Elders themselves, and a battle of wills commenced as they tried to read him, and he in turn examined them.

A truce was agreed, and through a device installed in the hall of the Elders—the Nordicassian Linkage—they and Steve joined mentally. For the next several hours, they each read the other's memories, seeing the truth of each other's experiences and knowing beyond all reasonable doubt that they could trust one another.

A deal was brokered: Steve would use the medical suites to unlock the nanites of the Elders, and only the Elders, for now, but they would give twenty percent of their nanites to Steve in exchange, to ascend his own people.

The remaining eighty percent, just as Scylla's had been, would be stripped from the Elders and retained in the medical suites. They would then be available for the medical suites to use to bring back the long-dead Arisen who were destroyed.

Astorian, the Speaker, was strangely unhappy about the deal, but the others were ecstatic. The negotiations were fortunately a lot quicker and easier than expected, thanks to the device that allowed mind-to-mind linking, eliminating the usual bargaining positions.

Steve was given basic access to the rest of the refuge, and proceeded to search out the old power systems—including tracking down hidden weapons emplacements—aided by Ingrid, who now had remote access, via Steve, into the system.

After significant exploration and mapping out of the local surviving technical systems, Steve had Ingrid confirm with Hans and Petros that the Elders had spread the word that they were officially off-limits to anyone who doesn't want to defy the Elders.

In the end, Ingrid, Scylla, Belle, and Oxus set off from the recycling facility—Dimi returning to collect them—and they were bringing some custodians with them to assist in the reworking needed.

Steve found the security RI for the facility, and assumed control of #4A, discovering in the process that this facility was the original production site for the various strains of humanity.

Although it was heavily damaged, it still had massive potential, especially as a base for the Arisen. Steve decided to push toward a full alliance with them, while also maintaining control over the facility until such a time as he felt comfortable relinquishing it, just in case.

As part of gaining control, Steve found the training facilities that humanity and its various sub-races were designed to use. Although they were trashed from long ages of inactivity, they were also innovative and could be easily reproduced.

Steve made a report to the Elders, making them aware that the facility that they'd lived in for millennia was in fact far larger than they knew, and that behind certain sections of walls lay entirely unexplored—by them—areas.

These sections were heavily damaged, and where most were lost to the gradual onslaught of nature and time, some were still intact, and could be repaired.

The power facilities were found to have originally been geothermal, with the power plant having been a short-term measure to keep the facility running while geothermal and solar systems were put in place.

The geo systems, unfortunately, had long since failed and become heavily irradiated, marking those entire sections of the facility as unusable.

Steve made the decision, and recommended to the Elders, that the best method of moving forward was to build an entirely new power plant, and use that to provide power for the short-term, then create a series of smaller factories, including one that would create custodians.

Artorian spotted the flaw in this plan, in that the custodians and any new systems that Steve developed here, in the heart of the Elders' seat of power, would be controllable by Steve alone, and insisted on a local control facility being created as the first step.

Unfortunately, Artorian convinced the Elders that was the priority, and that any custodians that Steve's companions brought must also be slaved to that control facility before they were allowed into the valley.

Steve argued, but eventually agreed that he could understand their perspective, and consented to create a full control system before Ingrid and the others arrived. The main problem with this was that it required Steve to use up most of the attuned nanites he had to create the required systems.

Arise: Conqueror

Steve and Jonas spent the next several hours working in the bowels of the ancient refuge, repairing systems where possible and building a small factory unit, as well as a controller system to enable the Elders to use the factory.

Steve was nearly finished with this, when he was interrupted by a draconid demanding he present himself to explain something that was unclear. Annoyed, Steve forced himself to comply, and when he was eventually brought to Artorian, deep in the hidden forest at the heart of the refuge, he was attacked.

Artorian, it turned out, was well aware that the return of the Elders to mobility and action would essentially remove the need for his role, and his own power would be massively reduced.

Rather than accept this, he planned to kill Steve and the Elders, and frame him as an assassin—twisting the narrative to prove that the outside world could not be trusted—and ruling in the Elders' place while they recover. Then he planned to "discover" that Steve's abilities meant that the Elders would not recover, at which point, he would already be ruling, leaving no reason for further dissent.

Steve fought the draconids, and Artorian, seeming to see his plan failing, fled, ordering the guards to defend the Elders, as he hides with them.

Steve gave chase, killing many of the draconids and some of the local guards in the fight, before he broke into the Elders' chambers. Artorian laughed that Steve, in his mad rampage to catch him, had provided all the evidence the twisted Speaker would ever need.

Artorian executed three of the Elders, murdering them as they lay trapped within their frozen forms.

Steve and he fought, only for Artorian to show that he'd truly planned for all contingencies: not only was he wearing an armored artifact, but he stunned Steve with cleverly placed projectors that were part of the original security system of the refuge.

Steve collapsed in agony, his nanites shutting down and crumbling under the security system's onslaught.

Cybele, the leader of the Elders, managed to force her body into action, bones shattering as she did, and lasted long enough to distract Artorian, before being gravely wounded.

At the same time, the other Elders used their telekinesis to break one of the three projectors, giving Steve a chance to counterattack.

Steve fought Artorian. Part of the way through the fight, Cybele, dying, offered him her nanites, and he drained some of the blood on the floor, before finally defeating Artorian, and against the Elders' demands, killed him.

Jonas and the guards broke in as he drained the corpse of Artorian, covered in blood, and Jonas barely managed to keep the guards from attacking Steve on the spot.

They broke the body free of Steve, and one of the guards used the linkage to speak with the surviving Elders.

They learned that Artorian was the traitor, and that Steve, now drunk on the nanites, had defended them.

Steve recovered, and accessed the linkage, expecting to be feted as a hero by the surviving Elders, only to find that even in this, Artorian had a backup plan.

Knowing that should his rebellion fail, he'd beg for death—and if it worked, he might need more scapegoats—he'd linked explosives to his suit. When he died, the defenses that the Elders had painstakingly built around the valley were robbed of power, and four of the leaders of the Blessed faction, with their forces, landed, attacking and trying to take the Great Refuge.

Artorian had gambled that should his rebellion fail, it was better that the valley fall as well, likely giving him a chance to escape.

Steve and Jonas took some of the defenders of the valley and defended the entrance, with Ingrid, Scylla, and the others arriving as the battle turned, enabling them to kill Zeus and his companions.

The Elders who were killed were inserted into the medical capsules; they were stripped of most of their nanites, and were ascended instead. Anders and Freja were also ascended, one by one.

Over the next several days, the Elders summoned the leaders of both the Blessed and the Accursed factions, as well as eliminating many of the more rabid of their supporters, showing that they were in fact always watching and ready to take action.

Both factions sent a single representative, concerned that they might be feeding that representative into the meat grinder, but in an attempt to broker peace, and a possible alliance with a now resurgent group of Elders…

Only to find that Steve and the rest of his "faction," now named as Gaia's Vengeance, had already formed such an alliance.

The factions attempted to cause issues, to drive a wedge between Steve and the Elders, only to run afoul of the Elders' mind-reading device, the Nordicassian Linkage.

Both factions attempted to manipulate Steve, finding that he holds them both in equal contempt. The representative for the Accursed, Coara, in league with one of the creators, released a nanite bioweapon upon the slowly recovering corpse of Artorian.

Artorian transformed, ripping his way free, reduced to a mindless beast, interested only in feeding, spreading the nanites' infection, and reaching a hidden device below the refuge.

While the creature that had been Artorian freed himself, Coara attempted to eliminate the Elders, only to find that Cybele, now very much awake, aware, and ready for a fight after Artorian's betrayal, took poorly to the attempt.

Steve and Ingrid were awoken by the mental screams and terror of Freja, caught unsuspecting in the corridors by the creature. As they head to her in panic, she was brutally torn limb from limb, and fed upon.

Steve and Ingrid chased the creature that had been Artorian, while Anders, broken by the death of his wife, and Belle, recovered some of her corpse.

The refuge was prepared for such an eventuality, nanite experiments having run amok before in the deep past. Unfortunately, millennia of degradation and cascading failures rendered the local solutions useless, and Steve had to order the custodians to cleanse the area.

Arise: Conqueror

They fell back on an automated routine, constructing specialist equipment and heading to follow the trail of death and destruction. Their nanite suppressors would destroy any nanites in the infected areas, rendering them unable to reconstitute their hosts, including Freja.

Steve ordered Belle to get herself, Anders, and a single fragment of Freja free of the infected area, explaining that it must have absolutely no trace of the infected nanites in the bloody mess, or else Freja would be lost forever.

Belle and Anders managed to escape the cleansing area and secured Freja inside a medical suite, but the limited remaining mass meant that she required a full rebuild from scratch.

While this was happening, Steve, Ingrid, and several others hunted down the corrupted creature that Artorian had become, exploring several buried sections of the facility as they went, and finally defeated it, securing an experimental gravity drive that had been hidden as well.

The Blessed faction were locked away, while the Elders attempted to figure out what happened and purge the remaining traitors in their ranks, the last of Artorian's servants having been involved in the last-ditch coup attempt.

By the time the Blessed were permitted access to their communications again, they found that one of their most secretive facilities was under attack, and as it had happened when they were being held incommunicado, Daversa, their leader, jumped to the conclusion this was some deep plot and refused to explain what was being held there, while simultaneously accusing Steve et al. of using the situation to somehow enrich himself.

Steve, realizing what the attack signifies after questioning the Blessed representative, was furious, the hours lost while what was now clearly a diversion made only worse by Daversa's refusal to explain anything.

Steve and Ingrid had already launched two satellites to try to track the rogue creator, and these were diverted to check out the attack site, while Steve and his people, joined by Cybele and Sanneth, another Elder, gathered their forces and set off.

The site, the island of Yuzhny in northern Russia, was a site that Steve was made aware of by the Erlking, as possibly holding materials that he could use to leave Earth, once his repair and rewilding efforts were complete.

Because of the multiple desperate calls on his time, Steve hadn't started to search the island yet, nor the other sites he suspected held similar troves of artifacts or damaged and abandoned ships.

The rogue creator, however, had launched a full-on assault of the area, eliminating the Blessed's encampment, which was, in turn, being used to try to eliminate the current inhabitants of the ship.

This third species had been there since time immemorial, and when the Blessed found it, they had battled to a standstill. Had the survivors of the Blessed team not retreated with verifiable artifacts, they would most likely have simply bombarded the site with bunker-busting munitions and moved on. But when artifacts were discovered? The potential gain was too great.

The creator's forces attacked the Blessed fortification from the rear, eliminating most of the defenders and driving off the survivors, before pushing ahead and boarding the buried facility, one that was later revealed to be a hidden ship.

The Xi-Ma—forced by their hulking size to crawl through the passages of the ship's hull, and unable to use their most powerful weapons for fear of damaging the ship—were slowed in their assault by sheer numbers.

The delay meant that Steve and his forces arrived in time to assault the Xi-Ma and the other forces of the creator from behind, although many of their own people were badly injured and killed in the fight. They eventually entered the ship, eliminated the remaining enemy forces, and confronted the creator: Varnock.

Varnock the Defiler, leader of the three who were banished here on Earth eons ago for the crime of unleashing humanity on the stars, unleashed the full fury of her presence on the group, forcing them to their knees.

Inbuilt into their nanites were kill codes, contingency plans that attempt to take over and shut down Steve and the others, only to be shut down a split second later, as counter commands were issued, by an unknown third party, the UC.

The UC declared that Varnock the Defiler was stripped of all authority, and named a bounty on her head. In the confusion, as their nanites battled internally and as Varnock regarded them all with disdain and hatred, Steve scented her nanites.

Unlike the forms of others, Varnock and others of her ilk consisted of nanites: nanites in their hundreds of millions restructured to form them in their entirety.

That sheer density, the unrelenting sense of the insane sheer mass of nanites within his reach, drove the Devourer into wakefulness. Knowing that this was a battle he needed every edge for, instead of fighting with it, Steve reveled in it and released the beast inside.

The Devourer rose, the most primal aspects of who and what Steve was coming to the fore; while the others cowered, confused, he attacked.

The fight was short and brutal. The field of confusion and hero-worship that was projected by Varnock faltered as she fought, and the others quickly took the opportunity to join the fight.

Varnock—after the fight turned against her and Steve's form morphed, his jaws extending as he began to feed on her—shifted, and a much less impressive form burst free of the main body.

In her pain and panic, she reverted to an earlier form, a vestigial one of her species, and as she ran…she ran headfirst into Sanneth's boot.

Kicked backward, she screamed in outrage, furious that one of her lowly creations dared to attack her, only to meet one of the weapons that the Elders had brought, this time wielded by Ingrid, who in righteous anger over what happened to her mother, killed one of the creators of her species.

Recovering from the battle, Steve and Ingrid, identified as the leaders of the raid, were given notifications from the UC, or United Confederation, identifying that not only were they "out there" still, and apparently paying close attention, but they were also well aware that the Ændari Council were as well.

Steve and Ingrid were informed that the Ændari had demanded their heads for killing a member of their race, and the only reason that the UC wasn't sharing what appeared to be clear knowledge of the location of Earth was that they, too, had an interest in the Devourer and his companions.

Hints were dropped that they wished to recruit them, and a demand was issued: either Steve and his party present themselves at a set of galactic coordinates in five solar cycles, or the limited protections that Steve—and Earth—currently enjoyed would be revoked.

The final communication from the UC brought even more confusion, as they advised that they'd now remove the security lockouts on the vessel, making it clear that unlike the rest of the ships and facilities scattered across Earth, this ship, that the companions were currently inside of, wasn't in fact an Ændari one.

Jez Cajiao

ARISE EXPLORER SYNOPSIS

Steve and his close-knit team had survived the fight with Varnock the Defiler, cleansing the ancient ship and indeed the world of her corrupting presence.

The ship that she had been so desperate to capture was revealed to not only be mainly intact—the AI core had refused her access and she had destroyed it in a fit of rage—but NOT an Ændari vessel.

After investigating the ship and doing their best to clean it of the funk of more than forty thousand years, both an armory and storage areas were discovered to have been looted. On checking out the tracks, the team found a concealed entrance to the ship that led out into a hidden and submerged cave.

Steve followed the tracks through several passages and out to the wider ocean, before returning, having learned that indeed someone not only knew about the ship's existence, but had both the technology and the knowledge to exploit it.

The team argued over the best course of action, having been given a highly limited timescale to meet representatives of the United Confederation. The UC had extended five days' grace before the meeting and offered to unlock the very ship that the team were aboard, making it easy for them to make the rendezvous.

Unfortunately, unknown to the UC, the ship was long buried, and although they might have sent authorization to unlock the AI for Steve and his allies' use…Varnock had destroyed it.

Zac pointed out that even if they could uncover the ship entirely in enough time to launch it and travel to the meeting, the ship was unlikely to be capable of interstellar travel after all this time.

Most importantly, without access to the AI, the coordinates to the meeting were meaningless.

The eventual decision was made to locate the original crew of the ship. Someone, after all, had to know about it and had been there recently enough that there was evidence of their existence.

After much consideration, it was decided that all clues pointed to Atlantis, and with that in mind, they questioned their ancient allies, Cybele and Sanneth.

Sanneth admitted to having been fascinated by the myths in his past, and to having tracked them to a location in the Azores, though due to the technology of the time and his rapidly deteriorating body, he was unable to explore the depths of the ocean and confirm his suspicions.

The team set off, and as Ingrid, Jonas, Scylla, and Steve dove into the depths, they were quickly hunted down and attacked by the last of the guardians of Atlantis to maintain its patrol.

Arise: Conqueror

The remains of the ancient sunken city were badly damaged during the fight, and when the guardian believed it had driven off or defeated Steve, it immediately headed home to report in.

Steve, attached to the hull, led the others, while examining the guardian, and shared that—as they had suspected, due to its lifetime, form, and weaponry—it was a construct, not a living creature.

The leviathan unknowingly guided Steve and his companions deep into lost caves miles below the surface, and far out to sea. Finally, after many hours of travelling, the leviathan settled into a docking cradle, entering standby, as Steve and his team explored the area.

At the bottom of another set of caves, a hidden habitat was revealed, ancient and oft-repaired, and the surviving members of the original ship's crew were discovered.

After much discussion and arguing, the crew shared their story, explaining that they were dispatched to watch over Varnock and her companions. After several centuries of observation, the crew settled into new lives, with a reduced watch due to the Erlking's apparent compliance, and Varnock having entered hibernation.

The third and final member of the trio was Tiamak, known colloquially as the Sculptor, and it was she who created Atlantis, guiding her creations in growing a sophisticated and civilized society.

After she became aware of the observers, she and one of their number, despite their positions, eventually fell in love and had children. The pair spent long years exploring Earth and delighting in each other's company, while the observation team essentially retired: two at a time maintained the watch and the others relaxed, having their own families and enjoying, for the first time, "real" lives.

That crashed to an end when one of their number, frustrated with his long centuries of isolation and stagnation, attacked his companion and claimed rulership of Atlantis.

When the pair returned, they found the city had devolved into anarchy, their own children had been put to the sword, and the once peaceful city-state had become an all-conquering tyrant state.

Diamos, the ship's navigator and Tiamak's lover, convinced her to wait, to trust him, and he attempted to find the other retired observers to do battle.

Instead, Tiamak, in a fit of rage and loss, had only placated her lover. As soon as he was gone, she used the ultimate weapon that she had designed, integrating its form with her own.

The hybrid creature destroyed Atlantis in a night and a day, driving the survivors to flee. When Diamos and the others returned, Tiamak fled, burying herself in the depths of the ocean, where they lulled her to dormancy.

The group had been there ever since, working to maintain the slumber of a creature now grown so impossibly large that even buried as she was, below the ocean, that should she wake and rise to the surface, the world as it existed today would be destroyed.

The leader of the small team of observers agreed that should the Ændari discover Earth and scan its depths, they would find Tiamak and disturb her rest, compounding their failure.

After much discussion, it was agreed that Steve and his team would hunt down and eliminate the surviving and faulty guardians, the last of Atlantis's ancient war machines, driven mad by the long ages and unable to carry out their duties.

In return, Diamos would provide the navigation data they required, but they would also need to provide a memory core to store the basic navigational memories.

Steve and his team travelled to Scotland to fight the first and nearest of these creations, a plesiosaur variant known locally as Nessie, and upon defeating it—barely—they realized that the time required to hunt all four down would mean they would miss the deadline for the meeting.

The observers reluctantly agreed to share the data now, along with the agreement that Cybele and Sanneth lead the hunt for the remaining three creatures.

Zac had adjusted and rebuilt the megayacht for what seemed the hundredth time after Steve changed his mind again. Although Zac was furious about this, the hull and systems were ready, and he agreed that using the already enclosed systems just made sense.

He attached the gravity drive to the bastardized megayacht/spaceship and set off to meet Steve, only to have the UN flex their muscles and open fire on him, in an attempt to show Steve that they were not afraid of him.

The resulting fight was short-lived, though vicious, and the UN panicked before surrendering.

The damage done to the ship slowed them sufficiently that after basic space trials, the group were late to the meeting, though only just.

Field Commander Aaronis Balthazar, their contact aboard the warship waiting for them, was a UC soldier. After he and his First Fist Leshan (roughly a high NCO role) met the group, they decided that conveying them to the nearest Forgeship was the best decision.

As they had some time before the Forgeship rendezvous, they agreed to show Steve and his group to a nearby moon, where they'd be able to harvest resources.

This was both because of the condition of the little ship that the group arrived in—the engines were highly damaged and were cut away by the warship—and because the UC soldiers wanted to test them.

The moon was in one of many systems that had been forbidden to all but the UC soldiers due to nanite contamination. The UC soldiers' armor provided the much-needed protection against such things, though the armor was in highly limited supply, as were soldiers capable of using it.

On exploring the moon, Steve and his group discovered that the corrupt—beings that have been taken over by their nanites, and reduced to a zombie-like state of desperate need to feed on viable nanites to fuel their recovery—were driven into a frenzy by the nearby "live" and attuned nanites that the group possessed.

Steve noticed that the corrupt were easily cleansed and wiped; a simple blockchain failure in the nanites created the issue. Quickly and quietly, pretending to fail in wiping a captured corrupt, he deployed the wiped and viable nanites, dumping them with orders to wait until he and the others have left, then begin wiping and reconfiguring all they can reach.

He included a basic command to create the facilities needed, then to build a ship as a "just in case" measure, granting Zac and a few others of his close team the right to adjust the design and take command if need be.

The group ended up aboard the UC vessel, being hosted—and subtly questioned—before finally making it to the local Forgeship.

The Forgeships are well named, they discover. Although badly damaged and ancient, they were once the heart of the UC's fleet, capable of ingesting entire asteroids and churning out viable, complete starships from their enormous makers.

Upon meeting with the local council representatives of the UC—Shanah, a saurian being; Clicqo, a four-figured gestalt entity; and Emberalis, from the Right Hand of Man—they were brought up to date on the current situation in the sector and those around it.

The discovery that a nanite plague, designed and released by unknown forces but believed to be the Ændari in the distant past, explained why Earth was left to languish in forgotten squalor.

The nanite plague not only reset the nanites connected to each user, rendering them inert or damaging them, they also erased the memories of almost all infected.

Billions awoke to find their past gone, struggling to feed themselves as entire fleets of ships vanished into deep space, their crews unable to guide or maintain them.

The vast majority of beings died in those early days, either from starvation, weakness and confusion, or from accidents. The Forgeships took more damage from their escorting fleets crashing into them than had ever been done by the enemy.

The Ændari were similarly afflicted, and the general consensus—though they denied it—was that they had created the plague as a biological weapon, and it was accidentally deployed.

The location of Earth and other important sites, already closely guarded, were lost, and only referred to obliquely and through partially recovered data.

That the nanite plague damaged all crystalline and biological memory units, both designed and organically grown, was pointed to as evidence that it was an intentional plague, and not a naturally occurring one.

The explanation of the past and local events was cut short by the arrival of the nearby Ændari ambassador and a significant portion of his sector fleet.

Rather than start a likely war by refusing the ambassador access, the trio agreed to his demands for access to the Earth contingent, and counseled Steve to say nothing. It was decided that Steve and Ingrid would play the part of bounty hunters, given that Varnock had a bounty on her head, should she ever leave Earth.

Steve and Ingrid agreed and adjusted their armor to appear more slipshod, mismatching and battered.

In the course of the Ændari ambassador's threats and demands, Steve claimed to be an independent hunter, but that he discovered Varnock in deep space, and that Earth and all its stored secrets were offered to him as a bribe in a last-ditch attempt to escape.

That started a bidding war for the data, which cumulated in the Ændari—who Steve had named Francine, to annoy them—attacking Steve.

In the process of the fight, Steve was revealed to be a Devourer, and he and Ingrid pretended that the Devourer condition was gained through an interaction with Varnock. The pair made it seem that it was her fault, and something that could be replicated, should either the UC or Ændari get her research.

Steve sold the data to both sides, at Clicqo's request, to prevent an immediate escalation to war, with Steve charging the Ændari, in addition to credits, his right hand and right horn.

This was done partly to shame the Ændari ambassador, but mostly because Steve was hungry and could sense the nanites before him and wanted to punish him for the attack, beyond killing his guards.

The Ændari fled the sector with the data—helpfully forged by Ingrid and the team while Steve bargained—and the group received from the UC side (albeit more as a bribe, as they knew the data wasn't real) a warship of their own and some more credits.

Steve and the others decided to repair the warship—it was a damaged model—and visit a local independent system.

Upon repairing and upgrading the ship at the independent starbase, the team recruited two more members, Benat and Malthus, a pair of devilkin mercenaries, and discovered a senagra infestation.

The senagra were explained to be a hive mind, spiderlike species that exceled in remaining hidden, then infecting people around their hive. The larval stage of their growth enabled them to puppet unwitting victims around to spread their infection.

The starbase was damaged as Steve and the team eliminated the infection. In the process of this, they took ownership of the shipyard that was carrying out the repair work on their ship.

Ingrid and Steve agreed to transfer ownership of the yard to the devilkin, provided all their repairs and upgrades were carried out first and they maintained a stake in it.

As such, the local devilkin populace became more or less allies to the team, who continued onto the Universal System Quadrant Node.

This was their only realistic option, as Steve had recently discovered that his nanites' higher functions, the quest system, the upgrades, and skill trees had all been disabled by attacking Varnock as he did.

Arise: Conqueror

She was unable to shut down the systems of others, being too busy fighting by then, but her revenge against him was significant. The UC soldiers on Earth had recommended that the quadrant council would be able to remove the "war crime" marker that he had been marked with and reactivate his systems. But due to the nanite plague—which was after their deployment to Earth, and therefore unknown to them—the council had lost the capability.

On arrival at the Scorpio system, to reach the node, they discovered that the recent warning from the Ændari about them taking ownership of the node "soon" was a cover.

The Ændari were already in the Scorpio system, and had blockaded it, placing ships at the Lagrange point and opening fire on any vessel that entered the system.

Steve was rendered unconscious in the final fight for the space station and awoke to find the ship under fire. In the process of helping Zac carry out repairs, they managed to drive off the attacking vessels, but could not call to the UC—or anyone—for aid.

They managed to board the system node after a running fight, but the Ændari had also driven the local inhabitants and visitors to the node from it, injuring many who had escaped aboard desperately overloaded and overcrowded ships.

Steve, Ingrid, Scylla, Jonas, and Belle were joined by Paul, Courtney, Malthus, and Benat, and they assaulted the node, while James took the warship and the remaining crew to help the injured.

The node had fallen to the Ændari, and while they too were locked out of the secure internal sections, they had basic access to the dock and entrance areas.

The node had been colonized by various groups, all convinced that they and they alone deserved access to it, and that on the other side of the impenetrable door lay the secrets of the galaxy.

Churches and other parasitical creations had sprung up to prey on the lost and deluded who visited, creating temporary shelters and hundreds of buildings.

When James dropped the team on the node, knowing from the escaping civilians that the Ændari had boarded in large numbers and massacred any who failed to flee fast enough, he opened fire with the ship's weapons into the massed buildings.

With the beachhead cleared, the team assaulted the node, killing the small Ændari force that held it, but not before an Ændari nanite disruptor weapon was used on Steve.

Steadily losing the last of his control over his nanites, Steve shared access with Ingrid through her mind, creating a bridge to question the AI controller of the node.

The AI accepted their access request, having desperate repair needs of its own. But as Ingrid released Steve from her mind, it decided it was fooled, and the request was invalid.

The group hurried through the open doors before they could be sealed; in response, the AI released some of its stores of another failed BWV, an earlier Ændari attempt that were known as the terminators.

Upon appealing to the AI, a middle ground was struck: If Steve and the others could fight their way to the control room and eliminate the terminators, then it would evaluate Steve directly. Should he pass the evaluation, it would reboot and activate his nanites; should he fail, then their death would serve as a reminder to any other trespassers.

The group fought their way through the node, being forced to go level by level and eliminate the enemy, before finally facing the remaining infestation and its leaders.

Steve was installed into the command facilities and studied, with long sections of his past revealed and examined, as the AI evaluated him.

In the end, it accepted his authority, partly as one of the only surviving nanite users who had unlocked their systems, and partly because the Erlking had long ago bequeathed him its authority.

When Steve left the command access point, he was horrified to discover that the memories that had been read and evaluated by the AI were shared on the walls nearby for all his companions to view as well.

Instead of them laughing at his naivety as a child, and his brutality as an adult, they were horrified by the past that shaped him, and demanded the right of redress against his parents. When Steve attempted to pass it off as not being worth it, the group refused, and he decided to leave them to enforce it as they desired.

The Ændari landed a stealth ship at the node. The activation and unlocking of the node meant that they, too, would be able to take control now, should they reach the control center, and a fight ensued for possession of the most precious location in the sector.

Should the Ændari gain control, their plan was revealed to be the elimination of all nanites in the sector. They intended to raid Earth, capture and convert any BWVs they could from the population, then flee, triggering a wipe that would eliminate all nanite users in range, or at least horrifically weaken them.

Then they would return and enact genocide against their now weakened rivals.

Steve and the others battled the Ændari troopers and their hybrid forces, eventually boarding the enemy ship and attempting to capture it.

In the process of taking control, the Ændari leadership aboard triggered the ship's reactors to go into meltdown, with the intention that it would either cover their retreat, or should they die, then they'd take the rest of the node and anything nearby with them.

In a last-ditch attempt to save Ingrid and the others, he ordered Scylla from the ship, and released the last of his personal controls over his nanites, converting all of himself from flesh into a nanite-based consciousness, and truly unleashing the Devourer.

He used his conversion ability to feed on the damaged ship, then triggered a jump through the huge reservoir of energy he gained from the conversion, jumping himself and the terminally damaged ship across the galaxy blindly.

Arise: Conqueror

<u>PROLOGUE</u>

The cold of space extended ahead of "Francine" as he sat, staring out at the dead system beyond in abject fury.

"I told you he lied," sneered Alberjeet, looking down at his former master.

The shorter Ændari had been making his beliefs clear since they'd reached this sector of space, and Francine was utterly sick of it.

A mere few days ago, the little shit would have never dared speak so to his superior; that he did now was a mark of how far Francine had fallen.

When the council had reviewed the logs of the interaction with the upstart of an abomination aboard the UC Forgeship, they'd remained entirely silent, making their position as clear as if they'd broadcast it for all.

They attached no blame nor praise to his actions, and they'd continue to do that right up until he proved that the records he'd procured were valuable or not.

Now, an hour after they'd reached the innermost system of the forbidden zone, having lost a pair of irreplaceable Skarn assault vessels when they fell afoul of a drifting cloud of corrupted builders, he stared down at what—according to the sensor returns—had once been a class-three, living and vibrant planet. The taste of ashes and despair filled his mouth.

The crew had taken one look at his mutilated and abused form, and they, too, had stayed silent. Each of them knew exactly what would happen to the first of them who stepped out of line, and yet…

"You were a fool," Alberjeet whispered caustically. "You brought us here, delaying our ascension, leaving the capture of the node to that worm Darr, and for what?" He gestured grandly at the tumbling rocks and shattered remains of another world. "Behold, the might of Earth. Our most valuable bargaining chip and conquest."

"Be silent," Francine snapped, distracted by the text that hovered before him. It had arrived on their final approach to the tumbling ruin, and it was incorrect. It *had* to be. He gnawed on a knuckle and stared ahead pensively.

Universal System Quadrant Node, designation #2 has been captured by the Devourer abomination.
All Ændari forces within Quadrant Six are ordered to submit to Overlord Renain; gathering point Vector Ten has been approved.
Any forces in Quadrants 2-5 are to make their way to rally point Tren-Seven and submit to Overlord Kriev.
Diplomatic forces are to maintain their current strategy.

For the Glory of the Empire!

It was both horrifying and unexpected. That the abomination had somehow managed to not only reach the node but force the node's accursed AI to accept it as its master was bad enough.

The lack of any reference to him, though, and the utter silence regarding the fleet that he was ostensibly in charge of? "Maintain current strategy" could only mean one thing.

There was no way the council would just leave him to search, to find whatever evidence he could, to save face, and hopefully his position.

No, they'd eliminate him.

They *had* to. And it'd be someone internal that they'd use to remove him. That he'd been in contact with the abomination and had not killed it outright would be held against him forever, he knew.

It didn't matter that an entire battalion of shock troopers had been stationed on the node, nor that there was a stealth vessel deployed in that system with a full complement of both troopers and the disgusting ACF wastrels to deal with any issues.

If they failed, it'd be on his head, and the dozens of personal messages he'd started to receive had made that clear.

"Francine" seems a fitting name for you. Let it be made permanent. –
Codex Keeper Athemaa

In normal times, for that message to be sent to a diplomat of the great Ændari Empire, a literal Hand of the Council, would have resulted in the foolish sender being slowly tortured to death over several centuries.

He'd ordered lower ranks jettisoned from his ship into suns for less than that, and yet… This had come from one of the codex keepers, an ordained librarian for the council.

His name had been physically changed in the Great Codex. It was an offense punishable by slow disintegration to so much as infer that the codex could be incorrect, so his name was now, and would forever more be—unless he earned a new name—*Francine.*

For a librarian to dare to do such a thing showed the direction the galactic wind was sailing. And for that fool Alberjeet to feel secure enough in his position to speak out so openly now?

Francine shifted slightly. His left hand twisted, and the needle-thin dirk that lay hidden beneath the golden bracer slid smoothly into the palm of that hand.

Without his right hand, he'd be slower, and the little shit had deliberately positioned himself on that side, no doubt to gloat over his master's fall.

No matter.

This was why he kept the existence of weapons such as the Aspen Heart hidden, even from his so-called protégé.

He shifted again, being careful not to so much as nick himself, as he unsheathed the encoded weapon. The shiver that his own builders gave off, being so close to an active destroyer blade, was both exciting and terrifying.

He let loose an involuntary hiss as the sheath fell free, sliding down the side of the chair. He froze, staring at the back of Alberjeet; then he let out a slow breath in relief as he in turn continued to stare down at the world before them.

Arise: Conqueror

"You know, I dreamt of this day," his minion said softly. "For six hundred cycles, I served you faithfully, earning my access to the upper ranks, and then you had to go and throw it all away with your incompetence."

"Go on…" Francine encouraged, licking his lips nervously. "Say it." He shifted the blade around, oh so slowly, gripping the hilt in his palm that, had it been capable of sweat, would have been soaked with it.

"You had to know this was coming." Alberjeet turned, sneering down at the incomplete form of his master. "As soon as you returned to the ship, you knew."

"I knew before then," Francine corrected. "I knew the day I agreed to become your master, that you were too weak, too small, and too foolish to do what had to be done. But very well. We both know what has to happen here."

"We do," Alberjeet agreed, almost jovially. "Farewell, my master, and remember this later. When you peer up at me, begging for my mercy from the floor of the Punishment Pit, I'll show you exactly as much as you'd have shown me, were our positions reversed."

With that, the younger Ændari drew his sidearm, an ancient weapon built for one use only: the stunning of prey to enable a comfortable feast.

Then he fired—three blasts when one should have been enough.

He fired them one after another, at almost point-blank range. The electrical blasts should have overwhelmed his meager personal shield and left him a drooling, defenseless mess on the floor.

The use of a ceremonial weapon like that was an insult of the highest order. But Francine had anticipated that would be Alberjeet's chosen weapon.

That was why when the blasts hit his shield, he *smiled*.

The crackling electrical discharge flooded the shield, then dissipated into the chair, the interwoven and well-hidden dispersant net doing its job perfectly.

"What…?" Alberjeet gasped, reflexively pulling the trigger a fourth and fifth time before the ancient weapon let loose a click that they both knew so well.

"Out of charge." Francine smirked at his former subordinate.

"I… I…" Alberjeet whispered, staring from Francine to the weapon in his hand, before lunging forward, hands rising like claws as he reached for Francine's throat.

Francine's right arm came up instinctively. The slowly regrowing nub of flesh barely slowed Alberjeet.

It did its job, though, distracting him long enough for the destroyer blade to punch through his armor.

Francine sneered, staring into the confused, then horrified face of his former subordinate.

"Why?" Alberjeet whispered.

"Believe me, it's better than you deserve," Francine hissed. "And I'll still have my makers and be reborn—I'll just have them torn from the bodies of your mate and spawn instead!"

With that, he shoved the body aside and dragged his blade free. The gritty feeling of the blade exiting the wound felt more like he'd dragged it free of a pile of sand, rather than from the body of one of the most glorious of species.

He stood, glancing down into the dying eyes of Alberjeet. Even as he triggered the alert, a bodyguard stepped in from outside the ambassador's office.

"Summon the captain. Pass word that Alberjeet's mate and spawn are to be brought before me and prepared to become the fuel of my rebirth. And dispose of *that*."

The bodyguard bowed his head, and Francine sneered again, knowing exactly how the lower ranks would take this. They'd be horrified, and yet relieved.

The Devourer had stolen his horn and hand, and no Ændari could regenerate a limb lost in such a way. No, the regrowth must be taken from another, and because the ignominy had been inflicted on him, the highest aboard the ship, that meant the lower ranks had all tread carefully.

They all knew that the first of them to cross him would end up stripped and bound to his table, and the relief that the victim had been chosen would battle with the shock that it'd been the family of his own protégé.

Instead of being stripped, drained, and broken but having a hope of recovery one day, that protégé had been destroyed utterly.

That would serve to keep the others in their place for now. Hopefully it'd last long enough that he could find the original Forgeworld and return in glory. But if not?

Well, all he had to do was wait until the fight was almost over, then return with his fleet.

"You summoned me, Ambassador?" came the captain's carefully deferential voice.

"Yes." Francine sighed, staring down at Alberjeet's face, as his body was dragged across the floor, the last light fading from his eyes.

He drew a deep breath, forcing himself to settle, to be present and aware. The challenge to his authority wasn't over. For the librarian to dare that much made it clear, and the council were unlikely to have only one knife in the dark waiting for him.

"Prepare the fleet. I want every system in the forbidden zone scoured for life signs. You have thirty rotations of the All-Star. By the time our home world has been graced by the light of rebirth twice, we will either have found the Forgeworld, or we will be on our way to the node, and every ship in this fleet will have a new captain."

"Lord Ambassador…" The captain gasped. "We have no way of knowing if the Forgeworld can even be found here—" He broke off suddenly. Apparently, he'd realized that he was either admitting that the ambassador had been fooled and that they'd all wasted their time in coming, or that he was incapable of his own role.

Either way, he clapped his fists to chest and bowed his head in supplication, before rushing from the room.

Francine drew a deep breath in the silence of his now private bridge, watching the dirty planet below spin slowly, as he contemplated the future.

There was only one way for him to be sure that his position was secure. He just had to rise atop a sea of blood.

Arise: Conqueror

Find the Forgeworld, find the renegade weapons and upgrade them, then use them to quell any resistance. Or, if they couldn't be found? Well, the node was already open. All he had to do was make sure that he arrived at the fight at the right time.

If the abomination was winning, he could always flee. And if the empire's council-led forces were? The Devourer wouldn't go down easily. And that it'd managed to destroy an entire battalion already? Well, history was written by the winners.

If the other fleets were foolish enough to not be on their guard when he arrived? That just proved they were unworthy of the highest of ranks.

He would not be so foolish as to make that mistake.

He smiled then, his mind moving to the exquisite set of tools he'd commissioned for feasts and wondering which he'd use first.

Somehow, the day didn't seem such a loss after all.

CHAPTER ONE

The world around me shifted, the field rippling as I did something I'd never dreamt I'd have the power to do.

The branes slid apart. A vortex appeared around me, pulling me and my mass inside, dragging me into the depths as the outer galaxy shivered, then vanished.

I felt the pressures, the needs.

Equalization was the natural process.

The gravity drives worked by "buying" access to the lower branes, forming a slipstream around the ship that dragged it down, then released it, allowing the equalizing pressure to return the vessel to the galaxy of our birth.

That was all well and good, and a tiny adjustment made on the slip in and out was enough to guide the rising vessel to another jump point, the universe naturally guiding the re-emerging vessel to the nearest point of neutrality.

As there were generally two points like that in any system, both Lagrange points, that made it easy. Simply put the correct amount of energy in, and you completed the jump to an easily discernable point.

That was gravity drives at their most basic point, but I'd just dragged the rapidly disintegrating ship backward into the branes, at a time when the reactor was about to go nuclear.

Or, to put it another way, I'd used all the energy I could summon to drag myself into a path that led between all the stars of the galaxies, using only energy as the payment of choice. In comparison, at least ten times that energy was about to be released, and I had literally no way to know where I'd come out, if I ever came out again.

I felt the reactor building even higher, and knowing that at any second it could blow, I did the only thing I could.

The Devourer armor was fully deployed. The sub-sentient mass that was at once me and something more primal covered everything around me, dragging me deeper into the superstructure of the ship as it flowed over it all, tearing the hull apart, molecule by molecule, realigning them, forcing them into a fast version of leaden armoring, then digging deeper.

I'd been on the bridge, one level from the outer hull when I started.

Arise: Conqueror

Now I was three decks lower down, my body cocooned in the middle of a mass of oily red and black as it fed on the walls, floors, and more around me.

If it'd been possible to make the Devourer invisible to see the effect, I imagined it'd have looked like those time lapse videos where fruit collapsed in on itself. The metal, rubber, ceramics, and more crumbled around me. My armor pressed against it all, and where the surfaces touched, they fed.

Everything and anything was torn free, fed into me—the molecules repurposed into the cloak that flowed across everything within reach, and the energy dragged into the only things that I'd not fed upon yet: the emergency power cells that had been reserved for the bridge.

I was charging them at a horrific rate. Every single thing I broke down in this way released more energy than it cost to do so. The perpetual flow of energy granted me levels of power I'd never dreamt of.

They also allowed me to build a reserve that was going to be my only chance.

The superstructure ahead of me crumbled, collapsing beneath the onslaught as I dragged my mass deeper, even as the last functional vestiges of the ship's Tsunami-infected control system triggered releases.

The ship's reactors were at the point of meltdown. One of them was dead and scrammed; I'd maintained complete control over it, but it was several decks and hundreds of meters away from me now, cooling and worthless.

The second reactor had flooded the grav drive with everything it had. Usually that would be a moderated supply of power, and it'd be guided. Instead, it'd been thrown at the drive in an attempt to overload it entirely.

What the hell the Ændari who were fleeing the ship had expected to happen, considering they were literally going to be doing the intergalactic equivalent of setting off a nuke and holding a bedsheet up between them and it, I didn't know.

They'd set it all to blow, though, and they'd fled.

The worst case was that the grav drive would explode, and sterilize the system after all, killing everyone and everything.

The second worst was that I'd waste all my time dealing with the gravity issue, and then I'd not have time to deal with the third and most distant of the reactors as it went nuclear.

That would have "merely" devastated the ship, unleashing a wash of "hard" radiation that would have at the very least badly fucked it up, and probably killed Scylla and me, as well as covering the only entrance and exit for the node in the remains of a burning and scourged starship.

As it was, I'd managed to divert that power into the grav drive and guide it so that rather than a massive sterilization blast, I'd instead sucked the ship—and me—into the depths of the branes.

I was able to perceive the passage of time in here, but only dimly. And that was in part because I was using my abilities to slow my perception of time already.

That meant that when I was thinking I had literally a few seconds to do something here, in reality I had far less.

The gravity drive was just ahead. The various systems that connected the secondary reactor to the ship were melting. The power output was still climbing as we were driven deeper…

I threw everything I had at it. The armor pressed against the bulkheads, eating its way through. The computer systems triggered automated meltdown procedures, jettisoning the farthest reactor into space, as the secondary, the one directly over my head, began to melt its way through the deck.

Explosive bolts triggered, and the ship shuddered as sections were ripped free. The reactors were powered into space through the galactic equivalent of a slingshot.

As they did that, though, the last of the power that had been feeding the gravity drive cut out.

I'd burned everything I had. Every single fragment of energy I could create, beg, borrow, or steal, I'd forced into the grav drive, guiding it, forming a stable bubble.

That had meant that as the drive engaged, rather than it being bombarded with a mass of power that would trigger an explosive result, the energy was accepted. It was used as the drive was intended, even if that had been to force the ship deeper into the branes than any vessel should ever go.

Now, as the reactors were jettisoned from the ship, they were forced free of the warp. So, too, the last vestiges of power left the drive, and the remnants of the ship shifted, rolling, buoyed up as it twisted.

I felt us starting to rise again, the ship literally designed to ride the flux between the branes.

Then I felt them.

I felt the incredible sentients that called the branes home—massive creatures, things I could barely guess at—and I felt the depths that were still below me, and the order of magnitude more masses that existed down there.

The explosions from the ship had sent it into a roll, and the heat and light energy being released by the reactors' emergency evacuation drew their attention.

The most distant had been the first to launch, for whatever reason, and it was also apparently the least damaged, as it rocketed from my senses, vanishing "upward" to presumably explode into our reality again, before, you know, exploding.

The other, though…that had been horrifically close, and the ship was barely behind it as it exploded.

The wash of energy was horrendous, and the fragments that tore into the hull made it clear that they should have ripped the vessel apart.

They didn't, though, as something else took the majority of the blast— something huge that had swum closer, examining the strange visitor to their realm.

When the reactor exploded, it tore into the curious form, shredding it, ripping it apart, and bathing it in alarming levels of radiation that was anathema to this realm.

Arise: Conqueror

I felt it—the shock, the pain, and the sudden horror that flashed from mind to mind—as one of their kind was injured, their body torn and battered, by the strange visitor…

No, by the *invader* from the higher realms.

My mind reeled. The psychic shock rendered me impotent, unable to function. I collapsed. My Devourer armor that had been rolling across everything nearby, desperately trying to eat its way to the drive, so that maybe there could have been a chance to guide the exit…failed.

My armor buckled in upon me and formed a desperately protective cocoon. I fell, stunned, as everything descended into blackness.

***

Screaming, I woke again, shaking as a horrific amount of power flooded me. Electrical discharge crackled and leapt from the walls, the floor…

It went on and on, and I had a transient memory of this happening before, of pain and shock and… I drifted and reeled, trying to comprehend what the hell was going on.

My armor covered me still. The metallic outer sheath peeled and crumbled as more and more power discharged into me. I looked around, panicked, trying to make sense of the world, as a memory of a plan came to me.

It wasn't a plan, though. There was no way in hell it was coherent enough to be a "plan"—fuck no. But I'd been trying everything else, and passing out eventually, so…

The pain ratcheted higher, and I was surrounded by a hazy cloud of disintegrating nanites—nanites I goddamn needed. So, with no better solution, I did it.

I retracted my armor.

The crackling, frantic pulsing cut out almost instantly. The relief was so great I almost passed out again, shaking as I tried to figure out the world around me.

I realized I was floating after a few uncertain seconds. There was something hard and cold to my right as I shifted. My fingers brushed against it and I flinched, almost expecting the discharge again to send me drifting in another direction.

Blinking, I tried to focus, my brain slow to piece together details as I attempted to figure out what had happened and where the hell I was.

It didn't help that I felt like I had the worst hangover of my life and…

That was wrong, I realized, still blinking and stirring as my back bumped against another wall. My head smacked off the arched stanchion overhead. I gritted my teeth, reaching up to rub at the back of my head.

Everything I did sent me moving again. Reaching up, I started to twist in the air, the…

The *air*.

I tried breathing and went into a panic.

There was *no air*.

Trying to breathe caused an uncomfortable pressure as my lungs tried to inflate. I tried to draw down a deep breath, only to find there was nothing there!

I thrashed, panicking, twisting around and trying to see anything: a mask, an oxygen tank, a…

The room around me—there was nothing here! The door nearby was sealed, but the walls, the floor, and the deck overhead…all of them were half eaten and sagging, falling apart.

They looked like something had been chewing on them. A split-second surge of memory roared up at me, seeing the Devourer armor spread everywhere around me.

More, I felt the coldness of the metal I'd just bumped into again.

The metal that had caught my bare flesh.

That almost sent me deeper into a panic, as I finally noticed three things.

First, I was bare-ass naked.

Literally, I was floating from side to side, barely remaining inside the same section of the ship that I had been, and that was probably only because of the damage to the overhead deck, meaning that it'd slumped sideways at some point, and I was resting in a small, blocked-off pocket of the room.

Secondly, it was pitch black. Not "hey, it's a bit dark in this room" and not even "fuck me, it's dark down this mineshaft."

No, it was as dark as I'd ever seen anything. And instead of with light, I'd been "seeing" since I opened my eyes using my other senses. I'd been feeling the world around me through minute gravitational pulses, at an instinctual level.

Lastly, as much as it was freaking me out, the only effect that me not breathing was having on me was the panic it was creating.

It was hardwired into my brain that I *needed* to breathe, and when I had realized I couldn't, that had triggered an instinctive mammalian reaction.

But I was still alive when I eventually got control of myself.

I floated slowly, reaching out and grabbing onto a twisted section of stanchion, arresting my drift. I looked around; then, with a thought, my armor flooded me again on instinct.

It was different, though, I realized as I looked down—seeing it, feeling it. My armor no longer needed to pool on the surface of my skin. No longer pouring out from hidden reserves deeper inside me, from hollowed-out bones and storage.

It was my skin.

I was it.

The last seconds before the jump, the decision I'd made—all of it crashed back to me. I hung there, transfixed as I tried to make sense of it all.

I'd not been capable of doing what I needed to, not and still be who and what I was, and so I'd accepted what I knew instinctively I had to do, to save the others.

The change—hell, I didn't even know what I'd done, not really…I'd just known that there was no way that a mortal form could survive long enough to do this.

Arise: Conqueror

I'd had to use my body as an energy conduit. And not just a conduit, but a converter as well.

I saw it now.

I felt it.

What I'd done was to convert everything that I was into the Devourer.

I *was* a Devourer, after all. I'd known that, and I'd been terrified of losing myself in the change, in the growth of that side of me. But instead of that happening, I felt more "me" than ever before.

Through the armor I now wore, I felt the ship around me.

I reached out, and I felt the wall under my armored fingertips as if they were flesh. And then, with a thought, the senses were reduced and it was like I was inside my armor again.

I was inside it, and yet not. To anyone looking at me from the outside, I was armored as I normally was. But for me? My skin wasn't covered in the Devourer armor. My skin *was* the armor.

There was no longer a difference. With a thought, my right hand morphed, becoming a blade.

It didn't extrude one; the nanites didn't flow out and form a blade, and my hand was attached to it.

The wrist slid narrower, as if my fingers had become quicksilver, reforming and growing into a gleaming longsword, then a dagger, then my hand.

I stared at my fingers: the hairs on the back of my hand, the old scars that I knew were cosmetic now and reformed because subconsciously I was used to them being there.

With a simple flex of my mind, my bare hand was smooth, the old scars gone. Then another flex and they were back. My hand was encased in armor; then it was bare.

There was no longer a difference, I knew.

I was no longer tied to the old rules that had bound me. And as I accepted that, I felt another little fragment of "me" fall away.

As my armor retracted, I straightened, floating forward, as more normal clothing appeared.

It was instinctive.

I no longer needed the armor, not here—and not now at least—but I still felt "wrong" being naked. It wasn't a self-conscious thing, as oh so many people— especially my old neighbors—would have confirmed.

I felt no inhibitions about being naked, but the remains of the ship here were torn and damaged. On an instinctual level, I felt I damn well needed some pants on at least.

Jeans, sneakers, and a short-sleeved T-shirt appeared, as insane as that seemed. I was dressed again, but I realized that this apparently cotton-appearing, almost silken top could provide a level of armoring that a main battle tank was incapable of.

I flexed my arms, stunned as I sensed the potential there. I could probably tear the turret off a tank barehanded now as well, not even needing the gravity ability.

I didn't understand all of it, and I was still struggling to not try to breathe. The impossibility of that act, thanks to the realities of vacuum, meant that every time I did, I nearly panicked.

For a few seconds, I struggled with wanting to summon the armor again, and at the same time the crackling hell of electrical discharge rang in my mind. It had to have been the armor.

That was what I'd dimly guessed at before, that the discharge was hammering off me over and over through the mixture of the metal all around me and the armor itself. That was why I'd given a last-ditch attempt to remove it, and there was no way I'd have even considered that if I'd realized that I was in literal fucking vacuum.

What I was realizing, though, was that I had another choice to make.

I'd made one when I'd gone down this route, and I didn't understand why others hadn't done this before me. I instinctually knew that only a tiny fraction of a fraction of all of those BWVs from the past had ever been capable of this. But the power? The potential?

They'd risen as Devourers, and they'd seemingly moved on, some of them remaining enough in contact that they'd reached out and had given the UC the ability to use some of their makers.

Makers…that was the term for the factory units, I remembered, and builders, the term that the Erlking and others had used for the nanites. That was going to get real confusing at some point, and I resolved to keep them as makers and nanites for the sake of my own sanity.

Regardless, though, the Devourers had unlocked some of the makers that had been left on the Forgeships and elsewhere, and then they'd seemingly fucked off and washed their hands of it all. That rankled, but I understood it as well.

I clambered out, hesitating, then stood at the bottom of the hole I'd eaten into the hull of the wrecked starship, staring upward into the darkness of space. For the first time, I guessed I was seeing what those other Devourers must have.

The universe was huge and wonderful. It was beautiful, and there was so much out there, so much that you'd miss, if you just stayed here.

I knew some things instinctively now, balls to bones. First, I was immortal, effectively. There was no such thing as true immortality, no matter what that cockgoblin the Erlking might think.

At some point, the universe would contract, and collapse into heat and light and radiation, and then into the depths of the gravity well that lay at the heart of creation.

There was nothing that would ultimately survive that, not even the creatures I sensed at the bottom of the branes.

But beyond that, in most ways, for any of the tests that mattered to me right now, I was immortal.

I could also probably kick the shit out of the Erlking like he'd done to me originally. At that thought, a little spark of "me" flared to life.

Arise: Conqueror

It wasn't pride in humanity's potential, or fear of the greater galaxy that flared it; it was the thought of taking some prick down a peg and beating him like a redheaded stepchild.

Then other memories flamed, fanning that tiny ember of me back to life.

Ingrid. I saw her sitting cross-legged on the bed in that hotel in Crete, puzzling over translations, a smudge of ink on her cheek where she'd accidentally caught herself with the pen in her hand. A lock of her hair fell free from the ponytail that she liked to wear, tumbling loose to fall down before her eyes, and as she worked, she was absently blowing it out of her line of sight.

I'd laughed, and the sound had distracted her, making her look up at me, wide-eyed. That she'd forgotten that I was even there, so recently after our gold attempt in the bedroom Olympics should have annoyed me, or hell, embarrassed me and made me wonder what the judges would say about my performance.

It didn't, though; it made me smile, staring at the woman I loved.

More memories flooded me then: silly ones, happy ones, proud ones. I remembered the look on the face of a small child, bawling their eyes out as their mother clung to them, on the stairs of that selfsame hotel.

I remembered being embarrassed, not wanting to look too close at the emotions that rose in me when I'd saved that mother and brought her back to her family.

I'd felt the need in my heart then—to do more, to be more—and it'd terrified me. Because I knew that if I was to devote myself to being that, to being the terror in the night for the assholes out there, there would be no end to it.

There was nowhere that I would ever be able to stop, and that I'd never not see things that I had to address.

I wasn't some "God of Justice"…I was a man. I was an asshole, in fact—a shallow, uncaring, arrogant fucker.

I'd allowed myself to go after the werewolves, the vamps, and the Arisen. I'd given myself that as my mission, mainly because I damn well knew that if I didn't? I was weak enough in morals that instead I'd give myself over to being the worst monster the world had ever seen.

I'd be lazy, I'd be greedy, and I'd be base.

I'd always been terrified that if I let myself "go," to just do whatever I wanted, I'd find myself taking tiny step after tiny step down that road, until my soul was black as pitch. And on my arrival into hell, the devil would step down from his throne, handing it over to his successor.

Those fears had always been there.

Always.

Now, though, after years of seeing the assholes, of seeing what those who were truly evil were capable of? Well, maybe I knew better.

I was still an asshole. I always would be. But the difference was that I didn't want to be. I didn't want to be the fucker who stole the last crust from a starving child, or who took what I wanted from others who couldn't stop me.

I was capable of it—oh hell, was I capable of it—and I'd broken enough laws in my time, as well as a lot of bones.

But maybe that was the difference? Maybe some people—hell, most people probably—were actually "good"…or at least bland as fuckin' oatmeal and not willing to risk being anything else. For them, it seemed so easy to just be that. Maybe all I needed, though, for me to not go to the dark side, was to accept that I didn't want to?

That seemed crazily simple and obvious, which meant that it couldn't be the real answer, but still.

I'd given myself a charge, though, that I'd only feed on the things that went bump in the night.

I'd face the things that others couldn't, and I'd leave those who could deal with the "lesser" crimes to deal with them.

That was where I'd gone wrong, and I saw it now, even as I saw where that path led.

It led me to be a Devourer, and it led from here into deep space. It led to exploring the galaxy, because no matter what I did, I couldn't be everywhere. I wasn't a god, after all, not a real one. While I'd been unconscious, there'd probably been a billion lives extinguished, and two billion more begun.

When you looked at it like that, and knowing that no matter what you did, you couldn't be there for everyone?

Worse, if I did? If I saved everyone and helped them to create a perfect society where everyone was happy? Eventually it'd all crash down when they consumed everything—every scrap of land, every crumb of food. The galaxy would end in fear and hunger and pain.

There was nothing you could do, not permanently, and the knowledge of that, when you realized at your core that you were literally destined to see the end of days, was crushing.

But it was also freeing.

That was why the Devourers had gone as they had, I guessed. I knew that they were still out there, and that one or more had unlocked things for the UC, giving them limited access to some of their old technologies.

Then they'd sailed on, serene in their exploration of reality, knowing that at the heart of things, it just didn't matter anymore.

I could be like that, I knew. I could be out there; I could go, to let myself revel in my wanderlust nature—the desire to walk away from it all, and to see what was out there.

I'd done it once already, after all, fucking off from my old life to party and hide in the Greek islands, only to end up here.

I *could* do it all over again, and it'd be so easy.

The change into my new form, the differences between a human body, a hormonally driven meat sack, into a machine that was based almost entirely on cold logic and silence in the depths of my soul meant that I could do it easily.

"I love you."

I'd heard it at the end, as I'd dragged the ship into the depths of the gravity well.

She'd reached out to me, her heart filled to bursting with horror that she was losing me, with pain that she might never see me again. I felt the understanding in her as well, the sheer knowledge that no matter what, I was hers and she was mine, and that what I was doing was literally fucking impossible.

There was certainly no way a mortal could do it, and certainly no way that one could ever do it twice. It should be impossible for me to get back to her now. I could be anywhere in the fucking galaxy, or any of the galaxies; I had a wreck of a ship, and I was barely sane at the best of times.

But I felt the pride in her. Pride that I could, and I damn well *would*, make it back to her.

It didn't matter that she *knew* it was impossible. She also knew it was impossible for me to do any one of a hundred other things I'd already done.

I'd damn well do it, and I'd make it back to her. I'd do it, and we'd be together. We'd flatten the Ændari empire, we'd burn their council to the ground, I'd piss on the ashes and we'd straighten out the cosmos as the first round, figuring shit out as we went, and then we'd go home.

We'd go there and fix that goddamn shithole of a wonderful world, and then I'd damn well marry her.

We'd have kids, we'd have a life together, and I'd be a husband to her and a parent to my children who they'd be proud of as well.

I'd be all of that, and I'd do it because I loved her.

It didn't matter that in the long run it'd all end.

Fuck that. It was the journey, not the destination, and that was where I was different, I knew.

I'd been shit on from a great height as a child, and so many times since, but right now, I'd fallen on my feet.

I had a woman I loved now, I had a *family* I loved, who loved me, *and* I had friends.

I was richer than I'd ever been in my life, in a way that had nothing to do with the incredible wealth I could lay my hands on. And if the only thing that stood between me and all of that was that something was impossible?

Fuck it.

I'd do it twice.

With that in mind, I turned my back on the depths of space, and started back inside.

It was time to sort this mess out.

CHAPTER TWO

I slid down, gravity flexing at my will to give me a more familiar effect. I landed on the deck, staring around the torn and battered remains of the ship.

The first thing I had to do was figure out what the hell had happened at the end and the condition of the ship; then I could try to figure out where the fuck I was.

The last seconds in the depths of the branes were a blur. I remembered little of it now, but something had been nearby, and pain and horror had filled me, and then it was all over.

I remembered the reactor being ejected. It'd exploded before it could be shoved out of the warp, the effect somehow shielded from doing too much damage to the ship, and I dimly felt that was important.

I needed to know what I was working with. If all I had was this damn room, and maybe a few fragments of the surrounding ones, then yeah, it might take me a bit longer to get home.

Looking around, I saw the section that I'd been in before, where I'd been drifting, unconscious.

The roof, or the floor of the deck overhead, had slipped at some point. Presumably something had hit it and smashed it downward. That had, in turn, basically cut off three-quarters of the room I'd been in, keeping me in the last section, surrounded by damaged and half-eaten walls.

I could see that I'd made it maybe halfway through that wall and into the next section, where the grav drive had been. I reached out with the Devourer, and I couldn't help but smile as it flowed effortlessly into being. The armor flooded the wall, wrapping around it.

It poured through holes, over lips and edges, and absorbed the mass with ease.

As I did it, I felt the difference now.

When I'd been doing it before, it'd been like I'd been using a toffee hammer to drive nails in. Now I was suddenly holding a sledge, and the nails knew it too.

The surrounding mass practically leapt into me joyously, terrified of displeasing me, and the energy…

I gasped, as strength and power flooded me.

Arise: Conqueror

I'd been feeding it into the power cells before, feeling them absorbing it, and I'd been using it as soon as I could generate it, emptying the ship's cells to keep the jump going.

Now that I was out the far side, the storage cells…they were gone.

A quick look around, stooping and looking under sections of the fallen deck, revealed absolutely no damn power cells, and I cursed. I flooded my body with more power as I fed on the walls, tearing them apart and making null coins instinctively as I went, but the power was being wasted.

I focused, exploring these new powers and knowing that with access to the mass that I had and my true abilities, I no longer needed to spend my nanites to build things.

Instead, they would use the mass that was all around me to rebuild whatever I wanted.

Sure, there was some breakage, but nowhere what I'd experienced before.

I resolved to make some power cells as soon as I could, but for now I'd learned what I needed to.

The room beyond the one I'd been in was still there, and in the middle of it—fortunately fully powered down, the warp having ripped what was left free— was the gravity drive.

As soon as I'd seen that the gravity drive was still there, I relaxed. I'd tried to let loose a relieved breath, all on instinct, and the sudden surge of panic as my diaphragm should have spasmed…

I shook myself instead.

I didn't *have* a diaphragm anymore. I was literally solid with nanites. All my internal structures were gone; I was one being, and as such…

I shifted my internal structure slightly, enabling me to "breathe" now, or at least for my chest to rise and fall on autopilot. That done, and feeling a little more like a real boy, I turned and headed back into the room I'd just left.

I grabbed onto the hanging deck and pulled myself up and over the edge, through the torn and shattered sections of the ship, and headed for the outer hull.

As I went, I stared at the decimation that I'd left behind. The walls and decks looked like the hand of God had reached down and torn its way into the heart of the ship.

It didn't take long to make it to the outside, not fully. I'd clambered out of the first room earlier, and I'd stared up through the hole I'd "eaten" in the decks to see higher floors that had been ravaged by the explosive blasts of the reactor's death.

Clearly the "armor" I'd made had done its job, as I'd survived, but it'd also apparently been torn loose.

Now I settled onto the surface of the ship, slowly turning as I stared at the devastation that had been wrought, starting with the ship whose hull I stood atop of.

It'd been a big fucker before, the ship: six levels high and several hundred meters long, maybe as much as a kilometer. I'd not really been able to tell. The sights I'd seen of it originally were when the stealth coating had been active, and now…

Well.

There was a lot less of it than it'd started with.

The rear section ended abruptly. A solid line that looked to have been burned through marked where the ship had once continued on.

Now as I stared out, I could see the slow rotation that, had I not had all the improvements to my inner ear or the massive changes to me more recently, would have sent me vomiting over the edge, earning the name "vomit comet."

Something, and I guessed it was the reactor's explosion, had carved deep lines of devastation through the ship.

The reason I was guessing it was that, though, and not that I damn well knew it was, were the other occupants of my immediate space.

The first of them tumbled nearby, both of us slowly separating from each other. As I stared at it, I knew there was only one place it could have come from.

It was part of one of the creatures that lived in the branes.

It had to be. There was no way that something like that just happened to be alongside the remains of my goddamn craft out here in…in…deep…space…

My mind stuttered to a halt as I stared, slowly looking out and up from the remains of my ship at the strange corpse that floated nearby.

Beyond it, beyond the mass of what I guessed had to have been a body—though I had no clue how it could have naturally evolved, considering what I could see from here was a fused mess of both metal and flesh—there were more.

More ships, more things, more…just more.

I was in deep space, I fucking knew I was, and yet everywhere I looked, I could see clouds. Clouds of red and orange, lit from within by crackling bursts of lightning. And we'd not long since exited one, from the looks of things.

Here and there, I could see more. Massive hulks drifted, dead in space. That was all I could see; I turned slowly, realizing that I was surrounded by the junk of a thousand spacefaring civilizations. Also, I guessed that although a million scientists would give their right nut to see the shit I was seeing right now, I had no clue where to start.

As I stared, I saw more, estimating the debris field as containing hundreds, if not thousands of ships. Where they weren't reduced to fragments of drifting debris, it was clear that almost all of them were differing designs.

The exit point of the branes was dependent on the energy input: a little and you jumped a little distance; a lot and you jumped farther. That was simple.

How the hell I'd ended up here, instead of a Lagrange point, I didn't understand. But looking at it, I guessed a lot of other ships in the past had made the same mistake.

That didn't bode well for me, considering the fuckers were still here. But there was also the bonus that there had to be a lot of recoverable tech around as well.

I needed to get back to the others, but for now I had no clue whether I needed to go left, right, straight past the last star and on 'til morning, or what. I needed to find a map, or make one, and to do that…well, I needed to figure out where the fuck I was.

Arise: Conqueror

Logically, to do that? All I needed to do was somehow resurrect some of the memory banks in these ships, then patch it all together.

And the first step in an attempt to do that?

I needed power.

Turning once more, I stared out, trying to figure out what my first target should be.

I needed to tear loose the power cells from this ship, that was a given. I'd had some that I'd been using before, but they'd gone, no clue where, and in every direction, all I could see was floating debris.

I might be ten meters from the cells, or ten thousand light-years. There was no way of knowing for sure, but I had the basic theory behind the Ændari ships and knowledge of their UC counterparts.

That, in turn, gave me a solid starting point, and it was logical. The bridge had a separate emergency battery of power cells, ready just in case. That was where I'd gotten the last set from.

If you were going to have that on the bridge, you'd need it elsewhere as well. Notably engineering, atmospherics, and presumably shields, as a minimum. I had to guess that Zac's idea of building them routed through a bank of power cells wasn't *that* revolutionary, surely?

Either way, I damn well knew that the reactors had some nearby as well. The one that had done the most damage wouldn't be recoverable, not judging from the devastation, and the other one…

I moved around an outcropping, comparing the details I could see to the map that I'd gotten access to earlier when my Tsunami had been still inside working systems…

And I nodded.

Yup. That made sense.

About ten meters before the area I guessed the power cells would be in…that was where the ship ended.

Fuck.

I set off jogging to the edge, feeling incredibly weird about this whole T-shirt and jeans thing. I reached the edge and peered over, suppressing the insane and entirely human reaction to consider peeing over it.

Then I remembered that as I was in space, any liquid would boil away, and I had to guess that would do Mr. Happy some damage.

I still considered doing it, because I was so different now, and wondering whether it could even affect me. Then I realized I'd have to convert nanites into liquid to do it, and it all became just a bit too much navel-gazing.

The ship ended at my feet. Some sections had apparently melted, run like warm caramel, and then had solidified again.

There was also absolutely bugger all that was of use.

I found that a dozen or so sections looked to be intact, with the original stealth coating clear, and that was it—the rest of the ship was a total wreck.

Seeing that, and forcing myself to accept that there was no way I could repair this ship, freed me up to move on.

There were two things off the top of my head that this ship had to have, hopefully still intact, beyond anything else.

That was Ændari bodies, because I damn well knew I'd not stripped them all, and at least the grav drive.

Beyond that, I was guessing that there'd be some memory banks. I'd gotten some of those from Nessie's bloody corpse, admittedly, but I'd not even considered trying to learn how they were made at that point.

Now I was regretting it.

Quest Uncovered!

Evolving Quest discovered: Building the Future

You have found yourself adrift in a graveyard of titans. Explore the local area, claim that which you need, and discover technologies long thought lost.

Investigate and access 10 separate ship technologies to receive the following rewards:

- **+2 Support Points**

- **+2 War Points**

- **+Access to Level 2 of the Evolving Quest**

I nodded to myself, reaching out, remembering the node and the way that it'd "felt" to me. Then I cursed as I found that there was nothing like that here.

That was fine. I'd not expected to be able to use it, but for the quest system to be working again, I guessed that either it could sense me still, or…

Or more likely, once the AI had reset my system, I was back on my own again. There was no way an AI hundreds of star systems away had been monitoring me before, after all.

It probably involved itself when certain things happened, but until then I was on autopilot. That would explain this as well. I had a need; it was judged something that I could use to grow, and the automated system saw it, marked it up, and I was good to go…no need to do more.

With that in mind, though, and because I'd not been able to access it for a long time before this, I pulled up my character sheet.

Identifier: Biological Weapon Variant #Steve				
Species: Human		**Nanites available**: ERROR		
Threat Level: Beta		**Corrupted Nanites**: ERROR		
		Weaponized Nanites: ERROR		
Stat	Current points	Description	Effect	Cost to Upgrade

Arise: Conqueror

Body	12	Physical strength and capacity to absorb damage	+110 resistance to damage	ERROR
Reactions	12	Mental and physical reactions	Time Dilation= 12*12*10= 1440+50%= 2160 seconds	ERROR
IQ	12	Intelligence and the capability to utilize it in the real world	+110 to Assimilation of new technologies and capabilities	ERROR
Nimbleness	12	The capacity to utilize tools, weapons, and small devices	+110 to success with devices	ERROR
Dexterity	12	The ability to dodge and utilize larger items/devices	+110 chance to dodge	ERROR
Karmic Luck	2.7	The likelihood of an action to spawn an adverse/ positive reaction	+17 chance to gain a favorable outcome in games of chance	ERROR
Perception	12	The ability to differentiate between details and spot threats at a distance	+110 likelihood to spot concealed items, details, or traps — see Reactions	ERROR
Control	12	The ability to control external systems		ERROR

Cybernetics	12	Integration of Cybernetic and Biogenetic augmentations and how likely they are to work		ERROR
Resonance	0	The capacity to use and integrate devices that require elemental resonances		ERROR

I stared in shock.

First, because whoo-boy, had I reached a new level.

I was twice the man I'd been before—according to the system, at least. Twelve was my new "standard," it seemed, though it couldn't figure out a way for me to upgrade that any further.

I guessed I was only able to upgrade myself now in the physical sense by rebuilding myself stronger. Like if I figured out how to make that diamond-hard marble-looking shit that the node was made out of, and I started building that into the outer layer of my skin.

I had an inkling how I'd do that, but it'd basically make me into a statue, so that was pointless.

The other thing I noticed, right after feeling entirely too pleased about my progress, was that my Karmic Luck was in the toilet. Literally, I'd been at seven or so last time—I couldn't actually remember for sure—but still!

Admittedly, I had absolutely no clue what that meant. Apparently it was a general luck stat, though that had never made sense to me.

I guessed maybe I'd burned up a load of my luck now? Maybe I'd gained a lot in the universe's POV from the years of torture, and now…

No, that was just crazy. That meant that someone, somewhere, was sitting with their thumb on the scales of chance and deciding whether they should lift or press down.

I refused to believe in that on general principles.

Though meeting Ingrid was a pretty big lucky point, I had to admit.

Screw it. I shook my head and moved on.

The other thing that had happened was my "elemental resonance." That was frustrating as well, because I'd supposedly had some before—something about sensing and being able to manipulate certain metals and shit at a distance, I dimly remembered.

Arise: Conqueror

The assholes who had been torturing me had been excited about it certainly, and so had Hans. I vaguely remembered that little wytch thing that had been able to throw flames around because it had used resonance as well. I instantly lamented the lost chance at flinging fireballs in a fight like a monkey flinging shit at the zoo, then I remembered that I could probably build a plasma caster to do that easily now, and that I could bench-press a rhino.

I'd take that trade-off.

"Okay, ten forms of tech…" I muttered to myself, focusing. I had the gravity drive here, and to figure it out, I'd need to take it apart, so I'd leave that for last. That way, if there wasn't another that was intact out here, well, no loss.

I could just lift it out and plug it into the cobbled-together wreck I was going to build.

Power storage cells, though, and memory cells I guessed. They were the first step.

I clambered around the torn edge of the ship, dropping a few levels, then catching myself and starting to really look. The engineering department had two stations, I vaguely remembered.

The main one had been farther back, much closer to the main engines, and was definitely gone now. The other one, though, was around here somewhere…

Ten minutes of looking and a little light cursing, and I found I'd been looking at the levels the wrong way around. Climbing two levels up, I found the section I needed, as well as a small memory core.

This one hadn't been important enough to have an AI—or hell, even a much cheaper to produce RI—but it had the capacity.

I laid one hand on it, and focusing, reached for my Engineering sub-mind; and, thinking at it that I needed to understand this, I then sighed in relief.

The nanites that pooled around my hand flowed down across its surface, searching and probing, before providing a pop-up.

Viable sample discovered! 16% chance of creating intact blueprint from sample. Continue? Yes/No…

"Fuck no!" I snapped, staring in horror at what could have been a damn expensive mistake.

Quest Uncovered!

Evolving Quest discovered: Building the Future: Sub Quest!

In order to correctly evaluate and assimilate the technological marvels that surround you, your engineering systems must be improved.

Level up your scanners and engineering knowledge by successfully scanning and integrating 10 designs to receive the following reward:

- **+1 Support Point**

I cursed again, before ripping the memory core out of its housing and sticking it to my back. A backpack formed around it as my armor flowed up instinctually.

Looking around, I saw a mess of scattered technology, piles of trashed systems, and bugger all that stood out to me as viable.

The next few rooms were the same, filled with trash and shattered tech, but nothing of use.

The first room, though—that was a goldmine, in more ways than one.

First, the steadily reforming body of an Ændari dickhead provided me with a nice burst of nanites. That was a relief, as was the speed that they integrated.

The other relief was that she'd clearly been a soldier or a warrior of some kind, considering she was wearing armor and had a rifle, a handgun and two grenades on her hip.

The armor, unfortunately, failed to generate a design plan in my first five attempts. I'd thought that between the dozens of parts that made it up and the sheer rolls of the dice that worked out, I'd probably be able to get the sub quest sorted with her corpse alone.

Hell was I wrong.

The first five goddamn attempts all ended in a failure as the armor crumbled and fractured, and worse was that there was still a cost in nanites! Each section needed a relative amount of nanites to scan it, with bigger bits needing more.

The breakthrough came when I realized that flooding it with nanites and waiting to see what happened was a fail every time.

I forced myself to sit on the edge of a low desk and think about it. Zac managed to do it virtually every time, after all.

Yeah, sure, he was the boy wonder of engineering, but he was also an Aussie asshole and he was drunk at least half the time. Add to that I'd been using these systems much longer than him, and I had a wider depth of skills, so how the hell did he do it?

Thinking about it, he'd done it with the makers as well, not with himself personally, and we'd done it with them…wait, *I'd* done it with them, scanning in systems before!

I'd patched and botched together things before, so why the hell wasn't it working now?

Then it hit me.

When I'd been doing this on the derelict ship originally, I'd been trying to learn it myself.

I'd not been relying on the system to figure it all out and to essentially spoon-feed me the knowledge. I'd been trying to figure out how everything worked, and just like that, as I started to pay attention to the armor before me, examining it and drawing simple comparisons in the way that it was layered?

It started to make sense.

There were three parts of the armor left by that point, and two worked. The rifle didn't, unfortunately. Stopping and considering things, I pulled the handgun apart, figuring out the battery pack, then the main projector, before losing the rest.

That was fine, though; I was learning.

The grenades were both successful, probably because I was insanely careful with them, having no desire to blow myself up.

Two hours later and I was done. It'd taken a shitload of failures still, but I felt like I'd learned a lot as well. Then, taking out the memory core, I tried again.

Viable sample discovered! 68% chance of creating intact blueprint from sample. Continue? Yes/No…

That was a hell of a difference, but it was still essentially a little over even odds. This was too important for that, and along with my newly awarded Support point, I still had a perk to spend.

Sod's Law, when I went looking through the system with that in mind, I found that it was actually a "lesser" perk, not a greater one. But still.

After ten minutes of searching through the perks, I was starting to curse at a level that would have made a sailor blush, as I'd made the stupid mistake of sorting by available capacity.

I'd done this before, and it'd always reduced the insane levels of perks that were available, down to a more manageable dozen or so.

Unfortunately, saying that my situation had changed slightly from then was like saying that an otter's pocket was damp.

It wasn't.

There was probably nothing in the world that was wetter than an otter's pocket, and this goddamn system had to know that.

I eventually stopped and just stared at the scrolling and constantly updating list with one thought uppermost in my mind: scan and blueprint.

The perk that eventually updated and was offered wasn't exactly what I had in mind, but it worked well enough.

__Stellar Engineer__: Travelling the depths of space requires an engineer to know their ship and its capabilities like no other. Gain 10% to instinctual understanding of your ship's capabilities.

I'd wanted something that could help me with the multitude of systems I was going to be working with, and I'd almost settled on another.

__Mechanic__: Intuitive knowledge of mechanical systems.

But after a little thinking, I'd gone for the Stellar Engineer, mainly because that at least gave me an overall boost to the chances of getting home.

I put the memory core back on my back and returned to searching.

Forty minutes later, I'd found another memory core, as well as a half-melted power cell. Taking the cell and using what I understood of them, which was more in the larger generation side of things, than the storage side, I eventually managed to repair the damaged unit. In doing so, I got enough of a comprehension to produce some of my own that were marked as "low grade" power cells.

Twenty minutes after that, and using the details I'd learned in repairing the power conduits aboard our ship, I'd managed to raise it to medium grade.

A quick experiment verified that I could create a simple variant of the power cell by layering them one over the other. Charging them by absorbing a section of wall and feeding the produced energy into the cells resulted in them keeping that energy more or less stable.

That was huge, knowing that I had a way to generate as much energy as I needed, and that I could make power cells to store it.

Gathering up my things, I turned and headed back, taking the time to make damn sure that there was nothing else of viable use aboard the ship.

That—of course—was when the ship entered another cloud.

The only warning I got was a feeling like the air around me—if there'd been any—was shaking. And then, as I stared, trying to make sense of it, the world exploded.

Literally, lightning flooded the corridors, slamming into me and through, driving me back against the wall, roaring in pain. My armor triggered on instinct, and just as the crackling wave had begun to pass, I was hit again and again.

The power cells I'd been building up exploded. The little energy that'd been held inside as a test ruined what I'd built as it discharged, and I was hit repeatedly with the crackling overload.

Long seconds seemed to become hours, as the world around me was filled with floating, fragmenting nanites. And that was what finally got through to me.

I pulled my armor into myself again, shaking and cursing. It felt as if my skin was rendered down to individual fats…then it was over, the last of the electrical backwash vanishing.

I collapsed, drifting in the dead corridor. I got control over myself again, catching my breath and swearing as I looked at the reforming skin, the burns, and the shattered cells.

Clearly, wherever the hell I was, I'd found out why the fuck nobody ever escaped to tell people about the wrecks.

The cells that hadn't had power stored in them had been fine—or, well, they'd taken damage, but it was because they were attached to the ones that had.

A little poking and prodding as I recovered, and I snarled, getting the hint at last. Whatever this place was, the energy discharge fucked with electricals like nothing else.

That could be a good thing, though, I realized. Because it might be that the ships weren't as fucked as I'd been worrying.

Arise: Conqueror

Sure, the outer layers were going to be toast. And anything that had held a charge was going to have gone boom, so the reactors and more were likely shit. *That* wasn't good at all, but the rest? The general systems would hopefully be more or less intact, if I could get deeper into the wrecks.

I tried to create a few power cells again, using some of my nanite and the null coins. This time, just in case, I left them entirely empty, gripping them with a tentacle and generating a simple crystal input device, feeding into the cell.

Fifteen minutes later, I was cursing as I stared at the blacked rubble that had been the storage cell. Clearly the input had worked, as there'd been bugger all in it originally, but whatever that red lightning was, it was fucking powerful.

The next bit passed with me fucking with the cells, making change after change until I finally got something that was more or less stable. And even then, when it was full, it exploded.

The point was, though, that until the input was attached, the cell were stable, and right up until they were full?

They worked.

That was a massive relief. Maybe, just maybe, I could generate the power I'd need for a single jump after all.

All told, I was three hours down in my experiments, but more importantly, I was also a hell of a lot closer to being able to start the grav drive up again, if nothing else.

I'd still need to be able to understand how the hell I "aimed" it, or guided it or whatever, but the quest prompt had made one point clear.

Somewhere, hidden in this debris-laden graveyard, there was tech that had been lost to the outside galaxy. That might be a super-advanced toenail clipper, but I was damn well hoping there was a laser rail gun setting to it.

We had three weeks at the most, and I was betting that as soon as the Ændari found out that Ingrid and the others were on the node, they'd speed things up.

Three weeks was how long the AI Argus had estimated, and I had no doubt that was the most optimistic way we could be looking at it. He'd said that it was in part due to the Ændari fleets and that they'd been getting ready to fuck off from this sector of space.

Some of the fleet that would have been used for this was off with Francine, meaning if they launched straightaway and came running, they'd be doing so with a much smaller force.

They were clearly willing to go from a "cold" war to a shooty-shooty one, so they had to make sure they had enough forces to try to take, as well as defend, the node.

What I guessed they'd been trying before was a smash-and-grab, then running out of the quadrant and triggering the node to kill everyone's nanites.

Now, they needed to take the node over to do that, and if they sent too small a force, they'd be defeated in detail.

No, they'd be awhile before they could take it; they knew the forces they'd sent had failed, so now they'd gather a fleet and do it properly.

In the meantime, I'd be frankly amazed if they didn't try to do something, like another stealth ship or something, but that'd be it, I was hoping.

It made me sick to my stomach as I considered that, and that Ingrid and the others could be fighting for their lives already, but there was nothing I could do.

I had to trust that they'd hold things together until James and the others could reach them, and I'd do my best to be there for them as well.

For now, Ingrid and the others would have to dig in and make whatever improvements were needed to the node to hold it.

The ship I'd taken with me and had fucking totaled? It was intended to be scrapped—not by the Ændari, admittedly, but Ingrid and I had been planning to use everything we could to make the node into a battle station to blood those bastards for every meter we could.

With that gone, I had no clue what the hell they'd be doing back on the station. But I had to hope they were making the most of the little time they had.

CHAPTER THREE

A handful of hours later, I was on the hull, sweat rolling down my back as I tried to guide not only the ship I was on, but the remains of the brane creature toward the biggest of the nearby hulks.

I'd searched my current ship from top to bottom. Although I'd not found anything else that was particularly viable, in terms of usable tech, I had discovered two things: there were more bodies, all of which I'd torn apart and absorbed, and there was a secondary bridge.

It was similar to the CIC, or Combat Information Centers, that I was familiar with from human ship designs. There wasn't a secondary set of power cells or anything so useful, but there had been the remains of a backup memory bank.

It was definitely trashed, but I hoped that some sections of it could be repowered and searched, and at the end of the day, the ship still had a fuckload of mass if not.

Then there were the torn-apart remains of the creature that I'd somehow brought with me back up and out of the branes.

It was mangled pretty badly, and as near as I could tell, it was something like a living starship, or a metallic whale or something. I genuinely couldn't decide, as the more I'd stared at it out there, slowly drifting away from me, the more I became convinced it was both.

I couldn't see any way that a creature could naturally evolve a fucking metal skin, nor how it'd survive in space, or at the bottom of a gravity well.

It even had nanites—or something like them, anyway. I managed to attune them, but they were weird, unresponsive in a way that I really didn't like, and that made me leave them alone, just in case.

None of that shit made sense, and yet, it damn well looked like it had.

I decided that it was at the very least worth dragging in close and trying to break down, if nothing else. Then I'd started to look elsewhere. There were thousands of fragments of ships out here, and most of them were trashed.

I knew that—looking at them, it was goddamn obvious—but several of them were so unbelievably huge that there had to be shit in there I could use, somewhere, as they slowly drifted out of the clouds, wreathed in crackling electrical discharge.

One of them looked a little something like a Forgeship, in that it was mind-bogglingly big.

So, being that I needed shit, and there was shit in the distance gradually drifting away, the obvious choice was to use my abilities to go play with it.

I'd triggered my gravity bubbles carefully, well aware that if there was anything here that could sense it then I was giving my presence away, and that inertia was a real thing.

I started small, a little blip of gravity here and there, slowing the drift of the chunk I was aboard first, then reversing it, gradually floating back toward the biggest ship in the distance.

The remains of the sky-whale, or whatever it was, I did the same with: a little pop, then another and another.

It was all going well, right up until I realized that the massive ship wasn't just a single ship.

Or that it was in fact once a ship, but that because mass has its own gravitational force, it was dragging more of the shattered hulks in toward itself.

This, I guessed, was how asteroids and so on formed in the first place: the mass of some of the larger rocks pulled in closer to the biggest bit, and as each bit was added to the mix, the gravity just grew stronger.

I'd probably read or heard about that somewhere, because the way it popped up as I focused and the hull of the massive starship resolved at the same time? It was just too obvious.

Had I *understood* it, and not just heard or read it, then I wouldn't have found myself in the shitty situation of trying to slow the impact of the trillions of tons of metal I was currently riding.

As soon as I tried to trigger smaller gravitational bubbles, thinking to cushion the impact, I found out just how many thousands of wrecks made up what I'd seen as a particularly bumpy hull from a distance.

I made the mistake of trying to create a bubble where I was aiming to strike, thinking to have it push "out" a bit, and slow the impact. Nice and simple.

Instead, the hull of the giant ship looked as if I'd set off a claymore mine on it. The debris fields that had settled over who knew what for who knew how long, went from powdery fine fragments of metal and rock, silica, and more, to entire ships, ancient ruins, what looked like space suit bits, armor, bent and crushed weapons, beer cans…

Anything and everything that had crashed together over hundreds or thousands of centuries here in deep space, and the dust that had been shattered free and that drifted everywhere here, had coated it all.

I swear I saw a coffeepot go flashing past at one point, and that was just crazy.

Underneath all the junk, it still might be useable, but the top layers? Hundreds of billions of separate parts, millions of which were now hurtling in all directions.

I panicked, ducking down and pulling hard on my armor on instinct, willing it to cover me, to be me, to keep me safe and…and the red-black void flowed out from me.

Arise: Conqueror

It formed up, reaching ahead to create a spreading wave. It pushed out, looking organic in the way that it flowed. But as soon as the dust hit it?

I gasped in shock.

There were organic and inorganic fragments mixed here, I suddenly knew, along with…it almost seemed like nanites, but utterly alien and weird. No matter what I tried, they remained dead. After a few minutes of effort, I dismissed it as coincidence and moved on. The Devourer did what it did best, tearing the mass apart, converting it, absorbing it, as I dragged it through the mess.

Thrusting a hand behind me, I extended a pseudopod that formed null coins as fast as thought, dropping them into a box that I was creating at the same time, frantically trying not to waste the bounty as more and more of my armor rippled out.

The ships were different, obviously.

They were too big, too heavy for me to just collect and process in seconds, but still they fell to me.

This time I was more careful, understanding slightly more, as I triggered more and more gravity bubbles.

I drew the mass in again, packing it tighter as I swept the armor around like a static cloth collecting dust, dragging the fragments in and processing them.

I created a new gravity bubble behind me, triggering it slowly, gently, as I slowed my approach, fine-tuning it as the distance fell.

Minutes passed in a blur, until finally, almost as gently as a butterfly alighting, the corpse and the remains of my ship touched down atop the junkyard surface.

The real work began as a second glimmering cloud of dust lifted from the surface.

I extruded a thick gelatin-like mass around me, all the while checking the skies for any more clouds that might arrive and fuck me up. My armor felt like literally warmed marshmallow that pushed out in all directions from me, pressing against everything, as I stepped off the edge of the ship I'd arrived on.

Walking forward was weird. I gradually sank inside the mass, my armor happily shredding and reforming it into coin after coin that dutifully dropped into the box that I dragged along behind me on a tentacle.

I made myself go deeper and deeper, sending out regular pulses of gravity to try to map everything around me, hoping against hope that what had appeared to be a huge ship genuinely was, and not a collection of billions of years of technological trash.

After an hour, at a point where my skin was crawling at the thought of just how much mass there was currently suspended over my head, I finally got the radar return that I'd been hoping for.

Solidity.

I dug down and down, working left and right on a gradually increasing angle until I finally found the hull, deliberately having left a path to follow back, I hoped, to the surface once I'd done this.

I'd lost track of the hours by now, but I was fairly sure it was still around halfway through the first day, when I finally reached the hull. Kneeling and pressing my palm to the surface, I let myself rest.

It wasn't the physical drain on me that was wearing me out—it was not knowing.

I didn't know whether the Ændari had responded already, and had dropped everything else to go and attack the node straight off.

I didn't know if I'd turned left rather than right as I dug down, instead of possibly finding a veritable treasure trove of technology, I'd found a virtual toilet dumping ground.

I didn't know whether I was still in the same galaxy as the people I cared about, or whether I was just on the other side of the gas giant in the same goddamn system that Ingrid and the others were in.

I didn't know *anything*, and it was making my mind race as I tried to figure out method after method to deal with it all.

Instead, I forced my mind to stillness and focused on the situation.

So far, I had a basic design for a power cell and its connective systems that was a hell of an improvement on where I had been.

I also had a gravity drive that was more or less intact, and that with the use of those cells, I could in theory jump at any time. I'd just not know where the hell I was going.

Lastly, I had a literal junkyard of ships and mass here, and with the limited tech I had access to, I could—in theory again—build a ship of my own in short order.

The only thing I didn't have was any kind of navigational system. One star looked the same as the next to me, so there was no way I was going to be able to eyeball this.

Hell, on Earth, I'd never been able to tell one star from the next when my ex took me stargazing, so out here, where every star looked different and I saw them from different angles anyway?

Not a chance.

That was why I was so desperate to find a ship that was more or less intact.

Hopefully it'd have something that I could use.

I opened my eyes, pushing the Devourer out in all directions, letting it feed on the metal and mess that lay everywhere, sending pulse after pulse. I was hoping to feel an air lock, a bump—hell, a fucking window or a section of damage…anything on the goddamn hull that might give me a hint—and I found nothing.

Trying to keep the pulses small, I kept going, shifting gradually, using a dozen frequencies and strengths, and again found nothing. But it was the movement of the mass overhead that made me accept what I had to do, and that I couldn't afford to go looking anywhere else.

I'd had to dig out a pocket under all this debris to send the pulses out, and I could feel the shifting and slithering of it all overhead as more and more of the path collapsed.

That made my mind up for me. I reached out, forming a structure around me to brace most of the bigger bits, before I pressed my hand to the hull and started to eat my way inside.

Arise: Conqueror

My first shock had been that this place, a literal space graveyard for ships, existed. I was in store for a second and third major shock, though.

Initially, the hull resisted me—not fully, but where I'd eaten my way through things easily before, this was more like pushing something hot through solid ice.

It went, and the mass that was being converted by me leapt upward as something about improved matter and "grade-three structures" flashed up.

I didn't care, though: I needed in, and I resolved to find the notification again later if I could. But the third surprise?

It was when the atmosphere inside blasted me backward and into the debris overhead, causing it all to come sliding down and bury me.

<u>INGRID</u>

"I appreciate that's your opinion," Ingrid said brightly, smiling in a way that definitely didn't reach her eyes as she stared at the figure on the screen before her. "But considering that it's wrong, I'm going to ignore it, and repeat my position. We are—"

"You are the holders of the node, and you maintain all rights as to who is permitted aboard." The Ændari on the screen before her rolled his eyes and waved a hand insultingly. "Yes, yes, I understand. You claim all rights to the node, *fine*. Whatever. I don't see why we can't return, though! You've asked for help from any ships in the system, as well as any and all forces that the Scorpio system will donate, but have the unmitigated gall and speciesism to refuse to allow *me* to dock!"

"You're Ændari," Ingrid replied cooly.

"I am, yes, and yet I'm here, aboard the *Lurksome Doubt*. I fled the station with the others when those Ændari troopers boarded it! They'd have killed me just as quickly as they did the others, as I've explained more than once!"

"And we don't care," Ingrid said. "Your entire species has been nothing but a blight on the galaxy in every single point of contact we've had. Therefore, no. You are not permitted to board the node. If you attempt to disembark from this, or any other ship, and board the node, you will be removed. If you somehow find your way aboard the node, you will be removed.

"If you somehow magically teleport to the node, you will be removed. Have I made my position absolutely clear yet? *Any* attempt to board will see you removed. If you *still* try to board this node, understand that I won't *ask* you to leave—we will physically throw you off the node and into space. You can try swimming home. Thank you for your call."

With that, she cut the connection, settling back into the seat with a groan as she dropped her face into her hands.

"Why the hell does he keep trying this shit?" she whispered.

"Attention, incoming communication request from—" Argus started to say, cutting off as Ingrid held up one hand to stop him.

"If it's that same idiot, I don't want to hear it!" she snapped. "Tell him all communication attempts from him are now blocked and to go attempt to mate with the star."

"Confirmed," Argus replied.

"Mate with a star?" Jonas smiled.

"He wouldn't get the cultural significance of telling him to go fuck himself or anything else, so hopefully that will—"

"Attention, incoming communication request from unknown sender aboard the *Lurksome Doubt*."

"Refuse it," Ingrid growled.

Arise: Conqueror

"Confirmed."

"He can't take a hint, can—" Jonas shook his head, then threw his hands up as Argus cut him off again.

"Attention, incoming communication request from the captain of the intersystem transport *Lurksome Doubt*," the AI announced.

"If this is him…" Ingrid growled.

"You know it will be." Jonas snorted. "Want me to take this one?"

"Please." Ingrid sighed.

"Put it through to my station please, Argus," Jonas called, before leaning close to the screen and staring at it, as a helmeted figure was pushed roughly to one side, the same asshole Ændari pushing his way into the pickup.

"At last!" he snapped. "How dare you refuse my connection! I was—"

"*Lurksome Doubt*, be aware that if you attempt to land at this node with any Ændari aboard, your ship will be confiscated, and all aboard will be ejected into space, without space suits. We have eradicated the entire Ændari presence aboard this station, and the stealth ship that docked here, eliminating the whole crew.

"Our spacecraft is currently battling the Ændari vessels that were holding your jump points. Can I make this any more clear to you? You cannot land here, and if you try, I will kill each and every one of you, if that asshole is aboard your ship. If he attempts communication with us again, our warship will receive orders that you are an Ændari sympathizer and will destroy you next. Now kindly fuck off."

Jonas cut the connection, then settled back and shook his head. "See, you've just got to be clear with them. If he doesn't get that—"

"Attention, incoming communication request from the captain of the intersystem transport *Lurksome Doubt*," Argus said.

"Refuse it," Jonas snapped.

"Attention, incoming communication request from the captain of the intersystem transport *Lurksome Doubt*. They claim they have an atmospheric leak and are demanding access to the node to prevent loss of life."

"Are you fucking…" Jonas snarled, lurching to his feet. "Fine! Connect them to me!"

"I'm sorry!" Those were the first panicked words out of the mouth of the captain when the connection was made. "Please don't kill us all!"

"Just fuck right off then!" Jonas snapped.

"We can't!" he wailed. "We're a glorified tug and that bastard is shooting holes in the hull!"

"What?!"

"The Ændari! He's gotten a gun from somewhere and he's blowing holes in the hull! I've got fifty-six refugees aboard we turned around to come help, before we knew that he wouldn't be allowed to dock. Now we can't make it to anywhere else before half of them are dead!"

"Motherfucker!" Jonas roared and shook his head, glaring first at the panicked figure on the screen, and then at Ingrid.

"Let them land," she said flatly. "Meet them at the dock with Scylla and make the situation *very* clear to them all."

"And the Ændari?"

"I'll kill him," Scylla interjected, shrugging. "You have warned him."

"Dock as soon as you can," Jonas told the terrified captain. "You'll be cross-loaded to another ship as soon as one's available. Until then, you'll stay in the dock, and if any of you attempt to leave there, you'll be executed." With that, he cut the connection; the frantically babbling captain's voice ended abruptly.

"What the hell do they think is going to happen?" Courtney shook her head. "I mean, they know we're going to be under attack again soon. Why the hell are they so desperate to get aboard?"

"The Ændari is probably a spy," Jonas guessed. "The others?" He shrugged.

"Most likely they're just desperate people who have nowhere else to be." Ingrid sighed. "If they're refugees from here, the people who lived here before, and now they know that we've gotten inside? We've got no clue what insanity they believe about the nodes. Half of them seem to think this is the first step on their path to replace their gods, others think it's a way to become a Devourer, more think…you know what, I don't care." She shrugged. "I just don't."

"Ingrid…" Jonas started.

"No. We've got far too much going on to care. Without Steve, we've got no way to build any of the weapons with the raw materials we were going to take from the ship. That leaves us with harvesting the bodies as best we can and sharing out those nanites," she said. "Our only options are to allow volunteers to land and hold the outer areas, while we close the doors and set up whatever traps we can figure out in here, or to give up, and after Steve…after everything! I'm NOT giving up this place without a fight!"

"We won't," Jonas agreed, putting a hand on Ingrid's shoulder as she struggled to keep the tears from flowing. "He'll come back. You know what he's like."

"He will." Scylla seemed to believe it beyond any doubt. "When has he failed?"

"He hasn't," Ingrid whispered.

"Then until he does, we will trust in him."

There were three ships already on approach, two of which were filled with "volunteers" from the refugees who had left, and one that had taken clear damage in its escape and apparently couldn't currently communicate.

They'd all been warned that if they attempted to board the node and were not in fact capable of defending themselves, they would regret it.

They'd also all been warned that the interior doors wouldn't be opened to them under any circumstances, and yet they were still coming. This asshole of an Ændari was only the latest scumbag to believe that things would be different for them.

Ingrid was *still* waiting for someone from the nearby world of Scorpio-3 to be available to discuss mutual defenses and them dispatching additional forces to help secure the node.

Arise: Conqueror

As soon as she made it clear that they wouldn't be permitted joint control of the node, they'd said that they'd consider their position and that someone would be available to discuss things "soon."

Ingrid and the others had talked, and the consensus was that between the local leadership who were boarding ships and waiting for the Lagrange point to be cleared, and the almost total lack of any armed ships in the system, help wasn't likely.

Short-range fighters and orbital defenses were all that was left now.

Most likely, if help ended up coming at all, it'd be at a steep price.

That was why Ingrid had reached out to the local mercenaries through Malthus instead. There weren't many of them, and those Malthus recommended as being either trustworthy or worth the expense were even smaller in number. But almost seventy were spread across three ships and on their way to the node now.

They were also bringing some additional "toys" that Malthus had ordered through them.

Or they damn well better be, she silently swore. Between hiring these mercenaries and the purchases that Malthus and Jonas had picked, their accounts were almost dry again—and that was after all the money that had come from the incidents on the Den.

It would all be worth it, though, she desperately hoped, glancing at the one screen on the wall of the command center that showed neither the system they were in, nor any details for the upcoming war. The text gently pulsed on it.

Contact Status: Biological Weapon Variant #Steve: Lost

Ingrid tore her eyes away from that damning detail and got back to work, knowing that the AI was monitoring its systems frantically, almost as desperate as she was to find Steve.

CHAPTER FOUR

The ship was a mess. Well, it'd probably not been as much of a mess before I made a fucking hole in the hull and let out a bunch of its atmosphere, admittedly, but still.

Once the jet of pressure that'd slammed me into the compressed debris and remains of hulls overhead had dissipated, the mass shifted and had driven me down into the hull headfirst.

It'd not been good.

First, the pressure was far, far higher than any human ship would have had, considering the force of it, and it was only the sheer density of the wrecks above me that had kept me, and them, from being fired out into space.

That didn't mean they stayed where they were, though. At first, they bounced around and I was crushed into and smacked around in them. Then, when I slid out of the main "thrust" of the jet and grabbed onto the hull that had been exposed?

Well.

I'd barely managed to get myself in close and out of the way of the pressurized outgassing when it stopped, and the mass overhead shifted, then drifted down to crush me.

I moved as fast as I could, grabbing sections of debris from nearby, yanking them inward, slapping the base against the hull and extruding patches of nanites to stick them there, even as I shifted more and more to form as solid a ceiling over that as I could.

I'd begun to form the Devourer, thinking to use it both to protect me and to absorb some of the mass. That was when I felt that same charge building in the air again.

Cursing, I forced myself to keep my armor away, and instead took the impact. Lightning flooded the hull again, and I hissed in pain.

I was driven to my knees, straining. The hull shivered beneath my knee…and that was it. I blinked, stunned, then couldn't help but smile.

The changes to my body were far more than I'd guessed. I needed to make sure I remembered that—that my armor was me now, and I was the armor. It wasn't worn over my skin; my skin was pure nanites now, and hardened. All I had to do was get that in my head, and I'd be an unholy terror to fight.

Arise: Conqueror

With that thought in mind, I waited until the pulsing lightning had almost all dissipated and I reached out with one hastily extruded tentacle, flooding the tip with the Devourer alone.

The charge built, as though it'd gone into reverse and was coming back to punish me for fucking around…then it was gone, and I let loose a sigh of relief.

I'd needed to know that, after all.

It wasn't the Devourer or my flesh that was the issue; it was something about the actual outer layer of my armor that attracted it. And now I knew that it was possible to extrude the Devourer without my armor.

Just as I could change my outer surface into the armor, I shifted it now, forming the outermost layer into the Devourer.

It felt strange, but also somehow more relaxing, as if I'd put down a weight I'd been carrying for far too long.

The armor ate through the hull steadily as I focused, expanding the hole until it was big enough for me to enter. Then I slid inside, grabbing more of the mass overhead and dragging it with me, reforming several of the null coins into a patch that sealed the hull again. Just in case.

Twenty minutes later, I was done, finally looking around the room I'd found myself in.

It was pretty boring actually, when I had a proper look. There were stacks of metal flakes—I didn't have a better name for them, when I examined one— stacked in the middle of the room in various sizes.

I checked several of them out. The Devourer happily consumed it, showing it as highly refined metals, but beyond that and the designation "unknown metal sheets" when I tried examining it, I knew nothing else.

Well, I did. For the system to not recognize them meant they'd come from either somewhere far away or from a long time ago, I guessed.

Then I had a horrible thought that maybe it was me that was from long ago, as gravity had been proved to bend space and time, after all.

I could have ended up in the Sol system, just in a billion years' time, and I'd never fucking know it.

That thought had me hesitating for a few seconds, then I tossed the sheets aside and headed for the door, shaking my head. That I'd travelled years into the future, or the past, was fucking unlikely. And even if I had? Nothing changed for me for now.

My first step was to learn about these ships, get some tech scanned, and get my arse in gear to make a viable ship that could get me out of here. Nothing else mattered.

The door from this room into the main corridor didn't want to open, and I cursed. As soon as I'd started to force the door, ancient and apparently cold- welded closed, the atmosphere on the other side slammed into me.

I was driven several steps back, and I grunted, feeling heavier than before. I paused, assessing, then shrugged. Beyond experiencing a bit more pressure than normal, there wasn't any real change—well, not once I dismissed the drifting gasses as unimportant.

As soon as the pressure had equalized, it'd dropped again. But as the atmo rushed to fill the room behind me—and I was glad that I'd thought to seal the hull—I was surrounded by thick, grey clouds.

It was like walking through heavy fog, but as soon as it equalized again, the fog slowed, then drifted downward.

I waved a hand through it, drawing up trails of silvery grey from a blanket that seemed to fill the hallways at roughly waist height, and I shook my head in bemusement.

Maybe it was something to do with the atmo having been here like this for so long? I'd probably have been a lot more freaked out, imagining all sorts of weird hidden creatures, if not for the fact I was still "seeing" by radar.

I was getting a hell of a lot better at it as well, as more and more of the ship became clear to me.

I could sense things all around me. The squarish form of the corridor was obvious, and yeah, highly metallic, so just in case, I was floating again.

The rest of the structure that I could sense, though, was weird. There were what felt like pools of mercury or something similar, scattered about, here and there.

In addition, there were crystals seemingly dropped everywhere at random. They weren't like the ones we used for weapons and transferring data or power; they were smaller and denser, and most were cracked. The few I found that weren't made me suspect they were empty.

The others had shattered, as there were either larger ones that felt empty, or piles of broken ones that were much smaller.

I guessed that meant that they'd once held a charge. Moving on, I found more.

Rooms that led off to the sides were invariably sealed, and more often than not, there were pools of liquid in them as well, some larger and some smaller, but generally strewn about in much the same way.

I passed carved divots in the rooms, wondering at their purpose, and areas where there had been technological devices that seemed to have exploded.

Most of the tech seemed to be crystal—discs of it on the walls, dishes…whatever I kept finding scattered about the corridors. Hell, when I looked at the doors, I found more embedded in them, presumably their equivalent of a doorbell and press button or something.

That was it, though: metal for the inert things, like the walls and floors, and crystal for everything else, and the halls filled with drifting gasses.

Here and there, I passed piled rocks that reached halfway to the passage's ceiling. It was almost as if there'd been a rockslide and someone forgot the minor detail of a fucking mountain to get it from.

As well as that, about every twenty meters or so, I passed small tubes set into the floor, about two inches across, that vanished downward.

Sending a pulse into them showed that they were all identical, and that they sank deeper into the superstructure, but nothing else.

Arise: Conqueror

The farther I went, the more confused I got, wondering what the hell the ship had been for.

I paused after I'd collected the fifth of the larger crystals from the corridor, and finding the fucker was seemingly endless, I sat on a pile of the rocks, having not found a single goddamn chair yet.

I pushed nanites into the crystals, focusing and looking for anything that felt like a storage lattice. After the first shattered, crumbling into dust in my hands, I tried a different method.

I searched for any kind of input device, finding several metallic nodules, but that was it. The only way I could describe the other end of the crystal was a "twist."

It looked straight, as though there was nothing different about it, but it just *felt* weird. I tried poking and prodding, turning—hell, I tried banging one of them with a rock, before giving up and trying something else.

I started off by absorbing and breaking down some of the rock I was sitting on. Then, after pausing to center myself and making sure I was paying attention to the feeling of it, I fed that energy directly into the metal at the base of the crystal.

When I forced myself back to consciousness, I felt like I'd gotten a really bad case of sunburn, and yet a-fucking-gain I was surrounded by a mess of shattered nanites.

Cursing, I brushed myself off by instinct, before shaking my head at the automatic actions and absorbed them all again.

This time, as I absorbed more of the rocks and the shattered crystal from before, I noticed a few things.

Firstly, the rocks had a hell of a high content of metal in them, like far higher than anything I'd ever seen on Earth, and some crystals as well. They were spread out throughout each of what I'd taken to be a pile of boulders until now.

I crouched, running a hand over the rock and focusing, before swearing as I realized what the damn thing was.

It was part of the ship's crew!

It *had* to be—the almost solid mass, the high-pressure zones in the ship, the metal goddamn flakes that were probably dinner! Then add in the crystal, which I was betting was a fucking weapon now that I thought about it.

When I'd gotten back up, I'd felt like I'd been hit by damn lightning again, despite having been searching for it and paying attention in case the ship drifted through more of it again, and…

And I'd not felt the lightning since I entered the ship, had I?

The more I looked at the "rocks," the more I was convinced that they were the former crew, and the patches of mercury or liquid metal?

A little further thought had me undecided. Maybe a form of food? Something to keep them lubricated? Hell, art installations and floating burgers, for all I knew.

It didn't make any sense, not until I considered the pipes.

The pipes would allow something that was fluid to reach other sections of the ship, I guessed, while the rocks…maybe they were only used to work on the outer ring?

I shrugged, pocketing the weapon, finding that I'd now learned another blueprint when I checked my notifications.

Storm Needle	Personal Weapon
An unknown variant of proton weaponry, the newly named "Storm Needle" creates a negative ion charge between point A and point B, then spins the electrical charge contained in the crystal to damaging results.	
Durability 59/100	Proton Weaponry

It wasn't particularly exciting, or impressive, but it counted as another one of the ten that I needed. At the end of the day, it was something that was unknown to the Ændari database, and a cool little weapon that, now that I'd figured out what it was, I'd noticed the minor mistake I'd made with it.

There wasn't a barrel, not for a solid bit of crystal, but where the twist was, and that I'd been looking at? Yeah, that was essentially it.

I'd been peering down the barrel with my thumb on the trigger and I was never going to live this shit down if there was anything like CCTV here.

Jonas and Zac would get their hands on it somehow; I just knew it.

Setting off jogging along the corridor now that I'd found a few more details, I started to ignore the rooms on either side. They were invariably the same, and after figuring out the rock monsters, I started to wonder a bit more as I went.

The rocks would barely fit through the doorways that I passed. And when I did finally find a door that was wide enough and that was different than all the rest?

I paused to search it, finding a dozen big dips in the floor that looked like dry pools, but that was it.

Beyond that, the rooms were identical, and the rocks I'd passed were few and far between.

Loads of small rooms with shallow depressions on the floor, crystal artifacts here and there, but barely enough space for a rock to squeeze through the door.

I'd also noted that the crystals that I found were almost always by the molten mercury. The big rocks had crystal in them, but...

No, after a little more thought, I was guessing that I'd had this the wrong way around, as I finally found a walkway that led deeper into the superstructure. If the rock monster was a high-pressure world denizen as the ship's atmo suggested, then there was nothing to say that there couldn't be sentient fuckin' metal, was there?

I mean, crystal was always being argued over by the hippies as being alive and in tune with the galaxy and shit. I thought it was rubbish, until I found that it could be used as a storage device for information, a transmission medium for power; it could be a weapon...

The more I thought about it, the more I worried that it genuinely *was* alive.

If crystal could do all of that, then yeah, liquid metal people didn't actually seem so ridiculous now.

Arise: Conqueror

The passageway that led deeper was wide and tall, and at the foot of the ramp that led down, I found another pile of rocks, before what I guessed was a sealed air lock.

As soon as I ate my way through that, though, it became clear that somewhere down on this level was a breach. The atmo behind me began to tear loose with a scream, and I cursed, pushing myself through the wall, finding it easier than I expected to patch it over once I was through.

The area beyond was both deeper into the ship and far more electrically charged. The crystal weapons started to shiver as soon as I passed through.

After the experiments so far, though, I formed a coating around them that was closer to flesh than metal and grinned to myself when they quieted instantly.

The next hour was a repeat of the higher levels, although this time there were only a few rocks, and where I found them, they were of markedly higher quality.

They were shot through with crystals, platinum, and other precious metals, as well as coated in something that crumbled when I touched it.

"Guards," I muttered to myself. "That makes the most sense. Either guards or guard dogs, with the silver fuckers being the crew and being armed."

An hour more, and I found a second ramp leading down. By now, I was convinced of the relationship. Each of the tubes that I'd found on the level above extended to this floor and others, exiting via small holes in the wall that, when I checked them, were just large enough for the crystals to pass through without issue as well.

It took a few more minutes to find the rupture, but when I did? Damn.

I guessed it'd been a sentinel power core or a reactor or whatever, and realizing the size of the explosion, I was struck by how goddamn lucky I'd been in that I'd already lost the reactors on my ship, and that I'd had to use all the power to do the jump.

If I'd arrived here with the reactors powered?

I looked out over a hole in the ship that had to be the size of a football field, if not two. There were piles of debris everywhere I looked, and the last few minutes, I'd been back to wading through knee-deep dust and metal fragments.

There were at least twenty decks exposed to the vacuum that I could see from here, staring out over the shattered hole, holding to the torn remains of the corridor.

It'd ended abruptly, with the levels below and above vaporized or torn loose, like a giant maw had bitten down and ripped half the hull free. There were exposed conduits, piled wrecks, impacts from meteors and ice, and dust coating everything in the harder to reach sections, while the debris of a spaceborne junkyard covered the rest.

Standing there, clinging onto the corridor out of instinct, I stared down, wondering how the hell I was going to get around this.

My first thought had been that when the ship's atmo was around, I'd not been able to feel the electrical discharge. But now? I could see drifting banks of clouds and roiling lightning all around.

I stared out across the debris field and fought the urge to despair. This ship had been fucking huge, okay—now that I was exploring it, it was clearly smaller than a goddamn Forgeship. But the scale? It was still bigger than most cities I'd spent time in.

For a ship this goddamn huge to have been destroyed, and so utterly? What the hell chance did I have? I could just about maintain my goddamn motorbike and little else beyond that. Sure, I could cobble together some drones and shit, but...

Drones.

Yeah... Drones could work.

The clouds drifted constantly, after all—a simple remote drone might be able to map the area. I mean, it could probably stay out of the clouds, couldn't it?

I hesitated; then, swearing to myself, I backed up a few steps, ran at the opening, and launched out into space.

It wasn't the brightest solution, and it sure as shit wasn't one that the others would have chosen to take, but I had advantages they didn't, and I needed to know.

The arc of my flight held steady for almost a minute, rising as I leapt free. Then slowly, oh so fucking slowly, I started to drift downward.

That was when I triggered a faint pulse of gravity—a heartbeat long, and ahead of me—to adjust the direction, keeping me rising.

The debris and crap all around me shifted with the gravity pulse as well, but I was ahead of it and headed for open space.

As soon as I cleared it, I twisted and headed back on in the direction I guessed I'd come from, flashing over the debris-filled gap in the huge hull, slowly drifting downward, until in the distance I saw what I'd been looking for.

The remains of the Ændari ship I'd used to get here.

I passed through the edges of two clouds on my way, each time gritting my teeth at the electrical sensation, but relaxing as I made sure there was no real pain.

It took another gravity pulse, and then an outstretched tentacle to snag the lip of the hull, but soon I was back on it and ready to start the next phase.

The Ændari didn't do much right, but they were lazy fuckers with style. The hybrids that they'd been using to puppet those mostly dead creatures around had been run by the Ændari, mainly, but they'd also been using a lobotomized senagra to form the core.

We'd killed that, but I had to assume that they'd have other tricks. After all, what did they do if they went somewhere they needed to fly to get to the fight?

There was no way the Ændari troopers would go out and do the work if there was any way they could get their slaves to do it, and it took less than ten minutes to find the first drone, hidden in an engineering crawl space.

It was small, less than half a meter overall, and I just knew that the repulsor engines that it was fitted with would be a problem. A few minutes of tinkering, and then half an hour of disgusting cutting and sticking, and I had a very simple drone ready to explore.

Arise: Conqueror

Admittedly, it was also "wearing" the senagra's skin, as I'd literally skinned the fucker and wrapped it in that. I was damn glad to have found that here, even if it did give me almost nothing in nanites.

A few minutes later—knowing that nobody was going to believe how fucking random my life was these days—I threw the drone at the gap by the approaching cloud.

Six seconds later, I was swearing thoroughly.

Even with the skin on the drone, it was a massive failure. A finger of lightning flashed out like a giant cosmic "Fuck you, Steve," and the drone detonated.

I spent the next few minutes doing the "Why do you hate me, oh God," dance on the hull of a starship out in a cloud in deep space, before calming down and coming up with plan F—for fuckup.

First, because it'd only really occurred to me when I'd set off from the alien ship before that I could have lost the corpse and the ship, I slathered a small number of nanites on them both then stepped back, watching as they shifted slightly. Their outer layer became more flesh-like to prevent damage from the clouds.

I waited, verified that they did indeed survive the clouds just fine, and that I could find them both again if I needed to; then I started moving again.

The drone idea was a bust for now, but the whole point of it was to help me search. To search for a more or less intact ship, and anything that I could liberate.

Now, I threw myself into the air again, and this time I unfurled my wings. They'd always been made in the image of a fallen angel, and here, anything that was metallic wouldn't do. So I doubled down on the image, making myself into a literal biblical nightmare for any fucker who saw me. Then I formed and cut the gravity as fast as I could, flinging myself into the orange and red clouds.

It didn't take long for me to see more of the hulks in the distance, drifting, often encased in the flickering lightning. The only light here came from that, or the occasional distant explosion.

The second one that I saw got my attention. I shifted, aiming for it, angling in and diving into a cloud. I squinted as I tried to make out anything; the clouds grew denser and denser, and liquids started to run across my wings. I shook myself.

It wasn't water, I could tell instantly, flowing too freely. Hell, it vanished as quickly as it hit me. But it existed out here? The denser the cloud got, the more of this strange liquid I saw, until finally…

Discovery Made! Helium-4 Superfluid.

Bose-Einstein condensates are forming locally, resulting in abnormally high levels of naturally occurring Helium-4.

Explore this event further to gain valuable insights and rewards from the Ændari Council.

"And just like that, I no longer give a fuck about it," I muttered to myself, before cursing. If something was important enough that the bellend council of cockwombles themselves had put in a promise of rewards into these nanites, then it was probably too significant to ignore.

I'd not understand what I saw, but hey, maybe I could get another perk. That'd be worth it, after all.

Unfortunately, twenty minutes of flying around in the cloud managed to get me thoroughly coated in the liquid, which then ran straight off me, and absolutely fuck all else.

I tried to catch some of the liquid in my hand, thinking to look at it, and frowned when it poured free. Cupping my palm around it, and then eventually forming a literal cup with nanites, failed to keep the liquid inside as well.

Focusing on the prompt gave me bugger all that was useful, except that I paid a little more attention this time and saw that the helium-4 was marked as a superfluid, which I guess meant that it did whatever the hell it wanted, considering it flowed out of the bottom of a cup created by nanites.

I did remember one thing then as I drifted, trying to understand it all.

Although helium-4 meant nothing to me, helium-3 was a fuel, I was sure. I'd pretty much tried to forget it all when I'd slid all the engineering knowledge into my sub-mind. As soon as I focused on it, the damn thing went nuts trying to update.

My mind was suddenly filled with graphs, data arcs, power fluctuation conversions, and covalent shear factors. Swearing, I shoved it all away mentally, focusing on the most basic principles and forcing myself to make sense of that alone.

First and foremost, it was rare as all hell, occurring naturally, and yeah, the energy that could be given off by it, and the chemical and atomic reactions from it, was probably what was causing the clouds and so on here.

That didn't mean much to me at first, until a second detail popped up— mainly that both helium and hydrogen were known to form "clouds" and drift through stellar nurseries. The only ones that I recognized the name for were the Magellanic Clouds. They were in our galaxy, which was a bit of a fuckin' relief, but still.

Then the detail that was important to me directly was brought up.

Helium-4 was usable as a fuel, just like He3, but it was a hell of a lot more volatile and explosive. Give it an electrical charge when it was in the tiny gap between gas and superfluid, and you got a massive boom.

That wasn't all, though, as the clouds apparently warped the local space as well. And then the constant explosions and the lightning combined to create an effect like a pea on a drum for gravity.

It was jumping over and over, and although it felt fine here, at the top of the gravity well, at the bottom? It was banging like a hooker's headboard.

That was why this was a goddamn ship graveyard. Anything that jumped nearby was being sucked inward, then essentially fired "up" through the branes.

Arise: Conqueror

Once it came into "real" space, the interaction from the helium-4 and the electrical bursts set off explosions that tore the ships apart.

The logical leap from there was easy, and the sudden notification made it clear that whatever the system that was local to me was, it agreed with my theory.

This was a graveyard for so many ships because anything that tried to cross this zone was probably fine when it calculated the energy needed to dip down and back up at a set point. But if you were essentially awash like a cork bobbing to the surface, without any kind of guidance?

That was how you ended up here.

That nobody then came looking for the ships? That would be, logically again, because nobody knew where to look. Anything that made it here would already be damaged, ships buggered in war or through other damage.

That, or they'd be the new ships, the ones that were first experimenting with grav drives, and when they went missing, there was nobody to send after them.

They'd be written off as a failure, when really they *had* worked. But when they'd gotten here, they just couldn't get back out.

Discovery Made! Helium-4 location marked in Magellanic Cloud.

Return this locational marker to the Ændari Council to receive your reward.

"Go fuck yourself." There was no goddamn way I was giving them anything, let alone this place, as tempting as it would be for them to arrive here with a fleet and get fucked up, though.

I snorted at that thought, wondering whether I could get them to actually jump here, and that was when it hit me.

Damaged ships.

The Ændari and the UC had been fighting each other for thousands of years, and the sheer number of ships that I could see here? There had to be hundreds of thousands of destroyed vessels.

That meant that there were bloody good chances that there were both Ændari and UC vessels, as well as everyone else.

That…

I burst from the clouds suddenly, frantically twisting as the wall of an ancient hull seemed to flow out of the void before me, the superfluid coating having hidden the closest approach from me. I arced up and around; the pitted surface flashed past below me, black and silent, torn from millennia of impacts and brittle with the cold.

It forced me to pay attention. I adjusted course, spotting shattered weapons mounts as the lightning nearby flashed, letting me see the ship in bursts.

The portholes and windows were dark, the inside long dead. Its hull was covered in tears and rips like a giant bird of prey had swooped in and mauled it to death. But as I turned, searching, I saw the same thing as before…

The hull breached outward from the reactor explosion.

That was the heart of this place, I guessed, remembering that the clouds were mobile, and that they were literally travelling across the Milky Way.

They were probably collecting ships from every civilization in the damn galaxy, and although it was a perfect place to search for the secrets of forgotten races, it was also a damn man trap.

Once you were in, it was impossible to get out.

You needed power and direction, as well as a working grav drive. Although I had access to one of those, as soon as I tried to get more than that, I was going to be fucked.

I forced myself to stop thinking like that. There *was* a way, at least half because it'd be a damn cold day in hell before I gave up on getting back to Ingrid or accepted that a damn cloud was kicking my ass.

So, instead of focusing on that, I decided to do the one thing I could do, and devoted the next few hours to searching the local area, maintaining a directional link to my nanites aboard the hulks I'd already visited.

CHAPTER FIVE

In the end, it took nearly a full day, going out farther and farther in increasing loops, before I found the first of them.

It was an Ændari vessel, long and narrow, or at least the section I found was. The reactor explosion looked to have cut the ship in half; then, a few more impacts and the ship was reduced to a shattered fragment of the original, one that wasn't identifiable as anything beyond "scrap" when I tried to scan it. But landing aboard it?

I'd almost flown past it, right up until I'd seen a twisted weapon mount that looked vaguely familiar.

Flying in and landing, I folded and absorbed my wings, blinking as my special senses realigned from the outside universe. The hull had been rolling as if it'd been flicked by an angry god. Now though, as I boarded, it changed into the universe outside being the weird bit, and the inside being normal.

I'd entered via a torn section of hull, and moving down the corridor, it was strange.

Everything felt so *old*.

I was used to Ændari wrecks and ships being old—hell, that was all they were most of the time, having been constructed before our ultimate ancestor "Lucy" discovered the dubious joys of anxiety. But this just felt…ancient.

Moving from room to room, I could not identify anything, so much having been destroyed. And when I finally reached the bridge, it was to curse; not even bodies had survived.

There was a memory module, though, and I tore that free, attaching it to my back before ripping my way out of the hull.

Ten minutes later, now knowing what I was looking for, I found two more similar sections that I guessed were from the original craft—a long, thin dagger of a ship.

Again, I was disappointed, almost ready to give up on the ship, when I finally found something worth the effort.

The medical suite.

It was buried in the heart of the ship, and as I stared at it in disbelief, I confirmed that most of it was still viable. That was gold as far as I was concerned, and I barely hesitated before ripping it free, then taking it back to the alien giant ship I'd found first.

That was how I was going to deal with this, I'd decided.

Something about the atmo in that ship had kept the lightning at bay when I'd been aboard. I could only hope that the reactor going up had been at least partly down to a leak or something, but for now, my plan was simple. That ship was huge and when I'd flown around it on my searching flights, I'd found three things that had kept it in my mind.

First, the damage was less than a quarter of the ship. Secondly, the overall superstructure was intact. And last, and most importantly, there were what looked to be massive docking areas.

At the very least, I'd found several doors, and scanning them even through the debris, they appeared airtight.

Paradoxically, by scanning the ship from a distance, I could see more details. When I was closer, all I got was a massively complicated return from all the individual parts.

Scan it from farther back and it was possible to see a lot more—from the layout of the trash, basically.

I dragged the cylinder from the medical suite back with me, taking care to keep it out of the clouds as much as possible, then landed, "ate" as much of the crap and debris on the hull as I had to, before cutting my way into the ship again, a level above what I'd guessed was a dock.

I manhandled the tube in with me once the outgassing had stopped, before sealing the hull with a patch again, and moving deeper.

It took me an hour of searching to find a way down, and of course, five minutes of going in the other direction to find my way back out of the dock again, but what I'd found was *perfect.*

There had apparently once been several levels of dock, with what looked like fighters in the outer sections. Then there was what I was guessing was a supply and armament section.

Seeing that they'd set up areas for replenishment of weapons and replacements made me think that the original inhabitants had apparently been warriors—or warlike, at least—although their fighters looked more grown than built.

Lastly, and this was the best bit as far as I was concerned, there was an entire level above and behind the docks. The floor of that level, of the ceiling on the dock, could be rotated out to allow access, presumably to ensure that if you needed more work doing on the craft, you could drag it inside and out of everyone's way.

That was why it'd taken me so goddamn long to get to the dock, and I loved it.

I'd not wanted to cut my way in originally, because I'd guessed that the dock would be big and if it was pressurized, the outgassing would have been insane, as would the loss of that atmo.

If I was going to follow through with my plan, I damn well needed as much of that atmo as possible.

Now that I'd found a way of opening the bay to the outside though, one section at a time? Brilliant.

Arise: Conqueror

That this bay was as deep inside the ship and as large as it was as well? I could have fit our warship in twice over, which meant that I had some room to work, even if I did only have a matter of days and weeks to do it all.

That meant that I needed to fucking *move*.

I'd put the medical tube on one side, then I got to work. Once again, I needed to start from scratch with making the basics here, but fortunately I'd learned a hell of a lot since the fight to claim Facility #6B.

I started small, by necessity, and because I was damn well hoping there wouldn't be a fucking explosion when I did it.

The converter didn't store energy, and that seemed to be key to the whole "everything fucking explodes here." Instead, it fed that energy into something else, or it converted one form of matter into another.

I made three converters, each with a hopper to hold scrap—there was a shitload of that around, after all—and a long cable that led, for the first one, to a tiny power cell.

The second one had the same setup, but led to a small maker, and the third converted scrap into null blocks.

Then I moved the fuck back and entertained myself by examining the roller function while I waited. The system to move the floor was pretty screwed up, having cold-welded itself in place where the metal touched, and there wasn't any power, *but*…most of it was stone, for some reason. Their equivalent of ball bearings, the roller itself—all of it was made of stone.

Only the locks that sealed it or worked to rotate it were metal, so I guessed that replacing just those sections should get it working again.

It wasn't long before I distantly felt the tingle of the approaching lightning, and although I didn't see or feel it inside here, not enough to be sure anyway, it definitely came and went.

That was a massive relief.

I quickly made copies of the three converter setups, leaving the first ones to work as I moved the new ones closer to the outer hull.

With the first maker unit, I immediately started to make a smaller version of the custodians.

I had access to the plans for the most basic AI and RIs, but I damn well knew that for what I needed, I didn't have time to go through the million details it'd take to make them into true functioning versions.

Or the brain I'd need to wipe and scan into the system to make an AI.

Instead, I would make the most basic possible workers, ones that were little more than drones following really simple and obvious orders.

They'd be working with a converter attached to power them, as I'd proved that either a very small power cell, a core or a constant stream of power was safe to use inside these pressurized areas.

For now, though, as the very first parts were printed up and rolled off the production line, I was moving through the lower areas, and then up to the room that I'd entered the wreck by and resealed after me.

The atmo in here was thinner than deeper in the ship, and the feeling of the lightning a lot closer.

When I set the systems up, I moved the fuck back before testing them. And, predictably, the power core exploded as soon as the storm arrived.

Surprisingly, the other two survived, though, and I waited until it'd passed, then built two more.

The first one was the same as before—a converter, a long cable to it, then a tiny power core—while the second was very different.

I used the remains of the space whale or whatever it was as inspiration and coated it in a solid surface that was as close to that as I could remember, then set the core to power up.

While I waited for the next cloud to come, I sealed the door, then opened the hull outward again, making sure that this time there was no atmo to protect at all.

Then, rather than just waiting passively, I got my arse in gear and went to look over the space whale corpse properly.

All I got when I examined it at first was a shitload of question marks. After a few minutes, the boxes started to populate, and I snorted as I realized why.

The species was totally unknown to the system, so anything I decided as I looked it over? That was the new text that anyone else that read this was going to see.

Space Whale	Unknown Deep Space Creature
A space whale, or whatever. Found at the bottom of the gravity branes, and killed. Ingrid is so going to be pissed at me over that. Also, the Ændari are dicks. If you're an Ændari and reading this, HAHAHA. <u>Capabilities:</u> *Dead*: It lies there, doing bugger all. *Lazy bastard.*	
HP 0/0	**Space Whale**

It might be a bit childish, but fuck it, how often did you get to do something like this?

With that out of the way, though, I did start to make a few "discoveries." Although, to be honest, they were very much wild-ass guesses more than actual discoveries.

First and most important was that yeah, the damn things were actual animals. There were a fuckload of weird little details: organs, and layers of what I guessed was the intergalactic equivalent of a layer of fat.

Looking it over, I soon realized it was lead.

That made a sort of sense, though, really. Radiation was a real issue in space, and so would be heat loss. If you got rid of that by adding in a layer of lead? I could see how these creatures might need that kind of thing.

There were a bunch of bits that made no sense to me, as a barely upright monkey, but there were others that I recognized on instinct or through the Engineering sub-mind.

Arise: Conqueror

That included something that was apparently an organic gravity scanner. It was more advanced than the ones that were in the engineering database.

I was just starting to make sense of the thing next to it, thinking it was some kind of gravity bladder, enabling it to tell how deep or high it was by the pressure on it, when there was an explosion behind me.

That made me jump, which sent me off into space. And instead of the small cuts I'd been making in the corpse, I sliced a hole three inches long, which sprayed some liquid out.

That liquid was insanely cold, coating my arm and freezing it solid for several seconds, further distracting me as the clouds rolled in again.

I landed, cursing and shaking my hand as whatever the liquid had been dissipated and the hand gradually returned to normal. I had to recover the corpse, unfortunately. The release of the liquid and its boiling away had sent it bouncing across the surface. Once that was done, though, I returned to the room.

As soon as I'd straightened up and sealed the hull again, I couldn't help but grin to myself as I worked through the damage.

The only one to explode this time had been the power core that hadn't been covered, which was a massive relief.

Basically, all I had to do was coat the fucker in thick enough armoring and I could build power cores as well as power storage cells after all.

I was betting that an actual full-on ship's reactor being powered up would go badly, but the smaller cores that powered the custodians and so on, or power cells, if they were coated and sealed, looked viable. I gathered up the bits I needed, then hauled ass back to the internal dock, separating everything from my experiments out and gathering up the parts I'd set the maker to produce.

Then I *really* got to work.

I spent the next two days working in a blur, barely stopping and being damn thankful that the changes the Devourer had wrought in me meant that although I could still eat and drink, I no longer needed to.

The first step was making a decent factory run. To make sure that there was no risk of a blowout, I built a solid frame around the converters, encasing them just to make goddamn sure, and then a massive hopper that I had a small drone refilling constantly from all the scrap in here.

There was a massive ship in the center of the dock that had apparently been in the middle of something—building, being taken apart, whatever.

It didn't matter, because as near as I could tell, there was no space internally for anything beyond a bunch of the liquid fuckers, and to convert it for my use would be a massive ballache.

Instead, I set a second drone the very, *very* clear task of cutting up just that one thing and moving it out of the way. I went through each step, each section that was fair game and what wasn't. Still, I kept watching the little fucker as it worked.

The converter unit was to feed the makers, and they, too, were built inside a massive box. I lined the outer walls in lead, encasing the cables, the transfer modules…everything.

It took three times as long as making normal ones should, but once it was done, I didn't have to worry about them exploding, and that was worth it.

Then I built the air lock.

Just in case anything that was produced in here was going to have to pass through an air lock to get into the main bay, from the lead-lined production center, for extra belt-and-braces safety.

The first "real" unit that stepped out, one of Zac's spiderbot construction models, was a wonder to behold. It was three meters high, by six long. Six legs enabled it to walk on almost any surface, and between magnetics and the near lack of any gravity in here, it could access anything it needed.

As soon as it was built, I started work on the second, with this fucker starting the real jobs. Without a proper RI or AI, it was a ballache at first controlling them, but between my Engineering sub-mind and simple processors that I already knew how to make, the orders could be queued and a rudimentary "if this, then that" set of instructions were created.

The spiderbot clambered straight onto the hull that the smaller drone was working on, and what it'd taken a day to achieve was done in minutes with the dedicated construction device.

I gave it a set of orders; then, with the test bed done, I downloaded a clone of the Engineering sub-mind into the memory unit of the "master builder."

This was going to be what changed things in here, I'd decided: a dedicated super-spiderbot that could guide all the others, like an AI but built from the sub-mind.

The first two would tear the old ship apart, then they'd build the big boss.

It'd start out as a spiderbot, just a bigger and much more advanced model, but as soon as I finished the final stage, it'd install itself in the frame of my new ship.

For the ship, well, that was where things got "fun" again.

When I was sure that things were stable inside, and the various systems I had in place were working safely and not about to fucking explode as soon as I turned my back? I was off.

I'd found three sections of an Ændari ship before. But for me to find them, both that quickly and "easily," meant that they weren't going to be the only ones out here.

And if there were Ændari, there were going to be UC ships as well.

The next stage took several more days, and I was constantly distracting myself with panicked thoughts about Ingrid and the others. I *knew* that the Ændari wouldn't be able to mount a large-scale assault too quickly, and I damn well knew they were lazy bastards, too.

Ingrid was way smarter than I was—and so were the others, really. I had to trust that she and they would be fine, but I damn well hated every second that I spent combing the wreckage or flying from one patch of hulks to the next.

Twice, I almost got lost before I learned to leave patches of nanites like breadcrumbs to lead my way back. But when I found what I'd been searching for, I knew it'd all been worth it.

Someone had clearly survived awhile out here, considering I'd expected to find a single vessel and instead I found five.

Arise: Conqueror

Three were UC, or at the very least, they were BWV's. The fourth was Ændari, and the fifth was a heavily patched alien vessel that had been raiding them, I guessed at first glance.

The UC vessels were attached to the rounded hull of the alien vessel by tubes that suggested that someone had been working back and forth for long enough that it'd been worth building them. The Ændari ship had been clamped to the hull as well but was clearly being torn up for parts.

I chose to land there first, figuring it was best to know for sure whether my fucking enemies were about. The ship was silent—yes, all right, they all were, unfortunately. The Ændari vessel, when I landed and walked around it, was almost hollowed out though, literally having been pulled apart for spare parts.

The grav drive was the first and most obvious victim, with the reactor close by having been melted by an explosion, and the hull ripped and torn by weapons fire.

The upper levels were open to space, and the stupid triangular hull design was clear, limiting the possible areas that anything could have survived inside.

I boarded the ship, climbing through air locks and hatches, searching quickly as I moved from the outer hull down to the main bridge.

It'd been stripped as well. In fact, the entire ship had been raided down to the hull, with the memory modules and any power cores and cells that hadn't exploded being clearly removed.

Weapons that had survived the fight that had gotten it here had been extracted as well, as had practically everything else…including the medical facility.

Finding that left me curious, but I noticed the lack of any corpses aboard the ship and the depth of the dust and collected debris on the hull of the ship, so it hadn't been there nearly as long as my new home.

Moving out onto the hull, I jumped from the Ændari vessel to the nearest UC one. It'd been sealed in several places; although it'd been holed somewhat recently by a micro-meteorite, ripping any atmo free, before that, it'd apparently been repressurized.

Seeing it was definitely open to space, and there was no reason not to, I pulled up my Devourer coating and burrowed through the outer layer of the air lock, retracting it when I got inside, moving slowly through the first of the UC warships.

Two of them were the same as our ship: wide and long, if not that tall, snub-nosed and heavily armed. That meant that it didn't take me long to move through the ship to the relevant areas, finding the first had been stripped as well.

The memory modules, the AI core, even the crystal pathways that carried the power from the ship's reactors were gone, though I couldn't help but grin when I found the armory was well stocked.

I made a mental note to come back for that, especially the four armored suits that were assembled, ready to be used.

The second warship was in slightly better outward condition, clearly not having been here as long as the first, but again, stripped down to the bones, with anything that could be used removed.

The third vessel was different. I'd never seen anything like it. Although it was old and battered, they'd been working hard to keep it intact.

There were additional layers of armoring all over it—literally. Entire slabs of hull that I guessed had been ripped from other hulks had been grafted onto the hull, providing it with additional armoring. It was longer than a warship, but the middle of the ship was skeletal.

I passed around and around it, pausing several times as the clouds drifted in and out, before it clicked and I understood the design.

It was an engineering and repair vessel for the warships. The main body was at the front, with a hollow middle that could take a warship inside a long bay that ran the length of the belly. Arms that must have been designed like cranes to work on the hull were opened out to maximum extension and the belly was exposed to space; the great doors opened and sealed to the alien craft below.

The engineering vessel was attached to the alien round ship, latched onto it, like a dragonfly landed on a peach, then gutted as well. The signs of masses of equipment being moved through it were clear when I boarded it. Then I followed them, passing through the boarding hatches, and into the heavily patched alien vessel.

The air lock here was sealed. I hesitated when I laid a hand on it, chewing on my lip in thought, before moving back and sealing the open air lock behind me, making sure it was as airtight as I could make it, before forcing the air lock to open inward.

The rushing air made it clear that it had been sealed and maintained airtight. But when I breathed it in, marveling that I could sense as easily as if I were still in my human body, the air tasted stale.

The passage before me was silent. The corridor vanished to the left and right; solid floor, walls, and ceiling reflected my own gravity pulse back at me. I stepped out into it; then, picking a direction at random, I headed to the right.

The corridor arced gently, following the curvature of the hull. It was only a few minutes before I found the first connecting passage.

It was either meant to be in zero-g, or for use by people who could fly, I guessed, considering it rose overhead smoothly, with another passage to the right and then dropping down. Clearly, they expected people to go in all directions.

I sent a pulse down and up, as well as a stronger one down the passage ahead. The up and down seemed to be almost solid, with the occasional hatches here and there, but mainly leading "out" onto the hull; the closest hatch that led inward was ahead.

The marks on the ground had gone in both directions. But as I reached the first hatch that led deeper into the ship, I could see signs of passage dropping off ahead of it, indicating this as at least one of the regularly used ones.

Again, the hatch fought me as I opened it—the creaking and cracking of the cold sealed metal as it gave way—but beyond absorbing the locking mechanism, I left it more or less intact.

Arise: Conqueror

Stepping through, I paused, for the first time finding signs of a struggle inside.

Three bodies lay broken. Two were clearly robotic, or droids or whatever, shattered and broken. The third was something else, presumably the owners of the ship. Shorter than a human, they were broad and clearly strong, with heavy shoulders, longer arms, and short legs.

They lay on their back; the machines around them were torn almost apart, and apparently that had been done by hand. The short figure stared unseeing at the ceiling overhead, eyes frozen open in death. The sterile air of the chamber had maintained him for presumably long years.

He wore solid boots, what looked like armored trousers and a cloth shirt that barely fit those shoulders, even in death. His short beard was matted with dried blood, and the lips drawn back from teeth that were surprisingly human.

If I didn't know better, I'd have said he was human—or one of our variants, at least—but the system quickly made it clear I was wrong.

Dwarfen	Stoneborn
A dead Dwarfen, one of the various clans of the Stoneborn alliance, long known to be extinct.	
Capabilities:	
Stone: The Stoneborn were elementally charged beings able to absorb nearby minerals to alter their outer layers, providing natural armoring.	
Natural Engineer: The Dwarfen were superlative engineers, though they proved impossible to tame, resulting in their extermination.	
HP 0/2000	Stoneborn

I stared at the screen, gritting my teeth as I realized what this meant. The fucking Ændari had killed them. An entire *race*, probably one of those numbers that Argus had so casually thrown out as victims of the Ændari pogroms.

I reached out, laying my hand on his face, trying on instinct to close his sightless eyes, and feeling the hardened impossibility of the corpse.

He was frozen solid. I had no clue how long it'd been since he died, but I'd not even thought about the cold here. His corpse was literally as hard as stone and cold as ice.

Standing again, I forced myself to look away, searching the room for anything of use, as I tried to make sense of it all.

The robots or whatever they were had been torn apart by the dwarfen, literally, but they'd burned holes in him. His blood glistened on the walls and floor, ice crystals reflecting the light as I blinked.

The light.

There was actual light in here. I'd grown so used to there not being light that I'd not even thought about it.

Looking around, I found them easy enough—four of them, in fact—recessed into the ceiling, glowing gently and keeping the room lit. That was interesting, sure, but the important point? They were fucking powered!

I searched properly then, no longer just curious, checking the walls and floor, cursing over just how good the engineers were in here that I couldn't find any goddamn trace of it.

Moving out of the room and into the next, I found more of the same: a single machine torn apart, and the remains of a hammer that looked like something Thor would have approved of—and that was without the clear indications of tech embedded in it.

I hefted it and swung it experimentally, surprising myself with the comfortable weight, then pressed it to my hip. A tentacle flowed out to form a loop and hold it in place.

I couldn't feel any power in it—electrical, I mean—and I guessed that its battery had long been drained, if it used one.

The machine in here had been hammered before the dwarfen turned to his bare hands, I guessed, reading the signs of the fight, before frowning.

Judging from the weapon being discarded here, and stepping into the next room to find two more machines, both shattered by what I guessed to be the hammer, I returned to the first room to stare at them again in confusion.

The dwarfen had fought them in there, battling them until he fell, having used his weapon in there. Presumably, either he'd been trying to escape, or judging from the fight, they had.

The battle was spread over a dozen rooms as I moved back inward, finding three more dwarfen bodies and eleven more of the machines, most bigger and clearly heavily armed.

I started to find burns, shattered panels, holes blasted in the structure, and more bodies. The first of the Ændari was a surprise, even if them being strapped to a medical table and dissected wasn't as horrifying as it should be.

The Ændari were almost entirely made of nanites, after all—or at least their higher ranks were.

The lower soldiers I'd fought on the ships and the node were biological still, and almost a different species than the others, which made me make a connection I'd missed before.

The lower ranks would all be Ændari born after the nanite plague. The older ones were those who had replaced their bodies with nanites, back when they could access the system and make decisions for their nanites.

Since then, most likely the lower ranks were stuck waiting for their nanites to make any changes as time passed. I smiled as a thought occurred to me. If I was really lucky?

There'd be entire planets full of these fuckers locked into place, trapped in their bodies by the buildup of corrupted nanites like the Elders had been.

That made me consider a trip to find out at some point, as I stepped closer, laying a hand on the Ændari corpse, and getting a much bigger shock.

He had no nanites.

Not dead ones, not corrupted or damaged nanites—the fucker had none at all.

Arise: Conqueror

I paid attention again as I saw that the table he'd been strapped to had tubes folded away under it, each tipped with a needle.

Following pipes attached to the needles, I traced them to a box that was full of machinery I didn't recognize. But after extending a pseudopod into it, mapping the interior, and then breaking it down section by section, I sat down heavily.

They'd been harvesting the fucker and purifying his nanites!

Five minutes of searching led me to half a dozen bodies, all stacked like cordwood in a nearby storeroom, all Ændari and all utterly devoid of nanites.

Moving from there, and this time opening my senses as wide as I could, I started to find traces of nanites, small ones locally, but deeper in? A fuckload.

I moved back to the entrance first, sensing them there, and resolved to make sure I missed none, fully intending to recover and damn well use them all.

The machines that the dwarfen had been fighting were the first places I found them. Each and every goddamn one had a central storage unit that was covered in nanites.

I ripped them free, absorbing them, and nodding in satisfaction as my number inched higher and higher. There weren't a lot in there, not compared to the normal numbers I got from slaughtering the Ændari, but there were enough that it was more than worth the effort. I gained anywhere from a few thousand to tens of thousands in the bigger ones.

The real surprise, though, was the dwarfen. Examining the bodies, I found that their brains were filled with them—though, strangely, not the rest of their bodies. When I checked the bodies more carefully, they'd each had an injection into the skull that hadn't had time to heal before death.

That was a bit weird, considering the bodies should have been healed anyway. After a few minutes of thought, I decided not to drain them.

There might be a reason they were like this, after all, and as frozen as they were, I'd have to literally smash their skulls apart to get them free.

Moving back into the interior more slowly, I found additional tech that'd been recovered from the UC vessels, memory modules stacked neatly, crystals…weapons!

The reason I'd only found one intact armory was that the others had been plundered, and it was all here, along with the suits!

This time, I took the opportunity as I discovered more equipment to work with. I gathered a dozen bits of kit, three of each, for an atmospheric generator, a control run, a mainframe interface unit and a scanner, all stacked neatly, and one after the other, they were accepted.

Quest Uncovered!

Evolving Quest discovered: Building the Future

You have found yourself adrift in a graveyard of titans. Explore the local area, claim that which you need, and discover technologies long thought lost.

Investigate and access 10 separate ship technologies to receive the following rewards:

- +2 Support Points

- +2 War Points

- +Access to Level 2 of the Evolving Quest

Current technologies: 7/10

Seven out of ten I'd gotten. As I moved deeper into the ship, I found that I'd barely scratched the surface. I passed room after room filled with stacked technology, weapons, random crystals, stacks of metal plates that I recognized from the ship I'd been on, *custodians*!

There was a supply room filled with a dozen of the little bastards. Every one of them had their cores ripped out, sure, but still!

I started to search more carefully, before grumbling. The only three things that I'd *not* found so far were universal: no power cores, cells or gravity drives.

I picked up speed as I realized that the path of damage, where the machines had stormed in and had fought the dwarfen, led to the greatest concentration of nanites.

Heading toward the last of the rooms, I found one where, when I entered it, I almost shit myself. It did have a goddamn intact reactor, one that was smaller than any I'd seen in a ship until now, and utterly surrounded by shielding.

I examined the room carefully, forcing myself to ignore the siren call of the nanites I sensed ahead as I did.

Whatever had been in here before had been a hell of a draw on the power systems, making me guess at the grav drive, because the reactor that was in here sure as shit wasn't what had originally been here, judging from the melted bulkheads and damaged walls.

They'd repaired it, sure, but as I moved from section to section, I saw evidence of replacements being fitted.

The next room was huge, and very obviously a workshop, one that'd presumably been used to rebuild the rest of the ship around the damage it'd taken on arrival.

It took me another fifteen minutes, but when I made it to the heart of the ship, I couldn't help but sit, staring in wonder at the treasure I'd found.

I didn't know whether the dwarfen had done it alone, or whether they'd had the help of the UC teams, but there were three rows of medical suites stacked side by side, and each and every one of them were full.

Ten tubes to a row, three rows deep—that was thirty figures frozen in the tubes, glittering frost covering the front. I moved closer, wiping the glass and staring in, seeing closed eyes before me.

Thirty people.

Arise: Conqueror

Looking at them, moving from tube to tube, I counted quickly, shaking my head as I returned to the front. Twelve UC soldiers or whatever variants they were. Eighteen dwarfen, each filled with nanites, and as near as I could tell, in perfect hibernation.

This changed *everything*.

CHAPTER SIX

I t took two full days in the end to move the central vessel close to my base of operations.

I almost didn't. Hell, I very nearly took over the dwarfen vessel—it needed a lot less doing to it at first glance. But after I'd toured the vessel twice more, and very carefully, I'd determined that there was just no point.

Much like the ship I'd found earlier, and that I'd set the drones and spiderbots to carve up, it needed so much work to make it usable, that it'd take twice as long to do it.

Instead, I used my gravity manipulation, and a horrific amount of effort and stress, to "pull" the ship through space, pushing the other hulks aside and slowly closing on the biggest of them.

By the time I stopped it on the much larger vessel's hull, I was fucking exhausted, and desperate for sleep.

I didn't dare, though.

Instead, I very, *very* carefully disconnected each of the medical tubes, one by one, and carried them to the outermost areas of the dwarfen vessel, then went level by level, stripping out every storeroom I could find.

I'd been torn—I knew I could probably power the reactor down and hopefully do it safely. Then I could have peeled the ship like a grape with my spiderbots, after covering them in new lead armoring.

That would have been the easiest and fastest way to do it, but…

If I made a single fuckup? Everyone died.

As much as I wanted to, I had to be realistic, and I forced myself to damn well do it carefully.

By the time I'd finished carrying everything to the outermost level, and I'd copied the dwarfen idea of linking the ships together by passages, I was even more tired.

I moved inside after completing the last air lock and headed all the way down to the heart of the dock, collapsing when I made it, forced to accept that as much as I'd changed, some things remained the same, and I slept.

Arise: Conqueror

Waking sometime later, I admitted, even if only to myself, that I'd damn well needed that. Staring at the piled gear all around me, I almost wept with relief.

At some point as I'd staggered down here, my brain so floppy I could have pulled it out of my ears and tied it beneath my chin like a pretty floral fuckin' bonnet, I'd still managed to give the drones orders that apparently made some sort of sense.

Then, as I checked over more of the area, I realized that it'd probably been the sub-mind, and I decided that totally counted as me, because it was based on me.

So fuck it. Still a win.

Getting an update and checking out the shipbuilding that was in progress, I winced. I altered the plans, making broad, sweeping changes that were reflected in the shape.

It'd been close to the original megayacht design when I'd first done it: a single main cabin, one that had no space for minor things like a toilet or a bed, but plenty of space for shield modules, a massive reactor that'd only be activated once I was out of here, and heavily shielded power cells.

There'd been a single rail gun, just in case, and powerful engines, but that was pretty much it. A small cargo hold for anything cool that I found, including a few artifacts I was planning to steal from the surrounding vessels for Ingrid as presents, but that was it.

Now, the design was layered over and over. The outer hull had originally been coated in lead and reflective antiradiation shielding, but I'd been relying as much on the shields as anything, figuring either I'd get out of here with the jump I was going to attempt, or I wouldn't.

Now the ship had quadrupled in size, and that meant I needed a lot more spiderbots working on it.

The original two had finished their larger sibling, and that had, I found quickly, been the one that had discovered the systems I'd been trying to drag down here.

It'd created a dozen smaller drones and sent them after the mass, and I'd thankfully awoken before it could make use of more than a third of it.

Unfortunately, it saw mass from an engineering point of view, and had come to a different conclusion than me.

It was pretty simple, really, when I considered it. This was a heavily refined and more available mass than the rest of the room had, and I'd made it clear I didn't want the walls, floor, and ceiling stripped, so when it'd detected that mass, it'd gone and got it.

It was mainly the metal sheets and refined ingots it'd used, but fuck me, that had been close. Had it decided to pull the weapons apart, or the medical tubes, it could have ended badly.

Instead, I settled into it, and adjusted the plans.

First and foremost, I needed space for those tubes, all of them.

Sure, I could have left them, or even decanted the people—maybe even shoot them in the head if I wasn't sure of them and stack their bodies, let them recover later or something when I was back, as that'd take up less space.

The thing was, I didn't know whether they'd come back.

I didn't know whether they were pre-plague or post. For all I knew, I'd found survivors of the first generation that would all be loyal to the Ændari, or both the BWVs and the dwarfen would attack me on sight.

If they didn't, though?

They could be allies. *Insanely* important ones.

They'd clearly had some engineers with them, considering they'd built the shit they had, and I had to guess that they'd been working on escaping this shithole when something had gone very wrong.

Actual engineers, with access to the original systems, and who owed me some damn loyalty? That could be all we needed to turn the tide of the war…not to mention possibly reviving a race that were accepted as extinct.

That had to carry some weight when I had to eventually do some UC council stuff, surely.

Either way, though, it meant that the original plan for the ship needed to be totally revamped.

Instead of changing everything, which I could have done, I suppose, I scaled up the design.

That gave me the space to add in the cargo hold that would store everything. And as I didn't need rooms that were fifteen meters high, I changed the interior section that led from the cockpit to the engine room into a sort of frozen test-tube barracks, just with the inhabitants kept upright in two rows of fifteen, one on either side of the passage.

Then I really got to work.

The new estimate on timescale, as so much of the ship I'd brought and left outside could be used, was six days. Although that had me gnashing my teeth, it also couldn't be sped up by much.

I tried, over and over, but the longest part was something that couldn't be hurried.

The thing that I was betting that had been protecting the interior of this ship, when I'd examined the surface more carefully, wasn't heavier armor.

It was whatever the atmo the previous inhabitants had been breathing.

The clouds that drifted around outside could only be sensed the farther out I went onto the hull, and where the dwarfen had gone with the lead coating option, I was doubling down on both.

The ship that was currently being built was as close to the center of the mercury dudes' ship as possible, surrounded by as dense an atmo as I could gather, but I needed more.

For whatever reason, the converters took forever to make this. Despite my plans including building three larger converters just for that purpose, it'd still take days. At best, I could shave a few hours off that timescale, and the changes I needed to accomplish that were already in motion.

We needed more spiderbots, first of all: two building a third, then three building another three, and those six then building six more.

Arise: Conqueror

With four spiderbots, we quickly tore apart the walls leading out to the hull, restructuring as they went, to make a passage wide enough for the medical suites to be brought down before their internal nanite reserves could run out of power.

Once that was done, and we had everything we needed inside, the secondary drones went to work. They'd been in progress for a while, and they used the discovered custodians' frames and a simple tank system and heavily shielded core to clank their way around the ship, collecting as much atmo as they could, then sealing each section back up as it was emptied.

They then moved into the rooms that surrounded the central dock, ejecting the atmo and layering it as heavily as possible. They did this repeatedly.

Their larger siblings sealed each level as they went, making damn sure the atmo didn't get wasted.

That, and three smaller drones that worked constantly with their own converters to line the walls of the dock in lead, effectively hid us from the clouds outside, and enabled the first reactor to come online.

I'd not planned to use it. I'd been thinking I'd use a load of power cells, and basically channel the jump enough to get the smaller ship out by sheer madness alone.

The discovery of the larger dwarfen vessel and all the tech it'd held had changed all of that.

Between the crystals I'd gotten, the AI cores, and the precious cargo I now had aboard, I'd accepted that I wasn't going to be flying my mad little botched-together vessel out of the docks here.

Instead, I was going to have to jump out from the depths of the massive ship.

That had two main problems. First, the gravity well.

Anything that was nearby when I warped space would be coming with me, and in order to "feel" the space out there as I went, I couldn't do it with shields.

That meant that I required enough power that not only could I take the ship around us with us if I had to, but I needed to be damn sure that I could get the shields up—and *fast*—on arrival at the other end.

After the Ændari had almost killed us all on jumping into the Scorpio system once already, there was no way I was leaving myself vulnerable.

Fortunately, that had an easy solution.

You know, beyond the whole "wearing the remains of this vessel as a shield."

The reactors I had access to were good, but the ones that the dwarfen ship had were an order of magnitude better.

They also didn't have issues like the Ændari and UC versions did with being in proximity to each other. Had the dwarfen had access to nanites originally, and converters, I had no doubt they'd have won their fight with the Ændari.

As soon as I powered it down and figured out the minor differences, I incorporated them into my design, allowing me to put four reactors in proximity, rather than the one my original design had.

That was one of the things that was drawing out the time until I could jump as well, because the reactors would need more time to charge and build up. But it'd mean I was much more likely to succeed.

The other advantage was that because of the time that building the reactors would take, I now could tackle a few extra projects.

The first of which was a maker in the heart of the ship that I had scanning every weapon I'd found so far into its memory, so we'd be able to reproduce them when I reached Ingrid and the others.

The second? *Well...*

Those spiderbots were just standing around, after all, so I had them work on an emergency evacuation protocol—mainly, a shaped charge of truly epic proportions.

The six spiderbots each had one attached, and they were going to sacrifice themselves to blast a path out of the dock for me, one at a time.

The biggest of them, the "master builder" as I'd named it, had a recess built into the ship itself. And as soon as its jobs were done, it attached itself and joined with the ship's memory cores, spreading out to form a dedicated AI engineer, ready to fix the ship whenever I needed.

The smaller drones each had assigned spots in the hull, ready to operate from there if they were needed.

All of those were cool, and they were all additions that'd make the ship both have a better chance of surviving and carrying out its main mission, which was to get me back to Ingrid and get my cargo there safely as well.

The real special project, though?

In order to power this jump—to take the savaged hull of a billion-ton super-starship with me—I needed a *lot* of power.

Once this jump was done, though, and hopefully I was back in "normal" space again, I wasn't going to need anywhere near so much power.

So, being the mad bastard that I was, I'd taken the sample of the crystal weapons I'd found, and between the supersized reproductions of them now being built on the hull, the lasers, and of course the pair of rail cannons the spiders had built, and the three shield modules?

The Ændari were in for a hell of a surprise when they tried to face me.

My ship might be ugly as sin, held together by the intergalactic equivalent of baling wire and duct tape, and definitely wasn't going to be winning any design awards, but the advantages it did have?

It'd be powerful and fast as fuck.

The UC engines had been better than the dwarfen ones, mainly because the dwarfen ones used some kind of inertial reactionless drive.

I couldn't figure it out, but they'd been capable of flying in any direction, and didn't need to be on the outside of the ship.

That was great and all, but when I didn't understand the basics of the engines, I sure as shit wasn't slapping them in place and praying for the best.

The ion engines I understood, at their most basic level: energy in, thrust out; boom. It was a bit more advanced than that, but the basics were there: electrical energy in, equals ionization pushed out.

Like the way that a combustion engine burned fuel to provide expansion and moved pistons. It was more complicated, but I could grasp the basics, even before I'd rebuilt my brain. Now things were coming much easier to me, I had to admit. The changes in my brain had helped me to just get shit easier, regardless.

The dwarfen engines I could probably figure out if I *had* to, but the basic details I had meant that there was no point. Instead, I had parts being printed up, and I moved them almost as easily as the damn spiders did, attaching them and building as I went.

Once you understood the general principles, and you tweaked the design on the fly, it was like building a really complex set of Lego, but when you'd memorized the parts: slot this bit here, press that bit there, add charge to this, add nanites to that.

I worked for three of the days straight, right up until I caught myself attaching a spar to support the engine and prevent buckling under pressure…backward.

Then I cursed myself and admitted I needed another goddamn rest.

I looked up at the ship overhead. The skeletal structure looked weirdly ominous as section by section was attached.

The overall shape now was more like a starfighter, I had to admit.

There were no turrets on this thing. That was more work than I had time to manage and would have cost more effort.

Instead, the overall body was a long cylinder. The top level had the cockpit, a corridor that led past all the popsicles in their stands and then to a cross corridor that ran out into the inside of the wings to access the engines…you know, if I needed to.

The new design had two wings, each with three engines on them, extending from the sides of the main body, with the next level down as storage of the massive windfall of tech and weapons.

The lower floor was four massive reactors staggered from the rear of the ship to the front, with an air lock at the back and a ramp down, just in case. Then the whole thing was wrapped in thick armoring. Three shield generators were spread out along its length, and the lasers, rail cannons, and the crystal lightning thrower things…fuck it.

The *storm casters*, I decided they were now called.

They were all built along the hull at the front of the ship, with slight adjustments to ensure that they all aimed in almost exactly the same area.

My plan was that although the ship was going to be strong and fast, in order to make it possible for one guy to fly and maintain, it had to be simple as well.

Adding in additional turrets, special weapons, all that shit would have been great, but there was just no way I could do it with everything that was going on, and I'd have needed to dedicate more time to it.

The AIs that I hoped were still in the memory cores I'd looted would have been able to run them without issue, I was sure. The minor issue was that if I powered the AI cores up and they were empty?

I was fucked.

Then I'd have spent days working on weapons that would be firing in any and all directions when I pulled the triggers, or that didn't *do* anything at all.

Instead, simple was best.

Fortunately thanks to the sheer number of parts I'd had to scan and understand, I'd earned a few notifications.

Quest Complete!

First level of Evolving Quest: Building the Future has been completed!

The graveyard of ancient titans has provided you with all you needed and more. Through exploring the local area, you have claimed all that you needed, and recovered technologies long thought lost.

Current technologies discovered: 23/10. You gain:

- **+2 Support Points**
- **+2 War Points**
- **+Access to Level 2 of the Evolving Quest**

***

Quest Uncovered!

Evolving Quest discovered: Building the Future (Part 2)

You have claimed all the technologies you need to return to the fight, but although knowledge is indeed the greatest weapon, stabbing an opponent with your brain is less useful.

Use all that you have learned to construct a viable vessel, then return to the Node to receive the following rewards:

[Bonus: Return with all living members of the dwarfen race to receive a bonus.]

- **+3 Support Points**
- **+3 War Points**
- **+Access to Level 3 of the Evolving Quest**

Viable Vessel: 0/1

Dwarfen survivors: 18/18

Return to the node: 0/1

Arise: Conqueror

I hesitated, wanting to spend the points more carefully and certainly in a more fun way, but I knew what I needed.

The two Support points went straight into power generation, unlocking two more levels and almost blowing my brains out with the backlash. The Engineering sub-mind redlined, stuttering as it tried to adjust, then finally, went almost mad trying to integrate the changes to the reactors I already had in progress.

I let it guide me, making a dozen small changes. There were sections that I still didn't understand, ones that made it look like they'd almost be really inefficient for the first month or so. That was the case if I was reading this right, but if so? Even four smaller and less efficient reactors were better than a single basic and only slightly more powerful one.

I slept for six hours, then got back to work. The hours blurred past as I clambered and dug, welded, riveted and smeared nanites here there and everywhere, making an unattractive abomination of a ship, but one that I was desperately hoping would work.

That was probably why I was so out of sorts, when three hours before I was expecting to fly out of the shithole nebula or whatever it was that I'd found my way into, I was hit from behind.

CHAPTER SEVEN

I staggered, the world erupting in light and pain. I'd been totally unprepared for the blow, focused on attaching tiny crystals in the correct order to make sure the reactors would charge and not explode.

I'd also been doing it under standard Earth gravity because that kept the damn things from floating away when I let go of them, which was why I didn't go bouncing off the bulkheads.

It did stop the wonderful rendition of the Christmas classic "Frosty the Pervert" I'd been singing to myself, though.

Spinning around, one of my hands rose to clutch at my reforming skull in pain. Fully expecting that a section of the overhead ceiling had given way or something, I was stunned to see a fucking dwarfen trying to breathe, coughing and choking, staring at me, then looking at the bent length of piping in his hand.

He tossed it aside and lunged at me. A fist swung at my stomach, making me gape in surprise at the sheer fucking slowness of it.

I stepped back a single pace, then swore as his blow missed me. It slammed into the housing of the reactor I'd been working on, buckling it inward.

"Oi, you fucking dick!" I roared, stepping in and deflecting his hand wide as he pulled back, then grabbing the back of his right wrist with my right hand.

I twisted, expecting to lock his arm into place, then snarled. Instead of locking him into an arm-bar as I'd done automatically, his elbow joint shifted and bent backward, apparently having no issue with flexing both ways as he almost went into a paroxysm coughing.

Fucking aliens.

That was when he grabbed my crotch with his left hand, though, reaching under his right, and squeezed as hard as he could before twisting.

I grunted, doubling over, the pain both uniquely male and horrific…and then he headbutted me.

He headbutted *me.*

It'd been years since someone had properly stuck a nut on me like that, and he made a terrible mistake in releasing my balls as I let go of his wrist. The pair of us staggered apart.

The rising fury over the downright underhanded and *nasty* tactics he was using filled me at the same time as my body reacted to my instinctive demands.

Arise: Conqueror

First, I was covered in armor. Not because it was any harder than my flesh could be now—when I wanted my "flesh" to be hard, that was—but because it was instinct to fight in armor.

Secondly, I felt my balls recovering, as the damaged areas were literally rebuilt in seconds. My nanites flowed to restructure as they should have been; the pain smoothed away as sections slid back into place again.

"You little shit," I growled, wiping my nose and sucking the blood back into me. My nose reformed with a pop and a click that brought tears to my eyes.

This time, when the dwarfen lunged at me, I was ready. I was struck again by the speed that he moved at. He *lumbered*—that was the word—the punches were slow as shit compared to fighting with someone like Paul or Jonas, and wouldn't have even registered against Scylla. But when they landed, it was like being hit by a truck.

I stepped forward, catching the incoming punch in my left hand and exerting myself properly for the first time. I'd been unconsciously limiting myself, still learning to use my new body, and now, encased in "armor," I automatically accepted that I was stronger than normal, and that now my armor would make me so.

The dwarfen was clearly used to being the strongest fucker in any fight. Although I was considerably taller than him, he had a clear expectation of how this fight was going to go.

That was why when his fist stopped dead and I squeezed, my fury injecting an extra level of power beyond whatever I'd normally manage, he certainly looked surprised as his bones broke.

Then I yanked him in close, grabbing him by the throat and lifting easily, smacking him into the wall and choking him as I stared into his eyes at point-blank range.

"You're a fucking dead man, pal!" I ground out, staring into his eyes. I closed my fist slowly, feeling first the shift in the cartilage of his neck, the spine moving, then the buckling of his trachea.

Or you know, the alien version.

I felt a triple spine beneath my fingers as it tried to flex and resist my squeeze. His left fist slammed into the side of my head, once, twice, then a third time; I took the hits and kept staring into his eyes, fury filling my own.

Panicked, he kicked at me, thrashing and trying to bludgeon me with his broken hand. I batted it aside as well, then yanked him forward and headbutted him in return. Bone crunched as I crushed the front of his skull in, before finally dropping him to the floor.

I stared down at him, seeing the broken-in forehead, the wide-open eyes, the sightless gaze fixed on the wall behind me. Thick black blood dribbled from his nose and mouth. His body twitched, the last fried messages from his spinal column shooting back and forth as I glared down.

It took long seconds for me to regain control of myself, to push the animal instinct to fight and to kill back far enough for me to think again, then search the ship.

A handful of minutes later, I was back in the room he'd found me in, staring down at the cooling body, now with a shitload of fresh questions. It was one of the dead dwarfen I'd found before, having somehow recovered and come exploring. And if he'd been just unconscious before, now he was definitely fucking dead.

I grabbed the body, dragging it back out of the way, thinking to finish the reactor setup, then shaking myself and leaving it. I was damn lucky that the little bastard had found me before he'd found the armory, all things considered.

I'd been so focused on the reactor and doing things right, as well as the consequences should I do it wrong, that I'd been oblivious to the fucker coming for me.

I should have heard him—hell, I should have *sensed* him—but I'd not, and now I stood over the fucking twice-dead corpse of an extinct dwarfen.

I hauled him out of the reactor room and into the hall beyond, then up a level to the storage areas. The door he'd come out of was clear, the other bodies of the dead dwarfen I'd found having been stacked neatly in there.

I looked them over, then sighed. They'd been moved, examined, and no doubt that had a little something to do with why he'd attacked me without warning.

I couldn't remember where I'd found this particular dwarfen, but it'd seemed right to bring his corpse back. I'd guessed that the others, if they survived being pulled out of the medical tubes, would be glad to see their friends' bodies.

Now, looking them over, I was torn between disposing of the corpses out of the air lock, and…

And another of them shifted suddenly.

I jerked back. My right hand came up and a punch dagger formed on it, just as I'd done so many times with my harvest blade, before I realized they were not attacking.

They laid there haltingly jerking, their body trying to adjust to the atmo and clearly struggling.

They *were* trying to breathe, though.

They sure as shit hadn't been when I'd dragged them down here.

Hell, they were all definitely dead before. But as I checked them over, I groaned in understanding.

They had nanites!

I'd seen that they'd been draining the goddamn Ændari, and I'd not considered what they'd done with the nanites. They'd ripped every single one out of them they could get, but in the cold of space, and then in the sterile atmo of their ship, there'd been nothing for the nanites to use as fuel, I guessed.

They must have been injecting themselves with the nanites, presumably in an attempt to make themselves immortal too, or at least capable of surviving until they could be recovered.

The robots had come then—I didn't know where they'd come from, or whether they were there all along and went haywire—but they were full of nanites too, and they and the dwarfen had fought to the death.

The nanites then hadn't been able to repair the bodies without cannibalizing them, so for whatever reason they'd all shut down, leaving them dead.

Arise: Conqueror

That sparked a load of questions, but for now they didn't matter.

No, what mattered was that they were in my ship, and the entire level was filled with that bloody atmo that the pressure dudes had been breathing. That was why he'd been coughing and choking, and I'd probably missed it with all the clattering and banging as the spiderbots built the ship around me.

I'd gotten so used to just ignoring the noises that I'd been virtually deaf to them, and now…

Now those selfsame nanites were repairing and recovering the damn dwarfen, and the first of them to wake up had found themselves stacked on a pile of their dead friends, the air choking, and a strange creature working on a reactor a level below.

I was just glad again that they'd decided to come and see who was about rather than going in the other direction and finding the damn armory.

Now, though, as the second body jerked and twisted, coughing harder, I had a definite problem.

I reached out, hesitated, then pressed my right hand over the figure's mouth, forming a seal of nanites and expanding a plug into their lungs.

It sounded terrible when I imagined how I'd explain this to anyone who asked about it. The last dwarfen had been attempting to breathe the air, but had been more or less managing it, and so was this one, even if they were struggling.

The atmo in their ship had been a lot lighter than this, the pressure being very different as well, but the dwarfen were apparently hardy fuckers.

I focused, using my new conversion abilities. I tried my best to mimic the atmo I'd encountered in the dwarfen ship, frowning as I tried to remember it.

I'd noticed it absently, that it was a bit like Earth air, but heavier; colder, sure, but it tasted sterile. I tried to reproduce that as best I could.

They started to shake and convulse, and I adjusted it, upping the oxygen level, then the nitrogen, lowering then raising the carbon dioxide…

Then sighing as they shuddered one last time, then went still.

"Fuck," I whispered, before examining the others with every sense I could.

As near as I could tell, I'd just smothered this one, meaning that I definitely didn't have the air mix right. But their nanites were definitely active now, and the ones I'd just killed were being slowly purified of the harmful mix and repaired, meaning that it was only a matter of time before they recovered again.

Twenty minutes later, the next one awoke. By this point, I was getting mightily annoyed, surrounded by the goddamn bodies in a closet space that I'd built for storage, not for a comfortable chat.

This one died as well, but they lasted almost a full minute, making it clear that I was moving in the right direction.

The fourth dwarfen that awoke did so much more gradually. I'd sat back, extruding a tentacle and using that rather than a hand over their mouth.

The converter ability that was now inbuilt in me was helping, as I'd compared the only two atmospheres I'd encountered the dwarfen in, and I'd found a few common points.

First, the pressure in here from the aliens didn't seem to affect them in the slightest, much as it no longer did me. I'd been wrong in using that for the last ones, and instead I stripped the helium out of the air and upped the nitrogen content.

That did it. They slowly awoke, blinking and staring around as if they were recovering from a hangover. When they saw me, they jerked suddenly; then, as the movement apparently tugged the tentacle, their eyes widened as they realized what was attached to their mouths.

I backed up, hand raised to show I was unarmed; they grabbed and yanked at it, and I disconnected it, pulling it back.

The dwarfen was male—or I guessed he was, anyway. I'd not noticed any distinguishing features of male or female, but the heavy beard meant I automatically saw him as such.

As soon as the connection was pulled free, he took a deep breath and started to cough. Ten seconds later, I extended the tentacle to him again, seeing the confusion, the horror, and the distrust in his eyes, surrounded by his dead friends.

He took it though, letting it attach to his face and feed him the same mix I'd been giving him before.

He took a few coughing breaths, then seemed to relax, slightly, as soon as he could breathe more easily again. He stared at me, obviously not liking what he saw, but not actively attacking me either. Then he checked the bodies near him, staring in dismay at their obvious death.

I tried talking to him, telling him my name, pressing my hand to my chest and repeating it.

"Steve," I said. "I'm Steve."

Either he wouldn't—or *couldn't*—speak. I cursed, realizing that of course he couldn't, being deep-throated by a fucking tube. I quickly reformed the tentacle from being halfway into his throat like a facehugger to cover his mouth and nose, creating a bubble, and waited as it filled with air.

He coughed and shuddered.

"Steve," I repeated, tapping my chest.

He just glared at me, pointing at the bodies around him, then at me.

I shook my head, then winced and tried to decide how to explain this one.

I pointed at the one with the crushed-in skull, now slowly pushing back out, and I pointed at him and mimed out him attacking me, and me headbutting him.

Apparently, I wasn't very convincing as he sneered at me, and I glared back.

The best I was getting here was careful distrust, I guessed. Still not sure whether he was hearing or understanding me, I realized that I now had a shitty decision to make and cursed.

My choices: I boot these fuckers off my ship, leaving them here to die. I could kill and drain them. Or I had to accept that my escape plan had just been fucked in the ass without lube or even being bought dinner first.

The one I'd fought before had been incredibly strong, strong enough that a missed punch, when he was choking and barely able to see, had still dented the side of the reactor I'd been working on.

Arise: Conqueror

That meant that if I tried locking them in here? They could just smash their way out if they were that strong.

I'd not been building a damn cell to contain Superman—it was a storeroom. And more and more, I was regretting that it was right next to the fucking armory!

If I tried to lock them away, they could break free easily enough. If I created a turret or something here to watch them and shoot them if they tried to escape? Well, there was no way that was going to end well for anyone.

The sheer distrust that'd engender would definitely start things off badly.

Alternatively, if I let them have the run of the place, what was to stop them doing something that fucked it all up?

What if, when we couldn't understand each other, one of them decided in all innocence to "help" by upping the reactors' power or whatever, and blew us all to hell?

They could decide they liked the ship, and try to take it, or maybe they liked fresh meat and I looked like it.

Hell, it might be that the BWVs were how they'd gone extinct and I'd totally misread the medical tube situation. Maybe they weren't being protected by the others—maybe that had been their goddamn pantry.

No. There was only one way I could see this working out now, besides killing them and ejecting them all, possibly making sure an extinct race stayed that way and committing literal genocide.

I needed to wake one of the BWVs in the tubes.

That gave me a whole other problem, though: how the hell did I pick one, and what did I do with this guy while I did it?

I sure as hell wasn't leaving him here to just look around and pick up some new toys.

I gave it a minute as I thought; then, moving to the door, I reached out to the side, hiding what I was doing. A tentacle flashed to the next room, opening the door and pulling one of the stored converters I'd not needed anymore and had put in there.

I dragged it back to me, along with a handful of coins to keep it running for a week or so, just in case. Then I brought it out and showed it to him, before putting it in the corner of the storeroom he still stood in with the other bodies. I triggered it, watching his face as he felt the sudden breeze that wafted out, displacing the current air and making it easier to breathe in there.

I waited, then mimed pulling the mask off, and slowly, he did.

He coughed almost instantly, of course, but when I pulled the mask on the end of the tentacle back from his reaching hand, he glared at me.

I waited as he struggled for a few seconds, then seemed to grow more confident breathing the air. I was doing this wrong, I had no doubt—Ingrid would have done it so much better—but I didn't have the time to screw around, and I needed him to understand that the air in here, at least, was breathable.

Then I stood, offering him the mask again, and gestured to the hallway outside, before making it clear I was headed that way.

He stayed where he was for several seconds, then stuck his head out into the corridor, glaring at me. He tried breathing the air, finding it was harder away from the converter, then made the point of sealing the door behind him and covering his mouth as he hurried to me, snatching the mask from my hand.

I was deliberately making it look like the tentacle was technology, and that I had to hand it over, or pull it back, rather than move it on its own. I'd gone so far as to form a box on my hip for it, even if it was just really a frame that held a few of the null coins in it.

Making it to the hole I'd left to reach the next floor, I jumped up to the next level, maintaining the gravity inside the ship as I had been all along, then offered a hand when the shorter figure clearly hesitated, searching for rungs.

He glared and waved me back before jumping and, hilariously, missing.

It took two more attempts before he accepted my hand, and he couldn't back away from me fast enough when I'd pulled him up.

"Make some rungs next time," I muttered, getting another glare from the fucker. "Do you understand me?" I tried again, before turning and pointing at the tubes. "Do you know what these are?"

He followed my pointing fingers, then gasped, the first sound out of him I'd heard beyond choking, and shoved past me, moving to the first of them.

He bypassed the ones with the BWVs in them, moving down to the dwarfen inhabitants, and checked the tubes, pulling up the control panel and shaking it as he tried to get it to work for him.

After a few experimental shakes and prods, he turned to me and pointed at the tube and then his people, apparently torn between asking and demanding they be freed.

That or some kind of interpretive dance-off. He was definitely stomping a lot, either way.

I shook my head, gesturing to him to follow me, then moving closer and grabbing the fucker by the arm when he stayed where he was and just glared.

"Here, you dumb fuck," I snapped, pointing at the tubes holding the transplanted humans. "I can speak to them, and if they vouch for you, then there's an option at least, but…but you don't understand me." I groaned, rubbing at the bridge of my nose.

"Fuck it," I snarled after a few seconds of looking at them and the dwarfen, and picked one of the only ones who didn't look likely to rip my head off and shit down my neck as a greeting.

The figure in the tube was human, or whatever they were classed as, but I was betting they were an Engineering subclass, judging from the attachments and the replaced right arm that ended with a handful of mechanical implements.

They were also considerably smaller than most of the others, showing as a Support class or BSV when I examined them.

Linking to the control panel, I approved the options, unlocking and ordering the system to wake them from their apparent hibernation.

I'd not known for sure that the tubes, nor us as a species were capable of it, but it was nice to know that they weren't just perfectly preserved rations.

Arise: Conqueror

The dwarfen glared at me, jerking a hand toward his people. I shook my head, trying to signal that this guy first, then we'd talk, but getting absolutely nowhere with it.

It took half an hour and a lot more power than I expected it to, to reboot or reawaken—or hell, *defrost*—the engineer. But when I finally got the fucker out, I nearly killed him.

In my defense, it really wasn't intentional, but that took awhile to explain to him.

First and foremost, the only reason he survived at all was that he had his own armor, inbuilt like ours were, but the fraction of nanites he had available to form it meant that it was highly limited in coverage.

When he awoke, it was to a pressure differential that was close to lethal even for one of our kind, and the air mix was pretty bad as well.

Mental notes were made as I formed an additional tentacle, then as he shook and convulsed, his armor only covering his face, and the extreme cold of space apparently not agreeing with him either.

I formed a second suit, one made entirely from my nanites, and flooded him with it, regulating his temperature and enveloping him in it, waiting as he slowly slid back from the brink of death and through the various levels of shock.

It took a few minutes, but by the time he was more or less awake and aware, I was getting some very strange looks from him.

"Identify."

When the connection request and question came through, I almost laughed in relief.

"Steve," I replied.

"Identity and rank," he demanded.

I snorted, stepping back from him, but making the point of keeping a string of nanites connected to him and the suit I was protecting him with, before flooding my skin—or the upper layer of my body, anyway—with the Devourer coating.

"Steve," I repeated. "Devourer."

That clearly changed things. He dropped to one knee fast enough that I nearly cut his head off on instinct, before realizing what he was doing.

"Lord Devourer," he said. "I meant no offense."

"None taken," I assured him. "Who are you, and do you know this one?" I gestured to the dwarfen, getting a glare from him.

"I am Maker Lieutenant First Class Zhonat. Second maker to the repair vessel *Krinzat*. We found the dwarfen on a search of a gravitational anomaly, and while only a few of them survived, we made it a priority to retrieve them."

"Why?"

"I…I don't understand?"

"Why was it a priority?"

"To recover the dwarfen?"

"Yeah. And can you talk to them?"

"I…" He hesitated, glancing up, then looked at the figure that stood glaring at us both, then back down to stare at the floor. "My apologies, Lord Devourer. There are standing orders to recover and protect the dwarfen at all costs."

"Whose orders?" I asked it on instinct before wincing, not really expecting to get an answer I'd understand. After all, it wasn't like "Field Marshal Bob" was going to help me much.

"The Devourers?" he responded, making it even clearer why I was confusing the fuck out of him.

"Damn, sorry, that was before my time." I shrugged. "Can you communicate with them?" I asked. "I can figure out languages usually, but this fucker isn't talking."

"He's a mute," Zhonat said. "Forgive me, Lord—"

"Steve," I snapped. "Just call me Steve, it's fine. Or Devourer. The 'lord' bit is a bit much."

"I thank you for your permission, Devourer," he replied. "May I stand?"

"Shit. Yeah, sorry."

"Thank you." He rose smoothly, glancing at his new armor then at the link between us, and down the hall of tubes. "May I ask as to our location and status, Devourer? And to the status of this armor?"

"You were going into shock." I shrugged. "So I gave you some armor. What happened to your own?"

"On finding the dwarfen, the decision was made to sacrifice our builders to enable as many of them to survive as possible."

"Okay. I saw the body of an Ændari as well?"

"Our enemies were also trapped while exploring the anomaly. We attempted a truce with them due to the situation, but when they inevitably betrayed us, we decided the best solution was to treat their impregnated bodies as an opportunity to save the dwarfen survivors."

"I'm not complaining," I assured him. "Okay, so you found an anomaly…the clouds, I assume?"

"Correct. Our ship was damaged, and when we emerged from our jump, instead of our destination, our ship underwent catastrophic decompression. Many of the crew were lost in the first seconds, while the majority died over the following months.

"When we first found the dwarfen, we were able to establish communication, and even agreed to a truce with our old enemies the Ændari. Over several months, we formed an uneasy alliance, mainly down to the fact that the dwarfen had been dragged into the field and trapped at a time that they were battling the Ændari still. Our advising them of the loss of their race…was not taken well."

"What happened?"

"The Ændari blamed us for manipulating the situation to our advantage, and claimed that they were in fact currently allies, against us. The dwarfen clan split, the majority siding with the Ændari, as they'd been there longer than we had.

"We retreated with our own smaller grouping of dwarfen, and began rebuilding, albeit cautiously. Several years passed in careful construction, and we developed close relationships with several of our companions. Eventually the Ændari led an assault on us, using their allies' abilities to supplement their ranks.

"We were, I am ashamed to admit, barely able to hold them off. The dwarfen make more use of drone servant classes than we were aware of, and with the Ændari technological backing, they almost defeated us.

"Both sides were heavily depleted, and in the end, the damage to our ship was judged too much. An agreement was made, and one of the dwarfen volunteered. They pretended to change sides. Instead, as soon as they were inside, they triggered an active reactor inside the enemy stronghold.

"We believe they eliminated most, if not all the enemy, and the single Ændari corpse that was able to be retrieved was drained. Their nanites, and the majority of our own, were used to grant some additional survivability to our allies."

"So why were you in the medical tubes?" I asked.

"Dwarfen reactors take several years to build in power," he said with a wry smile. "They're usually jump-started by a working reactor that was already in service—we'd lost access to ours in the fight. By the time the new ones would be ready, we'd have all run out of food and atmosphere, due to the destruction of so many of our tools. When we realized that, the simplest solution was the best.

"A small number of our group stayed out of the tubes. We were short by seven tubes in total anyway, so we rotated. One of our engineers and six others were left to work, drawing out the food and atmosphere that we had access to, and hopefully enabling us to last long enough to power the reactors again." He glanced at the dwarfen who glared at us both now.

"The reactors—" I started, only to be cut off as Zhonat spoke up hurriedly.

"My apologies, Devourer, but perhaps one of the others would be a better choice to explain the situation? While Yartiman is…well, he's less hostile than some of his peers, but his condition makes it much more difficult to communicate with him. He was unwilling to learn any sign languages we were aware of, speaking only through data link, and when that was unavailable…" He shrugged.

"Condition… Damn, you said he was mute, didn't you. I didn't think. You mean he can't talk?" I asked. "Not at all?"

"Indeed," he agreed. "Perhaps Lehman?"

"Who?"

"The clan elder. He was on rotation with Garnen. Is he…?"

"Dead." I sighed. "Look, when I found my way in here, I found your ships attached to the dwarfen vessel, three of them?"

"Yes, we found two older and lost vessels when combing the wrecks, and although their crews were long lost, the medical facilities were recovered and repaired, along with other usable systems."

"Were the crews able to be recovered from the medical units?" I asked.

"They weren't in them when we found them," he replied, as if I wasn't listening.

"Yeah, but…" I hesitated, then shook my head. "It doesn't matter. We can look at it later." The ones on Earth had been capable of literally reconstituting people from recordings but maybe these ones were different, and I didn't want to give hope that ended up being in vain. "Okay, so first off, are the dwarfen trustworthy?"

"More or less," he said carefully. "They have no love for us, not really. They're a pretty untrusting group, as apparently the first and only other species they ever met that was self-aware was the Ændari."

"Yeah, that's gonna give you trust issues, considering that they're almost all dicks," I agreed. "Okay, I'm going to go out on a limb here and trust you, but we're at war, and shit isn't going well. First off, what do you know about the Great Reset, or the nanite plague?"

"I've never heard of either," he answered, looking perplexed.

"Brilliant news." I smiled as I banished the Devourer coating and stood there in my jeans and T-shirt again. "Now, do I need to do anything to prove to you who I am?"

"You're standing in the corridor of a ship in deep space in what appears to be cloth, without needing to breathe, and you can manipulate the builders with a thought. If there's another being beyond the Devourers that can do that, and you're secretly hostile to us? We've already got massive problems. Also, you've saved us, instead of feeding on or killing us. I think I can extend a little trust."

"Good." I smiled again. "So, the war is a stalemate, and the shit just hit the fan. I'll explain everything soon, but you're going to be very popular when you get back to civilization, and I need these dwarfen to be kept under control while I get us out of the anomaly."

"We're still in it?"

"How were you planning to escape?" I asked.

"We were all to take turns in hibernation, with those who were aware working to finish the rebuilding of the ship. Once it was done, the dwarfen had a reactionless drive that could fly us out, but it'd take several centuries. The agreement was that we would attempt a jump, and if that failed, we would instead draw lots and one of the group would remain aware, watching over the ship while the rest hibernated."

"And the other six who there wasn't room for?" I asked.

"We would remain behind, searching the wreckage for another solution until we expired."

"Yeah…" I shrugged. "Well, I'm going to jump us out of here. Then, once we're clear, we'll power up the engines and see where the hell we end up. Then fly from there to the node. You don't have a pilot, do you? Someone who can figure out where the hell we are once we're back in normal space?"

"We have two, and the dwarfen had one, as well as the AI memory modules."

"That's the best news I've had all day." I sighed. "Okay, one last point. When I found the dwarfen, they were all dead, and there were none of your people there, just the five dwarfen and a shitload of dead robots."

"Then…the Ændari are most likely alive." He shook his head disgustedly. "They're vermin. No matter how hard you stomp on their necks, they just keep coming back!"

"Well, we're leaving them here, so fuck it. Can you sort out the dwarfen? Keep them from causing any issues and get them to stay in the room I put them in?"

"What room? And how many of them are there?" He straightened up. "Also, am I tied to your side with this?"

I glanced down at the nanite link from me to the armor I'd made for him then shook my head, cutting it and releasing control, letting him claim it.

"No, I can spare them…it's only a few million. Okay, like I said, I found five of the dwarfen, and they were all dead. You'd injected them with the nanites, or builders as you call them. As soon as they were near a bit of usable matter and air that hadn't been drained completely, they started recovering. Unfortunately, the first thing one of them did was attack me."

"I apologize, Lord," he said quickly, dropping to one knee again. "We had no opportunity to explain your kind to them, beyond the most basic of details. They will have meant no offense…"

"Oh, get up from there! One of them snuck up behind me, hit me with a pipe, then tried to crush my balls—oh, and he headbutted me," I pointed out.

There was a sudden very clear and uncomfortable silence from my new friend as he climbed to his feet again.

"So yeah, that fucker's dead. I headbutted him back, after all. Unfortunately, his friends all started waking up as well, and the air in here wasn't ready for them. Most choked to death while I attempted different atmospheres for them."

"I…" He paused, clearly thinking, then nodded. "In that case, I suggest we check the bodies, and if possible, we awaken their leader, Lehman, and allow him to keep his people in line?"

"Good plan. Which one is he?" I gestured to the tubes.

"He remained awake with his son Reman."

Of course.

Of fucking course, when we checked it out, it was Mr. Testicle Twister's father who turned out to be Lehman, and when I reawakened him with a burst of nanites and the electrical equivalent of a stiff drink and a taser up the arse, the first person he asked Zhonat about was his son.

CHAPTER EIGHT

It took a little discussion and a lot of arguing, followed by me pretty much going nuclear with the nanites, transforming into a cloud of tentacles and almost ripping Lehman's head, arms, and legs off before things were calmed down, but eventually it was.

It wasn't helped by the situation that Lehman and the others had intellectually known that the nanites could bring their BWV and BWS allies back from the grave, as well as the asshole Ændari, but as far as we knew, none of their kind had ever undergone it.

That meant that when he saw his son and friends all dead, he didn't take it well.

Hence the whole "Cthulhu" ass kicking that I started to give him and Yartiman.

Once I'd pinned them both and threatened to slowly remove their limbs like a really fucked-up medieval rack, another of the group had started to recover— and that changed things.

Also, having Zhonat explain the minor thing of me being the local cluster's equivalent of a dark god with unlimited power, and that I was trying to save them all, when Reman had jumped me from behind, and then tried to rip my balls off…

The dwarfen were currently staying as small and quiet as possible while I prepped for the jump outside in the alien bay, surrounded by the clouds of that weird atmo.

They'd confirmed that the thicker the gasses and pressure in here were, the less reactive the entire place became to the drifting lightning from outside. So after sending them inside to stay out of my way, I'd gone back to layering it over and over again.

I did a final round of tests, before doing a little "Night Fever" dance when it worked. I'd finally been able to create better storage devices for the power cells.

I'd still enveloped them in solid lead apart from the connections leading off, and even those crystals were sealed, just in case, but it meant that I could finally start.

I gathered everything together, and began.

Arise: Conqueror

The ship…well, it wasn't ready, not really, and certainly not for the bloody menagerie I currently had aboard. But the longer we were here, the less time I had on the far side to work with.

Dwarfen-based reactors apparently needed either a very slow buildup—much like the grav drives did—or a jump start from another running reactor. Although I could do that, trying to while in the middle of this mess was running a risk we didn't need.

Instead, the plan was that I'd jump us out using the power I got from converting the mass around me. Then, once outside, I'd tear a load more of the surrounding mass apart, and use that to build a big enough reserve to jump-start the reactors all at once.

That was what I was doing currently, absorbing ton after ton of scrap. Instead of going all out and plowing it into the power cells, though, I was reforming the mass into coins and charging the power storage cells more slowly with the additionally released energy.

I'd been ready to just go all in, until I'd seen the looks on both the dwarfen and BSV's faces when I'd said it aloud. Apparently the higher the charge in the cells, the more likely they'd still somehow spark a reaction and they really didn't want me risking that.

Admittedly, they were also trying to be polite, which when dealing with engineers was a new experience to me. Instead, I agreed that I'd build the charge slowly and drip feed the grav drive as well, warming it rather than shoving enough power into it that it'd likely tear open space and time and take a steaming shit on God's lawn.

Converting solid matter entirely to energy would be the final step to power the grav drive. Although I could possibly channel that energy myself all over again, I'd be a bloody fool not to have more easily converted metals and a load of storage cells ready for draining if I could.

The coins clinked into a box I'd made for them, keeping them ready and on hand for when I needed them, while the massive pile of rusted and broken machinery before me crumbled under my shroud.

The Devourer had flowed out with barely a thought, moving like sentient silk as it slid over the mass, digging in, then flowing like warm honey and absorbing matter.

I took a deep breath, feeling weird about the whole thing, as more and more of the matter around me was broken down.

Using my body as a conduit for the kind of power that could hurl starships through the vast distances in the void of space was both incredibly stupid and yet awesome.

Fragments of metal and rock, rubbish in many ways, having rusted and collapsed millennia ago, broke down like ice in the glare of the sun as the sleek Devourer flowed across it. The knowledge that I gained second by second came close to overwhelming me.

Somehow I was fracturing the world apart at a quantum level, literally shifting atoms and molecules in ways that should have required insane levels of energy, and I was using my gravity manipulation to help with it.

Now, as I grew more and more skilled and gained more experience with gravity and its manipulation, I found that I'd clearly been using it for this for ages.

All it required to discover more was fine-tuned control.

The tiny builders, the nanites as I always thought of them, were machines so small that they'd been assumed to be cells in our bodies all this time. That they were that small, and could interact with literal molecules and atoms was crazy, but that was life.

The more I looked at this, the more I realized that the changes to become a Devourer weren't just in "me." As I attuned the nanites to me, I didn't just get greater control over them.

I was gaining better control over gravity.

I'd thought it was just me, that they were growing better with gravity because of their link to me, but the more I thought about it, the more I saw that I had it in reverse. They'd always used gravity. They used it to fracture the molecules away from each other. They used it to move, to grow, to bind together.

I registered almost at the outer limit of my senses the shivering of gravitational fields. They were so small that I'd never noticed them before. But as I covered a larger and larger area with the Devourer form, I felt it more. It helped that the gravity here was so messed up, with the only pull literally being the ship's mass.

I decided that although "cloak" wasn't entirely inaccurate, "shroud" was definitely the better way to identify it.

The shroud was covering more and more mass. And as the nanites that made it up ate into the pile, there was a faint but definite gravity field building.

I didn't know whether this was unique to me or whether all Devourers had it, but either way, I was gaining energy faster and using steadily less to break the bonds apart.

I was growing more powerful, and I realized that I'd not even been building the tools I'd needed so long ago to manipulate gravity. I'd been doing it on my own, funneling the ability through the tools when I remembered. And when I didn't? I just did it on instinct.

Closing my eyes, I dug deeper, extending my senses as I got ready for the first phase.

The dock around me was huge.

I felt like I was constantly being overwhelmed in size and using "huge" this or "massive" that, but the dock was at least as long as a modern skyscraper was tall, two hundred plus meters from one side to the other, and another hundred or so high.

There just wasn't any other way to look at it. Although I used my gravity senses to "see" more often than not, between the energy that was being released by the constant breakdowns and the thickened atmosphere, it felt like I stood at the bottom of the ocean and was surrounded by clouds at the same time as it surged and eddied away.

Arise: Conqueror

The first of the power cells passed a third full, and I focused on them and the room around me, drilling down into the atoms as far as I could, searching for instabilities, for building patterns, anything that might show me that it was all about to go Pete-Tong.

I found small ripples flowing here and there as something reacted, but nothing that overly worried me. I opened the feed from the first one to the second and third, bleeding power off and starting the relay.

I'd set them up this way deliberately: a connection from each of them flowed inward to me, ready to deliver all the power I'd need, and from me out to the first in line.

I created a loop, one that could push or pull, but also a second connection, one that ran from the first in line, splitting to the second and third. Then each split again and again, forming a pyramid.

I'd done it so that if the overall charge built too high in one of the cells, I could bleed it off into the others, reducing the risks again. If there were effects from too much power building over say, three in one area, I could bleed all three as well.

It was complicated, but it was worth it, I'd decided. Better to do this stage right than have everything explode and send us back to the drawing board.

As soon as the second and third powered up to a third with no side effects, I felt a massive wave of relief that it was working this well.

Four more were unlocked, and the building charge dipped again, spreading out across more and more. Seven became fifteen, then fifteen became thirty-one. Each of the cells were able to carry two connections off to others, and one to me, direct, just in case.

With thirty-one cells all charging, I felt the first tremor in the clouds around me, the power reaching ten percent overall as I did.

I slowed, examining it, then nodded to myself. I lifted into the air, shifting around and landing on the hull of my mad little starship, getting ready for phase two.

Ten percent climbed to twelve, then fifteen. The clouds slowly shifted as pressure built from outside, and creaks rang through the ship all around us.

Fifteen became twenty. More and more atomic excitement built; the universe seemed to shiver as the tiny amount of the local elements started to react.

My armor was digging deeper now. Hundreds of tons of matter fragmented, breaking down, as coin after coin clinked into the box I kept nearby.

They were essentially high-density energy to me now—coins of solid atomic value that I could spend to create anything I needed. What I needed right now, though, was power—so much power it was mind-blowing.

I shifted, extending my right hand toward the ship beneath my feet. That hand reformed, narrowing and flowing out; the fingers melded together and locked onto the port I'd built onto the hull.

My world expanded infinitely as I poured my mind into the ship, gasping involuntarily as it shivered awake.

The storage cells dipped, dropping to fifteen, then twelve, before slowly stabilizing and starting to rise again as the ship hummed to life.

I bypassed the reactors entirely for now, feeding a little into the power cells I'd built inside, but most of it went directly into the grav drive.

I felt it then, in a way I'd not before all of this, as the grav drive started to warm. Fluctuations in the universe around me appeared, then vanished.

They grew, then fell, grew again, then fell. I searched the systems quickly, watching for a pattern, a hint, a—

Something on the crystals was sliding off, and each time it vanished, the building tremors vanished as well. Something was there…

Twenty-five percent across the power cells became twenty-seven, and a fresh wave ran through the clouds of atmo. They rippled, like something was moving sluggishly below the surface, and I felt the instabilities growing.

I couldn't increase the power I was feeding into the drive—it just wasn't ready—and the gravity was clearly a warning. I couldn't let the power build higher, though, not and have nowhere to bleed it off into.

I hesitated, then drew back the Devourer slightly. I slowed the intake, allowing the drive to draw steadily, not increasing it, but systematically warming it.

That dropped the cells level, going from twenty-seven to twenty-six, five, four…

As it slowly dropped, the building waves in the clouds around me died away, gently settling, even as the grav drive continued to generate instabilities.

For several seconds I watched, trying to make sense of the drive, of the way that the gravity rippled, the flows, the…

It couldn't be, surely.

I cocked my head unthinkingly, staring at the way the pulses rippled out; the clouds around me moved like the surface of a pond with the wind blowing across it.

It couldn't actually be *that* simple, could it?

Whatever it was on the crystals that made up the heart of the gravity drive, as it ramped up, the surface of the crystals grew cloudier, less clear and fuzzy, with the pulse building.

As soon as the cloudiness vanished, the engine stabilized; then it'd happen again, and again.

I slid a tentacle through the hull of the ship, extending it on and on, darting through the passages and down, latching onto the gravity drive's surface, and extended my senses even further.

Searching from side to side, then down and down, looking around at every joint, at every seal, I probed deeper. Examining each and every section bit by bit, until after a solid minute in which I'd done nothing else, I found it.

The cells were down to seventeen percent now, and I absently set the Devourer back to work as I stared at the shitty connection in mixed disgust and amusement.

The seal on the smallest fragment of the door that led into the crystal chamber wasn't solid.

Arise: Conqueror

It was literally the only way in and out of there, and inside, as I extended a pseudopod into the chamber, I felt it.

Water.

There were tiny water droplets in the vacuum inside, and as the gravity drive cooled to match the cold of space, the water molecules had settled on every surface.

As the crystals were fed power, they warmed, and the water began to condense as the pressure in the chamber increased.

The crystals were suddenly covered with a cloudy coating, much like the windshield of a car when it'd been too cold overnight and before the sun warmed the glass.

The crystals were designed to warm space, and when they were covered with a film, they weren't able to build the energy equally. Sections would have the energy trapped inside; then, as the pressure built, the molecules were forced off and into the rest of the chamber.

The crystal would settle down, and the water molecules would cool, then form again.

This went on and on until the chamber was warm enough and stable enough that the molecules were kept off it fully. When the gravity drive was powered down, though, then the cycle would start again.

That was it.

The great secret of why the drives had to be powered over weeks, rather than minutes—considering that if they blew up, they could form black-fuckin'-holes—was because the original quality control of the grav drives was so shit.

Then they'd fed that first working design into the makers, and it'd been faithfully reproduced again and again, as engineers and scientists worked desperately to figure out the mechanics of the jump, and why it kept going wrong.

It was a single fucking shitty weld that had done it, and because it was so incredibly tiny, it'd passed by all the examinations.

There were probably similar spots on the other ship versions that did the same, and as they were copied, it went on. Nobody wanted their drive to go off, so when they didn't have any bad experiences, they probably just celebrated and moved on.

Looking at this now, as I extended the pseudopod farther, gathering up everything in the chamber and sucking it all back out, before sealing the chamber again, I started to laugh.

It was something so stupid that only a welder would have seen it, because only someone with the same mentality would wonder how stupid the design engineers had to be, to make something fit so flush as that seal had.

It meant that there was almost no room for error, and although a welder would build in an extra layer for error, just in case, an engineer was obsessed with the perfect fit and would shave it down micron by micron.

Sucking those tiny water molecules out left the crystals suspended in a perfect vacuum, and as soon as that was achieved, the ripples in space around us died away.

The pressure was still building on the ship as the hostile environment of the helium-4 outside was drawn to the power cells.

That mattered a hell of a lot less, though, when I could feel the goddamn grav drive was stable.

I pushed more energy into it, knowing that I wasn't just jumping my ship, but everything around me, and the drive soaked it up effortlessly.

Ten percent came and went as I drew more and more power into the ship. Five percent and I started to dig deeper into the pile; then I switched to the coins as well.

I had hundreds by now, but as they crumbled, the energy levels leapt upward, and so did the pressure.

Fifteen percent, twenty, thirty… At forty percent, the pressure was high enough that the creaking and groans that rang through the ship got worse.

At fifty, something in the distance started to scream as the metal tore, and I swore.

I'd wanted it to be higher—I *really* wanted there to be a lot more power than this—but I clearly wasn't getting what I wanted without running insane risks.

It was time to start the jump.

I still didn't have the ship powered properly, and the reactors were cold and dead, meaning that the tiny amount of power I'd provided and that was sitting in the inbuilt power cells was nowhere near enough to activate the AI core.

Without that, I was doing it all on instinct again. I reached into the drive, gathering myself, then started to eat the null coins like they were peanuts.

The energy leapt into me, and I pushed it all into the drive. The field rippled slightly, then flashed outward, passing over and through me like a spectral wave and filling the universe around me.

I felt it then, the way that the drive did it, the pressure wave, the tear—all of it. The mass that was dipped into the lower branes was what you paid the energy penalty for, as well as the depth and the time spent there.

The mass around me…well, there was a lot of that.

I felt the energy levels that we expended on our very first jump out of the Sol system and into that asteroid field come and go. Those needs, which had dragged literal asteroids along with our ship, were suddenly tiny, childish almost in comparison.

The bubble pushed out and out, further and further rising through the lower levels of the enormous ship, before shuddering, as the energy I was pushing in passed the limit.

The amount I was consuming and feeding into the drive hit the maximum, and rather than try to push that point, with at least half the greater ship inside the bubble with us, I triggered the change from expansion of the field to driving us into the branes instead.

The universe around us tore and fractured. I felt and heard huge explosions ring out as the metal buckled inward. The force that had been pressing in on layer after layer of reinforced armoring and carefully built exploration vessel was suddenly pressing on an eggshell.

Arise: Conqueror

The ship crumpled. Explosions raged out of control. Gasses vented. The liquid metal corpses of the pressure creatures were ripped into space. The crackling red lightning and the raging clouds drove deep into the shattered hull, rabidly determined to dig out the foreign contamination of energy…

But we were already sinking from the universe of our birth.

The branes rose, fluttering past us as we dove deeper. I cursed as I felt the nearest of the creatures appear in the distance, swimming deeper, heading away from us as quickly as possible.

I'd brought a section of that corpse in here with me, and in doing so, I really hoped I'd not just pissed these creatures off.

We'd barely dipped through the third brane when I pushed forward, feeling the pressure around me.

It was almost as though there were paths here, between the stars, leading upward past thicker areas, and I selected one ahead and to the left, judging it to be a decent distance, and hoping that I'd not just bring us back out into the same damn cloud.

Rising slowly, I reached out—feeling pressure all around, the shivers of movement nearby, a sense of curiosity and concern, bone-deep weariness and shame from somewhere—and then we rose, faster and faster.

Things like cobwebs fractured around us as we passed through. More and more of them snagged on us, slowing the ascent, and I pushed more energy into the field, but in reverse this time, pushing the branes down.

We picked up speed again, flashing forward, juddering as something brushed against us. Then, with a jerk like a cork leaving a bottle, we exploded back into our own reality.

CHAPTER NINE

I shook uncontrollably as we burst back into space. The pressure around me suddenly ripped into reverse as the broken hull around us erupted into vacuum, and I staggered, eyes jerking open.

I'd done it!

The shattered outer hull around us, and the battered and twisted docks were still there, but somehow, in the jump, it'd been torn apart. I could see the cold and glorious light of the stars filtering through the rents torn in the metal, and I sank to my knees as relief overcame me.

The gasses that had surrounded us and the pressure were gone; the damage in the hull had been enough that it'd escaped already. And outside, the haze was vanishing by the second, the stars becoming brighter and brighter.

I kicked off the surface, dragging myself free of everything, leaving the box of coins behind. The Devourer flowed back into me, the tentacles flashing back as well; the last section remained on the hull of my little ship to seal the hole I'd made.

Then I reached out, grabbing a buckled support spar, and twisting myself around, grabbed it and launched myself upward again.

I hit the walls as I went. They buckled as I bounced, fingers extended to find purchase on the solid smooth surface as easily as a handhold.

The walls blurred as I went; passages appeared and vanished before I burst out into space. I had to pop a gravity bubble behind me to slow me down, then twisted, exulting in my newfound invincibility.

I hung there in space, staring at the glory that was revealed.

Sitting in a starship, looking through cameras or at a projection was nothing compared to this—the cold majesty of the deep dark, combined with the burning light of the stars.

I stared for long minutes, drinking it in before I even started to search for anything else, finding the nearest star in less than a minute, hanging there in brilliance.

Three worlds were easy to pick out, spinning silently in the distance. One rose behind the remains of the ship, and as I turned, looking down at it, I couldn't help but shake my head in amazement.

Arise: Conqueror

The damage we'd taken hadn't just been from the pressure, nor the explosions of atmo.

The ship was covered in glistening, evaporating strands. They crumbled, turning to gas as I watched, and yet the sheer number of them made it clear this hadn't been an accident.

Whatever lived "down there" had put up a fight, trying to make sure that either we didn't get away, or they'd tried to stop us entering again.

Either way, whatever the strands had been, they must have been both incredibly strong and savage, considering the lines torn and burnt into the surface.

It'd started to crack the hull, constricting, and that was where the tears had come from, making me wince as I saw how close we'd come to death.

Had I not made the decision to take the remains of that ship with us, we'd have been shredded.

My little ship was going to be fast and strong, but without the shields powered, it'd not have stood a chance against that. Had I been capable of sweating, I'd have been covered in it as I searched for any hints in the mess.

The system didn't recognize it as anything, just coming up with boxes full of question marks when I tried to examine it. After a few seconds, I darted back down to the hull, digging my way in and sliding through the gaps as quickly as I could.

By the time I fell through the hole in the ceiling of the dock, drifting down to land on the deck, the dwarfen and Zhonat were glaring at me out of the diamond-hard cockpit.

I moved inside, passing through the simplistic air lock as quickly as I could, before being subjected to a barrage of questions as soon as I was inside.

"Where…"

"When…"

"What…"

The questions all started like that, and although Zhonat wasn't shouting, the look on his face made it damn clear he was only holding his tongue because the dwarfen was asking the questions for him.

"We're out." I gestured at them to shut up. "When we went through the branes, though, something tried to attack us. That's what happened to the hull up there…"

I pointed upward vaguely, only to be pestered with more shouted—and in one case gestured—questions again.

"Shut the fuck up!" I barked at them. "We're out, all right? That's all I know for now. We need to get the ship powered, the reactors online and the damn AI awake. We need to figure out where we are, and we're not doing that from in here, so I'm going to start that. Then we'll get some warmth and possibly even some damn food sorted out for you all, okay? Just…chill out. I'm going as quickly as I can."

I started to push through the group, when the testicle tickler moved before me and braced himself in the doorway I was headed for, glaring at me.

"You really want to do that?" I asked him quietly.

"You listen to clan elder," he ground out, clearly having difficulty with the words.

"No," I said with a smile. My armor flared up around me and spikes extended slowly from all sides.

His eyes boggled, and he frantically backed up, trying to make as much room as he could. Then he started to panic as he found that because the ship was designed by me, for me, and with absolutely no expectation of me carrying goddamn passengers, there was nowhere for him to go. He crouched down, having hit the bulkhead that protected one of the reactors.

I jumped past him and up, dragging my spikes in as I caught the lip of the hatch to the next floor and pulled myself up and through.

The air lock I'd come through was on the lowest level of the ship, literally just there because I knew I might need one to dock with the warship or something.

The dwarfen had clearly not considered the location, nor that when I came back I'd be "turning on" the gravity again. The shouts suddenly rose from behind and below me as they realized that with no rungs down there, for them to get to the level I was on…

Well, they'd be standing on each other's shoulders, at the least.

Zhonat turned up a few minutes later, hesitating at the door to the room I was in as a dozen of my tentacles finished plugging sections in.

The AI memory core was more or less solid-state, but I'd not dared to hope that I could find more, so the five I had were all separated and kept powered down.

Right now, I was plugging the first two into the system, both UC models, and into each other.

"They're not bad people, you know," Zhonat said to me after a few seconds.

"Do you know I don't care?" I responded, still working.

"Lord Devourer…"

"Here it comes…"

"They're not trying to antagonize you. Their race was exterminated, then they were killed. They don't understand the position they're in, nor do they mean disrespect. In dwarfen culture, they reach consensus by arguing. The winning argument is wholeheartedly embraced by the group, and they work toward that with everything they have."

"What's your point?"

"In their culture, if you won't defend your position, you don't deserve to have it. If you use force to make them do something, they'll never respect you. If you wish to have the surviving and possibly last members of the dwarfen race curse your name for all of eternity, then you're going in the right direction."

I turned and glared at him, my armor retracting entirely as I did so. "I don't need them to make this work," I said after a few seconds.

"No, you probably don't," he agreed.

"They're out of that because of me. I fucking saved them, and all they've done is give me shit for it," I countered.

"I agree."

"They're fucking annoying as well, all this constant challenging me…"

"Very much so," he said, and I glared at him even more.

"You know I hate this kind of shit."

"I guessed so."

"My partner handles it normally."

"That's probably very wise."

I could feel his fucking grin even through the armor, and I tried to bury my rising irritation.

"I don't need this shit," I repeated. "They should be thankful!"

"They are."

"Shitty way of showing it."

"From their point of view, they're presenting you with the chance to argue with them. If they believed you weren't worth that chance, they'd leave you alone and leave as soon as possible. As it is, you've got a chance to earn their loyalty."

"I don't need it," I muttered. But even I knew I was acting like a petulant child. I lifted a hand, rubbing at the bridge of my nose and breathing deeply as I tried to get my annoyance under control.

"FINE!" I snapped aloud. "Fuck it, tell him to get up here."

I gestured; the gravity inside the ship suddenly lightened, and I struggled to keep a grin from my face as the dwarfen started to shout, and suddenly the deck shook.

One of them had clearly been trying to jump up at that point and had managed to drive themselves into the deck overhead.

That put me in a better mood as they struggled up and into the room. Reman glared at me as he rubbed at his bleeding nose.

"I'm going to fix the AI core, then start charging the power cells, bring them all online. Once that's done, I'll tear us out of the ruined hull. We'll power the shields and start jumping until the AI figures out where we are."

They stood there, silently glaring at me, and I twisted to look at Zhonat, who had retracted his helmet and was apparently trying not to curse at me.

"What?" I asked.

"You seek consensus?" Lehman asked suddenly in a gravelly voice.

"Sure," I replied.

"This plan explains nothing."

"What do you want to know?" I asked as politely as I could, while trying not to swear.

"Why should we help you?"

"Because I fucking freed you, and you owe me?"

"You seek material gain?"

"No, you… Fuck." I took a deep breath and tried again. "Look, I didn't know you were in there, okay? I'm in a war with the Ændari, and they've literally just tried to destroy everyone's nanites, as well as slaughtering probably billions of civilians.

"I've got a chance to kick the absolute shit out of them. Their fleet is weak, their soldiers slow and barely able to fight, apart from their elites, but the UC isn't much better. Both sides have been beaten down to their lowest point. They can barely access their makers. Neither side has been able to replace their losses in the elite soldiers for thousands of years…" I paused at the look of shock and disbelief on Zhonat's face at that.

"There was a nanite plague unleashed. It wiped memories, both biological and digital, and left both sides broken. They've had to start again from scratch, and the Ændari being, well, complete and utter cockwombles, they started a war again as soon as they could. There's been a cold war in the sector of space we're from, for like forever. My people and I left our home world…" I turned to look directly at Zhonat. "That's the Forgeworld, I think you call it, by the way."

His eyes bulged, and I nodded, pleased with the reaction.

"Anyway, we came from there, kicked the shit out of one of our original creators, Varnock the cockgoblin, then I started a fight with the local Ændari fleet. They're off somewhere in deep space now, looking for me. We boarded and captured the system node, and it's accepted me as its master. The Ændari are coming to try to take it back. They're planning to use it to kill billions, and I'm stuck out here with you, while the love of my life and our friends are trying to defend it."

"You…" Zhonat was trying to speak, clearly having difficulty, and kept glancing upward and back, obviously thinking how much he'd like to wake someone more senior from cryo. "I…you…"

"What you want from us?" Lehman rumbled.

"Right now?" I shrugged. "Stay the fuck out of the way unless you can help, and when we get to the node, help us defend it. The UC will be sending a fleet, and I sent some of our people to bring help as well. We just have to hold out."

"No. What you intend for us? Why you save us?"

"Seemed a bit shitty to leave you there, though I'm starting to regret that decision." I shot a glare at Reman, who had the good grace to look away.

"So you not want our help?" Lehman pressed suspiciously.

"I'd not refuse it. If you give it," I assured him. "But so far, you've not exactly shown as willing, or that you can be trusted or even useful. I need to get to Ingrid. I need to protect her and the others. I don't give two shits beyond that."

"We are dwarfen," he declared proudly, jabbing a thumb at his chest.

"That's nice," I told him.

"Lord Devourer—" Zhonat tried to speak.

"Steve." I cut him off.

"Steve. You don't understand. The dwarfen are engineers beyond any that I've seen. We assisted them, but they built that entire ship that you found us in, from scrap metal, in only a handful of years…"

"Good for them. Wanna guess how long it took me to build this ship?"

"Steve…" he tried again, looking flustered.

"How long?" Lehman asked, his thick eyebrows beetling.

"Less than a week."

"You lie."

Arise: Conqueror

"Nope…oh, shit, actually, sorry, it was about a week and a half. Maybe ten days, eleven? I wasn't sleeping much, so it blurred a bit."

"Not possible."

"Were you having a nap when I just dragged us across space with nothing more than duct tape and bad attitude?" I countered. "Could you do that? Perform a gravitational jump across star systems using nothing but scrap metal and your own body?"

Silence greeted that statement, and I went on.

"So, look, you might be brilliant engineers, gifted even, but if it takes you a fucking year or ten to build anything, it doesn't matter how good it is, because this fight will be over long before then. If you want to fight? I'll be happy to have you. You're an engineering group that can make better weapons and shit? Great! Love it. Feel free to help. But if it's going to be ages before you manage to make anything, then you're a burden, not a help. Either stay out of the way, or I'll drop you on the nearest world I can. You can make yourself something nice and do…I don't know, whatever."

"We help," Lehman grumbled, glaring at me.

"You sure?" I asked. "I've not seen that so far."

"We…" He took a deep breath, then tried again. "You fight the Ændari. We help."

"You sure, though? Don't want to interrupt your nap or whatever. I mean, you've been extinct for thousands of fucking years…another decade won't be noticed."

"We help!" He growled, glaring at me.

"Great. Well, in that case, you sort this shit out and get any of the ship working that you can. I'll jump-start the reactors in a few minutes and…"

***

"That shouldn't have worked," Zhonat sent to me an hour later, as I stood on the shattered deck, using my gravitational abilities and my blades to carve sections of the hull free.

"But it did."

"The dwarfen are…they're a proud people!" he blurted. *"Treating them like they weren't valuable should have driven them into a rage!"*

"It pretty much did."

"And yet they're in there now, arguing over how they can prove their worth to you! We spent seven months working on them in that hellhole before they agreed to trust us!"

"Yup."

"Are you listening to me?"

He snapped it out, the sending very clearly frustrated and pissed off, and I sighed, turning around and facing him as I absently continued to shift metal and stone through the void to clear a pathway out of the ruined hull.

I'd had a plan before to just blow my way out using the spiderbots, but with everything that'd happened to the hull, if I did that now?

I got the feeling it'd be like sitting in a carboard box and setting off a claymore mine strapped to my chest to open it up.

I could do it, sure, but the remains of the ship certainly wouldn't be explorable later, and I knew that'd upset Ingrid. And it was likely to do much more damage to me than just putting in an hour's work with a blade and a gravity bubble was worth.

"Look, you're pissed because it took you months and me a few minutes of arguing with them, right?"

"YES!"

"What did you do? I mean, they're proud people, so what did you try before?"

"We flattered them, and explained how the loss of their species was a crime against the galaxy. We—"

"Yeah, I don't need to hear any more." I snorted. *"Listen, they're proud, right? They know that they're great engineers, and they'd never seen you before—you'd heard of them, but they'd not heard of you?"*

"That's right."

"Then they thought they were better than you. You came to them and basically begged. They're proud—they needed an ally. They needed help and they can't ask for it, not from the sounds of their culture. Then you come along and tell them how great they are. How the hell are they going to respect you?"

"We were trying to make allies," he ground out.

"Well, you made a piss-poor job of that then." I shook my head. *"Listen, they got wiped out by the Ændari. You're a group of warrior fucking legends. Had you led with that, being respectful but cool and pointed out that you had your own engineers but they could maybe tag along if they behaved? They'd have joined you, no stress."*

"They were already working with the Ændari."

"Uh-huh," I agreed. *"And how was that working out for them? The Ændari are dicks. You know it—they know it. The only thing they do well is fucking arrogance, so you needed to beat them into the ground and then give the dwarfen a reason to trust you. Negotiate from a position of strength, not on a bended knee, for fuck's sake."*

"You have studied much of negotiation, I see."

He sighed, and I snorted a laugh.

"Fuck, no. I just bargained with bastards in the bazaars in Turkey and Egypt. Take no prisoners and fuck the other guy into the ground. Hell with it."

"I see..."

"That why you came out here?" I asked.

"No." He straightened, clearly nerving himself up, before sinking to one knee and speaking. *"Lord D—"*

"STEVE!" I shouted, shoving harder than I should have on a mass of metal I'd just cut free, sending it hurtling across the bay and into an already weakened wall. *"Fuck's sake, how many goddamn times! Whaddya want, Zhonat? Eh? I'm a bit goddamn busy here!"*

Arise: Conqueror

"I…I ask that you awaken some of my fellows." The words fell out in a rush. *"They have slumbered long, and the worlds we knew are no more. Our friends, families, and more are lost. Everything we had is gone. All that is left is each other, and—"*

"Yeah, sure." I cut him off.

"They would be formidable allies and would… What?"

"Sure, go for it," I repeated. *"I was going to hold off until the ship had a decent atmo and was a bit warmer—it's colder than a witch's tit in there—but if you think they'll be all right, sure. Wake them up."*

"And the dwarfen?"

"Not enough room for both parties," I said after a few seconds. *"As it is, it'll be standing room only. Maybe wake two of the dwarfen and a handful of your people, but only if you know they'll be okay and won't go all mental and trash the ship or try to steal it. Believe me, that won't work out well for you."*

"I would never…"

"Yeah, I'm sure you wouldn't," I agreed. *"Stick with me and you get to see the Ændari fed their own horns via their assholes, but I don't know that for sure, and the dwarfen are mental. Just making my position clear, that if anyone tries to steal my ship or fuck me over after everything that's happened, I'll rip their head off and shit down their necks, that's all."*

"I see." There was a brief hesitation, then he nodded. *"I understand the inflection and the warning, Steve. I will ensure everyone else I awaken does as well."*

"Good man. Now fuck off and help the dwarfen or whatever. I need to focus here."

With that—and a little cross-armed salute—he was off, and I turned back to the now-floating debris that was clogging up the far end of the dock again.

Swearing, I gathered it up as best I could, dragging it all back in toward myself with a gravity bubble, then crushing it to the floor and spreading my shroud over it.

While that continued to feed, creating more coins almost absently as I poured the energy it gave off into the power cells, I focused on floating upward and carving more of the deck above out of the way.

It would have been almost impossible to move such a large mass under normal circumstances without explosives or something incredibly powerful. Fortunately for me, I had gravitational abilities, and all I had to do was separate more and more of the deck from the more solid sections that I could afford to ignore.

A handful of minutes of cutting, admittedly having to release the metal that I'd been absorbing when I moved farther out and up, and I could carve another section free, and then another.

Once I'd reached midway, all I had to do was move to the sections that were actually intact between the great rents that had been cut in the shell, and sever them.

I did it with a mixture of bladework and Devourer capacity, eating my way through sections, then triggering gravitational "bumps" to shove the deck up and away.

Fifteen minutes more, and I could see the stars again, giving me a section that was almost a third of what I needed to clear, for us to be able to fly straight out.

I'd contemplated at one point trying to use the remains of the dock's opening and closing system to get out. That was when I realized that not only was the damage severe enough in those areas that it just wasn't going to happen, but that the ship I'd built...

It was too big.

It'd grown with each new addition, and I damn well knew I was going to have to create a toilet soon at this rate if I didn't hurry up. But for now, speed was of the essence.

"Steve, the dwarfen have confirmed their adjustments are complete. We can start the reactors anytime you're ready."

"Coming." I sighed, shaking my head at the gap I'd managed to create, then ducking back inside, travelling quickly to the main dock level and gathering up the power cells.

They were a little over half full. That should be more than enough to jump-start the reactors, I guessed, connecting them to me one at a time, then plugging myself into the port on the ship.

The crystal network was easy to use now that I'd had a little time to get used to it. The similarity between weapons-grade crystals, power and data transfer crystals, and gravitational crystals were starting to stand out for me.

Weapons grade was generally high capacity and storage, charging up and discharging rapidly without damage.

Power and data transfers were medium capacity, and significantly lower grade than weapons, and they were as clear as possible.

Gravitational... They were different. Something about the flecks of gold and the reflective quantities I could sense deep inside made them significantly more powerful, and yet directed the warp inward.

I didn't know why they were like this, not yet, but I was getting to the point that I could interact with them easily and identify them even easier.

It made it so I could plug myself into them and feed the power and intention in, feeling the subtle shifts that were needed to make sure the power went where I wanted.

The reactors were like giant wells in the darkness of the power relay system, the power pouring in and vanishing. Second by second, it poured into all four, making me worry that I might not, in fact, have enough stored, when the first contraction started.

The reactors were almost like piston engines in their startup: the more energy that was poured in, the faster it built, and the sooner they reached their "coasting speed."

When the first one slowly and sluggishly started to move, contracting the pistons and solidifying the "bottle" into place, the others weren't far behind.

Arise: Conqueror

Seconds became minutes, minutes became hours, but as the pressure increased, the energy debt grew less and less, until around the fourth hour, it reached equilibrium.

"Hour of your units." Lehman grunted, staring at the readouts. "No more, they gain power."

"Damn well hope so," I muttered.

I'd come inside at the end of the first hour, eager to meet some of the others, expecting that Zhonat would have decanted at least a handful of them by now, only to find that he'd spent that time prepping a new suit.

He'd halved the nanites I'd given him, making his suit essentially a vac-suit instead of a full-on basic nanite one. But, as he'd explained, it was better to make sure that whoever he broke free of the tube didn't freeze or suffocate in the first minutes.

I winced at that, remembering that I'd forgotten again to build the goddamn heaters.

He'd spent the next hour working on them, and making sure that the air was tweaked a bit more to be easily breathable for both races.

Then he went to one of the tubes and, with my approval, started the defrosting process.

Apparently, the way I'd done it was considered incredibly dangerous, and it was supposed to be done over a twelve-hour period, rather than practically pouring them out onto the floor and dropping them into a panicked state.

Zhonat was fine, but as an engineer, he had taken upgrades to enable him to deal with similar situations. The warrior variants didn't have those options, so he played it safe, and I got bored.

Once the reactors were online and the basic tests were being done, I went back outside and up a few levels, then started to cut and carve again, reluctant to waste any more time on this.

I was getting closer to Ingrid by the second, and I could feel it, having spent a few minutes thinking about her, about being with her again. That, of course, led to memories of certain views and things we'd enjoyed last time we'd had a little quality time alone together. That kept my brain busy while I carried out the monotonous task.

Unfortunately, when we'd erupted into this system, we'd done so with a slight momentum twist imparted by the explosions as we entered warp. We now spun gently on our axis; the light slid in from the distant stars, making its way across the floor and climbing the wall nearby.

That was why it took me a few seconds before I noticed the slowly vanishing starlight, as the shadow of something outside appeared. It was also why I just stood there, staring, as the first lasers opened fire.

CHAPTER TEN

The darkness was lit by terrible light as sections I'd been slowly pulling and carving free were eviscerated. Metal exploded into gasses that rocketed more of the scrap and general rubbish I'd been collecting out into the void.

The lasers carved through layer after layer of the metal decks, before hitting the stone layers and digging into them. Fractures appeared and spiderwebbed out, and I damn well *ran.*

"Get the fucking ship up!" I roared into the link with Zhonat.

"Up?" he replied, confused. *"What's wrong? I'm in the middle of awakening—"*

"We're under attack, you fucktard! Get the ship ready to fight!"

"What?! Who?"

I snarled, cutting the connection and sprinting across the level I was on. I threw myself into a sliding tackle, then popped a gravity bubble to drag me down into the gap.

I bounced off one side of the shattered hull, jarring loose some more fragments and then bounced off the other, before finally dropping almost straight down.

The dock appeared around me as I fell through the roof. My freshly built ship spilled light from a dozen open sections.

"What the fuck are you doing!" I screamed at a pair of dwarfen, in some botched-together space suits, arguing over a connection point on the side of the hull.

"Devourer! Power cells, we no waste…" one said at the same time as the other spoke up hurriedly.

"No room inside! We fit outside, yes?"

"The power cells?!" I gasped. Already, several were attached to the outer fucking hull of a *warship*, and I almost gibbered with fear and horror.

Fucking engineers!

I took it all in, in a literal second; my brain triggered time compression automatically to make sure I could get it all at once. They'd not wanted to waste the power cells I'd made to hold the charge, the additional thirty-one cells, so the mad bastards had started fitting them around the outer hull.

That was logical—presumably—from a specialist goddamn engineer's point of view, but from a warrior's point of view, it was insanity!

They were putting things that were responsible for powering the shields and more, right outside where they could be damaged and…

And if I had thirty-plus power cells all storing the charge for the shields, it'd take a laser the size of the Death Star to damage them.

It took me a few seconds of gaping as my brain rebooted, frazzled, then rebooted again, the Engineering sub-mind and my own butting heads and trying to make sense of it all.

It *could* work.

It could be *magnificent*.

Then another laser dug into the hull behind me and something exploded. The floor beneath my feet bounced.

"Get it finished!" I roared at them, "We're under attack!"

The pair started to argue, presumably swearing at each other in their own language, as they frantically attached things that looked to me like they were installing a damn radiator or something.

I sprinted for the open air lock, not giving them time to screw me around anymore, and cycled through as quickly as I could, finding three more of the dwarfen inside as soon as I entered.

One was working with a small handheld laser, crafting something that looked like a suit helmet from…I didn't know what. Scrap, I hoped.

Another was working on a backpack and…

I skidded to a halt.

It was the armored suits that I'd found and rescued for us to work on later. The fucking armor that I'd collected from the ship that the UC soldiers had been wearing.

That stuff that was the pinnacle of the UC's "recovered" tech—and irreplaceable—these dwarfen had cut up and were modifying so they could play outside the ship.

I nearly killed them all on instinct.

Then the ship lurched again. I screeched in fury, darting past them and the third, who looked confused but had been installing rungs to help them climb from level to level.

I leapt to the next floor, then sprinted, reaching out to the ship and feeling her coming alive around me.

The reactors were ticking over at between twenty and twenty-two percent, depending on the draw on them. Storage cells were powering, though none of the internals were past ten percent. The ship was warmer, cheery light spilling from installed crystals here and there, and the shields…weren't even active yet.

I shoved past a dwarfen I vaguely recognized who grinned maniacally at me, then waved two ends of a split cable at me and jabbered something about upgrading the weapons.

I whimpered, finally reaching the cockpit and skidding to a halt.

There was only supposed to be me in here.

I'd designed it for fucking me, that was it—everything within reach, all ready for me to be able to grab and use if I needed to. Sure, I needed more room than the dwarfen did—or Ingrid and the others, for that matter—but still, I didn't need *that* much space.

The cockpit was twice the size I'd had before, and looking back? They'd torn apart a storeroom to get the space.

They'd moved the goddamn door! It'd only been an hour! They'd only had a goddamn hour, and two of them had moved the door back and were arguing over a gunner's position behind the pilot's seat, and whether they should be upright and facing forward or laid down and facing back.

I grabbed them both and almost hurled them out of the way, shoving past and into my seat. Then I screamed curses as it collapsed under my weight.

An explanation rose from behind me as someone started saying they'd moved the chair for something; tentacles exploded out, bracing me, lifting me back into the position I wanted.

I rammed the Engineering sub-mind into primacy in a section of my mind without thinking about it and just mentally waved at everything that was going on, screaming at it to "fix this shit."

The whole "lie back and think of England" piloting couch that the other ships had really wasn't for me. I had a more traditional "Top Gun" style pilot's chair, with a control stick in my right hand and three triggers on it. Index finger was the rail guns, thumb on the top was the storm caster, with the lasers being on my middle finger. Easy to fire one at a time or all three that way.

Left hand was for the reactors for things like the engines, a literal throttle for the reactor that fed into them.

My feet each had pedals, rigged to control both sets of engines, going from a gentle press to a stomp depending on the need.

Then there were all the others. My tentacles were latched onto a dozen different levers and controls, all of which were there as more of a "just in case," as most important of all?

I was plugged into the ship. The Devourer armor flowed across the surfaces all around me and onto a pedestal of crystal I'd created just for this. It didn't feed on it. Instead, I connected to it all, and my skin shifted as I was no longer just a BWV in the cockpit. Now I *was* the ship.

I ignored the sensations, leaving the sub-mind to work on it entirely on its own. I plugged into the ship, expanding my mentality into the waiting memory modules and finding out exactly what it was like for James as a pilot.

More or less.

James was plugged into a working and heavily developed ship, with a hell of a lot of experience in sailing and commanding systems. Yes, it'd been mainly managing people, but still, it was all logical steps for him.

He understood the hierarchy of needs at an almost instinctual level, while I did everything by the seat of my pants. The difference was that his skills, when he'd unlocked the piloting options under Command, had been boosted by the implanted knowledge.

The ships he flew had at the very least been patched together by experienced engineers with an overall plan.

Arise: Conqueror

I didn't have that. And, worst of all, I didn't have any damn points to spend until I earned more.

I did have two War points, admittedly. And as I remembered that, I slammed both of them into my Basic Stationary Platforms, taking it from Basic to Intermediate.

The pop-up that tried to explain the details was banished to the depths of my brain. My right eye twitched uncontrollably for several seconds as the data download unlocked.

At any other point, it'd have been a waste, just punching two into something almost at random like that. But for me, my weapons systems on the ship were literally stationary platforms. Yeah, attached to something that'd be hurtling across star systems, but that wasn't the point!

Any change, even a slight improvement in the fire rate or control, was incredibly important considering what was to come, and I could always make some turrets or something later to defend the node.

It wasn't as big a difference as I'd hoped, not even close, but it did come with several attractive unlocks to look at in the future. As much as I wanted to go down the rabbit hole of upgrades, I just didn't have time to pay it any attention.

The weapons unlock helped a little with making the weapons systems even more automatic for me than they had been before.

No, it was a lot more difficult to integrate myself with the ship than I thought it should have been from conversations with James.

He'd explained it as becoming more instinctive the more experienced he got. Certainly, in moving from the cobbled-together mess that was our first ship, to the fully functional—more or less—warship had been a vast relief.

He'd compared it to swimming, flipping the ship almost like rolling over in the sea to stare up at the sun, effortless and just…wonderful.

For me, if that stage would ever be possible, it was a *long* way out. Just like learning to drive, I needed to take it step by step. Increase the power from the reactors to the engines; start the shields powering up; start swearing because those goddamn dwarfen were still on the fucking hull…

"I swear, Zhonat, if those dicks aren't back inside in thirty seconds, I'm fucking leaving them!" I screamed it through the link, then cut it off before he could respond, swearing constantly as I killed the power to the shields again.

If they charged too quickly, if they sealed the hull and those idiots were outside on it? They'd be blasted off the hull at the very least. Most likely, they'd be fried as well.

Right now, I was almost hoping they didn't stop working. The more cells they attached and the less dwarfen around…

I shook that thought off and continued to push my mind throughout the ship, muttering as I went, searching for anything else I needed.

This was the real problem: I didn't have a goddamn clue what I was doing.

Okay, think of it like a flying car. That was the best way.

What did I need? I needed power to the engines…they were warmed and ready, I guessed. They'd not exploded and they'd not sent me flying into a wall or anything yet, after all.

The landing gear! I paused, trying to remember whether I'd made any, then shrugged. Couldn't remember, didn't care.

Okay, engines, landing gear…doors? I focused and got a list of open doors throughout the ship, and that the air lock was in use currently. Interior doors…well, I didn't care about that; leave them be.

The exterior air lock? Dammit! I hadn't put a camera or anything down there. I didn't know whether that was Zhonat going outside to get the idiots in, or whether…

"We're inside!" he sent.

"Okay, that's better," I muttered. "So…engines, doors, landing gear…shields?" I pushed more energy into the shields, feeling a popping crackle and tasting something like ozone as the exterior of the ship was flooded with power.

I hesitated for a second, focusing on that weird sensation, the feeling of tightness across the ship…

A fresh beam of power tore through the deck a dozen meters ahead of me. Gold faded to red as the beam cut off, but it left a line carved through the deck, with the remains of the outer ship shuddering as something hit it from the outside repeatedly.

As it reached the far side of the dock, it hit the spiderbot crouched there, and my eyes widened. I'd totally forgotten about them.

As the beam petered out, it licked across the bot's back, barely missing the shaped charge that sat there, ready to be used.

"Idiot!" I gasped.

As shredded as the hull was, it didn't need the explosives. But now that there was someone outside who clearly didn't like me? Explosives were back on the menu.

I'd given the spiderbots high explosives, and I'd been planning to use them to blast our way out; then I'd rethought that plan because of the effect on me and my ship being inside the damn thing when they exploded.

I was clearly still too easily distracted, but as soon as it all flashed into the forefront of my mind, I grinned.

With the sections I'd cut out before and the damage the lasers were already doing, I didn't see how setting off the shaped charges could make things much worse.

I sent an updated order to the remaining spiderbots to get into new places, imagining the look on people's faces should they see the big bastards clambering around.

The light vanished, a burning afterimage of the beam printed on my retinas for split seconds as the nanites quickly shifted, realigning and fixing the view.

The remains of the dock were a mess now: sloping and torn sections of ceiling, uncovered paths that led out to the stars or deeper into the hull, and closer to the other side of the ship. The air—well, vacuum, really—but the damn space between me and all the walls was filled with fragments, molten metal dots that were cooling and rehardening, gasses that were escaping…

Arise: Conqueror

It was an utter mess, and that was just the little stuff. There were sheets of twisted metal, stone, half-eaten materials I'd been absorbing. Even several power cells still bounced off the walls, and a rippling, silvery liquid that I guessed was one of the previous crew floated on one side.

"Hold onto your butts!" I yelled over my shoulder at the closed door, then shrugged. It wasn't my fault if they got a little bounced around. This wasn't a pleasure cruise.

Then, making sure the shields felt tight and the engines were flooded with energy, I triggered the charges.

The far side of the dock was already damaged, the floors above shredded and sectioned up, levels carved free of each other, ready for me to trigger the gravitational warp and rip them free.

Instead, the explosion forced sections apart like a firecracker stuck in an ostrich's egg.

Fragments flew in all directions, bouncing off the walls, floor, and the overhead decks, and pinging into my shields. The detonations for the spiders continued on, splitting the hull along fault lines that I'd thought I'd identified before.

Now, with all the additional damage?

It was massive overkill and would have resulted in horrific damage to my hull, had I not had the shields up.

With them up, though, I was bombarded by the equivalent of hailstones, stinging slightly but bouncing off and vanishing.

The structure around me split. Scrap flew in all directions, and I pushed down on the gas, feeding the engines with more and more power, feeling them flare, build… Then I snarled, spotting a detail in the command lines—a kink that was holding the final stage from activating.

I undid it with a thought. Then, as the engine lockdowns cut off and grinning like an idiot, I flew the *Pheonix* out of the hull at incredible speed.

I twisted as we rocketed forward. A section of wall appeared, hitting the shield and bouncing off as I pulled up and to the right, aiming for the nearest more or less clear path.

The hull was hit over and over with scrap, small fragments and large. The shields dipped from full to ninety-eight, ninety-four, then back to full; the power cells did their job and automatically boosted them back up.

We burst into the light of the nearby sun, and I pulled up and right again, inverting us and frantically dodging the ship directly overhead.

It was vaguely familiar, but the first details that stood out were that it wasn't Ændari, and it was right in our path.

As I twisted and fired the engines again, the universe flipped. The shattered hull I'd just escaped now rotated around to be overhead for me, and I rocketed back along its length, headed in a one-eighty from the direction I'd launched.

Behind me, the ship I'd barely glimpsed started to rotate, and I felt the wash of alien energies across my hull. Radio, light, pings I had no words for…all of them streamed across me, followed by more weapons opening up.

Lasers impacted first, crackling across my hull as the shield dipped again and again, only a few points at a time. But as four, then six, then eight lasers hit, it dipped faster.

I twisted and rolled, then pulled up, arcing away from the chrysalis I'd just burst from, which was now an expanding ball of devastation.

The ship behind me continued to rotate, lasers flashing out and tracking me. Plasma washed past in the cold of space, great balls of fire encased in magnetic fields.

"Really?" I snarled, reaching out and returning the favor. I examined them, trying to parse the signals that washed across my hull, as well as looking at the ship itself.

The signals were weird, almost data, like a constant streaming call that washed across me, or a remote signal, but at the same time so much more, flooding back and forth. I could feel subtle attempts at hacking being easily rebuffed by my Hack sub-mind.

Their ship was circular, more or less, and dotted with dozens of turrets. Smaller lasers were set regularly around the hull, and the plasma casters powered up for another shot.

The hull was spotted with communications antennas, small and large turrets, docking blisters and armor—oh, *so* much armor.

The turrets for the lasers were small, or at least they were in comparison to the main hull: a handful of meters across and with a single triangular projection that slid around on a gimballed mount, tracking us.

Blasts of light filled the void, and I no longer knew whether I was making them visible through a trick of mental gymnastics and ability, or the spectrum they used was visible.

I didn't know and I didn't care, because the nearest plasma caster was lining up on me already.

They were much bigger—each roughly the size of my damn ship, if I had to guess. Four towers extended from a central point, spaced equidistantly around the mount and reaching out to one another with narrow lines of metallic wiring.

Lightning crackled from one to another, forming the plasma that built in the middle into a ball, compressing it, pulling it back like an ancient catapult, ready to fling it into space after me.

That was when I opened fire.

"My turn," I purred, squeezing the trigger. The ship around me shivered gently, the first time all my weapons were fired in anger.

The lasers were the fastest. Two blurs of light flashed out, followed by another two, and another, rapid-fire style, as the rail guns that I'd not thought to charge before this frantically tried to charge to the level of firing.

The storm casters, though? They were things of beauty.

Officially they were proton weapons, but to me they'd always be storm casters.

The lightning that screamed across the heavens to tear into my target was just wonderful.

Arise: Conqueror

I held the triggers as I rolled and pulled to the right, dragging the fire across the hull. Everywhere the lightning hit, there was blinding light and crackling discharges.

The first impact on the towers that surrounded and contained the plasma tore the carefully maintained and pressurized field apart. The plasma washed out to my left, melting the seemingly flimsy towers on that side and washing across the ship's shields, taking them from serene and invisible, to rippling and on the verge of failure.

The lasers punched into the shields and sent them further to redline. Lightning danced across the surface; then the storm casters tore lines along the hull.

The impact point tore through the disintegrating shields, digging into the deck and shredding the upper layer, explosive decompression left behind it. I rolled, just as the rail gun finally reached enough power to fire.

Twin slugs hummed down the rails and vanished into the void, totally missing the target. I growled, shifting my aim and opening fire repeatedly. Lasers reached out and touched the enemy in special ways.

Ways that involved the hull and the weapons that dotted it exploding.

I twisted and rolled again, arcing away from the surface of the ship, and aimed for deep space, planning to get free of the hull and come back for a strafing run. And that was when the shit hit the fan.

Chapter Eleven

First, as soon as I arced out from the ship I'd been targeting, I came into view of more and more of the ship's weapons. Sure, I'd taken four or five down, including a plasma caster, but it was, well, *big*.

There had to be dozens of laser turrets dotted around the hull, just in sight as I headed away, and they were all lining up on me and firing.

Five plasma casters came into view as I headed away. Every one of them glowed as they charged their fields.

Then the "meh" news met the bad news, as for the first time I saw the other ships.

When I'd arrived, I'd spent a few minutes staring at the stars, the local sun, and the planets I could see with my augmented vision. It'd all looked incredibly pretty.

The minor thing I'd not considered?

Space is *big*.

Planets stand out because they're pretty big as well. But in the grand scheme of things, something that really doesn't stand out well, unless you're close enough, are ships.

More specifically, as they drifted inward, these moved from "ships" in my mind, to "Lagrange point protecting fortresses."

Multiples of them.

And they all headed inward, with the little crackles on their hulls that suggested distant weapons being charged.

Moreso, they weren't all the same size.

I'd been fighting the quick response force, I realized as I turned around and dove for the surface to give myself some time. More specifically, I'd been fighting *one* of them.

The others were still busily carving up the mass I'd just apparently used to Trojan-horse my way into a heavily defended system.

I didn't know who these fuckers were or what they wanted, but I just knew there was no way this was going to end well for me.

Dozens of them were incoming. I reached out to Zhonat and fed the image into the link, getting a burst of disgust and hatred, as well as a single word that explained everything.

"Senagra."

"Motherfuckers."

That was why the system was so fortified. I opened fire almost absently at the damaged vessel as it came back into my line of sight. The senagra were universally despised as parasites, and most of the people I'd met believed they were almost extinct.

Finding that they had a star system here that they were protecting so heavily?

They couldn't allow anyone to know that they were here, so they'd created significant defenses at the Lagrange point. Kill anything that jumps in and boom, no worries. You could even capture any survivors and use them to learn about the outside galaxy, but I didn't doubt they'd have better means in place yet.

Once you held the Lagrange points, you'd work to capture the system. I had no clue what it was like, nor where—not yet—but if it was anything that was pre-industrial? It'd make a perfect breeding ground.

Nobody who would be missed, nothing that needed to be hidden: they could grow and breed and consume, preparing a fleet to take over the nearby systems and nobody would know.

Nobody but a single bloody idiot who leapt through space like a ping-pong ball with control issues, that was.

"I need that AI up!" I sent to Zhonat. *"We need to know where the hell we are so I don't jump us back into the damn clouds!"*

"Working on it!" he assured me. *"The dwarfen pilot Zasha is examining the system as well. She wants you to do a flyby of the gas giant. Says it looks familiar."*

"Tell her to get out and fucking walk!" I snapped, before cutting the connection and opening fire with the now-charged rail guns.

The lasers had kept the shields down, and the storm casters were tearing up the hull nicely as I came back into range for them. But for all the visual destruction I was doing, in terms of the overall ship, I was still in single percentage points of damage done.

They were returning fire. I twisted and rolled, desperately trying to avoid the fire, until I noticed the shield strength.

My shields were still rising, still coming online; two of them were active now, with the third flickering into life. And they were climbing faster than the staggered laser hits could take them down.

The first barrage of impacts that had lowered the shields originally?

I'd still been activating them at that point. They'd shrugged off the impacts, when only one of the shields was active. I couldn't help but smile viciously as I stopped dodging and lined up on a single point, pouring the fire in.

Lasers dug into the hull; lightning bored deeper, crackling and flaring additional tendrils that danced across the hole.

Then the rail guns fired again, and again.

Each impact dug deeper into the hull's surface, the outer armor stripped back. Fragments were flung free as atmo erupted, and struggling, thrashing spiderlike bodies were ejected into the cold of space.

I pulled up, strafing across the surface, and focused on the makers, specifically the ones that fed the rail guns, as I continued to tear the hull apart with the casters and lasers.

The makers were creating simple slugs for now, modeled on the upgraded version of the shells we'd used in tanks when I was in the army: a pointed end atop a cylinder, with a flat base.

Literally as simple as could be, considering they were solid. The rail gun wasn't all the way up to power when it was firing. I'd been launching these shots on the lowest, quickest-to-charge setting every time.

Now I changed the shot.

The tip was grooved, the pointed end solid enough that it would do terrible damage, but the section behind it was changed into a hundred smaller fragments. The null coins converted the simple metal into a much more complex weapon.

The outer shell was solid too, an incendiary section behind the tip, packed inside the fragment chamber, ready to fire them outward. Next was the high explosive, the zirconium powder, and finally, most fun of all, the tungsten penetrator, surrounded by more fragmentation spikes.

There were better materials, I knew—hell, there were better plans for these things in my memories—but right now, when I really wanted to bring the hurt?

I fell back on the basics I'd learned in the army. The shell didn't need to be incredibly sophisticated, after all. On impact, the forward-most point would explode, helped along by the conversion of kinetic energy into heat and light.

The next section would fill the area with fire and expanding fléchettes of sharpened metal. Then the high-ex would go off, massively enlarging the impact point and hurtling those fléchettes that were just released forward on a blast wave. The zirconium powder ignites and burns at both a high temperature and for an extended time, and that was when the penetrator would arrive.

The penetrator would rip through any remaining armor, digging deeper and deeper into the target, and dragging all those wonderful flames and shrapnel deeper into the target.

I uploaded the plans into the makers. In seconds, as I arced around, ignoring the incoming fire that barely warmed my hull, the first versions were being fed into the firing cradle.

I set the rail guns to charge, feeding more and more power in. On a whim, as I pulled up, still wanting to use this one I was close to as a shield, I targeted one of the more distant and massive vessels.

It wasn't like they were going to be dodging anytime soon, after all: they wanted to shoot me, and I was here.

Then I made sure I was at maximum charge and fired.

The ship shuddered. For a second, I was worried that I'd made a mistake, that something had gotten into the tubes and I was about to go out in a very short-lived blaze of glory… Then, silence.

That was the weirdest bit about space battles: I couldn't hear them. I couldn't hear the explosions and the impacts—I could just see them—and for this shot, it'd take anywhere from seconds to minutes to hours to hit yet.

Hell, it could be a gas giant size and take days to reach it for all I knew.

Instead, I shrugged and got back to it, loading the same shells again and again, lining up on the others and firing, then arcing around and shredding the hull of the nearest one with laser fire.

Three minutes it took for the AI to come online, three minutes of me starting to actually relax and enjoy bombarding the vessel below me. And when it did activate, it very nearly fucking killed us all.

The first thing the AI did was try to identify the system it'd been plugged into. To do that, it sent a massive burst of information out into the network, mapping responses, receiving expected and unexpected surges, and generally shouting "Hello, is there anyone there?" into the void.

The problem was, *I* was there.

The ship was plugged into my brain, and the sudden arrival of a billion screaming voices and a petabyte of data being dumped into my grey matter was not helpful.

Especially not when I was essentially the entirety of the computer that was running a spaceship, all using my sub-minds and the mainly unused brain that had failed school.

Also, I was actively involved in a strafing run.

With a super high-tech level ship that was being flown by me basically pulling cables and shouting "Guns go pew-pew!" to fire them.

Spoiler alert: it didn't go well.

I screamed, clutching at my head. The Devourer went mental, surging out and slamming into the walls of the cockpit around me, shoving and scrabbling, trying to find whatever was attacking us and tear it apart.

The engines fired suddenly at random. The shields flared, then cut out. Reactors redlined and dipped. Weapons fired in a panicked blur as the power that had been in the reactors, ready for an emergency, was basically dumped into the weapons.

The lasers ramped up to rapid-fire full power. As the ship careened around, flipped, spinning and twisting, they crept closer and closer to overload, filling space with a barrage of terrible light in all directions.

The storm casters lashed out at everything within range, tearing great holes in the nearby ship and gutting it.

The rail guns tried to fire. The magnetic fields reversed, then surged; the shells jerked back and forth in the tubes. I barely managed to get enough control to eject them before they detonated.

It took long seconds for me to regain anything like real control over myself, never mind the rest of the ship. And when I did, I found myself slumped over in the cockpit, half squished into the gap between my seat and the wall of the ship, panting, my body…

I'd shifted, somehow, in ways I'd never even considered I was capable of.

Now that my entire body was literally nanites, I could—in theory—shapeshift. I was fluid mass, after all, and here, pressed into the gap between the side of the seat and the wall.

It was like I was a size ten body crushed into a space for a size four, and then melted like candle-wax to make it fit.

I should have been incredibly uncomfortable at the very least. Instead, my chest and waist had shifted, the edge of the seat was currently wedged into the section that I usually kept my spine in, and I was fine.

One arm was back to front, fingers were longer and shorter seemingly at random, my right knee was on backward, and… I shook myself.

Dragging myself out from under the chair, flowing around it like water with a conscious act of will, I reformed myself, and glowered balefully at the dwarfen figure in the doorway, staring at me with his mouth open.

"Oops?" he offered, grinning and waving a component at me. "Me fix!" With that, he turned and ran.

I took one step after him, then gasped and shuddered, falling to my knees again. My hands clutched at my brain as the AI sent out another mapping pulse.

"Stop that!" I half screamed, half begged, broadcasting it into the connection with the ship as much as I did the air around me.

Instantly, the pulse froze and then vanished, with a much more cautious pulse being sent to me next.

I staggered to my feet, seeing two of everything, and slumped sideways, catching myself on that wall now, then pushing off and falling into my seat.

I shoved the Hack sub-mind at the problem, and dragged the Engineering one back up and split the ship between us. I'd check the overall situation; it was time to get the ship working again.

Shields first.

I grabbed the controls, focusing and feeling a migraine that I'd not even spotted arriving, as it surged and danced through my brain.

"Why…" I whimpered. "What the hell?"

I blinked, forcing myself to open my eyes and stare out of the cockpit, triggering time compression again. As the wildly flaring and spinning of the outside universe slowed, I managed to make out some of the shit we were in now.

Fortunately, the ship we'd been strafing had been pretty damaged by now, and the final insane blast of lasers and storm casters had basically gutted it.

Until now, we'd also been using it as a shield.

That was the good news.

The bad news was that the relative motion of it, compared to us, and the wildly flaring engines, meant that we were now drifting out of the protective shadow of the ship, and into clear sight.

The slightly worse news was that the senagra evidently had an equivalent of space marines, and they were launching themselves from the wreckage of their ship that someone had apparently very rudely torn a new arsehole.

Lastly, the *very* bad news, as I started to focus the sensors, with the sub-mind shoving energy at a panicked rate into the shields, showed that the bigger ships in the distance were vomiting fighters.

Literally hundreds, possibly thousands of them.

It was a swarm of epic proportions. The one thing that the senagra had going for them as a species was that they didn't give two shits about individual losses.

My shields had held up to the hits from the presumably more powerful lasers of the ship I'd gutted. But I just knew that thousands of smaller, repeated hits were going to be a different story.

If nothing else, the power transfer to keep the shields up wouldn't be able to keep up with that.

I was swearing constantly as I dug into the ship with my mind, checking the reactors and nodding to myself.

Arise: Conqueror

They were steadily slowing. The energy that had filled them like a puppy after a kilo of cocaine and a gallon of energy drinks was dying away.

That was a problem.

A big one.

The dwarfen version seemed to take forever to change direction. If they were building, they liked to keep doing that, and now, after an emergency redline, they were dipping, slowing, and I really didn't have time for that shit.

I pushed at them, demanding more, and they slowed, sluggishly responding. The dipping levels no longer sunk as fast, but I damn well knew they'd not be going back up in the short-term.

Checking it over, I had less than ten percent in the various power cores, and that was dropping as the sub-mind worked to get the shields up.

"Fuck it," I grunted, changing its orders and dumping everything into the engines, kicking the ship onto a straight level and firing the engines hard.

I needed to change the direction before anything could hit me, and really, the wonderful feeling as the ion engines flared and hurled us forward just before the first of the marines could reach the hull was worth it.

They vanished into deep space behind us as the speed built up. Lasers ripped out, but almost all of them fell short.

The few hits that landed barely stayed on target long enough to do any damage, but it was a sobering reminder, as I flared the engines again and again, getting us onto a more even keel.

"If we go too deep into the system, we'll be unable to jump." That was Zhonat, and I dismissed him with a shake of my head.

"We can jump wherever we are with enough power," I assured him, getting a distinct sense of concern at that.

"It is possible, in theory, but the power needed and the risk? Please, Steve, unless absolutely necessary, we should avoid it."

"Yadda, yadda, yadda."

I cut the link and went back to frantically working the ship, trying to figure out the damage that'd been done.

The report that came back finally from the damn sub-mind wasn't good.

The dwarfen reactors were good—seriously powerful and had no issues with space the way the normal reactors did. But in basically cloning a load of the tech the way I did, without understanding the individual underlying principles, I'd also cloned a weakness that they had.

Not only were they slow to power up, but when they were scrammed, they could be slowed on shutdown, but not stopped.

They were dipping still, slower than before, but steadily falling.

Worst of all, there was nothing that I could see that would prevent it. I searched and searched, the sub-mind and the AI comparing details and filling in more and more of the blanks by the second. Finally, the confirmation came back.

The ship's reactors were going offline, and we had, at best, an hour left.

They'd reboot and restart, but to get to the point they'd been at, we'd need at least a week of buildup or a massive jump-start.

Neither of which we could do now with what we had.

I gritted my teeth and frantically searched, checking the cells, finding they at least were slowly filling and were at eleven percent again. As the reactors slowed, the power stabilized. The amount they were putting out was enough to keep the engines at this point for now.

That was it.

I cut the engines, cut everything that I could, and fed everything that the reactors were providing into the cells, splitting them down the middle.

Half were to just store everything they could, literally. Any and all energy they could store, they had to. The others were split again, half to provide power to the engines, and the rest I drained into the first lot—portioned off for my exclusive use only.

That done, and with a tentacle flashing back into the main sections of the ship behind me, I sent a message to Zhonat, to pass to everyone.

"I need every bit of scrap and null coin you can find. Get them to this point." Then I formed the tentacle into a shallow-bottomed dish and filled it with the Devourer.

Those dicks could earn their keep chucking any random bits they could find into there, and I'd in turn feed the power through to the quarter of the cells I'd partitioned off.

With that done, I kicked the first of the ship's reactors back into an emergency—but controlled—shutdown.

The other three I slowed as far as possible, draining everything they had into the cells. I needed to get them as full as possible; then I'd use them to jump-start the flatlined one. Once that was up and running, I'd be able to use that to power the second. And then, from there we should be good. I just needed to keep us alive till then.

Checking the sensors, I swore and seriously considered telling the dwarfen to get out and push, because the swarm of ships was definitely closing on us.

I fired the engines, a solid burn, then cut them again, increasing the overall speed a little. What I really needed was a sustained burn, and I didn't have the power for that shit.

The next two minutes or so was spent explaining—impolitely—to the dwarfen that no, the goddamn weapons that I'd hoarded to help Ingrid and the others were not scrap, and therefore shouldn't be put into the Devourer.

Also yes, the motherfucking space armor that I'd been so pleased about saving were important, and no, the minor detail that they'd scrapped *all* of it to make their new suits was not an improvement.

Also yes, violence was my primary method of communication and now that they were immortal, I would like to murder each and every one of them.

Possibly several times a day.

I'd met them and I'd seen space dwarves. Cool, I'd thought.

Now, after a little experience with them, I was finding myself in the almost entirely unique position of sympathizing with the Ændari for the first time.

I wanted to exterminate the little bastards too.

Arise: Conqueror

More minutes passed as I built the energy levels as high as possible and literally ripped all that I could out of Reactor One, before seeing it flatline. There was a stage here that I couldn't effect, something to do with the vacuum bottle, which made no sense to me, but that meant the temperature had to reach absolute zero and equilibrium needed to be attained, then it could start again.

It took nearly an hour, and with the ships closing on me, I started to get to a gibbering panic stage again.

Just in case, I regularly fired the engines in bursts, both changing my position on the off chance they used a rail gun and increasing speed slightly. But I just couldn't afford to have the sensors powered all the time.

I couldn't have *anything* powered all the time, and that knowledge was galling, considering how powerful we'd been less than two hours ago.

Still, the reactor finally bounced back and started to power up, allowing me to dump the entire store that I had in the partitioned half of the storage.

It hit and the reactor stuttered, nearly making it brown trouser time, until the lights flickered again.

The reactor burst into life and the other three slowly wound down. I let loose a relieved sigh, before using the sensors to look back.

Then I punched the thrusters again.

The first wave—a mere forty or so ships, that's all—was nearly in range. As soon as I booted the engine, they blasted their missiles, clearly not planning to let me rock off on my merry way, and I fired the thrusters again, and again.

Fast burps of thrust sent us leaping forward, increasing speed, before I spun the ship, coasting backward as shields started to hum to life as well.

It was the lasers that I wanted, though.

There was still too big a distance between me and the missiles to hit with any degree of accuracy, but even a handful taken out could make the difference. I waited, aimed, and fired. The first three shots were solid misses. The fourth and fifth were lucky hits, exploding in short-lived pyrotechnics, before the next four shots all missed.

Then I spun again and fired the engines, darting a few degrees upward and angling slightly to the left, aiming for a distant cold world.

Slipping back around, I fired continually, taking out a handful more before cursing and spinning, dumping all the energy I could get into the shields.

They flared. The primary shield snapped into place at full power; the secondary layer started and reached seventeen percent before the first missile hit it.

That was when I realized that those point defense turrets would have been an amazing idea.

These missiles weren't just "bang" and a detonation. Oh, no—they were fléchettes packed into the head, so a single detonation provided dozens of tiny pinpricks that drained the shields more.

Explosions went off all around me. Fléchettes punched free and hammered my shields. Flames, light, and chaff: the universe outside vanished and I flew through clouds of madness for several seconds.

The secondary shield dropped fast, seventeen to four, then failed entirely. The primary dropped all the way to six percent before the wave was done, and I burst from the far side of the explosions with my ship streaming crackling red lightning as the shields tried to reform.

I could feel the shuddering of the hull as well. We were leaking atmo from somewhere, and as much as it boiled my piss, I had the trust the dwarfen or Zhonat to fix it.

The remaining three reactors were flatlined now, and I had nothing to throw at rebooting them—nothing beyond what I had for the engines or the section of emergency power I'd started to store to help with the next gravity jump.

I gritted my teeth and shoved that emergency energy into the storage cells.

It wasn't much, certainly not in comparison to the riches that the matter had been beforehand, but the various things I'd grabbed were worthless if we exploded in space, so fuck it.

I approved it, and the dwarfen started to strip the rooms for everything they could get. That was when I remembered the box.

The box of coins I'd been making earlier. I'd been doing it when I needed the energy before—what the hell had I done with it?!

The last time I remembered having it, I'd been on the roof of the ship, and although I didn't have cameras, I did have the shield's data.

Checking it quickly, I found the shields were surging up and around something on the hull, probably pinned there by the shields originally, and then by centrifugal force. Hell, I neither knew nor cared.

"Zhonat! You still got your suit?!" I asked him, getting a confused response. *"Here."* I sent a burst transmission to show him what I wanted and where I needed it, only to get a reply that showed he indeed still had his suit.

Some of it, at least.

He'd given a load of it, or more accurately the nanites, to another of the BWVs who was even now trying to make sense of the world they'd awoken into.

A dwarfen was quick to volunteer, though, and I let them do it, even knowing the risk that it was to us all.

For anyone or anything to survive on the hull, we needed the shields to be down. And if the shields were down…

I snarled in frustration and spent all the carefully hoarded power I'd been saving for the engines, boosting the speed for several seconds before bringing up the details for the nearest planet that I could see in the distance.

There were two plays here, I guessed. Glancing back at the ships that were tailing me, it was clear that the lead ones—forty or so as I'd seen before—had only one missile each, and they'd used them on me.

I knew that they were just outside the maximum range of the lasers I had, and I was guessing they had a similar restriction. The lasers that were fired and used beyond their maximum range were reduced to essentially warm light and that was it.

I also noticed that several of the bigger ships were now listing or outgassing, and had significant damage, all of which I was guessing had come from the rail gun shots I'd fired some time ago. They must have landed when I was a little busy or the sensors were down, considering that I'd totally missed it.

Regardless, where I was at the minute meant that I had two choices. Well, four really.

First, I could hammer it and just keep going. Now that I had a reactor working, all I needed to do was keep feeding the power into the engines. Sure, they were catching me at the minute, but if I dropped trying to store energy for a reactor bump and let it just build naturally, as well as pushing all that was generated into them, I'd outrun them. I was fairly confident of that.

Plus, these ships weren't likely to be recoverable beyond a certain range. Keep going and the ships chasing me would likely run out of atmo and fuel. Give it a day or so, and I'd be able to board them one by one, cannibalize them and then use that energy I recovered to jump out.

That was probably the best play here.

Option two: I could set the engines to go nova and take the express route out. Yes, I'd be reduced to my constituent atoms, but you know, that was always an option. Just a very bad one.

Option three: use the planet for a slingshot maneuver. I'd be able to either use it to loop around and send myself off toward another planet in the system without sacrificing any velocity—or delta-V, as they called it in the movies.

Then I could bypass those idiots chasing me and probably get onto a path to the system's second Lagrange point. Or, if I did it tight enough, I might be able to loop right around and fly back into the teeth of those following me, though it'd probably be a suicidal choice if they realized what I was doing and just spread out instead of pursuing me.

Any plan that relied on the enemy being utter idiots wasn't exactly a good one. Best to discard that and the nuclear option, as they'd both have the same result.

Most likely I'd just be trading the current situation for a worse one, given that there were hundreds more ships behind the first forty, and they'd no doubt have missiles as well.

Unless I could get all my shields up, and the reactors all charged, that wasn't likely to work out well for me.

The last option was the planet.

I could aim for the planet and try to lose them in the clouds and whatever was hidden in them.

Even from here, I could see the flashes of lightning and the mad swirls of hurricanes that had to be the size of England. Maybe that should be a last resort, considering I'd need to slow right down to enter the atmo.

I was pretty much decided on the "fire the engines and just outrun these dicks" as the safest option, while I got the reactors back up to speed, and it all went wrong.

Again.

CHAPTER TWELVE

The "bravely run away, away" plan wasn't exactly a proud one, but it'd worked for Brave Sir Robin, so I decided that was good enough for me. Right up until the bastards behind me peeled off, looping up and around, opening the path for the ones behind them.

It wasn't for them to wave and wish me good luck either.

The wave of missiles that appeared in the distance really made my mind up.

There was no way I could outrun this many missiles forever. They were smaller, faster, and lighter than me. Cursing, I twisted in tighter, hammering the engines as hard as I could, burning to get ahead of the incoming wave, before bringing up the details that I had on the world in front of me.

The AI was operational, and although it was still cross-referencing the system and location, the planet was similar enough to others in the database that it could make some estimates even from here.

It was far enough out from the primary sun that it was probably too cold to support life, and the atmo was cold. Clouds of various chemicals constantly filled the air with liquids that were closer to acid than water.

The temperature alone for the falling "rain" would kill a human as soon as it hit them; then the liquid would dissolve what was left.

For those reasons, I was definitely thinking a fast visit was best, and possibly no swimming. But now that there was an entire cosmos of flaring stars chasing me, entering the planet's atmo took on a whole new urgency.

Mainly because I seriously doubted missiles designed to chase people down in deep space would like planetary atmospheres.

"Get ready back there!" I bellowed over my shoulder at the still open door. "We're going into the planet!"

"INTO?" a dwarfen voice roared, and I waved them off.

"Just bite the fuckin' pillow," I shouted back distractedly. "Too many missiles to dodge at the minute. Gotta dip into the atmo and see if that takes them out."

"It should."

That was a new voice, and despite myself, I looked over my shoulder. A new figure stood in the doorway, clinging to the frame as if it was all that was keeping her upright.

"Who the hell are you?" I snapped before jerking back around to stare out of the cockpit.

"Saryet," she replied. "First Fist of—"

"BWV?" I cut her off as I got a surge of power from the left wing, third engine. "Dammit, that's not happy making…" I glanced out of the diamond glass at the engine, trying to make out the issues from here.

"Yes," she replied coldly, drawing herself up. "I apologize, Lord Devourer, but—"

"You don't like being called a BWV?" I glanced back over my shoulder, nodding. "No worries. Sorry. I don't mean anything by it. Everyone gets triggered by different shit. Best we can do is live with it."

"I see…" she replied after a few seconds.

"Look, I'm trying to be patient here, really I am, but I was kicking ass and taking names before, then the fucking AI came online and screwed everything up. Now we're going to have to enter the planet's atmo hard enough that the missiles explode on impact and fast enough we can stay ahead of them. I'm no pilot, and I need to focus. What do you want?"

"You seem to have engendered a level of respect from our dwarfen allies that is borderline fanaticism, considering one was willing to leave this ship in a battle. Did you intentionally risk their lives?"

"Really? Shit, I just want them to stay out of the way," I grunted. "Dammit, is he still outside? That's gonna cause some issues…"

She lifted the box into view, showing me that although it'd taken some damage, it was still at least half full of coins.

"Oh, thank fuckin' God. Gimmie," I gasped; a tentacle flashed back to latch onto it, making her flinch back before standing straight.

"Lord Devourer, we were charged to explore the cosmos by Lord Devourer Shan'Gai. One of our standing orders was to attempt to locate any of the survivors of the Ændari pogroms. Once we found them, we were to ensure their survival by any and all means. You ordering them onto the hull in the middle of a firefight is a direct contravention of those orders."

"Uh-huh," I agreed noncommittally. I'd formed a second tentacle that was latched onto the box, absorbing and tearing it apart. The tip covered in Devourer armor was happily breaking the mass down into energy, then feeding it through me and into the crystal pillar that connected me to the ship.

I couldn't help but sigh in relief as the percentage on the power cells bounced slightly, then started to slowly rise.

"Fuck, that's a relief." I glanced back at her and frowned at the look on her face, then remembered what she'd said.

"Ah, right. Look, I need mass. That was what he went out to get, and because he got that, I can strengthen the shields and kick the engine harder. That means we're not as fucked as we were ten seconds ago, and they just got a better chance at surviving this. You got anything you want to add, or you just standing there for shits and giggles?"

"You will not endanger my charges again without good reason, Lord Devourer," she said flatly, and I turned to squint at her.

"Seriously?" I asked. *"'Without good reason'?"* I quoted. "I found them dead, and you and your friends enjoying naptime. That I saved *any* of you, when I'm literally trying to save the entire goddamn quadrant, should have you on your knees worshipping me. I don't care what you think of me. Just stay out of the damn way and you can explain to the others later why you're such a fuckup."

I twisted back around, focusing on the planet ahead and the markers on the plot that showed the incoming missiles. The entire map directly behind me looked like the galaxy was on the move, a solid wall of light that was slowly catching up to me.

I'd always thought that missiles had to be fast, incredibly so, but in space that wasn't the case. They accelerated rapidly, sure, breaking away from their launch platform, but once they were up to speed, they reserved most of their fuel for maneuvering.

That was the Engineering sub-mind, explaining it as I stared, wondering why they'd not just overhauled me in seconds.

Then, looking at the intercept tracks around the planet, it made sense.

Most targets wouldn't be entering atmo; why the hell would you? Bigger ships couldn't. The gravity and the friction were death to them, and the smaller ships would generally break up unless they slowed right down, letting the missiles catch you. Why trade one death for another?

I was betting that the missiles were there to herd me as much as catch me: herd me around the planet, herd me back to the fleet—avoid the dogs nipping at your heels and be caught by the hunter instead.

To do that, they needed to be able to adjust their course constantly, to follow me, to close on me and either, sure, take me out, or more likely, drive me around to be collected.

A spaceship had reactors, it had storage cells, it could generate its own thrust indefinitely, and the distances in space were insane. A missile that went really fast then ran out of fuel was useless. One that chased and drove the prey where it was wanted?

That was *valuable*.

Instead, I was headed right for the planet, and not to do a slingshot.

It was only slightly less suicidal than heading for the missile swarm, admittedly, because if they slowed and dropped into orbit, the fighters could sit there and bombard me as I tried to leave again. But that was where the best bit about my ship came in.

The power cells were steadily ticking back up to decent levels, and I was eyeing the next reactor to boost it.

With two working at a decent level, I'd not be panicking so much. With three? I'd be ready to take the fight to the enemy.

At four?

Well. If I could find somewhere down there to land and get some mass to work with, an hour could make all the difference in the world.

Arise: Conqueror

I wanted to boost the shields, the reactor, everything, but the missiles were closing, and my one advantage currently was speed.

If I could get far enough ahead, I'd be able to slow before entering the atmo, I hoped. Otherwise, this was going to be a seriously one-way trip.

"Devour—"

"WHAT?" I practically screamed over my shoulder.

"The dwarfen wish to assist you. They claim they can increase the power to the shields—"

"How?"

"The explanation is complicated, but they assure me they can have the shields accepting power faster, provided they have time to work on them."

"How long?" I asked Zhonat.

"Ah…" He paused for a few seconds, then shrugged. "We need to discuss time to make that clear for you, but they can have them done by the time we approach the planet's upper layer."

"Fuck. And I guess the shields need to be down to do it?"

"Unfortunately."

I hesitated a few seconds, then cut the power to the shield and hammered that and the stored power into the secondary reactor, jumping it.

"Do it, but make sure they know if they don't get them up? We're all dead!"

Zhonat left the cockpit then and I bit my lip, focusing on the energy levels that were slowly creeping up.

The dwarfen upgrades were badly needed. The shields I'd installed were basically just normal shields. There was nothing over the standard issue about them, beyond that they had more power to draw on and the power cells to keep them up.

If we could make them stronger as well? That could be helpful, but normally that'd not change anything when I was this deep in the shit.

Using that power gave me a chance, though. As I watched the readings tick up fractionally, I forced out a breath I'd not realized I was holding.

The planet was slowly growing ahead of me, and a little mental gymnastics, with a lot less help than I expected being needed from the AI, showed me just how long I had.

Seven minutes for the missiles to reach me—thank fuck for space battles being over such insane distances—and six minutes and fifty-eight seconds to reach the upper atmo.

That wasn't good.

I needed time to slow down as well, or entering the atmo would be like flying headlong into the ground.

I looked at the power levels. I could increase speed slightly, but really not much.

I did it anyway: a tight little burn fed into the engines, dropping the available levels even further, and making me curse as the third and fourth reactors continued to build oh so slowly.

At this rate, they'd not be producing anything I could use until far too late in the fight, like next week. Reactor One was powered and producing at a decent rate. The power being produced was split between the engines and general ship's maintenance.

Reactor Two was at halfway now, starting to produce more than it cost, and all of that was going into the engines as well.

I struggled to make sense of the output details, before remembering that the entire thing was being fed into my mind and interpreted as I wanted.

With a single thought, I changed it all.

Reactor One was producing twenty units now; Reactor Two was producing five, with Three and Four still building up.

I needed five for the general ship's use, the AI, the warmth for the others, the goddamn air…considering there'd been the loss of it earlier—all of it.

That gave me twenty to shove into the engines, and I was making sure it all went in at full power.

With that in there, I was steadily pulling away from the missiles, and they were pouring in more power to try to catch up.

Looking at them, I had to think that their supplies were limited, or they'd be up my ass already.

If they kept pushing that hard…I'd not outrun them. I checked the records with a thought; they'd started to accelerate again as soon as I'd pulled too far ahead…

I cut the engine for a few seconds, hoping and praying that I was right, and fed the power into the power cells instead.

Three seconds, and the missiles cut out as well, making me nod. Okay, I could do this. I was seven seconds ahead of them now, closer to the planet. They were definitely herding me, instead of being sent out to kill me.

Seven seconds wasn't much time. But if instead of hitting it dead-on and trying to decelerate into the atmo like that, what if I arced around it?

Use the gravity to pull me in, turn in toward the planet, and hope that I'd gain a little time as I got closer?

No—what if I flipped the ship?

Wait until I'm close, literally starting a slingshot maneuver, but let the planet pull me in using its gravity. Flip the ship over, hammer the engines full power. If I waited until the missiles started to group together, closing on me and packing in tight to arc around the planet, I could open fire on them at the same time.

Take out as many as I could, power almost everything into the shields and roll into the atmo, then dive out of sight in the clouds.

I'd already tried scanning them and all I was getting back was a mess of static and occasional chemical markers.

I doubted a missile's sensors would have any more luck than I had.

All I had to do was get out of sight in those clouds and hope that the shields could hold while the reactors powered up.

Well, that and the ship didn't come apart on insertion.

Minor detail, that.

"Five minutes and counting till we hit the planet!" I shouted over my shoulder. "Those shields better be working!"

Arise: Conqueror

"Working on it!" came the response, just as movement out of the corner of my eye made me twist and look out of the cockpit.

A dwarfen stomped across the wing with a power cell clutched in one hand, making me gibber at the sheer balls this guy had to have, considering the missiles and micro meteorites that had to be out there.

Reactor Two reached seven units available, and that gave me twenty-two now.

My power cells could hold five hundred, I saw—the conversion leapt into my vision—and currently the cells were ticking up steadily. I'd diverted the power from the engines into there rather than wasting it, and it was sitting at thirty units. Once it hit a hundred, I could boost the next reactor as well.

The next few minutes passed in a blur, as I made minor adjustments to the trajectory, slowly twisting, making sure I was as close to the best path as I could figure.

The AI wasn't helping at all.

Not even slightly.

All I got from it when I fed in the path was a series of big red Xs and warnings of death and destruction coming.

I chose to ignore that, coming as it was from an AI that had already practically killed us all as soon as it'd come online.

Three minutes to insertion.

I was at fifty units now. The second reactor was up to eight units, and the dwarfen were still working.

I twisted the stick and maneuvered the ship. The planet rose in my view, eclipsing the stars as I rolled, shifting until the planet now hung overhead, growing by the second.

I checked the missiles. We'd managed to pick up another second, giving me eight until impact. I chewed my lip, starting to arc around and aiming for the far side. I wouldn't get a second chance at this.

My mind was different now, I knew that, both on an intellectual level and a real one. As I stared up, entranced at the swirling blue and white clouds, the spirals of hurricanes bigger than countries back home, and the flashing, deeply buried lightning, my mind ran calculations at an almost subliminal level.

I worked out insertion angles, impact points, visual tracking, the most likely trajectories for the missiles, and the chances of the following ships being able to track me as I did this.

All of it came together until, with a deep breath, I nodded to myself.

"Get them inside!" I roared over my shoulder. "We're heading in!"

"Six more millicycles!" a voice shouted back. "That's all we need!"

"We've not got it!" I returned. "Inside now, or they'll be on the hull when we enter!"

There was cursing, shouts, then the popping of pressure and more angry shouts. I counted down the last seconds. If it meant I lost a dwarfen off the hull, then at least the others would have a chance.

I glanced out...and swore long and loud.

The first one I'd seen was no longer there. He was stomping back across the hull, along with three others!

The mad little bastards had gone out to help him finish!

The horizon was coming up faster and faster now, the window I had closing tighter and tighter...

"Entering now!" came the shout, repeated over from those by the air lock.

Ten seconds and counting down before I missed the chance.

Seven.

Four.

One.

"Inside!" a voice shouted, and I wrenched the control yoke, flipped the ship, facing back the way I'd come, and gritted my teeth as the seventy units I'd managed to accumulate dropped savagely.

I'd made it to twenty-nine units produced between One and Two, with Three and Four still clawing their way back from the deficit. Twenty went into the engines, and I shifted another twenty from the power cells as well; five went into the general ship's systems, and four started the power-up cycle for the shields.

Ten was sunk into the lasers, just the lasers, and I opened fire, aiming for the general location of the incoming missiles.

I was out of sight of the following ships now, though not for long.

The lasers started to hit the incoming missiles as I pushed more and more power into the engines. The reserves dropped like a stone as I fed more to the shields: four going to six, to ten.

The crackling red lines danced across the ship's outer hull, even as the missiles closed. Bright blooms of light flared in the darkness as lucky shots took some down.

It wasn't enough, though.

The wall of light that the sensors reported seemed barely diminished, despite the lasers' rapid-fire draining of the cells. Eight seconds' lead dropped to six, to three.

Cursing, I flipped the ship again, focusing on the planet, and cut the power to the lasers. Twenty stayed in the engines, and everything else sank into the shields.

The lights in the ship flickered; the atmo production ceased. Everything nonessential was cut off as I hammered the engines, surging forward into the upper atmo.

I'd hoped to get enough distance to be able to take the shortest path, and maybe even make it entirely out of sight before I left the planet's shadow.

No such luck, though.

I was down to a second's lead now. The missiles, had I turned and looked out of the window, were probably in visual range, and I dipped the nose of the ship again.

I didn't know how long I could hold it for, but I popped four gravity bubbles in my wake, spreading them out slightly and pulling in for five times Earth's power each.

Arise: Conqueror

Explosions bloomed behind me, and I dove into the clouds. The nose of the ship shook as though it'd been hit by a trip hammer. The wings shuddered and swayed; creaks and groans filled the air.

Screams came from behind me; deeper into the ship, more rang out—warnings, cries of panic. I ignored it all and twisted the yoke, rolling the ship and dove headfirst into the nearest cloudbank, vanishing into the depths.

CHAPTER THIRTEEN

The storm was violent, like nothing I'd ever seen before.

The winds yanked and pulled at the wings of the ship. Pressure rose and fell as cracks opened in the hull. The shields barely held us together as we dove deeper and deeper.

Liquids poured across the cockpit—making it almost impossible to see, they were that thick. Then the first lightning bolt struck.

It hit the starboard wing. The entire ship bounced like I'd hit a speed bump at seventy. White lightning met red as the shields flared; the storage cells dipped as the shields pulled hard on them. Then the second bolt hit.

Then the third—and above us, the sky was suddenly blanketed in reds and yellows.

"What's happening!"

I didn't turn around. I recognized the voice as that of Saryet, and I didn't have time for her shit.

"We're in the atmo, and missiles are going off!" I snapped.

"I can see that!"

"Then don't—" The ship bucked again, hit hard. "Fuck! Then don't ask stupid questions and get out of here!"

"What can I do?"

"Nothing, unless you can get me more power!" I snapped, twisting and frantically searching.

I'd just gotten a burst of information back from the sensors. The missiles had started to impact the upper atmo, and when they'd done that, the pressure wave had given us a sudden picture of the ground.

It'd been a split second—a flash, then it was gone. But maybe…

I twisted the ship, aiming for the ground behind us, trying to bring it around. The hull screamed; the metal attracted the lightning as the shields flared and dipped again.

"What—"

"GET OUT!" I roared. A tentacle flashed and shoved her back through the doorway, then slammed it closed as I tried to make sense of the universe around us.

Arise: Conqueror

The sensors were whited out again. More missiles hit the atmo but they were too high and too far back; the world spun, making me curse as I reached out with the only other senses I had.

Gravity wasn't right here, either. The storms, the world… I "felt" floating islands somewhere below, huge mountains of rock and metal that were on a constant collision path.

I jerked the yoke and turned away from them as they grew more clear. They impacted incessantly, bouncing off each other, and continuing on.

There was no way that I could use them as cover from the storm. If they were strong enough to hit and bounce off each other continually… Focusing, I sensed more from them as the ship's sensors locked on at last.

They were the remains of ores, or so I guessed—melted, refined, and compressed into indestructible mountains and then flung into perpetual motion.

No, there was nothing we could use here.

The shields were dropping steadily. The hull shuddered under constant impacts of the storm now. I frantically searched, reaching down as far as I could, looking for somewhere I could land us—a cave, a fucking hole in the ground, a damn…

Something loomed out of the distance, tall, taller than I could believe for how narrow and thin, and yet it was being lashed constantly by the lightning.

It was drinking the power down into the depths, and the closer I got, the more I stared. It was an artifact! It had to be. There was no goddamn way it was natural, not out here, sunk into the depths of a planet that was warped and hounded by storms all day and night.

"Get up here!" I bellowed over my shoulder. The same tentacle that had locked them out now yanked the door open. "Fucking move!" I shouted as we closed on it.

"What do you…what is that?!" Saryet asked as it loomed out of the cloud-filled darkness.

"I don't know!" I snapped. "I was hoping you did!"

"I've never seen anything like it," she admitted as I twisted the yoke, turning the ship on its side and circling what I now saw was a tower.

Gleaming white and steel grey, it was wreathed in constant lightning, drinking it down as we arced around it, still fighting the winds and the rain.

That was when I realized that the lightning, although it was all around us, had dipped in its power.

We were no longer being struck, not like we had been. It'd ramped up to several impacts a second, mainly minor, but the larger and more powerful bolts that had been making the entire ship shake and the shields buckle had vanished.

Now, though, we were being hit only as an afterthought. The majority of the strikes impacted the giant needle.

"She did it."

The whisper that came from behind me made me turn, shooting a glance at Lehman, who stood in the doorway, staring wide-eyed at the structure before us.

"Who did what?" I asked grimly.

"Rosenblut." He shook his head. "Old ally. She think hide better than fight. Showed plans for this."

"Dude, it's a giant piece of metal in a fucking world covered in storms. What do you know and how do you know it?"

"Rosenblut, she old scientist. She say fighting Ændari be pointless. Too many them. Needed refuge, far from them. When we no longer threat, they leave us be."

"Yeah, that's not how the Ændari think," I muttered.

"No, they evil. But some our people wanted that be true. They go with her. She want we claim worlds the Ændari no want, places no one else live, and stay there."

"Sounds like a stupid plan," I snapped. "Why do you think this is her?"

"Spire. It draw energy, power shield. It be her suggesting."

"You think she's here?" I had a sudden surge of hope that maybe there were thousands of dwarfen down there that we could get to help us, or even if they were all pacifists now, that might help us to fix the ship at least.

"Not her," he admitted after a few seconds. "Long ages passed since we last free."

"Tens if not hundreds of thousands of years," I agreed, still staring at the spire as we lapped it again.

"She maybe dead. Others might live?" he suggested. "We land?"

"We need to," I said, looking at the engines and the power readouts. "We need to either land and do some fast repairs, or we need to head back into orbit. If we're lucky, the ships that were following us think we're dead and they've kept going, but…"

"But we can't know without exposing ourselves," Saryet finished when I left it hanging.

"Exactly."

"Have we got the power to check this tower out?" she asked, and I shrugged.

"Probably. If we can't land, then the shields will be slightly stronger than they are currently. Either way, the spire is drawing the lightning away from us."

"Then it only makes sense to try," she said flatly.

"We go," Lehman whispered. "Rather know if kin survive."

"How's the ship?" I asked him, and he hesitated.

"We vent. Some areas no strong. We fix."

I nodded, waiting as he went, before turning to Saryet. "You think it's likely?" I jerked my head in the direction of the spire. "Did they have time to build this during the war?"

"Possibly." She sighed. "The dwarfen and Ændari war lasted decades. They were poor fighters, strong but straightforward, and gifted engineers. If they were more cunning, they'd have won. But they believed the Ændari each time they offered peace, ceasefires, or excuses. They lost half their empire to the Ændari denying there was a war and claiming it was all pirates."

"How do you know?" I asked.

"The Ændari," she spat. "When we still served them., they laughed about it. They liked us to worship them. They liked to show off just how powerful and smart they were."

"I thought they told you that you were defending the galaxy?" I asked, turning back and arcing the ship in toward the spire, slowing it as we sank deeper into the clouds, sending more and more power into the shields.

"They did," she said flatly, clearly unwilling to discuss it. She straightened. "What's that?"

I looked where she indicated: a torn section of the spire, dozens of meters, maybe hundreds long, with open and blackened holes in the side.

"An explosion?" I guessed aloud.

"It looks old," she agreed, squinting. "Can you get closer? Could we land there?"

"No chance," I said firmly, checking the readings. "The shields are up still, but they look like they're cycling."

"Explain?"

"The shields are strong, like seriously strong. Make us look like we've got a piece of paper we're holding up in comparison. There's a tiny break in the shields, though, looking at this."

"How small? Could we dock?"

"About a tenth of a second…" I cursed. "Fucking timescales. Listen while I count, okay?" She nodded, and I counted to ten using the old "one Mississippi" method.

"That took me ten seconds to say that," I explained. "For reference, the gap we'd have is about a hundredth of that time, maybe less."

"So we're not landing through that gap."

"Definitely not," I agreed, shaking my head and watching as we sank lower and lower. Great towers of clouds obscured everything, then vanished again.

We were bouncing so frequently in the wash of the powerful winds that I was almost used to it by the time that Saryet suddenly jabbed a finger out, staring at the side of the tower.

"There!"

I twisted the ship, arcing around, moving closer, then peeling off.

"More damage." I shook my head. "That's not good."

"I thought it was an entrance." She muttered an apology, and I shrugged. "It's fine."

Ten minutes, we sank past the spire, before the first explosion sounded in the distance, and I realized I'd been hearing them for several seconds. The next one rocked us, swiftly followed by a second, then a third.

"What the hell is that?" I snarled, twisting the yoke and looking back as the pressure in the ship bucked and screamed again, guessing a seal or something had gone.

"It's not from back there!"

"What?" I stared at her for a second, then cursed, realizing what she meant, and looked up.

It took a few seconds, but I saw it.

Tiny dots were floating down and then exploding—and they were coming in their hundreds.

"Oh no," I whispered, shaking my head. "Oh, fuck no."

"They followed us!" she snarled. "You led them here!"

"I didn't know!" I snapped, flaring the engines. Rather than flying slowly and letting the reactors conserve energy in this pocket, storing it up and strengthening the shields, I gunned them hard.

The towering clouds flashed past as we dove into the depths; liquids screamed across the outside, the shields constantly working to repel them as we went almost straight down.

Saryet shouted out a warning over her shoulder, bracing herself as I did.

"Why the hell don't you have seats!" she snapped at me.

"Because you were all frozen and the dwarfen were dead!" I snapped back. "Now hang on and we might survive this yet."

"The dwarfen won't!" She growled, "They've been hidden here for who knows how long, and you just led the senagra to them!"

"Fuck!"

I dove faster, as more and more explosions rang out around us.

"They're targeting our engines!" she snapped. "They must be able to trace them!"

"Well, this day just got oh so much worse!" I cursed, arcing left, then twisting right, making a single pass as I saw what looked like a landing dock far below. "Is the dock intact?!" I shouted, hands dancing as I fed the stored power we'd managed to accumulate into the third reactor, boosting it all the way to generating energy at last.

"No..." she said slowly.

"You sure?"

"No!" she snapped. "I'm not sure at all, but it looks ruined!"

"Then if we live, we can get someone to come back later!" I snapped back, gunning the engines and pulling back up.

It wasn't that easy, of course. Missiles and bombs rained from the heavens, and as they went off over and over in the clouds around us, they flattened the storm.

As great rents were torn in the cloud cover, lasers and fire poured down. We flew on as fast as we could, drawing them away from the ancient spire.

The last I saw of it vanished into the clouds behind us as the shields continued to resist the barrage. "I hope they follow us..." I muttered.

"Because if not, perhaps you just condemned an entire spire full of peaceful dwarfen to death?" Saryet snapped. "Yes, I too would wish for that, were I not aboard this accursed vessel!"

"Then get out and fucking walk!" I snarled at her. The lightning started to hit us hard again. "All you've done is complain since you came up here, and I'm sick of it!"

The reactors were coming online much faster now. The first was generating a solid twenty units, the second was at fifteen, the third at three, and the fourth, although still not adding to the total, was slowly climbing.

Ten more units should be enough to get that one up and working now, I hoped.

Arise: Conqueror

Punching the engines, we barreled through the clouds. Hissing liquids poured from us and whipped away. The steel-grey and thunderous clouds gave way as new shadows appeared.

I shook my head in dismay. "What the hell does it take to get rid of these fuckers?" I whispered, seeing the first of the enemy ships roiling out of the darkness.

It vanished again almost a second later, exploding as a direct lightning strike hit the ship, tearing a hole from one side to the other and bathing the nearby clouds in yellows and oranges.

I twisted, avoiding a particularly powerful burst that stuttered through the sky, and another ship erupting from the cloud banks took it instead.

It fared no better, exploding, the hull rent apart and flames streaming from it as it fell. But dozens more appeared behind them.

The explosions behind me—the missiles or bombs or whatever—had been to drive me into this, and I'd run like a rabbit!

I rolled, pushing energy from the stored areas and powering up the lasers, firing a fast burst that barely singed the nearest ships, before I was past them.

"I hope you've got a plan!" Saryet snapped at me, and I swore again.

"Don't you have anything better to do?!" I pulled up and shunted power into the shields, checking them as we were hit from behind by something.

Twenty units into the shields was enough to keep them more or less solid as lightning hit us repeatedly, dipping then rebuilding, but never enough to spare anything to add to the stores.

Fifteen units were in the engines, giving us rolling blackouts of lights as I frantically tried to keep ahead of the incoming ships. The last three units we had were not quite enough to do anything, and the AI was offline again.

Then the first hits came in from overhead.

The air around us exploded with incoming shells, detonating here and there and filling the skies with shrapnel.

My shields dipped fast then. And when the lightning hit again and again, they dipped further.

"What the hell do we do now..." I muttered, frantically rolling and dipping, diving and rising, but always chased.

All we needed was time for the shields to recover, for the reactors to come online again, and then we'd be all right. That goddamn spire! If we could have just landed and repaired a little, or better yet charged up, plugged into it and...*plugged into it.*

Plugged into it!

"Get out!" I shouted at Saryet, who glared at me and opened her mouth to speak. "Now! I'm going to depressurize the cockpit!" I grinned at her, seeing confusion and growing horror.

"But, Lord—" she started, clearly thinking I was going mad.

"Trust me!" I said quickly. "Get out. Seal the doors. You're going to get all the air you need soon, but you need to get somewhere safe!"

"I...very well." She dipped her head suddenly, almost a bow, then she was gone, shouting something as she dragged the door shut behind her, and I grinned maniacally.

"Now it's my turn, assholes," I purred. A tentacle flashed out to impact the ceiling nearby, burrowing through it and out into the wild skies above.

I made sure the connection between me and the crystal pillar was solid and it was ready to receive. Then I flexed the tentacle, pouring more and more into it, as I deliberately disabled the shields around the spike that steadily grew.

"Please don't fuckin' shoot me now…" I muttered over and over, waiting, and cursing as the damn lightning seemed to have picked the stupidest time imaginable for a break.

Then I saw the second spire.

I'd not been fantastically lucky in finding the only spire on the entire goddamn planet, I'd just found the nearest one, I realized, as a much more ruined one drifted out of the clouds, cut off maybe halfway down its length. The battered and torn lower half was wreathed in frantic lightning.

"What's going on?" came Saryet's distant and muffled voice.

I cursed, ignoring her, and instead poured more energy into the engines.

It only cost us a few seconds, and while the shots flashed past us and the explosions continued to rain down, the lightning did its job before they could reach us again.

The first bolt that hit danced across the port wing, shedding power before leaping to the nanite spire I'd offered up. And as soon as it hit, I was reminded how goddamn glad I was that I was no longer flesh and blood.

The power that flowed through me hit the crystal and flooded the ship. Lights flared, the storage cells glowing as they began to refill.

Most of the power, though, I directed to Reactors' Three and Four. Three leapt all the way to full activation before the bolt died away, and Four was at eight units.

That was enough for me. I rolled fast, spinning the spire in the air, waiting and hoping.

Two seconds it took, as impacts hit the rear of the ship again, dropping the shields slightly.

Then the second bolt was joined by another, and another. I was clear of the spire's interference, and my nanite lightning rod dragged the power down into me.

The AI came back online, saw what was happening in milliseconds and reconfigured the shields, bringing them up and tightening them around the crackling spike.

Reactor Four flared and settled. The power levels showed solid as it started to churn out twenty units as well; a light touch on Reactor Two…and it was topped off as well.

I pulled up, arcing straight for space now, grinning maniacally. I pushed the engines. Additional strikes came in hard and fast. The power cells shivered as they were force-fed tremendous amounts of power. I cut the stream, yanking the tentacle back down; the hole I'd drilled in the ceiling reformed over as the last nanites devoted themselves to the task.

"Everyone okay back there?" I shouted. The door opened a few seconds later, light pouring in from the hallway.

"What the hell just happened?" Saryet gasped, looking shaken and more than a little battered. "We just got thrown off every wall in the ship!"

"Uh…a firefight," I lied. "Sorry, had to dodge a lot."

"Really? I didn't hear the guns…"

"Oh look, we've just got our shields back!" I said quickly. "Also, there's more spires down there!"

"More of my people?" Lehman rumbled, and I bit my lip.

"Ah! Uh, no, probably not. They looked abandoned," I said swiftly. "And the ships are chasing us, so better if we draw them away from there, right?"

"How?" Saryet asked. "I thought we needed repairs?"

"Oh yeah, we still do," I said. "But for now, we've got enough power to get by, so I think it's time we sorted these shits out, don't you?"

As I said that, the nose of the ship punched through the last wispy layers of cloud cover and out into the black of space.

Before me was what I'd been sensing for the last few seconds. I grinned evilly, as the ship's weapons hummed with power.

The ship that found itself ahead of me in the first seconds had already met me, or at least it'd tasted my anger once—as the rumpled devastation on one side attested.

It was long and ovoid, bristling with guns and bad attitude. Although several sections were now open to space, it looked more scarred and dangerous than out of the fight.

I decided it was time to change that.

The rail guns were charging, rounds forming and being fed into them as we closed; its own lasers rippled out, stabbing into our shields.

With a dedicated reactor just feeding the shields, another for the engines, one that was on standby to run everything else, and the overflow from that topping off the cells? The fourth was exclusively feeding power into the weapons.

The shields flickered, and that was all they did. They never even approached overload. I grinned ferally and squeezed, my response flying back up at the behemoth overhead.

It was a David and Goliath fight, or it would have been, if David had a shotgun and power armor and Goliath stood there flinging pebbles back.

Instead, the lasers bored through the shields in seconds. Then the rail guns chimed that they were ready, and I opened fire with them.

The distance was too great for the storm casters, but my God, they weren't needed.

Before I'd strafed, I'd spread the damage across the hull.

Now with the new penetrator rounds, I chewed through the upper levels. Explosions shook the ship as they dug deeper and deeper; secondary areas buckled. Flames roared out into space, before finally, as I let loose with the storm caster, then pulled up, the huge ship listed to the side. Explosions rocked it as it slowly fell toward the gravity well behind me.

I burst past it, rocketing into the dark of space. A mixture of elation, determination, and sick concern filled me.

Elation, because I'd just fucked up a ship that was chasing me and had clearly had no clue how overmatched it was by my tiny mad vessel.

Determination, because I'd fuck up anything I had to, to get back to Ingrid and the others, and sick concern, because if those spires were inhabited…well.

I'd just dropped a starship on their world.

"Uh, that world…" I said slowly, not sure where to go with it.

"The spires we saw were uninhabited," Saryet said firmly. "When we were leaving the planet, we were able to get a scan on them. There were no life signs I could detect."

I glanced over my shoulder, seeing her and Lehman standing there, before nodding and turning back to stare at the ships that were even now moving to follow us.

I wasn't sure whether she'd just covered my ass for a possible massive fuckup with Lehman, or whether she meant what she'd said, but I wasn't asking questions at this point. Instead, I floored it and twisted, loading the rail guns and firing again and again.

The nearest ships shuddered under the onslaught. I made sure to do several passes, letting them see just how useless their weapons were against us, as hit after hit made our shields bounce, and that was it.

The plasma casters would have done a lot worse, I had no doubt, but the lasers weren't on the same level. And as close as we were to the other ships of their fleet, they'd not fire the big guns.

I had no such inhibitions. I strafed and hammered them for almost ten minutes, before turning my back on a dozen of the behemoths, now leaking atmo, gouting flames, and clearly out of the fight.

Then I headed for the Lagrange point, waiting, as Lehman and his pilot argued with the AI over stellar drift, classes of stars, and something called parallax.

I was reminded that no matter how much my damn brain had been improved, unless I had the basics down, I couldn't make head nor tail of their discussions, until the AI suddenly burst back into life, filling my system with navigational data.

We were on the far side of the quadrant, in an area that was registered as worthless when I looked at the notes we had on it, but I didn't care.

Ten seconds after I had our location, I was feeding the destination into the AI, getting a few errors, then a solid plot, and I couldn't help but grin.

I knew where Ingrid was now, and where I was in comparison.

Best of all? The space I needed to pass through was all held by the Ændari.

They were getting ready to attack us, I had no doubt. Well, that was fine, because they were about to get a short, sharp lesson in not fucking with Earth.

CHAPTER FOURTEEN

As much as I wanted to shred the remainder of the senagra's forces, it'd take several hours to build up to speed and get back to the Lagrange point and the majority of the biggest vessels, even if I floored it all the way.

Instead, I fired a dozen long-distance shots at the three ships that were ostensibly holding position near the jump point, and gave it ten minutes, making damn sure that the ship was solid, that the holes in the hull were patched, and that everyone was ready before we jumped.

Then I smiled, watching as the rail gun rounds arrived, tearing the shit out of the lead vessel, before charging the grav drive as far as we could and jumping out.

This time, I let the AI manage it, given that it knew exactly where we were going, and that with the shields up, our signature was now almost totally different than the ship that the creatures at the bottom of the branes had tried to snare.

Also, I only really knew that I wanted to go "that way" vaguely, so my navigation abilities could be tested later.

It was longer this time, considering that we were literally jumping at the very maximum of the gravity drive's range. As we dipped in to the jump, the gravity branes seemed to hesitate. As we entered the warp, I reached out, slowing time for me and extending my senses, searching, focusing.

There was nothing, I found; it was as if there was nothing out there—no life, no movement. I guessed that I was right in that shields both protected and hid us, so I'd have to figure that out, I supposed.

It didn't matter in the long-term, though, because as soon as we exited the warp, the universe exploded with warnings and notifications. Two subjective seconds later, while space was still appearing all around us, the first mine went off.

The ship lurched sideways, and shields flared. Then another went off, and another. The universe seemed to fill with fire and warnings, before we burst from the field, shields registering alerts, down to a third even with everything we'd done.

I banished the notifications, frantically searching space around us as I tried to make sense of everything that I was seeing, panicking that I'd just fucked up massively.

Then the shields started to climb, and I almost collapsed into my chair, seeing the mines were mostly all gone, and then fixing a glare on the two ships that had clearly been left on picket duty.

One was a boxy affair, barely more than some engines and a cockpit slapped on a giant shipping container. I guessed that was the minelayer.

The other?

That looked like the love child of a snowblower and a jet: bulky, overengineered, and definitely only described as graceful in comparison with the shitty ship that it squatted next to.

They both hung there in space, apparently clearly utterly confused that we'd not exploded yet.

Then I opened fire.

The minelayer exploded like a beer can packed full of firecrackers. Its hold was certainly full of something that went boom happily. The second ship was already sent flying before my storm casters lashed out as well, peppered with shrapnel from its friend's death. The lightning tore and blackened the hull from one end to the other; its shields flickered, dipping then dropping out.

I flashed past it, pulling up and arcing around, cancelling the time dilation and focusing in, about to open fire, when Zhonat spoke up from somewhere behind me.

"Steve, are they Ændari?"

"Uh, they shot at us, so yeah, probably. Don't know, don't care." I lined the reticules up in the middle of the ship, ignoring the frantic turrets that were even now opening up on us.

"Could we capture them?"

"What?" I snapped, glancing over my shoulder, then cursing and rolling the ship as we flashed past them again, but this time holding my fire.

They desperately fired their engines; shields flickered as they tried to reestablish, and they twisted away from us. Their jump engine started to power up, the gravity warp clear to me even from here.

"They're fucking running…" I whispered, confused, then unable to keep from grinning at the insanity of it.

Here we were, jumping into their system, and rather than fight us, now they guessed they were overmatched. They were willing to run and leave their system defenseless if it meant that they'd escape.

I targeted them again, this time determined to finish the fight before they could escape.

Saryet spoke up quickly before I could fire. "Devourer, could you strip them of their builders?"

"What?" I snapped.

"Their builders!" She went on. "The Ændari, could you take their builders and make it so that we could use them? Armor, weapons—everything we need could be aboard that ship!"

"I…dammit," I growled. She was right; the chance to strip the Ændari was just too good to pass up.

Arise: Conqueror

I shifted the ship around, lining up on where I guessed the reactors were, and opened fire with the lasers, punching through the reforming shields and into the hull, grinning at how easily they did it.

There had to be loads of more powerful ships than mine out there, I had no doubt, or there *should* be. Before the nanite plague, there must have been. There was no way that my mad little slapped-together Frankenstein's monster of a ship was that impressive.

That the two great superpowers had to start from basically nothing again helped, admittedly. As did that there were genuine issues and reasons that there weren't reactors built in proximity normally. The risks of overload and contamination kept ship designers from putting so much power into small hulls, and that was a massive point in my favor.

Under normal circumstances, the more reactors and more power needed, the bigger the ship needed to be. The bigger the ship, the more meterage of the hull needed to be covered with shields—and the higher the cost in power. With us finding the dwarfen solution to that problem, we'd been able to pack the power that a battleship usually generated into a ship that was barely larger than a deep-space fighter or small transport.

The three layers of shields, the guns that I'd slapped on with barely more than a "this'll be fun" and a vague nod to physics and a dash of nanites?

All the madness combined to create a ship that was both smaller than my enemies would ever expect, and far more heavily armed and armored.

The Ændari ship was listing now. Flames belched free of the hole I'd just drilled in the hull. The lights that shone from the dozens of windows ringing the upper levels suddenly flickered.

Sections on the hull nearby exploded outward. Blowout panels deployed as sections vented; a reactor ejected into space bare seconds ahead of a meltdown.

It soared upward; gleaming red lines on the grey-black hull flared, running from the top to the bottom, rolling faster and faster. The ship twisted, engines firing as more of the lights flickered. The gravity distortions died away as the captain obviously realized they didn't have enough power to jump now and committed to running.

The reactor flashed faster and faster. Warnings pulsed wildly as I arced away, pushing my engines hard and increasing the power flowing to the shields, pulling the majority from the guns to make sure we were okay.

The reactor exploded, a bright-white flash that seemed to shake the world. My ship bounced as I rode the shock wave. Then it was over, dying away as my connection to the ship warned me of radiation spikes, debris, and more.

I ignored it all, curving around and lining up on the Ændari vessel, seeing the limping, broken hull ahead.

The shock wave had hit it harder than us: its shields were down, and the back third of the ship looked as if it'd been hit by Thor's hammer.

It was battered, broken, and the engines were clearly cooling, the light of the ion drives faltering, then dying away.

"My turn, I guess." I grinned, twisting and rolling my ship, inverting so that the Ændari seemed to hang overhead, a hundred meters or so away.

They were venting atmo heavily, and as I stood, releasing my bind to my ship, I took a deep breath and rolled my shoulders. I really needed this.

I'd checked the local area before I did this. Although the rest of the system was fairly empty, there were more ships deeper in, closer to the main planets.

For now, though, I had a little time.

My notifications started to rise once more and I dismissed them, glad that I was apparently back inside a quadrant node's range again, but not having the time to fuck with it yet.

I pushed past the others, shaking my head at the dwarfen volunteers who wanted to help board the enemy, and the offers from the BWV and BSV to assist as well.

They didn't have anywhere near enough nanites to really help, but they were clearly serious about coming with me, using any weapons the goddamn dwarfen hadn't already fed into the converters.

I shook my head again, this time banishing my armor entirely. I stood there in my jeans and T-shirt to make a point, before stepping into the air lock like that.

I forced myself to nod to the others, then turn my back on them as the air was sucked out, the outer door cycling.

It felt incredibly stupid, doing this and just wandering out onto the hull, as the air lock opened and I stepped out, but I had to do it.

I needed to prove, both to myself and to the others, what I was.

Also, fuck it, I needed more nanites, and so did the BWVs behind me.

My first instinct was to hold my breath, and I did it automatically, before forcing myself to remember that I only "breathed" now by habit anyway.

I had no need to do so. I wasn't flesh and blood: I was literally nanites. My entire "me" was distributed across the nanites that made me up, a shared intelligence that could become anything and anyone.

And right now?

I was going to be the specter of death to the Ændari.

I crouched, then launched myself from the hull, soaring across the gulf of space between the two ships. I popped a gravity bubble to guide me down to the right spot on the opposite hull.

As I landed hard, the impact reverberated through the hull; then I stepped over to the nearest laser turret, sitting still and dead.

"Time to make an impression…" I whispered, gripping the nearest barrel, bracing myself, then pulling. The metal held for a bare second; I strained harder, and with a creak, the metal started to tear.

I grinned then doubled down, realizing that I was, again, not using any of my "real" advantages. My feet shifted; the soles of my "boots" adjusted, binding me into the hull. As my arms shifted, on my back, pairs of nanites doubled and redoubled. No longer was I pulling with my biceps, back, and hips.

Instead, every nanite cluster assisted, and like paper, the turret ripped free.

Arise: Conqueror

I tossed it aside as atmo rushed free, then reached down to the narrow gap below the turret and dug my fingers in, pulling the hole wider and releasing the binding between my feet and the deck.

Below me, lights flashed. Depressurization warnings screamed and doors slid shut as I tore the hole open enough to admit me. I dropped in, landing in a corridor. Simple carvings lined the walls to either side as they vanished to the left and right.

Or they should have.

Currently, emergency bulkheads were sealed in place, with stubby yellow and red lights flaring warnings in the serene silence of the depressurized passage.

I stepped forward, reforming my right hand, then stabbing out. The blade I'd formed in place of my hand cut through the bulkhead easily, and I yanked it downward, carving a gap free.

Once that was done, I split the blade down the middle, separating to the left and right, folding down, latching onto the door and tearing the hole wider and wider.

As the atmosphere rushed past me, I grinned, seeing the horrified look on the faces of several Ændari as they backed away.

"Heeeeerrrrre's *Johnny*!" I called in my best *Shining* voice, before shredding more of the door to let me through. Stepping into the passage beyond, I shook my head in annoyance as more doors slammed into place, sealing the passage from me.

"You're no fun," I grumbled, before grinning and releasing the automatic locks I maintained on myself now.

Instantly my upper layers shimmered, shifting as the Devourer layer was set free, and I walked forward. A thought was all it took: tentacles flashed out, latching onto the next door, and ate through the metal and ceramics, consuming all that could be used and discarding the rest. I stepped through the gossamer curtains that were all that was left of the pressure doors.

More and more fell, the Ændari fleeing desperately as I bored in deeper, flashing out a hand to close over the nearest connection, pouring my Hack submind into an all-out assault on the ship.

It burned through the upper layers of defenses even as I walked deeper, absorbing my way through the walls. Screams and shouts rang out, lasers flashed, and I flinched, feeling…a sting.

That was all. I actually laughed. The weapons that the Ændari expected to use were clearly calibrated not to harm them, just in case. Presumably the kind of weapons that they used against the UC soldiers and my kind were kept under lock and key, because they sure as shit weren't in evidence yet.

The sub-mind reported back, deploying Tsunami against a protected system, then searching, finding a backdoor and slipping around the hardened sector, leaving it to fall as it dug deeper and deeper.

Secondary reactors were flagged and the emergency scram orders sent. The reactors themselves jettisoned—thankfully clear of my own ship—to float away into deep space.

Then the power cells cycled, draining their charge into the connections that led straight back to the now-missing reactors.

I grinned as the ship was suddenly plunged into darkness. Distant clangs and whirring fell silent as even the warning lights cut off.

"My turn…" I whispered, striding forward. I reached out for the next door and ate my way through that as well.

This time, there was no slamming shut of the pressure doors ahead, and the screaming of the atmo went on and on. I stood there, grinning, in jeans and a fucking T-shirt as frantic Ændari tried to gather masks and fired lasers at me, all while trying to breathe, trying to catch themselves now that gravity was gone, and, best of all, trying to see in the darkness of the ship's hull.

I had no such issues, seeing with my gravitational senses as they fired in all directions, trying to kill me—injuring their companions more often than they hit me.

I let them, feeling the first couple of hits sting slightly and that was it. The vast majority hit the walls and walkway in their panic. When they saw that, and the gleaming, roiling red and black surface of the Devourer, it was as if all their nightmares had come true, and I loved it.

These fuckers were responsible for everything that had been done to me, at its most basic level. They'd created my entire species. They monkeyed with our genes. They fucked with our evolution. They gave us a goddamn anxiety complex to make us easier to control and basically laughed about it.

Then they tried to use us as weapons. They tried to conquer the fucking galaxy using us, as their unwitting slaves, scapegoats, and walking terminators.

I suddenly realized just how much I fucking hated their entire species. And the fact they were impregnated with nanites? That was just a bonus!

I'd kill them all, each and every one of them. I'd bring the end of days to their entire species and make sure they knew why.

I reached out; tentacles flashed forward, latching onto the walls and floors to drag me down the corridor toward my panicking, asphyxiating prey.

These were inexperienced Ændari, I knew instinctively, ones that had gained a load of nanites but weren't yet evolved to the same level as the older ones. They were soldiers, but more than that, they were weak ones.

I grabbed onto them. My tentacles latched over their faces, digging in, and extended blades that pierced brains, then spread out, absorbing, consuming.

The ship didn't take long to board and strip, and because I was nice like that, I even grabbed a handful of their heavier weapons, ones that they had been desperately trying to get out of a locked armory, when I was finished harvesting.

In truth, the part of my visit that took the longest was hunting down the final crew member. It was the captain, and I found him trying to force himself into what I guessed was a toilet.

I didn't care, really. He was the only fully active and ascended member of the crew. Although he could shift himself in small ways, trying to break himself down enough to fit literally into a toilet wasn't one of those abilities.

Arise: Conqueror

I caught him, dragged him out, then ripped his arms and legs off, sealed the wounds and carried him back out of the ship with me, to snack on, on the way rather than wasting any more time. He spent his last minutes thrashing and panicking in the dark of space, asphyxiating and crumbling as I fed.

By the time I reboarded my ship, there was almost nothing left of him, but we'd gained over a hundred and fifty million nanites.

A simple breakdown of five million nanites put aside for the twelve BWVs was enough for each of them to form a basic level of armor. The first two already had that, of course, but adding five million more to each of them and giving them the weapons I'd recovered would make them feel a lot more ready for the fight that was to come.

I also decided I'd give each of the dwarfen a million nanites. There were twenty-four in total—most were still asleep, of course, frozen solid in cryogenic stasis like the BWVs—but the defrosting had begun now. As much as I wanted them all to stay nice and easy to manage as dwarfsicles, there was going to come a time real soon, I was betting, that we'd need them. For now, it was better to accept that we were getting cramped.

That came to eighty-four million clusters, and as my air lock hissed, flooding the chamber with atmo and warmth I barely registered, the other sixty-six million nanites were already tagged for my use.

It was insane, really.

As I ripped the nanites from my victims, I felt the change. The difference was that now when I was fully in Devourer mode, I no longer needed to attune the nanites.

They weren't needing to be slowly unlocked over days, wiped, reset, and commanded to obey me, not anymore. As I reached out, they seemed almost desperate to join with me. And as soon as they touched my own nanites?

Their old internal programming was shunted aside. In seconds, a rippling wave that poured through them, upgrading them to the level that I was at, resulted in the nanites seeming almost joyous to be a part of me.

To be what they were made for.

The air lock hissed open. The door rolled back and the brightly lit ship beyond came into view. Saryet stood there, waiting.

"Did it go well?" she asked slowly, one arm held behind her back.

"They're all dead and we have the nanites," I responded dryly. "So why don't you bring that arm out into the open and explain yourself."

She hesitated, then did, slowly. She had a heavily modified laser, clearly barely operational, but held at the ready.

"This where you demand the nanites or you'll kill me?" I asked, readying myself to kill her with a thought, a gravity bubble aimed between her eyes and three inches back.

"No." She sagged. "No, not at all."

Then she sank to her knees, pushing the laser aside and doing the whole fingers to the chest salute thing that the other soldiers had given me aboard the warship and the Forgeship.

"I beg forgiveness, Lord Devourer…" She went on quickly. "I was concerned that the influx had unsettled you, that you may need time to recover or to stabilize yourself. I am aware that we are small beside your magnificence, and yet—"

"Cut the crap," I snapped. A tentacle flashed out and grabbed the laser, lifting it and pulling it in close where I could see it better. I finally noticed the bulges around the room, all attached to the joints between this room and the rest of the ship. "What the hell's going on?"

"You…we were warned by Devourer Shan'Gai that when a Devourer feeds, they run the risk of losing themselves to the influx," she admitted in a rush. "That sometimes, until they regain their equilibrium, everything around them is seen as prey."

I glanced from her to the weapon, then to the bulging forms that were attached to the walls.

"So you were ready to try to fight me, to protect the dwarfen?"

"Yes."

"And those?" I indicated the bulges.

"Explosives. Shaped charges that would free this section of the ship from the rest, allowing Zhonat to attempt to take control of the ship and fly them away."

"Nice." I snorted. "Well, good luck taking control of the ship."

"We knew it was unlikely, but should you attempt to feed on me?" She shrugged. "It was all that we could do in the short-term."

"Fair enough." I sighed. "Here."

Before she could stand, a tentacle shot out, latching onto her thin armor, and pumped her five million nanites out, pouring them across her like water. Then, with a thought, I wiped their bond to me, unable to explain how I did it.

I just did. The nanites reacted to my will now, reforming as I directed, and in this case, they released their bond to me and latched onto her, making her gasp as they bonded to her, all five million, all ready for use.

I explained how many each of them would be getting, and that they weren't to give the dwarfen more than the million I'd already decided to donate to each. She started to open her mouth, clearly planning to volunteer some of hers to give them a better chance at survival, before I spoke over her.

"With a million nanites in them, unless they're killed by hard radiation or something like that, they'll always recover. Their best chance is if you grow strong enough again to defend them. Take the weapons, take the five million nanites each, get yourself and your people back on their feet and be ready. There's a hell of a fight coming."

As I spoke, I was creating boxes—literally boxes of nanites, blank, upgraded but prepared to attach and bond, spread out around the room, pressed to the wall and left there, joined and ready.

"Anyone who touches these will bond them, so make damn sure that the dwarfen understand which ones they can touch, and no more. If one of them tries to grab more, I'll rip them free, and they won't like that," I snapped, before shaking my head and forcing myself to go on in a more conciliatory tone.

"I'm sorry, Saryet. I know we've barely met and all I've done is argue with you, but the people I love are in danger. Although I needed to do these things—I needed to fight and to build the ship, to save your people and more—I don't regret any of it. It was the right thing to do, but…"

I paused. The terror that I'd wasted the last minutes of Ingrid's life, that she could have died already, all while I'd been playing with building a ship or something…it was just too much.

"We need to go," I told her. "We need to get back to the node. We're not even in the right damn quadrant. The best thing I can do right now is raid the Ændari systems as we go—fire on them, damage them all badly enough that they divert forces in this direction instead. But any time we waste here…"

"It could cost the lives of those you love," she finished for me, standing and nodding as her nanites flowed into new configurations. Armored bulges rose from the liquid nanites that covered her. "I understand. We all do. This is the burden of being a soldier, never knowing if what we do now is right or wrong, if those we love are being taken from us as we fight a meaningless battle somewhere far from the hubs of the galaxy. All we can do is fight the fight before us, though, Devourer. May I give you some advice?"

"Please." I nodded.

"If you fight as if all that matters is those you love, and you abandon the opportunities to address the greater war, then although you may win more time with them, you make their sacrifices worthless. You dishonor their fight, and you risk the entire war."

"I…wow." I glared at her.

"You can choose to ignore the fight before you and run to them, abandon all you could achieve, or you could earn your place by their side. Will they throw the war aside to run to you? Will they believe you are so weak that they must be by your side and protect you, or will they fight the battle before them?"

"They'll fight," I admitted.

"And when they hear that you abandoned the opportunity to weaken the engines of war for your enemy? Only to run to their side, allowing the Ændari to marshal their forces to face you all, instead of spreading them out to defend their systems?"

"I hate you," I muttered.

"I mean no offense, Devourer, but you have what? A hundred cycles of experience? Less? I doubt more. And yet I am of the second generation. I was created and flash grown to fight for the Ændari. I was among the first to rebel, to form the fleets and to strike down our false gods. I have over ten thousand battles behind me, many that took entire cycles to complete. I have trained many of our kind, and although you are a Devourer…"

"I'm new to it." I finished for her, sighing and nodding. "So shut up and do my job, don't panic and run to Ingrid and the others when we could do real damage to the Ændari first."

"Essentially, yes." She nodded seriously.

"Fuck. All right, you wake your people, get them as ready as you can." I took a breath. "We'll jump around a bit, hit some of the Ændari back worlds, but then we head for her."

"Of course, Devourer. We follow your lead."

"As long as I lead where you say," I muttered.

"As is the right of an experienced warrior," she replied, the edges of her lips in a slight smile. She stood aside, headed for the hatch to the next level.

It opened as I moved closer. Zhonat stepped back to give me room, and I leapt up, passing him and heading down the passage to the cockpit.

I had to twist and step carefully between the dwarfen. Several were already working on the medical tubes, trying to figure them out. With a wave of my hand, I unlocked them all, releasing the cryo lockouts and starting the warming cycle.

Lights lit on the tubes as I stepped here and there. Condensation on the glass made the faces within glimmer and seem coated in ice. Blinking lights strobed as I passed the last few, and outgassing of compressed atmo filled the passage and settled on the walls and floor.

I closed the door behind me, sliding into my chair, letting out a long breath and then shaking my head. I pulled up the system details, trying to make sense of what we had before us.

The notifications flashed again, and I hesitated, then pushed them aside. I'd read them soon, but first the system—pick a destination, then I'd look at them once I was on my way.

The Ændari system was weird, clearly a frontier one. The mine field on the jump point made me think they weren't expecting to use it much, or if they were, they must have a way to prevent them detonating when one of their own arrived.

A simple check on the sensors and the records that the ship had been making since we arrived showed that there were two similar sized and paired-up ships at the other jump point as well.

Beyond that, there were three planets that had structures in orbit. One looked like a small shipyard; the other two were probably mining and transshipment points, I guessed.

The AI helpfully pulled up sections, identifying smelting facilities, barracks, waste products being fired back down to the planet below… I shook my head, marking each of them up, picking the mining site first, then the smelter and shipment point, then…

Then I grinned as the AI helpfully pointed out that these sites were locked into geosynchronous orbit. They didn't move; they didn't change at all, and that made my intervention *much* faster.

I hesitated for a minute, thinking about it. Was I basically committing war crimes here? Knowing the Ændari, it wouldn't be them who were mining, etc. Then I shook my head.

Fuck it.

This was war, and as much as I didn't like it, I couldn't waste the time worrying about it either.

After all, I wasn't officially a soldier of the UC, so I'd take the Canadian approach to war crimes, which was that they were fun ways to pass the time.

Arise: Conqueror

The AI figured out the plots, measuring the rotation, the distances and more, and then gave me three vectors. I almost fired, then gave in and summoned Saryet to the cockpit, explaining the situation and my concerns to her.

"Give them a warning," she said. "Order them to evacuate the stations, and if they choose not to, then it's their responsibility. Stations that size won't be able to move quickly, if they're mobile at all. Time the launch to hit them all at the same time. Give them perhaps five hundred of your seconds to respond. Aim for the center of mass for the stations, and in that time, they cannot move it out of range.

"They'll have time to reach evacuation shuttles, though, or internal bunkers. What they choose to do with that time is their decision. This is war, and as much as you might wish differently, lives will be lost regardless." With that, she strode back out of the room.

I sighed, nodding that I agreed and made the changes to the AI plots, firing a barrage from the rail guns of high-explosive penetrator rounds, six shots each, as well as four more each aimed at the ships that hung silent at the far jump point.

I fully expected they'd move between now and the rounds arriving, but as Saryet had said, the stations weren't going to.

Sure, the planets would rotate, and the stations, being in geo-sync, they'd rotate around as well. But that just meant adjusting the plot a little so that they literally flew into the incoming fire.

I fired the engines again, focused, and started to search local space.

Sure enough, there were signal repeaters, strewn about, each ready to relay messages faster-than-light. To do that, they had significant reserves of tech aboard, as well as power.

Linking to one, I unleashed the Hack sub-mind, gaining control quickly, and used it to deposit two messages, each timed to release ten minutes before the shells would arrive.

The first was a standard one, basically me warning them to evacuate the stations as they were valid targets of war, and would be destroyed, as well as providing a countdown to impact.

The second?

Well, that was a little more fun.

"Greetings to the Ændari High Command, Council, and leadership," I started, not really sure about their internal command structure and not caring enough to get it right. "I am Steve, Devourer, ruler and defender of the Forgeworld Earth. For the crimes committed by the Ændari race against my people, I declare you to be war criminals, and deserving of no mercy.

"Your attempt to claim my node was laughable, and I have decided to eliminate your capability to wage war, starting here, at the outer edge of your empire, and working across to reclaim the next of my system nodes.

"If, on my arrival to each system, you do not immediately power down all structures, disable your warships, and surrender, I will kill you. Each and every one. I know of your plot to eliminate life in this quadrant, and it is for this reason that I have chosen to respond now.

"Surrender, accept your punishment, and repent of your sins. If you do all these things, then perhaps your maker will show you mercy, because I will not. Prepare to experience the true meaning of war."

With that, I cut the recording and sent it into the system, ready to be released in four hours when the shells arrived at their destinations. Sure, it was a bit corny, and a bit arrogant. I mean, a few years ago I was tending bar, with the biggest concern in my day-to-day life not being caught by a gang of criminals. Well, that and getting laid.

Now I was declaring war against the empire that had raised my species from the dirt and convinced us that flinging our poo at each other wasn't the height of culture.

Admittedly, some of us had regressed from that point, but still.

With that done, I set the next destination, and, making sure that the shields and all systems were powered and ready, I triggered the next jump, deeper into Ændari space.

Arise: Conqueror

Chapter Fifteen

Unfortunately, the next few systems were incredibly boring, and yet oh so dangerous, in all the wrong ways. The notifications were the first step.

Beyond them, the systems were cookie-cutter copies of the last, each set up with multiple stations. Some were apparently food production or shipyards. Most, once I was past the minefields, were both boringly empty and almost devoid of challenge.

The first tried to surrender as soon as we arrived, swearing that they were only Ændari by name, and that they were rebelling against the evil empire.

Thirty seconds of hacking their communications revealed the local leadership coming up with this plan, and the laughter as they assured each other that a mere weapon would never see through their deception.

I agreed, thanked them for their time, then opened fire, uploading a pre-recorded message in which I sent them the recording of themselves saying this, and then a much shorter countdown, one that referred directly to the rail gun rounds that were now targeted on their leadership's personal bunkers.

Neither their locations nor the limited effort that had been made to secure them were hard to find. Once again, Ændari arrogance made me smile.

I jumped out of the system before they'd receive the messages, but amused myself imagining the looks on their faces when they found out the truth.

I'd fed on the local ships, ripping another hundred million nanites free, and donating half to the BWVs, leaving them in "boxes" of ready nanites for them to divide up as they saw fit.

The notifications were a relief, though. As soon as I'd entered the next system, destroyed the next minefield, and shut their ships down, I pulled them up.

Devourer, there is little that can be gifted to you that you cannot and must not instead discover on your own. Each of our kind bring unique gifts to the galaxy, and as such, we cannot guide you, beyond this:

You are unique, and a power that is beholden to no other. The universe itself glories in your rise, because as a Devourer, you are both the Alpha and the Omega.

We are given, and have taken, the power to create and destroy the universe as we see fit. Remember your place is where you decide to stand.

None may command you.

None may hinder you.

The only barrier to your growth is you.

Arise, Devourer, and let the void reign free.

That was both fucking unhelpful and terrifying. Whoever was sending this shit had basically said I could do whatever I wanted, and that I shouldn't listen to anyone else.

That wasn't a good idea for any man or woman, because every single massive dickhead in the history of my world had decided that they and only they got to decide who lived and died, and that hadn't ended well for anyone.

Fuck that.

If I was a Devourer, then sure, I'd glory in some of it. It was my nature to be a brutal fucker when people pissed me off, and anyone who so much as looked at Ingrid sideways was going to be torn limb from limb. But more than that?

If I just did whatever I wanted, I knew myself too well. There was a darkness in me, and if one of the reasons I'd evolved to be a Devourer was because of that? Because of who and what I was? Then that meant that there were others with the same darkness out there, doing whatever they wanted.

It'd be too easy for me to just toss off all inhibitions and make the rules for those weaker than me to obey. Considering who and what I was, that could end up being, well…*everyone.*

No. For now at least, I'd focus on not being a shitehawk, and protecting Ingrid. That'd be enough. And maybe, with her help, I'd become more one day. I'd be a better man.

Or, if I was lucky, there'd always be dickheads out there for me to take my anger out on and I wouldn't have to grow up at all.

I moved onto the next notification.

Congratulations on your survival, Devourer!

Co-leader Ingrid rejoices in your survival also, and has been informed of your location.

Current node status:

Damaged: 22.4% operational capacity reached. Further processing power will be unlocked upon reaching 50%.

Syncing remote data…syncing remote data…sync complete.

Additional rewards unlocked.

3x General Specialization Points available

3x War Points available

3x Hack Points available

I'd frowned at that point, finding that the other notifications had been removed, but remembered that when the shit had been hitting the fan before I'd "left" the node, I'd ordered the AI Argus to discard any notifications, only telling me the points I had.

Clearly the fucker had defaulted to that, and although he could send me messages, nothing I tried in response worked to send one back.

Fuck it.

Arise: Conqueror

I still had nine points to spend.

I wasn't sure about the others, not yet, but the General points were an easy spend.

The three points for General System Specialization went into the Harvest tree, moving to System Replenishment, then investing them all in Growth. It wasn't a hard decision at all, considering it literally allowed me to reach out and spread "me" further.

I could do it regardless—stretch a tentacle or two—but the more I reached, the more difficult fine-tune control became. Spending three points in Growth allowed me to go from the "cape" I'd made before at a single point to the ability to spread across a medium-sized room at four points invested.

Now, at seven, I felt that same gnawing, desperate hunger rising again.

I needed more nanites, so many more that it was like I'd been cored out. For long minutes, I battled to maintain control, to bury the need.

At some point around then, Saryet had stepped up into the cockpit to discuss something. I'd slammed the door in her face again, the hunger at a few million nanites that she possessed almost making me attack her before I could get control.

Then I sealed the door and boarded the ships that I'd disabled, leaving my people aboard my ship, as I tore through the enemy indiscriminately.

Most of the fight wasn't enough to even get my attention. Each of the Ændari appeared to me as patches of heat and desire, glowing in the darkness as I stripped them, ripping their nanites free and into myself, before running onward.

There weren't enough of them, even when I'd finished every single Ændari on both the minelayer and the picket ship. I felt as if I'd been starving for years, and a feast was nearby, tantalizing me with the drifting smells.

Ignoring them as best I could, I'd launched myself from the gutted vessels, landing on my own, and opened fire again, this time barely taking a moment to upload the warnings and declaration before jumping back out of the system. The next two systems were much the same: a frantic battle as I launched myself at them, savaging their ships and scarcely keeping myself above the level of feral, before I regained enough control to think properly again.

When I did, I found myself deep in the bowels of a ship: sparks flying from a ruptured conduit, blackness all around me beyond that, and a single cage before me in the darkness.

The power had failed to it, and the prisoners it held were low on air, gasping, collapsed on the floor, all but one of them unconscious already.

It was in the eyes of that last prisoner that I'd found my sanity again. The Ændari who had been threatening to space them all unless I left him alone was shaking on his knees.

I'd thrown out a tentacle. The tip hit like a water bomb, flowing out and enveloping him, tearing him apart atom by atom and nanite by nanite as his constituent parts gloried in joining the Devourer.

He'd collapsed, shuddering as he was torn apart, and I'd stared at the weak numbers of nanites stored in the box ahead of me.

It'd taken long seconds for me to make sense of what I was seeing, feeling the gorging and desperate need that had filled me drain away at the look of horror and exhaustion in the eyes of the young child.

She couldn't be more than five Earth years old, clearly human, and the adults around her had already passed out.

She was half laid across their unconscious bodies, panting, struggling to draw breath and staring with eyes that were even now sliding closed. The last thing she'd seen was her "owners," her goddamn *slavers* being torn apart.

Then the look had gone from feral satisfaction to horror.

Sparks flew from the conduit behind me again, lighting the container they'd been kept in, and the glass side, presumably meant to show a prospective buyer what they were getting.

I saw it all and as my anger rose, the red hunger faded away.

That a child, an *innocent*, had looked at me with such horror was enough that I felt every scrap of self-loathing I'd ever experienced rising in me.

It wasn't just the condemnation in her eyes.

It was that until I'd focused, I'd seen her and her companions as resources, food, and nanites. I'd seen them as something to take, something that was mine by right, and I realized just how close I'd come to losing myself.

A simple fucking upgrade had nearly created a fresh plague on the galaxy, and it was a miracle that I'd managed to hold control as long as I had.

I remembered considering sneaking into the lower chambers of the ship and stealing the nanites that I'd put aside for the others, and wondering, if any of them died in the defrosting process, how I could force the others to accept me feeding on them.

It was dim, like the memory of a dream, but I'd damn well felt it, and I'd been contemplating it.

No, I needed to focus on control from now on, I vowed. The remains of the Ændari crumbled to the floor as I stepped forward, tentacles flashing out and latching onto the cage that held the humans.

One of the tentacles ate through the outer layers, sealing them tight behind itself as it dug in, until it pierced the box fully. Then I switched it to conversion. A nearby block of metal ripped free and sank into the tentacle to fuel it.

The air in their box freshened in seconds as I adjusted it, focusing and demanding it change to the air I remembered most clearly: that of the beach when I was growing up.

It'd been a place I ran to, when I was too young to do anything else, to breathe in the cold, clear, salt-tanged air of the coast, with the waves crashing against the shore at the foot of the cliffs, and I reproduced it as faithfully as I could.

They were out cold. The box was airtight, I presumed, because attached as I was now, I could sense the waste in there. The lack of a toilet or anything could only be to make their containment more unpleasant, and the air was foul with it.

When I'd attacked the ship, the first thing I'd done was cut off the reactors, then I'd drained their power entirely. So it was no surprise that the air in the box had grown foul quickly, especially not with eighteen of them crammed into a space that was less than three meters on a side.

The girl's body was slumped on a pile of them, pressed against the glass, and it enraged me.

I nearly pulled the cage apart there and then, barely keeping control as I instead tore the ship around me apart. I needed to latch this onto my ship to be able to get them out, and seeing what I'd almost done, I was now as determined as it was possible to be that I'd damn well save these people.

We were deep in the ship currently, the rearmost cargo hold, with two levels above and one below, making it more awkward as I ripped apart the structure below.

It didn't take long for me to lash out with the Devourer instead, covering the surfaces between me and the deep dark, tearing them apart and using the matter I liberated to strengthen and reform the box.

It was airtight, and it was secure enough to keep the prisoners inside, but how strong I had no way of knowing. So I ripped and tore and upgraded it. Seconds became minutes as I slammed the remaining points I had in Support into General Technology, unlocking more and more advanced materials: malmetals, forms of matter long since lost to both the Ændari and the UC.

As soon as they unlocked, a cascading update rippled out. The Engineering sub-mind locked up as it was overloaded by update after update, structural changes, matter restrictions, malmetal failures and successes, weaknesses and strengths…all of it.

I froze, then shook myself back awake, refusing to stop, refusing to give in, forcing myself to struggle through it, until the Engineering sub-mind rebooted.

When it came back, though, the ship was changed forever.

First and foremost, the discoveries made with malmetals had been part of the research path that had originally resulted in the Devourers, and I sensed more secrets ahead, somewhere.

The Devourers were originally a test project, something that got wildly out of control, before being pruned, stripped from the systems, the overall paths lost.

I'd discovered it only because the data storage devices literally transcended star systems and were embedded within everything, and it was therefore impossible to fully scrub them.

That and the nanites' innate need to adjust the path that lay before a user for maximum growth efficiency meant that the records were always going to exist somewhere.

Just like Rule 34 and porn.

Malmetals had eventually been scrapped and removed from the records as well, mainly because they were linked to the Devourers, and the Devourers had made their own discoveries using them.

They could be manipulated in ways that were similar to our own forms, and as a Devourer grew and evolved, so could they grow too.

My eyes twitched as more and more data poured into me. The structure of the ship around me collapsed as my Devourer form absorbed it, ripping every atom free that I could.

The secret wasn't that malmetals had failed—it was that they'd succeeded beyond all reasonable expectations. The Devourers had been envisaged as the next evolution of starship: living, breathing forms that could be grown and developed. Warships that could regrow damaged sections, or discard them. Weapons that could evolve, be upgraded indefinitely.

I saw it all in a thunderous rush, and I reached out to my ship, starting the upgrade as soon as I understood it.

No matter what we evolved into, there was always a hard limit on our nanites. Not because we couldn't control them, but because there was a literal mass limitation. As I absorbed more and more nanites, I needed to grow.

That'd been countered originally by using my bones as storage lacunas, then replacing sections of my body with smaller, more efficient ones and filling the spaces—first with power cores, and then with more and more nanites.

Then I'd gone full Devourer, and in my insane need for power to jump a starship across the galaxy, I'd transformed myself entirely into nanites.

That was fine and had made more room for a fuckload of nanites. But in growing further, in reaching out to control more and more, I needed to literally increase in size as well.

That or I needed to have the Devourer form extended at all times. They had to go somewhere when they weren't tearing the galaxy apart, after all.

This was the answer to that.

Instead of becoming bigger and bigger, I sensed that I could separate, although not permanently. The malmetal was how the first Devourers had existed, joining themselves to the malmetal by their nanites and embedding themselves in the ship's heart, becoming the ship as much as piloting it.

Then, as they'd absorbed more and more matter, they'd upgraded themselves. Their nanites were used to make the parts that needed to be high-tech presumably, and the frame and the rest of the ship was made of malmetal.

The Devourer then was enshrined and free to grow, roaming the cosmos, sentient starships that could grow from a fighter to a fucking battleship given enough matter.

Hell, I could see how the AI memory cores could be embedded and accessed, the entire ship growing into a hybrid creature.

I could become that, and with the ability to separate myself from it, I could still be "me." I didn't have to give up who and what I was to become a starship. I didn't have to make do with Ingrid roaming my halls and passages while we toured the galaxy. We could still be together in every sense of the word.

That was a massive relief, as was knowing that all I had to do was focus to split myself free of the ship. The nanites that made it up would sink into a sort of secondary state, but also not able to be taken by another.

If I was away from it for too long, the ship would revert to a "normal" ship, then awaken as I returned.

I couldn't do it forever—hell, as near as I could tell at the minute, maybe a couple of days was the maximum I could manage. But with the new level of growth? I could insert myself into the ship and be the ship now.

Arise: Conqueror

More to the point, if I converted the solid structures to malmetal now, I could attach new sections as I needed them.

The cage that held these people being a perfect example.

As more and more of the Ændari ship was torn apart, I started the transformation. My Devourer flesh flowed across the outside of the cage—absorbing, converting, and transforming it—shifting the simple iron and steel composite into malmetal.

By the time I emerged to stand on the hull of the ship, almost a third of its mass torn free now, it was done.

I strode to the edge, looking "down" and seeing my own ship there, glimmering in the black.

Launching myself into space and dragging the box with me, I twisted, falling toward my vessel, and landed at the rear, grinning as the stars around me started to spin. A face appeared at a nearby window, peering out in mixed fear and aggression.

I waved a tentacle to let them know it was fine, then frowned, staring at the structure of the ship. If I added this here, on the back of the air lock, the malmetal would flow to form a seal and they'd be able to disembark easily enough. But then I was stuck with a random cube on the back of the ship, and no damn air lock.

No, I needed to have the cube somewhere else. Maybe higher? I moved around slowly, searching, before deciding that the best option was a temporary one. Slap it on the top, convert the metal around it into malmetal as well, then absorb it into the frame once it was done, considering I was about to add another eighteen to twenty people at a rough guess to my ship…

Crap, I'd activated the damn tubes as well!

I was about to have real issues with space unless I could jam these people into the soon-to-be vacant tubes, I supposed, but either way, I'd saved them so far, and that was an improvement.

Certainly over the plan that had been to feed on them.

I fixed the cube into place, then slid back into the cockpit through the roof and reformed the seal there, repressurizing it, and opened the door into the rest of the ship…only to face Saryet with a now improved and much larger laser, and better armor.

She stood there, the laser aimed at my face, as she waited.

I waited, too, for several seconds.

"So, you going to shoot me or what?" I asked.

"Are you, you?" she replied.

"What kind of a goddamn question is that?" I snapped back. "Seriously, who the hell else would I be?"

"Are you in control again?" she ground out, and I sighed.

"Yeah, yeah…I am. Sorry about that. I take it you saw there was a change?"

"You were barely aware. The ship lurched from system to system, firing on unknown targets, and you refused to answer any questions, beyond screaming that you knew we weren't food and you were fine."

"Yeah…" I winced. "Okay, so I was a little out of it. Turns out that the risk in the Devourer path isn't the nanites, it's the upgrades. When you upgrade to the next level of growth, you need to have enough nanites ready, or you go mad trying to gather them. It's like starving but with less mental control."

"And the structure that you brought back? And the metal that glows?"

"Glows?"

"Behind me, on the ceiling, a section of the metal is spreading. It glows as it grows."

"Malmetal," I guessed, ducking slightly and staring past her down the corridor. "Huh, didn't realize it'd do that."

"That is not a reassuring thing to hear you say."

There was a literal patch in the ceiling roughly where I'd stuck the box, and it was steadily spreading, rippling slightly and leaving a gentle sparkle behind in the metal.

"I thought I'd have to do it section by section," I admitted. "Looks like the nanites do it automatically once they start. Wonder what'll happen when they hit the reactors?"

"The spreading patch is under your control?"

"It is." I hesitated, then waggled a hand back and forth. "Sort of," I admitted.

"Given that you do not understand the movement and that it may reach the reactors at some point, this is also not a comforting sentiment."

"Meh." I shrugged, actually feeling a little better now that I had a solution to a problem I'd not even realized was worrying me. I didn't have to grow beyond Ingrid.

"Look, you need to either shoot me, or put that down," I suggested after a few seconds of staring at each other. "I need to get to the people in there and help them, and I'm going to need you to look after them, so make a decision."

"What people?"

"Humans…uh, BWVs?" I guessed, shrugging. "I found a bunch of them in a box. They were unconscious from lack of oxygen—"

"And you left them in a box?!" She glared at me.

"Will you shut the fuck up and let me finish!" I snapped back. "I *found* them in a box. I needed to get them from there to here, so I put some fresh air in and brought them with me across to here. They weren't exactly going to swim it, and they had no armor, so yeah, I left them in the fucking box, all right?"

"And you left them out there?" she asked, clearly trying to be polite but still glaring at me as if I'd just punted her puppy.

"Yeah, I did, after I stuck them to the goddamn hull. Then I came inside to open a path through for them to get inside…you know, to safety. Unfortunately, someone got in the way and stopped me. I wonder who that could be!"

"You're wasting time," she replied flatly, stepping to the side and putting the laser down, resting it against the wall.

"Women," I muttered under my breath, stepping around her and moving back. As I passed several of the medical tubes, I looked at the ceiling and traced the start of the spreading change.

It wasn't hard to do. The center of the square where I'd pressed it to the frame hadn't been flat, making it easier to notice the edges by tracing the frame back.

Reaching up, pressing my hand against the hull, I felt the cool of the metal and the shifting possibilities held inside. I smiled, unthinking, tracing the edges, then willed it.

The metal contracted, flowing back to show the underside of the box. The second layer flexed and opened more slowly as I adjusted it. A shout in a language I didn't recognize rang out as the floor started to vanish for the prisoners.

I held it, waiting, the hole only a few inches wide. And sure enough, after a few seconds, the first eye appeared there.

I expanded the hole, only by a few inches, but the person on the other side drew back in fear.

"Your skin," Saryet muttered to me, and I frowned, looking down, seeing the Devourer was retracted. "Did they see you on the ship like this?"

I mentally cursed, nodding. The Devourer flowed back inside me, the black and red oily shimmer dying down. But even with that done, I was clearly inhuman, considering I'd been strolling around in space without armor, forming tentacles and ripping my enemies a new asshole with only a thought.

I hesitated, then turned and left, moving back out of sight while speaking quickly to Saryet.

"I was…distracted earlier. I didn't hurt them, but there was an Ændari. I killed him as he threatened them. I don't know how much they understood or saw, but it's probably best if I stay out of sight for a while."

"Probably." She sighed, before stepping past me, moving closer to the hole and wrinkling her nose as she did so. "Tell me you've been hiding a cleanser all this time?"

"Nope!" I grinned. "I'll put it on the list for the upgrades, though. Are your people okay now? Do they need more nanites?"

"We'll never refuse them," she admitted, turning away from me and showing the people on the other side that she was unarmed. "But for now we're stable. Why?"

"The more nanites I take, the less risk of the hunger overtaking me, and the stronger and faster I can make this ship," I said. "If you don't need them, then I'll keep them."

"What's the next step?" she asked.

I shrugged, already turning away and walking toward the cockpit. "What else? We're going to hammer the Ændari."

<u>INGRID</u>

"He's alive?" she whispered, sagging back in the chair and staring fixedly at the updated readout on the far wall. "You're sure?"

"Confirmed," Argus declared. "Commander Steve has entered the outer range of Node #04. Syncing…syncing…sync complete."

"Where is he? Show me on a map," Ingrid ordered, before standing, twisting around and leaning on the command desk as she raised her voice to shout to the others. "He's alive! Steve's alive!"

"Told you!" Jonas roared, more animated than he'd been in days as he bounded to his feet; Scylla rose by his side, blankets discarded. "Damn that man. Doesn't know when to quit…"

"He better not learn." Ingrid sighed, smiling wearily. The long days and nights of fighting the constant worry and being unable to sleep for fear of missing an update crashed down on her at once. She sagged back into the chair, fighting tears. "He's okay…" she whispered to herself, stifling a sniffle.

The nearest screen updated. The local cluster of stars showed first, then another, then three more. The view panned out farther and farther as dozens then hundreds of star systems were marked up. Finally, one at almost the farthest edge of Ændari-controlled space lit, pulsing green.

"How long until he can reach us?" Ingrid's heart sunk at the clear distance, even as she tucked her legs back under her in the chair, squinting at the details, counting the systems between her and Steve.

"Unknown. Current location is registering. Local information is limited. Unknown vessel located and identified. Multiple eliminated Ændari vessels confirmed…correction. Minefield deployed and identified, correction…updating…"

"What's the mad bastard done now?" Paul yawned, ambling over and squinting at the screen.

"Confirmed. Unknown vessel arrived in the midst of a minefield, triggering them."

"Oh no…" Ingrid whispered, hands flying to cover her mouth. "Argus, is he…?"

"Vessel appears undamaged, although identifying high-powered weapon deployment…confirmed. Ændari mine deployment vessel identified as test bed #1184 is destroyed. Ændari picket ship identified as test bed #55267 has received damage…"

"That's Steve, all right," Jonas muttered, unable to keep the proud smile from his face as he shook his head. "*Damn*, that boy can *fight*."

"Vessel disabled. Commander Steve is boarding…" Several minutes passed, broken only by updates like "Ændari eliminated."

Arise: Conqueror

Until eventually, Argus finished the report, still sounding barely interested. "Confirmed, Commander Steve has reentered unidentified vessel."

"What the hell are you doing there, my love?" Ingrid whispered, staring at the flashing system data, but getting no answer. "What do we do now?" She asked the question rhetorically, but Argus answered it anyway.

"Recommend continuing current course of repairs and defensive upgrades. Current Ændari vessel count in-system: seven. Local militia forces have strengthened docking area, and armoring project continues unabated."

"It was…you know what, it doesn't matter." Ingrid sighed. "Okay, I guess our break time is over. We need to—"

"You need to rest." Scylla stepped up and laid one hand on her shoulder, staring down at Ingrid. "You have permitted yourself the bare minimum of rest since we…since *I*…lost Steve and the ship. I will watch and alert you, should anything change. Jonas will lead the defensive teams, with the assistance of Paul."

Ingrid grinned, hearing the words that Scylla had chosen not to use as well as the one she had. "That idiot" was as likely to be used to describe Paul as praise, and she didn't think Scylla even realized she was doing it now.

They'd all changed over the last weeks. They'd had to.

One of the greatest changes was Paul, though—even Scylla had to admit, though she no doubt hated it. He'd gone from one of the most insane marines in his past unit for the United States, to a leader in his own right.

When Steve had been lost, along with all the mass that they'd planned to use to create the defenses for the node, they'd been forced to reach out to the local worlds and stations.

Most had ignored them or claimed that they needed everything they had, regardless of the sheer stupidity of that claim. That or they'd demanded control and access to the hidden sections of the node.

Ingrid had refused that, and had refused all requests by any Ændari asking to dock, regardless of the oaths they swore.

That had meant that the people who did turn up, ready to help and to risk their lives for the node and the future of this quadrant of the galaxy, were almost entirely poorly armed, ill-equipped, and inexperienced.

Several were out-and-out crazy, unable to decide whether Ingrid and the others being able to access the command sections of the node meant that they were defiling them with their unholy presence, or whether they were in fact holy themselves.

Paul had stepped up, and although Courtney flatly refused to speak to those she called "that bunch of twatwaffles," he'd formed them into teams, working hard around the clock to demolish more and more of the buildings, creating makeshift bunkers, firing emplacements, traps and more.

He'd also been the one to deal with the Ændari who had shot up the *Lurksome Doubt* he'd been on to try to force Ingrid to let him board. As soon as he'd arrived and tried to disembark, Paul had beaten the shit out of him. Then he used a collection of claws salvaged from the failed original terminator BWVs and a brick to literally nail him to one of the few partially standing walls on the dock.

When others had asked why, he'd explained that the original structure of the dock was so solid he could hardly nail him to that, so he'd done it out there.

That he said it as if it was such a common-sense approach left people nodding and confused still. But the one thing people were sure of, as he whistled merrily, hammering the "nails" through the Ændari using a brick as a hammer, was that Paul was *not* to be fucked with.

Scylla had laid claim to the Ændari as well, warning him that as soon as Paul was finished using him as an object lesson, she was going to kill him.

Belle had also drained the Ændari to within an inch of his life, breaking him down to a mewling mess a third of its original size prior to his nailing.

All things considered, it proved an efficient example, as the next ship that docked that had an Ændari aboard didn't have to fight to keep them there. If anything, they were hiding and begging not to be disembarked.

Ingrid nodded, smiling at Scylla, and took her hand, rising to her feet and hugging the shorter woman, who stiffened then relaxed.

"Thank you, Scylla," Ingrid said. "An hour, no more than two, then I'll—" A jaw-cracking yawn forced her to pause, before Jonas took her wrist, guiding her away.

Scylla slid into the command chair and adjusted the settings, bringing up more displays focused on the docks and the teams that trained or slept there now, depending on their rotation.

Glancing at the screen as Ingrid allowed herself to be led away by Jonas, the blankets that had held the sleeping pair only minutes before now called to her with a siren song, and she sighed in relief.

He was alive, and more than that, he was fighting. That meant he was safe and happy as Steve could be.

He'd come to her soon. One way or another, he'd come to her, and then at last, she could rest.

She settled down, wishing more than anything right now for a real bed and her love, but some reasonably warm blankets on the floor was what she had.

They'd more than do, she decided, her eyes slipping closed…

"Ingrid, devilkin subject 001 reactivation of nanites is confirmed." The voice of Argus, as he privately connected to her and shared the undoubtably good news, sounded inordinately proud of himself, even as she was jerked back from the brink of sleep. *"Activation is highly limited and will be restricted to the lowest level of attuned. However, with the data from subject Malthus and subject Benat, likelihood of activating all devilkin before the Ændari can storm the station now stands at 73%…"*

"That's…that's great news," she agreed, unable to stop the yawn. *"What about the refugees?"*

"Time required to research and make sufficient remote changes for the refugee group is estimated at five months and eleven days. There are sixteen different races, with four racial sub-groups, and…"

Arise: Conqueror

She stifled another yawn, lying on the floor, before forcing herself to open her eyes again, and looked at the ceiling overhead as Argus began to list potential issues, and she reconsidered those she could reactivate and reawaken.

CHAPTER SIXTEEN

The stars around the cockpit blurred as I gazed out, surprised to find that although I got bored, as long as I wasn't active mentally around the clock, I didn't need to sleep anymore. The hours passed and damn did they pass slowly. Space was insanely big in a way I'd never allowed myself to really contemplate before, but although I got bored, that was basically it.

There was plenty I wanted to do, most of them revolving around sexy time with Ingrid…and even a few including engineering experiments, which was new. But instead, as the hours blurred, I jumped from system to system, avoiding the direct route back to her, and pretended I was headed to the nearest node.

That was deep in Ændari space, and each jump showed the difference between frontier systems and more developed core worlds.

They also showed the goddamn difference in minefields, as leaping into the frontier systems was almost laughably easy in comparison.

The first of the more developed star systems I entered was an order of magnitude in difference. I'd barely exited the jump, "real" space rippling around me, when the first of the mines went off.

Nothing new or unusual there. I saw the readings; the sensor reports came in slowly, then faster and faster as the first explosions cleared and more could be seen, and the shields dipped then climbed over and over.

That was when I saw the defensive fortresses.

The senagra had struck me as being paranoid bastards, despite the fact that, yeah, everyone genuinely did want to murder them—and for good reason.

This, though? This was a whole different level.

Lagrange points aren't small. They're literally sections of space that have the lowest gravity interaction because of multiple fields cancelling each other out, and they move.

They literally move as the planets rotate, meaning that the point that today might be closer to say, Mars, might be closer to Earth tomorrow.

That meant that the minefields needed to be shepherded constantly. There was nothing to attach them to, after all.

Arise: Conqueror

That was understandable, common sense even, just like the "lesser" Lagrange points that each solar system had. Every planet had five, apparently: three that were unstable and two that were stable, one ahead of and one behind the planet's stella rotation, where the individual world's gravity was cancelled out by the sun, etc.

The two "greater" Lagrange points operated in similar ways, literally points where the entire solar system did the same thing.

Whereas that point for a single planet might be small, in terms of stellar mechanics, the solar system's version was a fuckton bigger.

That meant that when the first wave of mines vanished, their rolling explosions whiting out the sensors for several seconds, I was expecting to see a much busier system beyond.

When it came back as blank, I stared, confused. Then, what I'd unthinkingly registered as stars, oh *so* many stars, shifted and recalibrated.

Then I started to swear and triggered the engines, damn hard.

The Lagrange point for Earth was apparently about half a million miles wide; the solar system versions were hundreds of millions of miles across.

That was tiny in terms of the solar system, where most distances were measured in how long it took light to cross it. But in terms of a place to string with an absolute fuckton of satellites? It was insane.

The mines were bad enough—with even basic converters, you could make them from literal rocks, so it was only a matter of time. But the clusters of satellites that opened fire were terrifying.

I gunned the engines. The first lasers already flashed out, licking across the outer layer of shields, and dropped them at a far faster rate than the mines had.

There were tens of thousands of floating satellites, each simple creations: orbital engines to counter or follow stellar drift, a medium-grade laser, and a power cell, attached to a network of solar cells.

That popped into my mind, the Engineering sub-mind already parsing the data as I fired, aiming as fast as I could, before cursing and dropping the power into the shields instead.

The engines were pushing hard, but I was never going to escape this, not in time. Shields were dropping like a stone. The first was down already, the second at half power, and the power cells were barely able to keep up with the hammering.

Power levels were screaming warnings at me; lasers pounded the shields, dozens upon dozens of hits a second. They weren't powerful, but there were so many it was too much. Add that we'd been at a dead stop, having jumped straight from hovering over the shattered hulk of the last ship I'd raided, and the engines didn't even have real inertia behind them.

I'd massively fucked up.

I shunted all the power I could to the gravity drive, picking the next nearest non-Ændari "core" system I could, reaching out and helping the AI, stabilizing the gravity fluctuations, smoothing it, and letting out a relieved breath as space around us warped again.

We plunged into the branes, diving, and it felt like the rear of the ship could barely be out of sight before we were rising again, space rippling…then filling with explosions.

The ship shuddered. The stars outside rolled crazily; cries came from somewhere behind me. Creaks and warnings filled the air as the shields approached failure, counting down the seconds as the final one dropped from ten percent to seven, to four, then failed.

Then the lasers hit again.

I twisted the yoke. Engines flared, the universe barely resolving again as I frantically checked the readings, trying to find a way out, a weakness, a…

A target.

There!

A fucking picket ship had opened fire on us as soon as we'd emerged. The mines were already triggering; a rolling wave of explosions again blanketed us, hiding the system beyond from us. More and more of the local minefield poured inward, attracted to the emergence.

We weren't in a core system anymore, though.

We'd burst back into our universe from the branes. The mines had been repelled, and then they'd activated their position-keeping drives, pushing back in, attracted to the change in local space, and hammered into my shields, taking the final defenses and shredding them.

The picket ship had started to fire as well, tearing holes in the hull, stripping sections free of the stuttering shields, damaging the rail gun coils…

But there were only two ships there: the minelayer and the picket ship that the outer systems had. And they were gamely hammering on my ship as I twisted and dove, trying to get clear.

More mines fell in toward me as I gunned the engines. Energy allocation popped up in my vision as I transferred power from everywhere into the power cells, leaving literally three units for the general ship use to combat the damage already taken and replace the outgassing atmo, and five units in the engines.

That was it.

The other seventy-two points hammered into the cells, and from there, into the shields.

An explosion off the starboard side sent us rolling again. Lights flickered across the ship as something started a cascading ripple of detonations. Lasers tore another hole in the hull, and then silence fell.

The ship was dark, the cockpit unresponsive. I stared in horror. Distant shouts grew faint on the far side of the door, and I snarled, launching myself from my seat and tearing my way out of the nearest wall, onto the hull.

"Steve!" It was Zhonat. *"Steve, are you…?"*

"I'm alive!" I snapped back. *"How many did we lose?"*

"I don't know—some. We need to get the hull sealed!"

"We need to…" I started to correct him, knowing that getting the goddamn shields up was far more important, until I saw the lasers that were hitting them, and being absorbed. *"They're up,"* I whispered, relief flooding me.

Arise: Conqueror

"The control run to the cockpit...looks like that was taken out. I can fix it, but the hull has to come first."

"Seal the hull," I ordered. *"Seal that and save as many as you can. I'll help."*

With that, I tried to step back out onto the hull, only to cry out in pain as the shields hit me. Crackling lightning shoved me back inside, stunning me for long seconds.

"Fine, I'll do it from the inside," I muttered, then cursed. I had to repair the wall first. That wasted valuable seconds as the nanites sealed over the cracks, adjusting and upgrading the metal to malmetal as they went.

Opening the door, I was greeted by a scene of chaos, not overly helped by the rush of air as the cockpit equalized: screaming ex-prisoners, furious dwarfen, confused BWVs—all of it.

There were apparently two Support classes in the team now. The second was a tall, rawboned man in an armored suit that was closer to a spider on crack than a human. He had multiple legs that flashed, sealing a hole in one wall with two laser-like implements while three more were pressed to the hull around the damage. A glowing blue panel of light stretched between them, keeping the atmo from escaping as he worked.

Zhonat was missing, presumably deeper in the ship, considering I wasn't getting any screams from his connection. But the looks I got from basically everyone suggested that I wasn't high on the list of people they wanted to see right now.

Unless, that was, it was the list of people they wanted to see swinging by the neck from a branch.

I shouldered through the nearest few people, moving up to a section where a short, powerfully built woman was pressing a section of seat cushioning to a hole in the hull.

I reached over her, pressing my hand atop the cushion and pouring out a small number of nanites, their mission to reform the material into a new patch that would mesh with the wall.

She didn't look happy when I told her to move her hand, but when the nanites started moving, she jerked it clear with a nod and an attempt at a smile.

Clearly she was pissed at me, and I didn't know why, considering I'd hardly asked the goddamn Ændari to blow my ship up.

Also, they should be fucking thankful I'd bothered to rescue them!

I glared around, moving quickly, slapping my hand onto the walls and conduits, repairing as I went; tentacles reached, locking onto damage as I poured more and more of myself out.

It took minutes, that was all, thankfully. It should have taken much longer, but the malmetal meant that sections that were already converted had automatically repaired themselves, even if the cube was apparently long gone, having been a bump that allowed some of the worst damage through.

Ten minutes later, I was working with Alberene, the second Support class, who'd found the damaged conduit that led to the cockpit.

"What kind of an idiot puts a control conduit here?" she snarled, shaking her head. "We're lucky this is the only break. There must be dozens of chips in the crystal now, losing power by the second!"

It was in the floor between the upper and lower passages, and where I'd thought it'd be safest, but apparently the middle of the ship was the first place it'd get damaged. Go figure.

"Yeah…" I muttered, not looking at her as she went on and on. "Seems pretty obvious now."

"Obvious? Obvious? What kind of a fool would do this? It'd take utter stupidity to—"

"I didn't know, all right?!" I snapped at her. "I never had to build a fucking starship before, never mind in deep space with no help!"

"What?"

"*I* built it!" I glared at her. "I built it, and I damn well rescued you all, and them, and the dwarfen—and not one of you bunch of shitehawks has even said fucking thank you! I'm fighting every goddamn minute to survive and all I get is grief, so fuck you, fuck them, and fuck this galaxy!"

That was when the universe chose to send the ship quaking again as more mines hit. I lurched to my feet, my skin flashing red and black.

"YOU WANT SOME?!" I screamed at the walls and the suddenly silent passageway. "RIGHT! JUST YOU FUCKING WAIT RIGHT THERE!"

I was off, leaving Alberene staring after me open-mouthed, as I stomped off to the cockpit and slammed the door behind me.

The conduit wasn't fixed, not fully, but it was working again, and that meant that control was returned to the cockpit.

I could have plugged in anywhere, once we found that the conduit was the problem, but all the sensors were rigged to the cockpit and without them, I couldn't see anything anyway.

Now that some power had been brought back online, I threw myself into my chair and glared at the visions that filled my mind.

The minelayer had opened its doors and was pouring mines out. That was what had just hit us—a literal wave flowing at us.

On the other side of the ship, the picket ship fired on us constantly. Its lasers showed they were close to redline from the heat buildup. And thanks to the wonders of three and a half reactors all being poured into the power cells, the shields were holding in the nineties still—though the incoming mass wave of mines might change that.

Fortunately, though, the first of the new wave was just arriving.

I kicked the engines, flaring them and stopping the constant roll, smoothing it out until the incoming wave of mines looked like a tsunami sluicing down on me.

Then I diverted twenty units from the pool into the weapons and engines, slammed the ion engines into reverse and backed up, triggering more and more mines from all sides as we drew closer to them.

Arise: Conqueror

The shields dipped, then rose as my lasers ripped out, slashing lines of coherent light and hard radiation through the incoming wave. The mines detonated; more and more exploded as shrapnel caught others that were too close. Tens, then hundreds went up. The wave poured back to catch the leading edge of the last mines, as they exited the minelayer.

The ship vanished behind the rolling wave of detonations, and I turned, staring at the picket ship as its own guns went silent.

There was a long, drawn-out series of breaths as we watched each other over the gulf of space, before his engines flared.

He rolled, twisting to get away, firing the engines as hard as he could, pushing toward a section of the still-intact minefield, and I bared my teeth in a snarl as I followed.

The mines ignored him, making me glare as I locked onto him, desperately wanting to open fire and tear the fucker a new arsehole. But I couldn't.

That the mines didn't respond to him meant that there was something I was missing, something that the mines were attracted to, and I needed to damn well find it.

I scanned the ship as it fled, finding nothing particularly surprising: the usual mix of metals and more that almost all current ships were made from. The shields were up, so it wasn't that they attracted them. And the…

The signals it was sending.

It was broadcasting something, something over and over. When I locked onto the signal, it took literal seconds before I burst out laughing. I was torn between annoyance at myself and disbelief, but it was basically saying "not me, not me, not me" on a loop.

Literally.

The program was blasting out "not me" on a frequency I had to guess covered the targeting parameters for the mines, and that was all that I could find.

I hesitated, wondering whether this was a trap, something incredibly cunning that would set all the mines off and fire hidden missiles or something. Then I shook that thought clear.

If they'd thought ahead to do that, they'd have had the mines just launch them on my arrival anyway.

I copied the signal, then broadcasted it as well, snorting as the nearest mine that had been headed for me at speed suddenly diverted, warning lights across its hull blinking off.

As I blasted past it, literally weaving between the remaining mines, I altered the power draw and laughed despite everything.

The mad bastards had put lights on their mines.

Literally, I'd seen it at the last second as they shut off, but I had to guess that the lights were a "live" warning or whatever.

They'd put warning lights on the mines—helpful to their own people, presumably—but fuck me sideways with a running chainsaw, it changed my way of looking at the Ændari all over again.

I'd known they were lazy and bloody stupid, but who the hell came up with the plan of basically screaming "don't chase me" at the mines and putting lights on them "just in case"?

It had to have been a committee, I bet. Some utter wankstain sitting there complaining that they were offended by the ingredients in the provided cookies or something and then needing to justify their salary by adding in stupid suggestions.

I both hated and loved it.

And then, as I opened fire on the fleeing ship, dropping its shields under a heavy barrage, I grinned evilly. These fuckers just handed me a way to enter the Ændari core systems with impunity.

There was no way a group stupid enough to use "not me" as the only preventative to their mines going off was likely to have a second code to stop what I guessed were those automated lasers I'd been hit with on arrival.

For now, though, what I needed was a little snack…

It didn't take long to take out the engines, reactors, and then the grav drive on the fleeing picket ship, followed by a fast boarding. And, now that I had more and more nanites available, and a damaged ship nearby, it promised a much more impressive eviscerating of the Ændari.

I'd brought my ship in close enough that I could literally maintain several tentacles on it, as I poured the Devourer across the Ændari vessel's upper hull.

It ate through it steadily. The armoring and turrets went first. The armor and hull were absorbed and used to repair my ship. The turrets were transported across and held in position as the two Support classes worked feverishly.

They'd been overjoyed when I explained the plan, loving the idea of using the Ændari vessel as fuel to rebuild our own, making a few "minor" changes as we went as well.

The wings were extended, the two turrets inserted into the hollow hull. My tentacles formed new armored plates that the pair worked to seal into the structure, extending down and out.

New rooms were growing as atmo vented; screams and pleas from the Ændari fell on deaf ears as I literally peeled the upper layers of their ship free.

Lasers flashed out, hammering into me, but as before, the ship's armory was sealed away, and without power to open the doors, all they had were personal weapons.

They weren't enough.

Tentacles flashed out, latching onto the struggling Ændari, and ripped them free, dragging them into space and back to me. They were enveloped in a mass of red and black, and absorbed, everything that they were torn free and fed into my growing ship. I hovered there, encased in my own flesh between the two.

The Ændari vessel, thankfully, didn't have any prisoners aboard this time, and I tore through the second, and then third levels in short order.

It took less than two hours to entirely shred the ship. Although it'd take longer than that to fully integrate the changes to the superstructure of my new vessel, even in that time, we'd managed to seal two more rooms and pump them full of atmo.

Yeah, all right, there was nothing in there, literally—not so much as a space heater or a seat yet—but any space that people could move to was progress, considering a ship that was meant to hold basically me and some loot now had more than fifty people aboard.

Or it had.

I returned to the ship, now a third bigger and significantly heavier armored. I sealed the cockpit again, my newly expanded Devourer armor layered into the hull as well.

The malmetal shift meant that I could now integrate with it at a much more personal level. The ship felt more and more like my own body, the solid struts and supports like my bones had once felt.

My Devourer "me" was now layered beneath the new armoring and above the superstructure. In theory, it should enable me to make fast changes to the ship if I needed to, then reform the structure. But most of all, it let me "feel" the ship, responding to it and the universe around it at an instinctual level.

One day I'd not need any of the rest, I knew. I'd be able to generate shields, shift the surface of my skin to form whatever armor I needed, and the weapons… I could only guess at the level of weaponry I'd be able to bring to bear one day.

For now, though, I was able to seal away the cold of space, making the interior of the ship heat faster, and maintain a more comfortable temperature for my crew.

That thought gave me pause as I stood before the door from the cockpit into the ship proper. Did I need a crew?

Hell, did I *want* one?

I could operate the ship without them, after all. And did I really want people inside me? The thought brought a new level of *ick* with it, thinking of Jonas and Scylla getting busy inside my literal hull and me being unable to tune it out.

That almost decided me right then that I didn't need a crew, but the thought of not having Ingrid with me made me determined that if she wanted to explore the galaxy with me, she'd always be welcome.

Then I considered taking her away from her family and everyone she loved, *again.*

No, she'd need other people, even if I didn't, and I had to admit enjoying having people around at times.

Like James and that fucking magical coffee.

I shook it loose. This wasn't the time to get lost in stupid thoughts, but I knew why I was doing it.

We'd lost people.

I'd lost people, considering they were literally just passengers, without any way to help or hinder, and now I needed to go out and face them, face the survivors and look them in the eye.

I hesitated for a few more seconds, building my nerve. Then I opened the door, mentally cursing myself again as the rush of displaced air tore past me, filling the previously empty cockpit and drawing everyone's attention.

The air had filled with screams from the former prisoners, shouts of alarm from the BWVs, and both the dwarfen and the Support classes shouting for people to get out of the way and that they were coming.

"It's just me!" I shouted, getting glares and exasperated sighs, making me feel even more unwelcome in my own goddamn ship. "Well, fuck you all very much," I muttered, dropping my voice, then sighing as Saryet moved through the crowded passage, stepping up to me.

"Devourer, what do you need?" she asked me.

"I came to, well, to check on people," I admitted.

"I can give you a status report. There's no need for you to—"

"I don't need a status report," I snapped. "I need to see them, to make sure they're okay and to…to apologize."

"What for?"

"For the fight, for the damage and to see how many died."

"Why?"

"Whaddya you mean, why?" I snapped. "I need to. I—"

"Devourer, your inexperience is showing." She dropped her voice and inclined her head toward the cockpit. "Can we speak inside?"

"Fine," I grunted, seeing the looks on the faces of the people ahead. As much as I desperately wanted to run from them, this was as much to take her advice as that.

I led the way back into the cockpit, bracing myself against the back of my chair as she entered and closed the door.

"Why did you do that?" she asked, and I glared at her.

"I needed to check on them."

"You said that." She leaned back against the door and watched for a few seconds, before sighing and rubbing at her bare jaw with one armored hand. "I'm going to try to give you some advice, if you'll take it?"

"Go on."

"You're the leader here. Not just that, you're a Devourer. My people respect you automatically for that."

"Yeah, that shows," I muttered.

"I said respect, not like," she corrected. "If you're looking for parades and worship, don't come looking with the rank and file. We've lost too many to your kind's mistakes already. And no, that wasn't an attack on you. Too many died when Devourers failed, or when they drifted off and lost interest. We respect you, but we don't love or belong to you."

"Right." I grunted.

"You went out there looking to salve your conscience—to help, sure, but you know that some died, and you're there looking for someone to tell you it wasn't your fault."

"What? No, I was—"

"You were looking to check on the people you saved. You wanted to know how many died and you wanted to help—I believe that. But at its core, you were looking for reassurance that the people out there were still alive and that you hadn't failed them. You wanted reassurance, and that's not what you get from this. Maybe you fucked up, I don't know…none of us do—we've got no access to the ship's systems beyond basic repairs.

Arise: Conqueror

"We don't know where we are, where we're going, or what's happening. We're in fights where the ship is on the verge of destruction, then you order the Supports to help rebuild and patch the ship. You explain nothing, and wonder why you don't have their wholehearted support.

"In this, you're a Devourer. All those I've encountered have been the same, distracted by all that you are, and forgetting that the fight is down here and that we're dying. Too many of your kind have left us, when they could have made a difference. Only Devourer Shan'Gai stayed, or had when I last fought for the UC. Those soldiers expect you to grow bored at any time and leave. Maybe you'll drop us off somewhere first. Maybe you'll feed on us instead.

"The dwarfen don't know what to believe, but they know some of the legends that we shared with them over our years working together. They've seen you build and rebuild a ship in practically an eyeblink. They've seen the potential you have, and they've seen their friends die because you failed to live up to that. And don't get me started on the prisoners.

"They saw you rampaging through the ship and they thought you were a god come to deliver them. Then they saw you feeding, apparently, and looking at them like something that you'd save for a snack later. All they've seen of you is horror."

"And that's why I came out!" I snapped, cutting her off. "Literally, fuck's sake, I came to see how many we lost, to see if everyone was okay!"

"No, you came for reassurance," she corrected again determinedly. "You can either be a distant god to them, or you can be their leader and captain, but you can't be both. If you want to lead them, you need to earn that right, show them what's happening and why, teach them, earn that loyalty and show you trust them. Or..." She fixed me with a glare.

"Or you treat them and us as cargo. Disposable tools that you might use up or feed on at any time. If that's all we are to you, then keep going as you have, Lord Devourer, and we will obey your orders. Zhonat seems to think you could be more, but everything I'm seeing says that'd be beyond you. You don't care for my people or those I defend."

"Fuck you, Saryet." I straightened up. "You don't know me. I never had this shit handed to me. I wasn't trained, or led by the fucking hand and shown who to fight, who my people were. I had to figure it all out on my own. I've been stabbed in the back more times than you can fucking count and I'm still here! I'm taking my ship back to the node and I'm going to protect it! I'll save my people and I'll damn well save you all as well. Then you can fuck yourself with a double-ended dildo for all I care!"

"That sounds unpleasant."

"Yeah, well, you deserve it," I snapped, glaring at her as she smiled slightly, then nodded.

"Well, if that's what it takes to get you to unlock the ship's systems and share what we're doing, it'll be worth it. Is this double-ended dildo a beast of some kind?"

"Yeah, it's a variant of the one-eyed trouser snake. Spits at its enemies," I muttered, unable to help myself.

"Sounds amusing. Perhaps I'll fight one and send you the recording sometime."

I stared hard at her at that point, actually unsure whether she was fucking with me or not.

"Sure." I shrugged after a few seconds, shaking my head and moving on. "Whatever floats your boat."

"Now, are we done with this, and have you made a decision?"

"On?"

"Are we cargo or crew?"

"Crew." I grunted, deciding that if I damn well had to have them, at least they could earn their keep.

"Excellent. Will we have stations, or a way to keep up to date on the current situation?"

"What do you want?"

"Ideally access to the ship and the AI," she said.

"The AI? I ripped it from one of your damn ships—why wouldn't you have access to it?"

"As Devourer, you have primary authority over almost any of the UC forces. The AI is damaged and still integrating. Without your command to do anything, it won't."

"Fuck's sake." I reached out to the crystal pillar and latched onto it blindly with a tentacle. I locked eyes on Saryet and fed her profile as I had it into the AI, telling it that she was crew and leader of the shipboard defense force.

That gave her a predetermined level of access it apparently understood, and I designated the dwarfen as support staff, with Zhonat and Alberene as the leaders of that group.

I knew Lehman was the leader of the dwarfen officially, but I also didn't know whether they could integrate with the ship, and needed to be sure of that shit first.

That done, the others we'd rescued were marked as passengers. I blinked, focusing on the "real" world again, instead of the digital one, filling her in on the changes I'd made.

"Excellent. How do we interface with the ship?"

"How do you normally do it?" I frowned.

"We don't."

"Oh for…"

"We're a frontline force," she clarified quickly. "I was never in command of the ships I served and was attached to, nor was I in that chain of command. I can give you advice, but I've got no way of knowing what you've added into the ship by way of access points."

"Wi-Fi—" I started to say, then cursed. "Remote digital access—can you use it?" She nodded, and I sighed in relief.

"I have both a basic internal access device and one built into my suit."

"Great. That's your responsibility then." I gestured at the door to the section the others were in. "I…I'm going to leave you to sort them out and make them useful, seeing as you think I'm so fucking unwelcome."

"I will explain you have granted them access and your mission, with your permission?"

"Zhonat did that already."

"Zhonat had understanding as to your aims, and those details were not shared beyond myself, as I ordered him not to. I didn't know your position, but I'll share them now."

I glared at her, then turned my back and clambered into my chair, biting down on a snarled response. I didn't know whether I hated her or not, but she was fuckin' borderline, that was for sure. One minute, she was helping; then next, she treated me as if I were the greenest second lieutenant in the army.

I hated that. I goddamn hated it.

I hated that she had a damn point even more.

Then I decided that if I was in such a foul mood, I might as well spread it around. It was time to return to that damn system that just fucked us up, and going back in, we weren't going to be using lube.

"Time to bite the pillow," I growled, sending a series of messages through the AI to everyone aboard who had access. Five minutes and counting down to the visit to pound town.

CHAPTER SEVENTEEN

The second visit to the system was a marked difference from the first. This time, I was ready for the fight, had a return jump to the same system I'd just left plotted already, and the ship screaming the Ændari's super-secret code at the same time.

We burst from the depths of the brane, and I grinned evilly when, this time, we weren't greeted with rolling explosions and heavy fire.

Instead, the three picket ships that floated serenely nearby seemed to be asleep.

"They can't be that stupid, surely?" I whispered. My eyes flashed from one to another of the ships, before a signal was beamed to me, locking on.

I opened it, too surprised not to, and the image that filled my vision made me laugh.

It was an Ændari, presumably the second or third watch's commander. He looked all of twelve years old, maybe fifteen, and was slumped in his command chair, gazing disinterestedly at a tablet in his hand instead of at me as he spoke.

"Identity and reason for visit," he demanded, thumb flicking at the screen and still not looking up.

"Devourer, and to conquer and enslave," I said with a feral smile. I shunted power from the shields to the engines and weapons. The turrets wouldn't be online for a few hours yet, but the rest of the ship was.

"What?" he muttered, frowning and finally glancing up.

I waited until he actually saw me, eyes opening wide, and then I opened fire.

The first barrage was a burst of rapid-fire lasers followed by four shells ripping through the air toward his ship. Then I was moving; the engines flared to high power, guns tracking.

He stared at me, then at the readings that were showing on his side, and down at the tablet, then back up as alarms rang out on his side. The ship was clearly aware it was under fire, but the little idiot just stood there!

I shifted my fire to the second ship, firing off a barrage there as well, before fixing the first with an evil grin, as the initial rounds impacted.

He was thrown from his feet. The lighting of the bridge shifted from pleasant pastel colors to flashing red and yellow strobes, before gravity apparently failed and he started to float.

Arise: Conqueror

This was even better than I could have hoped. The mad little bastard was still trying to make sense of things when another door burst open and a wild-eyed, half-dressed Ændari staggered into sight, grabbing a chair and pulling himself forward.

"Status report!" he barked, looking anywhere but at me, clearly having no idea that the screen was even live.

I couldn't help it.

I quickly pulled the Hack sub-mind into primacy, feeding the images I could remember with perfect clarity from the Ændari I'd killed most recently.

The sub-mind adjusted them on the fly, and overlaid my own image with an amalgamation one, adding in the greater horns that seemed to denote status among these idiots.

"You attacked me!" I barked at the screen, and the frantic half-dressed commander flinched, twisting around and looking at the image, seeing the new me. "I'll see you all dead for this—a council representative, attacked!"

"Who…what?" He gasped. "No!"

"Your servant attacked me!"

"What…" He struggled, trying to make sense of it all when the kid spoke up, finally getting control of himself as his ship outgassed and tumbled.

"He said he was here to conquer us!"

That just added to the confusion, and I found that for the first time in ages, I was actually having a burst of fun.

"I said that he should be ashamed he was using his tablet instead of paying attention, and asked if he concurred! Then he fired on me! I'll be reporting this to the council, after I take your heads!"

"Honored representative…" the newcomer started, then he flinched. "That ship! You're supposed to be dead!" He looked up, staring in horror, and I glared at him.

"You fired upon me as soon as I appeared!" Then, to add to the confusion, I opened fire again. This time, as I gunned the engines as well, the other ships were coming to life.

They'd obviously celebrated what they thought was my death before. The differences between the ship I was in now compared to the last one, the damage it'd clearly suffered, and presumably the debris from the exploding mines had all combined to make them think that I was dead.

Now they were under fire, their shields down, the ship venting, and more fire incoming.

"We surrender!" he screamed, desperately. "Cease fire!"

"All of your ships?" I bit my lip, watching the shells as they closed on him.

"Yes! Please, we offer tribute!"

That threw me for a few seconds, but I held my fire, then nodded.

"Lower your shields, all of you!" I ordered. "If you survive the incoming barrage, I'll dock with you each and examine your tribute. If I decide that it's enough, then I'll let you live!"

Then I cut the connection and stared at them. A little giggle escaped as I shook my head in disbelief.

These fucking idiots actually believed that…

The first ship exploded then. The incoming fire tore through it and set off a cascading ripple of detonations. I hesitated; then, using the same image, I reached out to the other ships, including the minelayer some distance behind me and its escort.

"I was attacked on entry. Your leader offered tribute, but too late. What do you offer?"

"Tribute!" the first one barked, his ship already damaged from the barrage I'd unleashed on it.

"Tribute!" the others agreed quickly.

"Attach your ships together," I ordered after a few seconds. "I shall send my servants aboard one to collect the tribute and examine your ships. Gather it all together."

With that, I cut the connection and summoned Saryet, filling her in on my plan. Apparently, she'd been watching the fight and the general bullshittery with amusement.

"You want us to board them and collect your tribute?" One eyebrow arced as she folded her arms across her armored chest, leaning against the wall.

"Yeah, you take a team aboard, see if they have any prisoners or anything we want, then come back with it. Make them all gather together in one ship or as close as possible. Then I'll go in after you leave. It'll make it nice and convenient to slaughter them all."

"And their ships?" she asked, making me hesitate.

"What about them?"

"What do we do with them?"

"Nothing. I mean, I was just planning on trashing them a bit as I kill everyone, then blasting them as we move off. It's not like they hold a candle to this one."

"They don't, but if you're serious about saving as many lives as possible, you could place one of my team aboard the least damaged and take those we rescue aboard. They could follow us. As we raid the systems, if we capture bigger ships, then we can transfer them, upgrading each time."

"Can they jump as far as we can?" I asked, and she shrugged.

"I don't know, but you weren't planning on jumping at the maximum range, were you? Also, we can move the dwarfen across and they can work on upgrading the other ship."

"That's…that's a good point," I admitted, loving the idea that we'd be able to get most of the people off my ship and I'd not have to worry about them so much.

"Also, we need to be more predictable," she said, making me look at her in confusion. "You said that you want to raid the Ændari systems along the way, make them think they need to send forces in this direction to defend it, right?"

"Yeah?"

"Well, in that case, we need to be more predictable, and we need to leave some survivors. As it is, word isn't spreading, or that little show would never have worked. We need to leave survivors who spread the word."

"Okay, well, there's a load more ships in this sector, right?" I shrugged. "It's not like we're going to attack them all."

"That's a second issue. Have you examined the ships in the sector?"

"No?"

"Do so now," she advised.

I sighed but pulled up the details. It took a few minutes, looking from one to the next, to the next, before I finally thought I had what she was hinting at.

"There's no big ones."

"Correct. But more importantly, what class are the ships?" she asked, making me feel like that green officer again.

"Fucking annoying?" I tried, not understanding.

"What level of armoring and weaponry are you able to identify?" She clearly fought the urge to roll her eyes.

"Uh…minor," I admitted, flitting from one ship to the next, then comparing them to the ships near us that were even now arcing in closer, preparing to dock with each other. "Wait, most aren't really armed. Are these…they're fucking pleasure craft?"

"Most likely trade and transport vessels," she corrected, nodding. "There are only a handful of military-class vessels in the sector. And they, like in the last several sectors, are remaining at the jump point."

"Protecting it," I muttered.

"Possibly," she agreed, before going on. "You said before that the Ændari were preparing to unleash a weapon that would eliminate all builders…sorry, *nanites*."

"Yeah, that's right." I nodded, checking the details for the worlds in the system as I did. "But there's millions, no, billions down there, so that might be wrong? I mean, where's the evacuation ships? I was thinking the military would be on us, already pulling back, but they can't be."

"Why not?"

"They'd be leaving their civilians behind. They'll all die."

"Will they?"

"Well, no, not straightaway. We think their nanites would, though, so anyone who needs them would die, and everyone else would be weaker—like, much weaker."

"Ah. I see the heart of the confusion here. I must explain more of their kind, if you will hear it?" she asked, and I shrugged, gesturing for her to get on with it. "The Ændari of my time did not separate themselves into civilian and military. There were those who had power, and those who did not. Certain families retained control over facilities, gaining leadership more and more by commanding vessels that they caused to be built.

"The Ændari are ruled by three systems. The lowest is a house of nobility, where families have control over the local area as governors. The second is the Ændari Council, a smaller body that had, in my time, only the ten leaders of the most powerful solar systems in it. That may have changed, but they made the day-to-day decisions for the empire.

"Lastly, there's the imperial family, headed by the emperor. Largely a figurehead, stripped of most power by the council, the emperor maintained control of the largest estates and the Helio Guard, but was permitted no directly controlled fleets.

"The three groups battled and backstabbed one another almost as much as they did the rest of the galaxy, and it was because of that the original rebellion was even possible. If the Ændari of these times are anything like their forebears, they'd view eliminating the majority of their race to maintain an illusion or to gain a tactical advantage as a viable price to pay.

"Also, should they have any intention of returning to their territory, then to find their lower-caste enemies and the vast majority of their people reduced to a level that they could not fight back would be a cause for celebration among the nobility."

"Well, fuck me with a greased telephone pole," I muttered. "There's literally nothing about these fuckers that's worth saving, is there? They're scum from one side to the other."

"Their upper ranks are," she agreed. "They were raised to expect nothing but backstabbing from the lower ranks and bear hatred of those higher, spending their lives in fear of all around them. The lower ranks were…less. They made up most of the scientists, the more common soldiers, crafters, and workers. In the early days of the rebellion, many of them joined the uprising, fighting alongside us."

"And now they're being left behind." I shook my head.

"Perhaps," she corrected. "It may be that the Ændari have changed since my day and not for the better. The entire race may be beyond redemption now. I cannot know this, and neither can you. What will you do?"

"Tiamak." I clicked my fingers as the name suddenly came back to me. "The scientist, one of the scientists who helped to change us, to make us into BWVs. Varnock was a mental bitch and I had to gut her, but Tiamak tried to save our people. Shit, maybe they're not all mad."

"Varnock the Defiler?"

"Yeah, her and the Erlking as well, met them all on Earth…uh, the Forgeworld."

"You casually mention such things at the same time as dismissing the most hated of our enemies." She shook her head.

"Well, if it helps, we kicked the shit out of Varnock, and I ate her face?" I shrugged; then, because I could see the confusion, I went on. "We didn't actually eat her face. I mean, I ripped her nanites free and shared them around, that's all."

"But you killed her?"

"Ingrid, my partner, actually delivered the final blow, but I was named on the updates as killing her, weirdly."

"The majority of the damage is registered by the systems. Otherwise, you'd have people hiding until the end of the fight and then creeping out to deliver a final blow," she pointed out.

I snorted, thinking of all the kill-stealing fuckers in the old online games I'd played.

Arise: Conqueror

"So, what will you do?" She stared at me.

I sighed, nodding as I saw what she was getting at. We'd gone off on a tangent, but fuck it, she was right.

"We're raiders," I said. "Time to start stealing ships and shit."

It took the Ændari nearly half an hour to gather together and arrange their tribute, and we made the absolute most of that time that we could.

The first thing I did was bring up the Hack tree. I had three points earned and available there now, and damn was I using them. This was the first and possibly only chance we were going to get to hack an active enemy ship, and although, yeah, it wasn't a big one, it was clearly intended for the Ændari to be on station for extended periods of time.

The picket ship was built over three levels, with four turrets—two on the top and two on the bottom—and multiple areas that we could use to house people if need be. I'd savaged enough of these ships to know they were pretty basic inside, but the one thing they did have was space.

Clearly the Ændari weren't sociable fuckers; each required their own room and they weren't small. There were less than a dozen of the fuckers aboard each ship, but that added up.

Put in a few more air recyclers and a food maker, and the people aboard my ship would think they'd died and gone to heaven in comparison.

That meant that I couldn't afford to waste this chance.

The Hack tree was one that I had a bit of a love/hate relationship with, considering that it was both really useful and needlessly complicated.

The main system was split into three—Information, Stealth, and Control—and I quickly looked over them, thinking about what I needed to do.

Each section was named for the driving focus behind it. Information, for example, was literally all about getting the data I needed from the target. It didn't care how; it would just get it.

The issue was that it left traces behind and it wasn't subtle at all. As I upgraded each area, the skills I had access to changed over time; they evolved.

If I worked on the Information tree primarily, I'd be like a raging bull with party foghorns in place of feet as I accessed anything. There'd be no doubt I was there.

If I went mainly down the Stealth route, then it took me longer to get what I wanted, but the systems I was working on were far less likely to detect me.

Control was all about taking the entire system under my control, treating the enemy system much like the theory of heavy stealth. Namely, it couldn't report anything if it was on my side, or dead.

The issue with that? Systems that were connected to it almost certainly knew straightaway as the target one was nuked.

That'd been the case with Tsunami, certainly.

Now though, I needed to be a bit more subtle. There was no way that the Ændari were just going to roll over and take me raiding and killing them all. There had to be a backup plan in case we tried…well, exactly what we were intending to do.

It might be explosives, it might be a reactor overload, it might be anything—but nuking their ship with a blatant hack attempt had to get their attention.

I moved to Stealth, pulling up the data on Plague. It was an infection-based system—clearly, by the name—and when introduced to the target, it mimicked the basic data transfer system—not asking for anything, not broadcasting nor searching.

Instead, it started basic replication, leaving copies of itself everywhere and moving on, coating the surface of everything it touched with a time-activated program.

Once the timer elapsed, it'd go nuclear, spreading like wildfire. Each individual system would be basically nuked and stripped, the data transferred out through dedicated channels, and then the plague "burned itself out," leaving no traces to follow.

That was great, especially if I was targeting a bank or something, but it wasn't going to help here.

I focused on what I needed and more options started to spin up. Possible paths dropped away as more opened. I waited, watching the paths stabilize as the system took into account the upgrades and abilities I'd unlocked so far, before offering me three options.

First was a direct upgrade to the Plague path, essentially just doubling down on it, investing all three points I had available into the Plague, making it both harder to detect and enabling it to "jump" more.

The original version had a single system that it could jump to, literally detecting the first linked system it came to and cloning itself to infect that one as well.

This would enable another linked system to be hit as well, and then the infection would spread slightly faster and slightly farther. It also changed it from basically ignoring anything that presented any risk of being caught and instead sneaking for as long as it took to reach the target.

It introduced a risk evaluation system, where if the system met parameters that it judged worth the risk, then it'd still attack. Although that was a possibility and it was a good growth if I had nothing that needed to be done specifically, I dismissed it.

It wasn't enough of a solution to make it worth the effort, and I moved on.

The second option was to spend two points in Stealth as the overall tree, improving all my Stealth-based Hack abilities, and then spending the final point in Control.

That was an option, mainly because although it sure as shit still wasn't subtle, it was better than I had currently. And if Saryet could distract the Ændari, then maybe we could get away with it.

Maybe.

That wasn't a term I liked to consider, though, when there were reactor breaches and explosions in my near future if I fucked it up.

The third option was a little better.

First, I'd not been considering the War points I'd gained as well. There were three of them, after all, and using those three to improve my basic skills in the Assassin tree was an easy spend.

Arise: Conqueror

Rolling down that tree, I came to Conceal quickly enough. As soon as the War points had been pointed out to me, I'd thought of investing them generally into the Infiltration tree, to improve that skill set and everything that was linked to it all at once, even if only slightly. But this was actually better.

The Conceal ability was an assassin's bread and butter—along with sharp stabby-stabby shit, anyway—because it literally did what it said on the tin.

I had five points invested in it now, with true invisibility marked as hitting ten—though something happened once I hit twelve as well, which I sensed and was weirded out by. After all, what the hell did you get *after* invisibility?

Fuck it. I shook it free and accepted the recommendation, figuring it couldn't hurt.

I was wrong.

It damn well did hurt, though only for a few seconds as updated Stealth information was downloaded to my nanites.

That done, though, and only two points away from true invisibility, the options available to me in Hack adjusted, taking the upgrades into account, and offered a new ability. It'd need a single point in Control, one in Stealth, and then the third spent to unlock it.

Changeling: The Changeling is a Stealth-based infiltrator, first examining the system it's inserted into, then adopting the highest placed identity it encounters. The Changeling program utilizes both minor variants of Plague to examine its target, and aspects of Tsunami to crush any resistance, eliminating the target identity as it assumes it.

BEWARE: Changeling can be corrupted, copied, and used against creators. This program is highly dangerous. Recommended only for emergency use.

I liked it. I also noticed the warning, and that made me grin. As much as I liked the idea that I was trailblazing and that there'd never been another like me, ever, knowing that in the deep past another BWV had created this, had the same points invested in both Hack and War trees?

That made me feel better.

Also, knowing that the only ones of our kind who had survived multiple tree unlocks had ended up as Devourers as far as I knew, meant that there was a chance that I'd be able to meet the fucker one day.

I took it, then hurried to work on the armor of Saryet and the three soldiers she was taking across into the ships with her. I'd spent entirely too long upgrading my abilities, and not helping.

I used the information I had on the Ændari and their feedback to make small, mainly cosmetic changes to their armor, making them look more like the Helio Guard that I'd fought before, though with the heavy weapons I'd looted from one of the Ændari vessels.

Saryet seemed to think that as the Helio Guard in her day were known for both taking absolutely no shit and for killing with the slightest provocation, it'd even out that they were also only known to carry the proton lances.

If they were unarmed, the Ændari would know something was up. If they were carrying something that didn't look right, like smaller arms, then the Ændari would be suspicious.

If instead they boarded armed to the absolute teeth, and used uber violence on anyone who gave them the slightest grief, then things were much more likely to end how I wanted.

Also, Saryet admitted, she was bored and really needed to let off a little steam. The thing that probably took the longest was locking them into my communications link. Like Zhonat, their systems were so different that it had to be done one at a time.

The Ændari linked their ships up—the minelayer on the far side of the three, two picket ships side by side, connected by an extendable air lock—and then the pair physically docked to an upper hatch on the minelayer.

I slid my ship around and latched onto the upper hatch of the picket ship farthest from the minelayer—just in case—and hid, ready for the violence to come.

The first hint that things weren't going to go our way, though, was when the air locks opened and the pressure equalized, air rushing into the separate ships and combining.

"What is that stench!" I heard someone gag, and I winced, exchanging a look with Saryet, before she dropped through the hatch, landing easily despite the eight-meter drop from our level to their deck.

"The stench of WAR!" she roared at them. The sound echoed around as the other three followed her. "We fight on the front lines, unlike you scum, and your cowardly attack damaged our ship!"

I stayed where I was, ignoring the response and the subsequent apologies. Instead, I closed my eyes and focused, as I sent gentle, subtle pulses through the open hatch, mapping their ships as best I could.

I grinned at their stupidity, extending a subtle tendril, as thin as possible, and edging it down into the ship below. As soon as it reached the controls for their air lock, the tip morphed to spread out, covering the panel and sinking into it, branching and breaking down into smaller and smaller points until they connected to the electrical system.

"Go to the left. I can sense nanites that way…not many and spread out," I sent to her as I started the hack. Local systems accepted me on the outermost level easily, but a monitor program further in stirred.

"Looks like it's a storage area," she sent back. *"They've been taking 'tribute' or 'taxes' or whatever they call it, and there's several cases of it stacked here and there, mainly spices and luxuries, some crystals, and there's a pair of saa locked in a cage. They look badly wounded."*

"Fuckers. Anything worth taking besides them?"

"Not really. There's several small cases of precious stones, only valuable because they're difficult to reproduce in my day. But if they've lost access to the makers, then I suppose maybe it's currency now?"

"Anything we actually want?" I asked.

Arise: Conqueror

"Just the ship and their nanites," she assured me. *"We'll move to protect the saa and distract them when you're ready."*

"Have they gathered all their people?"

"Most," she said after a pause to question them. *"I've told them their tribute is offensive and demanded they bring all their crew here. They think I'm going to choose one of them to be a slave for us aboard our ship."*

"And they're okay with that?" I asked.

"The leadership are. They think they're getting to keep their shiny stones."

"Just tell me when and I'll make an impression," I sent to her, already sinking back into the ship, searching and activating my time compression ability.

I barely heard her response. The monitor program was fully active now, sniffing around the link to the air lock. I didn't want the crew to get a warning before it was time. I released the Changeling, sitting back and watching as it unfolded itself, flowing out and around, and sent back a link to me, establishing itself and its control parameters.

Time was already slowed, but in digital terms that was almost meaningless. The monitor slid closer and closer, sections that I'd already seen winking out as the program examined them, and the Changeling went dark automatically.

For long seconds, I wondered whether I'd fucked up—whether I'd deployed it too late or whether I'd made a mistake in the selection, that maybe this ship had better defenses.

I gathered myself, ready to launch myself through the hatch…then the Changeling pinged and went active.

It was like the monitor program was a shark, sliding distractedly past, swimming overhead as a giant fucking octopus reached out.

It was attacked from all sides, torn apart almost too fast to see. Tsunami ripped into the monitor; Plague, inserted into the connections that held the monitor, flashed out, tracing the limits of the program, and then deploying Tsunami again and again before it could go active.

The monitor program vanished with barely a whimper. The red warning light that I'd associated with its presence was replaced in an eyeblink with a comforting blue one. Then the Changeling reversed direction and started back into the depths of the ship, mimicking the patrolling monitor sentience.

"Fuck me…" I whispered, eyes wide.

That was both terrifyingly effective, and outright terrifying. If someone was to deploy that fucker against my ship… I didn't want to think about what could happen, especially because it killed the program or identity it assumed.

If I replaced my digital presence, even though it couldn't—I hoped—kill me directly, it'd supersede me. I'd not be able to log into something to try to fight it.

It'd be a full-on Tsunami battle of the titans that would decide who controlled the ship. For now, the only comfort was that the Changeling could only use Tsunami in limited ways.

I could pour it out into the target system and leave it to replicate, transforming the entirety of the ship to a replication of my neural cell structure. I would be both the key and the lock, so nobody else could try to hack it, but this…there was the potential to evolve this into something similar.

It kinda freaked me out, to be honest.

Either way, though, it was currently under my control. This version of the program was literally linked to my mind and had no desire to supplant me. The terror was that one day I might piss someone off who had the same program. Now, instead of wanting to meet them as I had been, I was damn well hoping they were long dead, and the program with them.

I blinked, forcing myself to look at the world around me again, and hearing the conversation from below.

"Leave?"

"You wish me to leave?" I distantly heard Saryet snarl. "You demand I leave your vessel, is that it?"

"No!" the other voice replied quickly. "I assure you, Great One, you are welcome here. I wondered if you were looking for something, as you'd examined all those who were here, and yet seemed distracted."

"Ready?" I sent to her, and the sense of "Yeah, about fucking time" that flowed back was palpable.

"Most certainly," she assured me. *"All that I have identified in the ships are gathered in the main hold. I'll keep their attention."*

"On my way."

I took a deep breath, standing straight and looking up. The dwarfen and BWVs above stared "down" at me; then I grinned and stepped out, dropping to the deck below.

CHAPTER EIGHTEEN

It'd taken an hour in the end, both the slaughter of the crew and then the transfer of our people across. The pair of saa that had been held in a box, apparently ready for sale by the Ændari, were terrified and then overjoyed when they realized what was happening.

I literally tore through the ship like a hungry ghost, finding each and every Ændari aboard, enveloping them, tearing them down to their smallest atoms, and feeding on them.

As I went, the Changeling ripped through every defense, overpowering and absorbing higher and higher placed programs until it hit the AI.

That slowed it down. But by the time I'd killed and absorbed the entire crew of all three ships, enough of the linked vessels had been taken over that there was nothing left for the AI to do but turtle up and cut its connections to the surrounding systems.

That made hunting it down and infecting it with Tsunami directly almost trivial.

Each of the ships fell to us. The programming that prevented the AI from being able to captain "itself" basically was removed, and the other ships separated.

The minelayer was already equipped with a small maker, deploying mines as it went. Basically, all you had to do was feed in an asteroid or chunk of whatever, and boom…it did the rest. So that made me smile.

We set it to restock from the ruin of the wrecked ships—there were two others in the area that had apparently fallen afoul of the minefield as well—and then it was to start deploying fresh mines and take out anything that showed up broadcasting the Ændari top-secret "not me" code.

Besides us, obviously.

I also set it to update all the mines as it went, so that they'd all be a wonderful surprise for the next visitor.

Also, just to fuck with them all the more, I installed a ten-second delay on the activation. I was thinking that when the ships arrived, they'd check, find the mines were ignoring them, then they'd start cruising in, and boom!

Literally.

They'd take their eye off the ball and lose their own.

We found a link to the laser battery system as well, and I was disgusted by the simplicity. There was literally a single point of contact between them and the mines, and that was the minelayer.

It provided the basic controls and any updates, as well as an override. Taking the minelayer gave us a backdoor into the system, and I set it to fuck up the Ændari next time they jumped into the system.

Then we moved everyone through and onto the two ships, deciding there was no reason to cram everyone into one ship when we had two here.

Then, with more and more strident and furious questions coming through from the military vessels at the far Lagrange point, I took the time to identify myself, and opened fire on every target we identified as probably military in the system. Some we'd miss. There was no doubt, they'd realize what was happening soon and they'd move the things that could be moved. That was fine, though, because we'd get at least some of them. And knowing that the Ændari were just as much of a bunch of bastards to their own people as they were to everyone else had left a bad taste in my mouth.

I didn't target any more of the various settlements and starbases around the system, just the ones that looked clearly military in nature. I also got a quest, which was nice.

Quest Uncovered!

Evolving Quest discovered: All Hail the Conquering Hero

You have discovered that far from the monolithic edifice the Ændari appear from the outside, they are truly an empire built atop a tower of cards.

Raid their solar systems, destroy ships, rescue prisoners, and force the Ændari to the bargaining table.

Rescue 10 prisoners and destroy 10 ships of the Ændari to receive the following rewards:

- **+1 War Point**

- **+Access to Level 2 of the Evolving Quest**

As it was something I'd been planning to do anyway, it wasn't exactly a hard choice, and I accepted it.

There was the section of "force the Ændari to the bargaining table" bit to consider, but I happily noted that it didn't say what I had to do once they were there.

If I could get their leadership gathered around in a nicely accessible location with a table?

I'd bend them over it.

That came out wrong, I decided.

Arise: Conqueror

I'd eat them on it.

Dammit.

Yeah, I missed Ingrid.

With our people spread out across the other two ships, they agreed to wait a short period—an hour, no more—so we could clear out the next system's entry point. I wasted no more time in declaring myself a Devourer and warned the Ændari that I was going to the sector #04 system node, and everyone better get the hell out of my way. Then I triggered the jump, wondering whether they'd noticed yet that although I kept saying node #04, I was actually getting closer and closer to #02.

Fuck it—it was their problem, really.

Space warped around my by now much quieter vessel, and I grunted as Zhonat stepped up, sinking into the seat behind me in the cockpit.

I'd not wanted seats up here at all, but the dwarfen had already been working on making them. And thanks to their fucking around with the door, there was enough room now for the remaining members of my "crew" to use them.

Zhonat had stayed. Saryet had gone, taking command of one of the picket ships with my enthusiastic blessing. And Lehman had taken command of the second.

Three of the dwarfen had died in the fight on our arrival in that system, apparently. It'd come out as their bodies were being carried off my ship, and I winced internally at the look that Reman had given me as he passed.

Clearly some of them blamed me for their losses.

Five of the prisoners I'd rescued had died as well, all humans, and unlike the dwarfen, none of them would recover. We set their bodies free into the dark of space with as much ceremony as we could allow.

The other member of the crew who had decided to stay with me was a soldier. I'd barely exchanged a word with him beyond "I need to get past— move your arse" in the hours that we'd been aboard the ship together. But apparently he was a firm believer that the Devourers were necessary for the advancement of the galaxy and the UC, as well as being loyal enough that when Saryet asked for a volunteer to help protect me—against what, I had no fucking clue—he'd jumped at the chance.

Bach was his name, and he barely spoke, nodding rather than speaking in general. That was all he'd done when he'd entered the cockpit…or the bridge, I should probably call it now.

It was no longer just for the main cock to hang out in, after all. Heh.

He sat behind me to the right, and Zhonat to the left. Both had been given basic access to the ship, Zhonat slightly more than Bach as he was an engineer, and that was that.

My ship that had been full of loot and spoils of war was now upgraded again slightly, and pretty much stripped to the damn rivets.

I'd seen the dwarfen clutching weapons that I'd either looted or that had been made from everything I'd grabbed, and I'd not had the heart to kick off about it.

They had nothing after all, *literally*.

Their species was functionally extinct, their home world apparently bombarded from orbit repeatedly until it was left broken and glowing with volcanic heat. Their friends, their families—hell, their ships that they'd been rebuilding—*everything* was gone, and all that was left were scattered remnants of legends.

I didn't begrudge them a bit of scrap and old weapons I'd already scanned.

I gave them unlocked makers, for both ships; then we sealed the air locks and disengaged.

Now we were rising from the warp again. The shimmering of stars appeared to blur as we arrived back in our own reality.

To confuse anyone trying to track us as much as possible, and to allow the others to follow, I'd shifted to smaller jumps. We were bouncing from system to system, never in a straight line, appearing, making sure the mines didn't target us, then opening fire.

As the minelayers exploded—always our first target—the picket ships roared into action, lasers flying as I gunned the engines. The lasers dotted around the emergence point opened fire as well, and our new turrets returned fire.

Bach was a natural with them. His enhanced reactions and upgraded skills made him a brilliant gunner, and as he took more and more down, I'd focus on the picket ships.

The first barrage taking out the minelayer was a tactical choice. I didn't want it changing the programming of the mines, after all. Next was disabling any of the laser satellites in range. They weren't much of a threat without the others moving in, and certainly without the mines as well, but I didn't want them activating when the others arrived.

Then came the picket ships.

They were generally there, hanging around, and now that I'd had the chance to think about it, I guessed I knew why.

They needed to make sure that nobody knew what they were doing, and that included their people, too. So, they couldn't take everything out of the systems and not have their oppressed masses rise up, I bet.

If their little plan for the system nodes didn't come off, they also probably didn't want to be trying to return and come back to a civil war. So, instead, they moved most of the ships out and left a few in-system to create the illusion that all was normal.

Thing was, they'd only leave the lowest grade and weakest of their ships to do this, considering the fights that they were expecting. And, most important of all, they'd not be leaving people they couldn't afford to lose if they didn't get out in time.

That was why this shit was working.

They'd left the military equivalent of the village idiot in charge of system defense, and they'd run off to wherever they were marshaling.

That was the *good* thing. We were able to attack before they'd even gotten their shields up half the time, knocking their ships out and capturing them again and again. Then we'd slaughter all the Ændari aboard and free their prisoners.

Arise: Conqueror

That was also the *bad* thing, though, as we jumped into the third system in two hours, and found only civilian craft, brain-dead third-watch rejects, and shite vessels.

"That thing had to be mothballed," I muttered, looking at the minelayer that was listing as its hold detonated under our fire. "Had to be."

"Mothballed?" Zhonat asked curiously.

"Uh, it means scrapped, like they're not getting rid of it entirely, but they'd put it aside, replaced it with a newer model and left it just in case."

"Not recycled?" he asked. "Turned into a new ship?"

"That would be a better idea," I agreed, "but on Earth, a lot of equipment is just left in case. Then, if you need to call for reinforcements, for fighters that aren't normally used, they can use that ship, for example."

"Seems wasteful. Why not recycle it and have a new ship waiting for them?"

"Yeah, you know that does make more sense, but we didn't have the technology to do that when we developed these terms. Looking at that…" I nodded at the minelayer as the final explosions ripped it apart. "I don't think the Ændari do either. Why use these shitty ships instead of the warship designs, after all?"

"It seems foolish," he agreed, checking his data over. "There is only one picket ship in this system, and it appears unaware of us… Do you wish to chase it?"

I checked the data he was seeing, grunting that he was right. In this system, only two medium-range jumps from the node, I'd expected we'd find much more to fight—at least a heavier Ændari presence, even if they were only picket ships.

Instead, we found even less. The entire system looked to have been stripped; one picket ship and two minelayers maintained the "defenses" for a system of four million souls.

"I don't like it," I muttered, biting my lip. "I don't like this at all."

"The raid strategy was a valid one, given all that we know of the Ændari intentions," Zhonat assured me, sounding more like he was trying to convince himself.

"Or…they might not be responding to the attacks we've made because nobody knows," Bach suggested blandly.

"What?" I asked sharply, squinting over my shoulder at him.

"Well, if they're afraid of their people rebelling, they can't have word getting out about our attacks, right?" he rumbled, scratching at his chin.

My stomach dropped. "Go on."

"They'd have to keep it quiet, because if they're all gone, and even the system picket ships are destroyed, the locals who have been waiting would rise up. If they don't want that, they'd need to keep things quiet."

"They couldn't," Zhonat replied, shaking his head. "Faster-than-light comms. There's no way they…oh…"

"Oh?" I asked sharply.

"Well, if they shut down the faster-than-light communication relays, they could make sure nobody could coordinate a rebellion. And then word of your attacks wouldn't be getting out either, except to maybe the rulers, and they're not going to warn their people. Not if they want to avoid another uprising, anyway."

"Oh shit," I whispered, my stomach now somewhere past my ankles and sinking faster by the second.

"That would mean that the time we've spent raiding here, it's not really effected the overall war at all," Bach added helpfully. "Well, not beyond that War point."

"Shit." I pulled up the notification that had started flashing on the destruction of the minelayer.

Quest Complete!

First level of Evolving Quest: All Hail the Conquering Hero has been completed!

After further investigation, your suspicion has been proved right: the Ændari are abandoning their empire, and far from beginning their flight, they've almost completed it!

Your assault on their backwaters and minor developed systems has had little effect. If anything, time has been lost! You receive the following rewards:

- **+1 War Point**
- **+Access to Level 2 of the Evolving Quest**

Quest Uncovered!

Evolving Quest discovered: All Hail the Conquering Hero (Part 2)

You have discovered that the majority of the local star systems have been ruthlessly stripped and abandoned, all major military vessels have been taken, and are being marshaled elsewhere...or are they?

Discover the location of the missing ships and disrupt their plans to receive the following rewards:

- **+5 War Points**
- **+5 Specialization Points**
- **+Access to Level 3 of the Evolving Quest**

There was only one place I suspected I could find them right now, and it was the last place that I wanted the goddamn ships to be. I hoped I was wrong, but knowing my luck, there was just no fucking way.

241

Arise: Conqueror

I barely kept myself from shouting, as I forced my anger and disappointment down, crushing it under the need to make sure I got there as fast as possible. I pulled up the last quest as well, checking it as I fed more power to the cells, making damn sure they were as full as I could make them.

Quest Uncovered!

Evolving Quest discovered: Building the Future (Part 2)

You have claimed all the technologies you need to return to the fight, but although knowledge is indeed the greatest weapon, stabbing an opponent with your brain is less useful.

Use all that you have learned to construct a viable vessel, then return to the Node to receive the following rewards:

[Bonus: Return with all living members of the dwarfen race to receive a bonus.]

- **+3 Support Points**

- **+3 War Points**

- **+Access to Level 3 of the Evolving Quest**

Viable Vessel: 3/1

Dwarfen survivors: 18/18

Return to the node: 0/1

The dwarfen survivors were back on their feet, I guessed, considering it showed them all as "survivors" again. I took a deep breath, wondering whether I'd evolved far enough to pull off what I'd been planning for a while.

If I jumped into the node system and it was as bad as I was worrying it could be? As soon as we'd arrive, we'd come under fire. Although we'd survived the fights we'd had so far, it'd been a close thing. It was too much to make me confident about jumping in and trusting to luck.

That left two choices.

First, I could jump in and try to adjust the emergence point. I could jump out from locations farther out than the Lagrange point after all, so surely I could jump in, in the same way?

The only issue was control. What was to stop me jumping into the system in the middle of an asteroid belt, or a debris field?

Hell, if all I had to guide me was the feeling of gravity, and from a distant solar system at that? I might emerge into a fucking planet, or the rings of a gas giant.

No, that wasn't much of a choice. And if I wasn't going to jump in and just hope the shields protected me long enough, then there was only one option:

stealth. And because of the nature of what I was going to do, that meant no shields at all; their power was too easy to detect.

I slid the War point I'd just gained into Conceal again, bringing me all the way to nine. Nine points in it, and I could definitely feel the changes now, reaching out to the ship.

"Uh, Steve?" Zhonat's eyes widened as he picked up both the changes in the ship's power output and saw the changes in me.

"We've fucked up." I gritted my teeth, reaching out further and further. It started with small strands that flashed out, almost spiderwebs, flashing from my form to stick to the surfaces nearby.

It didn't stay small, though.

I'd been absorbing nanites in their millions, tens of millions, and knowing that I couldn't physically "fit" them all inside me, I'd been attaching them to the ship instead.

The knowledge that I could become the ship had changed everything, as had the descriptions of the other Devourers that Saryet and her people had given me.

I'd heard conflicting descriptions, over and over again, being told that they were massive creatures, that they were warriors, that they would tour the interior of the Forgeships, and that they'd even helped build them. They were men and women, they were ships, and even that they were space stations.

When I'd learned that I could separate myself from the nanites, albeit only for a short period, and still retain control over them? That was the final hint. Although I wasn't ready for it entirely, I was getting closer.

The outer hull of the ship was entirely malmetal now. The interior rebuild was ongoing constantly, tiny shifts that filled the air with incessant creaking and groans.

More importantly, the hull was now covered, literally, in a thin coating of nanites, from one end to the other.

Thin was probably an understatement, and, well, it wasn't complete. I needed about another ten million nanites to cover the hull entirely, but what I had was what I had. Fuck it.

It'd have to be enough.

I reached out; connections formed as I fed power into the gravity drive, starting the power-up sequence. The skin of the ship shivered as I felt it come alive.

Conceal wasn't just a small skill—hell, none of them were, I'd realized. The changes rippled across the hull as they adjusted, changing, evolving by my will.

"Get ready." I grunted. "We can't wait. Leave a message on repeat. Reach out to the local signal repeaters, and set it to send it to Saryet when she arrives. We're going to Scorpio. She's to redirect and head to the Forgeship here…" I attached the coordinates for the Forgeship and waited until Bach nodded that he understood.

"By the maker and their mercy…" Bach whispered, fingers already flying as he quickly connected to the nearest satellite to leave the message.

Arise: Conqueror

Zhonat dove into the AI connections, working as fast as he could, trying to bring more and more of the ancient system back to life. "An hour…" he said quickly, holding one hand up. "Give me an hour, and I can get the turrets linked to the AI. You think Bach is good? A dedicated defensive AI with this many memory units for processing will be more than you can—"

"Jumping in two." I cut him off, shaking my head. "We've wasted too much time—no more!" I focused, feeling the potential, the links forming between me and the hull.

The matte silvery steel of the hull, barely reflective but clear enough on radar, shifted, blurred, and vanished. Pinpricks of light appeared, drifting across the hull; my Stealth abilities kicked in fully as the illusion tightened up.

I could feel the ship now in a way I'd not felt it before. Even when I'd ripped space open and I'd flung us across reality, I'd been joined to the ship, but I'd felt encased by it.

Now it was like being laid in the bath.

I could feel the water—space—around me, and yet…the feeling of twisting, diving into the branes. With each evolution, I felt it growing stronger and more natural.

I'd felt I was swimming through space before, but when I'd done it, I'd been contained, protected inside a vessel. Now I *was* the vessel. I felt the wash of solar radiation, the starlight that slid across my hull, the caress of the void.

I detected tens of thousands of tiny particles that flowed across my hull, smaller than a grain of sand, and yet rolling across the hull, too small to see, and somehow familiar. They seemed… No. I shook myself.

I'd never noticed them before, and that meant that they either didn't matter, or they'd not be affecting me today. They were a mystery for another time.

As I opened the rift, my nose angling forward, sinking into the depths, I triggered my time compression. I knew I needed every advantage.

And that was when I felt *them*.

Whatever the creatures were that lived at the bottom of the branes, they were there, and they were gathering, following…*watching*.

I felt them amassing, swarming.

The deeper I sank, the AI aligning me for emergence in the Scorpio system, dozens of light-years away, the more I felt them moving.

They'd apparently not been fooled even slightly by the changes in the shape of the ship, nor the way I'd tried to hide behind the shields.

I felt them converging, though, and I gritted my teeth, pushing deeper, faster.

This time, they saw it; their mighty bodies flowed in excitement as they sensed the changes in me, the way that we moved: less and less through the manipulation of the gravity drive, and more and more through my own power.

I felt them reaching out, strands lifting, touching.

The hull shivered under their touch, the incomplete covering scratching, and yet…

Where the webs touched my hull, touched *me*? I felt something familiar, and wonderful.

I could feel the truth, or the shape of it anyway, the reality-bending secret that…

The rift opened before me; space reappeared, and my heart lurched as it did. Something was wrong, *very* wrong. The local area was full of mass, metal, shifting gravitational fields…

I felt all the almost revealed truths being ripped free like the memory of a dream on waking, as space around me exploded in a frantic wash of lasers, debris, and fire.

CHAPTER NINETEEN

We burst into reality into the tail end of a firefight, my plan to appear stealthily and sneak away before anyone could tell we were there lost already.

I swore, stripping the hull of the stealth coating, powering the shields as fast as I could, even as the first impacts crashed into us.

I'd bet wrong, again! Goddamn Karmic Luck stat!

The solar system around me appeared in waves—sections hidden behind explosions, hard radiation blasts, debris, and more. I'd emerged into a fight, and although nobody was targeting us yet, that wouldn't last long.

Hell, the sheer mass of debris, the damaged ships, the destruction and the floating shit that was everywhere would be enough to fuck the ship if I didn't get us out of here, and goddamn fast.

I gunned the engines. All six flared and pushed forward as quickly as they could. The entire ship creaked and groaned under the sudden power.

The shields crackled wildly as they began to cycle, snapping into place. The third, and closest to the hull shield, hit five percent, ten, fifteen…

Then zero.

The first impact hit the hull, bouncing, rolling, and tearing a thin gash that broke loose sections of the armoring, hurtling them into space.

More debris hit us…then the first body. I saw them at the last second: the upper half intact, the lower half missing from the waist down—no legs—ropy entrails hardening in the vacuum…then shattering as they impacted the hull.

I almost hesitated—almost. Then a tentacle of my rapidly retreating nanites flashed out, latching onto their head, and yanked them in as fast as they could.

I sensed more bodies out there—dozens, maybe hundreds—then the first missile exploded.

I twisted and rolled, diving. The directional engines on my belly flared as I reached out, triggering a gravity bubble and pulling harder.

The nose arced around faster and faster. Engines flared and sent us back behind a massive section of a starship.

It sparked and rolled slowly. The external side looked almost intact, until the interior rotated into view.

Rooms flickered as their lighting gave up. Jets of fluids whipped out of severed cables and pipes. Melted and torn sections of hull exposed to vacuum. Bodies floated…

It was a UC vessel, I saw then.

I'd love to have lied, even to myself, and say that I'd been planning to try to save the body that had hit my ship, that had left drifting, crystallized blood floating across the void, but I hadn't. I checked quickly; the corpse was already half eaten, and I had to force myself to swing it around, flinging it free to drift with its brethren.

Hopefully they'd be found.

I knew that if they were, as impregnated with nanites as they'd been, they could be recovered. They could live again—as long as I didn't fucking eat them, that was.

Hell, even if they fucking crashed into a planet from orbit, there was a chance they'd recover and come back.

After me feeding on them? Nope.

The shields crackled again, snapping to life. The hull shivered as more and more of the debris that had been bouncing across my hull was shoved free, flung away as I twisted, diving and arcing, and aimed for clear space.

More of the battle became clear as I did so. Huge battleships, three of them, were positioned in a rough triangle. Hundreds of batteries faced inward, bombarding the shit out of the fleet that I'd just appeared in the middle of.

They were Ændari—the battleships, I mean—and beyond them, below and all around were hundreds of smaller ships. I'd appeared in the rear of the UC formation. Their own giants used their overlapping shields to provide limited cover for the smaller ships that hid behind them.

I sensed them as much as saw them, and shook my head at just how lucky we were. Had we emerged on the other side of the fleet, between the two sides and without the shields engaged? We'd have been blasted into atoms in seconds.

Looking at the power that was being unleashed by either side now, even if our shields were up fully, we'd last bare seconds if we'd arrived in the middle of that.

There was just no way.

The missile that had almost fucked us up?

One of thousands that were hurtling back and forth in the darkness—waves of EM interference, gravity bursts, some kind of warp weapons…

Missiles flashed across the distance that separated the two fleets. A section of space twisted and shifted, and hundreds of missiles that were headed to the Ændari fleet were suddenly gone, a tear in space opening to the side of the fleet.

Those same missiles ripped free, catapulting toward the side of the nearest UC capital ship. Shields that were already under strain flared. Defensive turrets were taken down, and a rolling wave of death hammered into the lead ship.

The shields buckled. Missiles that were incoming attempted to self-terminate; engines flared as they tried to redirect. Explosive charges detonated. The missiles tried to kill themselves before they could take out their own fleet, but it was too late.

They were too close, too many, and moving far too fast.

Arise: Conqueror

Almost a third of them impacted the lead ship. Its shields had already been under concentrated fire, the Ændari battleships having been prepared for this. Between the heavy, sustained fire and the storm of missiles that the Ændari had already launched, the massive cylindrical vessel came apart.

Explosions ran its length, ripping free sections. The shields in those sections that hadn't yet given out contained and redirected the fire, trapping it inside for precious seconds until they, too, failed.

Those extra seconds, though, ensured there could be no survivors.

As the capital craft came apart, more and more missiles hit it. Those that were too close to redirect spent themselves in an orgy of destruction, converting the larger sections of hull into smaller, more widely spaced and highly charged shrapnel.

Ships that hadn't been targets yet, that had been hiding in the shadow of the great behemoth, lost their shields and exploded in a firecracker ripple of destruction that sent the entire flank of the UC advance staggering.

The next capital ship in line, a blunt-nosed rectangle that sloped to a sharp point, shifted, arcing over to the side and shoving itself into the oncoming fire.

Its shields flared, shuddered, but held. The smaller vessels, like a school of fish dancing around a whale, dipped and slid under its protection as more and more lasers opened up.

There were hundreds of ships on both sides. Even as this side of the battle shifted and flowed, the other side unleashed hell.

There were so many missiles in flight it made my asshole pucker reflexively—and that was before the Ændari revealed their fucking warp weapon. The only hope I had was that whatever it was that they were using, it was apparently slow to charge and even slower to move.

The next one that flared into being missed most of the incoming missiles, capturing and rerouting barely forty.

That was enough to give the wedge's head a pounding, though, considering that the Ændari battleships were firing lasers as well.

The projectors that were in use had to be almost as big as my ship, and here and there…

The first outflow of controlled plasma hit the wedge full on the bow, exploding and washing over it. Shields flickered and failed. But whatever the Ændari had been expecting, it clearly wasn't for the ship to pick up speed.

The massive engines, four of them on a cross at the rear of the wedge, flared brighter and brighter, so bright I had to look away. It surged forward, as Bach started a litany from behind me.

"Bless their coming and their going. Honor their sacrifice and remember their names. Our brothers and sisters who go into the night, in the full and certain hope that rebirth, though never guaranteed, may be bestowed. They who ask nothing of the universe, save that they be a shield to the night, that they bring the light to the hidden places…"

It went on and on, a litany that repeated, and I heard Zhonat adding his voice to it as well.

The nearest of the Ændari battleships fired its own engines, even as all three focused their fire on the incoming vessel. The bow was shredded, then the main body. Shields failed in relay; the hull gained deep wounds that vomited atmo and bodies. Flames burst from section after section.

Doors and emergency air locks banged open. Escape pods launched in waves, bursting from the hull and rocketing backward as all three battleships focused on a central point in the hull, digging deeper and deeper. The targeted vessel desperately tried to move.

That was the secret to space warfare, I noted, almost absently.

Speed.

If they'd been moving already, they'd have had a chance. As it was, though, there was none.

The incoming fire slowed for a second. Then the impacts tracked back as they apparently gave up on that plan, focusing on two of the starboard engines, clearly trying to take them out to give the ship a twist, maybe even enough to throw it off course.

They were too late. The other engines flared to compensate as the first died, and the ship still closed.

Its massive banks of lasers and missile launchers switched targets. Those that still worked all focused on a single, second target. The rest of the UC vessels had been focused on the battleship as well, and as its shields failed, they too switched to the new target.

That had to be the worst bit, I guessed. Well, apart from the dying. When everyone switched targets, the mauled Ændari vessel was still trying to escape, but everyone knew it was done. That included the Ændari aboard as well, apparently. Like dandelion fluff, the ship was suddenly surrounded by thousands of pods, rocketing free into the void, desperately trying to escape the incoming impact.

Even as the titans of the battle fought it out, their smaller consorts vanished in bright flashes and darkness. Hundreds of missile boats darted forward, great blurs of light lifting into the void and creating miniature galaxies that danced and spun.

The warp weapon appeared, and this time the missiles that sank into it, reappearing on the far side and diving toward another UC behemoth, detonated as soon as they appeared.

The tactic had already been countered, and I shook my head in disgust. Not at the UC; it'd been a damn fast adjustment to make the missiles detonate as soon as they passed through the warp—no.

I was annoyed and dismayed by the usage in the first place.

"It was fucking amateurish." I said that thought aloud, not realizing I'd done so.

"The power it takes is horrific," Zhonat replied.

I frowned, cutting my time compression as his words dopplered. "Can't be that bad, surely?" I blinked as reality sped up again.

"The farther from the ship it activates, the more power and less control is available," he explained. "Everything that passes through the field destabilizes it. I'd bet it's all they can do to make the field appear where it was."

Arise: Conqueror

"Really?" I frowned. "How much power?"

"More than you could generate." He grinned. "No offense, Devourer, but if you could generate that much yourself? You'd not need a ship."

"Maybe not," I muttered. The first beams hit us, and communication requests activated.

"Identify!"

I wasn't willing to waste my time with more explanations. Instead, as Zhonat was still working on the turrets, I slid it to Bach and let him deal with it. I arced the ship sideways, rolling and diving again.

The battle had clearly been going for days, as more of the system finally registered with me.

The largest ships were here. What had been four UC vessels, true behemoths, were now reduced to two, and two of the Ændari were left out of three as the wedge impacted into the side of the third.

The two crumpled around each other for a brief second. Then the explosions started, rippling out from the point of impact, all the way until the reactors went critical. Brief-lived suns flared into existence and returned thousands to the star stuff they were made from.

I was diving into and around the giant hulks that littered the jump point, sensing as I did that the exit point had automatically come at the most "level" point of gravity, and I'd been damn lucky it was behind the current front line.

Elsewhere in the system were more ships. The nearest planet was being used for slingshot maneuvers, its twin moons adding complexity as ships that were barely bigger than fighters zipped and danced, flashing past each other at speeds that had to be AI controlled.

Deeper into the system, more battleships hammered each other. Great drifting hulks rolled, flames and venting atmo sending them off course.

Dozens of huge vessels were reduced to little more than drifting rubble. And even then, still searching the system, I found battles going on across the hulls of dead warships.

Thousands of warriors raced across the great hulls. Lasers and more fired at each other; bodies vanished in silence, as I stared, horrified.

Through it all, in the distance, the node hung. It appeared pristine, even this far out, and yet it was anything but.

The dock was full: two massive cruisers were docked, and a third was pushed to the side, reduced to smoking devastation. A glance was all that it took to identify them.

The original vessel was UC. The second pair, one of which was slowly backing up to make room for a third as I aligned on it, were clearly Ændari.

They had to be boarding the node—they had to be! *Was Ingrid okay? Was she hurt? Dead?* The damn system-wide comm link wasn't responding at all, and the more I tried, the more frustrated I got.

I reached out desperately, linking to the nearest ships, cutting off the conversation between Bach and whoever, as I tried to access the system comms, only to find them disrupted.

"Identify—" they started, and I cut them off.

"Are you jamming the node?"

"Unknown vessel, identify yourself."

"You can see my ship?" I asked grimly.

"I repeat, identify yourself, unknown vessel. You have attempted to claim holy—"

"CAN. YOU. SEE. ME?"

"Yes, unknown vessel." The comm technician sounded disgusted. "I can see you. Now you need to—"

"Then watch me!" I barked. "Watch me, decide which fucking side I'm on, then let me through your fucking jamming field so I can connect to the goddamn system comm link!"

With that, I pulled up, arcing around the end of the hulk I'd been hiding behind, then rocketed out into clear space.

Debris bounced off the shields, causing them to flare constantly. The ship practically looked like I'd installed strobe lighting for shits and giggles.

I locked onto one of the larger "medium" vessels on the far side, a cruiser that had to be three times the size of the warship that James was currently flying…wherever he was. It wasn't getting fired on currently and was only a little off the route I needed. I fired all engines and picked up speed.

"Fucking asshole, little stuck-up shitbag, daring to question *me*…" I muttered grimly. The ship shivered around me as I focused, the first lasers incoming as we picked up more and more speed.

The acceleration of my ship was far beyond the normal. The lasers that were hitting barely scratched the shields at this distance, and I diverted the secondary reactor entirely to the engines, making them flare with an insane brightness.

The speed we were going at doubled as the seconds passed; debris and smaller ships appeared and vanished almost as quickly.

Reactor One had been running the ship on arrival, keeping the standard ship's bits and bobs going with ten units, then ten into the engines. Reactor Two was now entirely pushing the engines as well, giving them thirty units and making it look as if I'd stuck stars on the verge of nova in each engine housing.

Reactor Three was sinking entirely into the cells, keeping them topped off, and they in turn kept the shields full.

Reactor Four was powering the guns, and Bach had come up with a few interesting adjustments for the rail gun shells.

I sank all the power into the adjustments he'd suggested. New shells slid into place, more being produced as the rails heated.

The latest shells weren't complicated—hell, they were probably too simple, really—but they worked.

They were basically nuclear warheads, just with a little tweaking. And yeah, admittedly the ability to create anything pretty much in any shape, as if it'd been done by a 3D printer? Well, that helped.

The lithium deuteride that surrounded the uranium-235 was apparently one of those things that you really didn't want close to you, especially unshielded and if you ever wanted to have children who didn't glow in the dark. But the neutron generator was the hardest part to get right.

Arise: Conqueror

There were several seconds where in the test phase I'd genuinely wondered whether we were going to blow the ship up, and yeah, possibly testing experimental munitions on distant Ændari military targets was a bit of a war crime. Especially when I fired them out of a rail gun that was already basically converting the impact into a nuclear hell storm, but hey.

What's a little war crime between friends?

I locked onto them and opened fire.

These shells were *much* bigger than the others, and they'd needed some changes to be made to the rail guns. So not only were they slower to fire, but they needed a shitload of null coins to make.

They also required a magnetic shield. Literally, a fucking shield for the shell, because otherwise the slightest impact, on say, a bit of space dust, would end the flight real fast.

The four paired shots I'd just launched were half of the remaining ammo we had, but to prove my point, I decided it was worth it.

My little presents took thirty-seven seconds to arrive. Despite launching four sets of two, only three hits actually made it.

Fortunately, the shields were fairly damaged by now, and thanks to the spread from having to individually make the shells, they arrived spread out.

That meant that the first impact took out the remaining shields on the starboard side. As it arrived, there was a bright, eye-shredding blast, and the entire ship rolled slightly off course.

The second shot hit the hull directly, the tip of the shell converting into energy on impact. The second level barely had time to explode, but it was enough to tear the ship a new arsehole.

The third hit the hole, sinking deep into the hull, before sending the ship into the next reality, Viking style.

That was when I noticed that the connection was still live to the comm technician, and he'd gone noticeably quiet.

Apparently, he'd been watching the result.

"Now," I said slowly and as patiently as I could. "Link me to the fucking system comm link. *Please.*"

"My…my c-commander—" he stuttered.

I cut him off. "Is busy, so just fucking do it, all right?" I forced a smile, trying to maintain my patience. My eyes were drawn back to the node, and the latest ship that was even now docking.

They had to be unloading troops. They *had* to be.

"Who is this?" A fresh voice barked into the comm link, and I snarled unthinkingly.

"Who am I? Fuck's sake, we've told your guy… Bach, you told them, right?" I shot him a glare over my shoulder.

"Confirmed, Lord Devourer." Bach nodded. "They chose not to believe me. Although, as this is the first time I have been a personal envoy for the Devourers, I'm afraid I may have been unclear."

"What did you say?"

"I'm the personal envoy of the Lord Devourer Steve. Get out of our way and stop pestering us."

"Seems simple enough," I muttered, glancing back at the link. An image had been included now.

It wasn't overly helpful, considering that the figure standing before me took up half my vision, and I was twisting my ship to avoid space debris, but that's life.

He wore an ornate military outfit, all burnished gold and platinum, white epaulettes and red accents on forest green.

"This is a military channel. If you've chosen to assist the UC military in this fight, you have our thanks, but—and understand this is the only warning you will get—you will make no further demands on my crew's time. The system comm links are blocked from all sides. And even if they were not, no civilian would be granted access to them in times of war. Contact your existing chain of command for further orders, and fall back. Resume your place in the fleet and hold the line. Serve with honor, and perhaps your claim of being a Devourer will be forgotten."

The little prick cut the line.

I stared at the "end transmission" symbol that rolled across the feed, before tearing the connection apart with a snarl of fury.

"He was correct on one point," Zhonat said suddenly, and I bit back a cutting comment.

"What?" I asked.

"The system comm link. I thought it was being jammed by the UC, but it's not. It's there—it's just not accepting any connections."

"And yet this asshole hangs up on me?" I muttered, shaking my head. "Fine, fuck this."

The shields were getting hit repeatedly, dipping slowly. But as I pulled ahead of the wave of the fleet, more and more of the larger ships targeted me.

That was when I found the mines.

The first read like debris, and I'd rolled to the side, flashing past it almost too fast for it to register. Then, as it vanished behind me, exploding a split second later, I realized what it was.

"Mines!" I snarled. "Fuck's sake, they're targeting us!"

"Starting transmission," Zhonat said quickly, and I bit down on the need to question him. Thankfully, he spoke up a second later. "Transmitting now. I cut the transmission when I saw we were behind UC lines. I didn't want them to identify the signal and think we were the enemy."

"Makes sense," I admitted grudgingly. "Send the code to the UC. Fuckers might at least listen to that…"

I rolled the ship sideways again, this time triggering gravity bubbles ahead of me, staggered to the left and right, holding them two seconds then cutting them. Anything in my direct path was dragged to the sides, giving me precious seconds as more and more fire tracked me.

The shields flared constantly now, the charge level bouncing like a hooker's headboard, and the power cells storage levels were being steadily depleted. I cut the power to the engines by ten units, feeding that into the cells instead, and saw them climbing again.

That was the "joy" of space travel: once you were up to speed, you didn't need to keep pouring energy into the engines. There was nothing but gravity to slow you, after all—or the debris and mines that filled the plot now, but that was a separate issue.

No, I could afford to cut the engine power, because even with less power feeding the engines now than before, I was still accelerating.

The other option, of course, would be to take power from the guns, but that was just crazy talk.

"Bach, you're on turrets. If they won't listen, then ignore those useless UC fuckheads and fire." I ordered him over my shoulder, hearing him halfway through the explanation about the mines.

He finished in a rush, then cut the connection, the turrets already all swinging around as he slaved them to his viewpoint.

"We're going to pass through the field to the right of that one…" I tagged a ship that was listing and spouting flames for him. "I want you to make sure the fuckers are dead."

He grunted.

A marker appeared in my vision to denote the distance, and I flicked the settings, changing the rounds to more normal tungsten penetrators, and reloaded the rail guns. The null coins I had left were seriously limited, and I cursed myself for letting them get so low.

Even changing to these instead of the massive nuclear rounds, I had less than fifty to go, but maybe…no. I shook myself and twisted again, dipping down around a particularly large section of hulk that was drifting past, figures still fighting on its hull.

There was so much I could do. These hulks, literally being abandoned in space, dead, could provide the matter we needed easily. I could cover them in nanites, order them to make a battleship that had twenty meters of solid nefindium armoring and cannons that could destroy the sun; then I could just take out the entire fleet on my own, no worries.

It would just take time. So. Much. Time.

That was the one thing I didn't have, and every second that passed, I was getting closer and closer to losing Ingrid, possibly forever.

I burst from cover again. The lasers that had lost me behind the wreck slid around to retarget again, and this time I was in range of some of the enemy smaller ships as well.

Two closed on me from ahead, clearly a standard design: three fins deployed equidistantly around the base of what looked like a rocket, and lasers spread around the nose firing directly ahead.

I pulled up, twisted and sighted on the nearest; its own lasers stitched their way across space, closing on me. I squeezed the trigger. Lasers flashed, then blinked as four more sets of laser light shot out, the turrets all synced in.

The first exploded. The second broke off and rolled, vanishing behind a wreck, and I twisted, diving after it.

There were more ahead, smaller UC fighters chasing them already, and mines exploded here and there as they got too close. I rolled, sighting in, firing and missing, snarling. The one I was chasing rolled again, moving back up and around into the shadow of another wreck.

"Devourer." Bach spoke up. "They appear to be drones, designed with limited offensive capabilities, but working to lead the UC vessels into the minefield. I recommend resuming course and I will track them with turrets."

I cursed, then broke off, nodding. The ship hummed as the turrets twisted and fired, still tracking them.

"Pass the word to the UC," I forced myself to say, not wanting to, but also not willing to let people die just because I was annoyed with their stupid bureaucracy.

Both sides had massive capital ships, large and medium cruisers, fighter and drone platforms. Those were the most concerning, because at this distance they were barely identifiable. But one of the larger ships, presumably a carrier, was vomiting more waves of tiny dots into space.

"Attention all vessels, prepare for incoming waves. Coordinate defensive turrets—"

It was another random communications officer, sounding harried and confused. I cut the transmission off with a snarl, seeing just how many ships were being deployed. As the seconds passed, I had less and less options now, and the Ændari continued to fill space with these tiny little bastards.

I could try to go around, or I could go through—that was it, basically… because there was fuck all chance I wasn't going to her.

CHAPTER TWENTY

The only other option was that I turn tail, head back to the UC formation and hide among them, and we use our automated turrets to take down the incoming waves of whatever they were.

I didn't see the Ændari just waiting for that to happen, and no doubt there'd be another trick behind it, then another. Both sides were hammering each other, and neither had a real advantage.

I wasn't exactly experienced in space combat, but even I could see that there were problems with this fight.

The UC BWVs were a tightly compressed cohesive force, but they were currently being sacrificed as rotating shields. The Ændari looked to have a similar design of ships, but only a few of them, and they were deeper into the system, currently chasing a handful of UC vessels that were being steadily overhauled.

The fleet here… I rolled and dove, twisting around another large collection of mines, space around me currently filled with them, and Zhonat spoke up from behind me, disgustedly.

"The outer edge of the fleet just hit the minefield."

"What?"

"The minefield. They hit it, and the lead ships are getting wiped out."

"Are you fucking kidding me?" I snarled. "They didn't listen?"

"Apparently not."

Bach bit the words off with such anger I almost turned around. For a handful of seconds, I fought with myself, weaving in and out as I tried to come up with another option.

"Bach, as Devourer…will the BWVs obey me?" I bit my lip.

"You have rank equal to the admiral of the fleet," he said after a few seconds. "I would not recommend a battle to take command of the fleet at this time."

"I know!" I bit out. It was bloody stupid to do so, but also the fleet here was getting wiped out. "They're flying into a damn minefield, though!" I snapped. "Are they broadcasting the code?"

"Negative."

"Fuck!" I roared. "Try again. No, hell with it, I'll try!"

I reached out. The communications links defaulted and redirected me as I targeted what I assumed was the flagship. Links connected and disengaged, valuable seconds being lost, until finally it connected, and the same harried comm technician from earlier appeared before me.

"This line is to be kept clear at all…eeep!" He'd not been looking, staring at something to one side, and when he'd seen me, he'd cut off, clearly not sure what to do.

I had to assume they'd seen the weapons I'd used before, and either this little bastard was now convinced that I was what I claimed, or they at least weren't willing to argue it, just in case.

In any event, the screen blinked, then I was staring at the same fancy-pants asshole I'd seen before. And now he was on the verge of spitting feathers.

"You *again*?!" he snarled. "I gave you an order, free-booter! Get back in line and obey the orders of your betters, or I swear I'll have you in the brig and that ship given to someone who can!"

With that, the connection cut off.

"Oh, you fucking did *not* just hang up on me *again*," I snarled. "Fuck this shit!"

Bach had been controlling the turrets in a blur. Lasers flashed in all directions; drones and occasional missiles vanished as I wove in and out. But now I pulled around hard, aiming for the nearest Ændari ship.

I took out my anger on it, snarling as I vented, ripple-firing the lasers over and over as my shields bounced from the incoming fire of others.

It wasn't as good as literally stabbing some fucker in the face, but it was still a little relief. I forced myself to get my anger under control before I reached out again, this time activating the Hack sub-mind and punching a break into the comm system.

It went haywire. The carefully choreographed filtering programs freaked out as they identified an enemy hack, attempting to shut it down.

Links started to go active, then targeting warnings came up—a shitload of them—and they were almost all coming from behind me as the UC fleet locked onto the intrusion.

"Fucking hell, all I wanted was someone with a goddamn brain!" I snarled.

A new face appeared, my own hack being torn out of the communications net in a sudden purge.

"This is Second Spear Raimos, Communications Commander of the UC deployment *Shield of the Union*, to all inhabitants of unknown vessel X-237. You will take your captain into custody immediately and—"

He stared at me as I flooded my skin with the Devourer coating and apparently noticed for the first time that the pair of figures seated behind me were clearly in UC soldier armor.

"Listen to me, you little prick," I hissed out between gritted teeth. "I am Steve, the Devourer who started this entire fight off and who summoned you all! I've been trying to give you the codes to stop the mines targeting the fleet, and to get linked into the communications net for the system and the fight, but your people keep threatening ME!"

Arise: Conqueror

His mouth hung slightly ajar as he clearly tried to decide whether this was a trick, or whether I really was a Devourer.

"You don't know me, and I don't give two shits about your opinion, but if my people die because I'm wasting time trying to protect your stupid arses, I'll rip your heads off and shit down your necks!"

"Lord Devourer—" He broke off to lick his lips. "Ah, if you could provide some proof—"

"You can see me?" I snapped.

"The visual record could be tampered with…" he pointed out.

Even as angry as I was, I got that. I'd done similar shit to the Ændari already, after all.

"Fine!" I snarled. "You want proof? Cut me a goddamn path into the middle of the enemy!"

I cut the communication link—hanging up on *them* this time—and cut the power to the guns, diverting it all to the shields and engines. The ship leapt forward again.

The incoming lasers were hammering me now, and flights of missiles were being flushed from the remaining battleship. The carriers that flanked it shifted and started to turn away, their own racks presumably already emptied as whatever they'd been launching dribbled to a stop.

"You want proof?" I muttered under my breath. "Proof that I'm not a fucking Ændari, that I'm a Devourer and you should never have fucked with me? Fine. I'll give you proof, all right!"

The Ændari battleship was almost eclipsed behind the swarm that rose up now. Tens of thousands of tiny ships, drones, missiles, and more filled space between us.

My shields had surged to full again, but as I closed with them, the incoming fire started to cut through them. The distances in space meant that only either the bigger ships could reach me out here, or the very closest of the smaller ones.

The lasers were only so powerful, after all, and the distances between them and me had meant that for every hundred shots fired at me, just a handful actually hit.

The closer I got, though, arcing up out of the debris fields and blasting through the remains of the minefield into the open, meant that the blasts that had been absorbed by everything else were finally free to get me.

The power cells were dropping again, and hard: ninety percent, eighty-three, seventy-six…

As soon as they ran dry, the shields would be next. At this rate, a speed that was only increasing as I got closer to the enemy fleet, they'd last seconds.

As much as my little ship was awesome, it wasn't invincible, and neither was it magic.

It was essentially a seriously strong heavy fighter. Although a heavy fighter might be able to take out a battleship, or even a weak fighter might take down a Death Star with a handy exhaust port and a proton torpedo…it wasn't going to survive this for long.

"Power cells are at forty percent," Zhonat announced, and I grunted. "Diverting additional power from ship general systems, shutting down non-essentials…"

Then I cut the engines from thirty units to five, rerouting all that glorious power into *me*.

"Time to play, bitches," I hissed.

The power that flooded the crystal pillar and then into me was almost enough to blow my mind. My nanites quaked as they tried to divert and accommodate it. But as quickly as it arrived, it was gone, fed into the building warp.

I could jump, I knew I could, but the system being as cluttered as it was, it was even odds I'd come out of the warp where I needed to be, or halfway through a planet or a ruined ship.

The risk was almost worth it. I could feel the potential, that making the jumps I needed were only just beyond me now, and that I was getting closer, but not yet. Right now, if I did it, I damn well knew I wasn't ready.

What I was ready for, though?

Gravity.

The power flooded into me at a horrific speed, and I was using it as fast as it came. I'd needed tools when I'd first started to control the gravity around me. Then, as time went on, I'd found that I was only consciously using those devices when I reached for bigger and bigger things.

I was entirely nanite-based now: my body, my mind… everything that made me, me. I was infused into every nanite that I controlled, and they were tiny, insanely small, and intensely powerful.

They each manipulated gravity to split apart the atoms and molecules they needed to work on. With that realization, I'd understood that when I'd been shifting things since my change, I'd done it all with my mind.

So, instead of forming a single giant gravitational manipulation device, I connected to the nanites that I'd pulled into the hull. I fed the power into them all, sending them out across its surface and setting them ready for the next phase.

The first gravity bubble that spun up started at ten, then quickly ramped up to a hundred gravities projected ahead of me, a bare dozen miles.

The ships and debris that were just entering that area, closing on me almost too fast to see, exploded in a vast, fiery wave.

Then the second and third appeared.

I shifted them and formed a triangle; each overlapped at the center, forming a nexus that shredded everything that came near it.

I kept the three points held in place ahead of me. As we flashed forward, more and more of the enemy fleet fell into it.

The gravitational nexus was building, accelerating, and in seconds, as both sides tore in toward the same point, the explosions grew.

The fleet behind me had ceased fire for several seconds, their comm link needing to reestablish. Then they'd started to fire again, focusing on the battleship, with a small number targeting the incoming waves.

Arise: Conqueror

As I shredded the wave in the center, the torn, battered, and compressed fragments of their former friends were flung out from the edges and back at them.

Shields failed, missiles exploded, and all around me, the wave was torn apart.

The warp grew as I punched through the middle, erupting into clear space. The nexus started to shift from taking the power I was feeding it, to starting to generate its own. I snarled, twisting the feed and cutting the three bubbles.

They resisted for a few seconds; a cold fist seemed to clamp around my heart, before they shivered and dissipated.

I'd nearly created a fucking wormhole, I realized.

A hole in space that led who knew where—and I'd nearly created it, trying to feed my enemies into a sausage grinder.

It'd worked, though. As I broke off the connection, the last of the gravitational distortion twisting space and time ahead of me, I cut the shields, rolling the ship onto a new course.

The ion engines were easily hidden. The nanites around them formed boxy structures that caught the stray emissions, tearing them apart and hiding the signal. As the expanding wave of devastation settled, we were on a new course, heading to the node at a horrific speed. My Conceal ability made me literally vanish into the black.

Then I sent a tight beam and private connection to the guy who had taken over the last attempt at communication, the "Second Spear," and damn, he looked at me differently as I glared at him now.

"Well?" I snapped.

"Lord Devourer…" He swallowed. "I regret that events required you to be contacted by one such as I. I am charged with maintaining the integrity of the fleet's communications, and—"

"And I don't blame you." I grunted. "I blame the stupid fuck who kept threatening me and refusing to listen when my people tried to explain the situation. Bach, you get the contact details for that prick?"

"Attaching to the link now, Lord," he said, deadpan. "I have also included the records of the communication by his officer, the codes for the mines, and the likely numbers of losses inflicted on our fleet by his apparent refusal to share such details."

"Good man. Right—you're Raimos, right?" I asked.

"Yes, Lord De—"

"No time for that shit," I snapped. "Is the system comm network down? We tried to access it."

"The Ændari have activated a suppression field around the node," he replied quickly. "One of the ships in its immediate vicinity is maintaining it, reducing the operational capacity of all in the system."

"Can the Ændari reach the network?" I asked, thinking fast.

"Unknown, but unlikely," he admitted. "We've lost contact with all inside the node."

"Who was there?"

"We dispatched a warship to the node with a full brigade of assault troops to assist in the node's defense. The warship was destroyed as it docked. A stealthed vessel unloaded a broadside of missiles as its shield dropped for landing. We have no way of knowing how many survived."

"And the people on the node?" I asked grimly.

"Again, unknown. My apologies, Lord Devourer, but the only contact we've had with your team aboard the node was prior to the suppression field's activation. They were—at that time—preparing defenses to hold the enemy back. I know no more."

I gritted my teeth, barely suppressing a need to scream swearwords as loudly as I could. Instead, I made small changes to the directions, and carefully kept the engines just below the point that the nanites wouldn't be able to hide their emissions.

We were going fast, insanely so. Probably the fastest any natural-born human from Earth for thousands of years had gone, and yet it wasn't enough.

I needed to go faster. More and more, I was thinking I needed to try to use the gravity jump.

I could warp space easily enough now, after all. *Could the wormholes help? Could I punch a hole in space here and direct it to there?*

No, that was madness. I had no clue what the hell I was doing with that shit, and neither did I have the faintest clue how I'd direct the other end.

Hell, for all I knew, the other end would come out at the edge of a black hole and that'd be that.

"Devourer Shan'Gai."

"What?" I asked, suddenly realizing I'd totally zoned out.

"Ah, I said that Lord Devourer Shan'Gai is due to arrive at any time, my lord. That was most likely why my technicians refused to believe you. They were aware that Devourer Shan'Gai was on their way, and that, my apologies, you were clearly not them."

"Shan'Gai is coming here?" I asked again, leaping onto that fact. A *real* Devourer. One who was around when Zhonat and Bach and the others were out doing whatever—one of them was coming, and that was fucking fantastic news. They'd be able to sort all this shite out; they could wipe the floor with the Ændari, and I could focus on the node.

"It has been confirmed. The Lord Devourer is coming. But alas, I cannot be sure they will arrive in time. All that we have is that they will arrive 'soon.'"

"Fuck. Well, I guess that's better than nothing," I muttered. "Okay, we know that the ships that have docked with the node will be unloading troops—no point in them docking otherwise. Can you deal with this?" I gestured vaguely at the fight I was soon to leave behind.

"Affirmative, Lord Devourer." He nodded. "The admiral has been holding back to lure the Ændari in close enough. Main weapons are powering, ready to fire now."

"Good. Wait, what's the—"

The main weapons of the fleet were apparently lasers.

Arise: Conqueror

Meh, a bit uninspired as far as that went, considering that we'd barely been a galactic menace for a month now and we already had much more creative weapons. But the minor difference between their lasers and ours?

Size.

I've heard people say that size doesn't matter before. Hell, I've heard it from men and women, in a variety of different ways and for different reasons.

I've said it myself. Although I'd never had an issue "there," if I was entirely honest with myself, I'd been tempted to add an extra inch—or three—now and then, since the upgrade.

I'd always been able to "helicopter" instead of merely "light switch," but what guy didn't consider that, right?

The only thing was, in comparison to this laser? Mine was pathetic. Hell, it wasn't even in the same league. This wasn't a laser; this was a star trapped and fed into a lens, then fired across the cosmos.

There was a single shot, that was all. The second ship that tried to fire suddenly shook, surrounded by gasses as something went wrong and an emergency feature activated. The ship went dark, drifting as the crew presumably scrambled to fix whatever had gone wrong. But the shot that they did get off?

It was one of the cylinder ships. One end had opened, and the blast that ripped across space to hammer into the remaining battleship was just terrifying.

The shields just…vanished. There wasn't a hint of them being active, and the beam tore from about two-thirds of the way down the hull on the starboard side, all the way through to the far side, in a heartbeat.

The remainder of the battleship held itself together for all of three seconds, before exploding.

With the center of their formation entirely missing, and the majority of their advance ships shredded by a mysterious—*ah thank you ver' much*—gravity weapon, the remainder of the fleet broke ranks in seconds.

Ships blinked out, warping out of the system. The Lagrange point covered just enough of space nearby for their gravity drives to enable their escape.

As more and more tried to run, the UC fleet disintegrated as well. Hundreds of ships rippled free of the cohesive whole, racing into the void to try to chase down their enemy.

"What the hell?" I muttered. "Uh, Raimos, what happened to the fleet?"

"We've dispersed the majority of it to aid the remaining UC vessels in-system," he assured me. "The core of the fleet will remain together, and we will assist survivors to face the larger Ændari ships. But most of the fleet will help to chase down the stragglers."

"But…" I struggled to put into words how wrong that felt, before shaking my head. "Whatever. It helps me, anyway. I need you to send more troops to the node."

"Ah… I can dispatch two additional assault brigades to assist, but not until the remaining capital ships of the Ændari have been eliminated, I'm afraid. The admiral has already made that clear to me, that no further troops are to be dispatched to the node. Those already aboard are it, unless…"

"Unless?"

"Those who held the node previously refused a…" He paused, clearly pulling up something and reading off the prompt. "A most reasonable request made by the Lord Emberalis, High Seat of the House of Paendrag, Guide of the Eastern Marches, He Who—"

"Oh, that dickhead," I muttered darkly. "What does he want?"

Raimos almost swallowed his tongue, clearing his throat before going on.

"High Admiral Emberalis has requested that due consideration be given to those who risk their immortal lives in an attempt to protect and preserve others, that's all. There was a most reasonable request—"

"Cut the bullshit and tell me what he wants," I snapped.

"Ah…ah…" His eyes darted from side to side.

I sighed as it finally all made sense. "He's there with you now or he's watching this transmission, isn't he?"

"Ah…"

"Emberalis, get your arse on here," I snarled. "I've got no time for this bullshit, and I'm already in a bad mood."

"When are you not?" the newcomer asked sourly. The screen flickered as Raimos vanished, only to be replaced with the image of Emberalis, slouched in a contoured chair, a bridge behind him clear.

I also noticed in the back of the image, what looked to be Raimos slumping in relief.

"I'm generally happy and cheerful, actually," I said flatly. "I tend to be in a bad mood when people try to take advantage of me. So, what do you want, Emberalis?"

"Very well, let us dispense with the pleasantries." Emberalis forced a smile. "So, despite your rudeness, we dispatched forces to assist you here, and even brought the fleet, choosing to back you, to protect our Forgeworld cousins. Then, despite all these horrific losses we sustained, co-leader Ingrid refused to permit my people to lay equal claim to the node, nor to even—"

"Of course." I shrugged.

"Of course?"

"Of course she said no."

"We have lost hundreds of ships and outrageous numbers of resources, as well as thousands of lives to defend you! The Right Hand of Man has been weakened horribly by this. Our choosing to assist our cousins may end us as a power in the galaxy, and all you have to say is 'of course'?" he hissed.

"Yeah." I leaned forward, making sure that he could see me clearly. "Listen, Emberalis, I've spent the last few weeks in a deep-space trap—no food, no water, barely any sleep. The first thing I find when I get here is that the goddamn fleet that *should* be helping to maintain the system and defending, literally, the one thing that stands between the Ændari and total victory, is getting mauled."

"We lost thousands!" he snapped.

"Yeah, you did. And, speaking as a soldier, and as someone who's fought on the front line all my fucking life, I *care* about those lives. You? The first thing you complained about was losing ships and resources. You complained about the cost and the possible loss of what you think is your 'rightful' fucking place. You don't give two shits about the people who died, you just want more power!"

"Will you share control of the node?" He glared at the screen.

"With you?" I asked, pretending to consider it.

"Yes!"

"Fuck no! I'd sooner slather my balls in meat paste and dip them in a tank of fucking piranha. I'd rather slide down a rusty sword and use my dick as a brake! I'd—"

He cut the connection.

I stared at the screen, seething inwardly, unable to believe that the little shit was so petty, so…

The reflection of the diamond glass that covered the cockpit shifted slightly. I glanced into it, seeing for the first time that both Zhonat and Bach were staring at me, and I drew in a haggard breath.

I forced myself to run the conversation I'd just had through my mind, and yeah.

I was out of line.

As much as I hated it, I was out of line. And although I wanted to rant and rave, to tell him exactly what I thought of the little bastard…I literally just had.

I'd let my anger, my irritation, and the fear that something had happened to Ingrid rear its head, and this was the result.

I forced myself to reach out, forming a new connection to the fleet. I was going to have to apologize, and—

"What the…?"

The connection had dropped, and all the ships back there were shifting.

Their formerly green markers, the "allied" tag that kept them from accidentally getting me in the crossfire, were vanishing.

"Shit," I whispered, eyes widening. "Oh no, no, you fucking didn't…"

I checked my notifications. Nothing was showing up, not even the notification for getting back to the Scorpio system, which I'd been expecting to have at least been there.

Then the fleet's signals started to ripple again, going from the grey of neutral…to the red of enemies.

CHAPTER TWENTY-ONE

If I'd not been stealthed to buggery already, I would be shitting myself a lot more, but I still twisted the ship and moved onto a new path just in case.

Then I sat there, cursing myself for my stupidity, as the entire system slowly turned red.

I was literally marked as an enemy for everyone here now, and I didn't know what to do. I tried to reach out to the nearest ship, thinking to bypass the dickhead and try to explain, only to have it automatically refuse the connection.

It didn't even ask for verification, or listen at all. It was like I was beaming a signal at a sheet of steel. Nothing, nada.

I was in so much trouble now.

"Umm, Steve?" Zhonat said after a few seconds. "I'm intercepting some communications…"

"Yeah?" My heart lifted slightly, thinking that maybe I'd just made a mistake and they were reaching out anyway.

"We've just been declared traitors."

"*WHAT?*" I gasped.

"The fleet are claiming that we're traitors, and we just attempted an attack. We apparently tried to take their shields down during the fight."

"That's bullshit!" I complained, outraged.

"They're saying that the attempt damaged the communications system and cost hundreds of lives."

My stomach sunk, ready to drop out of the bottom of the ship and be left behind.

The hot rise of my anger also chilled right down, and the forging heat grew cold and crystal calm.

"He's declared me a traitor," I repeated carefully. "The little… Emberalis has declared *me* a traitor? Fine."

"Lord Devourer?" Bach spoke up. "While I know that there is no way that anyone who knows you would believe this…" He trailed off, clearly unsure where to go from there.

Arise: Conqueror

"But the fleet doesn't know me," I said flatly. "And yeah, I hacked their communications because they wouldn't speak to me. Motherfuckers have got me there."

"What do we do?" Bach asked calmly. "Do we attempt to take control of the flagship?"

"Tempting," I admitted, nodding. "Fucking tempting."

"For three of us, that would be unlikely to be a success," Zhonat said firmly. "I mean no offense, Steve, but unless you are willing to kill the current crew, I don't see how we would take control of the ship. And should you be willing to take such a step, to attack our fellows in such a way…"

"You'd not stay with me," I finished for him, before holding up a hand to stop him as he started to speak. "Don't worry," I assured him. "I'm an asshole, and yeah, my mouth tends to be engaged before my brain, I know, but no. If I did that, I'd be no better than him, and that's not the best way to deal with this shit."

"Oh?"

"All we have to do is get to the node, get control of the system communications again, and I can bypass that little shit entirely, and show people what he's doing."

"And the ships between us and there, and the forces that are docked?"

"We kill them," I said, shrugging to get a bit more comfortable. "We kill them *all*."

"I approve of this plan," Bach muttered. "I know you do not require my approval, Lord De—"

"No, I like getting it. Let's go kill them all." I checked out the ships that were closest as we tore through space, almost silently.

The hull wasn't entirely hidden by the Conceal effect. I was too short of nanites to manage that, despite the insane numbers I had now at my disposal, but most of it was coated.

That meant that what did register for anyone looking was a collection of tiny fragments of hull, most likely appearing to be scrap.

That let us get past several lines of enemy ships that cut across our path, and close enough that the three ships that were currently surrounding the node were totally unprepared for me, as I pulled the nanite coating from the hull, activated the shields, and opened fire.

Or so I thought.

As soon as the stealth field dropped and I locked onto them, the nearest ship opened fire.

Lasers bit into the hull, even as my own tore out as well. Lasers battled across the short distance as I bore down on them, cursing. My shields were barely rising before they were knocked out, and their own were flaring but holding under my laser barrage.

The starboard rail gun shivered as it belched shell after shell downrange, hammering into the shields bare seconds after launch, making them flare, buckle, then finally fail.

The port rail gun exploded, enemy lasers having cut into it, and the released energy was probably all that kept us alive, as the ship was violently shoved sideways.

My own shots hammered into the enemy hull again, tearing a line of destruction as the lasers bored over and over. Their shields flickered as my own snapped into place and staved off a second round of hits, although only just.

The Ændari vessel shuddered as a shell hit something vulnerable, and then, finally, the range finder confirmed that the storm caster was ready.

I squeezed the trigger, and it tore free, digging into the hull and shredding it, drilling deeper and deeper. Lasers followed it, even as all four turrets shifted, no longer peppering the enemy hull, and instead locking onto and firing at seemingly empty space to our left.

It hit something, though. A second ship shivered into sight, its stealth field disrupted.

That was the real weakness of stealth, I knew, as I pivoted my ship, dragging the nose around to face the appearing enemy. To maintain stealth, you couldn't have shields active. They created a disruption of space that was all too clear to anyone looking. Although you could have the energy ready to slam into the weapons, as soon as they actually fired, that fucked up the stealth field as well.

I knew that there were more options down the Conceal path, and I was going to damn well take them until I could strike from the shadows fully.

Either way, though, the first target was listing, explosions rocking it as it turned, trying to get away from me. And thanks to Bach spotting the stealthed vessel, I had the second fucker in my sights before it could get its shields up.

The lasers were already ripping the hull up when the lightning storm was unleashed, tearing into the hull and blackening it. Then four of my remaining slugs punched into the hull, each exploding with incredible force.

The first hit the bulky, rectangular vessel on the port side, pounding in the thick armoring. Cracks cascaded out, atmo venting uncontrollably.

The bulkhead doors didn't get the chance to seal and save the crew; the second shell landed, smashing into the damaged side of the vessel and punching deeper.

It was mainly converted into energy on impact, but enough survived to release the tungsten penetrator, sinking further into the hull.

Walls and decks were destroyed; bright flashes of electrical energy escaped; screaming bodies were ripped out into the vacuum. And then the third shell hit.

It punched through the hull a meter or so from the first, converting itself into energy as it hit the inside, and damn. It was like someone had stuffed a firecracker into a Lego model.

The upper floor and the lower were blasted away from the impact. Cracks ran the length of the ship, walls were vaporized, and flesh-and-blood creatures…

They didn't fare well.

The fourth shell was probably overkill, as it practically hit the far side of the hull before going off. When it did, though, it was definitely the end of the stealth ship.

Arise: Conqueror

I twisted the ship further around, pointing the engines at the node, and fired them as hard as I could to try to decelerate.

There was no way this was going to be enough, I knew. The closeness of the ships to the node had meant that I couldn't just do this before the fight, and that meant that I wasn't even slightly surprised as the node shot past me.

I still damn well cursed, though, as I tried to slow, imagining that I could almost sense her.

Then I was past. The ship's engines were firing hard enough that the entire ship creaked and groaned as I triggered gravity bubble after bubble, using them both to repulse and to attract, the former behind me, and the latter between me and the node.

It helped, but not enough.

Space was still blurring, and as the speed came down, farther and farther, I saw the second of the ships docked on the node launching.

There was one staying there, presumably to provide support. Then, as I watched, it too started to move.

I opened fire, not too much, and aimed—more carefully than I normally did—for mid-ships, planning to do enough damage as quick as possible that it'd be out of the fight, but not damage the node by exploding…hopefully.

That, of course, was when I found the second minefield.

They went off.

My ship bucked wildly. Pyramidical metal flew inward from all sides as more and more mines activated. The entire field went live in a spreading wave of pinpricks of light.

"We're broadcasting!" Zhonat assured me, sounding stressed. "They've changed the code!"

My shots hit the side of the rearmost ship then, and were absorbed by the shield, making me curse even more.

"She's doubled strength to the port shield," Zhonat barked. "We'll need time or concentrated fire to wear them down. They were already at full power."

"Who the hell keeps their shields up waiting in dock?" I shook my head. "Or puts a goddamn second minefield around the node?"

"Someone who's expecting us," Bach growled suddenly. "I'm detecting scatter from a high-powered laser communication."

"Where?" Zhonat asked, as I fought with my ship, robbing from the power cells against my better judgment to feed it into the lasers. I was already out of range for the storm casters, and I was down to a handful of matter, barely enough to make a dozen penetrators, or…

I cursed, feeding the plan for the nuclear shell into the maker, confirming the shell was loaded into the rail gun ten seconds later.

I was almost out of range of the lasers, and my enemies' shields were borderline—still up, but only just.

I hesitated, then fired, putting everything into the last barrage.

The ship shuddered. It was maybe a hundred meters off the dock now, turning to face me. The shields flickered and crackled as they teetered along the edge of failure…

Then the single remaining shell arrived.

It hit high on the front-port quadrant, and the entire front section of the ship vanished in a bright-white flare. The ship reeled as though it'd been hit with the hammer of the gods.

I grinned savagely as it spun, venting and failing, and crashed into the second ship, as it tried to leave the dock as well.

I pushed harder and harder at the engines; then, cursing, let up the pressure.

The engines were redlining; stress markers and warnings proliferated through my vision. I gritted my teeth, watching as my speed decreased.

Three minutes it took to reach zero, and another ten to make it back to the node. By that point, the last ship had left the dock entirely, firing a barrage of three balls of plasma, making me curse again as it also deployed something else.

Behind the rapidly approaching balls of plasma, a flash of light filled space. Dozens of small devices were fired in a halo pattern by the ship, before they exploded.

Whatever they were, they released waves of disruption, light, electrical bursts, radiation…everything.

The third plasma blast was caught in the rear by it and exploded, adding to the confusion. I opened fire on the incoming first and second ball, focusing on them with laser fire and then, when they were within range, the storm casters.

I managed to break the foremost blast apart. The dissipating cloud spread out, before the second, which I'd only managed to weaken, hit the nose.

The ship was hurtled off course. Electrical discharge fried the hull, and plasma burned into the shields and dropped them faster and harder than underwear at 4AM.

The blast dug into the armoring, and I howled. My nanites that still coated the hull died in great swathes. The sticky, horrific plasma seemed to burn into me…before finally, blessedly, it died away.

The ship that had fired it, though? That fucker was gone.

I seethed, staring and speaking fast as I started to search, my remaining nanites out on the hull flowing around to repair as much as they could.

"Find them," I snarled. "I want those fuckers…"

"Searching now," Zhonat said quickly, and with a grunt, Bach agreed as well, speaking up a few seconds later.

"It's a different kind of stealth," he declared.

"What?"

"The stealth—I spotted the last one because it leaked. The hull was coated in something, but it was thin. This one? It's different. No emissions, nothing I can see above the background radiation yet anyway."

"Motherfuckers," I growled. "What about that scattered comm laser? Where was that coming from?"

"It…it came from the fleet," Zhonat admitted. "Someone was sending data to the Ændari."

"Oh, you fucking shitbag," I whispered, shaking my head. "Emberalis, I'm going to fucking gut you, slowly."

Arise: Conqueror

"Regardless of who did it, we're not going to catch them easily," Zhonat said a few seconds later as I slowly pushed the engines higher and higher, approaching the node again. "You need to decide, Steve—do we hunt the stealth ship, or do we dock?"

"I…" I hesitated, for the first time torn. The all-consuming need to reach Ingrid was almost overpowering. If we docked now while that fucker was out there, that left not only my ship defenseless, as we'd need to leave it docked while we roamed the station, but the jamming field would still be active.

If I docked, I could go to Ingrid, but I might lose the war if somehow Emberalis managed to turn the entire fleet against us all.

If I stayed out here? Not only could Ingrid and the others die—if they hadn't already, that was—but the Ændari might take the node and find a way to shut down all our nanites.

I was damned if I did and damned if I didn't. That left me one choice, and it was a shitty one.

"I'm boarding the node," I said flatly, before turning to face the other two. "But you're not."

"What?" Zhonat asked, confused.

"Are we to fight in your stead?" Bach asked, and I nodded.

"The ship is capable of being piloted like a normal one, more or less, and you know the power transfer systems already, Zhonat. If you work together, you should be able to fly the ship, Bach, and find that bastard."

"Lord Devourer…" Bach started, shaking his head. "I'm no pilot…"

"Then you'll learn," I said. "If we dock, they'll pound the ship to rubble. They've already done it once."

We all looked at the remains of the shattered UC warship that took up a third of the dock, heavily damaged and still blazing in places.

"If we land and they do that to this ship? We can't send out any signals. If we can't do that…the fleet out here thinks we're all traitors, and with that, if Saryet and the dwarfen jump and don't get the message and instead jump into the system in Ændari vessels?

"They're not due for hours yet, maybe even a day, but when they do get here? The fleet won't ask them if they're Ændari or not. At best, they'll fire on them and they'll be forced to run. At worst? They declare they're loyal to me, and then they're taken entirely by surprise when the fleet opens fire on them. Not to mention showing up aboard Ændari vessels just adds another nail in my fucking coffin with the fleet," I finished bitterly.

"No, there's no choice. Hopefully you'll be able to come for me. You'll find that ship, blast the shit out of it, and we can sort all this out; then the fleet comes screaming in and helps us to kick the rest of the Ændari out of here. But at worst, you can at least keep them from trying to board and make things even harder."

"What about the stealth coating?" Zhonat asked after a few seconds. "Will that still work?"

"No," I admitted. "It was too badly damaged. There's less than fifty million left, and it's nowhere near enough, unfortunately. I'll leave half aboard the ship, set to carry out emergency repairs, and I'll take the rest."

"I'm not sure about docking the ship," Bach admitted in a low rumble as I stood. "Perhaps you should, and I'll take over then?"

"You're not docking," I said. "Get me close and I'll jump."

"Jump…" He snorted, then shook his head. "Ah, Lord, you get more and more like the assault brigades by the hour. At this rate, we'll have to adopt you."

I grinned at him, seeing that was probably as far as he could bring himself to unbend around the "Lord Devourer" and I clapped him on the shoulder, transferring command authority to the pair, just in case.

I waited a few seconds as they pulled their helmets up, then opened the door; the last of the atmo aboard the ship ripped free. I reached out, gripping Zhonat's shoulder as I passed him, taking the nod of respect and squeezing once, before stepping through the door and closing it behind me.

Their voices were cut off by the sealing of the pressure door, and I hesitated, then started to move again.

It felt wrong.

It felt wrong to leave them here, to leave anyone in command of the ship I'd damn well built practically from scratch. Add to that the entire ship felt wrong now because it was so quiet. The nanites were flowing in, holes in the hull being patched as they went; streams of sentient snakes flowed to me, climbing my body and forming my armor as I strode through the passages, passing the scuffed, battered tubes that were worth more than any king's ransom.

Not only could they bring the dead back to life, but they could literally bring back anyone who was stored in their memory banks. They could bring back hundreds more of the greatest warriors of the UC, given the chance, and yet here they stood, silent, forgotten aboard a ship destined for another fight.

I patted one of them as I passed it, more and more of my nanites flowing up to coat my frame.

The hatch to the next level was open ahead of me. The cold, crisp perfection of the vacuum of space filled the passage as I stepped up, then dropped through the hole. Gravity took me and dropped me to the lowest level because I damn well decided it should.

Landing with my knees slightly bent, I took the impact, then strode forward. The air lock was already cycling, inner and outer doors opening at once.

It wasn't like there was a problem with that now—no atmo to be lost after all the damage the ship had sustained.

I moved to stand in the air lock, reaching a hand up and grabbing an overhead stanchion, holding onto it as I leaned out by instinct.

The node was clear ahead, glittering in the distance—almost glowing, it was so pristine.

"I'm coming for you, my love," I whispered, seeing her in the silence of my mind. Then, taking a deep breath, I counted down.

I couldn't jump too soon—I'd be a sitting duck for the Ændari if they were waiting—and I couldn't jump too late—I'd streak straight past it. No, I needed to wait, to be ready… I watched, listening to the combination of the engineering knowledge, the upgrades that had been crammed into my mind, and finally, to my heart.

Then I threw myself out into the cold of space.

CHAPTER TWENTY-TWO

I'd heard before that it's not the fall that kills you, it's the stop at the end, and damn was that going through my mind as I fell…flew—fuck, who knew what it qualified as. It wasn't like English had a damn definition for "idiot throws himself out of a starship at an enemy-filled floating citadel in deep space."

I squinted on instinct. My improved eyes sharpened their focus—rods shifting and lenses adjusting, zooming in.

The node was, as always, beautiful.

It rose high and low, a long, almost needle-like extension by the uppermost point. The bottom sharpened to a similar tip, and the dock in the middle extended out in a gentle crescent for ships to arrive.

A single ship was docked now—or, more accurately, there were three, and each were fucking wrecks.

The two larger vessels that had been there now floated out here with me somewhere, one shredded and one stealthed, maintaining the jamming field.

I tried again to reach Ingrid, sensing something…then nothing. I was getting closer, though: the sense of oppressive pressure that the jamming field exuded felt almost like the heavy air right before a massive storm.

Now and then, I recognized something in it—a shifting of the field—and as I approached the node, I felt that more and more strongly.

My ship vanished ahead as I set off the first gravity bubble, slowing myself as much as possible before releasing it and triggering another, and another.

Gritting my teeth as my speed decreased second by second, I fought with the insane urge to get there as fast as possible, and the resultant splat that I'd end the day with.

As the saying went, the last thing to go through a fly's mind as it hit the windshield was its arse. I damn well knew I was approaching too fast, and yet couldn't bring myself to slow too much.

Ingrid was just ahead, my friends were there, and I had no damn clue how many of the enemy were there too. All I could hope was that my people were okay.

273

Arise: Conqueror

That was why the node seemed to go from barely visible in the distance to slowly growing closer, to practically screaming through space right at me as I frantically popped more and more bubbles.

I was decelerating—at an insane rate—but I still almost overshot the landing, barely managing to slow enough to crash into the dock as if I'd been fired from a cannon.

It appeared before me literally like I was parachuting in, minus the parachute. The dock raced up to meet me as I frantically tried not to miss and impact the sides of the spire.

Or, you know, flash past into deep space.

Instead, I hit the gleaming white marble-like ground at terrible speed, bouncing hard, rolling, then slamming into the side of the remains of the smaller ship.

It crumpled in around me. A hull designed to withstand impacts from meteors and space debris, atmospheric reentry and more, buckled in around me. The blackened and partially melted metal rung like a bell.

It was several seconds before I could shake off the impact, and when I did, it was to the most wonderful of messages.

"Steve?" Ingrid's voice rang in my ears, and I felt her reaching out; mental fingers ran over the lock over my mind, desperately searching for the key to unlock access to all my senses. *"Steve, is that you? Are you okay? Oh my God, how hard did he hit that..."*

"Ingrid," I said, unable to help the grin that split my face. I approved her access, feeling the shift as her mind took up residence in my own, the desperate need to check me over, the worry, the anger that I'd been gone so, so long, and most of all?

The love.

The absolute knowledge that she loved me, and I her. That we were the center of each other's universes, and that nothing could change that.

I gripped the sides of the hull and braced myself. The metal creaked, then squealed as I bent it back from me, forcing it out and up, freeing me from the battered prison.

One foot hit the ground, and I shifted the bottom of it, bonding myself to the dock and grinning as the metal of the ship bent backward easier with a little leverage.

"Where are you?" I frowned when she didn't respond. *"Ingrid, you okay?"*

I could feel her still, nestled there in the center of my mind, so...

"Steve, what happened to you?" she whispered, disbelief clear as she examined me.

"I evolved," I admitted. *"I'm a Devourer now, fully."*

"I... What does that mean?"

Instead of answering, I poured into the bond all the knowledge of who and what I was, everything that I'd been through since the jump.

It took her long seconds to adjust, to sort through it all and to get it straight in her mind. And when she did speak again, I felt the sadness that filled her, and the worries that she tried to hide.

"Can you make it to us?" She provided a link to her location, three floors up, with the space between heavily contested.

I heard her words, and I felt the worry, and I felt her giving up on a dream that I hadn't even considered.

Children.

She'd been thinking that once all of this was over, somehow, we'd be able to go home, and that one day we'd be married and have children.

I'd sort of thought that would happen as well, but not more than that vague "maybe one day."

Now, with all the changes I'd had to make to myself, I felt the uncertainty, and that she didn't think it was an option anymore.

I didn't know what to say. I didn't know how to make her feel better, nor if I could, you know, procreate.

I could definitely do the deed, or practice a lot—we'd done that plenty. I felt the capability in me still, as well as the hunger when I thought about it. But kids?

Shaking my head, I banished the thought. I could create anything I wanted in me, so there was no damn way that I couldn't literally encode the ability into me…to adjust…

I kept seeing an image of me selecting traits, genetic tweaks, selecting upgrades for my own child, programming them to be "perfect" and what might be lost in the process.

I was still standing there, my mind racing when the first shots landed, hitting the side of the ship nearby. I snarled, twisting around the ship and glaring at the incoming enemy.

"Steve, can you get to us?" Ingrid asked again, and I nodded, not needing to think about it.

"I'm coming," I assured her, glaring across at the incoming troops, then shivering and stepping back into the dubious shelter of the battered shadow of the ship, as she returned the favor, sinking the memories of the last few weeks into my mind in a single concentrated burst.

I closed my eyes. My right hand extended into a blade, and I cut a section of the hull free, ripping it out and holding it as a shield before me, as I unpacked the memories.

As soon as I'd been lost to the void, Ingrid and the others had started work. There'd been a bit of a panic, frantic searching, guilt and remorse, mourning and more, but through it all, they'd worked.

Ingrid had reached out to the local worlds, asking for help. Some had answered and agreed, seeing who and what she was, that she was a leader of a planet and a member of the UC.

Some had seen that as a way to improve their lives, to run away from their issues wherever they were, and make a fresh start on some unknown but apparently powerful world.

Others had believed, *again*, that we were from a Shadow World, some kind of top-secret military training camp that spanned a whole, or multiple, worlds.

Arise: Conqueror

They wanted access to that, though fuck knew why anyone would want access to the worlds that produced supposedly the most insane, violent, and unprincipled warriors in the galaxy.

The ships in the system at that point had all apparently remembered that they had people aboard, or that they liked credits, as they repurposed themselves to transport volunteers to the node.

There'd been three main groups—well, four, if you counted the Ændari. There'd been five caught so far, including one who had shot up his own ship to force Ingrid and the others to let him land, for fear of innocent refugees being killed otherwise.

He'd been nailed to a structure Paul had made, to make an example of him, then Belle had drained him. Then Scylla had apparently done something to the body, really going all in on making an example of the fucker.

Another had hidden aboard a vessel that had docked, and he'd literally begged not to be taken to the "insane ones" and killed. He'd been allowed to leave on the ship when it took off for Scorpio-3, the nearest inhabited world, and he'd not returned when the ship did.

The remaining three had launched themselves from a stealthed ship—a much, much smaller one that had landed on the node three days ago.

It wasn't up here but had apparently landed at the tip of the spire that extended downward from the dock, with only Argus being able to identify that it was even there.

The three that had landed had used some kind of stealth coating, enabling them to make it past the lower defenses. They'd activated a hidden system, opening access to the lower spire for their ship; then they'd tried to assassinate the others and take control.

As soon as they'd accessed the node control system, Argus had been able to spot them, something about their armor hiding even their nanites' signatures, and he'd directed the others.

The fight would have been much harder, with them being fully stealthed, if the last major battle hadn't given the team a massive surplus of weapons.

Jonas and Paul had made a competition of throwing as many grenades into the midst of the stealthy bastard's position, then Courtney had opened fire, and Scylla…well.

Scylla had then danced into the middle and shredded the fuckers even as their stealth systems failed and rebooted, making them appear and vanish constantly.

Those who had come to the rescue, though—not just the Ændari trying to fuck things up—were split into three groups.

First and foremost, those who were looking for an "out." They were willing to fight to get that chance, and most of them had nothing to lose.

The issue was, most of them were also utterly inexperienced in war, or they'd have been working as mercenaries already. And they had neither the money for weapons and armor, nor the money for passage to the node.

That meant that although we could have had hundreds of thousands of those, they were instead the smallest group.

Most of them were the lunatics who had been on the node already and then were forced to flee, with the ships they were aboard using a planet to slingshot around and returning.

The second group were the most professional, and they were both the ones we'd wanted most of all and were the most experienced.

Seventy-six BWVs had made it off the warship before the Ændari blew it apart, and they were ready for payback. About half were armed and fully armored. The rest had been preparing still when the ship came under attack, had been killed and since had revived, or their bodies had been recovered and were still reviving.

They were the steel core of our forces, and I winced as I realized I was going to have to explain myself to them, considering the damn situation with Emberalis.

The third group was the largest and most heavily armed, as well as the most mental. At first, they'd also looked as if they were the only real support we were getting.

Ingrid had taken the funds we'd managed to get together, and she'd spent all of it—and the goodwill we'd earned with the devilkin—to basically hire almost every one of their mercenaries who could carry a gun and get to us in time. There were almost a hundred of them, all heavily armed, experienced, and willing to spend their lives to make a difference.

That was the best thing about the devilkin. They'd been shit on from a great height by the UC already, and although they knew we were allied with them, they also knew that we were their best chance at improving their situation.

Also, we'd given a maligned group their own dock and access to massive contracts, so they kinda owed us.

The devilkin and BWVs were cautious around each other, having had little real contact before. But both had heard about a reputation for excessive brutality and rule-following on one side, and rule breaking, piracy, and theft from the other.

I was hoping that distance would vanish once they bled together a bit.

The main issue was that once the Ændari had hit that control panel, they'd managed to open the lower levels, and lock open the main access to the control center.

I saw it all in seconds, literally.

Weeks of preparations, followed by the forced opening of the main access…and at least half of the work everyone had done was wasted.

Also, even more annoyingly, the one rule that Ingrid had held to with everyone was that unless they were one of our small group, they were being restricted to certain areas.

The refugee and lunatic contingent, for example, were kept outside, between the dock and the main entrance hall.

They were mainly made up of the lunatic fringe who thought that the nodes were some kind of way to contact the gods, and that all the secrets of the universe could be gained by getting inside.

Arise: Conqueror

That the Ændari had once built them, and they clearly weren't fucking gods and were instead utter dickheads was glossed over for most of them. Apparently, some of them actually believed that the Ændari were fallen angels, and that the nodes were ways that they communed with the "upper realms" and that was why they were locked now.

The main upshot was that these were people who should never be allowed past the entrance. As religious nutjobs, they'd keep poking and prodding until they blew the place up.

Now, with the doors being forced and locked open, they'd been allowed inside, because otherwise they'd be slaughtered on the approaches.

The BWV soldiers and the devilkin were trusted a bit more, and were restricted to the first three floors. Both teams had to split off people to watch for the first group, as people continually assumed that "none of you, not any of you, not even you, you prick," as Paul explained it to them, actually meant that everyone except them should stay out. For some reason, they were all convinced they were responsible for uplifting the entire galaxy, provided they could just…

Scylla had been forced to kill three of them already.

The Ændari had landed in the place of the destroyed UC warship, and they'd attacked instantly, disgorging hundreds of assault troopers and literally thousands of "lesser" troops as well.

The fights for the lower areas had been hard and brutal. Jonas had fallen, as had Benat as well.

Malthus had gone literally mental at that, having only gotten her back recently. He and Benat were an item, and they weren't used to the fact that they could literally come back from the dead yet.

He'd stormed the Ændari position, almost falling himself, and had personally captured the Ændari advance commander.

He'd cut his arms and legs off; then he'd dragged the wriggling, screaming body back through the lines and had crushed his skull with a hammer.

The last thing the Ændari had seen before that was the furious glare that Belle was giving him, tendrils already extending to his body, as Malthus explained that he was literally going to make things right for those who had fallen.

The Ændari had screamed, realizing that they were going to rip the nanites— or builders, as the Ændari called them—from him, using them to repair and reawaken our people, while making sure that he died for good.

The battle had been insanely brutal, but it'd settled into a stalemate.

That was when Argus discovered what the Ændari were doing in the base of the node.

The upper spire was the communication and control section, controlling the signal for the nanites that was sent out, while the bottom was the power generation and storage areas.

The storage being the massive banks of crystal memory modules that were required to house all the records that the AI had access to.

The control area in the upper section was more heavily protected than the lower section, but the lower section couldn't be accessed without access already gained to the upper, as the emergency panels were located there.

That was how the entire system had been kept safe. The Ændari, if they gained access to the lower systems and memory modules, could rip the details of how to access the node from the records easily enough. But they couldn't get to it without access to the upper levels, and why would you access the lower levels to do anything dodgy, when you already had access to the higher ones, etc.?

The truth was that if the Ændari got access to all the records and memory cores in the lower spire, then they could break into another node, and this one be damned.

They could blow it up if they had to. Or just power it down and sort it out later.

Either way, though, they'd have won.

That was why the Ændari had split their forces. And where I was currently? I was right in the damn middle of them.

That was me back up to date. And with the mental images of Jonas and Benat dead, and the tear-streaked face of Belle slumped over, exhaustedly trying to repair their bodies and resurrect them, I opened my eyes again, filled with righteous fucking rage.

CHAPTER TWENTY-THREE

I gripped the section of hull I'd carved free and stepped out into sight on the dock, glaring around the edges of the torn steel, counting, even as I triggered my time compression again.

The incoming Ændari seemed to float as they ran toward me. Eight of them bounded up the stairs with weapons raised. Their white armor gleamed; shoulder-mounted thrusters were deployed and ready, clearly expecting to move around to be able to get at me.

I read the bloodlust in their movements, the excitement as they fired on me, and I sneered at them.

Their nanites were barely double those of the average Blessed, and I could break them over my knee without effort now.

Starting to run at them, I held the slab of battered metal up between us, keeping it there as dozens of hits slammed into it, burning holes deeper and deeper.

They raced across the upper ring. The dock was constructed of three concentric half discs, each larger than the one below, with a set of stairs leading up from the bottom to the top.

The ship that I'd crashed into and had hidden me had landed on the upper ring at some point; then it'd been trashed. Heavy weapons fire had torn it up.

Then the ships that had docked had needed more space, and rather than get out and drag the ship out of the way—or, you know, wait—they'd presumably used the nose of one of the much larger ships and they'd just shoved it aside.

I ran at them as well, boots thudding across the perfect marble as Ingrid spoke into my mind.

"Steve, your armor!"

"I don't need it," I growled. The last shots sizzled into the makeshift shield before I threw it.

It had to look insane, considering I wore what looked to be jeans and a T-shirt. But the fact that I was carrying a two-meter by one-meter section of hull armoring that was at least a half a meter deep, one-handed? That I then threw it across the last ten meters like it was nothing? Well, that probably should have given them a hint they were in deep shit.

The slab hit one of the lead runners full-on. The crash and a pained scream rung out as he hurtled backward. That, finally, seemed to be when the other seven got a faint sense of their own mortality.

The firing slowed for a second, and in that time, I leapt.

Three lasers hit me, burning shallow holes in my upper chest, right shoulder, and throat.

I'd have loved to have seen their faces when the wounds closed over, the underlying sections of me that were exposed being solid nanites, instead of flesh.

I triggered three gravity bubbles with barely a thought, flared them to a hundred gravities and then cut them. Three figures gasped and fell as one. Each had a fist-sized warp in space appear in their chests, compressing their hearts to the size of a fingernail, then vanishing again.

They were down to four, and the remaining ones were bunched up close in the middle, lasers lifted, firing on full auto at me.

I hit the middle one full-on with a flying kick to the chest that liquified his internal organs and cratered the armor inward. My right arm morphed into a three-meter blade that slashed out, cutting the nearest on that side into two roughly even halves.

Two tentacles flashed out from my back, hitting their chests at almost the same instant. The tips seemed to splash like waterbombs, the liquid flowing across their armor…

Then it flashed from grey to oily red and black, and dragged them in toward me. Their armor was already crumbling, flesh following as they screamed.

More tentacles flashed out, latching onto the bodies around me, even as they fell, enveloping them and dragging them close. Spikes jutted from the mass, punching through the quivering bodies, burrowing deeper and deeper.

The bodies were hoisted into the air or dragged along, bloody trails left behind as I strode forward, seizing the stunned remaining trooper by the throat and lifting him into the air.

He seemed to wake at that, struggling, grabbing my hand and stabbing out with a dagger he pulled from his belt.

I let him. The blade hit my cheek and bounced off, not leaving so much as a scratch.

"Do we need him?" I asked aloud, knowing that Ingrid was watching through my eyes.

"No, but we need the nanites," she said grimly, clearly not liking the necessity, but also not telling me to stop. *"Steve, we need a* lot *of nanites."*

"Fair enough." I shrugged. My hand, wrapped around his neck, spawned a ring of spikes that jutted up and down, digging and consuming.

I ripped their nanites free, from all eight of them, in less than a minute while staring out across the devastation.

When we'd first arrived, we'd blasted the shit out of the dozens of warehouses and buildings that had been built here, because the Ændari had been hiding in them, waiting to ambush us.

Even with the damage that was done by the point defense lasers of our warship, the buildings had still stood—more or less—they'd just been missing walls and roofs here and there.

Arise: Conqueror

Now there was rubble.

Literally, that was it: half a wrecked UC warship was covering one side of the deck, reduced to absolute scrap, buildings around it smashed into rubble.

The ruined buildings had been torn down; defensive walls had been raised in their place. Destroyed turret emplacements, the remains of razor wire and traps, as well as hundreds of bodies were all clear from here, as were the lines of "wounded."

That was the best term, I guessed.

Ændari or UC troops who came from before the nanite plague had limited access to their systems, their nanites rebuilding them and bringing them back from death's cold embrace again and again.

In situations like this, both sides had to live in terror.

The UC's forces who had been salvaged from the warship were stacked like corded wood. Machines were connected to them, draining them of nanites and feeding them into a mixture of storage tanks and the "dead" Ændari.

The winners of the fight would recover their side's bodies, bringing them back to fight again. The losers would have their bodies stripped, and their remains presumably either thrown into space or similarly destroyed.

Well, the eight I'd already fought looked to have been the rear guard, although I could see troopers on the far side, across the bridge that led into the spire itself, were now moving.

Clearly the first ones had reported something, so I didn't have as long as I'd like.

I triggered a gravity bubble in the doorway where I could see movement, a powerful one, pulling in at a hundred gravities and ten meters across. I felt the impacts and heard the distant screams of pain and confusion as I did so.

Then I lifted into the air, marveling at the difference between when I was last here, and now.

Tentacles flashed out. The sheer number of nanites and the improvements to my intelligence and control stats meant that I could control as many tentacles as I had the nanites for now.

Before, I'd had difficulty with longer linkages, or more than six, preferring, when possible, to stick to four that I could control easier.

Now I had a dozen, all stabbing out, collecting bodies and ripping them into the air, dragging them close.

The Devourer was coating me entirely now, and everything I touched vanished into the unfillable mass.

I could feel the need to grow, to expand, building in me.

It wasn't uncontrollable yet, but as I absorbed more and more, they had to go somewhere…

Then I smiled.

I'd found that I could separate the nanites for short periods of time, should I need to. I'd been able to shed literally hundreds of millions into the ship's hold, after all.

All I needed was somewhere to keep them. I'd always liked the power armor that the UC soldiers wore—it was just a little, well, *subtle* for my tastes.

I focused, knowing that for now I didn't have enough to do this and do it justice, but I had enough for the frame.

I continued toward the bodies of the UC soldiers. Tentacles discarded broken husks behind me as they finished, then flashed out and snatched up another body, then another.

What I needed was something that screamed "don't fuck with me," that increased my power, gave me some actual armoring because why not, and somewhere to mount weapons.

My first plan had been to go down the power armor route—admittedly, partly because I'd loved movies with that kind of mental shit over the years…games, too. Then I'd been looking at my ship, thinking I'd continue to add nanites to it over time.

Now I was thinking that I'd been too conservative in my plans.

No, with what I had in mind, I'd need an absolute fuckton of nanites. But if I could pull it off? Damn.

The first step was the nanites, though, and we needed them.

As I drew close enough to the UC bodies, a tentacle flashed out, slicing the machine that was draining them apart with a single blow.

Then it latched onto the nearby reservoir, tearing it open and dragging the nanites free.

Half of all the nanites I was gathering were mine, I decided on the spot. I'd need them for the project. But the other half? I was going to have access to hundreds of millions soon. I could afford to be generous with my people.

Additional tentacles, needle thin and dozens of meters long, flashed out, covering the distance as if they'd been fired from a cannon.

They stabbed into the dead UC BWVs, and they pumped them full of active, fully primed nanites.

I reached out, finding Argus waiting, clearly ready.

"Argus," I said aloud, feeling his acknowledgment. "I want them back on their feet, unlocked, and able to access their systems as fast as possible."

"Current reawakening estimates vary from fifteen minutes to seven hours and eleven minutes. Due to repeated requests by co-leader Ingrid and others, I have refrained from adding the exact number of seconds."

"Good." I grunted. "The fifteen-minutes one—can you let them know to stay here, to gather up weapons and defend the others as they recover?"

"Confirmed."

"Dammit, and did you get the memo from that wanker Emberalis that we were now enemies? Did any of our people here?"

"Negative."

With that wonderfully expansive response, I pulled the needles back, firing out more to those who needed them, injecting fresh nanites that were wiped and upgraded with a thought, ready to serve their new masters.

"Well, that's a relief, I guess. I'll let them know what happened when I reach the others."

Arise: Conqueror

That done, with more bodies breaking down, I turned, flitting through the air toward the far side, summoning another two gravity bubbles, one on the left of the door ahead and the other to the right.

They appeared about a meter back from it. The left, spinning up to a hundred gravities, pushed out; the other pulled in.

That meant that anything in the middle was subjected to two hundred gravities of shear. I held it for a slow count of three so that they knew where it was, and to stay back… Then, grinning evilly, I shoved both bubbles backward, and spun them around in a little dance, out of my sight.

The screams this time were louder, as at least another dozen of the enemy were sucked in and shredded.

I continued to float over as more and more of the bodies between me and the door were grabbed, yanked into the air and fed upon, then discarded.

I didn't know what I looked like, but I had to imagine for an Ændari, it was pretty fucking horrifying. Not least because I was coated in Devourer armor.

As more and more nanites were ripped free and absorbed into me, I came up with a quick and dirty plan for now.

I needed room to store more nanites, but I didn't want to tower over people more than I already did. I wanted to be able to pass for human still as well. I wasn't ready to entirely discard that. Not yet.

No, for now, I needed a halfway solution, somewhere to keep the nanites, near at hand and safe, while still being useful.

I picked up speed, flowing across the dock, my feet a good three meters from the ground. Gravity now floated me along without effort or conscious thought.

Remains were grabbed, ripped upward and dumped into a new shape that grew, a billowing swarm of flowing nanites. With each body that hit the swarm, the nanites would envelop it. The bodies were stabbed through, then the pikes expanded, branching, punching free, then reformed, flowing back inside, across the surface, from spike to spike…

In less than a minute, a body was entirely stripped and whatever was left, that was deemed useless, too much effort even to break down for biological reformatting, was then discarded.

As soon as the bodies were flung into the mass, the tentacles stabbed out again. As their nanites were co-opted into my form, more tentacles were created. I went from six to twelve, to twenty, thirty…

The tentacles only stopped forming when I ran out of bodies. Two ahead of me flashed down to grab a section of metal, once a wall, now warped and battered, then dragged it back up, holding it before me. I launched myself upward, separating from my tentacled mass.

The gravity bubbles cut off. I grinned evilly, as I blurred upward, my skin shifting. Conceal activated, before I arced over and headed back downward toward the entrance.

Whatever else they might be, the lower ranks of the Ændari weren't slouches when it came to war. As soon as the gravity bubbles vanished, they raced forward. A handful at first, then more.

They rushed through the entrance, ten of them in a matter of seconds, activating their shoulder-mounted jets and launching into the air.

They arced to the left and right, rising fast, lasers already locked onto the mass and firing. They clearly knew the risk that it posed, if they let it get close enough…and they had the guts to do what they needed to.

I tore into them from above, arms flexing into blades and striking left and right. The first didn't even see me coming. The second barely had time to notice something was wrong; then they were impaled.

The third?

It was a bloodbath. They'd been gathered together as they came through the doorway by its restricted space. Now I was there, carving down from above and slamming into them as they rose.

Their armor barely slowed my blades. I struck left and right, killing with almost impunity, until I flipped over, landing in a crouch, bracing myself as bodies rained down, then launching forward.

The room beyond was the main chamber, once the only inner section of the node that could be reached. Hundreds of small buildings had been crammed in here, everything from temples to barracks, whorehouses to baths.

The baths had probably been a mistake, I'd guessed last time I was here, as the first thing that religious nutcases seemed to develop was a powerful aversion to soap and water, and a hatred of deodorant.

Now, as I burst through the doorway, I saw what was left of the buildings, mainly battered and damaged last time I'd been here, had been entirely razed.

The Ændari had come through like a tidal wave, smashing apart anything and everything that lay in their path.

The walls that still stood were riddled with holes. Blood, burned bodies, and shredded armor lay everywhere—and it wasn't just from me, although the first few meters were dominated by sprayed blood that ran down the walls and a solid mass that had once been dozens of Ændari.

The mass rocked gently, coming to a halt. The effect of compressing multiple bodies with a hundred gravities and jerking it around and around was clearly not a healthy one for anyone caught in it.

My Conceal was still active, but the forces ahead weren't stupid.

As soon as I'd landed, blood from those I'd literally just cut my way through had splattered down atop me, making me partly visible. Even as I leapt forward, someone screamed from my right.

"Stealth!" the voice rang out. "Assassin! There's an—"

I shot to that side; my right blade arced up and around, cutting them off midsentence. I spun, pivoting on my right foot, and thrust out with the left blade, punching through a figure that had been setting up a tripod-mounted weapon.

The blade took her in the chest, high on the left and then up and through the neck, ripping their head free. Then I spun again, ducking down. My right blade reformed into a hand that I braced on the floor as my left foot shot out, catching the third of this little grouping under the chin, snapping their jaw shut on their tongue.

I felt the jaw break; blood gushed from the severed tongue as they catapulted backward.

Arise: Conqueror

Then I launched myself forward again.

I didn't know how they'd been laid out before, but by the time I'd burst through the entrance, the remaining Ændari were fairly spread out.

The closest lot had been in an arc, surrounding the doorway, with the remains of dozens I'd caught in my gravity trap broken and bleeding nearby.

Blood was still raining down as the first laser blasts flashed out. The far side of the arc had heard the warning and presumably seen something, then decided that "fuck it—if they die, they die" was the best way to deal with the risk firing imposed on their fellow troopers.

The tripod-mounted laser opened fire. Powerful blasts pounded into me, as I reached for the next closest, burning through the upper layer of my skin and then deeper.

I twisted, right hand reforming and lancing forward. It became a spear of barely visible nanites, coated in blood that made my Stealth pointless.

I reformed my left arm into a shield. Null blocks flowed across the upper surface, even as a tentacle latched onto a nearby body and started the conversion.

The upper layer was thin, too thin, and shots from such a powerful laser pounded holes over and over. But as I shimmered into existence, they grew thicker and thicker by the second.

I flexed the spear as it punched through the armor of the figure before me; the head erupted from his back, and then eight spikes flicked out from the base of the head.

They connected to each other, forming a wide, flat ring below the head and on the far side of the gasping Ændari. Then I yanked him in close. The spear shrunk back into an arm at will, as I held him up, using him as a human—well, Ændari—shield.

Between him and my actual shield, which was now reaching a thickness that was holding against the laser fire, though others were joining it by the second, I'd gained a brief respite.

I used it well.

Three gravity bubbles burst into being, ramped up, then vanished—the first at the end of the tri-barreled laser that a second team was manhandling into position. Better not to let them add that fucker to the firepower, after all.

The second was right behind the brow of the helmet of that tripod-mounted gunner. His brain vanished, crushed into a fraction of its size, in a heartbeat; then the field cut out again. The fire stopped as his hands released the triggers, body dropping limply to the floor.

The third and final bubble?

The crotch of what I guessed was an Ændari officer.

He was shouting orders, anyway—right up until I reduced his pelvis to ground bonemeal and bloody mincemeat.

I'd probably just improved the entire Ændari gene pool in a single strike.

His orders went from curt and to the point into a high-pitched scream of agonized horror and disbelief. Then he collapsed, hands reaching down at the crushed inward remnants of his armor, shock setting in almost instantly.

I conjured four more, then six.

As each of the bubbles appeared, they ramped up to a hundred, then cut out, vanishing in a tiny implosion of gravitational force, and reality quickly raced to equalize things out again.

That meant, unfortunately for most, that because nature apparently abhors a vacuum, the surrounding matter would rush in.

If that bubble had appeared in flesh, then whatever had been there before was now a fraction of the size it had been. Therefore all the surrounding "meat" would be ripped inward to spread out and fill that space.

It happened with anything and everything, but when it happened in flesh, the effect was very clear. If I completely missed someone beyond their ear, and just ripped that into a compressed bubble, they'd die.

Losing an ear shouldn't kill you, sure, but the combination of a hundred gravities ripping from you would tear the blood from the brain at the same time in a term called exsanguinating hemorrhage.

The improvement to my mind was weird at times, but when I needed a damn word, sometimes it just came to me like that: a flash from a class in the army when we were taught about high-powered rifle impacts.

Now I was seeing it in the real world. And fuck me, it was a wonderful sight.

Staggering, screaming Ændari filled the air with their blood—or the closest batch were, anyway, as those farther ahead closed ranks.

The buildings here had been laid out in a spiral, one that was designed to maximize the space available to fit in literally as much as possible, all centered around the doors that led into the main spire.

Those doors were visible—just—even from here. The buildings between me and them had been shredded and torn down to such a degree that I could walk straight through.

The bodies and shattered weapons emplacements, broken armor and defensive formations made it clear that the fight had been a hard one. And now the Ændari who stood between me and that door were hunkering down behind rubble, aiming.

I flashed from partly visible, coated in bloody remains a few seconds ago, to coated in the Devourer; then my armor shifted again. Now that the Devourer had absorbed everything, Conceal triggered again. I flashed to the right, vanishing as lasers streaked through the space I'd just occupied.

On the other side of the door, the floating mass of nanites grew steadily larger, discarding the remains and shifting. Tentacles flowed back inside, the outer layer blurring as it, too, activated Conceal, focusing everything inward as the second stage went active.

I lunged forward. The nearest Ændari peered over the remains of a low wall and took a blade to the face. Then I flipped over it and crouched next to him, dragging him down and out of sight, waiting.

I rammed another blade into the body, ripping it apart almost absently as I drained and absorbed him. While I did that, I grabbed the helmet, cracking it apart and feeding in connections, linking to their communications network and starting a hack, before Ingrid spoke up again.

Arise: Conqueror

"We're holding our position on the third floor, and... Steve, we have full access to their communications. Do you need something?"

I cursed, then discarded the helmet.

"I was wondering what they were planning," I admitted.

"It's mainly 'run and shoot them all,' when it comes to us, and 'fall back, shoot him' and 'where did he go' when it comes to you. They're almost disgustingly simple."

"Why?" I asked, annoyed by it instead of pleased.

"They know that they'll come back, so when they fight anything that's not the UC BWV soldiers, they win. They'll spend their lower ranks and conscripted forces without thought for them, and the higher Ændari believe themselves to be effectively immortal. They've not had to actually learn tactics beyond running at each other and shooting for so long it's ingrained.

"Also, as much as it galls me, having grown up watching cunning tactics in movies all my life, sometimes that's the right approach. Here we have the upper ground; we have defensive perimeters and weapons emplacements. Both sides' technology is roughly equal, and the structure can't be damaged or worked around, so it comes down to them needing to break our lines.

"The only real way they can do that is to pour bodies in until they overwhelm us, and as the Ændari will come back from death with little more than an annoying time-out and a bit of pain... it's their best plan," she finished, a clear sigh in her mental voice.

"Seriously?" I asked. *"Thousands of years of technological advancement over us, and they're basically rerunning D-day all over again?"*

"Yeah, pretty much," she said. *"If it wasn't for the heavy weapons, it'd have worked. Thankfully, the devilkin like really big guns, and even the UC are impressed with them so far."*

"How big?"

"Like miniguns, the kind that you saw in all the eighties and nineties movies, loaded onto vehicles. That's their version of personal weapons. And the stuff they set up for fixed-place weapons? I'm oh so glad they're on our side."

"Well, look at you, loving heavy artillery." I grinned as I sent it, rising to a crouch and creeping along to the shattered doorway, the body discarded behind me now.

"I always liked heavy artillery!" Ingrid replied haughtily.

"Yeah, mine," I sent her with a laugh, and she replied with an image of a middle finger raised.

"I'm a lady, thank you very much. I was referring to all the movies that Far used to make me watch growing up. He loved the old war movies and eighties hero films. These miniguns remind me of that. Also, the Ændari are a plague on the galaxy, and seeing them charge a fortified emplacement with these ready? I used to hate violence—now I'm wondering if I'd have actually enjoyed life in the army."

"You wouldn't," I told her. *"Using weapons like that against real people rather than scum like these would be a lot harder. Here? It's goddamn pest control."*

"That's a fair point." She sighed. *"So, what's the plan?"*

"I'm thinking kill everyone, let God sort them out," I suggested with another mental smile, listening to a dim noise on the other side of the wall from me. I sent out a very faint radar pulse, listened, then sent another…

Then dropped to lie as flat as possible, barely having time to get down as the wall where I'd just been crouched exploded inward. A heavy blast of lasers from another tripod tore the wall apart.

I stayed prone, waiting. Then, as the lasers slowed, the Ændari searching, waiting to see whether they'd gotten me, I made the floating mass of nanites, totally overlooked, slide slowly to the left of the entrance.

It lifted, stealthily shifting along the wall, until it was almost directly overhead, looking down on four of the Ændari.

They were on what was left of a rooftop, rifles raised, watching the drifting smoke above me and waiting for movement, any kind of movement, to fire again.

I grinned, extending four, then five tentacles. The first four all moved into place over the standing Ændari. The fifth—well, that gently reached out and plucked a grenade from the belt of the leader.

It was a model I recognized, proving that the goddamn corpo scumbags we'd dealt with back on that space station were indeed selling to both sides. It was that super-awesome grenade that we'd only had five of before.

It was a three-part weapon. The base was both weighted and magnetic, supposedly to make sure it landed that way down; then the top third would fire off. A small magnet in the top activated through a charge as it fired upward on a spring-loaded release.

The top would stick to a passageway ceiling ideally, locking down, then fire out eighteen darts, in a circle, each attached to a monomolecular razor wire.

The darts would stab into anything nearby, and anyone who tried to run through the area would be shredded.

That was nasty enough.

But the second stage? That released a napalm compound—gaseous at first, odorless and silent—forced out under pressure, that would be ignited as soon as the storage chamber was empty.

Then, if being stabbed by darts, shredded by razor wire, and then set on fucking fire with napalm wasn't enough? The final, bottom stage went off, exploding and hurling a hundred tightly compressed metal slivers in all directions.

It was gloriously excessive, and we'd only had five, so I'd been fucking wounded when Ingrid gave them out to other people.

Jonas, that rat bastard, had gotten two. Paul—fucking Paul, a man so insane that he tried to claim that a hatchet and combat knife large enough to qualify as a fucking short sword was a "cultural weapon" and that I was oppressing him— got one, and Scylla did too.

Scylla.

The woman who was so insane and bloodthirsty that she was literally confused with a mythical whirlpool that was inescapable for the ancient Greeks.

Arise: Conqueror

The last one? It was given to Zac to make sure that we could make more.

I hadn't been given a single goddamn one. And now? Looking down as the smoke cleared from the Ændari blasting the shit out of the tiny apartment I'd been in, my tentacle monster struck.

The first four all latched onto the heads of the four Ændari. The inside of the "hand" turned red with Devourer nanites and chewed into the armor, before extruding a spike.

That spike, six inches of Devourer-coated null metal, punched through the weakened armor and into their brains.

The four fell with barely a second to react. A few stray shots fired as they collapsed.

That was it.

As the Ændari were moving, dozens of those scattered around the ruins now convinced that they'd been firing at the wrong place, that wonderful fifth tentacle primed and activated the grenade. I flung it over the ruins, across the plaza, and into the main mass of Ændari gathering there, staging for another push out at me on the higher levels.

The doors were open still, thanks to the Ændari stealth fighters reaching that panel. They'd not been able to be closed, and the first hall was apparently the perfect place for them to stage their people.

It was long, reasonably defensible, and had doors at either end that they controlled, allowing them to close them off and be potentially safe from counterattack.

All things considered, it was a great place for the Ændari to set up, right up until the grenade went off in the middle of it.

The first stage was unfortunately a bit of a bust. The walls weren't metal—neither was the roof or floor—so although the top of the disc exploded free, it shot up and then hit the nearby wall—it'd not been flat when it went off, instead having landed on the back of an Ændari armor plate.

The top hit the wall, bounced off, then crashed down onto the leg of another trooper.

He apparently recognized it, because he screamed and tried to run.

The minor and rather pertinent detail that was missed at this point, was that not only were the top and bottom connected, but they were connected by dozens of strands of *razor wire*.

It was monomolecular and designed to be deployed against heavy battlefield armor.

That meant that despite the advanced nature of the Ændari systems, it still worked against them—when there was a decent bit of effort used, anyway.

That probably would have been fine, if the pair who found themselves involuntarily wedded together in domestic destruction had remained calm.

They didn't.

They both tried to run. In opposite directions.

They reached the end of the lead and were jerked back off their feet. Those caught in the wires between the two screamed as those wires were jerked taut and sliced into them.

Blood filled the air along with the screams, and that was when one of those nearby spotted the telltale mist of the advanced chemical napalm in the air.

It sparked to life just as that wonderfully observant individual had been wiping his fingers down the front of his helmet, frowning at the sticky residue that had been accumulating.

Then everything in the hall experienced the joy that is napalm in the morning.

Or afternoon, really.

It's a wonderfully warming experience, especially for your enemies. The sight of them all screaming and running about, covered in flames that no water would extinguish, was one I'd treasure always.

Then, just as things reached the crescendo of madness…the final stage went active. A hundred tiny fléchettes of sharpened nefindium were fired out in all directions, shredding anything nearby.

Between the strange screams from above a nearby house, the random gunshots, and yes, all right, the total overkill in an enclosed space, the Ændari had collectively taken their eye off the ball.

Or more importantly, they'd taken their eyes off *me*.

I was up in all the madness, unseen and stalking. Both arms extended into blades; my armor was back to full Conceal, making me almost invisible, and I started to run.

Blades spinning, I dove into the largest concentration of the enemy I could reach, hacking left and right. Blood sprayed and more screams echoed.

The tentacle monster was almost finished its transformation now, and the first of my little darlings was released, flying on its maiden voyage as a test bed.

The plan was that as I could rejoin them to my body at any time, and because I now had sufficient control over my nanites to wipe them and upgrade them almost instantly, or re-wipe and prepare them for handover to another with only a thought, there was no need to keep them inactive.

Therefore, the first drone that slid free of the mass of stealthed nanites was the prototype. The assembly coding was already in place, and it was prepared to build more.

Dart One had a sharp, pointed nose, and four stubby fins at the rear, each extending out into sharp wings. The drone was a little over half a meter across, with a dedicated antigravity engine in the rear, a small power core in the middle, and reinforced blades that ran from the nose to the tips of the wings.

The darts, as that was the best way for me to think of them, were going to be fast, stealthy, and strong. They weren't complicated in any way. And if they received damage to the level that the engine or core was at risk, the nanites could disassociate.

They'd either release the power that was stored in a single blast, like a handful of high-powered grenades going off at once, or they could shut down and vent the energy, doing little to no damage.

Then the nanites would become liquid, splashing down and basically being ready for recovery.

Arise: Conqueror

The best bit, though, was that the tentacle monster—Bob…I was going to call him Bob, I decided—would follow along behind, collecting all the corpses and stripping them of nanites, making more and more of my little darts.

I believed I was finally starting to grasp the potential of the nanites, and it was about time.

Dart One, like all its brothers and sisters to come, was also making the most of my Conceal ability, and lined up on a target creeping along a rooftop, searching for me.

The dart slammed into his chest two seconds later, carrying him off the roof and into the next building, buried deep in his chest, caught in his armor. The Ændari gasped and choked, drowning on his own blood.

Tentacles exploded out from me, slamming into those around me and yanking them in close. Spikes punched into them, tearing them limb from limb.

Bob slid down from hovering near the wall, updating the design and yanking Dart One free of its victim, before picking the corpse up—along with fifteen others within reach—and drew it into the devouring mass.

Walking forward, I discarded most of the bodies, keeping two at hand for a personal "snack" and portable "body" armor. I'd already torn their arms and legs off, and them screaming in panic and dismay really added to the whole ambiance as I stepped up to the tri-barreled heavy laser that they'd been mounting on a tripod before.

A little magic with gravity, and a bit of excessive strength, and I was carrying the laser comfortably. A tentacle attached to the rear of the battery pack and fed additional power into it as another tentacle plucked a chunk of nearby metal free of the debris.

It was held behind my back, ready to be broken down and to provide additional power to the weapon. I climbed the steps, grinning evilly at the screams and smoking bodies ahead…

Then I opened fire.

CHAPTER TWENTY-FOUR

"**S**teve!"

Ingrid shouted down at me from two floors above, and I grinned at her, kicking a smoking corpse aside.

I was halfway up the first stairwell, and damn, the last ten minutes had been bloody.

The tri-barreled laser was designed to be a squad-served weapon, and it was a heavy one, both in weight and in terms of the firepower it could produce.

I'd scanned it, examined it, and I had some plans for the future that could only be described as cruel and unusual punishment. But for now, it'd done the job.

Striding through the mass of dead and dying in the ground floor hall, I'd fired almost constantly, tearing through the massed ranks of injured as they tried to get their bearings after the madness of that grenade.

That was probably bad enough for them, but that was also when I made a slight change to the dart drones and fired them into the room.

I connected two of them to each other and strung a monofilament cable between them.

Yeah, all right, so there'd probably be someone somewhere who would be complaining that dragging cables a molecule thick through the air, invisible and through a heavily populated area full of wounded was a "war crime" and other minor complaints…

But the screams were fucking *awesome*.

Bob had floated in behind me as I strode in, grabbing corpses and firing drones into the survivors out in the plaza. Anyone left alive now probably had the good sense to fucking hide.

Those in the hall were torn apart. Some managed to get some good hits on me, and a few grenades damn well did some damage a time or two, admittedly.

Between the original packed nature of the hall, the power of the grenade and the laser, and the invisible razor wire, though, it was a foregone conclusion.

It didn't take long to carve my way through the hall, dispatching anything that moved, or at least moaned weakly, followed by Bob, who harvested everything he found.

Arise: Conqueror

I occasionally marked a fallen corpse as not to be touched—they were UC or devilkin—but beyond that, everything was free game.

When I hit the far side of the hall, I had fifty dart drones flying in pairs. They scythed through the remaining Ændari on the stairwells from behind, causing mayhem in their ranks as blurred high-speed streaks carved limbs, weapons, and heads free.

By the time I was halfway up the first stairwell, the Ændari advance hadn't just been stalled—it had almost been eradicated.

Fifteen "true" Ændari were left, the elite core old enough and impregnated enough that they were able to shift their bodies to a degree.

Three were forming some kind of suckers, trying to climb down the walls and somehow get around us. One tried to form wings. Two more formed shields, though considering they were made of their flesh, due to them not having the degree of control over themselves I had, that was probably a bad idea.

The remainder either loudly tried to surrender, or had shrunk themselves as far as possible and made a run for it.

The one with the wings was the funniest overall to watch—flapping into the air in panic and trying to make it up through the open section between us all.

He made it half a floor before meeting Ingrid's insurance policy against the Ændari troopers who flew with armor. The firepower of five dedicated turrets opened up on the panicking fucker.

Spoiler: it didn't go well for him.

It took four more minutes to finish off enough of the Ændari left who were only dead or had surrendered in the upper spire. By then, I'd gotten sick of the shit and launched myself into the air.

I flew up into the space that'd just been filled with heavy laser fire, grinning to myself as the controllers of the turrets frantically loaded in stops and identification methods to make sure they didn't accidentally kill their boss. Then I was landing, and she was in my arms.

We held each other for a long minute, saying nothing, doing nothing, as the tail end of the fight wound down. The devilkin and UC soldiers charged down to finish the job.

"I missed you," Ingrid whispered, and I smiled, kissing the top of her head and squeezing her tight.

She wore her armor, the helmet retracted, but beyond that she was fully dressed for war, and I just held her.

"So, you gonna go get a room, or you saying hi to the rest of us?" Paul leaned against one wall nearby.

"Hi." I smiled at him, then looked around, seeing the others. Courtney was there, as was Malthus and a couple of UC commanders I didn't recognize.

Beyond that, there were about a dozen soldiers and devilkin, five civilians by their dress and hand-me-down weapons and armor, and that was it.

Most of the devilkin were down below now, looting new weapons and toys from the Ændari. The UC soldiers were checking the bodies as well, but beyond that, they were moving to secure the stairs and hall again.

"Lord Devourer." One of the UC commanders stepped forward, pressing fingertips to his armored chest and bowing in reverence. "My soldiers and I stand ready for your orders."

"Thank you, Commander...?" I paused.

"Captain," Ingrid corrected, smiling at him as she released me with one arm, turning to make the introductions and holding onto me still with the other. "This is Captain Shemer, leader of the surviving UC soldiers. Argus said that you'd updated some nanites for the dead UC soldiers?"

She asked that, looking up at me in question, and I nodded.

"Yeah, sorry, Captain. Good to meet you. There were some of your dead who had been recovered down below. They'd been set up to be harvested by an Ændari device. I wiped their nanites—builders, you call them—and upgraded them, before injecting them with the fresh batch. The first of their number is probably back on their feet now. They'll be weak for a few hours as they upgrade and update, but give it a day and they'll be better than before."

"Thank you, Devourer. Will they have access to their memories?" he asked me cautiously, clearly unsure.

I paused, frowning. "The ones from before the plague? Probably not. I think they were entirely wiped, weren't they?" I asked, nonplussed.

"I think he means will they still be themselves, or have you done anything to their minds?" Ingrid said carefully, and I winced.

"Sorry...didn't get that. Yes, they'll be fine. Have you unlocked their nanites?" I glanced down at Ingrid, and she nodded.

"It was the first thing we did," she said. "Their engineer was knocked out for three hours by the unlock, but since then, he's been incredibly busy."

"I bet. Good to meet you, Captain." I nodded at the soldier, who bowed again and then stepped back, eyeing me, as were all the others.

"This is Choni." Ingrid introduced the apparent leader of the devilkin, and I nodded to her as well, accepting the bow and muttered "Lord Devourer" without stopping her.

I guessed it was best to let them believe I was some kind of mystical god, after all.

"Good to meet you, Choni, and thank you for coming, both...*all* of you," I said. "Malthus, good to see you again, mate. And yeah, I should have known you'd be here avoiding the real work, Paul. Courtney! You still not shot this one and upgraded to someone smarter yet?"

"I'm tempted," Courtney admitted laconically. "Just waiting for the right one. He might not be very bright, after all, but he's got his uses."

"Hey!" Paul grunted, pressing a hand to his chest as if wounded. "How could you?!"

"He's actually been really solid," Ingrid said in a low voice, glancing up at me, her right arm wrapped around my waist now.

"I bet. Seriously, thank you all. I'm sorry I wasn't here sooner. Where's everyone else?" I looked around.

"Up on the top floor. We set up a triage area on the floor below, and then Belle is at the entrance to the command center, along with Scylla and four of the soldiers. They're making sure nobody enters the command center without a damn good reason."

"Good!" I approved. "Shit, we need to tell your people down there…" I started, turning to the devilkin and soldiers. "I've got a harvester in motion, so tell them not to fire. I'll make it visible."

"Of course, sir. One moment please." Shemer stiffened and turned slightly aside, clearly speaking into a comm link, mirrored by Choni, who seemed to be swearing as much as breathing.

"A harvester?" Ingrid asked, one eyebrow raised, and I nodded.

"Literally that," I admitted. "The changes in me… Ingrid, I don't understand a lot of it—hell, most of it in fact—but the changes I've felt? I don't understand how the war lasted the way it has. The Devourer…shit, I need to start from the beginning, to explain this to everyone…but I can control nanites in a totally different way now. I *am* nanites—I guess that's the best way to say it.

"I'm no longer flesh and blood. I'm…different." I struggled with the words, then shook my head. "I'll have to show you all, but for a start, the harvester is literally a part of me. It's a nanite structure, one I'm controlling, like when we create our armor, but the difference is, I can separate from it and still control it without effort.

"I can guide it. I had it harvesting the dead—not our people; I saw there were fallen of our side in there and I told it to leave them alone—" I explained quickly, getting a grateful nod from the UC and devilkin both. "But the nanites I recover? I don't have to spend months attuning them, weeks cleaning them or splitting them and losing half in an Emergency Wipe. They respond to me instantly now.

"I created drones, coated them in my Conceal ability and drew monomolecular wires between them, then flew them through the Ændari. They literally shredded their armor, sliced limbs off, killed them in their dozens, and all with just a thought. I could create ships like this. Literally, I could make *starships*. There's a Devourer out there, Shan'Gai, and that's the one who's kept the Ændari at bay all this time, who unlocked the facilities for the UC to build new devices, and yet…" I hesitated, not wanting to speak ill of one of the UC's "gods" right after meeting some of the soldiers. But the more I unlocked of my abilities, the more I was stunned that the Ændari had survived at all.

"Look, I'll fill you in on everything soon, but for now, we need to clear the node, then figure a way of taking out that fucking stealth ship."

"The fleet could hunt it down, or at least drive it off," Shemer offered.

"If they can get their head out of their arse for thirty seconds," Choni muttered, barely loud enough to be heard.

Shemer's cheeks mottled. He had clearly heard it, and stifled a harsh response, choosing to speak in as measured a tone as possible. "There are hundreds of thousands dying out there this very second. We cannot always see the logic of fleet maneuvers, but they would not spend their lives needlessly. Trust in the command decisions made."

"Yeah, command…" I winced. "Look, there's some issues there we need to discuss."

"Steve?" Ingrid frowned, closing her eyes and taking a deep breath. "You're happy to see Steve. You're not going to get frustrated or complain, not yet. You're going to listen to his side of the story first, then you're going to hurt people…" That last was whispered as she clearly dreaded what I was about to say.

"Let's take this up to the control room," I suggested. "It's not so interesting a story that I want to repeat it twice."

"Do you wish Choni and me to attend?" Shemer asked.

I hesitated, almost taking the opportunity to get them out of the conversation, then nodded. "Yeah, you'll need to hear this," I said flatly. "And I need to know where you stand."

"He's fuckin' done it again," Paul muttered. "Fucker's probably found God havin' a nap and pissed in his apple juice or somethin'."

"Yeah, yeah. Look, this time it wasn't my fault, all right?" I waved it off and swallowed hard as Ingrid quirked one eyebrow at me.

"Let's go up to the top floor," she agreed slowly, and I nodded.

"This harvester…" Shemer suddenly spoke up, apparently in the middle of a conversation with another until now. "Is it removing the Ændari bodies?"

"Yeah." I nodded, realizing I never described what it looked like. "Here…"

I made it flow out of the hall, moving into the middle of the empty space that rose to the top of the spire, and hovered there, as I mentally admitted that yeah, it was starting to look a little freaky as I made it visible.

It was entirely nanites, and without giving them direction, they'd reverted to a free-form, flowing, amorphous blob. It was like a cloud given intent and solidity: red and black oil slicked, with struggling lumps that had apparently been Ændari playing dead.

They were getting smaller by the second as the cloud grew.

There were over three hundred million nanite clusters in the cloud now that I could feel, and they were increasing by the second. Tentacles were retracted, but as soon as I told it to return to the harvest, they flashed out, latching onto bodies and ripping them into the mass.

They vanished with barely a ripple, enveloped, with even their armor being taken now. A slight change in the orders, and there was a nice little heart of null coins growing, ready for later.

"Wow," Ingrid said slowly, eyes wide as she stared down at it.

"Yup. There's an actual risk of being raped by a tentacle monster now. I'm out." Paul shook his head.

"Seriously, it's fine. That's part of me," I assured them all.

"I'm now more concerned than I was before," Courtney admitted. "I mean, you do you, Ingrid, but that's a level beyond my normal kinks." She patted Ingrid on the shoulder.

"I'm so proud of you right now." Paul grinned.

"Thanks, hun." She grinned at him, and I shook my head, sighing.

"Look, you fucks, it's a harvester, that's all. It's, well, it's like you're staring at my leg or something."

"Your third leg looks like that? All bumpy, and lumpy with tentacles?" Paul suggested.

"Really, dude? That was weak," I shot back. "There were so many better lines available there. You could have made a million better ones."

"I've got a better one," he assured us all. "Courtney knows."

"Sure, hun." She sighed, patting him on one shoulder.

"Fuckers," he muttered.

I gestured up the stairs, before pausing. "Two minutes," I said distractedly, reaching out.

There were fifty dart drones hovering now—stealthed, admittedly, but they were also covered in blood and viscera, so yeah, they weren't *that* stealthy currently.

With a thought, they rippled. Their outer surface shifted to the Devourer, absorbing the mess that was splattered across them, and then back to concealed.

I set ten pairs, twenty individual drones, to watch the open passage down into the depths of the node, then ordered the other fifteen to follow us, albeit at a safe distance.

I might need the nanites, after all.

"What happened to your armor then?" Paul asked. "Just not feelin' it these days?"

"Don't need it anymore, mate." I smirked at him.

"Show-off."

I bit back on the need to do something at those words. *Anything* I did would be literally me showing off now, so I forced a smile instead, inwardly cursing as I headed up the stairs with the others.

I'd been planning to fly, but yeah, couldn't do that now. Fuckers.

It didn't take long, to be fair, striding up the stairs. With Ingrid's hand in mine, I reached out to Argus, accessing the system easily now.

The node was heavily "contaminated," as he saw it, with biological matter, but he was happy that the harvester was working as well as it was.

A quick suggestion from him led to it splitting into two halves, with the first focusing on harvesting bodies, then the second unit splitting again.

The first focused on bodies as well, though moving back out into the outer section and starting to harvest the bodies out there—Argus requested access to guide it away from our people's bodies, and I gave him that happily.

The last section was pushing out a solid mass instead of tentacles. It literally landed on the ground and oozed across it, absorbing the spilled blood, the shattered armor plates, weapons—all of it. I instructed it to leave "viable" weapons behind, intact. Whenever it came across a grenade, a gun, blades—anything like that—it cleaned it and left it behind, sitting pretty on the gleaming, spotless floor.

Changing the orders for the three of them took less than a second, and then tweaking it was barely more.

That they were linked to my mind still meant that although they weren't sapient in their own right, they understood all the underlying context behind my orders instantly.

They picked up the dead from our side, setting them aside and moving to the next, absorbing and tearing the Ændari apart, ensuring that they'd never rise again, and injecting an upgraded booster shot into the UC soldiers who were found dead.

The others, the devilkin and the volunteers…for them, death was permanent, if they'd not yet been upgraded and ascended. Their bodies had never been awakened, and as such, when they died, that couldn't be reversed.

The others, though? As we climbed to the top floor, passing weapons emplacements, more soldiers and the masses of injured, that lay recovering.

They'd taken the brunt of the losses, Shemer had admitted, and although Choni looked pissed at that, she didn't disagree.

They could recover, and their weapons and armor were the best in the business, so they'd had the others supporting them. Although they'd taken a lot of punishments, they were still rotating in and out of the front lines.

The devilkin, who'd responded to Ingrid's call and had basically viewed this as a last-ditch attempt to rehabilitate their image, had done all the setup of the positions. Then they'd been pushed aside by the professionals, and I could see instantly it rankled.

Worst of all, as Argus burst-replayed the waves that had come over and over, the fights and the losses, I could see that the devilkin knew they'd been relegated, and knew it was the right thing to do.

The problem was, they'd either win here or all die, and if they won, it'd be the invincible super soldiers of the UC who won, with their help.

Not them proving themselves.

I saw people running as if on a screen: thousands racing back and forth, the deaths in the halls, on the stairs and in the air.

I saw weapons emplacements taken out by lucky shots or falling to waves of attacks, killing hundreds before they fell. There were stealthed Ændari assassins battling their UC counterparts; drones, explosives, mixed forces, and insane gambles taken over and over.

Each time I passed the UC soldiers who were recovering, I paused, and provided they gave permission, I injected them with a booster.

It was half a million nanites each, enough that a year ago I'd have been doing cartwheels at the massive boost to my power. And now? It was barely noticeable to me.

The fifteen pairs of drones that floated up behind us were mainly stealthed, but with a thought, another pair would slide forward. I'd lift a hand, reaching up, and the pair would land, touching my hand and then rippling, flowing down onto and into me like water added to a bathtub.

They'd vanish into me, seemingly gone without a trace, and I'd feel my mass "topped up," ready to keep giving them out.

Arise: Conqueror

Choni watched me, as I came to the first of the wounded devilkin, and hesitated.

"Can't you do it for them?" she asked.

I bit my lip, thinking. "I'm not sure," I admitted. "If they'd been ascended? Yeah, I could no problem. As they are, I might hurt them more. I know I can do it with humans, though, so I should be able to. Has Belle been healing them?" I turned to Ingrid.

"She has," she assured me. "She said there were some changes she needed to make to the commands, though, and it's both painful and takes a lot longer."

"Okay, give me a minute…" I crouched, looking into the blood-covered face of a slumped devilkin, his breathing ragged as he sat, back pressed to the wall, watching us. "I can try and heal you," I said to him. A tentacle slid out and collected some of the scattered ruined armor and scrap, converting it into null coins, just in case. "Do you want me to try?"

"What'll…it cost…me?" he asked gruffly, one hand pressed to his side. The armor on that side was cracked and burned by a high-powered blast from something, and steam rose from his wounds.

I'd forgotten just how hot the devilkin were. Literally, his internal temperature was at least fifty degrees higher than anything I'd have expected to be alive.

"Nothing," I assured him. "You came here at Ingrid's request. You came to help us, so I'm not going to charge you anything, but it'll probably be painful."

"So's life." He grunted. "What…do you need?" He was clearly having problems breathing, and I nodded.

"Can I do it?" I asked, wanting to be very clear about this.

"Yeah…"

I didn't wait. My right hand speared forward to press over the hole in his side and the shattered armor. I poured a finger of nanites around his own hand that was pressed there, flowing like the blood that was still slipping free.

I slid into his body—weird to say that about anyone but Ingrid, but still—and grunted as I saw the damage and felt the heat.

Whatever had hit him was a solid projectile, and although it'd passed straight through, the fragments of armor hadn't. The impact had shattered ceramic plates that were under the main outer layer, turning them into a claymore-like detonation that had shredded deeper into his body.

He'd injected himself with a medical kit, a fast-acting foam that would have probably had him back on his feet and fighting, possibly even without needing anything else, had the ceramic plates not been turned into shrapnel that had torn up his insides even more.

His body was a mess: dozens of old half-healed wounds, hundreds of scars and general deformities, sections where he didn't bend right from twisted and burned muscles, old injuries…

I shook my head, forcing myself to focus on the current wounds only.

"Are we giving them access to ascension?" I asked Ingrid privately, who squeezed my shoulder as she responded in kind.

"I think they've earned it," she said. *"They knew this was an all-or-nothing mission, and although I spent everything we had…we got a lot more for those*

credits than we should have, I think. Choni admitted this is a rehabilitation mission as much as anything else. And after our actions with the dock, they were willing to offer a little trust."

"They've been shit on from a great height by the UC," I pointed out.

"They have, and from the sounds of Emberalis, so have we."

"That's not over yet," I assured her. *"The little shit is trying, that's for sure, but fuck it—as soon as we've got the Ændari stealth ship with its signal blocker driven off, then we'll be able to reach the fleet directly. See how many of them actually listen to him when they see why we've been marked as an enemy."*

"Do you think Choni and Shemer will care?" she asked. *"They've fought and bled beside us for days, so I hope not, but they might be upset when you tell them."*

"I hope not, but just in case..."

"I'll make sure the others are ready," she assured me, and I smiled, thinking how lucky I was to have her.

"You enjoying this?" the devilkin before me hissed, glaring.

"This?" The smile dropped as I looked at him properly, seeing the pain and anger written large in his face, the blood that still flowed from a dozen minor wounds and the pain that racked him.

"I'm damn glad to have fighters like you on my side," I said. "But you look like shit, mate. You've been shot a dozen times, burned, blown up, stabbed… Shit, what's your name?"

"Lucky."

"Lucky?!"

"I'm…alive ain't…I?"

"Fucking hell."

"His name's Mikhael. He's unkillable, though, so they call him Lucky Lightning." Choni spoke over my shoulder.

"Well, you're not going to like this," I assured him, getting the final burst of data back and setting the nanites to work.

"Wh…aaaaargh!" His question was cut off by a scream that ripped through him as I pulled my arm back, wincing.

"What did you do?!" Choni snarled, lunging forward.

"I fixed him," I snapped at her, gripping his arms and holding him still. "Or, you know, I *am* fixing him."

"He's in pain!" she bit out.

"He had nearly thirty bits of shrapnel scattered through his body. They need to come out and the wounds be healed—of fucking course he's in pain!" I snapped back, holding the massive warrior as he thrashed and twisted, gritting his teeth.

It took less than thirty seconds in the end, but for him, that had to have felt far longer. By the time he collapsed, panting and trying to recover, it was all he could do to stay upright when I gently eased him back against the wall.

"What…what did you do?" His skin was flushed even more than normal and his helmet sat askance.

301

Arise: Conqueror

"Just catch your breath." I pressed a hand to the armor plate that had been shattered over his lower left side. I scanned the armor, then spent a bare thousand nanites and half a null coin, reforming and repairing the damage, front and back.

"How…?" he whispered, staring at the reformed armor plate, before gingerly sliding a hand up under his armor and touching the wound.

It was a third of the size now, and rapidly healing. The shrapnel had already been pushed out through the nearest skin. That'd been a lot of the pain he'd felt, unfortunately, as the most efficient and least damaging method was literally that.

I'd guided the shards through his body, pushed out by tendrils of nanites that had flexed and burrowed through his body, before healing over and retreating, exiting and leaving the entrance as the last to be healed.

By the time I'd stepped back and Choni had helped him to his feet again, I was shaking my head at the looks on the nearby wounded's faces.

"I can't heal everyone," I said to Choni and Shemer. "I just can't, as much as I'd like to. We've got too much to sort first, but if you bring the worst injured to the triage point…" I turned to Ingrid, who nodded and took over, her mind and mine linked, as we both agreed on a course of action.

"If you can rotate those who need healing—and I mean *need* it, not who have gotten wounds that are minor, as each healing he does weakens him—then bring them in batches of ten to the triage point on the level below the control center. Anyone we can heal, we will."

"Thank you," both said at almost the same time, and I nodded, starting to move again.

"That was a lot faster than we could do it before," Ingrid pointed out to me, on private mode. *"Much, much faster."*

"The difference in having full control over your nanites is insane," I assured her. *"Like night and day compared to how I was before."*

"You were already powerful," she said. *"How much of a difference?"*

"I could have walked through most of the Ændari without bothering to stop if I'd not wanted them dead," I admitted. *"The strongest of them…well, you remember the Erlking?"*

"Yes?"

"We don't have to leave Earth and never return," I said firmly. *"If he's got a problem with me now, I'll rip his horns off and feed them to him through his butthole."*

"You…are you serious?" she asked, and I felt the hope rising in her.

"Deadly serious," I assured her. *"The plans we had for building a citadel on Earth, a fortress for our people and making sure they're safe? We can live there too. I don't know what the future holds, but when it comes to anyone, and I mean fucking* anyone, *forcing us to leave Earth? Those days are over."*

CHAPTER TWENTY-FIVE

By the time we reached the triage point, word had already been sent, and the most wounded—mainly devilkin—were gathering.

"Why hadn't they been checked over already?" I asked Ingrid, who shook her head, looking annoyed that so many hadn't admitted they were injured.

"Because they didn't trust you." Malthus spoke up, getting a glare from Choni that washed off him like water off a duck's back as he grinned. "I told you, you need to start listening to me."

"Really?" she snapped. "Where's Benat?"

"In the control room." He shrugged.

"And yet we're not allowed up there, but should trust people to 'heal' us, when we can't stop them, or have any way to be sure of what's happening," she replied flatly.

"You and Shemer are allowed up." Ingrid sighed. "I told you this. You as the leader of your forces are allowed to go up, but not with more than two of your people."

"And why is that?" Choni snapped. "We came to help when you asked."

"You did," Ingrid replied firmly. "And you charged us for it. That's fine. I understand how mercenary contracts work. But I told you the rules when you accepted the contract, and again when you landed. The control room is highly dangerous and although you're allowed to access it to see it, and to understand that we're not hiding anything from you, you cannot enter the command ring, nor go there without a good reason."

"Because you don't trust us," Choni snapped. "But he's like you, so you trust him." She nodded at Shemer, who snorted.

"Yeah, cut the shit," I ordered, looking from one to another. "Listen, Ingrid might put up with it, because she's a nicer person than I am, but I'll tell you how it's going to be. When I've healed these, we're going up there. I'm going to check on our people, then I'll tell you exactly what's happening, and why he…" I nodded at Shemer. "Might be pissed at me. But regardless, you can stop this shit right now. There's two sides here—us or the Ændari. And if you're working with one, you're the enemy of the other. Are you working with them?"

"Never!" Choni hissed, glaring at me.

"Never," Shemer agreed.

"Then there you go." I shrugged. "That means we're all fighting them, and we're all friends, because we'd have to be fucking stupid to be wasting time and effort on arguments right now, all right?"

I got a round of glares and grumbles. Predictably, Shemer nodded and showed almost no emotion, while Paul and Courtney hid laughs at my "let's all be friends" tree hugger crap.

With that wonderful endorsement, I reached out, focusing on the wounded around me. They were laid on the floor. At least thirty were badly wounded, with another twenty who were almost healed.

"Belle comes down as she's needed and makes sure to heal them, but the devilkin need a lot of nanites to heal and…"

"And she's having to harvest the nanites, then purify them." I nodded. "It'll take much longer than for me."

"Exactly, especially when we can't get the bodies." Ingrid smiled. "Well, at least that problem is done."

She had a point: the one thing we had in excess currently was bodies.

That made a lot of sense as well. If they'd been fighting as hard as they had, it'd be a nightmare trying to grab bodies to harvest, so…

"How did you manage?" I asked.

"We grabbed them when we could, when we pushed them back or when they sent stealthed fighters creeping around. But beyond that…" She shrugged. "We donated our own."

"And that's the people you weren't sure about trusting," Malthus said to Choni, who frowned at the admission.

"Why did you not tell us this?" she asked.

"I did. You didn't believe us that the healing we could do was limited," Ingrid replied, forcing a wan smile.

"I saw you heal them…" Choni pointed out, indicating the UC soldiers.

"Because they were already full of nanites," Ingrid explained. "Look, we didn't stress it, because you made it clear you didn't trust us. Would it have been better if we explained it that way? We took some of their nanites, upgraded and unlocked them, then repaired them with their own nanites."

"That's not so—" Choni started.

"In doing so, we weakened them in the short-term, as it takes time to cleanse and ready the nanites. If we need them fast, to save someone's life? We can do it, but we lose half of the harvested nanites."

"And then you need to harvest more, which makes us weaker and weaker each time," Shemer rumbled, nodding. "As soldiers, we're aware that there are costs, and the Lady Ingrid explained the need for the 'nanites'…" He stumbled over the word, clearly forcing himself to use it instead of the builders he was used to using. "But I asked her to maintain secrecy regarding the use of them, as it is something not generally known outside of our forces."

"Why not?" I asked.

"Safety," he replied. "When people have discovered this in the past, we've lost soldiers to kidnapping and harvesting missions. We don't age. We heal from almost everything, given enough time, so we stress that everyone has the nanites in them, and we make out that we just have the same as everyone else. We make it look like it's something that's done in secret at our bases."

"And nobody tries to raid them?" I asked.

"Oh, they *try*," he assured me with a wry smile. "Regularly, someone tries to raid our bases. We even leak the location of a base now and then to the various pirate clans."

"And when they come to visit?" I couldn't help but smile as well.

"Well, we've had to recruit trainees over the years, the most skilled we could, but they don't have all our advantages. Instead, we use them to let our limited soldier numbers be used to best effect. That means that they need training, though, and we need to be able to harvest nanites for them to be injected with."

"So you harvest the pirates?" Choni sounded a lot less sure of things than she had been earlier, as well as a lot more conciliatory.

"Well, they've demonstrated that they think they're raiding a training camp for our teams and younger recruits…what would you do?"

"I'd kill them all, slowly," she admitted.

"So do we." He nodded. "We just don't waste the bodies afterward. And the ships can be used as well."

"How?"

"We usually use them and a pirate or two who surrenders to return to their bases and raid them in turn," he acknowledged. "Then we generally sell or donate what's left to the UC special missions teams, keeping a small number of the best equipment to outfit our teams for specific missions."

"Nice," I grunted absently. "Okay, I'm going to need a minute here. Might want to step back."

As the others moved aside, I stepped into a small space in the middle of the injured, reaching both hands up into the air. I closed my eyes, hearing the indrawn breaths as all but five of the remaining drone pairs became visible and flew to me.

Ten drones, five pairs, were still on watch below, ready to attack if any of the Ændari from the lower spire tried to counterattack. But the rest, all those left out of the remaining forty, came to me, sinking into and swelling a ball I held in my hands, inch by inch.

When I had them gathered, I started a new build—ten small machines, figuring a less organic design would be more likely to be accepted.

They slid out of the ball, one at a time, a "bulb" of nanites held atop a small pack of thrusters and a pair of tentacles, with three lenses, spaced equidistantly around the exterior.

It looked suitably high-tech, especially as the bulb that was on the top, or perhaps tank would be more accurate, was filled with a silvery liquid that was apparently feeding the tentacles.

The first of them slid across to a nearby soldier, his right arm clearly shattered; the armor leaked blood and mangled seemingly beyond repair.

Arise: Conqueror

The lens scanned the soldier, taking a sample of his DNA, injecting a small number of nanites and assessing him as I guided it, then scanned the armor.

It was mass-produced, not "real" nanite armor, and I marked that up to be repaired as well.

It completed the examination, made its choice on the correct steps to be taken, and I reviewed it, making sure that the decisions made were right; then I approved it.

"Are you ready?" I asked him, opening my eyes and waiting.

He nodded, pale from the blood loss but beyond that seemingly fine.

That lasted three seconds as a second floater approached from behind. The pair quickly cut the remains of his armor away, removing sections of the arm as well…to his stunned horror.

"Trust me, this is the quickest way to do this, and you're a hell of a soldier. You've got this," I told him, deliberately shifting my upper layers to show the Devourer armor, taking advantage of the whole "living god" image the Devourers had with the UC.

He swallowed hard, gritting his teeth, and nodded, forcing himself to stay still.

Blood ran freely as the wounds were opened further, before his own newly awakened nanites could stop them; then the tentacles blurred.

I'd taken inspiration from the 3D printers I'd seen, and the insane abilities of the nanites, combined with a movie I'd seen years ago, as the heroine was rebuilt from scratch by robotic arms.

It took literally minutes to do, to bring her fully back to life, memories and everything else intact, because rather than building her atom by atom and molecule by molecule, the system rebuilt her with specialist parts that were produced as needed.

The arm bones were first in that film, and although they were here in reality, they'd been badly damaged, so were entirely removed, with the arm left open and flensed.

The first two moved on then. The soldier looked confused as his arm was left mangled and now entirely stripped, while the third and fourth units floated up to take their place.

The third unit extruded an additional tentacle, sliding down and starting to print the replacement bones, as the other arms held the wound open. As they went, the next floater followed along behind, weaving fresh muscle and sinew, taking over and sealing the wounds.

A fifth floater approached and started to print the soldier's under-armor uniform again, binding it to the remains of the old one. The next two units reprinted his armor, literally, printing a replacement armor that matched the original.

The units used a mixture of nanites and a built-in maker, with the first two being dedicated to assessing the wounds, triage, and removing the damaged and broken matter.

It'd have been more effective and efficient to make it into a factory production line, and have everyone laid on rollers, sliding along the line, but then they'd have to be carried in some cases and laid in place.

This way, the units could be moved to wherever they were needed.

As soon as the first units were full of the damaged biological and armor parts, they broke them down, floating back to the units that followed them, and connected to their tanks, pumping the liquid matter in to refuel them.

All told, it took less than three minutes, from the first unit touching him, to him staring in wonder at the freshly printed armor that covered his arm. He reached hesitantly, touching the armor lightly, then squeezing it, running his fingers over it, then disconnecting the glove and feeling his hand.

"It's real," he whispered, shaking his head. "I'm whole again, already."

"Damn right you are." I smiled. "Tell the last models what you need to rearm."

The last three units of the ten were slightly larger, and took up a lot more matter, but they also had a screen each, and a scanner.

"Scan your weapon into the unit and pay the cost in mass. They'll print up whatever weapons, ammo, or anything else you need."

"Cost in mass?" Choni asked me, frowning.

"Yeah, if your gun is fucked, for example, give it the gun and a working one. It'll scan the working model, assess the fucked one, and if it can repair that one, it will. If not, it'll break the gun down for mass and use that, plus a little more—conversion costs an energy penalty, after all—and then it'll make a new one."

"They can do this for my people as well?" She pointed to the floating units that were now working their way along the wounded.

"Easily," I assured her. "That's why they take the DNA sample first, so that the arm, for example, matches the rest of the body. You're not going to want one of my arms on you, after all."

"And you can do any weapon?" she asked slowly. "Anything at all?"

"As long as we've got the mass." I nodded.

"How can you be so sure?"

"It took me two weeks to build a starship and fly across Ændari space," I said flatly. "Believe me, I raided and blew the shit out of everything I could on the way, and I'm here now. Making something that can recreate an already existing and scannable weapon really isn't hard for me anymore."

"What about improving on the design?" Malthus asked suddenly. "I've heard the legends, that the Devourers could make anything—that true?"

"Depends on what you mean." I shrugged, absorbing the mass that was left over and arranging it into blocks of solid, fully unlocked nanites.

A backpack flowed into being on my back. Blocks of nanites and null coins slid into place as the last of the spare nanites I had on me settled.

"Could you improve this?" He showed me his battered tri-barreled laser.

"Let's go upstairs," I suggested, not wanting our people to be injured for any longer than absolutely necessary but reaching out to take the massive cannon from him.

He carried it two-handed, generally, and it clearly made a hell of an impression on him and the others as I lifted it seemingly effortlessly with one.

Arise: Conqueror

I scanned it as we walked, using both my nanites and my gravitational senses to map it all out, before nodding and glancing over my shoulder at him.

"What do you want it to do?" I asked, having already seen a better design in the Ændari models I'd seen below, not to mention the more powerful reactors that the dwarfen designs used. Combining their improvements wouldn't be hard, and the weapon's actual frame was just…weak.

"Anything." He shrugged. "If you can improve the charge, that'd be great?"

"The power of the shots or the number you can make?" I asked.

"Yes!" He grinned, and I snorted.

"Should have known," I muttered, striding up the stairs with the rest in tow, only to find a good twenty people huddling three stairs from the top. "What the hell?" I frowned.

"Cestus, I've warned you and your people about this," Ingrid said grimly, her voice hard and clearly angry.

"You told us that we weren't permitted on the top floor." The whining voice of presumably Cestus carried from the middle of the huddle of beings, making no move to step forward, and clearly positioning themselves so that the only way we could get past was to let them go up and onto the floor ahead. "You never said we weren't allowed in the stairwell!"

"You know you're not, and you're twisting my words to try to get what you want." Ingrid snapped, "Cestus, we let you land—"

"And fight!" he bit out, moving slightly closer to the front of the group, but clearly not wanting to face our group fully. "You were happy enough to get some of us killed!"

He was humanoid, with clearly aquatic origins, green skin that looked slightly transparent, the organs and what looked to be cartilage beneath the skin dimly visible. His ears were scalloped, eyes shutting from right to left as he blinked, membranes slashing across them. As he shivered, flakes of skin peeled free and drifted to the floor.

"We asked for volunteers to help defend the node," Ingrid said firmly. "You volunteered, you came to fight, and then despite you being kept back from the majority of the fight, as soon as your people were injured, you refused to fight again, claiming that we'd misrepresented the danger."

"People died!" he spat. His friends surrounding him nodded, the jangling of bracelets and bouncing of unwashed hair sending a palpable wave of funk into the air.

"And the UC and devilkin have lost hundreds. You lost five," she growled.

"Eleven!" he shot back.

"Those six tried to surrender to the Ændari," Choni spat. "We don't count traitors."

"They fought for—"

"They didn't fight. They saw the Ændari and tried to surrender, and that was only because they couldn't defect."

"They sacrificed for the gods!" He hissed, "They came here like us, to defend the node and to serve the gods! Not to scrabble over meaningless lines drawn on a map by warmongers. You disgust us, insisting on war, when all you have to do is reach out to the stars to end this!"

"Reach out how?" I asked coldly.

"To the gods!" he cried, finally stepping forward and speaking quickly. "Repent of your sins, embrace the light of the stars, and you will be reborn!"

"And how will that help us now?" I stared at the literally frothing little shit, as foam appeared at the corners of his lipless mouth.

"The gods wait for their chosen to take the node!" He went on, words falling over themselves as he hurried to get it all out. "They've unlocked the way, but the Ændari and you insist on fighting! Only the chosen can open the path, the path for us all to become starlight!"

"You want to become starlight?" I lifted the tri-barreled laser and pointed it nonchalantly at the ceiling. "You sure about that?"

"The gods will come when the chosen reach the sacred space…" He ranted on. Half of his friends nodded vigorously, as the others started to speak up as well, apparently worried that he was going to be allowed to go somewhere they couldn't.

"No, it's the *faithful* who will be allowed…" another interjected, shaking his squat frame, skin grey like concrete and bald head recessed into his shoulders.

"The Starborn will…"

"The Secret Keepers of Prague…"

"Felis and her followers know the truth…"

They were all speaking up now, seemingly a dozen different beliefs spread across twenty people, and not one of them willing to admit they could be wrong.

"So which is it?" I smiled tightly. "Which of you is the chosen one who the door opened for? Which of you has been accepted as the commander of the node, is immortal and already accepted as a god rising?"

"You blaspheme!" Cestus cried, brandishing a laser handgun that looked like it'd have difficulty lighting a child's birthday cake. "Speak not of which you do not—urk!"

I raised my left hand ostentatiously, manipulating gravity to lift them all into the air. Watching them, I stepped forward. My skin flushed with the Devourer and grew by almost half again in size.

"I AM THE DEVOURER," I boomed. "I HAVE BEEN NAMED MASTER OF THE NODE. THE DOORS OPENED FOR ME, AND ME ALONE… YET YOU DARE OPPOSE THE WILL OF THE SHADOW GODS! BEGONE!"

Then I floated them all down the stairwell as fast as I could, literally filling the air with screams and flaking falling skin.

I used the mental map of the node, along with the points of view of the floating repair units, to carry them down and into the triage hall, and then over the heads of the mainly now healed warriors. I threw them unceremoniously to the floor at the top of the flight of stairs leading down to the next level.

"The shadow gods?" Paul asked.

"Just made it up to confuse them even more," I conceded, shaking my head.

"What did you do to them?" Shemer asked, clearly not happy, but also not willing to try to stop me.

"Just dumped them on the floor by the stairs at the far side of the hall," I admitted. "Choni, Shemer, could you make sure they know that they're not allowed to enter that hall unless injured? And if I catch them in this stairwell, or trying to access the control room again, I'll either throw them into space without a space suit, or crush them to paste with a thousand gravities, depending on how generous I'm feeling."

"Malthus." Choni jerked her head back the way they'd all just gone. "Go sort that out."

"After you," he growled. "Benat's up there, remember?" He nodded to the doorway, and the pair glared at each other.

"What am I missing?" I asked Ingrid as the pair kept staring at each other; then Choni grunted an order to her companion, who glared at Malthus and stomped off.

"Malthus and Choni hate each other. They're also brother and sister, so they're constantly trying to outdo each other."

"I didn't know he had a sister," I admitted.

"He denies she's his sister over and over. She keeps calling him little brother. I can't get the story from either of them, so I just accept it."

"Fair enough."

"So how about that upgrade?" Malthus nodded to his gun, and I grinned at him, lifting it to where he could see the nanites that were rolling across it already.

Sections were melting into each other; bumps smoothed out and regrown; the magazine shifted around and increased in size as a miniature power core was assembled. The barrels shifted, melding into a new layout.

I handed it over to him, telling him that it'd take a few more minutes to finish the changes—then, for shits and giggles, told him to tell me if it started smoking or looked like it was about to explode.

Then I followed Ingrid out onto the top floor of the spire, and to the rest of our people.

The top floor was a mess, especially compared to how I'd seen it before, but also not quite as much of a mess as it'd been on occasion, considering that the whole "hundreds of dead and slaughtered monsters" motif that had been left over after our first visit was gone.

Belle was slumped to one side, asleep in Jonas's arms as we trooped out onto the upper floor. The rangy ex-soldier had clearly heard the argument in the stairwell, judging from the glare he gave us all. When he saw who it was, he nodded, a tired smile on his face.

Scylla stepped out from her hiding place nearby, lowering the proton lance and favoring me with a nod of greeting.

"Well, it's about goddamn time, boy." Jonas sighed, gently moving one arm free of Belle, who was apparently out for the count. He reached up, and I gripped his hand in mine, having shrunk back down to my normal size once the religious nutters were all out of sight. "What's been going on then? Picked a fight with God yet?"

"Nearly." I smiled. "I'm building up to that. Thought I'd start with the UC first."

"What?" Shemer frowned.

"Yeah, real talk time." I nodded to him. "Okay, people, grab a section of floor and relax. Get comfy and I'll explain what the hell's gone wrong now. Yes, Malthus, don't worry, I've got Benat."

He nodded, clearly relieved as I moved over to sit near the unconscious woman.

As I sat, starting to talk and explain the situation with Emberalis to the others, I slid a tentacle of nanites out, plucking two blocks each of upgraded and unlocked nanites. I handed them over to Ingrid, Jonas, Scylla, Paul and Courtney, and Malthus, with the remaining four blocks being handed over to Belle as she roused herself, smiling at me in greeting.

The blocks fuzzed and collapsed into the skin of my friends, while a second tentacle slid across to rest on Benat's shoulder. A pseudopod extended and gently plugged the wound, pumping her new nanites in as the remaining few wounds were dealt with.

I barely had to focus now, pulling up the notifications and smiling. The healing challenges had been reset as well. I glanced at and dismissed the next notifications as they appeared.

Quest Uncovered!

Evolving Quest discovered: Do No Harm Level 1

Deployed Biological Weapon and Support Variants in the local area have been rendered non-operational by the enemy. Repair 10 units to receive the following rewards:

- **+1 Support Point**

- **+1 Espionage Point**

- **+Access to Level 2 of the Evolving Quest**

I still didn't know why the hell it granted a damn Espionage point for that, considering it was one of the rarest points I could get, but I sure as shit wasn't going to complain about it.

Quest Complete!

You have successfully healed 10 of the local Weapon or Support Class and receive the following rewards:

- **+1 Support Point**

- **+1 Espionage Point**

- **+Access to Level 2 of the Evolving Quest**

Quest Updated!

Evolving Quest: Do No Harm: Level 2 has been unlocked

The local Support class is deteriorating due to mismanagement and poor quality control on their systems. Repair 25 Biological Weapon Variants to receive the following rewards:

- **+1 Support Point**

- **+Access to Level 3 of the Evolving Quest**

I read through them quickly. Not only was this level done, but the next level was almost complete already, going from twenty-five to fifty, and I was at thirty-eight.

Not bad—I'd basically just gotten an Espionage point and two Support points for literally doing what I'd have done anyway.

I checked on Benat. The damage that had kept her out of the fight this time around had been mostly reversed before I'd come, between Belle's work and her own nanites, meaning that the two blocks I'd just pumped into her—half a million nanite clusters in each—would be more than enough to get her back up to kicking Malthus's ass in minutes.

Most of the delay had been down to the fact that Belle had been forced to harvest the nanites from the rest of the team to keep our allies alive.

Had Benat had the nanites she'd had when I'd left them before, she'd have already been up and fighting again.

Now, as I explained the shit that Emberalis was trying to pull, I was finishing off the last of her repairs—or healing—and I relaxed.

Not only were my friends okay—more or less—but the look on Shemer's face made it abundantly clear which side he was on.

"So, now you know why there's no more forces landing with me," I finished. "I asked Emberalis for them, and he agreed, but only on the condition that he got control over the node and we relinquished rights to him to share leadership."

"You thought about it, didn't you?" Ingrid asked shrewdly.

I hesitated, then nodded. "I did," I admitted. "If it'd have saved more lives, and I didn't think he'd just waste the opportunity, yeah, I probably would have. But considering he thought that in the middle of a fight he'd already fucked up was the time to try to negotiate? Then add in that the fucker literally decided to try to kill me to ensure he gained out of this during the same damn fight? Nah."

"So, what's the plan then, boss?" Jonas asked, and I couldn't help but grin at him.

"What else?" I asked. "We're going to fuck them all up and take their lunch money."

CHAPTER TWENTY-SIX

"Argus, are you online?" I asked aloud. He was there, but I felt it was the right thing to say to start the conversation, knowing that the others like Choni who couldn't access the node were watching.

It was a few minutes after the last conversation, and as soon as Benat had started to stir, that'd derailed the last details pretty thoroughly.

The massive devilkin Malthus might not seem the emotional type, but he didn't waste any time sweeping his much more slender partner up and crushing her to him.

By the time she'd been brought up to date, we'd all had a few minutes to relax, and I'd made the most of them by kissing Ingrid deeply, and damn well holding her, too. I'd missed her, and no matter how often I thought I'd gotten used to having someone who mattered to me like that, all I needed was a kiss from her, a touch, and I was amazed again.

"I am online," Argus responded.

"What do we need to do to reach the fleet, and to reconnect you to the rest of the galaxy?" I asked.

"I require either a much increased power reserve, or to remove the signal dampening field located around my node."

Nice and simple, and fucking common sense so far, I reflected.

"Can we increase the signal strength?" I asked.

"Affirmative."

"Okay, do it," I said after a few seconds of silence.

"I cannot. Maximum signal strength is dependent on available power reserves. Current power reserves are insufficient to overcome the dampening field."

"You just said…" I forced myself to take a deep breath, then tried again. "Okay, Argus, what do we need to do to increase the power reserves?"

"Emergency reserves must be approved for use."

"Okay, I approve of using the emergency reserves."

Silence.

"Use the emergency reserves and connect to the fleet, Argus," I ordered, taking another deep breath as I focused on what I was going to say.

"Negative."

"Mother…" I stifled the swearing and took a third deep breath, as Ingrid spoke up for me.

"Argus, what do we need to do to provide you with the power needed?" she asked carefully.

"Ændari forces have taken control of the lower spire, limiting power generation and ongoing repairs, in their attempt to gain access to restricted memory banks. Removing this interruption and securing the lower spire will enable repairs to resume. Once three more reactors are online, this location will possess the power necessary to overcome the signal dampening field."

"And how long will it take to get those reactors online again?" I asked suspiciously.

"Unknown. Too many variables to predict."

"Can we do it in a day?" I asked.

"Unknown. Too many variables to predict."

"An hour?"

"Unknown…"

"Steve, Argus can't tell you what he doesn't know." She smiled at me.

"Fucker better try," I muttered.

"Argus, can you identify the source of the signal dampening field, and project it onto the wall there?" That was Jonas, and I grinned evilly as the ship was outlined suddenly in the local space, hovering there, completely convinced it was invisible.

"How did you know Argus could sense them?" Scylla asked him, and Jonas shrugged.

"If he can contact their nanites, he has to know where they are. The dampening field stops him reaching out, sure, but there had to be ways he could see them still, even if he can't reach past them to the ships."

"Are there more in the system?" I asked quickly. "More stealthed ones, I mean?"

"Unknown."

"I hate computers," I muttered. "Okay, can they use shields at the same time as the stealth field?"

"No," Ingrid said firmly. "We tried looking for them originally, when they first attacked the warship. If they had the shields up, they'd be easy to spot still."

"Then maybe I should go introduce myself…" I started to say, only to be shot down by the rest of the room.

"If you leave the node, they'll use heavy lasers on you," Choni said.

"You're going nowhere without me," Ingrid said firmly.

"They'll fry you before you've gotten out of the dock," Jonas pointed out.

"A well-placed shot can injure even a Devourer." Shemer shook his head. "I mean no offense, Lord, but…"

"But it's a damn stupid idea." Malthus grunted. "You go out there and they'll shoot you with a laser. You think you can take shipboard lasers firing on you? You invincible now, are you?"

"I could stealth…" I pointed out, but I already knew the fight was lost.

"You'd be a fool…"

"It'd be suicide…"

"What would you say if I was going to do that?" Ingrid said flatly, and I winced, accepting that point.

"All right, then we go for option B," I suggested. The plan had already been in the back of my mind anyway. "How do you all feel about slaughtering the Ændari and blowing their ship up?"

"I like this plan," Scylla said firmly.

"Glad to hear it!" I grinned at her. "What we do is clear out the node, make sure they're all dead. But before we do that, I fire a few nanite missiles out into space. Like the drones, I make them stealthy and fire them at the ship. They'll take some time to get there, anyway. Then, when they arrive, they deploy a hack against the ship, get control, but stay hidden. When we're ready, they open all the blast doors and air locks at once. Flush the Ændari out into space."

"That does not slaughter them," Scylla said unhappily.

"That's because that's not the end," I hurriedly added. "As soon as the ship's vented, they're going to be too busy to pay attention to what's happening, so while they're all trying to get air and shit, and rescue their friends—if they have any—we set the ship on an intercept course with the sun, full speed, lock in the controls and then shut the whole thing down once it's moving. Purge the reactors—make sure they can't do anything about it."

"Why not just blow the reactors up?" Paul asked.

"Because they're not that far from the node, and they'd kill a lot of people still," Ingrid answered absently, chewing on her lip. "You can do this?" she asked me. "Take control of the ship like that?"

"Unless they've got a damn good AI that's watching for us? Sure."

"What if they do?"

"Then we make sure the missiles are nanites that I fully control." I shrugged. "Once they get to the hull, if they can't hack it or lose contact with me, they'll start converting the local mass into a nuke. As soon as it's ready, they detonate it on the hull. That'll fuck up their Tuesday, even if nothing else does."

"It's simple, and I like it." Ingrid smiled at me.

"That's just me," I replied.

"No, you're incredibly simple, yet complicated, and I love you. The nuke plan…meh, I like." She wrinkled her nose as she put her hands on either side of my face and then kissed me.

"Hey, get a room!" Jonas called over.

Without skipping a beat, I formed another arm, then another, flowing them all up around Ingrid.

The room went silent as I did this. Then they all proceeded to give him the finger. I grinned as the kiss ended and Ingrid looked up, seeing them all, then back at me, shaking her head in disbelief…

Then Courtney was there, her hand over Paul's already open mouth. "Not a word," she warned him. "Don't you say it."

That was it for the next half hour as we talked, getting one another caught up on the details of what had happened, until I got to the point of revealing the dwarfen's existence, and Shemer swore.

"What's wrong?" I asked him, and he shot me a glare.

"What's wrong?" he repeated, as if amazed I didn't get it. "You've found the remnants of an extinct race, one we've been charged with locating and protecting for thousands of years, as well as several of our ancestors. Then you put them aboard enemy vessels, and they could jump into the middle of a battlefield at any time?"

"Yeah." I winced. "Not my finest moment, I'll admit, but they needed the ships. There were more people than I had room for aboard my vessel."

"And speaking of that vessel, where is it?"

"It's out there, doing laps," I said.

Argus updated the plot with the ship, slowly orbiting the node, scanning space.

"What is it doing? Can we communicate with it?" he asked.

"They're searching for the enemy, and keeping them off guard." I shrugged. "We can't communicate with them with the field in effect, but as soon as we hit them with the nanite missiles, they'll be able to hunt them down as well."

"Then they will dock?"

"Ah…maybe," I said. "The pilot, well, he's a soldier and it's his first time as a pilot. He's learning on the job."

"So, can he interface with your vessel?"

"Meh." I shrugged. "Honestly, that they're even flying it is a massive achievement. I designed the ship for me and me alone to fly. I never even considered the dwarfen would awaken. Then I had to wake one of the BSVs to act as a translator because the one who was still alive hated me. It was really a collection of shit that turned out all right, more than a plan."

"That sums up the last few years, all right," Jonas muttered. "So, why'd he hate you, boss?"

"I killed some of his people."

"And there we go!" Jonas groaned as Courtney turned to Paul.

"You owe me a dollar." That was all she said, but I glared around at them all.

"Steve, they're an extinct people, and you killed some of them?"

"I was trying to help them!" I answered quickly, turning to Ingrid to explain.

"Yeah, helping to keep them extinct," Paul muttered, just loud enough to be heard.

"There was no atmo aboard my ship, all right?" I snarled. "I was trying to make one that they could breathe, and I accidentally smothered a few."

"A few," Jonas quipped.

"Hey! They got better!"

"Okay, so it was an accident." Ingrid sighed, then frowned as she saw my face. "Steve? It *was* an accident, right?"

"Yeah," I assured her.

"Good."

"Mostly…"

"What?" she growled.

"Look, I'd just finished one of the damn reactors—I was building them from scratch—and that little shit not only jumped me from behind, but he dented the damn reactor and grabbed my plums and twisted!"

"Oh damn." Paul winced, and Jonas instinctively covered his own with a hand.

"I take it back. That's wrong," Jonas agreed.

"Right?" I nodded as I glanced from one to another of the group for support. "Then he nutted me, so I just nutted him back."

"You headbutted him?" Shemer asked. "To be clear, that's what I mean, that you hit him with your forehead?"

"Yeah." I nodded. "A Glasgow kiss."

"Okay, well, the dwarfen were famously strong of bone. Perhaps he survived…?"

"Not with the front of his skull smashed in he didn't," I assured them all. "I mean, don't get me wrong, he did get better, but yeah. I killed him for that. Fucker."

"Okay, I think we're getting sidetracked." Ingrid smiled brightly. "So, first and foremost, are you both on our side still or not?" she asked Shemer and Choni.

"He headbutted the surviving member of a lost race to death." Choni snorted. "We're getting paid for this, and I'd almost do it for free to see the Ændari wiped out. This…?" She gestured to us all. "This is cabaret as far as I'm concerned. I just wish I had a stiff water to go with it."

"Water?" I started to ask, then nodded. I'd forgotten that to the devilkin, water was as strong as high-proof alcohol was to a human.

"And you, Captain Shemer?" Ingrid asked.

"I…am uncomfortable with the situation, but I see no alternative. Devourer, you command us by right, and yet we are bound to the UC as well. That a politician, one of our own species no less, has declared you to be a traitor and has risked everything, is a shame that will follow us until the taint has been removed. We are loyal to you, and to the UC. All I ask in return is that when the politician is captured, you do not let him weasel his way out of his punishment."

"Oh, don't you worry." I snorted. "Me and politicians get along famously. In fact, you know what? Scylla?"

"Yes?"

"How would you like to deal with Emberalis?" I offered. "I know you're good with politics and subtlety."

"Steve…" Ingrid whispered, covering her eyes with one hand. "That's a spectacularly bad idea."

"I accept." Scylla nodded. "I am gifted at diplomacy. I shall deal with this personally."

"Fantastic." I smiled, dusting my hands off. "So, that's all sorted. How about we deal with any upgrades, then go slaughter the Ændari?"

"Sounds like a plan." Ingrid smiled. "So, these nanites you've been harvesting…"

Arise: Conqueror

"Yeah?"

"What are they for?" she asked curiously.

"Honestly, I don't know," I admitted, smiling as I sat down against the wall, getting comfortable.

She immediately plopped down into my lap, shifting around to sit with her back against my chest.

"I've been without you for too long," she whispered as I wrapped my arms around her. "And before you get your dirty mind going, I don't mean like that."

"No?"

"Well, not *just* like that," she amended, and I could feel her smile as she said it. "I missed you."

"I missed you too." I kissed her cheek. She leaned in and we both enjoyed the hug for a few seconds, before she spoke up again.

"So, these nanites?"

"No plan," I admitted. "I've got another twenty-five million or so aboard my ship. It'll take a few hundred million to coat it entirely again, and get the full stealth systems working, or a few days of rebuilding the hull so that it can do it without the nanites. Truthfully, though, they're part of me now.

"I realized it when I was making the ship—the Devourers are talked about as these massive creatures, gods almost, living starships that explore the galaxy and are practically invincible."

"Yes?" she prompted when I fell silent, thinking.

"Well, first, I realized that I could split from them, so I could make the ship more and more 'me.' And then when I'm aboard it, it's like it's me flying through space. We can have as much room or whatever we need. It'll be literally as easy as this."

I lifted my right hand so that she could see it, then shifted it, flowing into a blade, a hammer, a shield, then a cannon, before shifting back.

"I'm surprised you stopped at those." She snorted, knowing me too well.

"Well, I did consider making a—"

"That's enough!" She bumped me with her shoulder, laughing before going on. "Okay, so you can change your form, and you can do that with the entire ship?"

"Yeah, basically." I sighed, making myself a bit more comfortable as I tried to get my thoughts in order. "Okay, so if the Devourers are so powerful, how the hell are the Ændari even still a thing?"

"What do you mean?"

"Well, you know my gravity cannon?" I asked, and she nodded. "Well, with my hull fully under my control, I could shift the ship into a giant one of those. We grab an asteroid, and boom. No more Ændari. Literally, I could pick a planet and snuff it out—dinosaur-level interventions—at will, and I could jump into the system and then back out. I'm close to being able to control the jumps now, and I've barely scratched the surface of my abilities.

"How the hell hasn't Shan'Gai or one of the others just dealt with this stuff already?" I shook my head. "I mean, I get it—genuinely, I do for the rest. Once those you know have died, and your friends and family are all gone, there's nothing to tie you to this sector of the galaxy, or this galaxy.

"Why wouldn't you just rock off and explore, leave the people behind to live their lives if they don't mean anything to you anymore? But Shan'Gai was here before the nanite plague. He's still here somewhere, supposedly. Hell, he's on his way now—or her way I guess...no clue. But if they've not gone, if they're still here, why? Why not take action, especially knowing that the Ændari were brain fucked for a while? It wasn't like he didn't have the time to fix the Forgeships. He, she, they...whatever...they could have fixed a single Forgeship without that much effort, right? A few months or even years at most."

"Then the UC would have rolled over the surviving Ændari. They could have ended the war in a matter of days," Ingrid whispered. "Steve, does Shan'Gai know you're here?"

"I think so, yeah?" I shrugged. "I mean, someone welcomed me to the Devourers. I assumed that was them, but maybe not?"

"Steve, how likely is it that they know about you?" she repeated carefully, and I hesitated, thinking.

"They probably do," I said after a few seconds. "And if they don't, as soon as the dampening fields and signal jammers are taken down, they will. If they arrive close to Emberalis, they'll get it all, no doubt."

"We need to get control of the system, and quickly," she said firmly, before raising her voice and calling out. "Argus, unlock as many points for our people to use as possible, please. Any soldiers aboard the station who are active, grant them any and all quests you can."

"Activating," he agreed.

"What...?" I asked her, and she shook her head, shutting me up and speaking aloud for everyone else's benefit, before sending a message to me privately.

"I just want everyone ready, that's all," she said aloud, before continuing privately. *"Steve, if Shan'Gai is that powerful, and there's no reason to believe they aren't, then there's only one reason this war is still ongoing. They want it like that."*

"Okay," I replied, mind spinning. *"If that's true, though..."*

"Then they won't want you changing the power dynamic. They'll want you gone, and everyone who knows about you," she sent in a rush. *"Argus, is it possible that the nanite plague was tampered with?"*

"Yes, Ingrid. It is highly likely."

"Why didn't you tell us this before?" I asked, barely stifling swearing.

"Because I cannot act against the will of a fully risen Devourer," Argus replied.

"Why not?" I asked.

Silence was the only response.

"Argus, are there systems or rules in place that prevent you discussing the Devourers?"

Silence.

"Argus, are there systems in place that could prevent you discussing the actions of individual groups or beings?" She tried again.

"Affirmative."

319

Arise: Conqueror

"Would these groups be involved in the local sector?"
Silence.
"Okay, location and identity are blocked out." Ingrid sent to me privately.
"Most likely by the Devourers, or by Shan'Gai directly."
"Shit."
"It's a computer system, remember," she assured me. *"That means it can be helpful. It's already led us to this point; it just can't answer direct questions that touch on the locked-out data. We just need to ask the right questions."*
"Joy." I sighed.
"This is my fight then, I think." She looked up at me, then leaned in again as I kissed her forehead. *"I'm still coming with you. You're not getting away from me after what happened last time I let you out of my sight. But I'll stay at the back of the group as you all kill the Ændari. Sort out your upgrades, and I'll focus on this…"*

"Five minutes, everyone!" I called out, holding her close and pulling up the upgrades. The damn quest to return to the node still hadn't completed. I checked it quickly, then nodded, seeing why.

Evolving Quest: Building the Future (Part 2)

You have claimed all the technologies you need to return to the fight, but although knowledge is indeed the greatest weapon, stabbing an opponent with your brain is less useful.

Use all that you have learned to construct a viable vessel, then return to the Node to receive the following rewards:

[Bonus: Return with all living members of the dwarfen race to receive a bonus.]

- **+3 Support Points**

- **+3 War Points**

- **+Access to Level 3 of the Evolving Quest**

Viable Vessel: 1/1

Dwarfen survivors: 18/18 – deferred

Return to the node: 1/1

It was the dwarfen. I'd completed the damn quest stage by stage, but the dwarfen hadn't arrived at the node yet. And until they did, it'd not be done. At least, looking at the eighteen out of eighteen, I still had hope that they were all alive.

It was time to spend some more points.

I pulled up the Espionage tree first, scanning over it with the current situation clear in my mind, hoping I'd be guided to something. When nothing popped up, I grinned and spent the point on something I'd been eyeing for a while.

Counterterrorism and Terrorism.

The Espionage tree was all about focuses, and I'd invested points into the defensive side already, Internal, making sure that I was able to counterattack and understand the defender's role as much as possible.

Now, though, with the last point I'd invested being in the general External section, granting a little tweak to the way that I saw everything, this latest point I put in Counterterrorism and Terrorism.

It wasn't "freedom fighting" or any such euphemisms that assholes liked to stick on it, to try to justify their actions. No, this was pure terrorism to the hilt. It was all about spotting opportunities for maximum damage, and destruction, and understanding that was the aim.

As with the rest of the Espionage tree, it wasn't a direct "do this" update. Instead, it was a highlighting of a million minor details, making them stand out, clear as day, to make sure that where other people saw nothing, I saw opportunity.

I shivered as it linked up a thousand details in my past, a million minor things I'd seen and read over the years, that suddenly when taken from an overview made me damn aware why the cyber security guys were so paranoid.

This shit was terrifying.

The next two points were both in the Support tree, and I pulled that up next, searching over the top layers and wondering where would be best to invest them.

Really, all things considered at this point, there wasn't actually a bad place for them.

The first three trees were split into Augment, Creation, and Repair, which were fairly self-evident. Augment was taking what was already there and improving it. Creation was building from scratch. And Repair…well, that was fucking repairing shit, wasn't it.

That was broken down further into Cellular and Cybernetics: basically, was I repairing—or healing—a biological entity or a machine. Not exactly hard to understand. Is the reactor fucked? Yes. Well, this is how you repair it.

Creation was literally understanding the machinery from scratch, and knowing how the reactors worked, for example, so that when I had no reactor at all, I could build one still from raw materials.

Augment was taking a working reactor and rebuilding it, upgrading it and using the baseline tech level to do whatever. I could improve on the tech, but I couldn't create it from nothing.

I could definitely see the advantages and disadvantages of each path, but for me it'd unquestionably paid off being able to do all of the various things.

I knew that specialization was the path to "true" power, but that was also for fucking insects and glass cannons.

Arise: Conqueror

The reason I'd survived as long as I had was because I was a cockroach and frankly unkillable. Looking at the three trees, there wasn't a wrong one to invest in. But just in case, I forced myself to take the time and check them all out.

Augment moved down into Efficiency, Effective, and Cost. Basically…put a point in Efficiency and it did more with less. Effective and it did more overall. And Cost meant it was cheaper to make it in the first place.

Again, not exactly rocket science.

There were bonuses to each, though Cost was the least important to me. In terms of building anything now, I'd rather do it right the first time around and build on that, as essentially I could now make anything I wanted.

Making it cheaper to build was nice, but I'd rather it was stronger or more efficient, so that was out the window. When it came to Efficiency and Effectiveness, they were two sides of the same coin, really.

Comparing it to the shields on my ship: would I rather that they were stronger, or I could make my reactors operate more smoothly, my storage cells be able to hold a greater charge, or conduits power things more efficiently?

When I looked at them in those terms, well, the power cells being more efficient meant that the entire ship was better. If they could store more energy but were slowed down in response times, I'd be fucked.

Stopping to think about things, I now had a dedicated healer in Belle and the ability to create machines like the floaters. They might not be fantastic healers, but from a mechanical point of view, they were marvelous.

All they needed were nanites and mass, and then they were easy to use. I could dismiss the Repair tree with that in mind.

Then it was either Creation or Augment.

Basically, did I want access to the plans for more powerful technologies right now, or did I want to be able to develop my own in Augment?

With that in mind, and taking into account the tech I'd already scanned into my sub-mind and still hadn't really had the chance to assess, it was an easy choice.

I already had access to the basics of Ændari tech, and I'd also scanned in a load of the dwarfen designs as well.

Mixing them up and using the limited abilities I had in both Creation and Augment meant that I'd made my ship already, so it was time to look at upgrades.

Augment meant I could take the current level I had and climb higher, so fuck it.

I sank both points into Efficiency, knowing it wasn't the sexy choice, and doing it anyway. Ideally? I'd have liked to go all in on, say, the Gravity Manipulation Technology.

That was *waaaay* more fun and gave me access to the awesome tech that could make things explode. I liked doing that.

Making my designs one percent more efficient or whatever in comparison? Nowhere near as much fun.

The overall improvement of one percent—or hell, ten or fifty; it changed depending on what I was working on, after all—wasn't much when you looked at it like that. But in terms of making a starship that little bit faster?

In making the engines, the shields, the power transfer systems, all of it that little bit better, that would be massive.

It still sucked, though, that I could have improved my laser designs or something.

The sub-mind flickered, stalling for long seconds as literally all its abilities crept that little bit closer to the height of Ændari tech. Then it was back, and I sighed.

Malthus alternated between stroking the nearly complete laser and Benat's hand.

"I'm going to need that back," I told him almost sadly. The tech update had unlocked a detail that could increase the overall power of the core, and with it, a small increase to the efficiency of the cooling systems and the metal. He could fire three times as fast, for half again as long as he used to, with just a little improvement.

The look he gave me at first, when I explained I needed to make some more changes to it, wasn't happy. By the time I'd finished explaining the changes and potential, he was practically shoving it into my hands and demanding I hurry up and work on it.

By the time it was finished and the others had completed their own upgrades, I found that I had a queue forming. First in line was Choni, who apparently fought with two carbine lasers and a pair of short spears, depending on the range.

Her attitude toward working with me and staying attached to us in the long-term was massively improved when I explained that these kind of "little" upgrades would always be at cost for "our" fighters.

She liked it even more that the cost was in Ændari bodies.

I spent ten minutes as we walked down to the "ground" level and main hall, upgrading everyone else's weapons. But by the time we made it to the hall, I'd barely scratched the surface of the weapons and armor upgrades I was now capable of.

Minor things—really little…like the improvements that reworking the elbow armor joints on Shemer's suit would bring—were now glaringly obvious and they itched, like seeing a light left on in the next room when there was nobody in.

It was inbuilt in me now that I needed to turn that fuckin' light off—save the planet and all that—and fix his goddamn elbow joint!

It was incredibly frustrating, but there was one small silver lining, in the form of a fresh notification.

Quest Uncovered!

New Quest discovered: Clear out the Rats

Rats have infested the basement. Perhaps it's time to call in an exterminator?

Arise: Conqueror

Eliminate all remaining Ændari aboard Node #02 to receive the following rewards:

- **+2 War Points**

- **+1 Ændari "Varrn" scout ship**

That was why by the time we took our first steps into the stairwell that led down to the lower levels, I was more than ready to unleash holy murder on any Ændari I saw.

CHAPTER TWENTY-SEVEN

The lower levels were clearly intended to be visited by less important Ændari and presumably less regularly, considering that where the stairs leading upward were gleaming and wide, with high ceilings and occasional portals letting you look out into space in all its wonders…going down was much tighter and darker.

The walls were lit by a solid red glow, much closer in and barely wide enough for two of us to walk abreast, where six could manage it going up.

And two was only if you were very close friends.

The steps descended in a straight line, stomping down about a hundred meters before we reached a sealed door, seemingly just waiting for us to knock.

That wasn't exactly a surprise—the Ændari were nothing if not fucking awkward to deal with. Pressing a hand to the door, I reformed a finger and sent it questing down to the bottom.

There was a tiny gap between the bottom of the door and the floor. The nanites flowed through it easily, pausing as they reached the far side and sending out a gentle gravitational pulse in all directions.

The room beyond was the upper access for the machinery hidden below, along with what looked like some kind of basic storage, from the image I could feel.

There was also a veritable shitload of explosives, judging from the mass packed around the door, that were there to ruin my damn morning if we forced our way in.

The door was as wide as the stairwell, squared off at the bottom, but rising to a point about a half meter over my head. Packed in, all around the upper third, were small devices, angled inward.

A little further scanning showed that the Ændari had apparently learned from someone, because they were basically claymore mines.

Step inside, they'd go off, and they'd fire their payload into the hall beyond. Not only would the first through the door get a nasty surprise, but the others who followed would as well.

The issue was, as I scanned it and then the rest of the room, there were monitors trained on the door, and three Ændari, all armed and all ready.

Arise: Conqueror

I relayed the issues to the rest of the team, getting a snort from Choni, who asked that we all back up, and let two of her people through.

The first was a figure I'd seen before: squat, armored to a frankly insane level, and almost medieval in his style.

Frette wore the heaviest armor I'd ever seen. As we all flattened ourselves against the wall, he creaked past, taking up station by the door.

He was devilkin, that much was clear by the covered horns and mad musculature, but the armor had to be two inches thick all around.

His helmet was like the ones worn by old knights you'd see in the really mad sword-and-sorcery movies, where it wasn't adjusted for style, and it wasn't painted or designed to show off. It was literally a circular bucket-style helmet, two raised sections that were designed to hold his horns, and a thin diamond-hard section of glass for him to see through.

He opened his helm and turned back to us, making me stare in wonder as it did a *Total Recall* head moment, splitting down a seamless joint to slide open, then sealing again when he was finished speaking.

"Choni, standard terms apply, right?" He waited as she sighed and nodded. "Yeah, all covered."

"Glad to hear it." He grunted, sealing the helmet, and moved up. The back of his battered and scratched armor lit as something activated underneath it.

"Standard terms?" I asked her, as he started to count down.

"Twenty…nineteen…eighteen…"

"You're up, Jotun." She clapped the next figure on the shoulder as he moved up to stand behind Frette, lifting a massive shield into place and securing it to the walls. "Yeah, sorry, standard terms for shield teams are that their equipment is covered. If his armor is fucked up by this, it'll take a chunk out of the profits for the job, but it means that we don't lose anyone."

"Impressive," I admitted, scanning the armor as Jotun deployed more and more sections that were attached to his own armor, to seal off the stairwell from what was clearly going to be a very big bang.

I pulled back the thread that I'd been maintaining to the bottom of the door, then stepped back behind Jotun.

"There's three in there still, far side of the room, heavily armed. They're waiting—must have triggered an alarm or something when we started down the stairs, because they're definitely ready for us," I told Choni.

"Anything you can do about that?" Choni asked, and I nodded.

"There's a lot of gravitational interference from here down. The walls are heavily shielded, but I can feel it," I said. "I can send a gravity field into the middle of them and throw them back, but I won't be able to do much more as we get lower. Not without risking the node with a reaction from the reactors."

"Yeah." She shook her head. "Don't do that. I'd hate to win, only to lose again straightaway."

"My point exactly," I agreed. "Okay, we ready?"

"We are." Shemer stood behind me. "I'd suggest we step up and take the lead once the door is secured. Is that acceptable?"

"You want to take the lead and the losses? Be my guest." Choni snorted. "If you want to take Frette's place, you'll save me a fortune in repairs too?"

"I think not," Shemer said firmly. "Your specialist is the best suited for this work."

"Remember that when we're asking for tips after the contract's done." Choni grunted, and I grinned, moving back farther so that the big soldiers could move up and get ready as well.

Frette reached zero, then triggered his armor. Shields snapped into place as he shoved forward, hitting the door with his shoulder and bursting through, into the room beyond.

He'd not even managed a half step in when the explosives went off. A small number were aimed forward, where they hammered into his armor from the sides and behind, and the rest were aimed into the stairwell.

He roared and kept going, shoved forward by the blast and hundreds of small impacts. His shield flickered and failed, even as the armor rang like a bell. He managed a few steps, then collapsed, falling forward to hit the floor and skid. The squealing of broken metal filled the air.

The majority hammered into the shielding that had been assembled in the stairwell—literally metal sheets that had been locked into place and shields activated over them. That solid barrier caught most of the incoming blast and neutralized it before it, too, failed.

Jotun shouted out in pain as a dozen sections that made it through the shields, now depleted and shredded, then hit his armor. Flames washed over, the impacts staggering him.

Then he was yanking levers. The hanging, torn mass of shields that had taken and broken the majority of the trap came free of the walls and crashed to the floor, where he dragged them aside.

Blood ran down from his right side, wetting his armor and making him hiss in pain. But he didn't hesitate, and neither did the soldiers.

Shemer was third in line behind two of his people racing forward, rifles raised, running in a staggered formation due to the size of their armor. They filled the air with the crack of supersonic projectiles as they went.

I'd triggered a gravity burst as well, aimed as closely as I could to the middle of the three ambushers. But with the reactors already being able to be felt below me, I didn't make the field strong.

Instead, I made it a simple three gravities, in the middle of them and slightly above, yanking them off-balance and up, then cutting it out.

Frette stayed down as the soldiers raced ahead, and as soon as they were into the room, I moved. I'd kept closer to the front, feeling a little weird, considering everyone else wore all their prettiest prom dresses…well, armor, but still.

I wore my signature jeans and T-shirt, and I was probably the most impervious of the lot.

I moved forward with the others, but by the time I reached the room, there was nothing for me to do. Well, not in terms of the fight, anyway.

The Ændari were dead. Their armor was designed to protect them in general terms, but there was a reason they developed the BWVs in the first place.

Arise: Conqueror

The three soldiers before me, and the five behind who had spread out, were the premier fighting force in the galaxy these days. And even with the element of protection that the Ændari had been enjoying behind the barriers they'd erected, the room was ours.

I crouched by Frette, laying a hand on his back and injecting a small burst of nanites into him, searching.

There were seventeen shards of whatever the bombs had fired embedded in his back. I cursed, seeing the telltale traces that came off the metal as I worked.

"They're poisoned," I said grimly. "Some kind of coded attack…"

The nanites that he had and that had interacted with the wounds were solidifying, breaking down and attaching to the nearest cells, taking them with them as they changed.

"Looks like they're petrifying," I muttered, sensing the changes all around the mass. "Hold him," I directed Choni as the big, armored man started to thrash. "The more you move or panic, the faster this gets spread," I snapped at him. "Stay fuckin' still."

"I've got this one," Belle called over to me, already working on the smaller number of injuries that Jotun had received. "When my nanites touch his, they're being contaminated," she admitted after a second, and I grunted.

"Rip them out," I said after a quick check. "I can repair them, but better to cut the infection out."

"On it," she agreed. Malthus stepped up and pinned the smaller shield bearer against the wall, while Belle ripped at the release catches on Jotun's armor.

I was doing the same, but more brutally. The sheer number of infected sections meant that I needed to act fast or we'd lose him. I trusted Shemer to deal with things, as farther ahead, in the next room that led off this one, I distantly heard shouts and more gunfire.

"Go!" Choni snapped at the others of her people who had paused, and they quickly followed the soldiers. "You need me here?" She glanced from me to Frette and then the distant sounds of fighting.

"No, I've got this," Jonas assured her, dropping down and pinning the larger man as easily as a kitten. "You go."

She didn't need telling twice. Smacking a hand down on Frette's armor in a silent good luck, she jumped up and raced after her people, as I ripped the last armor sections free.

I'd not had time to find the clasps and connections. Instead, with the shields being down, I grabbed the armor and flooded it with the Devourer, eating my way through the sections I needed to and deploying tentacles to peel back and discard the metal.

The nanites inside him were shifting rapidly, contaminated into shutting down, attaching to anything nearby and locking up. I enveloped a mass of them, hacking them faster than they could counter-infect. But, not having the time to fuck around, I lifted sections free as well.

As I enveloped the sites of infection, the Devourer "ate" into the new screaming devilkin like acid-coated teeth, tearing sections free, then absorbing them.

As I'd done with the floaters, two more tentacles were working, creating and repairing the flesh, stitching it together with the new synthetic version I was extruding.

Ingrid was there then, reaching out and laying a hand on the back of his head, injecting her own version of Hijack into his bloodstream and shutting him down.

He collapsed, unconscious, as she started to speak, more for Jotun and Malthus's sake than anything else.

"He's alive, just unconscious. Two, maybe three minutes and he'll come back around, but for now he's not feeling anything."

"He's out of the fight." I said firmly, "And so are you." I looked at Jotun, who was looking waxy-skinned now, as Belle removed small sections of his body, pushing nanites into the spaces and setting them to stabilize him, until I could take over.

"I... I..."

"You'll live," I assured him. "But you'll need to rest, that's all. Same for him."

The wounds were shrinking already. The patches I'd eaten out now filled as fresh flesh was replaced. The incredible heat of the devilkin raised the temperature of the small room by dozens, if not hundreds of degrees as I worked.

Three times his body shook and reached the border of death, shutting down out of sheer shock as much as anything. But after the third, it was clear we'd passed the worst, and as he slowly started to awaken again, I finished the rebuild.

I'd also summoned one of the harvesters, instructing it to clean up the room. I watched it for a minute, making sure that it was okay with the poisoned nanites, then nodded to myself. I stood, then followed the others through the next door, stepping over the torn and laser-riddled bodies of the Ændari.

The last room had been more oblong than square, with five hexagonal tubs rising from the group to the ceiling. Each held space suits of different designs. They took up the left side of the room, and the right had been covered in small honeycomb holes.

Hundreds of them covered the walls, each with crystal sections ending in the room, clearly connecting to sections that extended from here on out.

As I went, my Engineering sub-mind catalogued and evaluated everything I saw, making guesses as more and more was exposed.

The crystals were simple enough.

They were connection points, presumably to the deeper systems, places that an engineer or whatever could connect to various things, probably to test and do repairs.

The suits? Similar thing. The Ændari were usually melded to their suits through their nanites, able to summon and dismiss them like I could—or they had been like that when the node was built, as far as I knew.

Arise: Conqueror

That meant that these suits were probably for specialist areas, or special equipment. The last one that I passed was heavily coated in null coins; something reflective had been sealed over the top, presumably for high radiation areas that the nanites wouldn't be able to protect the user in.

Those damn traps had made sure that these suits weren't going to be used for a while, though, considering that a load of the poisoned shards had shattered through the storage tubes and had embedded themselves in them.

The next room was a second command center, totally unpowered. I assumed that when the main one had come online, Argus had been able to prevent this one being used.

I hoped so, anyway.

The systems all looked intact, more or less, save for some that were blackened and battered, where someone had clearly taken out their frustration on them.

Moving on, I passed several more bodies and picked up speed. The gunfire ahead shifted from sporadic and controlled, into heavy and sustained.

Two more rooms were ahead: a storage area, literally blocks of metals and null coins in their hundreds, then a small barracks, hastily abandoned.

After that was a stairwell leading down again, and at the foot of that...

Was glory.

I didn't know how else to describe it, but it was fucking beautiful.

The spire leading down had been explained as memory housing and reactors, but the sheer scale of it was astounding.

The main reactors on my ship, and on the warship, were the size of a small car. The ones that I had access to in the plans and data I'd unlocked in engineering?

They ranged from small enough to fit into my damn stomach in a power core, to big enough to send battleships through warp, and those were barely larger than a large luxury 4x4. Sure, they needed room around them to access them for maintenance and for shielding, etc., but the units themselves weren't that big.

These were...incredible.

The floor below me was visible through sections of glass—probably diamond, I guessed again—and holographic paneling. The left side fell several hundred meters, with three massive reactors each spinning constantly. Glimmering shields that could have constrained stars kept everything contained, somehow allowing such huge reactors to be set so close together, despite everything.

The reactors were laid on their side, shimmering fields of glass and the blazing light of atomic reactions spinning, flexing, and dimming. The levels were separated by great staircases and control sections, presumably for the reactors.

Then, on the righthand side, were huge towers of crystal, glistening gently, like a thousand years of glitter production had been trapped in amber. Great hexagonal towers rose, pressed one against another, barely ten meters from the level I was on now.

I realized what they were: these were the records, the memories of all those who the system had accessed. They grew at an almost infinitesimally slow rate, but they grew. In a few more centuries, they'd start to run out of space.

There were multiple sections where equipment was attached to the crystals and the reactors, with five teams having been working on them—all trying to gain access, I guessed.

That'd come to a screaming halt when we'd attacked. Now there were teams pinned down under fire, while Ændari troopers tried to leapfrog the soldiers.

Both sides were engaged in a heavy firefight, one made much easier on the Ændari as they could hide behind the stations and we had to stop firing. We couldn't risk damaging the reactors or crystals, after all.

Courtney moved up quickly, taking a place in one of the few sections not already claimed by the UC and devilkin snipers, while Jonas stepped up to my shoulder, Malthus ready with Paul.

"I'll wait here." Ingrid took one look at the fight below. "If you need me, let me know."

I nodded. Really, we should have left her to work on things back up in the control room, instead of leaving just Scylla and the still recovering Benat there. But she'd been adamant, and in truth, I'd not argued that hard. I wanted her nearby.

She was becoming a hell of a fighter, and her Hijack darts were a hell of a trick when they were needed. But she was right: as a Command variant, she was at her best overseeing and tying us all into one.

As soon as she brought her main systems online and activated her own abilities, the fight changed tempo.

She tied Shemer and his people into the basic command network, and our usual team, now including Malthus, in at a much deeper level.

Even for the UC soldiers still getting used to, or still unlocking their long-forgotten systems, there was a noticeable improvement in skill, as enemies were highlighted. Figures hiding around posts, for example, that were only in sight from one angle, were now visible to all and highlighted.

Weapons data that was relayed to her was shared in turn with the entire force, and a simple "I'm aiming here" or "cover me" was relayed to the whole group, but without being overwhelming.

It helped us all to operate as a single gestalt entity, improving our prowess in a hundred little ways.

For me, it was more about highlighting everyone. I grinned to myself and slid the remaining dart drones into the main chamber, keeping them in stealth, while highlighting them for our forces.

They seemed to glow blue as they entered the upper section, floating up and around, before diving in pairs.

There were only five of them left, ten drones in total with the monomolecular wire trailing between them, but they were more than enough to turn the tide.

Arise: Conqueror

The first of them dove down a level and looped around the far side of a
pillar. The loop of cable slipped easily under the Ændari trooper's chin and then
jerked upward, the drones' engines firing.

The cable snagged for a second on the armor, lifting the surprised figure off
his feet. But before he could make sense of what was happening, his armor gave,
and the cable sheared upward.

The loop had not only been caught under his chin but against his throat. As it
broke through the thickest section of armor, it slid upward. Moving almost too
fast to see, it cut the skull in half, then exited through the top of the head. The
front of his face fell free.

The body collapsed backward, blood spraying, and thrashed as panicked
signals tore through the brain. But with half of it no longer attached, his fight
was over.

Shouts rose from another nearby trooper who had seen their companion fall.
The air was suddenly filled with a variety of quickly set off grenades.
Everything from chaff to shredders, explosive fragmentary to napalm went off in
a wave. Through it all, my drones flashed and tumbled.

The only ones that affected them were the few magnetics, ripping the nanites
free in a confused streak that saved two of my targets. But the other troopers fell
back as quickly as the lost companions.

Our people stepped up their fire, pinning those they could and sniping, until
a sudden barrage of heavy laser fire went off, forcing us back.

That was when the sneaky bastards set off the concealed mines, shredding
half the UC soldiers as they'd moved up to push the line.

The explosions went off in a staggered line. Booming roars of pain and
screams as limbs were severed reverberated in the air.

"Advance!" bellowed Shemer, echoed by Choni.

Paul and I grinned at each other, Jonas a heartbeat behind as we ran in as
well.

"Steve!" Ingrid shouted, pinging something down below to get my attention.
"They're retreating to their ship!"

"No they're not!" I shouted, diverting to the side and picking up speed.

Where the others were primarily taking the fight to the enemy by sprinting
from cover to cover, leaping down the platforms and rolling to avoid the
incoming fire, I ran straight at the edge of the uppermost platform, then dove
off, arms spread wide, leaping into space.

There was a second where I could just imagine the stunned looks on people's
faces. Then I was flipping over, kicking out and redirecting midflight by
planting a foot against the wall.

Lasers peppered the walls near me; auto tracking systems zeroed in and
hammered me repeatedly, blackening my skin and clothes…then the damaged
nanites cascaded free, and fresh ones rose in their place.

I twisted again, a tiny pop of gravity there long enough to flip my feet
around. Then I grunted, grinning. I landed over a hundred meters down and
straightened, as I stood between the majority of the Ændari and their escape.

Two who had made it past me already skidded, twisting around and raising
weapons, sighting in and opening fire…before vanishing in a blur of blood and

spiraling meat as the drones flashed past, diving into the ship through the open air lock.

The group that had been rushing toward me stumbled to a halt. The leaders looked at me in furious confusion and contempt, before ordering their dozens of followers to slaughter me "like the fool I am."

I lifted both hands, waved them like a magician, showing that I held nothing in them, then flicked my wrists out. Twin broadswords slid out of my palms to extend into reality.

The hilts locked into my grip. Then just for shits and giggles I flushed my exterior red and black as I pulled up the Devourer. Then I strode forward, enjoying the look of horror on the enemy's faces.

The first of the Ændari was too close to flee, or even to change direction, and I lashed both blades across my front, passing them through his fully armored form like a paper mâché outline. The gleaming blades fed even as they passed through, intersecting mid-chest to render him into four unequal sections that collapsed to the ground on a wash of blood.

The Ændari were no fools, as much as I'd have liked them to be. Although their masters might be relentless dickheads, these lower ranks were warriors, even if they did primarily face only those weaker.

Guns were lifted. Heavy lasers were carried two-handed; tripods dangled as crew-served weapons were transported. And they all opened fire.

The world around me vanished in a barrage of lasers. The searing light chewed into me, as my upper layers flexed and shifted again. The gleaming oily red and black reformed as gleaming mirrored bronze.

The upper layer was suddenly reflective, glinting and deflecting, as the next layer down shifted. Ceramic plates formed, gel-like layers flowing into place to wick away heat. Dissipation panels opened down my back as I rebuilt my skin on the fly.

In three seconds, I'd finished, the glimmering bronze glowing with heat before fragmenting.

Cheers rose from the frontlines as they thought they'd gotten through, only to falter as the gleaming white of the ceramic plates floated up.

I'd found this before, but I'd thought that the design was just unrealistic for space.

It was a coating that I'd considered for the spaceship, similar to the ones that our own Earth-built space shuttles used, absorbing and redirecting the heat on reentry.

They worked there, and yeah, against small arms fire, they were perfect. But for shipboard weapons, they were just impractical. They'd deflect and dissipate lasers generally, but for the magnitude of power they'd need in space...if a rock got through at the wrong time and cracked the armor—which was, let's face it, goddamn *ceramic*—you were fucked.

Here, though, facing the Ændari and a massive, concentrated barrage of laser fire? It was perfect.

Arise: Conqueror

I'd crossed my blades over my chest in reflex, holding them before me, letting the idiots fire on them. Now I pulled them back, grinning evilly at the stunned collection.

Behind me, more screams and gunfire rang out. The drones flashed back and forth in the small ship, tearing the remaining crew apart, as I held the attention of the Ændari before me.

That was when the first of the UC soldiers landed like a comet in their midst.

Shemer had leapt from the edge of a platform fifty meters or so overhead—not that far off from an augmented human, and nothing to one of his kind. But when the enemy were firing lasers, it was an unnecessary risk.

Now, he landed like the angel of retribution.

The incredible armor he wore crushed his first target to the floor, cracking their armor and slamming them down, stunned. Then he started to fight.

He'd landed in the middle of a group of five. One was down and out of action; he probably didn't know what planet he was on after the multi-ton monstrosity had just landed on him.

The first to the right had his laser smashed aside by a swinging fist; then that same fist clamped closed over his face, yanking him in as Shemer brought the stubby fléchette handgun up, jamming it into his opponent's stomach and opening fire.

He jerked and bounced. Muffled screams sounded as the ammunition detonated inside him. Blood and viscera flew, and Shemer dropped him.

Lasers punched into his armor, blackening and digging into it. Glowing cracks appeared, and he grabbed the next on his right by a shoulder harness, yanking him around and spinning to throw the smaller Ændari into his companions, firing into them all as he did so.

Others dropped from above—UC and devilkin—firing as they came. Then Paul was there, landing lightly, rolling and coming to his feet so fast he blurred, his gun holstered. Instead, the long combat knife and tomahawk flashed as he severed hamstrings and biceps.

The leader shouted orders to the others; then Paul was there, hacking down.

The leader caught the tomahawk, then sneered, lashing up with a kick that Paul folded around, before ripping the tomahawk free and hacking downward, aiming for the back of Paul's head.

A split second before the blade could connect, there was another hand there—or, more to the point, a forearm.

Jonas hissed in pain as the blade sank into his armored flesh. But before he could say anything, a supersonic crack rang out. The Ændari leader staggered as his armor failed when encountering a rail gun firing a round from a very, very pissed woman.

"That's my husband, dickhead!" I heard from above, as his left shoulder vanished in an explosion of gore and armor fragments.

Jonas ripped the tomahawk free, tossing it underarmed to Paul, who caught it and drove forward, wrapping his arms around the Ændari's waist and hefting him into the air, before ramming him into a nearby pillar.

The missing shoulder was sealing quickly, his evolution to a fully nanite-based creature still in progress, but it didn't save him. Paul kneed him in the crotch, brought his head up under his chin, stunning the ancient creature, and then slashed his tomahawk across his opponent's stomach—once, twice. Then a left-handed punch to the chin snapped his head in that direction. The leader tried to snarl something, his body reforming.

He'd barely got a syllable out before Paul flipped the tomahawk over and whipped back around, the spiked tip slamming into his crotch.

Paul grabbed him by the throat, headbutted him—staggering as the Ændari's horns blocked some of the force—then snarled, punching him over and over.

"Just…"—*punch*—"fucking…"—*punch*—"die…"—*punch*—"already!"

I lunged forward, extending my blades to take the next nearest in the stomach. The tips cut deep enough that they emerged from their back. Then I dragged them sideways, carving the rat bastard in half.

Spinning, I threw my left-handed blade at a figure out of range. The blade extended, a tentacle driving it free of my palm. The blade sank into his chest, then dragged him back to me. I rolled my right wrist; the blade whistled as it spun through the air, then whipped around into a figure of eight.

I knew Paul was having fun with the leader—hell, the solid evolutions that he'd undergone in such a short period of time, to be able to go toe-to-toe with one of these fuckers in bare weeks since the admittedly higher-leveled and stronger Varnock had nearly killed us all, was insane.

We didn't have time for this shit, though, and I needed to make sure the enemy didn't pull out a last-minute win.

I slammed my fists together. Knuckles cracked and blades rang as they crashed against each other. Then I rippled: my nanites shifted, gathered—then struck. A dozen tentacles speared out like striking cobras, latching onto the Ændari all around, burrowing in, and starting their conversion.

The nanites, encoded to their user, shivered. Then, in a great swell, they started to convert, flowing out from the impact in ever expanding waves. They screamed as their bodies crumbled, collapsing inward, and I couldn't help but grin.

The last tentacles wove through the nearest enemies as the air cracked and hummed with lasers and rail gun fire, screams, flashing metal and spraying blood, until finally, the quest from Argus dinged. I stood for a second, glorying in the words that printed across my vision, the last bodies falling all around us.

Quest Complete!

Quest completed: Clear out the Rats

The Ændari aboard Node #02 have been eliminated, returning complete control over the station to you.

You receive the following rewards:

- **+2 War Points**

- **+1 Ændari "Varrn" scout ship**

Arise: Conqueror

The scout ship might not be much use to me in general terms, but it certainly made one thing easier. I'd been planning to launch missiles to take out the Ændari stealth ship, and that had been next on my interminable list of "honey-do's."

Now I had a new "missile," and it was a bit bigger than normal.

CHAPTER TWENTY-EIGHT

I don't care what anyone said later—I definitely did *not* giggle like a schoolgirl as the stealthed Ændari vessel that had been maintaining the dampening field around the node let my little Trojan horse dock.

It'd taken ten minutes of hurried and very messy work, boarding the ship and searching it from stern to keel to make sure that there definitely wasn't anyone alive aboard, then "mopping up" the nanites and creating an effigy that sat in the main command chair of the ship as it "fled" the node.

I'd hated having to do it, but just in case the Ændari had some way of accessing the bridge on their vessels that I didn't know about, Ingrid had insisted.

I'd used scrap as the underlying layer, literally absorbing and breaking down random shit I found in the ship, as the others looted it for anything and everything they could.

Then I'd made an effigy of the Ændari leader.

I'd printed his flesh-appearing nanites across the surface of the scaffolding I'd just created, imparting a limited sentience to the automaton with Argus's help. Then I'd gotten to work, tearing some of the structure of the ship apart.

The RI that controlled the ship was fortunately pretty much the most basic model it could be. It was almost entirely consumed with the management of the stealth systems, meaning that the interactions it had with the crew were limited to "stealth on" and "jump," etc.

As such, a little work by Argus and a bit more violence by me driving a spear of encoded nanites into its heart was all that was required to make it do as it was told.

Then we'd packed the hold with as much as I could create in a short time.

It was almost all explosives—omni-directional shredders, laser mines…all that good stuff—and the ship was set to open fire with its lasers as soon as it was inside its bigger sister's dock, just to make sure of maximum damage.

Paul had tried to convince me to run the little ship's reactors up to critical and detonate them as soon as it was aboard. I'd considered it, but the fear was that either the explosion would be too big or it'd set off the other ship's reactors. That damn well could happen—and it'd damage *us*.

Arise: Conqueror

Instead, even if the smaller vessel did damage the larger one, but not too much, just enough to fuck up the internals a bit and then exploded, they'd be forced to run.

Probably, anyway.

There was a risk that the smaller stealth ship would be scanned and they'd realize that it was a trap first, of course. In that case, they'd probably vaporize the smaller vessel and then we'd lost an opportunity, but fuck it.

I'd also considered just ramming the fucker with the little ship but wasn't sure that the damage would be enough.

It only needed to be minor, Shemer had promised me, when I'd explained my plan to him—the stealth coating was highly vulnerable—and so I'd gone with this plan.

If we damaged one side of the vessel, it could still turn and present the undamaged side to Bach and Zhonat, and maybe stay hidden.

With the dock exploding, though, and lasers going off in all directions, punching through the hull? That'd be damn obvious. And if the pair couldn't get them after that, they didn't deserve to be called UC soldiers, Shemer had assured me.

We gathered around the lower level's control station. Argus activated it and used the screens there to zoom in, letting us all watch as the ship inched closer and closer to its "friend."

It took less than three seconds after the larger vessel's doors closed, before the side of it erupted in flames and debris.

Atmo vented; flames gouted out into the vacuum. Random materials and sparking illuminated the hull as the stealth coating wavered and failed.

As luck would have it, my ship was on the far side of the node at that point, because that's just how karma likes to work, but the damage was enough that there was no way for the Ændari to still hide.

They fired their engines, shields flickering as they tried to come online, damage still clear as the ship vented, and I grinned, watching the chase as it began.

Then I turned back to the reactors, looking them over.

"What's the verdict, Argus?" I asked aloud.

"Thirty-eight percent and climbing," the AI responded happily. "I estimate the last ten percent will take the longest, due to the magnitude of the repairs required, but reserves are climbing, as is signal strength."

"How long until we can send a signal to the fleet, or out of the system?" I asked.

"The fleet will receive any signal sent to activated nanite management systems in approximately one hour, though this timescale may change if—"

He broke off as an image of my ship—lasers firing, rail guns pulsing— screamed past the node, firing everything it had at the now visible stealth vessel.

The stealthed ship jerked, the starboard side of the hull suddenly lit by dozens of damage markers, as flames wreathed it.

Most of the shots, though, the rail guns especially, ripped straight past, and as they did…it returned fire.

Whoever was in charge was no slouch. They had shields trying to boot in seconds. Engines flared as they shifted, and then they were turning, spinning in place as my ship jetted past.

They tracked it; turrets opened up and hit the shields, sending them flickering but barely more than that. Then the stealth ship was off.

"Stealthed vessel is deploying mines," Argus warned us all.

I nodded, opening my mouth to order him to warn them…and then remembering that we couldn't, thanks to those fuckers and their jamming field.

"Come on… See them. You've got to see them, right?" I muttered, watching as the stealthed vessel shifted, lining the track of mines they were deploying in a specific pattern.

"There are no signs that the allied vessel is aware of the growing minefield."

"Fuuuck." I groaned. "Okay, how bad are these going to be?"

"Unknown. Stealth vessels, by their nature, have limited storage options. Therefore, the minefield is likely to be highly compact, and yet more powerful than regular versions."

"Double buttfuck," I muttered, staring at the details, the flickering distance markers, and the projected track that my ship was following. "There has to be something," I almost pleaded with Argus. "Something we can do?"

"There are no options existing to enable contact between the allied vessel and this node at this time. Power levels are climbing, but too slowly to enable countering the dampening field. Time to impact: seventeen seconds."

I threw myself at the problem, trying to think of a way, but there just wasn't one. They were far enough away that they weren't even visible to the naked eye from here.

I could try to create a gravity field, but to reach them there? I'd be more likely to hit them with it than help at all, never mind manage to affect the minefields.

My gravity cannon? I could fire it, if I could get to the dock and outside in the next…eleven seconds. But even if I used all my available nanites and reformed them into a cannon that could fuck up the moon, the time it'd take to fire, then get from here to the minefield, not counting the chances of me managing to hit a mine from here?

Nope.

I kept frantically thinking, coming up with plans and discarding them, second by second, right up until they hit the mines.

The stealthed mines exploded around the ship, rocking it and sending it careening. Shields failed as the ship hit the concentrated collection at high speed.

It'd opened fire at the last second, presumably seeing something was ahead and trying to clear them out of the way. But by then it was too late.

When the whiteout of the explosions faded and we could see it again, my ship was tumbling out of control, venting gasses. Flames battled with the shields that were totally down; crackling lines popped into reality then vanished as they tried to reactivate.

A dozen new holes covered it, and the engines…well. The engines were still attached. That was the best that could be said about them.

The stealth ship arced around slowly, or so it seemed to us, closing on the tumbling craft as lights dimmed and the venting stopped, whatever gasses that were left having been extinguished and… Gasses?

We'd had the ship vented already, hadn't we? Why the hell had they repressurized it?

The Ændari swooped in again, their own engines flaring and their stealth fields utterly broken as they slowed, waiting as Bach and Zhonat fought the tumble, levelling the ship out.

Then Argus spoke up again.

"Reactors are undergoing emergency shutdown. Energy readings lowering in correlated…weapons fire detected."

"Weapons?" Ingrid asked.

I burst out laughing as the engines suddenly flared, kicking the nose around to line up on the Ændari ship. The storm casters, lasers, and one of the rail guns all opened fire at once, at point-blank range.

The Ændari ship vanished in lightning, flames, and destruction, coming apart under the hellfire.

I stared in wonder as my little ship's engines flared again. Shields flickered before snapping into place as it righted itself and started to limp away from the incoming rain of destruction.

"You sneaky fucks!" I shouted, loving it.

"They goaded them, lured them in." Jonas snorted, shaking his head. "Damn, they've got balls of steel. How the hell did they know they'd not be killed?"

"They didn't." Shemer nodded in respect as he spoke. "They knew that they were damaged and judged it the most likely route to eliminate the Ændari vessel. Impressive."

"Fucked my ship up, in the end," I muttered, then shook my head. "No. That's not fair. They're not pilots, and I left them to learn to operate the ship on the fly. They did a hell of a job with that."

"They did," Ingrid agreed, smiling at me as she took my hand in hers. "Argus, are we still being jammed?"

"The fleet will receive any messages you desire now," Argus deadpanned.

"Good to know. And getting signals outside of the system?" I replied.

"Additional jamming fields are still being detected, directed entirely at this node. Extra-system communication is not currently possible, but this may be circumvented through elimination of the remaining enemy stealth platforms."

"So, we can talk in-system now, but not outside, until we slaughter every fucker," I summarized. "I like it." I straightened, then looked about. The others gave me a little space, but I was still under the watchful eye of them all to make sure I didn't run off or teleport or whatever. "Argus, can we talk to Zhonat and Bach please?"

"They are currently dealing with a possible reactor leak. I recommend allowing them to deal with it without distraction," Argus pointed out, and I winced.

"Fair point. We'll talk to them when they get here." I shut the lower control center down, and looked around to make sure there wasn't anything I was forgetting.

Ingrid especially wasn't letting me get too far away. Even as she worked on the systems, trying to make sense of the blind spots Argus had, she was watching me.

"You ready?" I asked her, moving over and holding a hand out to her. She looked up, then nodded, her helmet retracted. She smiled, taking my hand and letting me help her to her feet, as I looked around at the others. "Everyone ready?" I called out.

"We are," Shemer agreed.

"Us too." Choni nodded.

"Ready." Jonas shrugged. "What's the plan, boss?"

"Repairs are begun in here." I nodded to the custodian that I'd made, as well as the vat of nanites and the pile of coins that stood ready. "Argus can make his own from that now, and it's time I sorted that little bastard Emberalis out."

"You want anyone to keep an eye on things down here?" Jonas asked me, and I shook my head.

"No, as soon as we're all out of here, I'm resealing it. The only way in is through that panel, and I'm damn well sealing that too for now. With those sealed off, the Ændari are fucked if they try accessing the lower areas again.

"Once we've got full control of the system, I'm going to reseal the entire node, make it so that no matter what the fuckers pull, there's no chance of them fucking us all over again."

"I thought you couldn't reseal it?" Jonas asked, and I smiled.

"I couldn't, before," I admitted. "Now, though, the changes in me? I don't think there's much of anything I can't do. It'll just be difficult at worst."

"So, what now?" he repeated.

"We get out of here. We call the fleet and sort this shit out. Then we kill the Ændari, tidy up the galaxy, and maybe take the weekend off," I quipped, before looking around, making sure that everyone was up and moving.

The majority were already on the stairs between the platforms, moving from section to section and gathering up weapons or loot they fancied.

Apparently they'd not expected me to offer it. The devilkin mercenaries were used to quietly grabbing anything they could but being subtle. The UC soldiers were trained to gather up something if it looked valuable or interesting, but they expected to hand it in. Their commanders would make a final decision on anything collected.

Here we'd told them to grab what they wanted, then move out. The various tech wasn't particularly interesting to me anymore, having seen most of it before several times, and what I'd not already scanned?

Arise: Conqueror

Well, it was mainly reverse engineered and shittier versions of the systems I had access to in my Engineering tree. I asked them to show me things as they went, but everything I'd seen so far was crap.

As we went—I was walking with Ingrid and the team rather than flying ahead because I wanted to make damn sure nobody and nothing was left behind—I watched the plot for the system that Argus sent me.

The fight was a stalemate again, with more ships jumping in all the time. The UC were up to five battleships, with a dozen cruisers and hundreds of smaller ships, ranging from small and medium fighters to larger but heavily armed transports and destroyers.

They'd apparently held the upper hand for a little while; then more of the Ændari had jumped in, driving them from the jump point and sealing the system again.

The UC had allowed themselves to be driven inward and were working to consolidate their forces now. Those who had been involved in dogfights around the system broke off and moved to join up.

The Ændari were up to seven battleships, but they'd lost the majority of their smaller vessels, leaving them vulnerable to hit-and-run tactics while the larger vessels soaked up the punishment.

"Do we have anything on the Devourers?" I asked Ingrid.

"Nothing concrete," she admitted. *"But there's a lot that doesn't match up. Anything that references the Devourers is…well, it's oblique, like the main details were removed, but clumsily, and it's just the secondary mentions that are left. It's like if you used a CTRL+F search on a document, and found all the references to something specific, then removed those and never went looking properly. All the mentions that don't use those exact words are there still. Am I explaining this right?"*

"I think so. So when was the last visit by any of the Devourers?"

"If I'm reading this right, they're fairly regular, and they're not good for the node."

"What?"

"The effectiveness of the node massively drops after each visit. There's been some significant updates sent out in the past, to all attached nanites at certain times…then at other times, to just those in a local area. We're missing something, because this really doesn't make sense."

"Can you figure out how many Devourers there are?" I asked, curiously.

"According to the data I've found—and remember, this has been tampered with, so it might be wrong—but there are five, or there were. None but Shan'Gai has been here in a long, long time. The others jumped, but as soon as they left, they vanished, never seen again."

"No signals picked up? No return visits?"

"Nothing at all." She shook her head, ponytail bouncing, and she caught it absently, running her armored fingers through it as the band that tethered it shifted, retightening. *"It's like once they leave, they don't return. Only Shan'Gai does. But I could have sworn we'd been told before that there were other Devourers still."*

"Yeah, we were told they patrolled the border systems, weren't we?" I asked, opening my mouth to speak, thinking to ask Shemer about them.

"Don't," Ingrid said quickly, squeezing my hand hard. *"Anything you say aloud Argus will hear. He might be able to hear this too, but I'm not sure."*

"You don't trust him, it…whatever?" I asked.

"It's not that," she said slowly. *"It's not that I don't trust him, but he's had his memory altered, sections edited, and I can't tell if that's all. I think there might be more going on here than we can see."*

"Yeah, if Shan'Gai has been able to access the node all this time, they should have been able to update the UC's systems at least, reboot them and get them into the fight. If they'd been able to access everything and the Ændari couldn't? They'd have won the war easily."

"Exactly."

"Maybe Argus wouldn't allow Shan'Gai to dock?" I tried, thinking through it.

"From the records, something has had direct access to the memory crystals and erased records from there," she admitted. *"It means that either Shan'Gai had full access to the lower systems, if nothing else, or someone else did."*

"That's not good."

"Definitely not. Someone wanted both sides to remain equal. And it gets worse. As near as I can tell, they've been eliminating anyone who got access to anything that would change the status quo. The lack of anyone finding outstanding technology? Old records, anything like that? You did, after all. And don't take this the wrong way, Steve, but unless it's me naked or a fight, you're generally not looking for it. For you to stumble across this, and for the UC to never manage to recover anything from the contaminated zones? Something has to be happening to keep things in balance."

"Is it possible there's more hidden in there?" I asked after a few seconds. *"Like, we've been thinking they're idiots for not exploring the contaminated and forbidden zones more, but have we just been lucky? Were there things there that we've just missed?"*

"It's possible, but if that happened to us, it'd have happened to more as well. Technology would have to leak out somehow. Maybe it's because so many smaller shipyards and tech companies are developing tech that's approaching the old levels now. Maybe there's a tipping point approaching, I don't know. But that the Ændari are as ready to flee as they are, it just seems crazy…"

"Crazy that it's all happening at once," I finished for her.

She nodded, squeezing my hand, and we climbed the last few levels in silence, our minds miles away.

It didn't take long for us to clear out the lower sections. For the first time in ages, it didn't feel like we were totally fucked for time. The two fleets had pulled back from each other: the Ændari now held the jump point, and the UC were grouping up again.

Arise: Conqueror

Zhonat and Bach had hammered the shit out of the stealth vessel, and as its remains flashed and sparked, drifting with their dead crew, they were on their way back to the node now, clearly planning to land.

I reached out and confirmed with them, as well as reassuring them both that if anything, the Ændari holding the jump point as they were was a relief when it came to the others I'd picked up recently jumping in.

They were far less likely to be fired upon as soon as they arrived, giving them a chance to get out of range, hopefully.

That being said, it was a fuckload more concerning for James and the others, as if they and the rest of the reinforcements arrived currently, they'd be trapped by the battleships and fired on instantly.

I didn't know what to do, but the first step had to be sorting the fleet out. If I could get them to accept that I wasn't a traitor, and instead that Emberalis needed to be nailed to the bow of the ship like a figurehead, then I could get them to hunt down the remaining stealthed signal-jamming ships.

Once they were down? Then we'd be able to find out where our people were, and make sure they knew not to jump in yet.

It was all starting to move in the right direction, at last.

The harvesters and drones were ahead of me as I tugged the door to the lower levels shut finally. I let out a long breath, glad that we could reseal that section away.

I smeared a small group of nanites across the access to the panel, making sure that nobody without access to their nanites could reopen it. I ordered one of the harvesters to head for the dock, joining the other that was already out there to make sure all the bodies that were viable targets were disposed of, then wait for the ship to arrive.

Then our small command group, along with Shemer and Choni, headed up to the control room at the apex of the node.

The others spread out across the node. The mercenaries made the most of the limited looting opportunities, and the UC soldiers checked on their recovering people, eating or sleeping when they could.

By the time I was ready for the signal to be sent out, I had a plan. Ingrid stood to my right, and the solid and imposing, heavily armored figure of Captain Shemer on the left, ready for broadcast.

The signal was sent out a minute behind the connection that was established to all active nanite systems embedded in the UC ships, sending a text and recording update.

That meant that every single unlocked soldier or member of the UC aboard all those ships received a notification, then a minute later the ships themselves received my broadcast.

Every single member of the UC that was, *except* Emberalis.

The system settings meant that you couldn't just cut off a specific load of people. The Ændari, for example, weren't able to select all the UC soldiers and turn them off because of the nature of the system's setup. But that was also heavily because of the way they interacted with it. They essentially ordered the AI to do it, and when that AI, who'd been charged with the survival of the

Ændari as a species, decided that this was a bad idea and lied that it wasn't possible, they'd just moved on.

They'd not tried to find a workaround.

It'd taken me a few minutes to lock down the bridge of the flagship, then barely a minute after that to go through the most recent upgrades unlocked and activated by the crew.

They were literally simple and straightforward—upgrades to their piloting abilities, improvements to targeting, and things like that. Then the last?

Attempts to unlock control abilities, queries that appeared to be all aimed at manipulating those around them, and basically trying to alter records.

Everything was aimed at improving their control of the world around them and their place in it, rather than being better at their job at all.

They'd unlocked a variant of the Assassin tree, but that aimed at capturing and manipulation of prisoners.

The fleet didn't have any prisoners, as far as I could tell, but this user was leveling that tree steadily, through coercion, blackmail, and attempted bribery. And that meant that the only people they were using it on were their own.

If that wasn't Emberalis, they needed fucking cutting out like a cancer regardless.

I created a loop in their system, making it unable to update; then I pushed out the message to everyone else. If I'd made a mistake? I could manually force a reboot now that I had access to the memory modules below in the lower spire, after all, so fuck it. It was worth the risk.

The notification that the rest of the UC personnel received was this:

Attention members of the UC forces in the Scorpio system. I am Steve, Lord Devourer, Joint leader of the Gaia's Vengeance faction, one of the leaders of the Unified Federation of Earth, and commander of the Universal System Quadrant Node #02.

On my arrival into the Scorpio system, I was refused access to the UC command network, and ordered to submit to local authority or be destroyed. When I accessed the main communications network directly, I was accused of attempting to hack the network, and was again threatened with death, before being finally recognized and granted access to the leader of the Fleet, Admiral Emberalis.

Emberalis has demanded access to systems that he cannot control, and when I refused this, he opened fire on my ship, marking me as a traitor and ordering my destruction.

Rather than damage the fleet in the middle of a war, I left, and instead continued to my own objective: assuming full control over the node and preventing the Ændari from eliminating all life in this sector.

On my authority as Devourer, I order the traitor Emberalis be taken into custody by UC soldiers directly. He is to be locked in the most secure cell

Arise: Conqueror

available and prevented from any access to the fleet until he can be tried for his crimes.
Prepare for a recorded transmission…

I didn't know what to say, not really, so I said it as well as I could, then attached a recording of his demands. Sure, Ingrid could have done it better, but there wasn't much she didn't do better than me.

This had to come from me. As soon as I'd given the soldiers who I knew were aboard the battleships time to even start moving, I connected to the fleet.

The bridge of the flagship shimmered into being before me—Argus accessed my senses to create a replica in my mind's eye—and I almost snorted in contempt.

The bridge was ornate, all white plastic and gleaming marble, polished wood and glass. A huge flag was painted across the rear of the bridge on the back wall, with the screens for those who faced that way shoehorned in at angles to prevent the flag being covered at all.

Emberalis squatted, toadlike, in an ornate throne-like chair. His feet barely reached the floor, and gold and red robes swamped him. The remains of a meal were on a carved table that was being removed by a servant who seemed, like the rest of the bridge staff, to be frozen in place, uncertain.

"Said explain yourself!" Emberalis was roaring in fury. "How dare you ignore me!" Emberalis snapped at someone off to one side, as I, Ingrid, and Shemer were holographically projected aboard the bridge of every single UC ship at once.

"Emberalis," I greeted the smaller man flatly.

"What…?" He grunted, jerking around, and then fixed me with a glare. "You. I suppose you've had something to do with this?" He settled back in the chair, plucking a napkin from an inner pocket and wiping his mouth, while his other hand gestured at the figures all around.

"UC personnel, I order you to take the traitor Emberalis prisoner," I said clearly. Around the outside of the room, I could see the looks on the faces of the command staff.

They glanced from one to another, clearly waiting for one of the others to make the first move, until the door behind them opened suddenly.

Two soldiers in full power armor stomped onto the bridge, rifles slung but handguns drawn, clearly ready for a fight if need be. They marched across the deck, stopping on either side of Emberalis's chair, and inclined their heads to my projection.

"Lord Devourer. I am Second Fist Conagh. The soldier corps accept your authority and stand ready for orders."

"Thank you, Second Fist." I nodded to the armored figure. "I want one of you to escort Emberalis to the most secure cell you have aboard the flagship. Be aware he's upgraded his abilities with access to various forms of manipulation. If he tries to escape or subvert you or your companion, you are to shoot him in the face as a warning."

"In…the face?" he asked carefully, lifting his handgun slightly to be sure I could see it. It was large enough that it'd be capable of anti-aircraft fire on Earth, and would clearly be overkill. "The prisoner is…*was* a member of the ruling House of Paendrag, one of the leaders of the Right Hand of Man—"

"So shoot him respectfully," I said firmly.

"Respectfully…" He hesitated, and I suddenly realized by the way that he held himself, by the tone in his voice, that he wasn't confused at all. He was fucking enjoying this. "We are to shoot him in the face, *respectfully*, should he attempt to subvert us or escape. I fully understand my orders, Lord Devourer."

With that, he nodded to his companion, who grabbed Emberalis and yanked him from his seat, pressing the barrel of her massive handgun against Emberalis's forehead and speaking calmly.

"I have been given my orders, prisoner Emberalis. I recommend you do not attempt to move, speak, or influence anyone, or else I will be forced to fire. Respectfully."

That last was said in an almost gloating tone, and I had to fight to keep the smile from my own face.

For the soldiers of the UC, the majority of whom were literally thousands of years old, each loss due to shipboard weapons and fleet battles was a horror beyond the imagining of most.

The nature of the power levels of a laser that could cut through shields and hulls of warships meant that it was one of the few things that even they couldn't come back from. So when an arrogant little fuckstick like Emberalis had already lost dozens, possible hundreds of ships and crews, it must have been driving them insane with horror. Especially as he'd been blatantly trying to set himself up to gain from their deaths.

Now, as his fellow soldier stomped from the bridge, Conagh bowed his head and holstered his gun, before removing his helmet and setting it on Emberalis's chair.

"How may I continue to serve, Lord Devourer?"

"Is the next in command of the fleet an actual fleet officer, or a political appointee who's there to line their own pockets?" I asked bluntly.

Conagh looked about, assessing those in the room, before looking back at me. "Political, Lord Devourer," he said firmly.

"Okay, is there an officer there who's actually capable of doing their job? Someone who can command the fleet and fight?"

"There are three aboard ship who are known to my corps as honorable and skilled fleet officers."

"Who's the best of them?" I asked. "I mean, who is both the best at their job and the one who should be actively leading the fleet, in place of a political appointee who's going to waste lives?"

"Commander Dolfing," he replied after a slight hesitation. "He took command of the flagship when the admiral suffered an unfortunate accident."

"How unfortunate?" I asked.

"Terminal."

"And Dolfing wasn't involved?" I asked shrewdly.

"Unlikely, sir. He was already second-in-command and maintained the fleet while requesting replacement by a superior officer. Instead, Emberalis arrived and took direct command. Dolfing was the previous admiral's right hand and commanded the fleet in his absence."

"And where is he now?"

"He disagreed with Emberalis's fleet actions, and was placed under arrest, to be ejected from the fleet upon the end of the battle."

"Why the end?" I asked, then frowned. "You don't mean ordered home, do you?"

"Ejected from an air lock," Shemer said from behind me, still standing at parade rest, and I gritted my teeth.

"Thank you, Shemer. Conagh, get Dolfing and confirm him as admiral, please. He's to take full command of the fleet until I say otherwise."

"As you command." He paused, clearly sending an order through his own systems, then nodded. "Admiral Dolfing is being brought to the bridge, Lord. Do you need any other assistance?"

"Not right now." I shook my head. "Captain Shemer is familiar with the situation here and will make sure the soldiers across the fleet are brought up to date."

"As you command."

"Do you know if there are more reinforcements incoming?" I glanced at the fleet details and the massive Ændari battleships.

He smiled suddenly, nodding once. "We received confirmation from the last ships to jump into the system, Lord Devourer Steve. Lord Devourer Shan'Gai himself is incoming and is expected to arrive in-system at any time. All other incoming ships have been ordered to avoid the system, under pain of death."

"Death...?" I blinked.

"As you are no doubt aware, Lord, when a Devourer unleashes their nature in defense of the UC, there can be casualties, so to prevent any risk of that, we have been ordered to stand down and maintain our distance from the Ændari fleet and the jump point."

"Okay..." I said slowly, wincing and understanding the risk if Shan'Gai might have invested too heavily in Hunger or Growth. "In that case, I'll have targeting data sent to you. We've located the stealthed jamming platforms scattered across the system. We need to take them down."

"The fleet stands ready."

That sounded fairly formal, and I nodded, pausing, speaking up before cutting the link.

"Thank you, Conagh," I said before the transmission ended.

It might be ten seconds before the new admiral got there, or it might be two hours or more, depending on the state and size of the ship. No sense in waiting. And knowing that the risk of the others jumping into the system and getting fucked over by the Ændari fleet was now gone? Well, it was time to damn well relax for the first time in forever.

CHAPTER TWENTY-NINE

I managed nearly three hours of "relaxing" before the first argument broke out. Unsurprisingly, it was literally as Ingrid and I had just started to get a bit more cheerful that we were interrupted.

I'd given up on finding a place to sneak away to just spend some time with her, and instead had created my own, picking her up in my arms and flying the pair of us up to a space near the ceiling.

The spire itself extended up and out over a large empty central space, the stairwells flowing up around it. It was clearly meant to represent some airy and impressive concept, but to me, it was exactly what I needed. I'd grinned, flying Ingrid and me up to a section that was well out of anyone else's reach. Then I created a literal love nest for the two of us, using the nanites I'd harvested from my enemies to form walls, a floor…even a comfortable seat.

It was everything we needed.

Hell, I even had a null coin slowly breaking down to provide fresh air for her. And because the entire room was "me," I could adjust it however I wanted to ensure we had perfect privacy.

It wasn't intended as a bedroom, not at first.

I'd genuinely just wanted a little time away from everyone else, with the woman I loved, just somewhere we could stop for five goddamn minutes and not be interrupted with some asshole asking a stupid fucking question.

Once we'd gotten there, and we'd been finally relaxing in a room that with a thought appeared to be an exact copy of the bedroom of the hotel in Athens that we'd loved so much?

Well.

We'd relaxed on the "couch"—which was actually me—while looking out of the "window"—yup, me—at the sights beyond—also part of me—and it'd been perfectly natural to have my arm around her shoulder and have her snuggle in close.

That had led to a perfectly natural cuddle, and an innocent kiss, which had led to a few more. Suddenly we were laid on a perfectly innocent bed, no longer a couch. Ingrid's armor was already gone; my clothes were vanishing and she was peeling her one-piece undersuit off, while I planted kisses down the ample slope of one breast.

Arise: Conqueror

That, naturally, was when Jonas shot me.

I should clarify that slightly. When the first bullet hit me, I barely noticed, considering the focus of my attention was growing hard under my wandering kisses, so I basically ignored that first hit.

Then he fired again, and again.

"What's that?" Ingrid growled distractedly, while arching her back and pressing me deeper into her cleavage.

"Don't know," I mumbled, trailing more kisses. "Don't care!"

More shots followed, and general shouting that the pair of us tried to ignore, before eventually laser shots started to land, burning through several layers of nanites and making me actually notice the losses.

"What the hell?!" I snarled, pushing myself up and looking around. My senses shifted to see "out" of the room as easily as I now saw my almost fully naked girlfriend below me. She'd just reached out to take hold of me, and was, judging from the grip that she was maintaining, *not* amused by the interruption, nor change of my attention's direction.

I shifted the room slightly, letting the sounds from outside pass more clearly, so that we could both hear them.

"Her!" Jonas was shouting. "Fuck's sake, you two! Get out here or someone's gonna die!"

"Yeah, you shitehawk," I snapped, projecting my voice to him. "It's gonna be YOU!"

Ingrid was nodding at the same time, releasing me, reaching for her undersuit, and growling as she unrolled it, getting the legs the right way around.

It took us a few seconds to make ourselves decent. Ingrid had to hop in place, dragging the skintight suit up and down over her generous curves, all the way muttering about that bastard Jonas.

When I paid attention to what she was saying, I had to nod. It was all about how she had the good grace to not interrupt him and Scylla when they snuck off, but oh no, he clearly wanted his next job to be scrubbing the outside of the damn node clean for the next ten years.

With his *toothbrush*.

I watched her armor flow up out of her body and seal over her beautiful figure. That was when I contemplated seeing just how far I could throw Jonas from the dock, wondering whether I could hit the Ændari fleet from here, given enough effort, while I shifted the outside of our little love nest to show an image to our friend.

It was Jonas, cartoon-like, being beaten by a stick, and he grinned and stopped firing, knowing he'd gotten our attention.

When I split one "wall" so that we could step out, he'd just raised his rifle again, clearly contemplating firing some more, and had to quickly jerk the barrel aside.

I took Ingrid's hand and launched the pair of us across the thirty or so meters to the platform he stood on, landing easily, before creating a hammer that looked like it was used to forge Mjolnir.

"You better have a goddamn *amazing* excuse ready," I said with a fake smile, already hefting the hammer.

"Sorry you two, but I do." He held his hand up in apology, shaking his head. "Seriously, I might be a dick at times, but I'd have at least given you a little time if I didn't need you."

"What's wrong?" Ingrid's anger and frustration melted away as we both saw the genuine regret on his face.

"It's the hippies," he said. "They're killing each other."

"*What*?" Ingrid asked, stunned.

"We've sent them all to the dock and we're holding them there for now, but…I don't know what to do," he admitted. "Look, this started like an hour ago, and whatever it is, they're seriously fucked up, and they're looking for you."

"Take us to them, and damn well explain that," I snapped, all thoughts of sex gone. I reabsorbed the hammer and clapped him on the shoulder. "You were right to interrupt. I'm sorry."

"It started about an hour ago," he repeated, gesturing to the stairs and setting off, leading the way to the edge. "Can you float us down? I don't trust that lift thing…"

It was one of the systems that had been designed to travel the spire. Presumably, when you didn't want to go level by level, stair by stair, there was a lift, a tube that reversed gravity and whooshed you up to where you wanted.

It'd been one of the systems that had failed in the past, though, and when we'd fought our way through the node, we'd been warned not to try to skip the stage-by-stage approach or we'd regret it.

It was more or less working, Argus had assured people, but it was the "or less" part, when you had to trust the gravity control under another's command. Jonas was one of those who chose not to trust it, being witness to some of the tricks I'd pulled with gravity already.

There wasn't the room in the free space to be able to fly properly, and although I had the experience to not care about how close the walls were here and the power to ignore things like that, he'd traditionally decided that the stairs were just fine for him.

That meant that if he was asking me to fly us, it really wasn't a good sign.

"So, an hour ago?" Ingrid asked, and he nodded as I picked us all up, gravity adjusting easily to carry us all into the air and over the side, falling fast.

The only sign she gave that she was even slightly uncomfortable was to rest one of her feet atop mine, and I couldn't help but smile at that show of trust.

"Yeah, the whole lot of them just went quiet at first. Look, you know what they're like, right? There's always one dingbat trying to convert the others, two more arguing over the sacred scriptures, and three others pointing out that they didn't say that last week.

"As a group, they're *never* quiet. As soon as I realized that the general complaining and haranguing had stopped, my first thought was to celebrate, thinking the fuckers had finally decided to jump over the side of the dock or something."

"Understandable," I grunted as the levels flashed past us, and people wandering back and forth jerked or swore at our sudden passage.

"Yeah, well, after a few minutes, it was like having a toddler, and it went from 'silence is golden' to 'silence is fucking suspicious' and I went looking for them, finding them all quietly tooling up."

"Tooling up?" Ingrid asked, frowning prettily.

"Yeah, getting their gear on. Guns...the lot." He nodded, and I slowed us as we approached the floor, dropping us gently and cutting the gravity warping. "Thanks, Steve. Man, I hate that shit," he admitted, shaking his head. "Okay, so they see me, and I asked them what they were doing. They just say that they're checking their gear over, making sure it's all good, you know?"

"Right?" I agreed, not getting it.

Ingrid looked more confused than before.

"Yeah, well, that'd not be suspicious, except that they've *never* done that before."

"Never?" I frowned.

"*Never,*" Ingrid confirmed. "We had to check their weapons for them before the fights started, they were that clueless. And most were unwilling to use them. Half of those who did still couldn't fire for the safeties they kept forgetting."

"Yeah, and that was after going over classes with them all," Jonas grumbled. "Anyway, suddenly they're all determined to make sure their weapons are working, and any that have got low-powered weapons?

"They're asking for more powerful ones, generally the most powerful we've got. I think okay, this is a bit weird, but let's face it—it's the whole apocalypse and we're in deep space fighting our makers thing...the end of days. We're all living through mad shit, so maybe they've just finally woken up to it all.

"I sorted them out with some of the captured Ændari weapons, the general assault rifles and shit, but I drew the line at the heavy lasers and any form of explosives. They're too unstable for the good stuff."

"Good point," I agreed, nodding.

"Well, that's where it gets weird. Theres a few of them who aren't as mad as the rest, right? Like, one of them has said before—a young lad—that he'd just come along following his lover; he wanted to help, so he came with. No stress."

"Uh-huh," I agreed, the three of us jogging along the hall.

"Well, he's been staying at the back more and more. And when this is happening, he's looking well and truly freaked out. He comes to have a word with me, says he wants to talk, but not near the others. And his boyfriend? He just walks up and shoots him in the back of the head, boom. Lifts his gun and pulls the trigger like it's nothing."

"Why?" I asked.

"No clue, seriously." He shook his head. "I'm standing there, this guy's brains scattered across the fucking hall, and they're totally uninterested. They didn't want to fire on the Ændari when they first attacked because of the 'sanctity of life' and shit."

"But one of their own being shot in front of them was fine?"

"The rest of the group? Only one of them even reacts, and he's the only other one who's less crazy than the rest. He starts to back away, and they fucking turned on him, all at once, and shot him."

"All at once?"

"You ever see those coordinated dances? The flash mobs that used to pop up for a while, all doing the same shit? It was just like that." Jonas shook his head. "I mean it, boss, something's wrong. And when I started shouting and questioning them? I got the feeling I was next. I just stopped, man…even started to hint that there might be something wrong. They all stared at me, guns held ready."

"You think…wait—they'd have attacked *you*?" I frowned.

"It felt like it," he admitted. "I told them that we needed to guard the ruins, that there were enemies out there, and they just stared at me. Then, when I said we needed to make sure the weapons caches were secure? They went toddling off happily to search for them."

"What weapons caches?" I asked.

"There's none out there, don't worry," he assured me. "I just figured that if what they really wanted were powerful weapons, they'd happily go looking."

"So, they're doing that now?" I asked. "They just head-shotted two of their own, and you let them stroll off with guns?"

"Honestly, I did." He nodded. "Because had I tried to take them off them, I'd have been victim three. There's no doubt in my mind that I was right on the edge of being shot. But the real kicker?"

"Yeah?"

"Right before this, they'd been looking for *you.*"

"Me?"

"Him?" Ingrid echoed grimly.

"Yeah. I'd seen a few wandering about prior to the whole silence thing and thought nothing of it. Then, when I came looking for you, Shemer tells me that you're probably with them, because they've all been looking for you."

"Okay." I drew the word out slowly, nodding. "So they're tooling up and they want to know where I am. That's not happy making."

"Yeah," he agreed. "That's why the first thing I did was warn Shemer. You know he's got a real hard-on for you, right? All the UC do. So his first words were that he'd sort it out. I had to stop him from booting them over the side of the dock."

"A hard-on?" I snorted.

"Ah, yeah, not like that. I mean they're all focused on you, you know? Damn Brits, not understanding simple shit."

"I understand. I just wanted to make sure you knew what you'd said, that's all." I shook my head. "All right, so what the hell happened? I've barely met these fuckers, and sure, I threw them out of the stairwell, but switching sides and getting ready to try to kill me seems…excessive?"

"It's not that." Ingrid shook her head as she shifted her hair, smoothing it in a way that let me know she was trying to contain her anger. "I've thrown them out of there and worse several times already. The leaders of the group are the real troublemakers…actually, no, let me rephrase. The real troublemakers are the *loudest*, that's all. They've not really got leaders. The group is made up of individuals who had small temples, houses, or businesses here, and the most fervent of the 'true believers.'

"None of them can agree on what they believe, except that they were forced along by the rest, when they ran for it from the Ændari. They lost everything, mainly their believers and their businesses, so when they heard that we'd gotten inside, they seemed to think they had some rights to the node, and that they hadn't wanted to leave, but were dragged out, kicking and screaming, somehow."

"All of them?" I looked at her, seeing the way she rolled her eyes hard enough to hurt.

"Yeah, apparently all the others were cowards who dragged them along, and whichever you're talking to at a given time were dragged by them. I'm not sure how that works, but okay. So, what do we do now?"

"Argus?" I asked aloud, already reaching out and directing my query at the AI.

"There are no confirmed outside influences operating within my boundaries of control at this time." Argus sounded a little stilted.

"Okay, well thanks for—" I started to say, only to be cut off by Ingrid.

"Argus, are there any signals that may not be confirmed as affecting the node, but that started around the same time as the disturbances?"

"I cannot answer that."

"Well, why the hell not?" Jonas glared around at the walls as we jogged out of the hall and started down the steps toward the main plaza.

"Just accept it," Ingrid said quickly. "Don't question."

"But—" He nodded, confused but trusting us.

"There's something hinky going on with the node. Lots of weird half-deleted files and shit," I sent to him, making him glance from Ingrid to me and nod at us both.

I grinned as Ingrid's message came through at the same time.

"I just gave him a quick explanation," she told me.

"So did I." I sent her a mental smile, and she grinned back at me as we hit the plaza. But it melted away upon hearing shouting in the distance.

"Let's pick it up!" I ordered, lifting us all into the air and rocketing over the buildings between us and the entrance to the dock.

"Dammit, Steve!" Jonas shouted, jerking and almost flipping over in his shock. "Warn a body before you do that shit!"

"Where's the fun in that?" I quipped distractedly.

The buildings between us and the dock were almost all shattered and reduced to slag now. Some sections had been rebuilt into cover for our people.

When I'd come through this way before, there'd been hundreds of bodies scattered everywhere. Now most of them were gone. A small number of them remained, all our own, and laid to rest in a mainly undamaged building at the edge of the plaza, with "The Honored Dead" carved into the granite over the door.

The walls that still stood between us and the docks now were battered and broken. Sections that were made of metal—everything had been scrounged from the surrounding planets and systems—had run like candle wax, melting and blackened.

It flashed past beneath us, and the shouting changed. The smaller oval doors set to the right and left of the dock were open again—the larger one in the middle, long sealed still—and it was from the left that the reflected flicker of lasers suddenly glowed.

"Shiiit!" I cursed, angling us over in that direction, reaching out and doing what I should have damn well done in the first place, and using the senses that I had access to as the commander of the node.

The dock came into view in my mind instantly, a full panorama scene, that I could manipulate to see from all angles. I cursed again, long and loud.

The loony fringe were firing. Most of them stood out in the open, and not a single one of them showed any remorse, hesitation, or concern.

Their target was the battered remains of my ship as it came in for a landing. The hull, coated in nanites that were frantically trying to repair it, was pocked and burned suddenly by small arms fire. But beyond that, the barrage did almost nothing.

Shemer yelled at them to stop, running forward, and they utterly ignored him, their faces blank, staring straight at the ship and firing.

The others in the dock were mainly devilkin, though there were still some recovering or rebuilding soldiers scattered about too. The sight of the generally unstable refugee volunteer force firing on the incoming ship was confusing everyone, especially as the small arms fire they were using against it wasn't doing much damage. But considering the literal holes in the hull, a lucky shot didn't have to be big or powerful.

As soon as Shemer reached the closest of them, grabbing his rifle and using his enhanced strength and armor to jerk the gun out of his hands, the entire group shifted their aim, opening fire on him instead.

The huge warrior was in his armor, but his helm was attached to his hip, there having been no need to be fully armored and locked away in here, or so he'd thought.

Most of the shots were stopped by his armor, or the figure that he'd grabbed, as the rest of the group unconcernedly unleashed hell on one of their own again as well.

There were a lot of shots being fired, though, and many were from automatic weapons.

"Shit, Shemer!" I gasped as we ducked down under the arched doorway. My attention was so taken up by the sight of the captain being mowed down that I nearly flew us into the wall, then the floor.

He fell; several shots hit him in the head all at once and took the experienced leader out.

Then all hell broke loose.

Arise: Conqueror

Bach and Zhonat, aboard the ship, had seen the incoming fire. They were used to doing contested landings in war; knowing the difference between small arms and actual weapons capable damaging a ship, they'd been shocked and pissed, but they'd clearly written it up as a mistake.

That changed drastically as they watched a figure they recognized as one of their own, dressed in their armor, who was trying to stop the attack, get killed before their eyes.

The devilkin were generally already pissed at the refugees, them having spent most of their time either trying to convert the mercenaries to this week's religion of choice, or trying to steal weapons and refusing to fight. That meant that when the firing kicked off, they were already ready to shoot, only being held back by the sight of the respected soldier stepping in first.

The soldiers in sight? All under the command of Captain Shemer. Most had been with him for centuries, and seeing him being cut down by their supposed allies was both shocking and deeply angering for them.

That being said, they were professionals, and used to being stabbed in the back—several had even been married more than once—so they returned fire without hesitation.

Lastly, adding to the confusion, one of my harvesters had been working on the wreckage of the UC ship, and as it floated out of the side of the wreckage, that seemed to confuse the entire lunatic group beyond anything else.

As Shemer fell, the group split, ignoring the shouting, the pointed weapons, and the now incoming fire that cut their friends down.

Instead, the dozens of refugee volunteers split their focus: diverting half of their fire back at the ship and the rest at my harvester.

We rocketed into the dock, seeing them already falling. Ingrid, Jonas, and I shouted at everyone, demanding they stop firing.

It worked, but only for the devilkin and the UC soldiers.

If anything, our appearance seemed to anger and confuse the lunatics more, considering they turned and started firing at us as well.

"Motherfuckers!" I roared in anger, twisting in the air and releasing Ingrid and Jonas, letting them land on the dock nearby. I punched forward, flashing across the distance that separated us.

I landed in the middle of the group. All of them switched from firing on the ship and harvester to focus on me, as I shifted my arms.

My feet skidded across the deck, the speed too much to catch easily. I shoulder charged the nearest off his feet, sending him flying. I lifted my hands, elongating and reforming into a shield on my left and a big fuck-off hammer on the right.

Half of them had been cut down by the fire of our allies already, and those still standing ignored anything else, all in their determination to shoot me.

It made no sense. As I lashed out, I saw their faces. There was no anger, no fear, no emotion at all. If anything, I'd have said they were bored, like they were watching a shitty movie and internally they were plotting tomorrow's shopping list.

For a brief moment, it also reminded me of an ex's face more than once as well, but then I instantly dismissed it. After all, she'd told me I was definitely the best.

My hammer swung left and right. Bones broke, and they fell, eyes still glazed, not even breathing hard at the impacts.

I shifted, crouching slightly and increasing the size of my shield.

Ingrid barked out an order I barely heard above the incoming fire. "Soldiers! Execute them!"

The words were barely out of her mouth when the incoming sound of fire suddenly ramped up, then dropped off. In three seconds of frantic swinging and blocking, the fight was over, and damn it still made absolutely fuck all sense to me.

Most of them were dead, that was clear, and those who weren't dead wouldn't last long. But damn! I couldn't help but look from their shiny goddamn clothes, bangles, crystals, and jewelry to their filth-laden skin, and then to the nearby body of Shemer.

He was a soldier who had fought for the UC for literally centuries. He'd lost his memories; he'd been blocked from accessing most of his abilities, and yet, regardless of hundreds, maybe thousands of years of battles, he'd still fought to protect people.

Then he'd been shot in the head by a group he'd been fighting to defend, when instead of being his allies as they'd agreed, they'd all been hiding and criticizing him.

I checked the bodies closest, grabbing a corpse and dragging it off a groaning figure that lay beneath, his right shoulder shattered by a hammer blow and several burned holes clear in his leg and chest.

He stared up at the spire overhead, his face blank and seemingly mindless, before he finally focused on me, as I grabbed him.

I lifted him, planning to demand some answers, until he grabbed a blade off his hip and drove it at my face. I blocked it on instinct, batting it aside, as Ingrid shouted over to me.

"Don't kill him!"

"Fucker just killed Shemer!" I growled.

"We need to find out why!" She cut across my protest. "Steve, don't! Just let Jonas and me talk to him."

I didn't like it. I didn't want to listen to reason. Hell, I barely knew Shemer, but he was a soldier and he was on my side. All these fuckers had done was complain and lessen our strength because we had to keep an eye on them. My eyes wandered to the edge of the dock, the open space, kept at bay by an ion shield.

My first instinct as he struggled and tried to stab me again was to throw him out there. I'd thought about doing it with Jonas interrupting me earlier, but that was an idle thought. For this fucker, though? That I could do.

"Steve…" Ingrid called, the rising and falling of her voice a warning as much as an entreaty to behave.

I grunted, then dropped him. He bounced on the corpses of his friends. Then the cheeky bastard immediately tried to stab me again.

For that, I kicked his arm, snapping it at the wrist and sending the interwoven bones of his forearm shattering.

Blood sprayed free, and for the first time I saw a new expression beyond indifference and hatred when he saw me. I saw pain, and I damn well wanted to stomp on him more.

Then she was there, grabbing his arm and shouting for Belle. She shook her head at me as her own nanites flowed forward, sealing the arm wound to give her time to save him.

"We need to question him," she repeated.

I forced myself to nod to her. The rage inside still burned as I thought of the way these fuckers had just taken a soldier we damn well needed from us.

"What happened?" Choni called from across the dock, and I waved at her, before cursing as I heard a creaking scream of tortured metal that rang out through the air.

Looking in the direction of my ship, I gritted my teeth, then forced a smile and a thumbs-up for Zhonat and Bach, as they tried to settle the ship a bit better.

"What the hell are they doing?" Jonas winced, looking up and over as well.

"First time they've landed a starship," I admitted.

"Well, any landing you can walk away from is a good one then," he said philosophically. "But damn, that sucks." He'd stepped up to stand next to me, and we both looked down from the battered and smoking ruins of my ship and the general chaos of the dock, to Shemer.

A significant section of his skull was missing, and just looking at it, I knew that meant he was out of the fight for a while now.

With other injuries, using the designs I'd come up with—the nanite capabilities and the printers and tech—I could literally reprint their missing limb or whatever.

The skull I could do, no stress, but the brain that was housed within? I had no way of knowing how the hell the nanites reprocessed our memories to give us everything back on reawakening. And I had a very strong suspicion that if I tried that? He'd not recover.

Instead, I knelt, placing one hand on his shoulder, and looked into his remaining eye, seeing it filmed in death.

"Lord Devourer…"

The voice came from above, and I looked up. Several other of Shemer's soldiers had arrived. Before, only a few had been about, and although they had their weapons close by, they were supposedly in a more or less secure base, surrounded by allies.

That was why the lunatics had managed to do what they'd done, and why when Ingrid had ordered them to kill them all, they'd fallen so quickly.

By the time she'd given that order, the soldiers in sight had the time to aim and coordinate targets; before that, they'd been caught flatfooted.

Now they stood over me, with the body of their leader on the floor by their feet, mown down by their own "allies."

"We'll take him," one of the soldiers said firmly. Two of them knelt and reached out, dragging their captain's body back from me, as others moved to stand between him and me.

For a second, I thought they were blaming me for his death. Then my stomach twisted as I realized what it was even more.

Death was a normal thing for these soldiers; everyone died, all the time, and if they were lucky, their friends came back. They didn't blame me for his death, I guessed, but they were quick to move him away, because there was one thing they *did* know.

The Devourers were named that for a fucking reason.

I gritted my teeth, standing and nodding to the soldiers who stood between him and me, speaking in as steady and calm a voice as I could.

"I can give him active nanites, like I did for all of you," I assured them. "He's in no danger from me."

"Thank you, Lord." The speaker stayed between us still.

"I mean it, dammit," I snapped. "I'm a Devourer but I'm under control. I didn't attack any of you before and I'll not start now!"

I wondered whether it was the drop in my Karmic Luck that sent my harvester floating past at just that fucking second, moving to clean up the blood that had been spilled and recover the nanites from the dead lunatics.

Either way, though, we both turned to watch it pass, and I cursed again. "It's cleaning up those fucks, that's all," I ground out. "I'll give one of your own an injection kit, something to give him active blank nanites, okay? That way I'm not near him and he's not at risk from me, and we get him back as soon as possible."

"Thank you, Lord," the unnamed figure said, once again not moving at all.

"Who's his next in line?" I asked.

"In line?"

"In command," I clarified.

"First Fist Zaren." He nodded in the direction of the main structure. "He's on his way."

"Thank fuck," I whispered, knowing that as a "first fist" he was roughly the equivalent of a sergeant major, with second fist being a sergeant's billet.

For a few seconds, I'd thought I was going to have a massive problem with the UC soldiers. I could still have one, I knew, but that there was still an active leader among them meant I at least had a chance.

"Lord Devourer," came the call, and I glanced to my left.

Zhonat and Bach jogged across the dock toward us, both armed and in full armor deployed mode.

The difference between these older soldier models and the younger, much more "modern" ones was stark.

The armor that the UC soldiers wore was essentially a replacement for the one that the older soldiers earned. Like me, the BWVs were intended to wear nanite armor. The powered armor that ninety percent had access to these days was more of a basic loadout.

Arise: Conqueror

As the BWVs earned their nanites, they were expected to adjust their own armor to the situation—although a lot less fluid than mine was.

The Ændari had built us all to be their weapons, and they'd fully intended that once we evolved, we'd be the perfect protectors and servants. Once the majority lost access to their full systems in the nanite plague, and obviously long after the Ændari rebellion, all that the local soldiers had was an undersuit. It was a sort of form-fitting stretchy layer that regulated and maintained the body, keeping you clean and alive in more extreme environments.

The basic-issue powered armor was worn over this, with the original expectation being that the BWVs would earn their own more specialized armor that would grow with them.

That meant that for the soldiers before me, seeing their ancestors jog up in fully active nanite armor, it was like a religious experience.

Seeing them, and comparing the armor that Yeshin and the others under the Atlantic Ocean had been wearing, it made it obvious, now that I could access my own nanites so fully, that the difference was night and day.

Powered armor looked awesome: full-on space soldiers who could storm alien worlds like the old tabletop games had imagined, taking the fight to the enemy and killing thousands in battle.

It was also a hell of a lot less powerful than the really good shit that Bach and Zhonat wore, and I, as I was now, could kick their asses without anything like it.

The soldiers around me—their armor cracked, broken, and frequently missing sections—looked at the others in shock.

Bach slowed, glancing from them to me and the body they were moving as quickly as they could. "Lord Devourer, we apologize for the delay in eliminating the stealthed ship. Orders?"

"You did good, don't worry. That ambush was a thing of beauty. But for now, I need you both to help the soldiers here," I said firmly. "There's a first fist inside the node somewhere, heading this way, I think. But the captain just got killed. Our supposed allies opened fire on him when he tried to stop them shooting at you."

"Murdered?" Zhonat asked, and I nodded. "Damn them."

"Yeah, and Captain Shemer was a good man." Then, deciding to get it out in the open, I went on. "We don't know why they attacked, but when we killed them, the soldiers here are worried I'll attack and absorb Shemer, so they're keeping him back from me."

"Ah…" Zhonat nodded as if this was fine and expected. "How can we help?"

"I'll give you a set of blank and upgraded nanites, just like the ones I gave you earlier to reconstitute your armor. Can you verify that they're fine to use to the team here, and inject Shemer with them?"

"I could…" He hesitated. "Or we could load him into the tubes? They're empty now."

"Shit, of course!" I grinned as it came back to me. I had thirty of the damn things on my ship, and each one of them had the patterns of lost soldiers stored in them. "We can heal him, and maybe even recover your friends as well! Did they survive the fight?"

"They did. The internal damage is less severe than it may appear. We repressurized and replaced the atmosphere to ensure it would seem more damaged, should we need it, though the outside—"

He broke off as one of the wings creaked, cracked, and then fell, crashing to the floor with a boom that resounded across the dock.

"May need some repairs," he finished with calm aplomb.

"Lord, tubes?" The apparent current spokesman of the other soldiers asked, eyes still flickering from his ancestors to me and back.

"Medical tubes…you've got them, right?" I asked, then went on before he could respond. "They're old tech, but they repair and heal much faster than the nanites can do on their own. Shit, I can't believe I'd forgotten about them. Ingrid!" I called, turning to her. My mood dropped as I saw the bodies scattered around. "These fuckers can help bring the others back," I finished with a mutter.

"No." Ingrid stepped across to me, hearing the last thing I said, even as the figure behind her struggled, then went limp in Belle's grip, her head bowed as she snapped his neck with a tendril.

"What?" I frowned.

"No, they won't be stripped of their nanites to be reused by others."

"They just fucking—" I started to growl, gesturing at the now vanished body of Shemer, before she cut me off.

"They were victims," she said firmly. "They're victims of something. We don't know what caused it, but we can prove that it wasn't their fault."

"How?"

"Hijack," she said. "A much more powerful and simpler variant than my own. But for me it's clear, and it was as soon as I started looking closer at him."

"Hijack? But who?" I asked, confused, thinking of it as she used it, the darts that she could fire and embed into her target.

"Digital only," she said flatly, before going on, in a private connection to me. *"Something accessed their nanites, using the node, and it shows the same markers as the files that were erased from Argus's memory. Something has access to the node and hacked their nanites while they were here. They were under its control when they attacked. I don't know how long it took to establish, but the changes began in them recently, I could tell that much. I'd bet it was done right before they tried getting the guns."*

"Anything else?" I wondered who the hell could have done it.

"The target was you."

"Me?" I asked, confused. *"I was the last one they attacked, not the first."*

"They were looking for you. They were looking for heavier weapons, specifically explosives, high-powered lasers, and, according to Jonas, the high-powered EMP grenades as well."

"The EMPs?" I shrugged, confused. *"Why bother with them?"*

"I think they're more dangerous to you than we thought," she said. *"You've been exposed to them before, but that was when you were flesh and blood. As you are now? If they were powerful enough, they could kill you."*

Arise: Conqueror

"I..." I paused, thinking it through and examining myself and my nanites against the Engineering sub-mind's evaluation. *"They're dangerous,"* I agreed. *"Shit, I'd never even considered it, but how the hell did anyone else?"*

"They knew." She moved on quickly as she grabbed my hand in hers, looking me in the eye. *"Steve, they attacked the ship, because it was you. They attacked the harvester, because it was you. They killed their friends and Shemer because they got in the way."*

"Me?" My mind raced. Sure, the harvester was, more or less, part of me now. Although I thought about "me" as being me in my body, the harvester was definitely part of me, and attached mentally at least, but still...

"The ship." I looked at her. *"I ordered my nanites aboard her to repair the ship if it got damaged. There weren't enough to conceal it, so I set them for that instead. But how the hell did they know?"*

"I Hijacked him." She looked concerned. *"Whoever did this changed them— and massively. They were dying. Their internal organs were being changed by their nanites. Their eyes were altered, and I...I don't even have words for the things I saw in them, but you can't harvest them."*

"Because they were victims?" I asked, understanding what she was saying, but not agreeing. *"Ingrid, they're dead, but their nanites could still help."*

"They could," she agreed. *"And I felt the nanites counterattacking my Hijack. He's dead because we can't be sure of what they were trying to do. They're a risk. Their nanites are entirely active, I think, but they're changing the bodies into something else. I think we need to dispose of them."*

"You said we weren't going to drain them?" I asked.

"Well, I didn't know what to say, okay?" she snapped. *"I just got my Hijack counterattacked, and I heard you planning to harvest them—I had to stop you somehow."*

"It's okay," I assured her. *"Okay, Belle's already had contact with him. She's strong enough to deal with most things. We have her monitor herself, make sure she's not been contaminated, and we have her pitch them over the edge into space. In fact..."* I almost facepalmed, shaking my head as I gestured absently. A small gravity denial bubble warped around Belle and the others, as the dead bodies lifted almost as one, propelled into the air.

"Why the hell didn't I just do this in the first place?" I muttered to myself.

"Because you can't think of everything all the time," she replied. *"Okay, the other reason we needed to talk like this..."*

"It's Argus, isn't it?" I asked her.

"Yes and no," she said worriedly. *"I think it's him controlling them, him that made the changes, but I think he also tried to warn us as well...all that 'I cannot confirm' and so on. I think he said it that way to make sure we paid attention."*

"Yeah..." I agreed, having totally missed it the first time around.

"I think it's whoever is deleting the logs, whoever hacked the plague nanites and made them as virulent and vicious as they were. I think there's a third player in the game."

CHAPTER THIRTY

That wasn't good news, and as much as I'd pressed her on it, there was nothing more that Ingrid had to add to it. Instead, she told me to consider it all and come back to her once I had, to make sure that my conclusions were my own.

There were minor hints here and there—like the deleted logs—and separately there wasn't enough to make anything of it, really.

The problem was when you looked at it more and more.

One of these details was just a bit weird. The deleted logs, for example—if that was all it was, it'd be nothing. Two?

The plague was insanely virulent, and it was altered on the fly to erase the memories and lock down both sides. It was created by a bunch of dedicated AIs that were trying to restore order and fucking peace to the galaxy, and that was the second thing, strange as it was.

That was where it got peculiar, though. Something had gone wrong with the plague. Something that was created by a dozen of the greatest AIs that existed at that time in the known fucking galaxy, and it just fucked up?

That seemed weird, sure, but that the nodes all just went "Oh well, never mind," that screamed *tampering* to me. If I was watching a movie, I'd have been saying something about "plot armor" at the very least, but as it was?

The nodes were looking for someone to help, and they seemed fucking ecstatic that I was here. Argus was doing anything he could to help, to the point of literally telling us where to go and warning us that he'd have to release the original BWV terminators if we broke the rules, when really? He should have kept the damn door locked or set them all on us without warning.

I was getting greeted and welcomed by something that wanted me to "rise" as a Devourer, to punish the wicked and to protect the innocent, and yet…that wasn't held up by anything I was seeing regularly.

The universe was a mad, bad place. People kept fucking me over, or trying to. These assholes were trying to slaughter us. Every step we took, it seemed like someone was stacking the deck against us.

It felt like…

Arise: Conqueror

I paused, as I searched and searched. My improved perception and IQ worked hand in hand. My eyes widened as I slowed time on instinct, triggering my abilities to try to keep up with my racing brain.

It felt like someone was keeping both sides at roughly the same point. Every time the UC managed to make a technological breakthrough, the Ændari caught up.

Thinking about it, even with both sides at a point of parity before the nanite plague, there was no way that should have happened.

The Ændari were shitbags at the best of times, from what I'd seen, but if I discounted the asshats I kept running into, they still discovered all this shit and were good enough scientists in their own right that they managed to pull all of this off, right?

Also, even if both sides were exactly equal in terms of potential, how the hell had nobody pulled off finding a cache of tech before now? I mean, we knew that there had been pirates who had made it down to contaminated worlds. And it wasn't that big a leap to imagine that somewhere along the line a corpo scumbag would hire pirates to grab stuff, right?

And the Ændari would just send people down to raid them. I mean, there had to be places in their territory that were like this, and I didn't see them going "Oh no, that'd be wrong under the Geneva convention" or something.

No, for there to be no sudden leaps or jumps by one side over the other, there had to be a reason. No tech discovered by one side that the other didn't get, no wholescale raids of contaminated space…nothing.

I knew there were third parties, the independents, but this was mad. There was no way that they could pull this off, surely?

Thinking about a shadowy third party, a cartel that was selling weapons to both sides or something seemed insane. And yet…the more and more I looked at this, there were too many little details that were wrong. This felt like I had a bit of the puzzle, like the blind people in the room describing the elephant, touching different places and identifying the whole animal.

The only thing I knew for sure was that the UC and Ændari had been reduced to barely able to make *fire*, the last time they were about to fight it all out in a galaxy-wide conflict.

Now, with me showing up and bringing literally the head of that snake Varnock, and all the tech secrets that Earth represented, had kicked off another war.

There was no way that this would stay as a border conflict after all. There were tens of thousands, maybe millions dead already on both sides. Even with those assholes like Emberalis in this for themselves and not caring about the losses in lives, they'd be pissed about the loss of control and power that the destroyed ships would bring.

The galaxy was fast approaching another war, and it had—even with the best will in the world—a hell of a lot to do with me. If I'd just been a good boy and I'd done as the Blessed and the Accursed had told me? I'd have been sitting in a low-ranked lieutenant's position somewhere.

Hell, I'd probably be sitting on a yacht with Hans, arguing over something stupid like wine or fucking crème desserts or something with those weird little hats on all the letters in the name.

Instead, I was leading a faction to war, conquering shit and stirring up the galaxy. I didn't blame someone for wanting to "off" me when I looked at it like that.

Shut the howler monkey up and see if everything goes back to peace…or the version of peace we'd had—considering that millions were still dying and being tortured every day.

I blinked, seeing the little connections, all of them, and "feeling" that there were more, dozens of them that simply *had* to be there. Someone was pulling the strings in all of this, and they'd just taken a direct hand, going after me personally.

I glanced at the loony party's bodies. My mind still raced as the others seemed to move at a third or less of their normal speed.

They'd been altered with a nanite virus, the difference being that it'd been a digital version this time around, Ingrid thought, and that was logical. They'd started acting up as soon as the dampening field around the node had been taken out. So it'd been a hack then, most likely.

It was too implausible that the group had just stumbled across a live needle of plague nanites and passed it around for shits and giggles, after all.

No, they had to have been hacked when the connection from them to the outside galaxy had resumed. Why them, over the devilkin or the soldiers?

The soldiers were active—their nanites, at least—and Ingrid had Argus work on unlocking the most basic functions of the devilkin's nanites already.

She'd made the hard decision that due to the number of different species that made up the refugee group, she'd have Argus focus on awakening only the devilkin, as he'd apparently thought he could do that before the Ændari arrived.

He'd not managed to do it to that timescale, in the end, but he'd proceeded to unlock and activate enough of them that, by the time I arrived, the survivors were all active.

That was enough to prevent the takeover by this hack, it seemed. I saw what Ingrid meant by it being more powerful and yet more limited than her own version.

It'd been sent over a digital connection, I had to agree with her, and even the most basically activated systems had cleared it out. That it'd tried to counterattack Ingrid's own Hijack attempt said that it had some protective programming, though. And that it had deleted the logs of its own transmission, as well as rendering Argus unable to comment directly?

That was insanely worrying.

More so was that the original versions of the nanite plague had gotten through fully active systems. So this? This was the diet version—the cheap shop rip-off, I'd have said, if not for the fact that it'd been transmitted digitally, instead of infected physically.

Arise: Conqueror

If Ingrid hadn't insisted on Argus trying to unlock the devilkin's nanites? Or making sure that the soldiers' nanites were active? This would have ended much sooner. I'd have been slaughtered if the entire station had turned against us, considering they were all around me and my defenses had been down.

The worst part, though?

It read like an evolution of a skill unlock. Like my own Hijack, just a few ranks down the road. And as much as I instinctively wanted to blame this on Emberalis or someone like that?

This wasn't them.

This was someone with access to the goddamn nodes. I didn't want to think about who that could be, though I forced myself to keep going.

Okay, considering they were steadily removing the evidence of the Devourers from the records, that meant it could be the Ændari. Yet…

It didn't make a great deal of sense, as they'd have to have access to the node for that, and if they had it, they'd be doing worse, I bet. But still.

They were trying to release a nanite killer, after all, to reduce the population of this section of the galaxy to a weakened and broken version of themselves. It could be that it was them trying to make sure that even the last evidence of the Devourers' existence was gone…

Or…it *was* a Devourer.

That wasn't something I wanted to consider, that they might have turned one of… *No.* I stopped that line of questioning as I realized a much more likely scenario. There was little chance a Devourer would join them. And if they did? I'd deal with it when I had to.

No, what was much more likely was that fact that these skills, these abilities—all of them came from one place.

The Ændari.

Conceivably, they'd seen the abilities of the Devourers and other versions that must have arisen, and they'd made themselves their own version.

They were crap at war, being too individualistic, aggressive, and self-centered in themselves, which was why they'd turned to uplifting other races. But they'd been annihilating other races long before they'd experimented with us.

The dwarfen were proof of that.

"We need to get rid of them all," I said aloud, nodding to Ingrid as I cut my boosted perception of time and manipulated gravity quickly.

Anyone who wasn't active at the least in the system was a risk, I'd realized, and while aboard the node, we were safe. That didn't mean that the fleet was.

"We need to reach the control center," I cursed. "Zhonat!"

"Yes, Devourer?" He straightened then nodded in understanding.

I held my hand out to him, focusing on the nanites I'd need, splitting a hundred thousand off like it was nothing, making them clean and ready to work for a new master.

"Check this however you want so that you can confirm they're safe, then give them to Shemer regardless. They'll help him to recover either way, and the day or so of downtime while he recoups will be cut down. Then take him to the ship. Take any of his team who want to go as well, and load him into a medical pod. They're unlocked for you. Hell, you probably know what you're doing with them better than I do anyway. Get him in and recovered as fast as possible."

He nodded, clapping his fingers to heart, then stepped back, as I turned to Bach.

"Bach, the shit is hitting the fan. I don't know what's happening for sure, but you're probably the strongest on the node we have, so you're staying with Ingrid and me."

"Lord." He nodded. "Bodyguard?"

"Maybe." I shook my head as I reconsidered it. "Most likely not, though. This was an attack. Someone twisted their minds to try to kill me, and in case they try that shit again, I want to know that you're there, ready for me to send wherever I need you."

"It will be my honor," Bach intoned, stepping back, as Ingrid sent me a look.

"He's one of the people I found out there." I said it in private mode to her, probably unnecessarily. *"He's unlikely to have had any kind of new updates to his nanites, but if whatever it is tries again, I'd make him the favorite target for it."*

"What do you mean?" Ingrid asked suspiciously.

"Well, you can call me a paranoid bastard if you want, but he's the strongest and most experienced here, probably by a massive margin, and has thousands of years of memories of fighting. If he goes rogue? I want it to be right in front of us where I can stab the fucker in the face before he can do any more damage."

"I don't know if I'm more impressed or appalled by that reasoning," Ingrid said, before smiling at me. *"I'll let the others know, and make sure that if they start to feel anything strange, they tell us."*

"Good plan." I led the way as we headed for the control center, and reached out to Argus as I did so.

"Argus, for Zhonat and Bach, have they earned points or whatever since they came back into range? Have they had whatever updates they were due?"

"Negative. Due to the sheer number of updates required, their conscious mind will be rendered unable to process fresh input when this begins. Standard procedure for such situations is to maintain the current system access, and update over a period of offline rest."

"So you'll be updating them when they're asleep. Okay, can they spend points or earn any currently?"

"Negative. As stated, standard procedure maintains their system at current level until update is completed. Once updates are complete, then their advancement system will be reactivated and unlocked."

"Do they know?"

"Confirmed. Standard procedure."

Well, that scuppered my plan of hopefully having Zhonat guide me in upgrades or share points, but I still had the others.

As I went, I changed the harvester's orders, making sure that all the drones were absorbed back into the mass or into me now, then ordered the various sections of the harvester to join together again, before latching onto the remains of the UC warship.

The harvester had been stripping the internals of the ship up till now—it was a total wreck, after all—and all that could have been damaged or destroyed pretty much had been. But in searching it, the harvester had been scooping up any random bits of crap and converting them into null coins.

Now it went one better, as the remaining sections rejoined, and it flowed across the outer hull, blackened and twisted as it was.

The surface of the harvester shimmered, sinking into the ship's hull, beginning to feed and burrowing deeper. The only commands given were to recover any biologicals and set them aside, safe to retrieve, and to break the entire ship down to coins.

I'd need those if I was to fix my ship, after all.

By the time we reached the control center, things had changed in the system again, with a handful of new arrivals that only served to make the conversation with Admiral Dolfing that much simpler.

"Kill them all, Admiral," I said after I'd explained that there may be a risk from the Ændari vessels of a new version of the nanite plague. "Kill each and every fucking Ændari until space runs with rivers of their fucking blood."

"An admirable sentiment, Lord Devourer. But perhaps a little more guidance?" he asked after staring at me in disbelief.

"Admiral, I've never commanded a fleet," I said. "I could try to lead you, and I'd be shit at it. Is commanding a fleet something I can pick up in an hour, or did you train and learn much before you took over the fleet?"

"I studied my entire life," he admitted.

"Then why the hell should I try to tell you what to do?" I grunted. "Look, Admiral—you know your ships, you know your sailors, you know your enemy. That dickhead Emberalis tried to fight the fleet, and you've suffered losses, probably bad ones."

"Horrendous."

"Exactly, so how's about this? I'll give you some basic direction, and then I trust you to decide how to carry those orders out?"

"That would be refreshing," he agreed.

"Wonderful. So, I repeat, kill them all, Admiral." I smiled. "Kill each and every fucking Ændari until space runs with their blood and there's not so much as a fucking whisper of this nanite plague again."

"As you command, Lord Devourer." He bowed. "And my thanks for the promotion."

"I had no idea who you were," I admitted. "Thank Second Fist Conagh. He spoke up for you. Until then, I was going to put him in charge, or fly out and do it myself."

"I…thank you," he practically whimpered. "Thank you, and yes, perhaps I was a better choice."

"Glad we agree, Admiral…" I paused, looking at the plot, then back at him. "Can you win this?" I asked him outright.

"If nothing changes?" He then nodded. "The enemy outnumber us again, but our shields, weapons, and armor are better, as are our forces. They are highly limited with screening forces, as well as smaller vessels. This will be a battle of titans, but given the alternatives, we can win it."

"Good to hear. Now, there's a Devourer coming, Shan'Gai, so you need to keep your distance from them. But I expect to hear that you've killed a fuckload of Ændari next time we speak, all right?"

"As you say, Lord Devourer." He nodded. "The secondary jamming platforms around the system have all been targeted. Missiles are en route."

"See, I knew you were the man for the job. Blood, Admiral. Rivers of it," I reminded him, before disconnecting the feed, really not knowing what else I could have suggested. I wanted to help; I wanted to be out there and to be doing something, but seriously? I didn't have the training, I didn't have the mentality, and I didn't have the ship, dammit.

I stared at the plot, shaking my head as I tried to count them all.

As we'd been flying back to the command center, Argus had reached out, and I could feel that he was having some issues. He knew something was wrong, and was clearly trying to help, having accepted me as the commander of the node. But he was also well aware of the mistakes and hidden details…he definitely wasn't happy, that was clear.

The warning that additional Ændari ships had jumped in was taken almost as a personal attack, and he was not fucking amused.

There were three of them: two smaller Skarn class, which were apparently the Ændari version of the warships, and a single fatter, longer ship that he couldn't tell us anything about.

That sent the alarm bells ringing, that he was blocked from talking about it. He could *see* it, considering he showed it to me, but when I asked what it was, he started identifying the Skarn.

When I asked about the other vessel, he'd switch to describing the second Skarn. Pushed again? I got the description of the first ship.

Ingrid grabbed my hand as I started to push harder and shook her head, instead asking oblique questions, like "For a random vessel that matches these dimensions, what are the likely capabilities?"

It was incredibly frustrating, but there was also fuck all that I could see that we could do about it, so I seethed in silence.

Using those parameters, the ship was tentatively identified as a carrier, or a massive transport of some kind. He really couldn't tell me anything I couldn't see for myself, considering it was damn big and slow as shit.

The UC fleet had gathered again and were doing a slow route around the system to get on course—or it seemed slow from here, anyway.

They were travelling at tens of thousands of miles a minute, a speed that could take them from Earth to the moon in about ten minutes, which was crazy, and they were accelerating still.

They'd fallen into a pre-planned formation, the battleships in a circle when seen from directly on, a five-pointed star that was going to spread the pain, with the rest of the fleet moving in close to the leaders, tucking in behind and preparing for the fight.

Arise: Conqueror

The next four hours as the Ændari left the jump point and headed directly at the UC fleet were both boring and scary as hell at the same time. For me, they were filled by me working on repairs to my own ship, and answering Zhonat's questions as he made alterations and improvements to the design, making the malmetal follow them.

I'd settled Ingrid into the command chair, made sure everyone else was okay; then I'd run for it, getting my arse back to the dock and starting work, desperately hoping I could get the ship usable again before anything else went wrong.

I also made sure to take Bach with me, just in case, leaving the others to maintain the control center and protect Ingrid.

She spent her time working through the AI, examining the memory cores and everything that she could find. At her request to Argus—and my order—her Espionage and Hack trees were unlocked. Despite the pain it inflicted on her, she still powered through the lower-level tests and gained point after point on dedicated anti-espionage quests.

She worked to counter trace and hack the intrusion that she was now convinced had originated from one of the cloaked jamming stations, connecting to them one by one, working her way through them and following the next link and the next.

The harvester chunked through the warship minute by minute, depositing materials that the devilkin and soldiers helped lug across the deck, pressing them into place on the conveyor belt I established to carry them up.

Where I worked on the main structure of the ship, reattaching the goddamn wing and so on, Zhonat spent hours working on the control runs and identifying issues for the reactors and more.

The plan was that with them all marked up and shared with me, I could literally run from job to job, slap the nanites on them, give them their orders, and move on.

It was a weird way of working, more like slapping stuff on the hull and running than anything else, but with him providing me with detailed images, repairs, and plans, I could then hit and run.

It probably shouldn't have worked, and it wouldn't have, had we not had so many nanites to use. But the dead bodies of my enemies were fortunately a readily accessed resource.

The giant spiderbot would be an amazing tool to help with the rebuild as well, if not for the fact that a laser had pretty much slagged its heart. So that was undergoing repairs now, as well as some upgrades that the ancient engineer had recommended.

Zhonat and I argued constantly over the design for the ship, too, making little changes. Although he might be respectful everywhere else, as an engineer, he took absolutely no shit.

The rail cannons were examined and found wanting, marked up to be ripped out one at a time and replaced by dedicated gravity cannons.

They were far more powerful and took up less space, but would interfere with the reactors to an insane degree, limiting the fire rate to once every ten seconds.

I hated that, but as he pointed out, the lasers and storm casters were almost continuous fire with the levels of power we had, so I could suck it up for an insane level of damage.

For a nearly two hundred percent increase in potential damage, it was worth it, and the null coins were currently being stacked in their hundreds, ready to be transformed into new ammunition.

Admittedly, it still wasn't a planet killer weapon, which you know, everyone who's anyone secretly wants, even if they'd never use it…*honest*.

It'd more than do for now though, considering it gave me more power than the average battleship.

That was my argument for going out there and joining the fight as soon as the ship was repaired, and why Ingrid flatly refused me, along with everyone else.

Zhonat volunteered to go out there with Bach, swearing that the two of them had more or less got all the bugs worked out now—even if everything from the landing gear up told a very different story.

Even they had to be entirely scrapped and rebuilt.

Ingrid promised to come and look at my ship when she had some time, telling me that I was the "bestest boy ever and to stop sulking."

That made a bit of an impression, finally getting through my self-imposed funk, as I continued working.

All in all, what I was doing was keeping myself busy more than anything else, waiting, while better men and women than me went to their deaths.

They had a point—and Argus had made it as well—that as a Devourer, if I went out there and got my arse handed to me, and was killed permanently or if I was overcome with hunger in the middle of the fight, then I could screw everything.

It didn't make it any easier to bear, though.

"Steve, this is what they do!" Ingrid snapped at me eventually. "Either you trust them to go and fight, or you don't. This is where their training and skills lie. You? You're wonderful—don't get me wrong. You're kind and caring and an unholy terror in melee range, but unless you can slug it out at point-blank range, you've got to admit that you'd be useless out there!

"You survived the fights on the way here—by your own admission—by underhanded trickery and being in too close for the enemy for them to use anything like their normal tactics. You managed to make interstellar combat into a no-holds-barred ring fight, and that was amazing…incredible even. Now they're fighting in an arena where the distances are worked out using the time it takes light to cover hundreds of thousands of miles.

"You've built insane weapons that are frankly terrifying, not to mention shouldn't work by almost any reasonable stretch of the imagination. But the speeds you'd need to be aiming and using them, Argus says you'd be more of a risk to the UC fleet than the enemy, and I have to agree.

Arise: Conqueror

"So, please, Steve, sit this one out. Trust in them to do their job, trust in us to do ours, and just accept that this, this right here, is how you leave us feeling *all the damn time.*"

That ended that discussion pretty fast. And as much as it pissed me off, I had to admit it was fair. The ship was…well, it was fucked. Let's be honest.

There were sections where I could put a tentacle through one side and out the other without touching anything. The wing was back on, but the engines were screwed, needing massive rebuilds. The reactors were down, *again*, and would need a full reboot.

I'd been begged by Zhonat to not jump-start the engines again, as apparently there were more stress fractures than actual solid matter in them by now.

That meant that we needed to take them all entirely offline, power them down, repair them, and then rebuild from scratch.

As the first few hours passed, it became clear that the chances of me fixing the ship in time to join the fight were slightly less than me being named ballerina of the year and taking part in that swan thingy that an ex had tried to talk me into going to see.

Also, karma apparently hated me, as a small group of additional Ændari vessels arrived at the Lagrange point, immediately gunning their engines and starting to head for the fleet from behind.

There were only seven of them, and they were clearly one of the newer and much more "manufactured" designs than the older organic-looking ones. But they bristled with guns, had powerful shields, and were going to add to our problems no end.

The fleet screamed into battle eventually, and with ten minutes remaining before the first shots landed, I returned to the control center, watching with the others.

The fight was over faster than I could believe, with both sides having gone from the close-range slugfest into something that was basically a half a second flash of light to me. Then, it was done.

"What the hell just happened?" I stared as the two fleets continued on, slowly shifting their course, each headed toward a nearby world.

"That," Ingrid said firmly, "is why I didn't want you out there."

"Seriously, what the hell just happened?" I asked again, scanning the records then nodding my thanks as Argus projected a large-screen, slowed-down replay.

Both fleets had opened fire as they approached, filling space with a plethora of madness. Everything from missiles to lasers to pointy sticks had been thrown at either side. The battleships had soaked it all up, coming out the far side smoking and with their shields damaged, but that was pretty much it.

"This is the reality of interstellar conflict," Argus said. *"The speeds required mean that all weapons are automated and there are several passes before the likely outcome can be determined."*

"And did it go well?" I asked, searching the data.

"The UC fleet acquitted themselves admirably. Their battleships maintained their formation and took minor damage, with shields pushed close to, but not into overload. The remainder of the fleet then used the cover of their larger brethren to focus fire on this battleship."

The screen shifted, focusing in on the most damaged of the Ændari ships.

It slowly fell out of formation, its engines flickering and flaring, as Argus threw details up on the screen alongside the image, showing falling reactor levels, damaged shields, and that if anything, it was now drifting, while the others shifted course.

"This ship is now likely out of the immediate fight, giving the enemy admiral a dilemma. They can either choose to reduce speed and surround the vessel, protecting it while it makes repairs, and maintain their overall strength as much as possible.

"To do this, they must accept a significant drop in their speed and maneuverability, and an increase in likely damage to the rest. Or they will leave the damaged vessel.

"Should they choose this course, they will keep the majority of the fleet safer, and maintain the advantages they have. But they open themselves to being picked off piecemeal, as well as losing the strength that this battleship represented."

"So, damned if they do and damned if they don't?" I summarized, and Ingrid snorted.

"The UC fleet's shields were pushed close to failure, but where Admiral Dolfing chose to focus fire on a single vessel as both forces clashed, the Ændari forces each fired on their own targets, reducing their effectiveness."

"And that…other vessel?" I asked, not knowing how else I should refer to it, as the biggest damn ship there and yet the only one that Argus couldn't apparently discuss.

Silence reigned, and I looked at Ingrid, one eyebrow raised in question as she shook her head that I needed to let it go.

"Argus, how long until the fleet reengages?" Ingrid asked aloud.

"Two hours, fourteen minutes, and—"

"And I'm going back to the dock," I grumbled. "Seriously, it's going to all be like this?"

"This is actually an improvement on the usual fleet engagement," Bach admitted, standing to one side by First Fist Zaren, who seemed to be as silent a man as I'd ever encountered.

"Oh?" I asked him, and he nodded.

"Usually we're restricted to our bunks, staying the hell out of the way during these things."

"You're kept in your bunks?" I asked. "Do they pipe the fight through or anything?"

"Pipe?"

"He means, are you shown the progress of the fight?" Ingrid asked.

"No, we are generally restricted to quarters to enable the fleet crew to reach damaged sections faster," Bach said. "Only at the end are we informed of the condition of the fleet."

"Okay, yeah, that'd drive me fucking mad." I winced. "Just sitting there in your room, waiting to see if you're going to be killed or the ship's going to blow up or whatever…"

"It is testing, but the reality of fleet engagements," Zaren admitted, speaking up for the first time since introducing himself and thanking me for the invite to see what was happening.

I nodded that I could totally understand that. Then, with a sigh, we left Ingrid and the others to it, heading back to work.

CHAPTER THIRTY-ONE

The next two days were almost identical to that first pass, with the times between fights only growing longer as the Ændari started to lose ships.

Instead of fighting it out, they turned and headed for the most inhabited planet in the system. Within minutes, its leadership was screaming at Ingrid and the fleet.

Apparently the Ændari had issued them an ultimatum. Either they renounced their membership of the UC and capitulated to the Ændari Empire, with any and all vessels and space defenses around the planet joining the fight against the UC, or they'd bombard the planet from orbit as they passed, with god-rods.

They didn't call them that, of course. "Spears of the creator's merciful light" was the term, but relativistic fuckin' orbital death spears was what they meant.

The planet wanted the fleet to stop them, and the fleet, clearly knowing what was going on and that they couldn't intercept the bastards, passed on their regrets and recommended that the planet speak to the local UC leadership, which was Ingrid and me.

It was all a bit shit, really.

She explained the realities of life to the apoplectic leadership, and despite the fact they'd refused to help us before, she still ended up coming to me in tears after the call concluded.

They'd trooped out a school full of innocent-looking children and shown them to her, telling her that these were the ones she was failing.

They would all die, because of our actions and ignorance.

The kids had been terrified, wailing as the leadership said all of this. Then the connection had been cut, with the promise that the recordings of the fleet's failure would be shared with all the UC.

I spent a few minutes holding her as she sobbed her heart out, all the while plotting the fucking murder of those assholes who had done this to her, and the goddamn Ændari.

Every one of those dickbags deserved to be nailed to a barn door by their bollocks and have it kicked by wild horses until they died.

I spent those few minutes as I reassured her fantasizing about killing them all, while the fleet assured me they were doing all they could.

Arise: Conqueror

They were already in a stern chase, and the Ændari were faster. There was no way that they'd be able to catch them, nor stop them from firing on the planet. So when the leadership announced their surrender and the capitulation of the sector to Ændari control, nobody was surprised.

The immediate effect on the surrounding systems would have been a terrible situation in more general terms, had anything changed.

The war between the Ændari and the UC in times past would have been massively disrupted by the UC losing one of their border systems. But considering it'd already been cut off from the UC for several weeks, there was pretty much bugger all difference.

What was worse, was the Ændari being reinforced by the small fleet of weaker vessels that had been holding back around the planet, and them launching for the fleet.

The asshole leadership contacted us again, me taking the connection this time, in full Devourer and armor-plated mode. They were a lot more apologetic as they gave us the shitty news, and demanded we find a solution.

The Ændari had ordered the minute space force that had been protecting their world to attack the UC fleet and were watching, they'd warned. If the "home guard," as they were called, didn't attack the UC, then the Ændari would bombard their planet.

If the UC ignored the home guard's attack—which although small, was still armed with nuclear and proton weapons, and so could cause significant damage—then they'd be weakened to face the Ændari.

The home guard wasn't a serious threat to the fleet, but what they lost in individual strength, they made up in numbers.

There were hundreds of fighters, dozens of small freighters and independent ships that were as armed as the owner could manage, and three previously mothballed destroyers.

The real issue, though?

The biggest and weirdest of the Ændari ships, that one that Argus couldn't talk about, was headed straight for the planet, while the others set up for what looked to be a slingshot maneuverer around it, to then head back and hit the fleet as soon as they'd been weakened by the sacrificial lambs.

The enemy fleet was already braking, slowing as much as possible to enable them to duke it out, while using the planet as a shield.

I couldn't stop cursing them, seeing that it was goddamn true what they said: there was no level the Ændari wouldn't stoop to.

"What can we do?" Ingrid asked me, broken, and I shook my head.

"Honestly? I don't know," I said. "It's two hours' flight time from here, and that would be if we had the damn ship working. As it is? There's nothing we can do."

"An hour until the first engagement," she whispered, closing her eyes again.

We stood in the lower bay of the ship. The giant spiderbot that I'd made ages ago was finally fixed, and the whole ship shook as it clanked and clanged around on the exterior, ripping panels free and replacing them with newly forged ones.

We spent a few more minutes in the hold, just relaxing and holding each other, before the sheer horror of what was likely to happen to the world of Scorpio-3.

Soon enough, though, we were forced apart: her to return to the control room and the deep dive she was doing in the node, and me to hour after hour of frenzied work to repair a ship that'd never known anything but battle and being rebuilt.

The others were helping. Jonas and Paul had enlisted help from the soldiers and devilkin. The medical suite was being moved, torn out of the ship and carried, inch by painful inch, across the dock to the first hall.

That'd been decided to be the site of the new hospital, with Captain Shemer due out of the "tank" in an hour, and the systems being set up, ready to be hardwired into the node.

Although I might be pissed about the stuff that Argus apparently couldn't control, I couldn't fault his effort on the things that weren't locked out.

He'd been issuing quests to the UC soldiers like a goddamn legend. "Reposition medical suite," for example, got a single point, each, and that was the first level of the quest.

There were five levels, all ranging in levels of difficulty from "carry X across the floor to Y," up to "activate the new medical facility and revive lost comrades."

That was level five, for five War points and five Support.

My entire soldier force was getting unlocked as the hours passed, and I wasn't doing too badly out of it as well.

Evolving Quest: Building the Future (Part 2-[A])

You have claimed all the technologies you need to return to the fight, but although knowledge is indeed the greatest weapon, stabbing an opponent with your brain is less useful.

Use all that you have learned to construct a viable vessel, then return to the Node to receive the following rewards:

[Bonus: Return with all living members of the dwarfen race to receive a bonus.]

- **+3 Support Points**

- **+3 War Points**

- **+Access to Level 3 of the Evolving Quest**

Viable Vessel: 1/1

Dwarfen survivors: 18/18 – deferred

Arise: Conqueror

That was a hell of a bonus, considering that I needed to fix it anyway. But the best was yet to come, and appeared after a seemingly minor question.

"Argus, when I was on Earth, the medical suites had a memory unit, one that the people who had access to them could use to bring people back from the dead. They were un-Awakened, and they had only the most basic access to their nanites, but they could still do it. Why was that?"

"I cannot answer."

"Fuck's sake!" I'd sworn, until Ingrid had reached out a few minutes later, excited and concerned.

"Steve, did you do something?"

"No...?" I lied, thinking of the solid five minutes of abuse I'd been shouting while kicking the walls in my ship.

"Steve?" she asked, clearly aware I was hiding something.

"Okay, maybe I lost my temper a bit, that's all. I'm trying, all right and..."

"Do it again."

"It's not my fault, okay? I'm not built to goddamn wait around and... Uh, what?"

"Do it again," she said firmly. *"Whatever you did, do it again."*

I tried kicking the walls, a little shouting, and then I facepalmed and reached out to Argus, connecting to him and asking the same question over and over.

"That's it!" she sent, excitement clear in her voice.

"What?"

"Meet me in the lower hall. We're going to the crystal memories!"

"Okay?" I agreed, confused but happy that she was happy again.

It took a few minutes to uncover the passage down to the lower spire. Once inside, she had me seal it up behind us again as well.

"Is there a way that you can seal this entirely?" she called over her shoulder at me as we went down the stairs, two at a time.

"Maybe?" I hedged. "I mean, what if we need to get back down here?"

"I mean so that nobody else can do it, not even someone with your abilities?" she clarified. "We can come back, but nobody except you can open it?"

"Maybe," I repeated, thinking about it. "I could probably use the same trick that the node is made from, but I'd have to unlock that level of building first. Might take awhile."

"What if we had the soldiers unlock sections for you?"

"How?" I asked, then nodded as I understood it. "Crap, you mean that dodgy boosting method we figured out before? Having them unlock sections by spending their points instead of me doing it? Sounds a bit shitty…"

"Can you do it?" she asked grimly.

"Probably. Why? What's happened?"

"The questions you were asking Argus," she replied. "I was in the system examining things, trying to find anything that could explain it, and when you asked him something, there was a difference."

"Okay?"

"Look, I'm probably not going to explain this very well, but think of the memory crystals as his neural network. Every thought he has is based on who he is and what his experiences are. That was how he was designed. But the weakness to this is that his AI core is in the upper spire."

"Right." I'd seen that before when we'd been exploring and learning about the place.

"Okay, well, his core is up there, but the memory storage is down here!"

"Right, that seems a bit bloody stupid," I said as we reached the bottom of the stairs, moving out on the upper platform and staring out.

The lower spire was a hell of a lot more breathtaking when it wasn't full of assholes trying to kill me. For a few seconds, I stood by Ingrid's side, as we looked out over the area.

There were hundreds of crystal hexagonal towers, each slowly growing upward, suffused by billions of gleaming fragments. They contained the basic memories of hundreds of trillions of users, those who had been active over millennia. As we stared out over them, I wondered just how much of their memories were stored.

"There!" she said excitedly, pointing to one of the crystals that looked exactly the damn same as the others. "Can you get us to that one? There's no room to fly."

I nodded and stepped over the barrier, a narrow railing that was more functional than ornate. Clearly the engineers' areas hadn't been deemed as important.

The narrow ledge on the far side was barely enough for me to stand on, but that wasn't really an issue. I took Ingrid into my arms in a princess carry, then crouched.

I leapt free, soaring over the distance between the highest point and the crystal tower she wanted. Only a touch of gravity manipulation guided me and lightened us. I kicked off the others as I passed them, using them to my advantage. I dropped, landing lightly, and set her down as she struggled free.

She'd had to link the one that she'd wanted to see in the command link for me. The hundreds of towers were all differing heights, with some only six inches across, and others thirty or more. It meant that when we'd gotten closer, we'd had to drop down and down, before we finally landed atop a small collection that were roughly the same height.

"There," she breathed, sinking to her knees and peering straight down at a crack between three of the pillars.

What I'd have taken to be a tiny gap between them was actually a recess, one that led down deeper and deeper, until it reached a gleaming black crystal.

One that made me stare in confusion.

"That's it," she told me. "Can you get it?"

"What are we doing?" I asked, already able to feel it now that I was fixated on it.

"It's what's causing the issues with Argus," she told me. "That's what keeps acting, sending out signals and deleting data, or forcing him to ignore us."

"That?" I asked absently, crouching and squinting, before extending a finger.

"Yeah. Can you get it?"

"I'll be able to reach it," I assured her, extending the finger and waiting as it flowed down, farther and farther.

"That's so weird." She shook her head, and I grinned up at her.

"The finger?"

"Yeah."

"Wanna see what else I can extend?" I offered, jokingly.

"Behave." She smiled, but neither of our hearts were in the flirting; there was too much going on.

I turned, feeling the pseudopod sinking deeper and deeper until it reached the crystal. I hesitated, then touched it gently, thinking to pick it up and pull it free.

Instead, it attacked.

I froze, totally shocked. Then the first vestiges of panic rose as something started to convert my nanites, forcing them to change their allegiance.

It wasn't many at first. The ones that were pressed flat against what I now knew was actually a goddamn nanite block were incredibly compressed.

Then, as more and more changed, the conversion rate picked up speed.

My shock shattered. I dove in mentally, triggering Tsunami and ordering the nanites to counterattack, to hack their former brethren and bring them back under my control.

The world before me erupted into a digital battlefield.

The usual three-dimensional dice were gone. In their place were tens of thousands of symbols, and by the second, they were pressing closer, changing.

They rained from the heavens, seeming to hit a glass dome over my head, sliding down it all akimbo.

My Hack sub-mind slid up into primacy as I called, with the dome slowly sliding closer by the second.

"S...T...E...V...E..." Ingrid intoned distantly.

A tiny fragment of my mind noted that I'd slowed time already, on instinct. It seemed to have no effect on the streaming numbers, and I stared, at a loss, considering most of them weren't even recognizable.

There were letters, symbols, equations and concepts; almost none were so simple as numbers. I frantically looked for something I could use, jerking to a halt as I almost missed a tiny golden zero, sliding quickly down on its way to the ground.

A zero.

The symbols around me were a riot of colors, but I'd seen that before.

I touched it with my mind and it froze. The symbols nearby shimmered into immobility as well.

A reaction! Spinning and searching, I spotted one, near the ground, almost lost in the pile of numbers that was steadily building.

Tagging that, a handful more symbols froze. Even as I started looking for the two, the Hack sub-mind was hard at work, linking with the Engineering one to compare the first and second groupings.

Similarities were found. Green equation symbols in both flexed when it pressed them, and I searched as quick as I could.

More were found—three, five, four finally being spotted. Then I was back to the five, tagging that as well.

The seconds spun away, but I moved faster now. My increased perception made the task easier as quadratic equations popped up and were solved.

I'd never so much as chewed a book that'd explained them, but at some point, I'd heard the name, and for my Engineering sub-mind, they were there, ready to be used.

Then I felt her. The command link pulsed as she linked her mind to me, giving me access to her abilities, to her mind, and the extra processing power that came with it, as well as her much more augmented capabilities.

Time slowed even further as I battled the morass. Tens of thousands of calculations were performed second by second. I battled on, the tide slowly turning. Tsunami caught the incoming wave, then began to convert the nanites before it back into my own.

The first few were slow to respond, but as more and more fell to my counterattack, the conversion picked up speed.

Five became ten, became twenty…then forty, eighty. And suddenly it was washing back in the other direction, an unstoppable wave that slammed into the tiny crystal that lay buried at the heart of the mass.

It shattered, a separate layer of nanites set below it. Sensing the loss of those above triggered a pulse, a twist in space that shattered the crystal irreparably. The remaining fragments cascaded down as dust.

I blinked, then shook myself, seeing Ingrid's worried face staring into my own.

"That…was beautiful," she whispered, shaking her head as the hack vanished and the extruded nanite grouping flowed back up to me.

"It was a hack," I explained, shaking my head. "A good one."

"Mine aren't like that," she admitted.

"No?"

"We create a system we can work with," she said. "For me, it's a language flow, a record of ancient words, all unknown to me. But by the time I finish it?" She smiled. "One of my last hacks, I gained an understanding of Vedic-Sanskrit."

"Okay…?" I shook my head. "No clue what that is."

"When you're hacking anything, it uses something that you can figure your way through," she explained. "For me, it was a basic language system. I wanted to understand it, so I started comparing it to others, and I'd studied Sanskrit in the past.

"I was a month into the course when I came on holiday to Greece, so when I considered that, the system decided it was fine to use that. It means I hack things as normal, probably as you do, but all the time, I'm learning the language model as well."

She smiled at me, seeming almost embarrassed, and I stared at her for several heartbeats in shock, working that out in my head.

It wasn't enough that she'd learned to goddamn hack to help in the fight, but she'd added in levels of difficulty to goddamn teach herself languages while she was at it?

I couldn't help but shake my head that she was so intelligent, so amazing, and yet she'd climbed on the back of my goddamn bike, all those years ago.

"Everything okay?" she asked, and I nodded, dismissing the wonder as I spoke up.

"We lost the crystal," I started to apologize.

"I know." She nodded. "I was there with you. But as much as that's a shame, it's not important."

"Why not?" I asked. "I thought that was the whole point of this?"

"No. That crystal might have had the memories in it that were stolen, but I doubt it. The nanites were left under it as a trap to make sure that nobody could identify the user. But the ones over the top? They were there to be used."

"Right?" I nodded. "I felt something, like an echo of intent…" I said it even as it came to me.

"Exactly." She nodded. "While you were cleaning up the last fragments, I was focusing on that, and I felt…something. It wasn't clear, but there was a sensation of movement, of distance and connection."

"Right." I understood exactly what she meant.

"I think they were here to form a link. The crystal controlled them, and they connected to the towers they needed to. When they were told to erase a memory, this was what was doing it."

"Okay, so now what?"

"Well, in theory, with that gone, if you can make sure there's no backup ones, then we can seal this away, and Argus can start to fix the gaps, to recompile it all. It'd also make sense as to why this was happening."

"Oh?"

"Sorry, I was thinking ahead there, but this makes sense as to why we kept finding oblique comments, references that led us to here."

"How's that?" I asked, before nodding. "Because it's a program, basically. Someone put a basic 'do this' script in here, and just left it to work. They never worried about checking it or tweaking it."

"Why would they?" she agreed, smiling. "After all, we only started looking because there were little discrepancies, and we only saw them because we're holed up here. How many times over history do you think anyone was squatting in the nodes?"

"Probably never," I agreed. "Okay, what now?"

"Now, we ask Argus about that ship."

"Warning, warning!" Argus blared to us, nearly making me shit myself. "Catastrophic loss of life occurring on local life-bearing world designation Scorpio-3."

"Well, fuck!" I snarled and spat. "Fucking Ændari!"

The pair of us set off running as I brought up the link to Argus, borrowing his senses to see what he'd seen, and stumbled, appalled by what I was seeing.

"That's…not the Ændari." Ingrid gasped, seeing the same thing that I was. "What the hell is that thing?"

"Warning! Warning!" Argus blared. "Catastrophic loss of life—"

"We know!" I roared, seeing the horror that was engulfing the planet. "What the hell is it!"

"Potential classified identification: Ouroboros class harvester in action. Beware, beware, beware…"

CHAPTER THIRTY-TWO

The world of Scorpio-3 was a green and verdant one, though much of it was locked in snow-capped sheets currently, the last ice age having ended recently.

The poles were thickly coated in ice, but the seas and thousands of smaller islands that dotted the archipelagos of the tropics were stippled with great patterns of light.

Cities floated across the oceans and dotted the islands. A single space-elevator that fell from orbit down to the largest of these gleamed red in the reflected sunlight of the dying day.

All those details paled into insignificance, though, as the massive ship that the Ændari had escorted into orbit had begun its transformation.

Argus ran a sped-up version of the ship's arrival into orbit for us, even as the second, current time image played, the pair merging as they caught up to each other.

The ship slid into a geosynchronous orbit, then waited, as the surrounding orbital defenses all shifted subtly in the digital realm. Argus marked them up in a wave as more and more flickered and changed colors, tagging them as falling under the Ændari's control.

As soon as the local area was highlighted as no longer a threat, though, it was as if the ship just couldn't wait anymore.

It was long, almost cigar shaped, then squashed slightly, making it more of an oval when seen from the ends. It had a raised bridge that sloped up from the main body by a small degree and ridges that ran along its length.

It was from the underside that the changes first came, as the hull split in a line that led to the end. A single thin section that ran front to back, forming the middle of the bottom layer, swung down, tail-like. As soon as that was clear, both sides slid out as well, opening the ship up from below.

At first, the segments that extended out looked almost like bomb bay doors, each an individual section of the hull, and although massive, were solid and manufactured.

Then they started to change.

The panels that opened out were thick. Glancing at the details for the overall ship gave me their dimensions, and I winced at them.

The ship was a hundred and twenty-three *miles* long. That sheer mass had been mind-blowing to me. I'd seen that such massive structures could exist—

like the Forgeship—but seeing the ships lost to the void when I'd found the dwarfen?

That made it clear that not only did many species subscribe to the "bigger is better" ethos, some had really big issues with it.

This ship was huge, sure, but seen in comparison to the battleships, which were each fifty miles plus, it'd seemed an insanely huge transport or whatever.

Now, as the segments opened out, each thirty miles long and ten miles thick, the true size of the horror show was revealed.

The segments extended, thirty miles becoming forty, fifty—*seventy*…

That was when *they* opened in turn. Ten of them extended from the underside of the ship like a monstrous squid with issues. The upper half of the ship flexed as the sides continued to open out. The underside of the ship glowed with heat as it began to enter the atmosphere, sinking down toward the planet.

As it went, the longest section, and the first to move and what had to be a solid hundred plus miles long, extended farther. Its tip crashed into one of the cities that floated serenely across the gleaming blue oceans, then into the water, and finally into the bedrock beneath it.

Earthquakes began as the construction continued to lower from orbit. The "legs" burrowed into the planet and destroyed huge swathes of inhabited land and sea.

The impact as the ship continued to lower was horrific, sparking devastating firestorms, tsunamis, and earthquakes. It was that impact that had started the full-on warning from Argus.

Time sped up as the ship continued to lower. The legs of the harvester lengthened as more and more segments unfolded, extending out below to carve into the now terrified world.

"Argus, what the fuck is that!" I shouted, grabbing Ingrid around the waist and pinning her to me, as I launched myself upward. Gravity twisted and rocketed us up and into the stairwell.

The steps flashed past in a blur almost too fast to resolve. Then we were banking hard, barely scraping through the gap and into the hall, arcing around and flashing over the heads of the devilkin helping to set a medical tube into place, two of the soldiers working to connect them up with their newly unlocked Support capabilities.

I rolled, then pulled up. The minute calculations to produce gravity fields that acted on us, and only us, the line of differential space-time that enfolded us, the counter charge that created a "safe" buffer around us…

All of it was as natural as breathing now, and as I dug deeper, the air shook with our passage.

Arcing around and up, rising into the air and closing on the upper floors, I watched, horrified as the "tail" of the harvester unlocked further. Additional panels extended, punching into the ravaged city, then pulled inward, dragging more and more matter into the central section.

"The Ouroboros class harvester has been theorized, but the majority of records to the location, design, or feasibility of the device have been expunged.

The Ouroboros was discussed as a response to the Devourer contamination feared by upper echelons of the Ændari. But, to my knowledge, the only prototype was destroyed."

"Because it's a fucking nightmare!" I snapped. "What the hell? It's a harvester?"

"Not only was it theorized as a response to the rise of the Devourers, but it was postulated as a way to deal with enemy planets at the same time. If the builders were sufficiently dispersed throughout the population, then upon securing the orbitals, the Ouroboros platform could be deployed to harvest the enemy world.

"There were several unsuccessful attempts to harvest enemy and unclaimed locations that led to the final tests, and these in great part led to the decision that I and the other node AI made to reduce the Ændari.

"The Ouroboros platform was designed as a replacement to the failed Jörmungandr test bed. The Jörmungandr prototype was designed to force conversion of a target world into viable unlocked builders. But upon deployment, the theorized minimum required builder population to begin a self-replicating chain reaction through standard mass was deemed too high for viable usage.

"Instead, the Ouroboros platform was designed to harvest sufficient builders from the target population and, using them as a seed, begin an exponential conversion process, with its primary systems providing the required mass, power, and printing capacity.

"When used in conjunction with a dedicated production facility, the paired units could both harvest entire worlds, and replace fleet losses in short order."

"Fleet losses…" I gritted my teeth. "Argus, can the Ændari be reborn through the medical tubes, brought back the way that humans have been on Earth in the past using those tubes?"

"Negative," Argus assured us. "Humanity's ability to be replicated and the original guiding sentience reinstalled through such systems was theorized, and one of the reasons that humanity was selected to be the next generation of Biological Weapon Variants."

"So we *can* bring people back using them?" I asked firmly.

"Theoretically," Argus said. "There were experiments conducted with limited success, before being entirely disbanded. Those brought 'back' through this method required an inordinately large number of resources, as well as time to recover. The process was deemed wasteful, and further investigation into its potential was curtailed by the uprising and subsequent cancellation of the BWV program."

"So we can come back but they can't." I grunted, twisting and rolling again as we flashed along the last hall and up the final set of stairs.

I burst into the control room, twisting around and landing hard, bracing my feet. I skidded across the polished floor, Ingrid clinging to me, her eyes screwed shut against the world flashing around us.

"Ouroboros class harvesting confirmed," Argus said, his voice filling the air as I stalked forward, setting Ingrid down.

Scylla stood from the command chair, relinquishing it to her.

"Harvesting of the planet is confirmed in progress, though no paired production facility has been detected in proximity."

"Could it be coming?" I asked, as Ingrid gasped, bringing up the numbers that she could see on the screens for everyone.

"This is given a strong probability, as the original Ouroboros platform has highly limited internal storage capabilities. Please wait…confirming incoming system entry…"

"What the hell is coming now?" I growled, reaching out and pulling up the jump point. I stared in wonder as a new player arrived to even the field.

"Identity confirmed. Devourer Shan'Gai has entered the system."

I froze, looking at the ship that had burst from the warping of space, tearing into the Lagrange point, before roaring to life.

Shan'Gai was huge, pointed at one end, looking more like a broadsword, viewed from the tip, with the last section all being bulging engines. Narrow wings that curled almost like a stingray flexed as he shifted around. Engines glowed with life and power as he started forward, already in pursuit of the nearest Ændari ships.

"Oh thank *fuck*!" I gasped, almost going weak at the knees as I realized that for the first time, there was another here to take over. I had another like me, someone these bastards looked up to and expected to have all the answers.

I had someone I could hopefully ask questions of that I couldn't ask anyone else.

"Connection request from Devourer Shan'Gai," Argus called out, and I nodded, approving it instantly.

The largest, central screen flickered for those who needed it. For Ingrid and me, we were suddenly seeing the projection of Shan'Gai's bridge.

It was dark, the room before us suddenly dimly lit and extending back. The walls, floor, and ceiling were all a deep red. Lights glimmered on sections here and there that were technological in origin, seemingly embedded into what looked to be an organic hull.

The real focus, though?

That was Shan'Gai himself. Or itself—I had no clue what I was supposed to call them. But the Devourer appeared half propped up in a crystal throne; connections flowed down from the roof, up from the ground, and all around, sinking into the figure.

He was embedded in the crystal from the waist down, with a heavily muscled upper body on display, and a mask that seemed to show a Chinese-style devil covering his mouth and lower jaw.

It was ornate in white and gold, while everything else, him included, was in tones of striated red and black, with sections that shifted and altered, changing by the second.

"Devourer…" he whispered, his voice cracked and uncertain, sounding confused as his head lolled to one side. "You are…"

"I am." I nodded, stepping forward. "I'm Steve."

"I am… am…" He nodded.

"Are you okay?"

"Am."

"Okay…well, uh, this is Ingrid." I introduced her, reaching back and taking her hand, drawing her up to stand by my side.

"Not…Devourer."

"No," I said softly. My earlier good feeling dimmed as I stared at the seemingly confused and distracted ancient Devourer.

"Not Devourer," he repeated, nodding as if that was all that needed to be said. "Ændari. Mine. Stay clear. Do not approach feeding."

"Okay." I nodded, relief rising again. "And the harvester?"

"Harvester."

"The harvester…the Ouroboros harvester that's attacking the planet," I clarified. "What do we do?"

"You do not." He said after a few seconds, "It is for me."

That was it; the connection was severed. I stared as the projected reality vanished, and I tried to make sense of everything that had happened.

"Steve, I don't like this," Ingrid said after a few seconds. "That was all kinds of wrong."

"Yeah, I don't like it either. Maybe, I don't know, but maybe he's just been alone for a long time?" I tried.

"Devourer Shan'Gai instructs that you are to remain here," Argus said suddenly. "They are unused to verbal communication, I suspect, and are picking up speed."

"Fuck, that's a relief. Show me them," I ordered, staring at the long shape as it increased speed steadily.

The shape remained the same, the outer hull gleaming gently in the reflected starlight as Argus spoke again.

"Ændari vessels in the system are continuing to fight. The UC have demanded their surrender."

"Tell the UC fleet to break off," I ordered after a quick consultation with Ingrid. "If they get too close to Shan'Gai, they might be too tempting to resist. Can they dock here?"

"They are able to dock one at a time, but due to their size and the dock's available mass, no more than a single battleship is capable of being hosted at a time."

"Okay. Can they, I don't know, break off and get around Shan'Gai? Stay clear so that they're safe from him?"

"Admiral Dolfing is requesting a communication link."

"Okay, put him through," I ordered, looking down at Ingrid as she squeezed my hand reassuringly.

"Lord Devourer," the admiral greeted. The bridge of his ship appeared on the screen, people racing here and there in a scene of organized chaos in the background. "I've received your orders, and those of Devourer Shan'Gai."

"Good. Can you do it?" I asked.

"Are you aware of the orders I've received?" he asked carefully.

"Uh, to break off the fight and come to the node?" I suggested.

"Those are the orders from *you*. Devourer Shan'Gai has ordered us to cripple the Ændari, making them easier to access, and then to take up station between you and Scorpio-3."

"Between us?" I asked. "Wait, he said that he'd take care of the harvester. What did he tell you?"

"A harvester…is that what it is? What the hell harvests a *planet?* Millions of lives have been lost already, and if that thing isn't stopped soon—"

"I know," I interrupted. "Shan'Gai told us to stay clear. As a Devourer, he doesn't want me close, but he's sorting it."

"He… Lord, you know your business better than I do, and your kind, but the orders I got from the Devourer, they didn't actually say that Lord Shan'Gai would stop the harvester. Did the lord confirm that with you?"

"He said…" I paused, thinking through what had actually been said, then nodding. "I'll confirm that. For now, do any damage you can to the Ændari in passing, but get your people clear. I don't want you too close to Shan'Gai when he, it…fuck's sake! Just get out of there!" I ordered, getting a grateful nod from him. I gestured to the screen with one hand in a cutting motion.

I spoke quickly, turning around as everyone started to ask questions.

"Quiet!" I ordered, focusing on the system link and reaching out to Shan'Gai.

"You," he grumbled, and I nodded.

"Me," I agreed. "Shan'Gai, I need to confirm that you're going to stop the harvester."

"Begun already."

"Yeah, it has. Sorry, I don't mean to go on, but you *are* going to stop the harvester, right? That's why you're here?"

"Harvest begun."

"I fuckin' know the damn thing's begun!" I snapped. "I need to know you're gonna fuckin' stop it!"

"Harvest begun. Do not interfere!" he snarled. The connection grew darker as for the first time, he no longer seemed distant or confused. Instead he was angry, and stared at me in warning. "Mine!"

"Yours…" I said slowly. A sinking feeling bloomed in the pit of my stomach. "Shan'Gai, you have to stop it! I'm not trying to claim it. I don't want to share it or anything—I just want you to make it the priority!"

"Ændari mine."

"Sure!" I agreed, nodding. "They can be yours and whatever you get in the system is yours. Just don't waste time, all right? Get the harvester first!" I paused, running my right hand through my hair as I thought quickly. Clearly we weren't getting through to each other, what with the language barrier or whatever it was. "Maybe I could attack it and buy you some time…" I muttered unthinkingly.

"MINE!" he roared. The connection shook with fury, before a final demand was thrown at me. "STAY AWAY!" The connection cut.

Arise: Conqueror

I stood frozen, staring at the screen, my mouth open as details finally clicked into place.

It wasn't all there, not yet, but there were enough fragments that were lining up, and cold fear filled me.

"Steve…?" Ingrid asked, seeing the change in me and afraid that what she was suspecting was what I'd seen as well.

"He's not going to stop it," I whispered.

"Oh no…"

"He's here for the harvester," I continued in a low voice. "He's letting it harvest the planet. Even if he might have stopped it at some point, now that it's started? All he cares about is feeding. It's making food for him, so he's going to let it work."

"He *can't*," Ingrid whispered.

The others all started talking at once.

"You shitting me?" Jonas grunted.

"Well, fuck *that*," Paul said. "Nobody fucking does that shit!"

"It cannot be borne," Scylla growled.

"There has to be something we can do," Courtney agreed.

"Lord, this is the will of the Devourer." The voice came from the screen to the side of me.

I turned, seeing Admiral Dolfing standing there. I suddenly realized that the "cutting" gesture I'd used? It was a human, and more to the point, an *Earth* motion. It meant nothing to him, so he'd just shut up, assuming that was what I wanted.

"Explain," I snapped grimly, thinking he might as well make himself useful as long as he was there.

"The Devourers, they change when they feed," he said slowly. "You know this?"

"I know the hunger," I snapped. "Yes, I know that we can get…a bit tetchy." That was, perhaps, the understatement of the goddamn century.

"Lord, Shan'Gai protects our borders, offers us protection, but the lord makes it clear, when it feeds, we must not be there."

"Because he'll get out of control," I guessed. "I know, so just…I don't know, you stay clear, all right? That's why I ordered you here."

"No." His voice rose. "No, you don't understand, Steve." He dropped the honorific and went on, even as the bridge behind him looked on. "When a Devourer comes across a battlefield, they lose all reason. They stay out in deep space because if they come into the populated sectors? It ends badly for everyone.

"The Ændari don't want a fight with a Devourer, not under any circumstances, because it won't stop. *You* won't stop. They can't be reasoned with. The Ændari might threaten and bluster, but knowing that the Devourer is here? They should be running."

"Right?"

"They're not."

"I get that, but why?"

"Steve, they're trying to gain that harvester more time to break down the world. They're killing millions by the minute, and as more and more food is gathered, Shan'Gai will go mad. He'll enter a feeding frenzy, and there's nothing we can do to stop him."

"Why!" I barked. "Why the hell would they do that?"

"I don't know. I've never heard of a harvester, not like this, not outside of the old legends, and frankly, 'why' doesn't matter anymore."

"Because?" I asked grimly.

"The only question we can ask at this point is what do we do next?" he said sternly. "The incoming planetary defense force has surrendered. They know the Ændari are killing their world. They have an uplift available of just under eleven thousand an hour, between them all."

"Uplift?" I asked dumbly.

"If they land, load up everyone they can cram in and launch again, they can bring eleven thousand civilians an hour to the fleet. We can increase that to nearly twenty, if we use every shuttle we have."

"And you can save twenty thousand people an hour, from a planet that holds hundreds of millions," Ingrid whispered in horror.

"We can only do that once we get there," he went on, nodding that we finally understood. "We can punch through the Ændari forces, overload our weapons and shields. We'll take significant damage, but if we go at them as hard as possible rather than focusing on a longer battle with less damage taken, we can punch through, I have no doubt."

"Okay, but?" I asked, knowing it was coming.

"But Shan'Gai will feed on us," he finished. "If we use orbital weaponry to stop the harvester, it'll be almost as devastating as if we leave it to work. The weapons impact, the debris, the collateral damage…all of it—Scorpio-3 won't survive."

"So what do we do?" I asked, and he smiled sadly.

"I was really hoping that you knew," he admitted. "I can take my ship and we can gain the fleet some time, break off and try to draw his attention, but…" He shrugged.

"It's not likely to work," I finished for him. "Has this happened before?"

"This situation or the harvester?"

"Either."

"We… *I* think so." He reached up, rubbing at the side of his head. "There's worlds in the registry that should be viable, that when the first recovery teams went looking for them after the nanite plague, they just weren't there anymore. Only great fields of debris and rubble. Something like this could have done it."

"But the Ændari would have had a massive number of nanites—sorry, builders as you call them—and they'd have had everything they needed to make new ships and more if they'd done it," Ingrid said. "They could have built entire fleets from a harvested world, surely?"

"Most likely," he agreed. "But the damage we can see before us now is an exact match for the debris found on occasion in systems with missing worlds.

There weren't many, a few dozen, but nothing else that's been found could explain the missing and devastated planets. If this was deployed, it would explain it."

"But not where the hell the mass went," I said grimly, as more and more pieces fell into place. "Zhonat?" I barked, reaching into the node's systems and demanding a new connection. He popped up, an avatar of him appearing as he stood to attention.

"Lord." He greeted me formally, seeing that there were others present. "How may I serve?"

"My ship." I ground out the words. "How long until it's ready?"

"To fly?" He paused, thinking. "A day, maybe slightly less?"

"I need it."

"When?"

"Now."

"Steve, it's not ready." He dropped all formality as he tried to explain. "We powered the engines all the way down—the grav drive, the reactors…everything."

"Can it be made to fly?" I ground out, and he hesitated, seeing my clothing rippling as it shifted. The comfortable and almost mentally automatic jeans and T-shirt blurred as more and more nanites floated up, reforming until layers of armor covered my body.

"We could jump-start the reactors, and I could work on the guns on the way?" he suggested. "I could… I don't know." He sagged. "Steve, the ship is barely intact. The frame is solid again, but almost everything else? From the control runs to the guns to the engines, everything is borderline able to be powered, but that's it. The engines might rip free. The grav drive can't be used—it needs a full power cycle. And as to the weapons…"

I stopped listening, staring at the plot and at the image of Shan'Gai as he increased speed again and again. We were at the halfway point in the system, he at the outside. The node was as secure a place as I could imagine right now, but it was too small to serve as a lifeboat for millions.

Shan'Gai was determined to feed, to not lose those nanites. He was going to leave millions of people to die, all because he could then feed on them. He couldn't see that…

Shan'Gai…

Shan'Gai was the key here. Take him out of the fight and everything else was doable. The Ændari were a pain, but they were manageable. The fleet could take them…probably.

They'd already been winning, after all. But why the hell did the Ændari bring that thing here? That, and Shan'Gai were the two bits that didn't make any goddamn sense.

They were attacking the UC fleet; everything else they did made a twisted sort of sense—but that? That didn't. If they punched through the UC forces, they knew they'd be weakened. Then they'd be facing the Devourer, and as old and strong as he had to be? They had no chance.

They *had* to know that. They could have done a loop of the system and used the harvester to make us focus on the world—they could still escape.

"Why commit suicide?" I muttered aloud. The sudden silence broke the spell as I blinked again, seeing that my eyes had tracked back to Shan'Gai unthinkingly.

The sheer acceleration he was showing? He'd be able to overtake the smaller Ændari fleet easily enough, but that didn't make sense either. They had to know he was coming, so why keep going in that direction?

Turn and go to the side and either he'd follow them and they gain their battleships some time, or they'd be ignored in favor of the planet and the fight to come.

It was almost like…

"They're not afraid of him," I whispered. Everything suddenly made sense; the last pieces of the puzzle clicked into place. "Fuck my life, that's it. They're not afraid of Shan'Gai. They're not trying to run from him, or to raid the planet and escape with it all! It's an offering!"

"What?" Jonas growled.

"The damn Ændari aren't his enemy—they're *feeding* him!"

"Lord, you cannot be suggesting what this sounds like," Dolfing said, triggering something out of sight. A barrier of light sprung up around him, presumably cutting off the conversation from being overheard by the rest of his bridge. "He is a Devourer."

"He is," I agreed grimly. "And the Ændari aren't afraid of him. That transmission that you got, that said he was coming and that ordered you not to call in reinforcements…what did it say exactly?"

"I-I don't know," he admitted. "It was locked by the previous admiral."

"Get him to unlock it, right goddamn now," I snapped. "Nail his fucking balls to his forehead if you have to—I don't care. Just make him talk."

"Lord." He nodded, twisting quickly and speaking as the barrier dropped, then reestablished itself.

"Zhonat, power my ship, I don't care how. Then get the fuck out. You've got three minutes to get as many of those coins aboard as you can, then get everyone back from it."

He blanched, then saluted, fingers to chest, head bowed. The connection broke, and I turned to face the others.

"Ingrid, I need you to work with the others. No time to explain. I'll tell you more when I'm moving, but I need you to work to upgrade your connections to us all. You link to them, and you link them all into me as well. You'll be able to share the load that way."

"The load?" she asked, and I shook my head.

"There's no time!" I snapped. "Do you trust me?"

"Yes," she said firmly, without hesitation.

"Then you need to do this, and now. Get everyone ready. Get them linked up as we talked about, as we've done before to share the mental load, but also the soldiers! I need anyone who's ascended and unlocked. Get them all. They need to share their points with me, as you'd suggested before.

Arise: Conqueror

"Argus!" I barked, spinning and fixing the screen nearby with a grim stare as I went on. "I need you to do whatever the fuck you need to do to unlock me more points, more everything! You've got hard lockouts, I know. Well, break them. Break what you can. Give everyone points for scratching their goddamn arses and picking their noses if you have to. Then link them with Ingrid and to me."

"Understood," the AI agreed.

I spun back to the others, taking a deep breath and gathering everything together, and explaining.

"We've had this backward," I said, knowing it was right, and that this changed everything. "Shan'Gai, he's not here to help—he's not here to stop the Ændari. They're not running from him because they're not afraid of him. They're going to slow the fleet down, stop it from reaching the harvester if they can, because that's what Shan'Gai wants.

"I don't know it all, but that harvester is stripping the planet, and it's all he can see. There's no construction vessel attached to it because that's not why it's here. It's here to feed him. That's all, and the Ændari are making sure that the fleet don't stop it. Beyond that, they don't give a shit.

"We know the Ændari are self-centered cowards. The only way they'd not be running for their lives when a Devourer comes for them is if they believed it wasn't a threat. They're feeding him, and all the records we're finding? Ingrid's found traces of Devourers visiting the node in the past, of records being erased. Argus was tampered with to stop him seeing things, to stop him recognizing the ship.

"The Ændari sealed the system to make sure nobody could get in or out. Then they made sure it was under a comms blackout. Why do that? It's not like anyone isn't going to know that the Ændari were here, after all. If they lose, there'd be bodies, ships…the works. If they'd won and got control of the node, they'd have been killing us all, so it's not like they have to hide it. Hell, they'd want to rub our noses in it!

"No, they did this to hide something, some*one*. Shan'Gai ordered our reinforcements to stay out, to 'protect' them. But if he was trying to protect everyone, he'd have wanted all our forces in here to smash the fuckers flat. He's had access to the node all this time, literally, and something was erasing the memories in the lower spire. He had that level of access, so he could have damn well reactivated all the UC's nanites at any time!"

"Shit…" Jonas whispered as it all started to fall into place for him. "I knew something was off!"

"Exactly," I growled. "He wasn't protecting the UC and keeping the Ændari back… He's been keeping his fucking larder stocked and playing both sides against each other! All that tech out there that should have been recovered? What's the chances he's been making damn sure it stays lost? The dwarfen and any 'extinct' races that the soldiers encountered? They were to bring them to him. It was a mission to fucking bring him anything that might see the pattern, and we've been keeping it in check for him!"

"The missing worlds, the missing technology and records… Ships go missing all the time, entire colonies sometimes," Dolfing whispered, closing his eyes. "We've been sent to search for evidence before, finding nothing…"

"And that's why we've got no records of the harvester," I finished grimly. "It was probably hidden by that fucker, and he's been keeping it safe until he could use it again and again."

Quest Uncovered!

Evolving Quest discovered: Harvest the Past, to Save the Future.

You have gained control of Universal System Quadrant Node, designation #02. In the process of securing the local system, you have discovered the terrible secret that lies at the heart of the UC and Ændari conflict.

Evolve to receive the following rewards:

- **+5 Points of Specialization**

- **+Access to Level 2 of the Evolving Quest**

"Argus, what does this mean, 'evolve'?" I stared at the screen.

"As stated. Evolve."

That was it, clearly all I was fucking getting. I nodded; I'd figure it out.

"Hardline blockages prevent this system from enabling faster access to underlying capacity than the entity can process."

"So I can only go so fast, because if you make it possible to go faster I'll break?" I growled. "Do you think I care? You see what's fucking happening out there, Argus? Millions of people are dying, fucking *millions*! That bastard is harvesting a world! You want us to help the Ændari? That bastard's probably been feeding on them as well for millennia!"

"Argus, with your lockouts removed, can you contact the other Devourers?" Ingrid asked suddenly. "Can they help?"

"Attempting… Processing request… Negative."

"Okay, how many are there?" she tried again.

"Negative…"

"Dammit, he's still got a lock in place…" she muttered, rubbing at her face as she thought.

"Negative…"

"Does he mean he can't answer, or he can't contact them?" Dolfing spoke up carefully. "On occasion, our ship's AI will default to simple responses if it's overloaded by other tasks."

"Argus?" I asked. "Are there other Devourers out there?"

"There aren't many, but—" Dolfing had been explaining, but he broke off as Argus responded.

"Confirmed. Search complete. Zero extant Devourers located."

"Extant?" Paul asked Courtney in a low voice.

"There aren't any out there," Ingrid said flatly. "Or if there are, they're out of Argus's range."

"Records indicate additional Devourers were located in nearby sectors, but upon further examination of locations, only one identity was identified thereafter."

"What?" Paul asked again.

"He killed them," Ingrid said hollowly. "Shan'Gai is a cannibal, feeding on his own kind."

"No. Wait, he'd have to be huge, though, right?" Jonas said suddenly. "No offense, boss, and I fucking see that look on your face, so I know you're looking for a goddamn fight with him, but he should be like the size of a solar system now, right? You can't win that shit."

"Not if he had to fight to kill the others." Ingrid pulled up a list of system data and the oblique references to the Devourers being sighted as we argued. "Each time they met up and there was only one after? That's when a world goes silent. He's feeding on entire planets to repair himself after a fight."

"When was the last one?" I asked.

"Two and a half weeks ago," she said softly. "The last Devourer… There's a message logged as being sent to this location, to…you?"

I pulled it up, knowing exactly which message it was, and I read it aloud as I did so.

Be welcomed to the fold, Devourer. The universe glories in your rise.

Let the wicked tremble, and the good rejoice; let the void reign free.

Arise, Conqueror.

"So that was the last," Jonas said softly. "The last one welcomed you, then this fucker killed him for it."

"Probably," I agreed.

"We don't know everything. We might be wrong about all of this, but the records that we found?" Ingrid said, looking at one of them. "They all show regular interference up to a certain point, hundreds of years ago, then nothing. No more."

"Right?"

"The earlier records were checked, it looks like…they were more carefully scrubbed. But after the plague, it's all automated."

"And?"

"What if—" She turned and addressed the AI again. "Argus, the war crimes, the way that Steve got locked out of his systems for fighting Varnock, do you see that? When it happens, is there a record?"

"Negative. All links between sanctioned individuals and relay stations are locked out."

"That's it!" She gasped. "Argus, is Shan'Gai connected to you by his nanites? Are they active?"

"Processing… Negative," Argus confirmed. "Devourer Shan'Gai has made a connection via alternative means."

"It's the tech," Jonas grunted. "His ship, him…fuck me—he's been locked out! That's why he's killing the others and he's feeding on everyone. He needs their nanites. He can't upgrade any more. He's been cut off from the system and he's integrating everything into himself."

"The engines." I brought up the image of his ship. "They're normal engines, like the ones on my ship."

"Exactly." He pointed at me. "Do you need to do that…build engines, I mean? Or could you move your ship without them?"

"I could do it without," I admitted. "But I wasn't there yet when I made it. I'd have to create gravity bubbles all the time, so using normal engines just made sense. I didn't have enough nanites to make a ship that I could just alter at will, so I needed to make a normal one, more or less."

"So, if Shan'Gai is locked out…when it happened to you, your nanites started to fail, didn't they, Steve?" Ingrid asked. "You couldn't use some of your abilities. You were reduced to more basic functions."

"That's why he's got normal engines, and other bits to his ship—his body, I mean. He's reduced to looting whatever he needs and forming the basic links with his nanites to keep the ship together. It's probably why he's so shit at communicating. He's using something he's ripped out of another ship and trying to make it work," Jonas suggested.

"And why he's better at sending orders through a simple laser link, rather than a face-to-face conversation. He's not got to focus as hard as all he'd have to do is send an order, rather than a complex signal," Ingrid agreed. "That means, Steve, if the jamming platforms can be taken out, we could call for reinforcements!"

"We need them." I nodded.

"All we'd need to do is hold him off for a bit, slow him somehow. If he's not got access to everything, then there's a chance still."

"Exactly," I agreed. "I lost the identification, the upgrades—hell, everything was set back to the basic level. I could form simple shapes but not much more."

"Okay, logically, if that is what's happened to Shan'Gai, what does that mean? If he's been locked out of things forever, could he have docked with the node? Could he have taken command here if he'd tried?" Ingrid asked Argus.

"Negative," the AI replied firmly. "Upon initial examination, the memory read would have revealed his unsuitability, and no node would surrender control. However…" There was a pause. "Node designation #07 does not respond to queries and has not functioned since the plague. I cannot confirm nor verify more."

"So he might have tried this shit with the Ændari before." I shook my head. "Fuck this."

"Steve," Ingrid said warningly, reaching out and gripping my forearms. "You can't do this."

"I don't have a choice," I snapped, trying again. "I'm sorry, Ingrid, but you know I have to. He'll have to make sure there aren't any witnesses to what he's been doing, or all this falls apart. Once he's raided the harvester, I'm betting he'll turn on us, on the fleet, the node—all of it. He might leave the Ændari. They're as unprincipled as he is, and he'll need someone to help him. But everyone else?" I shook my head. "He needs to die."

"You can't fight him." She held on tightly.

"I don't have a choice," I repeated. "If he's locked out of his systems? That gives us a chance. It means he probably can't recover or absorb new nanites properly. Shit, it's probably why he's feeding so frantically. He'll be trying to unlock them, to figure a way around the lockout."

"I don't care! He's tens of thousands of years old, and he's killed the other Devourers. They'll have had hundreds of systems more than you do, and thousands of years to get used to using them!"

"Argus, is that true?" I asked.

"Partially accurate," he confirmed. "The time difference does indeed mean that many of the Devourers had access to much greater reserves of data then you possess."

"But you reset me," I pointed out. "You reset my connection. Every single quest you get, the next in line is harder to unlock, so it makes sense that the further you go down that line, the longer it takes to earn more points."

"Confirmed. The time differential will be affected by this."

"Can you do it again?"

"Confirmed, but this would require several hours of updates to be rolled back."

"Okay, fuck it—well, looks like you've got a problem, Argus. I don't care how much you need to break me, I need those points," I said flatly. "With those points, my ship, and the nanites we've got, we stand a chance."

"Negative. Time required to reset updates and rollback system integration would result in your removal from the battlespace for a minimum of several hours."

"Goddammit!" I cursed. "Well…"

"Perhaps a bonus could be arranged, although this will have the effect of limiting upgrades further down the line."

"Do it," I snapped. "No point in saving for a rainy day if we all die now."

"This is madness!" Ingrid snapped. "Steve, if you go out there, Shan'Gai will kill you. He's fully grown, you're not and—"

Her eyes searched mine as our minds meshed; images, details, plans and half-formed ideas, hunches and more were pushed at each other.

They swarmed, plans formed and discarded in fragments of a second—my half-formed plan to basically try to take out the harvester, then throw myself at him and try to tear him a new asshole replaced with a much more realistic and nuanced one.

"The harvester," she said slowly, nodding, but still looking horrified.

"If I can get to the harvester first, if I can unlock my nanites all the way, we can still win this. The harvester is harvesting a fucking planet. The people it's killed already are dead—there's nothing we can do about that. But if I can get there before him?" I nodded. "I can do this," I said. "I have to."

"Steve…"

"There's no choice, Ingrid. Because if I do this and I fucking win? I can stop all of this. I can break the cycle and not just save the millions of innocents left on that planet, I can leapfrog my way to a form that *can* fight Shan'Gai. The other Devourers protected the UC—hell, they tried to protect the galaxy. This fucker probably killed them. He's turned both sides in this war into his personal game reserve, and it's cost him his abilities. It's driven him mad, if he wasn't before, but we can still fix this." We stared into each other's eyes, waiting.

"I'm going with you."

"You can't," I said softly.

"Steve…!"

"I need you to tie the others in," I explained quickly. "Ingrid, the changes…I'll need help. I'm going to need all of you. I need those who I can trust totally. I'll be linking you all into my mind, literally. When you link us all together and they unlock their levels, I'm going to need the processing power. I'll need you to tie us all together, and you can't do that from there, because you'll have to get everyone organized first. You need to link to the others—the UC forces, our people…everyone."

"It'll cost twice as much, maybe ten times as much to unlock with everyone attached." She shook her head. "It won't be enough."

"Even a single extra point will help, because I'm going to be unlocking a hell of a lot more," I said, finally letting the flashing at the edge of my vision catch up.

The notifications had appeared suddenly, flickering for attention, then dying away into a solid "we're here" pulse that I mentally dismissed for now.

I could feel them, and I knew that it was Argus, doing exactly what I needed.

"I have to go," I said softly, shaking her gently and staring into her eyes; tears had sprung up as she fought with what we both knew was coming. "You know that."

"I could—" She broke off. "Steve, I could come. I could help." She tried again, but we both knew it couldn't be.

"No. For anyone else, the ship would need life support, atmospherics, gravity, physical connections and control systems—all things I won't have time to make."

"It has them now!" she snapped.

"It won't for much longer," I told her. "Ingrid, you know I have to do this, and you know you have to let me go."

"No I don't. You…you just got back!" she finished in a broken voice.

"And after this? I'll never leave you again. But you have to let me go." I let go of her left arm, closing my fist, then opening it again as I formed something from my nanites, then offered it to her. "I'll come back," I promised.

"You better," she replied, seeing what I held, and dashing her tears aside. "You're not getting out of this that easily."

Arise: Conqueror

"When we get back," I agreed, pressing the simple band of gleaming platinum and diamond into her hand, then folding her fingers closed over it. "When all this is over, we'll do this properly, but for now, at least you have it." I kissed her, holding her for long seconds as my companions looked on silently.

She shuddered against my chest, trying to contain the sobs that racked her body. When we broke apart, she drew a deep breath, then nodded.

The plot behind us updated. A handful more Ændari vessels jumped in behind Shan'Gai, powering up.

"Go," she forced out. "This isn't over, Steve, so you damn well come back to me and finish this!"

"I will," I promised, before drawing in a deep breath and squared my shoulders. "All right, it's time to end this. Dolfing?"

"Devourer?" He straightened. "The fleet is yours to command."

"Buy me some time, then get the hell out. I need those jamming platforms down, and fast. Use the fleet to keep the Ændari busy, but be ready—I'm going to take the harvester out. If, and this is a big *if*, but if I can take control of it, then I'll try to pull it from the planet. Those who are left will have a better chance, but that's all we can do."

"We could take twenty-thou—"

I cut him off with a shake of my head. "No. You're to keep the fleet off my back, then turn and burn. You get the hell out of the way and head for the jump point. If we can get the jamming down, we broadcast everything to the UC; we pull in reinforcements and you goddamn lead them."

"The newly arrived may not accept my authority."

"Did I fuckin' stutter, Admiral? No? Good. *YOU* lead them. That's an order direct from me. Tell anyone who disagrees that I will personally visit them after the battle to discuss it, and that I'm likely to be fucking hungry when I do it. So, until then, you're in fucking command. I want someone I can trust to do what needs to be done. I don't have time to explain all this shit. Ingrid is my second. She will be linked to my mind throughout this fight, so if she speaks, you listen as if it were from me, understand?"

"As you say." He nodded.

"Right—you get out of the way, and if you have to, then you head to the jump point. You jump out, get reinforced, and then you lead them back. I'll need you and all the firepower you can get me. I'll lead him as deep into the system as I can, away from anything we can break, and make sure the fucker can't run. We end this here and now."

"Time to kill a fucking god," Paul called from behind me. "*Oorah!*"

CHAPTER THIRTY-THREE

The flight from the control center was one of the fastest I've ever made. Every second I'd spent talking, planning, holding Ingrid—each and every one came with a cost in lives, and I was determined to make up for them now.

I reached out as I flashed down the stairs, arched out across the halls and then dove over the railing, headed to the floor far below at a speed that shook the people I passed.

My own harvester flexed, grabbing every coin it could, flinging them into my damaged ship. The spiderbot shuddered to a halt, then about-faced and clambered up the side of the ship again, headed for the upper hull.

Anything and everything that could be used to give me an advantage would, and I'd damn well need them all. But I needed the last medical tubes out of the ship, and right goddamn now, because in five minutes even the corridor that held them wasn't going to be there.

As I went, I felt the connection establishing with Ingrid as she linked with the others, their hands pressed to the orb I'd formed and left behind.

It wasn't a complicated process. I'd have much rather not have had to do this, but the simple fact was that every stage that I could unlock was a slight improvement in our chances.

Partitions formed as Ingrid, with the help of Argus, set the system, and I pulled up, rolling as I flew through the now busier lower hall. A few whoops and shouts followed me as I twisted and rolled, soaring across the gap to the ship.

I flipped over, landing feetfirst, skidding slightly as I killed my momentum. The ship looked like a kicked anthill as dozens of soldiers ran in all directions.

"Shemer!" I barked, noting the grim-faced captain spouting orders nearby. "Good to see you're out of the tank."

"Just," he admitted. "I got out and heard the commotion. Care to bring me up to date?"

"Not really," I said. "Sorry, but there's no time."

"Short version?" he asked as I strode through the air lock, crouching and jumping up to the next level.

Arise: Conqueror

"You know all those legends you've got about not fucking with the Devourers?" I asked as I clapped a soldier on his shoulder, letting him move past and acknowledging his nod.

"Yes?"

"I'm about to add to them," I said. "Shan'Gai is harvesting a *planet*, and he's somehow working with the Ændari. He's the reason you've all been restricted to no working nanites forever, and the Ændari too. Near as we can tell, he's been killing and eating all the other Devourers, and a bunch of fucking planets as well."

"Planets?" He closed his eyes, clearly centering himself, and then stared at me.

"The others will explain. Right now, I'm going to do what I swore I wouldn't and let your soldiers share their quest rewards with me. I'm going to restrict the growth they damn well earned to make myself stronger, and then I'm going to take everything I can and rip that fucking rat bastard a new asshole. Oh." I paused, looking over my shoulder at him as I sat in my pilot seat.

"I had Emberalis arrested, promoted Dolfing to admiral. The UC fleet is in a fight with the Ændari. They're going to be fucking running soon, though, because they're going for reinforcements. Then there's a giant planet stripper tearing Scorpio-3 apart and I'm off to kill it. You like the short and sweet version?"

"Not particularly," he said. "A little more in the way of details would be nice, but it makes my wondering about why the previous inhabitants of the node attacked the ship and me a bit meaningless."

"We think it was a hack—probably Shan'Gai as well. He had the most to gain from them attacking me. The ship was coated in my nanites, as was my harvester. Looking back at it, beyond killing anyone trying to stop them attacking me, they didn't care about anything or anyone. You interrupted them, so they attacked.

"For more info than that, you'll need to go and see Ingrid. She'll share the evidence, though it's more circumstantial than I'd like."

"You're going to attack another Devourer on circumstantial evidence?" He winced. "Steve, perhaps—"

"No, I'm going to attack the supposedly Ændari harvester that's eating a planet. If he's innocent in all of this, he'll be pissed that I've taken those nanites; I apologize and we all have a good laugh as how stupid we were to think this. If not..." I shrugged. "If not, then at least I'll have what I need to fight him, one-on-one."

"It's madness," he said.

"Well, look on the bright side. At least we'll not live long enough to regret it if I'm wrong." I shrugged again. "Shemer?"

"Yes?"

"Get the fuck off my ship."

"I could help," he offered, after pausing for a few seconds.

"Thank you, mate. Yes, we need it, but go see Ingrid. She'll need all the help she can get. And frankly, you can't be on this ship with the shit I'm going to pull."

"Good luck," he said after another brief hesitation. Then he was gone.

I blew out a long breath, glancing over the screens and systems before me. It was all the readouts and basic bits that I'd installed so that if anyone bar me needed to fly the ship, as I'd needed to with Bach and Zhonat, it was possible.

I'd not done it for them originally, of course. It was a crutch for me, a way for me to interact with the ship before I was ready or strong enough to do what I was going to be attempting today.

Then I cracked my knuckles, slapped a palm over the crystal pillar before me, and closed my eyes.

The ship stuttered to life all around me in my awakened mind. The readouts slowly revealed details, but in here, I *felt* it all.

The engines were cold and dead, the reactors still firing. Power slowly increased by the second, as I searched, working through the repowering sequence.

Three tubes were left to move, and I growled at the delay, flicking through stage by stage, testing the ship. More often than not, I was reduced to swearing over just how much needed to be replaced.

The ship worked still, mainly, but the engines being dead, the power cells powered down and the multiple holes in the hull all combined to make it a wreck more than a viable ship.

Seconds stretched out as the spiderbot clanked and clattered its way back up from the pile of tubes resting on the hull and stomped across the back of my ship. I could feel its passage through the hull, even as it triggered its laser again, arms reaching down to lock onto the hull, malmetal flowing aside.

The structural supports were a mix of old school steel and advanced malmetal. I stifled my cursing as it took the time to carve one out, finally getting access to the last in line for removal.

The harvester was flowing up and into the ship around the spiderbot now. Its amorphous nature allowed it to shift and slide through gaps that the massive creation couldn't help but leave.

The last little while, it'd been devoted to dropping all the null coins it could get into the ship, literally stuffing every nook and cranny with them.

Now, as the spiderbot lifted the final tube free, locked it into place on its back, then turned to clank and clatter its way down the side of the hull, the harvester pressed itself into its place. It poured itself into the torn hull and expanded out to fill the interior of the ship entirely.

Before, I'd believed that a million nanites was a high number. Hell, I'd been down to draining a handful of viable nanites from corpses at one point. Now the sheer madness of just under a billion nanites available and under my control made me stare, then grin.

The harvester had fully collapsed now, connecting to me, its own form no longer locked, and instead I *was* the ship. I filled the corridors and the hold, the air lock and under the seats—everywhere, I was there. I reached out, feeling the frame of my ship buckle and twist at my command.

Arise: Conqueror

I was going to be entering atmosphere, I knew, so I'd need to survive the entry, and I needed to get there *fast*. Beyond those two details, there wasn't much else that I needed.

Well, besides the memory cores and AI, that was. I'd need those solidly protected and connected for what was to come, and I deliberately made space near my core for them.

I could create pretty much anything I could imagine, so I started to work as gravity flexed and danced around my new form, lifting me up and sliding backward.

The vessel that had become my ship-body lifted smoothly. The small figures of the UC soldiers rushed away from me as I slid back. The massive spiderbot clanked away as I approached the field that kept the atmo inside, and, well, *space* outside.

The ion curtain felt peculiar rolling over me, and I shivered unconsciously, even as at the edge of my awareness I collapsed internal corridors, their material being absorbed. The matter that had formed the walls and internal bulkheads were then broken down and converted into massive amounts of energy.

That energy was then pumped by the exajoule into the reactors, forcing them to jump-start their production at an insane rate.

I flexed my fingers, or what had been fingers, feeling the surface of my form flow. The new shape resolved both in my mind's eye and out in space, where all could see it.

My form was liquid quicksilver on the outside now, a split of malmetal and pure nanites with the engines sliding inward and back. The short wings that had held them previously now flexed, absorbed into the gleaming metal. The output of each engine was gathered together and pointed aft, before finally a ring of silvery steel wrapped around them.

The forming ship's new teardrop shape flowed from a simple bulge at the back to a tight spike at the front, looking almost organic, dotted with small bulges here and there that rolled back and forth as more sections moved.

The lasers folded into the body, crumbling as nanites ate them. The storm caster crystals shifted around and clumped together into new, more powerful layouts.

The now larger teardrop shape of the hull flexed as a dip formed in the top, flowing forward. Additional sections curved up and around, forming a depression that would hold the new gravity cannon.

This would be the new main gun; I didn't have the time or the patience to deal with anything else, and still my reactors burned brighter by the second. While the changes grew and continued, I slid around, my nose aligning on the intercept point that the AI's navigational data was predicting for Scorpio-3.

Then I punched it. The engines flared bright as they tried to outshine the stars, and I did what was as natural as breathing.

Gravity twisted before me. At first it was minor, a simple tunneling effect that I'd done a million times by now. Then, with the push from the engines building slowly, I diverted a little more power from the reactors, feeding that in as well.

Space before me warped, rippling outward. The push of the engines propelled me , as all resistance vanished.

For any ship to pass through the void of space, at the most basic point they just needed a push, or a pull, to get them started. Here, I was taking advantage of both. My engines were pushing, and with the sheer amount of energy I had access to these days, I could now create tunnels in gravity large enough for my ship to "fall" down as well.

They weren't tunnels down into the branes—or, at least, that wasn't what I was trying to do. I was careful to keep the warp from forming, the tunnel from sinking through the upper layer entirely. The last thing I needed was to end up in the wrong star system.

The pull of gravity dragged me faster and faster. The light of the stars seemed to stretch as I focused on the planet ahead, feeling its signature in the gravitational pattern.

That was it, I realized as I pushed harder, fighting to get as close to the lip of the warp as I could, but no further, forcing the forming ripples to flatten each time.

The nose of my ship started to shudder. Each ripple passed through me; power pulsed through me, making the stars seem to shiver.

Focusing on the world ahead, I couldn't help but nod to myself. It *was* a signature, one that felt unique, made up of its exact size, the composition of the world, the speed. It included the draw of the other nearby planets and moons on it and more. It was all distinct, twisting in space and time that lay ahead. And as the ripples built, it seemed that I could almost reach out and touch it.

Extending the "tunnel" of gravity ahead of me until it blurred and I almost lost control over it, I guided it to the bulge in the universe that I felt was Scorpio-3, then shifted it to account for the navigational system's predictions, feeling the signature.

Then I pushed harder, gritting my teeth as I forced myself to go as fast and hard as I could. The thought of the millions of people on that world who were dying by the second while I bumbled along here drove me on.

I was getting right to the lip of the warp now. The ripples of space-time that shivered across me seemed to come faster and faster, until it was all I could do to make one out from the other. I could just about feel the planet in the distance. The tunnel I was forming stunned me as my own senses and reach seemed to flow along it and out so much farther.

Scorpio-3 was there, seemingly barely beyond my reach. I pushed even harder, reaching with faltering fingers of gravity to inch closer and closer to the world.

I…could…almost…

The universe twisted; it wobbled all around me. I felt a shuddering lurch, even as I released the energy in a rising panic, terrified that I'd just sent myself out of the damn system and into the next in my stupidity, pushing too hard.

I cut the power, drifting for a few seconds. The universe seemed to slide back into crisp, clear focus, and the shivering walls of the warp faded away.

Arise: Conqueror

It took those few seconds—then another several minutes as I checked, double-checked and scanned the limited data that the AI had collected automatically—to realize that in my focus, I'd done something that I'd never done before.

It was something that everything I knew about the gravity drive said was impossible, and as far as the records I had access to, had never been done before.

To travel with the gravity drive, you needed to dig down; you needed to aim in the general direction you wanted, but all you got was "that way" and the next weak spot in space.

I'd just reached out and identified a unique pattern—the pattern of the planet before me—distant yet, but I'd locked the tunneling ability I'd been using onto it, and I'd *pulled*.

Instead of "falling" down the well of altered gravity, essentially just giving my ship an easier path and a hole that was helping me to build my speed as I'd intended? I'd created an effect like skimming a stone across the surface of a lake.

Checking the distance I'd travelled, I grunted, amazed.

I'd travelled nearly twenty minutes' flight time down the road toward that planet, and the power it'd needed?

It was nothing compared to the amount a gravity drive needed. And most interesting of all?

The grav drive wasn't even online.

I'd not had a need for it, not yet. If I poured in enough energy to overcome space-time's gravity drag as I needed to, the very best I'd get would be a jump to the Lagrange point in this system. Most likely, I'd end up in another, possibly light-years away.

Instead, I'd done it alone, unaided and on instinct, just trying to eke out an extra few fractions of a percent of speed.

It was impossible, insane even, but I'd done it. The link that I had to Ingrid weakened as the distance increased.

I banished the thoughts, determined that I'd come back to them later as I reached back to her and locked the connection.

"Steve!"

"Ingrid." I couldn't help but smile. Who the hell else did she think it would be?

"Don't start," she snapped, a hint of anger and amusement warring with each other as she went on. *"Okay, Argus managed to give thirty-five of the soldiers secondary Support classes, and they've all been grinding as you'd told them to.*

"They've got an average of four points each, but obviously if all they have are low-level skills, then you can't use them, so, we've come up with a pyramid structure."

"Don't try and sell me shit—I've got no money," I responded on autopilot.

"Ha-ha. Okay, so two engineers work in tandem. The first spends all his points to unlock the first two skills, the general Support tree and Creation. That costs him four points—two for him and two for the other. Then the first, who has

no points left, returns to work and a new soldier moves in. He does the same, except that he's unlocked the first tier already, and so has our lead engineer.

"This one unlocks his two sections, on his own, then a single point into unlocking Creation systems upgrades. That costs two points, to get him to there, then two points further—one for him, and one for the lead."

"Got it." I nodded to myself.

"We've done this eight times. That's sixteen of the soldiers all at the lower levels of Creation, Augment, and Repair, respectively. Now, that leaves us with eight people with four points each to spend to unlock the trees ahead. We can take this one more level if you want, then you'll have four more people with up to two more ranks unlocked?"

"Yes. Take them all down the route of Creation, General Technology and then Gravity Manipulation Technology," I ordered, waiting a few minutes as she did that.

"Okay, that's four people, each with four ranks available. Are you ready?"

"Do it," I requested, feeling the first one as an unfamiliar mind touched my own.

"Lord," he greeted me. *"I stand ready."*

"Thank you," I said, feeling it as he opened his system to me, allowing me to "reach through" and see his options using a small pearl-like device that Argus had helped me to craft prior to launch.

It was essentially a link, a bit like the way the Nordicassian Linkage had worked, but smaller and more specialized, allowing a mental link to be formed through it with a third party at great distance.

The first was the obvious one—Gravity Manipulation Technology I'd taken forever ago. But beyond unlocking it, and the bonuses it'd brought, I'd done nothing with it. I pulled it up, glancing over the details to refresh my mind.

It was fairly simple, the description, for something that was inordinately difficult to manage and explain.

Gravity, at its heart, was the curvature of space-time around mass. That was obvious, or it seemed so to me now, but thinking about it as I read it over, I knew I'd changed a lot since the early days of upgrades.

Gravity was another name for the pull that mass exerted on everything around it—that, I decided, was an easier way to describe it. And gravity manipulation? Well, that was just evening the force out.

Have a friend lean forward and put their weight against your hand, then push up. You're resisting the gravity of their action, added to the gravity of the planet round you.

If you can push up with more force than they push down? You cancel out and lift them. Congratulations, you just beat gravity.

The issue was that to do that further, you needed to cancel out each individual occurrence of it.

To fly? You needed to be light enough that your effort could outweigh the planet's pull—or strong enough to lift yourself, anyway. Planes weighed hundreds of tons, sometimes thousands, and they did it through forming the pull of air to lift them, at the most basic level. As soon as they ran out of fuel—or strength—then they crashed down.

To manipulate more than just the gravity of another, or an item physically, you needed a method of altering that—a way to push, beyond your hands.

In my case, it'd started off built into my armor as a modest upgrade, something that had been simple enough to unlock and minor, as the Ændari thought of it—just a localized force generator.

In my case, a bubble was formed through the input of energy to push against space-time around me.

It wasn't hugely powerful at first, but the more I used it, the more I understood it, and the more I came to rely on it at an instinctual level.

Because I did that, I found myself using it more and more. Over time, I found that I could use my nanites to generate the force, without an external focus beyond them, as they too used that ability.

From there, the step to using the gravity drive?

Well, it was massive, but also small.

The gravity drive was a supersized version of the same technology.

I had a single point in the tech already, and I had him spend three points in it: one for him to unlock it, and two for both of us to get the next level.

The data unlocked, and I felt a tiny shift in the cosmos. This wasn't about understanding the huge fields of gravity; this was focused on the little ones, the very smallest interactions between atoms.

Learning a little more about that enabled me to do it further, to guide the molecules and nuclei to wobble with a touch of power, that was all.

He left the link, a sense of reverence from him left behind.

The next joined and repeated the process. But this time, we managed to unlock the next level past those two. I asked Ingrid to do the same as before, to have the remaining three teams boost each other.

That got them all to the same point that I was, with three people available to me, each with four points.

The first gained me two more ranks in gravity control, bringing me to five, and that was when the world changed.

Options unlocked, and I grinned. This was indeed where I needed to be.

Generally, once I took a section, I could choose to invest further in it, or take the paths that were unlocked beyond. For Gravity Manipulation, those additional paths didn't unlock until I reached level five, and that meant that the tech was, frankly, insanely complicated.

As each point invested had unlocked more, cold data had poured into my mind.

I knew of long-ago tests—hell, I'd seen memories at times of star systems being literally eradicated. Prototypes that went wrong and annihilated everything for hundreds of light-years as black holes were formed and supercharged.

I'd known about them before, and I'd thought I understood them. But now, as more and more data unlocked, I felt it as my unknown companion started to shake.

His meat-based brain was shuddering, sections tearing loose as I felt the sheer mass that was being downloaded begin to overwrite details already stored.

I reached out, mentally forcing a channel to the side, splitting the data, preventing it from sinking into him, erasing what I could feel, and sensing both Argus and Ingrid working to manage and mitigate the effects.

For me, I had a slight fuzziness, a level of overload that was more weird than painful or frustrating. But for him?

I winced, scanning him, and shook my head as I found the brain red raw and bleeding in a hundred places. The need, the terrible shit that was happening had led me to forget the most basic of my experiences with the data downloads: that the data came in packets and unfurled into a meat-based computer. One that had limited bandwidth and storage options.

The human brain, even as augmented as that of the Awakened and upgraded BWV's brains were, was still only human. They were much more advanced than I'd been when I'd undergone the same thing. These soldiers, although they'd lost access to their memories and abilities, had spent hundreds and even thousands of years upgrading before the nanite plague had cost them everything.

That was the only reason they were still alive after the insane level of data and access upgrades that had been dumped into them. But even for them, we'd reached the limit. I retreated, feeling the convulsions that the unknown soldier was experiencing slow slightly, and I reached out to Ingrid and Argus.

"We can't stop, but we can't break them either. Argus, this... what's happening to him now, was this the final levels of the gravity tech that he took?"

"Confirmed. Data download has been deemed too detailed and large for user."

"How the hell does that happen?" I asked. *"I mean, we're designed to be able to unlock this, right?"*

"The system that you access is an Ændari design. It was intended and expected that the BWV and BSV program would be overseen by its makers, restricting access to higher levels of information. Therefore, limiting access to these areas was deemed unnecessary. By the time of the rebellion, this system was so heavily interwoven that it was impossible to separate access levels beyond the original intended supplicants."

"You're saying that they didn't expect humans to ever get access to enough points to unlock the higher levels, and I can handle it because I'm entirely nanite-based now?"

"Confirmed."

"Will he be okay?" I asked, checking the speed and distance markers, and made a slight correction after finding myself a little farther along than the AI had expected in the planetary intercept path when it'd been calculated.

I lined up again on the new path and reached out, checking the power levels and beginning more changes. If I had more power, I could do that again. That jump, or skip—fuck it, it was a gravity skip now, I decided—if I could do that at will? I could cross the entire system in an hour or two instead of twenty, from one end to the other.

Maybe even faster.

Either way, though, I had my own points to spend. I needed to make sure that I had everything I could from the others, without wiping them out.

"It is likely that BWV #664351221 will make a full recovery within thirty hours. He has been rendered unconscious for his own safety while the cerebellum is reformatted and prior programming is replaced from storage."

"WHAT?"

"His brain must be rewritten from stored data to replicate the original identity due to excessive damage. Was this not clear?"

"Fuck." I groaned. *"Dammit, no, that wasn't clear! Okay, the others, can they access more or is it going to do the same?"*

"Steve, we can't!" Ingrid said, shocked. *"You could kill them!"*

"We need anything and every advantage we can get," I replied grimly. *"Argus, was it the level of data that he just unlocked that did the damage, or was it the cumulative effect?"*

"Ongoing data unlocks and upgrades have resulted in noticeable deterioration of the BWV and BSV. However, this can be remedied through normal system interactions."

"So their nanites will fix them and they'll be fine," I grunted. *"Okay, moving forward...they've got points. Can I use them? I mean, if we unlock lower levels of technology, will that cause more issues, or will they be okay?"*

"Tree dependent," came the answer.

"Okay, there's three of them left, and four points each. Hook up the next volunteer." I gave the order grimly, knowing that we couldn't afford to not take the chance, if they were still willing to do it.

There was a brief pause, then another mind joined us, one filled with steely determination as they slid in.

"Lord Devourer."

I felt the respect and the need in them. They knew people on the world ahead of us, old friends who had retired from the more "normal" fighting forces, and they were determined to protect them if they could.

"Thank you," I said, feeling their acknowledgment as the risk and my new plan was shared with them, as it pertained to them.

"I accept and am honored." That was all they said, and I took a deep breath, before going on.

Okay, I couldn't go further into gravity tech without wiping them out, and the data download that was shared... I suspected that because they were leading the way, that the download was forwarded like a download from them.

I'd felt the data stuttering, and I suspected I'd lost some of it, but I'd address that when the time came.

Instead, I began to search, thinking about what I needed, and the need for it to be lower-leveled data than I'd already received. Options were limited, considering the things that they'd have access to now and the paths that I'd unlocked.

I had power cores at level three, after all. I really needed better power systems, but the best that I could do with these people now was have them go for something simple that I'd not taken yet. It was that or work as a team to upgrade one of their number again and the risk...

That was what I needed to do, I decided. Have the remaining other two boost this person. There was a risk still, and it was climbing, but I couldn't make that choice for them.

"Lord?"

I blinked, shocked out of my thoughts as the soldier—Hestia, I realized as they pushed their identity out to me—spoke.

"Lord, if this will help, I'd rather take the risk and be out of the fight a few hours while I'm rebuilt. My friends won't come back, not the way we do. And if this helps you to get there sooner? It's worth it."

I hesitated, having not realized that my mind was open to them through this link until now. I thought it was just Ingrid who could read me, but it made sense, considering what we were doing.

"I mean it, Lord. If this will help? Please, do it."

I nodded, not liking it, but accepting that at the end of the day, it was their choice.

"Argus, how bad will this be?" I asked. *"If the other two boost Hestia's understanding so that she gets access to the first three levels of power cores, then uses all four of her own points to buy us both two levels in it?"*

"The damage to their cerebellum will be significant. Risk of personality loss is low, though long-term memories may be affected by the update."

"Give me the worst-case scenario."

"Death, with significant long-term memory erasure and limited recall of the upgrade data. This would require the brain to be entirely rebuilt from storage data and the unlocked data would be lost, resulting in the loss of points invested and preventing the user from attempting further investment in the Support tree."

"I accept," Hestia said firmly.

"Hestia—" I started to warn them, only to be spoken over.

"Lord, I don't want to be an engineer. I'm a soldier. I'm happy as a soldier. I've learned an incredible amount, and thank you for the chance to grow, but I like being a soldier. If I lose access to the Support tree after this, I don't care. If this goes wrong, but I've helped you save millions of people? That's an incredible win for me."

"Thank you." I paused briefly to think, before speaking again. There wasn't really anything else I could say to that. And if the situation were reversed? Yeah. Even not knowing them, to possibly save millions of lives in exchange for just becoming a soldier again, especially when I wasn't interested in that tree in the future? I'd not consider it a loss of any kind either.

"Do it," I ordered, sensing Ingrid leaving the link with Hestia, before returning a few minutes later, clearly injured and straining.

"Are you sure about this?" I asked her, even as Ingrid started to speak as well.

"Steve, Argus has linked me into the remaining orbiting satellites around Scorpio-3. We're working with the planet-side authorities who are still responding. We're getting a clearer picture of the harvester, and comparing them against the blueprints we had. I'm going to be in and out as I focus on

getting you the information you're going to need on the target, but I think we shouldn't continue with this. Hestia..."

Instead of answering, I felt it as Hestia initiated it on her side, determined that any risk she could take to improve the chances for an entire planet were worth it.

I swallowed hard, as the data washed over me.

The first level had been the most basic, of course. It was essentially a blueprint that the nanites could build, but the actual understanding of nuclear fusion, vacuum management, and zero-point energy principles that were required to advance on that, and to make any kind of meaningful change, were viewed as well beyond the vast majority of us.

The first level was assumed to be all that the BSVs and other more general engineers would ever need to unlock. It covered making the cores and maintaining them to the highly limited amount they could be interacted with.

The second level introduced making small power cores from scratch, unlocking a hell of a difference in understanding. The third? That was where things got more complicated, literally making it a possibility to scale them up or down, including the issues that came from multiple units being built too close together, and the main differences between reactors and power cores.

More and more data flooded me on the reasons they were split into two distinct units here, cores being left at this stage and replaced with reactors.

The fourth level and fifth unlocked at almost the same time; the points slammed in and the data was shoved aside, toward me.

I took it like a professional hooker with a habit to feed, a two-week bender ahead, and a single trick left to play—going all in and taking one for the team.

CHAPTER THIRTY-FOUR

The sheer level of data was mind-blowing: everything from the study of zero-point energy and the implications for vacuum transmission and loss, to the uses for what humanity had termed "dark" energy.

Thousands of years of experiments, of findings that contradicted each other, of resolutions that changed the Ændari's outlook on power and the universe all poured in. For long seconds, I lay there, my ship frozen still halfway through the process of restructuring and engines stuttering as it drifted.

It was the reactors in the end that forced me out of my mental freeze. My need to tend to them, to improve them, at almost an instinctive level, overcame the loop I'd been stuck in.

Reactors were a level of technology that led in one direction. Power cores were similar, less constrained in terms of size and fuel, but generally weaker, pound for pound, as well.

Both used vacuum principles to maintain and guide the stream of energy that was released, and both used light as a perfect medium for it.

Zero-point energy was essentially the theory that everything always moved. The atoms and electrons that made up the universe, even at absolute zero, never fuckin' stopped. They were always in motion, and that motion required and released energy.

If you could harness it, you had, although not a perpetual energy store, at least the most stable and self-regenerating version that it was possible to create.

The issues came when you scaled them up.

The larger the system for cores, the more space you needed for them, as they tended to warp space and time.

Have two large ones next to each other? You were fucked in short order, and people in the next solar system ran a risk of gaining an extra star in their night sky.

Reactors weren't quite as touchy. They could be powered by a huge number of different forms of fuel and could be stacked much closer together, but they generally had a lower maximum ceiling and again, didn't like being too close together.

Arise: Conqueror

If the options were to have a single power core that could produce twenty units of power, or four reactors that could produce ten each? It really wasn't a hard decision to make.

Now there were decisions to make, though, because it was the dwarfen improvements to the reactors that had made them viable and so powerful.

The Ændari had dismissed that line of reasoning and had gone in the other direction, making damn big single reactors or cores and just accepting that they needed the space between them. With my new levels of understanding that opened entire new paths to me, and linked to Argus and with my own AI cores in the ship?

I saw parallels, and with access to the AI's capacity, I could even run some fast and dirty tests.

Normally those weren't words that should be put together with the word "reactors," especially when I was looking at power levels that exceeded the annual output of Earth. But what was life without a little risk?

The AI memory cores I had were massive—and mostly empty, unfortunately. Out of the four memory cores I'd looted and connected up, I'd managed to get a single AI to boot. Unfortunately, in its unthinking expansion into the connected units, it'd essentially erased everything in them.

It'd seen the data that was connected to it in its own core directly as data, and the secondary, interconnected memory units that held other AI that were struggling to awaken and their individual data as merely room to expand.

It'd formatted them, wiping them of everything, I now saw. And as much as that boiled my piss, considering the information that had been lost? It was a gain for me for now.

The AI had a massive overabundance of space, and little to do, so I plugged in all the data on the power cores, the reactors, and dark energy, then my plans and my intentions, while directing the Engineering sub-mind to do its thing.

I'd evolved past the need for the sub-minds now, and I knew it. I could reabsorb those I had and have a slightly increased level of understanding and speed on everything they dealt with, rather than connecting them up and giving them orders, but I decided not to.

They were still me, so I knew they'd never act against me. And in having separate sub-minds that were still part of me, I could split my focus when I needed to.

The experiments blurred along. As they ran, I reached out again to Ingrid.

"How is she?" I asked, dreading the answer.

"Oh, thank the gods!" Ingrid gasped. *"Steve, you asshole! You scared the hell out of me!"*

"I'm sorry," I sent back, along with a wry smile. *"I needed to assimilate the information."*

"Was it worth it?"

"Is Hestia okay?" I countered.

"She's unconscious. Argus knocked her out but said that no lasting damage was inflicted. Basically, it was the mid-range scenario—she survived and didn't lose her memories or her access to the tree, but she wasn't capable of retaining

the knowledge. The cross-contamination of data means that she lost some of the higher power core levels and some of the gravity tech.

"Essentially, she'd make a really gifted engineer with all she knows now, but the advanced stuff she'd need to learn again from scratch. Argus has said both of those lines are locked out for her, but the three in General are still available. She even earned two extra points on top of her quest rewards for going above and beyond in the completion of an assistance quest he'd issued to her for you."

"That's a relief," I admitted. *"I was worried I'd erased her mind or something."*

"That was a risk. I'm really not happy that it was my idea from weeks ago that led us to do all of this, but was it worth it?"

As she asked that, the AI pinged, and my sub-mind updated, pushing out data to me that made me smile.

"It really was. I need to go. I've got changes I need to make, but I love you."

"I love you too."

Then she was gone, and I took a deep breath, before focusing. I read the data over, seeing the hundreds of tests, the thousands of alterations and guides, the theoretical improvements, and the final flagged note.

Test Viable.

That—that was a *massive* thing.

I couldn't use the others' skills, and access to any more points was unlikely; even those from my friends in the team weren't likely to be usable. A very quick query to Argus made it clear that the only one who it would have been worth sharing the risk with—which was Belle, for her access to the Harvest tree— didn't have enough points to be useful anyway.

No, from here on in, I was on my own. But that was okay, because as I'd seen earlier, I'd been receiving notifications off and on all this time; I'd just not had the opportunity to read them.

I knew they were quest unlocks and notifications, and I had to admit, even if only to myself, that one of the reasons I'd not looked until now?

I'd have felt shitty as hell if the people who were risking their very sanity to help me unlock higher levels were to see that I had a load of points I was holding back.

Besides, from a purely logical standpoint, it was for the best. Get to the level others could push me to, and then climb higher on my own. Otherwise, I'd never reach as high.

It still all felt shitty, though.

I pulled up the notifications, scanning them quickly.

Quest Complete: Building the Future (Part 2-[B])

Arise: Conqueror

Due to the considerable damage inflicted on your vessel, a sub quest has been issued! Return your vessel to full operation status, to receive the following rewards:

+2 Support Points

+2 War Points

(+Access to Level 3 of the Evolving Quest)

Viable Vessel: 1/1

Dwarfen survivors: 18/18 – deferred

Return to the node: 1/1 – complete

My ship was viable again, apparently—more or less, at least—and as such, I'd gained both sets of points, along with the two War points I'd received for cleaning out the Ændari from the station. That brought me to four War and two Support, but that wasn't the end of them.

Quest Complete!

<u>Evolving Quest</u>: Protective Detail 4

The Elders' power has been exposed. No longer are they, as many believed, a "paper tiger." Instead, they are as powerful as either of the factions, if not more so.

Originally, this quest was given to ensure that the enemy factions were eliminated or brought under your direct rule.

Your forces have grown in power to such a degree that there is no longer a risk from the lesser Earth factions of a successful rebellion against you.

You receive the following rewards:

+5 Support Points

+5 Points of Specialization

That…*that* got my attention. I'd not known it was possible to complete quests without *actually* completing them, though it was kinda obvious as well.

As I was now? The various factions on Earth would be a bit pathetic to fight. More to the point, though…this was one of the quests that I'd lost access to before, and Argus had sworn that once they were gone, they were gone.

Argus was clearly taking a hand and bending the rules, I guessed. But considering the hidden chains we'd taken off him and the systems we'd found that were damaging him, I'd call that a fair deal.

That gave me four War, seven Support, and five General. And again, that wasn't the end of them.

The Harvest notifications went on for a while, and with everything that was going on, I just focused and minimized them, breaking it down to the results.

That'd been the majority that were flickering when I'd looked earlier. Apparently there'd been Harvest quests offered and accepted retroactively. Again, Argus's work, I was betting, but for harvesting one, then ten, then a hundred, then a thousand Ændari in the last day or so, I'd earned five more points.

That was far and away the weirdest thing, I found.

Harvest points were the hardest for me to earn, considering until now I'd earned literally three of them. That was it. General points could be spent in any of the trees, and I'd earned a buttload of those, but the specific Harvest ones?

They were strangely hard to get considering how much harvesting I actually did.

I didn't give a shit, though, because I had a load of points to spend now.

Twenty-one points spread across the trees, and I knew where I needed to start. Five points in Harvest meant five points that I could invest in my greatest weapon and ability, upgrading myself as a Devourer.

The risk was the hunger, the need to consume more, and I'd felt that so strongly last time I'd increased in size—the need to gather those nanites, to be all that I fuckin' could be. It'd been overwhelming.

I hesitated, sinking three points into Growth, then waiting as the changes rolled out.

It took a few seconds, then I hissed, barely stifling the scream as it finally kicked in.

The Devourer was a peculiar beast, no matter how you looked at it. It was limited in size and needed upgrades to grow. The limit wasn't just the number of nanites I had, but also the skills themselves. If I had ten nanites but had unlocked all of the skill, I still couldn't create the shroud. But if I'd not unlocked the shroud level of Devourer, I couldn't create it with a billion of the little blighters.

As it was, I'd been at the seventh level of the Devourer growth unlock, which gave me a damn good size to reach to. The next three took me to ten—pretty obvious that, really—but the changes that came at ten were more than I'd bargained for.

The sheer magnitude of nanites I'd had gathered and stockpiled were enough to cover the exponential growth that came next as the entire outside of the ship shivered and rippled into the red and oily black of the Devourer.

I felt it—the press of the radiation of the stars, the energy of the light as it slid across my hull—being absorbed and converted. Tiny fragments of dust stuck to me and crumbled, their energy flowing inward. I opened my eyes, seeing the options before me again.

I blinked suddenly, half twisting, feeling *something* that was familiar in the dust? The cold of space? As soon as I thought about it, it was gone. I'd not been paying enough attention to get more than a split second's hit, but it made me think. I hesitated then moved on. No time to try to figure it out now.

Arise: Conqueror

I almost spent the next two points in Growth as well, then forced myself not to. Ten points in Devourer were enough that I could reform the entire ship into a living form now, one that I could fly through anything.

If I was to end up in that cloud again as I was now? I'd ignore it and just consume it, flying through to the other side with impunity, using the lightning strikes to charge my damn cells.

I'd not have to care about the electrical feedback, the lightning that tore and burned; it'd be pulled into me, strengthening and helping me to grow.

No, ten points in that was enough for now. And they came with some pretty nice benefits.

The starlight was the first one. Before, it'd rolled across my hull…nothing about it particularly of interest beyond how pretty it was or the navigation capabilities. Now, it fed me. I felt the tiny trickle of energy that was being dragged into me, that was helping to offset the energy that everything needed to grow and to live.

It wasn't enough, of course—it was far too little for it to be much of a viable change—but it was enough to help, in an infinitesimal way.

The second change was the Devourer's ability to literally devour. It sounded stupid, even when I said it to myself, but the speed and flexibility that I could feel was significantly greater.

I'd already invested a single point into Phago, which was the literal act of devouring; with only a brief hesitation, I sank the remaining two into that.

I was tempted by the third of the trio of options as well, Hunger, as it'd both increase my control over my hunger and make it more enjoyable and easier to lose myself in it should I need to. But as tempting as it was to gain the control, the risks just felt wrong.

Also, I was damn sure it'd be like turning myself into a mix of a blood-obsessed fucking vampire and a berserker, should I lose control, and that didn't sound like it'd be healthy for my long-term relationship.

Or the universe.

Instead, I approved the changes. The alterations flowed out, and minute shifts rolled across my skin.

I'd gained a twenty percent increase to the speed I could feed. Considering the fight that was ahead of me, that was a massive improvement.

Moving on from there, and taking into account the changes I'd found in me and the newfound control over nanites, I decided to leave the Harvest tree.

It was powerful, sure, and needed in many ways, but…

If I could get access to the nanites being harvested from the planet and they weren't protected against me now, then they were mine. The speed of feeding covered eating my way through armor as well, so that was worth it, as I damn well knew I'd be doing a lot of fighting very soon.

But I'd improved those areas enough, and the fight ahead would be a fight.

If I could figure out the gravity skips, then I could reach the planet in time to not only stop that fucking harvester, but I could do it before Captain Cockwomble could make it and try to feed on the nanites still.

I might be wrong about him—I prayed I was, and that he was just confused—but honestly, there was so much that didn't add up here, and it was the only part of the puzzle that fit.

Better to take this as the worst-case scenario, and after, if I had to split the nanites off, hand them over and apologize, then I would.

Probably.

Instead, I pulled up the Support tree and rolled through it again. The early levels were great and all, but to make sure I wasn't missing anything, I quickly flew through. It was either Creation or Augment that mattered to me currently. As much as I wanted to be a better healer, it was only in case my people got hurt.

Out here, I wasn't expecting there to be an option to heal anyone, so I dismissed that.

Creation meant that I needed to understand the basics to make the item from scratch. Augment meant understanding enough of the basics that you could build on the platform. With my massively expanded knowledge of power generation, that was a place to start.

It'd help me to tie the various schools of thought together to improve the engines, the…fuck it. *Everything.*

I'd already come up with an improvement in the reactors, though, and with seven Support points, and then the five General use ones to fall back on? I had enough to invest, if I did it wisely.

I'd put two points into Efficiency already, and three more made a big difference again—a thirty percent increase in general systems, and that was great. In theory, that would make everything significantly better. But in reality, it was the least sexy option available.

I'd done it to be realistic and to make sure that I had enough power available for the next points I was going to spend.

Pulling up the Gravity Manipulation Technology, I stared at the new options, having seen them, oh so briefly, before as I unlocked level five.

There were three, as these things were so often and weirdly laid out, and I went through them quickly.

Gravitation Transitionary Systems was the most obvious. As soon as I looked at it, I got the standard "hint" layout, letting me know that it was literally all about the drives, about the classified theory behind them, most of which I already knew, and the actual use of them. Again, a lot of which I knew already from my own experimentation, but… I'd probably have to take at least one rank in it to make sure I understood it as thoroughly as possible.

Gravitational Navigational Marking was another obviously named one, and a skill that I saw immediate and fantastic uses for. Looking at it, I got the sense of truncation—that it'd been started, that there'd been experiments in it, but that there wasn't much there. I hesitated, then tagged it. I had four points left in Support, and five General, so I could afford one, to see whether it was what I thought it was.

It was. Oh, my fucking God, it was.

Arise: Conqueror

I did a little mental dance that would have probably looked like I was having a fit to the music of *Saturday Night Fever* to anyone who saw it.

The Ændari had experimented with locational marking, triggering beacons that could be sensed through the gravity fields to direct a jump, but when the "soft spots" in space at the Lagrange points had been discovered, they'd essentially stopped researching it. They'd abandoned the entire line of research, and just moved on.

The data that I got from the download wasn't even that complex. It was like a sand thumper from the old movies, sending a constant, gentle pulse that fired into the depths of the gravity branes to act as a guide.

They'd intended to set them up at the locations they'd use to jump from one system to the next, literally forming guides. The early ships had flown sub-light to the destination; then they'd set them up, and planned on it being the next wave of exploration.

They'd then found that if they were too close to a gravity well, they were shunted aside to arrive at the Lagrange point anyway, making it entirely pointless. Especially because to jump "out," they'd already been using the Lagrange points anyway.

But that single point in marking birthed a thousand half-formed ideas for me. I forced myself to go on. There was no need to invest other points in the tech; there was nothing there to unlock!

The third and final in the field of Gravity Manipulation Technology was Weaponry. And the fact that it was available as a weapon so much earlier in other areas made me pause.

I reached out and tagged it, curious and sensing a load of additional data there, before grunting as I was hit with it.

There was an absolute shitload of research that had been done on gravitational weapons. Although most of it was useless, a few nuggets were hidden within.

The seismic ablation impactor was essentially a giant projector. You fired it from orbit at a planet that you didn't like very much, and you forced a section of it into pancake, or smaller.

It was done through a constant hammering of gravity waves, manipulating the strength and depth to ensure that earthquakes and more formed.

The planet's gravitational field was forced to shift, adjusting in unexpected ways. Unexpected by the people who had annoyed the Ændari, anyway. They would be specifying it, forcing new mountains to rise, the planet's mantle to crack, and worse.

All of it done from a ship that, although it had to be a specialized vessel—the energy requirements were huge, after all—wouldn't be that much larger than a normal Skarn class cruiser.

It needed no port for the weapon, and due to the nature of it, there wasn't even a pulse that was traceable back to the vessel. The worst it would be, was that it was clearly using a lot of energy and was in orbit.

The seismic exterminator was another entirely Ændari weapon: a torpedo that could be fired into a planet's core to force out random pulses of energy that started a building gravity field that continued until it ran out of energy.

Join it to a specialist heat-to-energy conversion device, and a pool of magma could be used to power-flatten a planet until the surface was a shattered mess.

The main difference between the two was that the first one resulted in the Ændari being able to hang around and watch, probably while eating canapes and wanking each other off.

The second was for when they wanted to hit it and quit it.

My gravity cannon was there, as were others, though the vast majority were marked as dead-end research or were already mainly unlocked, thanks to the points I'd spent prior to this in the cannon realm.

Disturbingly, some were also marked as having viable *entertainment* uses.

One even had a link that I followed to a War tree, and as it appeared, I found it was an entire new tree…but not one I wanted. It was marked PWD, and a brief glance leaked that the Psychological Warfare Division was anything but what I wanted to spend my points in.

I could just imagine the uses for entertainment that an Ændari who worked for the Psychological Warfare Division of an already fucked-up species would do, and I damn well backed away from that.

Moving back into the Support tree, I selected Transitionary Systems, unlocking it and basking in the final details of gravity drives being provided.

The details we'd found before were right, I realized, shaking my head in wonder as it all linked up, connections forming that just made goddamn sense.

The Ændari had forbidden all additional research into gravity drives after so many worlds and systems were destroyed. They'd basically just kept using the bog-standard variants way past the point that they should have been upgraded as they learned more.

That the main reason behind the massive rate of failures in the gravity technology was shitty quality control would have been hilarious, considering the poor design I'd discovered before, if not for the literal billions of lives that had been lost because of it.

Life-bearing worlds, places that made Earth look like a slum, even before we fucked the place up, were lost forever, shattered and compacted into black holes because the Ændari were too arrogant and self-assured to believe that they could ever fuck things up.

It made me want to kick someone's teeth in, and at exactly the same time, I was making a thousand associations a second, working on connecting up the dots.

The connections I made gave birth to more and more. Before I knew it, I was spending additional points, triggering upgrade after upgrade.

Specialized Technologies was the first. I'd unlocked it before, and as I'd found last time, if I focused on what I needed, there were significantly more options available than what the system suggested I needed.

They were hidden for the most part. Not being an engineer by trade, I'd accepted what was shown to me as all there was, until Zac had laughed and explained the realities of life.

Arise: Conqueror

No engineer felt that a system had enough features until it was too broken to perform them. So, they were either utterly simplistic, a stick or something basically, or they made a garage door lock that was capable of landing the space shuttle, changing the TV channel, and making you a bacon sandwich at the same time.

Using that mentality, whoever had designed the system had included literally everything. But knowing that only the engineers would be mad enough to tinker with the system and find the rest, they'd provided an idiot's guide for the rest of us.

When I'd opened the main system before, I'd been utterly overwhelmed. Now? After all these upgrades to my own mind, it was simple. Graceful even, as I searched for the things I knew I needed to create what I wanted.

Gravitational Projectors were a specialized field; the general details were available in the systems I'd already unlocked.

If you wanted everything that the Ændari knew on it? You selected the specific registry item and unlocked that as well.

Once I had that, I was off again, this time to the War tree, pulling up the Command and Control sub-tree, then into Drone, and from there, Function.

The same text that I'd gotten oh so long ago popped up. I read it over, nodding to myself and selecting it.

There were three tiers. I'd never gone deeper than the Espionage overview, but that was with good reason.

The systems I'd been unlocking at the time were specific to a drone that was probably gathering dust on a shelf in the hotel back in Greece. Once I'd unlocked the basic functions, it no longer needed further points to unlock, instead giving me a general use package, and then requiring me to spend nanites to make the drone capable of carrying out the various things I wanted.

Now things were reversed. I didn't need to spend nanites to unlock the facilities. Instead, I wanted a hell of a lot more advanced ones than the "basic package" had gotten me.

A little focusing, and the required options were highlighted.

It was an entirely new layer of the Command and Control tree called Autonomous Remote Systems, which I automatically broke down into ARS—or arse, for ease of thinking.

The arse systems were basically to be used to augment the command and control teams. It was a weaker version of Ingrid's own ability to link with me and see through my senses.

In this case, it wasn't just that, as it provided autonomous options as well, rather than as she did it where she needed to access a living host with their permission.

This gave me that ability but with drones. And the reason it was in the War tree instead of anywhere else? Well, it was entirely geared toward creating and commanding drone swarms for battle.

This was a new skill set, like the Assault Trooper, but a big step closer to the leadership path, as it was entirely based around securing or killing targets with autonomous drones.

I took that, then flitted up to Assault, then all the way to Advanced Tactical Systems, and down to Saboteur. I'd unlocked it before, and I liked the millions of minor upgrades it'd brought. But like ninety percent of the abilities and improvements I'd gotten, they were pointless now that I'd evolved.

The additional cushioning to my joints to allow for smoother movements and less grinding? That had made me quieter in movement when I was human, more or less. Now? I could turn my joints into liquid with a thought.

There was no grind of bones, etc., unless I created the bones and wanted that to happen, so fuck it.

The additional smaller changes that it'd brought were great—improvements in stealth and so on—so it wasn't a waste, but still.

Now, though? The unlocking of the arse had unlocked a sabotage arse option, and that was exactly what I needed.

This was an evolution of the regular Saboteur into one that was more designed to use drones and autonomous systems to perform their goals.

"Why bother with that" would have likely been a question I'd have asked…if it didn't come with a slew of upgrades to the stealth systems, as well as improved third-party targeting.

The final point I had available in War, I spent on unlocking the last option that popped up, only available now that I'd spent enough points in the various trees of War to earn it.

Expert.

The Expert Tactical System upgrade was slightly more powerful than the lower-level models. But what it lacked in overall level increase, it made up for in versatility.

It was an AI upgrade, one that I'd seen hints of before as I'd climbed the ranks to get to here. The way that I could select the levels of violence and punishment further down the tree, and it'd guide me through, step by step, was great. But here? At this level?

If I needed to, it provided a full-on AI clone of my capacity, one that could be deployed.

It was literally a War tree AI sub-mind, something that I'd not needed until now, because it was primarily my focus. But in guiding the drones I was already halfway through designing?

That would be magnificent.

I was down to two Support points, bugger all War and five Specialization, and I flowed to the next that was screaming to me.

Data scrolled past in a blur as I searched for the things that I felt more than saw. The trees flickered as more and more unlocked, and new options populated.

Light was a new subsection of Specialized Technologies that appeared at my demand, mainly dealing with the various projectors and receivers. In providing that, it also covered the basics of each wavelength, the theories about light, and why it was possible to bend it, and so on.

That kicked off a slight upgrade in my Conceal and other Stealth abilities as well, and I kept going.

Arise: Conqueror

From Gravity and Light, I unlocked research into Time, as a subsection of Light-Speed Travel. Although most of the research into it was useless, it had hints and suggestions that weren't.

They'd attempted time travel, several times over. The connected data said it was to deal with the "Great Betrayal" and other shite. I ignored their reasoning; it was likely to be slightly less logical and carefully thought-out than a demented toddler on energy drinks and cocaine could manage.

No, the important details were found in the bending of space and light as the test subjects moved closer and closer to light speed, before surpassing it.

It was another tree that was abandoned. After all, why bother with the speed of light inside a star system, when you'd only need to slow down again when you reached the next planet and hitting a micro-meteorite at that speed could fuck up your Tuesday?

No, they'd seen gravity jumps and scrapped anything else.

That was my War and Support points spent, but my five General ones were there still, ready and waiting.

There wasn't any more data in the system for Gravity, Light or Time. My mind was swimming in madness as I tried to come to terms with thousands of years of research and arrogance all hitting at once.

I forced myself to focus, leaving two of the reactors working, then draining the other two into the power storage cells and venting them, shifting the design around, and rebuilding them from scratch.

The two remaining reactors were torn into fragments, as what had been my primary body slid deeper into the ship.

The hull bulged up slightly around me, a toroid—or a ring doughnut—forming; then a pair of nodules grew out at the north and south points. I designated the shape, size, and density, and then stretched them like putty, elongating them and reforming the new tokamak ring.

As soon as the shape began to grow, I split off a section of my awareness. I created two more shapes to the east and west of me, then four more, split equidistantly around the remaining points of the compass.

With eight nodules forming, all spaced around the main toroid, I started the infusion of plasma, draining some of the power from the cells and starting the process up, trying to do a million things at once like any true mad scientist.

The plasma formed slowly as the nanites that made up the walls of the toroid converted the raw fuel from the null coins and filtered it in. Each of the additional eight tokamaks made smaller infinity loops around the main outer toroid.

It was difficult to explain, but the main toroid was a simple device to create magnetically enforced fusion. Essentially, put the plasma in, turn up the temperature, and slam the individual molecules together with a hell of a lot of force and speed to overcome the electrical resistance.

The Ændari had mastered fusion plants while we were still deciding whether we should hit that hairy fella in that tree over there with the stick and claim his tree as well, and they'd done little with it since.

They'd moved from reactors to power cores, which were far more advanced, though smaller, fusion cores. Then they'd adjusted to use vacuum energy, and eventually, they'd replaced the standard deuterium and tritium with dark matter, but that was it.

That was why they had such issues with them being close together as well, as dark matter generators were *really* unfriendly fuckers.

The thing was, though, they were still using the basic same principles of the toroid design. Scale that up and imagine a loop of plasma running around the inside—that's the basic setup. Get things moving damn fast and engineer a loop into it, somewhere that the flow turns back on itself to ensure regular impacts, etc.—that was fusion.

Add in that you use the magnetic fields to ensure the vacuum containment cells prevent the loss of any energy, and more and more efficient collection devices—a special section of the toroid that collected and contained the fusion reaction—and you had zero-point energy creation.

Even attempting to lay it all out in my mind, my brain stuttered, trying to argue with the steps. But it worked. I didn't comprehend all of why…just that the systems that I did understand could make it work.

I didn't have to understand every step; I just had to grasp the technology and steps required to make it work, and that I did.

The area that I took it further with, though, was the introduction of the eight minor tokamak, spaced around the ring.

The plasma flowed into the individual spear-like protrusions, being compressed tighter and forced to flow faster. A fragment would split off as the majority flowed on, and it was magnetically accelerated into a new loop.

That loop was linked to the next miniature tokamak, which did the same, feeding the now faster stream of plasma onto the next.

The result was a larger loop that ran around the main toroid, then into and around each of the smaller models, picking up speed. The secondary loop split off pre-fusion particles and accelerated them into each other over and over, containing them with a magnetic field that was basically keeping a barely controlled, nuclear explosion ongoing.

The power this new version could put out was tremendous. Still in design mode, I shifted the remaining two reactors into backup positions, forcing them around to feed their power directly into the shields from now on instead.

That gave me a tremendous amount of power for the rest of the ship: twenty units of power per smaller tokamak and forty from the main toroid, giving me a grand total of two hundred units. Before, I'd felt that the ship was overpowered with eighty.

The hull was sleeker now, stretching out into a knife-edge tip, the teardrop shape of earlier now solidified. The engines blazed with new energy, throwing me forward again. I reached out; the grav drive was already spinning up, giving me just enough of an insertion that I could mentally "tag" the planet that was my destination.

Now, with all the data that I'd unlocked and the thousands of slight alterations that I was feeding into the control systems, the drives, the shields, and more? Well…I couldn't help but grin as I recalculated the time that this was going to take for me to get to the planet.

I had a chance. And more than that, so did that planet.

The changes to the engines, the reactors, and the tokamak—all of it would take time. There was no way around that. But the differences that were already coming through were sufficient to let me know that I was almost ready for phase two.

I just had to get more mass first.

I could feel it there, that and other gravity signatures that appeared for me. I reached through the warp, locked onto the planet, and *pulled*.

CHAPTER THIRTY-FIVE

Space blurred around me. Stars turned to streaks of white, reds, and yellows. The universe seemed to stutter as if in shock; then it was there, rising before me in all its glory and horror.

The planet below me slammed into position. The bow of my ship, of "me" almost scraped the upper atmosphere as the draining of all that power tore a hole in my reserves.

I'd used far more than I'd expected to, but I'd also saved hours of travel. As I twisted, rolling and arcing, firing engines and flattening the pull of Scorpio-3's gravity on me, I felt the furious, yet distant mental scream.

It was Shan'Gai. And that he knew what I was doing was impossible to ignore now.

It was a wordless one, and yet its meaning was oh so clear.

The transmission that locked onto me was a shriek of absolute rage and denial—a threat and a promise, that should I touch that which was "his," then he'd tear me apart, atom by atom.

The sensation of fury, the barrage of half-formed memories, screaming of betrayal most foul, and of his terrible madness-filled hunger ended any doubt I might have had left.

No matter what had happened to Shan'Gai to make him as he was now, he couldn't be allowed to live.

The Ændari were already firing their engines and scattering. Their carefully controlled pattern of ships that had been hurtling straight at the incoming UC force twisted, to arc and break up, determined to obey and come after me, even as the UC, boring down on them, couldn't believe their luck.

The two sides opened fire on their ancient enemies. Lances of fire and light caressed shields; explosions, missiles, and screams filled the void as both the UC and Ændari fleet unleashed hell on one another.

The Ændari took the majority of the damage, their careful formation broken by some lunatic demand of the Devourer. And more crazy was the fact that right before impact with their enemies, they'd actually tried to follow it.

I twisted, rolling and fired engines, shoving with all my might against the pull of gravity to create a ripple that slowed me. That shoved and buoyed me up, allowing me to arc around the planet rather than spearing into it. I let loose a mental groan of relief, before stiffening as I felt the sudden shuddering and distant tearing of space-time inflicted elsewhere.

Something changed, as I fought to slow my crazy speed. A ripple flowed across the system and left its presumed originator, Shan'Gai, silent—drifting and exhausted, to my mind.

A ripple of twisted space-time tore across the system. The effect of more and more space being shoved back and forth made everything shudder in my senses, as Shan'Gai somehow—and the power needed to do this reduced my mind to gibbering—but somehow, he'd flattened the gravitational curve in a specific area.

He'd altered the influence of every planet, stone, and goddamn bit of dust in the entire sector across a section of space that was large enough it just made me want to change my goddamn pants.

The power that he'd just unleashed was still far more than I could bring to bear. But whatever he'd done, it was on seeing me closing on "his" larder that had driven him to do it.

I focused on slowing, on entering high orbit rather than plunging into the world below or skipping across it like a thrown stone and vanishing into deep space. By the time I'd managed it, and I was able to look around again, I felt Ingrid's connection reaching out.

"Do you see it?" she asked me, and I stared in horror, before whispering that I did.

"How did he do it?" she continued in stunned disbelief.

It was all I could do to shake my head and stare.

Shan'Gai was about a third of the way across the system from the Lagrange point now. Before, he'd been spearing across it at a horrific rate, ostensibly encouraging the UC to battle the Ændari, to reduce their numbers despite the injuries the UC would take. Now it was clear that the balance of power in the system had changed again; for anyone who could trace the power surge he'd unleashed to accomplish it, the secret was out as to who was really in charge of the Ændari.

The ripple of space-time compression hadn't been small, and whatever, *however* he'd done it, what he'd managed to do was flatten a large enough area of the galactic plane that a ship jumping in no longer landed in the Lagrange point on the far side of the sector. Instead, he'd targeted a space that was far closer to me. And it wasn't a single goddamn ship that had jumped in.

It was a new Ændari *fleet* that dwarfed the already damaged UC one.

"Fuuuck!" I growled, rolling until the world was visible overhead rather than below me. I bit back a growl as I started separation, forcing myself to accept that the ships "out there" weren't mine to deal with.

My own ship was still in the middle of construction, and I'd just used a serious amount of the nanites I had available to form the new power systems. I'd not expected that the damn things would be so efficient, nor that I'd have enough energy to launch myself so far. I was totally unprepared for the effect, but I sure as hell wasn't going to complain.

I couldn't power the toroid down—not in any realistic timescale, when it was as powerful as it was. Looking at the fleet, I was going to need as much power as I could get anyway, so I had a decision to make.

I could split the power section and most of the nanites off and leave them here, forming the rest of the ship's systems and continuing the build that I'd designated. Or I could pull the majority of the nanites free to come with me, trigger the engines and send it hurtling across space as a kamikaze attack.

One that would almost certainly not work. But if it could…

That felt insanely wasteful. And even as I thought of it, I banished the idea. Until I got down there and actually secured all the nanites, I knew anything could change, so sending off the vast majority of mine would be a damn stupid idea.

I paused, reassessed to make sure I'd thought it through instead of just going balls to the wall on instinct again, then nodded, feeling a strange sense of seeping apart, like kids' play dough that was pulled too far, snapping, separating. Then I blinked. The world around me reduced from the star-studded wonder to the interior of the hull.

It slid back, expanding out to give me room as I re-coalesced from the amalgamation of nanites. The hull split over my head as a bier beneath my reforming body raised me up.

I stared at the world below me, at the striated patterns of torn earth, raging firestorms, and warring seas. There were huge, shattered plains of ice where the harvester had touched down. Its immense weight crushed through glaciers and shattered mountains.

The legs were slowly gouging out great lines in the planet's surface. Visible even from orbit were the billions of smaller legs that extended out in fractal patterns, digging into what had until recently been a lush and vibrant world.

Now there were scars that would take millennia to heal, and that wasn't even counting the untold millions of lives that had been torn screaming free to feed the forges.

I could feel them, though; from here, I could feel them in their billions as the nanites that had once made up the millions of people on the world far below were ripped from their torn bodies and fed into huge vats. Miles upon miles above the ravaged world that slowly spun below me, I could feel the raw potential of such numbers.

There was enough there to kick-start my evolution to… I didn't know what, not really. But for long seconds I hung there, staring down, bewitched by that siren call of the nanites.

It was Ingrid who woke me, then, reaching out and filling my vision with details.

The harvester was almost insect-like in its design now: a long main body, a tail that was almost as long as the body that trailed behind it, and multiple legs that dug in and dragged more of the planet inward toward the processing fields beneath the abomination.

Arise: Conqueror

A raised bridge, or control center, lay about a third of the way from the back, rising into the air and overlooking the monstrosity. Ingrid had highlighted it, and a dozen other points.

The bridge shimmered behind the highest concentration of shields I'd ever seen. Although I might be able to break through with the insertion method that Ingrid and Argus were suggesting, it was far from a guarantee.

It was also slightly terrifying how quickly Ingrid had gone from "You're the love of my life, keep out of danger" and into "If you do this, it'll be the most efficient way to reach the planet."

A section of the upper left side of the hull was marked out as ever so slightly more damaged than the rest. A comparison to the suggested blueprints showed that it was likely that, from there, I could find my way down into the hold easier.

The hold. I could sense the nanites from *here*, and that meant that millions were dead already, stripped and being fed into the main processors, then being used to kick-start the production of new, blank, and fully upgraded nanites that were ready to be deployed.

There had to be the equivalent of a hundred billion clusters in production already, and that many… I swallowed hard, imagining the sheer madness of that, the reality that I could upgrade everything—and I mean *everything*—about myself into the stratosphere with so many.

I might not be able to "buy" the points in my individual stats anymore, but I had to think that my intelligence score, for example, would change when I was expanding my mentality into a neuron cluster that was entirely perfect and the size of a small house.

Strength? Well…

"Steve!" Ingrid snapped.

I jerked aware again, then cursed my wandering mind. I propelled myself forward, warping gravity before me into a funnel, sucking me down faster and faster, along with the dozen smaller spears that launched after me.

The first I knew of the atmosphere was a slight bump as I hit it. Wisps of turbulence built quickly, then heat, the feeling of being hit by a thousand tiny hammers as I tore through pockets of low or no atmo, then denser gatherings.

The heat buildup was the easiest to deal with. Dragging the heat into myself and converting it into energy was the effort of barely a second; then I was staring as more and more details crept into focus.

The world-eater Ouroboros was mind-bogglingly huge. Its legs were covered by sheets of metal that were larger than capital cities I'd once visited on Earth. The underside was a mess of moving parts: great arms that slid out, digging into the ground and sea, and tearing everything it found upward, funneling inward.

There were short tracks from behind it, burned and torn into the land, visible through the shallow seas from here, with clouds of poisoned water rushing outward to the rear.

Clearly this fucker was slowly moving forward to find fresh prey, tearing the world apart.

As I plunged down toward it, the wind whipping all around me, I could feel her there in my mind with me.

"Can you do it?" Ingrid asked me quietly.

The sheer size of the machine below me brought doubts. *"I have to,"* I answered grimly. *"I've got no choice."*

"I know," she whispered, before taking a deep breath and apparently forcing herself to straighten, a sensation I felt distantly and couldn't help but smile at, as she gripped her ponytail and tugged it into a tighter braid, her nanites working to re-tie it.

"Okay, Dolfing says the last platform is under fire now. We should have access to the outer galaxy at any second, and I'm calling for reinforcements."

"We could lose anything that jumps in," I warned her.

"We could," she agreed. *"We could lose everyone, or we could kill this shit once and for all."*

"I'm not disagreeing," I pointed out, blinking on instinct as the whipping wind tore over and past my eyes. *"I'm just worried that we could lose more than we save. If that fucker turns around and attacks everyone..."*

"Steve, there's an Ændari fleet that's at least as big as anything that the UC can bring to bear here. They're headed for you and the fleet currently. That Shan'Gai brought them into the system is undeniable, and that means that either they're working for him, or he's working for them.

"Either way, though, as soon as the fleet is taken care of, they'll be heading to the node. If the Ændari manage to board it, and reach the control center, then the war is over. Argus can't refuse his creators, and we can't stop them entering. The best he can do is delay them, and not by much.

"The future of the UC, the independent worlds, and the Ændari empire is going to be decided in this system in the next few hours. No matter what happens, we have to win."

"I know that," I said softly. I passed through the thin upper clouds, staring at the glittering waves that swirled and beat against the mighty legs ahead.

"I know you do, Steve, but you need to acknowledge this, because you can't let what happens to me and the others stop you."

"What?"

"The fleet has launched assault ships, their Skarn, Argus calls them," she said. *"They'll be at our gates in two hours, and we'll hold them off with everything we have."*

"I'll be there," I promised on instinct.

"No, you won't," she disagreed. *"We can't let them take the node. But Steve? If you let Shan'Gai get past you, if he manages to win this? He'll go on with his insane plans. We don't know why he's not used this harvester more than he has, but he's clearly been trying to keep it and what he truly is hidden. When the barrier comes down, we'll be shouting far and wide what he's done, because they need to know, to fight him, to stop him."*

"But when you do that, he'll have no reason to hide anymore," I whispered, understanding.

"Exactly. When he can't hide it anymore, he'll have to defeat the UC—that or flee and be hunted forever."

"You're not selling this to me," I pointed out.

Arise: Conqueror

"Steve, I've spoken with the others here. Our group, the devilkin, and the UC soldiers have all agreed..." She took a deep breath, then went on. *"If we can't hold the Ændari off, then we'll take them with us."*

"Take...what?" A horrible feeling rose.

"There are enough of the soldiers who have engineering access now that they can manipulate the reactors. And Argus, well, he can't allow us to do it and he can't help us, but he's made it clear where and how many actions he can counter to prevent us. It's as good as giving us permission."

"You can't." My head jerked up, staring at the clouds overhead and the stars that were now hidden below a field of gentle blue and white. *"Ingrid, you can't mean..."*

"If we trigger a full overload, it'll sterilize the entire system. Nothing will survive, and that includes Shan'Gai," she said resolutely. *"So listen to me, Steve. If we can't hold, we won't let the node fall into their hands. If I tell you that we're going to do this—"*

"I won't leave you!" I snapped.

"No," she agreed. *"You can't, my love. And I'm not sorry because at least it means that we'll die here together. You'll have to stop Shan'Gai. If he realizes what we're doing, he'll try to escape. And now that he's shown he can do that, to create a jump point anywhere..."*

"He can't." I shook my head, inducing a fresh wobble as I plunged through another bank of clouds. *"He flattened the twist of gravity, that's all, and I think he bottomed out his reserves doing it. He's just drifting now."*

"Do you know that he can't do it again?" she asked. *"Would you risk my life on it? My family's?"*

"No," I admitted.

"Then you need to be sure. We need to be sure. Steve, if the Ændari break through, if we can't hold them, then we blow the node. It'll cut everyone in the nearby systems off from their abilities and upgrades, but they only just unlocked them anyway, so it's no great loss. It's better that we do this than they all die, and that's what'll happen if we don't stop Shan'Gai. Possibly hundreds of worlds, thousands of space stations, millions of ships, and hundreds of trillions of lives—all lost in exchange for our few thousand up here and the population of a world that's already close to being lost. It's simple math, Steve. It's not a choice we can make to do anything else."

"There has to be another way," I growled.

"There is," she assured me. *"This is the last resort, Steve. But you need to know what's at stake, in case you have to cross a line."* She drew in a deep breath and went on quickly. *"As soon as the barrier goes down, I'm going to send the truth about what's happened here, the records, the proof we have, and the live images of Shan'Gai and what he's doing. Then I'll call for reinforcements. I'll make sure they all know what they're getting into, that they'll be at a serious risk of death, and that it'll be forever, not just for a few years or whatever.*

"They'll have the choice, to come and fight, to be the heroes they always knew they could be, or to hide and lose access to their systems."

I sensed Ingrid grinning evilly.

"We gave them a taste of the future as it could be. Now, if they want more? They need to come and fight for it. Shan'Gai ordered them to stay back, to stay clear, so if they're all still gathered? I'll offer them the choice. Jump in, fight, help us and save millions, or lose everything and know that we fought for them and the debt that's owed to Earth. Either way, Mor and Far will be able to hold our home, and the Ændari fleet can't be allowed to escape."

"And if you lose, you're going to blow the node?" I asked, not liking it at all, but starting to understand where she was coming from.

"Basically," she admitted.

"There's ships that are closer to you than the UC can jump in. No way you can stop them boarding if they try," I pointed out.

"No, we can't," she agreed. *"But we can make them bleed for every single inch, and the time we hold on gives you time to face Shan'Gai. Steve, there's no plan B here—no escape and come back to fight another day. Either we win, or we take them all with us. Your job will be to fight and kill, or trap Shan'Gai, to hold him and keep him from escaping. Nobody else can do that. The UC fleet is injured, but they've got the Ændari to fight—the original battered fleet and this new one."*

"Send a monster to fight a monster," I said softly.

"Send a hero to slay a monster," she corrected. *"Steve, I know you, what you are, and what you're capable of. Could you be a monster? Yes, you could. You've got the anger, you've more than got the ability, and when push comes to shove? You're probably capable of anything you need to do, to get the job done."*

My heart constricted a little at that.

"I'm not you, Steve. I have to force myself to kill, to hurt people. Does that make me a better person? No. No, it doesn't, especially when what we need is someone to stand between the dark and the light. You kill without compunction, without regret and with a natural level of skill that's frankly terrifying, not to mention that I know you enjoy it."

That hurt, but damn it was accurate.

"But that's the point, Steve. I'm finally understanding that in a real war, you don't want a paladin standing tall in shining armor, quoting the rules of conduct at the enemy. I thought that was the way it was supposed to be.

"I grew up fantasizing about a knight to come and sweep me off my feet. I'm older now, and I've seen more of the real world and the realities of the universe than I ever imagined was possible. I see it differently now. We don't need a white knight, Steve..." Her words almost fell over themselves as she spoke, so full of passion and certainty, pride, and love.

"We are a race of weapons. We were genetically created to be the most vicious and skilled warriors in the galaxy, and we need an Alpha to lead us. Our Dark Crusader. We need a Reclaimer to tear our past free of those who would hide it. We need a Devourer to tear our enemies down and raise us up. And we need an Explorer to lead us. Most of all, we need a Conqueror to teach the galaxy that we're not their prey, that humanity is the greatest predator of all."

Arise: Conqueror

I felt her pushing her love at me, her respect and her faith, and that behind her, there were the others, distantly felt, all spread out, preparing for the final fight.

"We don't need some golden-haired prick in tinfoil armor to tell us all that something is right or wrong, Steve. That's what I've realized that I've always seen in history as well. All those thousands of years of tales told in artifacts, tablets, and carvings...they all had one thing in common, and you know what it was?"

"No?"

"It was that for the white knight to be able to last long enough to make the pretty rules that everyone agreed on, that for civilization to have the time to grow and the safety for people to develop and decide that the past was right or wrong? What had to come first was a true Alpha. A leader who stood up and tore the head off the shoulders of anyone who looked at them sideways and earned their people that time to breathe.

"You're not the golden-haired leader who everyone cheers, Steve. You're the one who makes it possible for them to come after. You're the one who kills everything until the werewolves, the vampires, and the other things that hide in the dark places damn well learn they need to stay hidden there. You might not be human anymore, but that doesn't mean you're less.

"It's the ones like you who make the monsters afraid, who keep the evil in society under control and afraid of the consequences. We need YOU, Steve. I need you. And don't you dare say you can't do it, because you and I both know that you're going to do what needs to be done, no matter what it is."

"I will," I whispered.

"What?"

"I said I will."

"I can't hear you, Steve!"

"I WILL!" I roared at her, feeling her smile and the kiss that she pushed to my cheek.

"Then do it. Do what you need to do to save that world. Millions of people are down there with nothing and nobody who can save them, so you do what you can. You give them hope. And Steve?"

"Yeah?"

"You need to hear this, I know, and it hurts to say it, but it's reality. If you can't save them, and if you have to, then to save trillions, you'll have to kill millions. I'll be there with you, afterward, if we survive."

My heart froze at that, as I heard what she was saying, what she was promising.

The words might not be clear, but they didn't need to be; I read her meaning in her mind. She knew the risk I was running as a Devourer, exposing myself to an insane amount of "food." That there was a chance, a good one, I'd not be able to stop myself.

What she was saying was that she understood that, and she accepted it. That if I was to become that monster, she'd not turn me away. Instead, she'd go with me.

I drew a deep breath, throwing my love to her, my understanding, my pride in her that she understood that it was possible that no matter how hard I tried, I might finally give in and lose myself, and that she was strong enough to see the galaxy for what it really was.

"It's a shitty game…" I whispered aloud. "But it's the best game in town."

"It is. And if we have to do things that burn our soul to ashes so that trillions of others get to live free? What kind of a cost is that?"

"I'll not fail," I promised her.

"Neither will we. I love you, Steve."

"I love you too, Ingrid." I sent that to her, then felt her backing up, taking up space at the back of my mind where we were dimly aware of each other, but no more.

The final whisps of cloud streamed past and I burst free, plummeting toward the enormous harvester directly below. I growled. I wasn't human anymore. Ingrid was right.

It was time to embrace that.

It was time to become a god.

CHAPTER THIRTY-SIX

I angled to the left, tightening up on my approach as sections of the hull opened. Anti-aircraft or similar weapons deployed, tracking me and opening fire.

I wasn't human anymore, and that needed to be in the front of my mind as I tried to do this. I was a one-man, nanite-fueled nightmare, and it was time to fully embrace that.

I'd left the ship in orbit, but that didn't mean I was defenseless. I'd learned, I'd studied, and I'd damn well rebuilt myself for this fight.

I had a power core in my stomach now—it wasn't like I needed room for a small intestine—and as the first shells went off nearby, their starburst payloads ripping out in all directions to take out incoming fliers, my first personal shield rippled out across my skin.

It'd taken a weird shift in my mind to do this, to change how I actually saw myself. I knew I wasn't human anymore, but I'd been thinking that I was, well, I was human, just with new abilities. New and improved.

Human version 3.0, rather than the standard, if impressive version 2.0 that was the soldier class of the UC.

I wasn't, though, and forcing myself to accept that changed everything.

I'd been planning to slow, to adjust my flight path, to reverse gravity so that I could land carefully…

Then I realized it was absolutely fucking pointless.

Would a god-rod fired from orbit slow itself down on impact? No, because it was a weapon, and so was I. It was designed to punch through the upper layers of the mantle and release incredible force. Well, me too, bitch—me too.

My shield rippled and flickered. Impacts came closer and closer as they tracked me. From over my shoulders, two rail guns flowed up, arcing around and tracking as I designated the targets.

They popped up in my vision; a ruby-red crosshairs locked onto each, zooming in and picking exactly where the shot needed to land before moving on.

My new War AI tracked more, selecting them all, and waited for my approval, before opening fire.

For three seconds, my shoulders and the following spears hummed, fired, retargeted, then fired again. Then, in a burst, I was through the latest cloud of shrapnel, falling free, and I grinned.

There'd been hundreds of turrets and firing positions that had opened up. Here and there in the sea around me, I could see the drifting and smoking remains of the locals' attempts to take them out.

Now those that surrounded the patch I was aiming for were smoking ruins, every one shattered, smoking or just plain gone, depending on their size.

The spears that had launched with me had changed, no longer simple lances of nanites. Eight had formed into self-targeting orbital rail cannons, firing their own mass until they were down to a quarter of their size, before rolling in and attaching to my body.

The remaining four had shifted forward, taking up position and locking onto their targets. Three aimed directly for the bridge, thrusters firing and driving them ahead; additional gravity fields spun up and angled them in, increasing their speed as they lanced forward.

The last was locked on my intended breach point. It, too, pulled ahead, hurtling like the fist of God to hit the shield at almost the same time the others hit the bridge.

The shields flared; the heavier ones held, despite the one-after-the-other impact from orbital weapons. The thing they did accomplish, though? The flaring out of the shields hid my course corrections.

I reached out, connecting to my ship in orbit and then to the local planetary net, forming the link to whatever leadership survived. Nobody answered the goddamn calls.

A blink, and I accessed a thousand cameras in public places, the eerie sights of millions of people staring spellbound at the local news equivalent as their world burned.

They weren't even running. For a split second, although that seemed wrong, I realized that for many of these cities, the harvester was visible hundreds of miles away, towering to the heavens.

After all, where the hell would you run from something that was literally eating your world?

I saw lines that were hastily being assembled, mobile batteries that were firing at the huge legs, missiles, troops on foot that ran forward with shoulder and handheld lasers, emptying their charge into the steel without visible effect.

I heard calls that were ongoing, pleas that were being screamed out into the void, for someone to come and save them, and I answered.

My words rang out from every speaker and overlaid their calls. My view was broadcast to their screens; with a thought, I invited their world to watch its last defender fight for it.

"Hold on," I called. "Hold the line…you've not been forgotten or abandoned. I'm here."

I saw the reaction to it: a thousand, thousand people who flinched, who spun to stare at the screens, their speakers, the billboards and adverts or glass data projection panels.

Arise: Conqueror

I saw the children who asked their parents what it meant, and who had come. Then I felt Ingrid taking over the connection, linking to a satellite that had recently arced over the edge of the horizon to show my arrival to them all.

I saw the shock, the hope, and the terror on their faces superimposed over my vision as I hit the weakened shield and upper armored deck of the harvester without slowing.

Feetfirst, I punched through it. The secondary armoring buckled, tearing like paper beneath the impact. I drove deeper, shattering through the uppermost floors and bringing devastation with me.

The first three upper floors were all armoring and mobility sections, areas for fuck knew what to be stored. But below them? I tore through the final barrier and into the interior proper. Only then did I flex the gravity fields, landing hard on the deck below with a boom that echoed around the great open space, buckling the floor and making the entire creation shudder.

Sections of the floors above cascaded down around me, debris and shattered marble shards. A ring of force blasted outward, hurling a dozen nearby Ændari from their feet with screams of shock and outrage, even as alarms sounded and lights began to flash in warning.

I straightened, looking around, and sensed Ingrid freezing as I started to search for a connection to the various systems that surrounded me.

"Barrier is down!" she called, before vanishing to send messages out to the wider galaxy. *"Good luck!"*

"Good luck, my love," I sent to her, stepping forward and scanning the area I'd emerged into.

It looked to be a processing area, hundreds of meters on a side, with barriers of light that reached twenty meters high. Each formed glowing walls that popped and fizzed, crackling as drifting dust and debris touched them. Off to one side, a bare handful of different species lay semi-conscious.

I strode toward them, seeing them laid in a box formed of the light. Each were battered and bloody, though wearing identical uniforms of dark grey and black.

Survivors, I guessed. Presumably from some kind of assault on the harvester.

As I stepped over an Ændari, she spat and reached out, grabbing at my foot and squeezing with what would have been a bone-shattering amount of pressure under normal circumstances.

Then she slashed at me with a growl and a crystal dagger held in her other hand.

I paused, curiously watching her as the blade hit my armored calf and bounced off. I waited for the split second of shock to break and for her to look up; then I reformed my outer layer into the Devourer and flowed it out around her hand.

She jerked back instinctively—or she tried to, anyway. The fingers of her right hand were already locked into the outer layers of my armor. Like sentient ooze, the Devourer swarmed up, over the back of her hand, flowing along the arm.

She screamed, yanking her dagger around and cutting downward into her forearm, hacking through it in two swift movements that barely separated her arm in time before I could take it all in.

The others were moving now. Half of them threw themselves at me. Two more crawled in circles, dazed, still stunned as they'd been the closest to my arrival and were clearly in shock.

Three more were up and were running as fast as they could get away from me. Lastly, a handful drew weapons where they lay, taking aim at me.

It made no difference in the end.

Tentacles flashed out, latching onto those closest. Short globules of nanites, connected to me by almost invisibly thin cables, grew and then launched at those farther out, splashing into the back of runners, the chests of those standing, and maws latched onto the faces of the nearest.

They screamed as I ripped them in closer. The Devourer fed, and all but the woman who had tried to kill me were lost in seconds. She shook her head, on her back now and scooting herself backward. Her feet skidded on the marble floor as another tentacle speared out, hitting her in the chest like a waterbomb of red jelly.

It spread across her armored torso, eating its way through until it hit flesh, lifting her into the air and dragging her to face me, stopping against her bare skin and making it clear that I was a heartbeat from tearing through that as well.

Her horns stood proud and true, but one of the spikes…the prongs? Points? I didn't know and I didn't care—but one of the fractal patterns of bones that jutted from her temples was splintered. A bloody line ran from it, rolling down her cheek as I held her before me.

"Shut it down," I ordered, staring into her eyes.

"Can't…" she wheezed.

I grimaced as she fought for air; her heart labored as I examined her. The system provided me all the data I needed, making me snort at how shitty her luck truly was.

"Your armor didn't protect you very well," I pointed out. The signs of a recent break in a dozen of her bones was clear as I looked her over; nanites were still integrating with her, still working to repair a line of broken ribs. "So tell me, what use are you to me if you can't stop this?"

"Kill…you…" She struggled, kicking and punching out at me.

"If you could have, you already would have," I grunted. I grabbed her by the throat, twisting with my right hand as the tentacle that latched onto her chest twisted her in another direction.

Her neck snapped with a loud *crrrackkk*. My armor flowed up and down, pouring over her as my shroud expanded. The others were mostly gone already; only two of them still showed any signs of life, and the rest were already covered by the flowing mass.

I drew in a deep breath, dropping her as I strode forward. A pillow of nanites poured out to catch the corpse as it fell, enveloping it and wrapping around it, tearing into her from all angles.

Arise: Conqueror

She'd been of the new generation, clearly, her nanites barely more heavily entrenched than an advanced ascended human. But she'd sure as shit been as vicious as her elders, judging from the snarl on her face. And as I looked back over to the survivors cowering inside the prison of light, I guessed she'd already shown them that side.

They were huddled back as far as they could get from me, drawn in around the fallen body of one of their own, a massive figure of stone and oily grey skin that leaked a glowing green fluid onto the floor.

"Are you okay?" I asked aloud, glancing from one to the next of them, even as I searched the ether for any kind of electronic signal I could hack.

"Do we look okay?" one of them replied in a shaking voice. "What the hell!"

"Point." I nodded. "Are there more prisoners?"

"I don't know. There were more who attacked but I don't know if any survived... Who—*what* are you?"

"Really?" I glanced down at the no longer struggling Ændari bodies that were even now shrinking, breaking down and being absorbed into my shroud. "Does it matter?"

"No?"

"De...vour...er..." the bleeding figure behind the speaker whispered, and I nodded to them. "Lord...we beg."

"For what?" I reformed my right hand into a long blade, drawing it down the crackling wall of light. The wall and those around seemed to scream with released energy, flickering and glowing brighter and dimmer in waves. I hissed and drew my blade back, staring.

It was a shield, a literal shield, the kind that should be protecting a ship in space—and they were using them for crowd control?

I almost missed their response, so surprised was I by the shields, and I flicked my gaze back to them.

"Children."

"What?" I asked.

"Forgive them."

"Forgive?" I asked, totally confused for a second. "The Ændari?"

"No!" another barked, then shook his head and tried again, lowering his voice and trying for a more conciliatory tone. "Lord, we ask that you forgive our children our sins." He awkwardly bowed, one hand to heart, the other clutching a gash in his side and trying to keep it closed.

"The innocent have no sins," I said instinctively, then winced, glad I was wearing a helm and thinking about just how fucking arrogant and pompous that sounded.

"They will die with us on our world, but if you could forgive them, rescue them..." he said quickly.

"Rescue them yourselves," I said. "I'm here to remove the harvester. If I can do this, take the ship off the world and kill the Ændari, can you rescue them yourselves?"

"Can you do that? Can you free us?" Another stepped forward, one hand rising to the glowing walls before being snatched back.

"One way or another," I assured them, before stepping back and staring up at the glowing barriers.

There wasn't anything I could see nearby to form or project them, and certainly no control mechanism. The only access points of controls I could see in the entire room were on the far side of it, and I sure as shit wasn't going to try to overwhelm…

That was a point.

The energy requirements of a system like this had to be *insane*. To create a hundred shields individually arranged as panels like a queuing system, forming literal lines and cells out of force field projectors had to be horrifically expensive. And for them to maintain them all like this when only a single cell was needed?

"How did you end up in there?" I asked.

"They dropped the wall there, and pushed us in, one by one," another of them, a red and yellow skinned woman with eyebrows that ran off the sides of her face and curled down to connect to the underside of her chin called. "That one, the…the one by your feet. She had a controller on her belt."

"Not anymore," I grunted in annoyance, pulling back the shroud to reveal a body that looked like a famine victim after a wolf attack. There was nothing that had been usable remaining beyond meat now. "Okay, plan B." I reached out to the local area and searched more carefully.

"Lord, they'll be sending more Ændari. There's hundreds aboard. Our children, our families…" another called, and I waved them to silence as the alarms blared and screeched in the distance.

For there to be a controller on her belt, there needed to be a remote mechanism for it to connect to. But after ten seconds of searching, I'd found nothing. And considering the sheer number of lives being lost by the second right now, I didn't have time to do anything more finessed.

"Okay, fuck it, plan C it is," I growled, reaching out and tracing the connections I could sense. Projector lines were buried into the floor, running back and forth across the entire room. I guessed that even though only a small section of the room was active, they could scale it up for…for processing.

This had to be a holding cell and processing facility, presumably designed so that they could capture people and split them up into groups for later.

That meant that if you were grabbing people and ramming them in here, you had to be ready for them to have tech hidden that you weren't able to find on a fast search. You had to be ready for them to try to hack the barriers, so they couldn't be easily accessed by remote systems…

I looked at the floor, tracing the lines, then forced myself to stop and think. This was an insane waste of my goddamn time, and that was limited to all hell. Time for plan F—for fuck it.

I reached out, forming and focusing. My fingers slid back into my palm; my forearm bubbled outward, swelling up and widening. I couldn't help grinning to myself as I reformed my left arm into a laser, shifting it further and further, moving from a small test bed version to a larger, *much* more powerful one in seconds, then finally to something that should have been attached to a ship's hull to take on incoming craft.

I could hear running feet in the distance. I pointed my left arm and its nozzle in that direction, even as I crouched, then reached out with my right hand.

"Lord, no!" one of them shouted, horrified as I slapped my palm onto the steel of the mechanism that protected the bottom of the shield.

The panels were each marked out on the floor by raised sections that could presumably be lowered back down when they weren't needed. The marble that glistened and gleamed across the edges of its expanse was littered with lines of metal, and to my new senses, they shone with power.

The lines that ran this way and that were directly over connections that drew incredible amounts of power from somewhere deeper in the harvester. And, well, it wasn't like I had to be careful with things right now, was it?

The panel exploded in light. The shields trying to prevent my access sparked and screamed. The first level of nanites that touched them overloaded, blackening and failing as they were shorted out by the influx of such energies.

More took their place, frantically building connections that burrowed into the superconductors, dragging the power out and into my body. I roared in pain as power that should have been used to send starships vaulting across the heavens poured through me instead.

I funneled it through me, pouring it up my arm, across my chest—careful to maintain a barrier between it and my stomach, where that core now lay—and down my other arm.

The power levels that hit the newly formed laser and were converted into searing radiant energy were sufficient to carve my name in the hull of a battleship. So the handful of screaming Ændari that raced into the room in the distance didn't stand a goddamn chance.

The beam tore across them, vaporizing them and continuing onward, tearing through internal bulkheads, gouging through marble and carvings, through support struts, communication cabling, more power lines…

The list was endless, and they all suffered the same fate: vanishing as the beam with a sound like the universe stuttering tore through the internals of the harvester, before cutting off as the local power failed.

The world around me collapsed into darkness as the shields fell. I sagged forward, catching myself on the floor, panting, my eyes wide at the feeling that had just torn through me.

It'd been insane, scouring, and maddeningly wonderful. I felt like I'd been reborn, a new man. I slowly rose to my feet, staring down at the huddling collection of beings who regarded me in utter terror.

I forced myself to remember how to walk, to take a few steps forward, reaching out with my right hand and seeing the way they flinched, terrified that I was going to attack them. A lance of nanites ripped free of my right hand, piercing the rock-like figure that lay slumped in the middle of the group, and I stared.

Their details lay open to me: their design, the wasted and failing DNA linkages, the repeated and misaligned genetics, the… I shook myself as they panicked, shouting to make myself heard over them.

"I'm healing her!" I declared, only thinking to actually start doing that now, as my frazzled brain rebooted and focused me in again. The wounds were many, and probably major in the situation they'd found themselves in. But for me, with my nanites, they were simplicity itself to address.

Swelling? Simple: calm the tissue, repair, smooth back. Shattered coatings, skin or stone or whatever it was? Easy: just break up this section, fold it back in, reform, reseal. The bones that lay in the center were metal already, and they'd taken the injuries well, so no work needed there.

Damage to the lungs, internal bleeding in that organ, something acidic that was scalding this one, something liquid that was bloating that…

Ten seconds of my time, and I pulled the lance back. The others were all apparently injured as well, but mobile at the least, so I left them as they were, speaking over the shocked exclamations as their friend writhed and twisted in pain as they were rebuilt.

"As soon as they stop, you need to run," I said firmly. "I'm going to destroy the harvester, and if I can, I'll take it back up into orbit. But if I can't, you need to get clear. Take the Ændari ships…they're bound to have some somewhere."

"Where?" one asked.

"I've got no fucking clue, but I've wasted too much time here already. You want to live? To escape? Make it fucking happen!"

With that, I turned on my heel and set off, reaching out to Ingrid as I felt her returning to the back of my mind.

"Ingrid?" I sent to her, both hopeful and concerned.

"The UC are coming," she said in a rush. *"So are the independents I spoke to. And Steve? Mor and Far are as well. James made it. They ferried them to the forbidden moon and dug out that mess of a ship. They're coming to help!"*

"That's wonderful!" I sent to her, and I meant it, though I couldn't help but be less than confident considering the ship that she meant.

When I'd torn the nanites free of the corrupt that roamed that very first moon, I'd not trusted the UC or anyone else outside of our own little group. As a little insurance policy, I'd released a batch of nanites with a very specific purpose.

They were to burrow down into the bedrock below and create a converter; then they were to begin feeding in everything that it could find to make a half dozen custodians. And then, they were to start building a backup ship.

It wasn't going to be anything special. It'd be massive and heavily armored, but lower in tech level than the warship that we'd gotten a few days later and far less powerful than the ship I'd later amalgamated into my body. It was built to collect and make use of the corrupt nanites, spreading like a virus whenever their nanites were encountered, cleansing them and adding those new nanites to the pool to continue building.

I'd done it almost on a whim, and I'd set them to accept any orders Zac gave them if it wasn't me who went back for them, which was probably a big fucking mistake as well.

Arise: Conqueror

The thing was, they were a Hail Mary pass. The design I'd loaded and specified into the single storage the nanites had access to couldn't be complicated, so I'd gone all in on simple instead.

It'd need a horrific number of improvements to make it into a viable spaceship under normal circumstances. It had a single basic gravity drive, no atmospheric generators, and not even so much as crew quarters. It had a control room that was buried under literally dozens of meters of solid armoring. It had a massive space for a reactor, but with only a basic one designed to be put in. It'd really need a lot more doing once it had access to a shipyard.

It had engines—my God, did it have engines. But again, they were simple. And the shields? Nope.

It was basically a flying cannon, because the one thing it did have, and it had in abundance, was a bloody huge rail gun in the middle that the rest of the ship was essentially wrapped around.

The final design was a tube, the control room buried in armor on the topside, space for a great big power core behind it and engines stuck to the sides.

That was it. But I'd figured that if I needed that ship, then I'd really need it, and a big stick was likely to be a wonderful solution to any shit that I was to encounter.

Another ship with more control and power could latch onto the side and perform the jumps needed to get it anywhere, and Earth now had a big gun, even if it'd need ammo to be produced to order.

As it was, it'd fire *anything* metal, though. Put a missile in there and pull the trigger, and you'd have it across the system in what would seem like a heartbeat.

It was just…*uninspired*, basic. And when I looked at the things I could create now? It barely seemed like it was worth the effort of bringing it to the fight.

That Ingrid's mother and father were there in that or the warship? That fucking terrified me, thinking of them being lost to a mistake I'd made all those weeks ago in my orders when I barely had access to half my systems.

I started to run again, searching for a way down to the lower levels, then snorted. I lifted myself into the air, rocketing forward and crossing the holding area like a bullet. I sent a pulse out ahead of me, mapping the corridors and sections of the harvester as I searched.

I could feel the nanites—my God, could I feel them. Billions were below me somewhere, and more and more of them were being sucked up and forced into a central area by the second.

The problem was that the sheer amount was mind-blowing; the wash of them from somewhere nearby was so strong that I couldn't focus on it, and all I could sense was generally "down."

I knew it was below me. I swallowed hard as I forced myself to remember that the nanites I was lusting after, that were so close, weren't all free.

They weren't even mostly freshly built, or I didn't think they would be yet.

No, these were stolen from hundreds of thousands or even millions of people. Literally, there had to have been at least several thousand little children in there. Babies, toddlers, little fucking kids, and they'd all been rendered down to…

I couldn't think of it like that.

I didn't have kids, and I really wasn't sure I wanted them ever, but I'd had friends who had them, and they always terrified me. Kids were so small, so weak, and far too easily broken…and they were *innocent*. They were pure in a way I was fairly sure I'd never actually been.

They deserved to be able to fuck up their lives on their own terms. That was one red line that I'd always had: that you never, ever let someone hurt kids and get away with it.

I might be a shitbag in every other area of my life, but that was a golden rule, in-vio*late* because it resulted in-vio*lence*.

Ingrid was telling me details, ship numbers, locations, UC troops and more. She poured them all in, and for me, they all poured out the far side like my earholes were lubed up and there was even less between them than normal as that one thought went through and around and around.

That fucker Shan'Gai was harvesting *kids*.

Movement.

I twisted, lashing out instinctively as a pair of laser cannons slid out of a recess in the wall nearby at my approach. A gravity bubble crushed them into unusable wreckage on instinct.

I changed direction, almost crashing into a wall, bracing myself and kicking off. Then I sprinted over to the wall. My right arm extended into a blade and I cut deep into the stone and metal…carving, looking for the controls, and finding…

Finding fuck all.

It was a damn self-contained unit! There wasn't any comm links that I could identify, and I'd smashed it to pieces in my fast blast. I snarled and slashed at it once more, then started looking again. This time, I hurled a bubble when I saw another laser sliding out again but ignored it beyond that.

I needed to be faster; I needed to be quick, to make it through all this time-wasting crap!

The anger that was building in me was normally an issue. Usually, it had to be constrained, be held back. I could never unleash it fully, that red rage, because that was when people got hurt, and badly.

Sometimes the wrong ones.

It was rising, though, second by second and inch by inch that I covered in my search, forcing myself to drop signal repeaters each time I ventured too far from the last. As I went, furious at the delay, somewhere below me the bodies of the innocent and the guilty alike were strip-mined for their second-most precious resource.

The corridors of the ship flashed past me, moving faster and faster. Lasers were crushed, and Ændari lunged out of rooms, ran toward or away from me. Sometimes they even hid. But the one thing they all did was die.

I lashed out in rising rage as I tore past them. Bubbles of gravity snatched them, ripping them free of the floor and lifting them to where a tentacle could grab, stabbing into them. Great explosions of blood and tissue ruptured as they were hit with the force of my furious passage.

Arise: Conqueror

Each one of them was torn apart, fed upon and discarded, their individual nanites dragged free and added to me.

Miles of the ship ran in all directions. I snarled, frantically trying to find my way down, ripping and tearing with gravity as I went. Sections exploded behind me in cascading fountains of sparks and twisted metal.

I heard Ingrid's voice calling to me, then falling silent, accepting that what was happening had to be, and that I was better off cocooned in my anger than sane.

I could feel more nanites getting closer. All I could think was that maybe I'd found a storage area, a pipeline, a vat or *something*. It was building below me. Yet, try as I might, I just couldn't find a damn way down!

I eventually gave up, flipping over and landing hard, skidding. Both my arms flexed into long blades that gleamed in the bright light of the harvester's abandoned halls.

I drove the right one down into the floor, feeling the resistance of the stone and some kind of molecular bonding device. I snarled, pushing harder, digging deeper.

I stabbed the left blade in as well, sawing it up and down. The monomolecular edge enabled it to stay intact and sharp even in this. But to get through as quickly as possible, nanites bled from the blade as well, digging into the cut behind the blade and eating outward.

It took me nearly a minute to cut a straight line all the way through. And all that time, I shouted in fury at the designers, knowing that every second I wasted could be hundreds of lives lost.

The floor was heavily reinforced; each cut cost me long minutes to carve through, and that slowed me horrifically.

Clearly, I'd given the Ændari too much time and notice in the effort of doing this. By the time I'd cut through, instead of finding a vat of ready-to-use nanites as a reward, I'd found a *barracks*.

CHAPTER THIRTY-SEVEN

I was greeted by a barrage of lasers; I cursed, then shouted in fury, working on as they continued to pour fire into me. I tore the last section up, then dropped through.

I landed hard. Desperation filled me as I lashed out at the goddamn battalion that awaited me. The front rows were on their knees, lasers cycling, with their companions behind them, standing in line as well, firing over their heads.

Manipulating gravity, I threw out fields, breaking up their lines. Dozens flipped end over end as gravity reversed and they found themselves upside down or suddenly standing on the ceiling. Others were crushed from their feet, or cried out as sheer tidal forces caught them, hurtling them this way and that.

I staggered back, then forced myself forward. Each step was like I climbed a mountain, with a howling headwind shoving me back. My layers were failing under the barrage faster than I could rebuild them, forcing more and more up, until a wave of warning rolled through me.

I'd used so many nanites that I was getting close to losing a cohesive form, I suddenly realized. Horror rose in me as I was shocked back to sanity from the roaring beast I'd devolved to in my desperation.

I pulled at them, flipping gravity ninety degrees, making them fall. More and more of the firing died as they tried to catch themselves. But all too soon, they were stomping; magnetic clamps activated where they were close enough to metal to make it work.

Others triggered shoulder-mounted jets, twisting around to hover, catching themselves and raising rifles again.

I launched myself forward. The War AI that I'd literally fucking ignored until now came online with my demand to *"Help me!!"* as I slowed time subjectively.

Targets were assessed, probable predictive paths for lasers, targeting recommendations, and the old familiar prompt popped back up, even as tentacles flashed out, stabbing into the nearest bodies that hadn't been kept clear.

I yanked them up and between me and the incoming blasts, holding them in place and tearing nanites free at the same time, fueling my desperate recovery.

Arise: Conqueror

The Devourer dug in, expanding through them and feasting as I made my selection.

Response Level:

Non-Lethal: 1-5

Lethal: 6-10

Please select required response.

"Fucking ten!" I snarled. The entire room pulsed. A prompt popped up and requested "full dimensional access." I approved it. And fuck me sideways with a gerbil dipped in ghost chilies, was *that* an experience.

What the AI had meant by "dimensional access," it turned out, was approval to interact with my armor to move me. I felt it start up, along with the knowledge that I could override it at any time.

I forced myself to trust it, being reduced to a back-seat passenger in my own body for several seconds as gravity on all sides went haywire.

Six fields burst into being, rolling left to right in the hold ahead of me. Then six more, staggered and slightly offset behind and above the first ones.

The first rolled right to left, the second row left to right, and a third group of six more flared into being at the back of the group. They slid forward, then back, dragged through the narrow gaps in the fields that were left by the others' movements.

The result was a gravitational shredder that had only one route to escape, and that was forward, toward me.

As the first of them realized this, I was already closing on them. The bodies I'd lifted into place as shields collapsed as I cored them out from the inside.

The new nanites were great, flooding into me in waves. But there were too few to fight as I normally would, and instead I was down to my own limbs, modified as they were, and a single tentacle.

I lashed out with the tentacle, latching onto the barrel of a rifle the nearest held and yanked. The laser fired repeatedly and burned into my side, digging deeper and deeper and getting dangerously close to the power core before he was in range of my blade.

As soon as he was, though, the tentacle ripped the rifle sideways, pointing it clear as I struck out. My left hand grabbed his shoulder and dragged him forward as my right came up. A high-frequency vibrational punch dagger flowed out to cover my right knuckles.

I punched him in the stomach—once, twice, three times. His armor, designed as it was for ranged combat and to protect against intransient civilians, barely slowed the blade.

Ripping it upward, from the stomach to bisect the heart, I tossed the corpse behind me. A narrow lance of nanites flashed out to tether me to the body and drag it in as I moved for the next.

I reformed my left arm into a shield, angling it to catch as much as possible as the top layers shifted, becoming highly reflective. But in the seconds it took to change, more and more were lost.

The Ændari knew their only chance was to get in close and kill me, and damn, they were working hard at achieving that. They seemed to come from all sides, lasers firing. I flicked my wrist, throwing a glob of nanites over the short distance to splatter across the faceplate of an enemy helmet.

It began to move, running like mercury down the hardened cover and pouring around the chin, arcing up and eating into the armor. It reformed into a spike, lancing up through the underside of the jaw and into his brain.

Concept proven, the AI went mad. A pair of launchers spun up over each shoulder, firing small nanite packages in a blur, even as replacement nanites were siphoned in from the body behind me.

More and more lasers hit me, burning in, slowing my regeneration and rebuilding. But the fight was far from over. As time slowed even further, targets were highlighted in reds for the primary targets, those carrying the heaviest weapons.

Next were the oranges and yellows—assault rifles, grenades, and more.

Last were the greens. And it was almost laughable that the AI viewed those as the ones closest to me, with literal guns pointed at my face, blades stabbing out and more, as the lowest threat to my existence.

An Ændari crashed into my shield arm, clearly more determined than sensible. He wrapped his arms around it, planted a foot on my knee, and fired his shoulder-mounted maneuvering jets, trying to wrench the shield out of the way.

I'd give him an A+ for sheer balls, but the F- for intelligence was really going to be the more memorable of his awards.

As he did that, and I passed a certain threshold in available nanites, three more tentacles slid out of my armor. The tips gleamed and vibrated in a way that only the most fucked-up hentai lover could appreciate…then they started to stab into the surrounding bodies—and not in a fun way.

I read terror in the movement as he wrenched at my arm, kicking and twisting. Then, when he wasn't getting anywhere, he tried to let go, to presumably grab a weapon.

That was when he found that the opposite side of the shield where his fingers were pressed, and the top of my knee where his foot was braced, had now sealed him to me, as the Devourer mauled its way through and into his fingers and feet.

He howled, trying to tear himself free, only to stiffen as a spike of nanites on the front of my shield reformed and punched out, piercing his armor over the heart and spreading, shredding his internals.

He collapsed with a wet grunt. A tearing noise came from his lungs as they were torn into, the last sound he'd ever make.

As they closed the distance, the gravity shredders making sure they couldn't just stay back and pound me, my armor grew more spikes, hurling them outward and into the nearest enemies.

My shoulders fired over and over again; the nanite packets hit, bursting and running to the nearest joints, burrowing through armor and clothing, then flesh.

Arise: Conqueror

Through it all, as the Ændari screamed and fell, I watched with a sense of bemusement.

More and more of them fell by the second. And as they did, Ingrid reached out and spoke to me.

"Steve, so you trust me?"

"You know I do," I replied, almost offended by the question.

"Then I want you to hack the cameras nearby. I need footage of the fight."

"Why?" I asked, confused.

"I don't have time to explain it all, too much to do, but these people need to see this. They need to know that not all hope is lost. Please."

I let the armor and AI continue to lead the fight, and instead started searching, checking the various frequencies and systems that were in sight, before cursing.

Whatever the encryption the Ændari were using to keep their version of Wi-Fi secure, it was goddamn spotless. I knew that there had to be some form of wireless communication going on nearby—there damn well had to be. And yet, despite knowing it had to be here, there was nothing I could see or sense.

I checked myself; I was up to nearly as many nanites as I'd had before I'd entered this goddamn laser-grater, and ordered the production and splitting off of the first autonomous drone.

They were something I'd gained access to with the new drone command and controller route I'd taken. Rather than the larger War variants, which varied from essentially darts to small tanks, to fighters and finally things that would have made the US military en masse propose marriage to me, I went for one of the Sabotage variants.

The larger models were lethal, and now that I was starting to get more and more nanites available, I was definitely going to treat myself to some new toys. But the one I needed right now was a simpler model.

It was the size of a closed fist and was named a "strategic enhanced recon probe." And as well as the small size, it was a simple build, fortunately.

Cheap, too—there'd be a hell of a lot of people in Hollywood who'd be sending me checks when I got back and started selling these fuckers, I thought distractedly, as it lifted free, flew to my right, then slammed into the face of an incoming Ændari.

Neither of us had seen that coming. As his knees went weak, his gun slipping from his hand, I designated him as a prisoner, and watched as the AI adjusted the spinning, death-dealing terror to include that in its plans.

The probe, or drone or whatever, flipped around and banked hard, rocketing off to the side as I designated access to it for Ingrid, feeling it as she linked up and started to guide it.

I also noted the swearing as she tried to aim it, not having the required skillset downloaded, and rammed it into a wall at high speed instead.

"Here!" I sent. A fragment of my Engineering AI download helped me as I wrote a horrifically fast and dirty code to maintain the damn thing and keep it nearby.

By the time I'd done that, the last three Ændari were running for it. A door on the far side of the chamber was already sliding closed, as they panicked and tried to reach it first.

"What are you doing?" Ingrid asked me, seeing the second drone boiling free of my left arm, swelling up like a tumor, only to float free a heartbeat later, still forming its internals.

"Testing!" I replied, grinning to myself as I created another, and another.

The first was morphing now. The simpler internal structures shifted around to create a swept wing design, a power core in the middle, a short rail gun on the top…and best of all? A small pulse generator.

It wasn't powerful, but it didn't need to be.

The main use for the drone as it shimmered, the Conceal ability kicking in, was as a fast recon. And with the various systems still fully forming, it tore off after the fleeing trio, happy to watch and follow them, finding out more about the layout.

I sent a powerful gravitational pulse out in all directions, mapping the floor as best I could. But from here, far too much of the inside looked exactly the damn same.

"Argus, this is a nightmare to navigate," I sent to him. *"You said you've got blueprints. Can you direct me?"*

"Negative," he replied. *"Internal blueprints that have been recovered appear to be inaccurate. Insertion target recommended previously should have delivered you to a central processing area, with quick access to lower levels. The internal layout has been heavily adjusted and reinforced, rendering most details stored as moot."*

"Joy. Okay, well, how the hell do I get down?" I snapped.

"Steve, it looks like there's a passage farther to the west, about fifteen rooms along," Ingrid interrupted. *"That might be where the Ændari are running to as well. I'm not sure. We need to get access to the harvester's internal systems, though. There's definitely something strange here. It's like—"*

"Like what?" I asked after a handful of seconds in silence as I popped three more drones free for a total of six.

Silence.

"Ingrid?" I swallowed hard, reaching back along the connection. The majority of the individual signal repeaters were working fine, but that one had dropped out entirely.

That was both the best-case and worst-case scenario. First, because my automatic instinct was to worry that something had happened to Ingrid, rather than just the signal. Finding that there was a logical and straightforward reason for the connection to fail?

That was a massive relief. It meant Ingrid hadn't just set off an overload and blown herself up or anything on the node. Probably.

The concern?

Something just got close enough to one of the relays, found it, and destroyed it without me sensing anything.

Arise: Conqueror

That wasn't good.

I sent the next of the drones off in that direction, slaving the camera drone to hover near me—stealthed again—and to follow along, recording and ready to broadcast to Ingrid when she connected again.

Then I forced myself to pay attention to the overall layout of the Ouroboros platform so far, dispatching another drone and another as soon as they were complete. Their orders were to map the entire floor as fast as they could, and to report when they found another way down.

I could cut through, and I probably would again at this rate, but if all it did was take me to the next random room, what was the point?

There had to be control facilities somewhere nearby or…

Or did there? The control center I'd seen on approach was heavily shielded—too heavily shielded for me to have punched through and not destroy it with the level of energy released.

That was why I'd picked a theoretically easier path, and I'd landed where I had. Now I was discovering the entire place was a maze, one that was heavily armored to keep me from just cutting my way through. No matter how hard I looked, I wasn't finding anything I could damn well use.

It was like someone had set out to make a city, with each level full of all the things it could possibly ever need. Then they'd wrapped the whole thing in a layer of armoring that was frankly insane, and made it mobile, but left it empty of everything but assholes.

If this hadn't been deployed to literally eat worlds, and had instead been used to say, harvest asteroids and so on? This could have been an amazing invention, one that could change the flow of any civilization.

It was large enough and from the details that Argus had shared, it was certainly powerful enough, not to mention advanced to the level that it could literally take a rocky asteroid in and churn out high-tech machinery at the other end.

Something that could do that, and was basically automated? There was no end to the possibilities. And even knowing that to kick-start the nanite production needed nanites?

There had to be a better way than it was using. But even if there wasn't, if the only way was this, then how the hell had the damn thing ever stopped? After all, once it was kick-started and working, you'd just grab another moon or whatever, right?

Surely once it had enough nanites, and it was chewing its way through a goddamn planet, it'd be able to make more continually from there. It was one of the last pieces of the puzzle that didn't quite fit, and it niggled at me.

Either way, though, trying to find my way through the maze of corridors, the halls with their massive, vaulted ceilings, and the strange, twisting passages that seemed to lead nowhere was infuriating.

It was like trying to find a specific door to a party in an entire city, without a map, and all the time there was music from the damn party seeping up through the rocks below you.

Fortunately, though, I might have a guide now.

I lifted him into the air. The minute changes in gravity that were required to make him float at my will were unconscious and automatic now, and he screamed as he felt himself being moved.

He'd been struggling with his helm on the floor, the front bashed in. Clearly, whatever systems they had inside to let him see out weren't working anymore.

Reaching out a hand, I slapped it onto the front of the helm. Nanites boiled up and poured forth to coat it, as tentacles grabbed his wrists and ankles, bending them back and immobilizing him.

My nanites ate through the armoring of the helmet, breaking it down, then the underlayers, section by section, stripping it away until the hate-filled face of an Ændari who could barely be out of his teens stared back at me.

"You'll suffer for this." Those were the first words out of his mouth. Facing a creature out of his legends that had him pinned and at its mercy…and the first thing he did was threaten me?

There really was no hope for the race.

I worked a dozen needles through his armor and into his flesh, ripping nanites free. As I waited, my drones mapped the floor out at high speed.

"Where's the nearest control facility?" I asked him, getting a glare, then having him spit at me in response. "All right." I nodded. "You want to play it that way?"

I grasped the stubby horns on either side of his head. They each had barely four inches of growth from his temple, and I twisted slowly, watching as his almost humanoid, almost deerlike face distorted in pain. His eyes bulged, and the weird double pupils shifted, one swelling as another shrank to a pinprick.

He whimpered as I fed my own nanites back into him, burning through his defenses and claiming more and more of his in exchange. My own spread, infiltrating his body, filtering into and surrounding major muscle groups.

"Tell me," I demanded. Starting with his feet, my nanites began to break layers of muscles and fat free, making his skin curl away from the flesh beneath.

I peeled him, layer by layer, making his own muscles tear themselves free as I stared into his eyes. "The control center!" I roared at him.

"Above!" he howled, when he couldn't take anymore. "It's above!"

"How do I get down to the lower floors!" I demanded, and he half laughed, half sobbed in response.

"You can't!" he wailed.

"What?"

"You can't!" he repeated. "It's a maze, a trap and storage—" His voice rose into an inarticulate screech as both of his lower leg bones, longer and finer than a human's, split lengthways, fragmenting under the punishment I was inflicting.

I stopped the nanites and shook him. "What do you mean?" I barked.

"It's a trap!" he admitted. "It's designed to hold you, to slow you so you can't…"

"So I can't stop the harvest!" I snarled. Understanding filled me. That was why the walls, the floors, and ceiling were so goddamn hard to break through.

Arise: Conqueror

That was why I couldn't find anything, or any damn controls or systems I could hack.

They had to be buried deep, because something like this needed to have them. But if this section—hell, if most of these levels were just mazes to trap and trick the world's defenders?

Those sneaky bastards!

It'd worked on me, and that pissed me off an insane amount, even as I reached out for the drones that I'd already dispatched.

The Ændari they'd been following hadn't gone into a goddamn room, either, or used a goddamn door. They'd run at a sodding wall and it'd split open for them! No wonder I wasn't finding things—this fucking place was a labyrinth!

Cursing, I looked down at the figure I'd been clutching and ground my teeth together. Distracted as I'd been, I'd clearly been communicating with my nanites on a more basic level, because not only was he dead…he was *very* dead.

I'd twisted a time or two too hard, so, yeah…

I dropped the bleeding mess onto the floor, recalling four of the drones, and lifted back into the air. Then I tore back up through the hole I'd made in the roof, heading straight for the entrance I'd smashed into the floor.

It was time to goddamn finish this!

The corridors and passages flashed past in a blur, almost too fast to see as the drones fell in behind and ahead of me. I'd stripped the battalion below of their nanites, and despite how close the fight had been, I was now feeling better.

I had a plan, I had a fuckload of nanites, and—

The corner I took should have led into a passage that then led to a huge hall, one that, according to the mental map I'd made as I went, was circular. From there, there were eight doors that led off in different directions: two leading up and two down, with four seemingly flat.

That was when I found out why the hell I'd been cut off from Ingrid, and why I'd not had any warning.

The passage I took that led into the hall seemed tighter. But it wasn't until I was more than halfway through it that I realized that it wasn't my imagination.

The walls were literally closing in! I sent a pulse ahead, even as one of the rearmost drones behind me reported the gap between it and the nearby wall as being in the danger zone, and the one that'd been in the lead burst out the far side of the room and reported the same thing happening behind it.

Thirty-seven millimeters, thirty-four, thirty…

I poured more speed in on instinct, bursting into the circular hall, and flipped over as I saw what waited for me ahead, even as the connections behind me grew fainter and fainter.

With half a second left, I ordered the remaining drones that weren't in the passage yet to stop and to trigger their pulse generators. I landed hard, skidding to a halt, and stared at the figure that stood before me.

The remaining passages slammed shut with a thunderous boom, the one directly behind me filled with a tortured crunching of metal as well, until the power core of the pair of drones caught inside detonated.

The blast of superheated plasma barely made it out of the wall before it was cut off. A shield flickered on around the room, pressing inward.

All those details were background, though, compared to the figure that stood in the center of the room.

My repeater was by its feet, fortunately now shut off from the rest of the signal. But even as I watched the nanites puddle up and flow like liquid quicksilver across their boot and up their leg, I couldn't help but curse.

I'd forgotten the most important detail of this fight.

I wasn't just facing the Ændari.

The figure that stood across from me looked like an Ændari warrior, all right: tall, muscular, but thinner than a human, with a pair of antlers that grew from either temple. Stretching out, they must have reached half a meter each. And if the Ændari worked out rank like the stags of Earth did, this fucker must have been a king at least.

He had twenty prongs or points or whatever, curling up and down, out and back, and strung between them were golden chains and gleaming red rubies.

His face was a mixture of human and deer, teeth smaller but pointed—clearly, he was a meat eater—with double pupiled eyes, and a skin tone that was just the wrong side of cream, looking unhealthy and closer to green than anything.

The armor he wore was bone-white and black as pitch, depending on where you looked. All the overlapping plates gleamed, seeming to float atop the undersuit he wore.

Twin longswords stood upright atop their tips, with his hands wrapped around the hilts. As he waited for me, the grin that covered his face showed he was excited for the fight.

All in all, he'd have barely registered to me, under other circumstances, considering he was clearly an enemy combatant and ready for a fight.

No, the detail that stood out for me was when the puddle of nanites—*my goddamn nanites*—flowed up and into him, causing a slight ripple as the armor over his leg absorbed it all.

"You," I said softly.

"Me," Shan'Gai agreed, nodding almost amiably.

CHAPTER THIRTY-EIGHT

"How the fuck did you get here?" I asked him, stepping to the right, moving to slowly circle him, examining him from every angle as he watched in amusement.

"I've been here all along," he responded.

"And out in space?"

He nodded. "There too."

"So."

"So."

"You mad?" I asked him.

He cocked his head to one side. "Point of clarification; do you mean as in insane, or angry?"

He seemed far too fucking calm considering everything that'd happened so far.

"Both."

"Angry? Well, *yes*. You've ruined plans that took millennia to enact, and for you to come along right now? To rise just as I'm weakened by hibernation and hunger? It's almost poetic, as if the metaverse has a sense of honor after all."

"Honor?"

"You don't know it? Pity. Most of your kind do. It makes them laughably easy to manipulate."

"I know what honor is, you dickbag. I don't understand why you think the universe has a sense of it," I snapped.

"Because just as I remove the last of my competition, ready to throw off the old shackles, it gives the beleaguered fools a final chance. A last vague hope for their future, before I harvest them all."

"You think the universe brought me forward just to fuck with your plans?" I asked.

"Metaverse," he corrected, baring his teeth in what definitely wasn't a smile. "Universe is one, little creature—meta is all."

"Meta is an attempt at shitty rebranding and to make people think you're smarter than you are." I snorted. "The meaning of 'universe' is the sum of everything, everything seen, believed and conceived of, all in one. Call it creation, reality, or a fucking cheese sandwich, though…I don't give two fucks. Why are you here, why aren't you insane, and why are you doing this?"

"Am I insane?" he mused, then shrugged, the action snakelike in the flow of muscles and armor. "Perhaps, some of me always was, certainly."

"Some?"

"You wish to know or are you playing for time?" A sly smile curled the edge of his mouth. "Because I'm here to stop you. You can stand here and talk to me, or you can fight me, but you cannot escape this room. Either way, we win."

"Brave of you to think I give a shit about your opinion," I replied. "But go on then. I'll tear you a new arsehole in a minute, but before I do, let's have an evil villain monologue."

"We're not evil," he replied. "That you believe so shows just how flawed you are, young one."

"Go on." I gestured in encouragement, waving my hand for him to go on, even as he apparently missed the single raised finger that I was waving with.

"When our primary body was young and foolish, it too believed in honor and depravity, in good and evil. Now we know better. There is only hunger."

His eyes flashed, and I noticed the ripple that had been the nanites that had flowed up to join his lower leg now reached his jaw, seeming to move through him as they slid up and into his head.

He let loose an almost sexual groan, then smiled, relaxing and shaking his head.

"One day, you could have understood, young one. Perhaps we would have even taught you, have shared. Certainly, we'd hoped that you could be reasoned with, and even sent out into the dark to raise up your own territories.

"Unfortunately, you chose to try to steal, to poach, rather than raise, and now you must pay for that transgression. Either way, though, this is for the best."

"Territories…" I nodded. "That's what the UC and the Ændari are to you, aren't they?"

"Food," he agreed.

"Why?" I asked. "Is it the Devourer tree? Did you unlock too much too quick, and it did this to you? Were you sane and fucking reasonable before you…I don't know, got your dick stuck in the plug socket of life?"

"We were sane, and certainly parts of us still are now, though others are far from it," he agreed. Only his head moved to watch me as I circled him. "Others are less so. You contacted our primary body. After all, usually we'd not permit that. One of us is always aboard, and ready to communicate with the lesser beings, but now? With our fleets dispatched and our feast at hand? Even we cannot be everywhere at once."

"Why?" The word came out harder and more desperate than I intended. "Why the hell did you do this?"

"Because we can," he replied, teeth bared. "Because we want to, and because we *hunger*."

With that, he spun to his right and lunged at me. The tip of the longsword flashed toward my face.

I twisted; my right arm came up and batted it aside, even as I punched out, slamming a fist into his side.

Arise: Conqueror

That was where it all went wrong.

The blade ran like liquid, reforming and twisting into a khopesh, then hooking around the back of my arm and yanking me in closer. The armor where I'd punched crackled like tinfoil, flexing inward and letting my fist sink deeper, before the "flesh" and body of Shan'Gai locked in around me, biting down.

"Such a shame," he murmured. His own body flowed like quicksilver, as instead of being half turned away from me, in a heartbeat he reformed, to face me straight on. "You're too young, little one. Too attached to one form, to a body that is ultimately meaningless."

I yanked, twisted, then snarled; my fist reformed into a blade. I shoved forward, digging it deeper into the figure before me and ripped upward. Tentacles flashed out, forming solid barriers that blocked the incoming khopesh as he tried to dig it into my back.

As I did that, his second longsword stabbed forward. For a heartbeat, I saw it coming, aimed right for my heart.

Then I was moving, forcing myself to change as he did, opening a passage through my chest, and letting the sword plunge through. When it met no resistance, he tore it sideways instead, trying to cut me, only to have my form part and reknit ahead and behind it.

For a handful of seconds, we were a blur. My time compression kicked in and the War AI sprang to life on instinct. Fists flew, morphing into blades, hammers, flails, hooks, and more. Tentacles latched on and were attacked; spears of nanites surged forward into each other's bodies as we tried to tear sections free and inject our own control into the other, while cutting the enemy out.

After almost a solid minute, he stepped back. I did the same, eyes darting, mind racing as I tried to process everything that had just happened.

If I'd not had the AI, that fight would have been over—and as it was, it'd come close. Far too close, considering that the blur of injecting nanites on my side were inexperienced at this level, and on his...

"You should have beaten me," I whispered, staring at him and seeing the curl of the lip in pleasure at my admission.

He took it for an admission of defeat, I saw, rather than what it was. A fuckin' question.

"Of course," he agreed. "And I will yet, but I was testing you."

"No," I disagreed. "No, you weren't. You attacked me because you couldn't help yourself. You couldn't say no to a meal, no matter how stupid it was to try to grab it."

"You barely survived—was it really 'stupid'?" His lip curled in derision.

"Yeah." I nodded. "Yeah, it was, because now I know what you are."

"Oh?"

"You're a shadow." I said it even as the realization came to me. A half second behind the words coming out, my mind made more connections. "You're literally just a shadow of Shan'Gai, not really him. That's how you've been manipulating the Ændari and the UC. You said that you're usually aboard him, that you don't 'let' anyone communicate with him without one of you to do it. There's not enough of you to be with him and to guide the Ændari fleet, or to control the harvester… Fuck, that's why there's no control runs or systems for me to goddamn hack!"

The look on his face made it clear that he wasn't happy I was putting this together, but he stayed silent.

"It's you! You're in control of the harvester, or one of you is! You can change your form, you have control over your nanites like that, but…you're locked out of full access!"

It was all falling into place, and I couldn't help but say it as I saw it. "One of you here to control the harvester, one aboard him to keep him under control, one on the fleet… Why not the UC—" I shook my head as I went on.

"You don't *need* one of you aboard the UC fleet because you always planned to kill them all. Why have one of you on their flagship in command or whatever, and then lose them? Also, the UC would ask too many questions!"

"They would have all died anyway." He shrugged nonchalantly. "If we left them to fight it out, they'd have killed each other. Perhaps one of them would rise to the top, but either way, most would die. Why permit the losses? Instead, we cull the herd, raise one up here, create a threat there, feed them both information, and drain them both of all they can use to fight the other.

"Then tell their leaders that they won, but that almost all died in the process, create a heroic tale, deposit a few life pods that were too far out to see anything or broken remains, and then leave them. They spend the next century or two frantically rebuilding, and they blame each other over and over again. When they rise too far? A plague to push them all back down." His face twisted in anger. "For thousands of years, it worked! I fed, I raised and protected my herds, and then Ort'a-Me'Ach returned!"

"Ort…" I shook myself and shut up, knowing this was important. Sure, it was the hidden history of the fucking galaxy, but what was more important was that the prick kept talking.

I had a plan, and time to waste until it was ready.

"Another Devourer!" he snapped. "She returned unexpectedly, injured, telling tales of the dark places and begging for my help. I gave it. I healed her, and I shared my stores, allowing her access to my vats to feed, only to have her throw it all in my face as she read the memories of food!"

He spat, gesturing wildly.

"What did it matter where the food came from, where my builders had once been? I was sharing them, an act that went against every instinct, and still I did it. When she confronted me, weak as she was, I told her what I'd done and why, explained the waste that the two sides were leaving, showed the numbers! The numbers *never* lie! Trillions dead and almost nothing left to be recovered from the battlefields. But after I'd had the time to insert my controls in the fleets? I could shut them down! Render their ships cold and dead, then feed on them as they tried to recover. Food that was being wasted was now useful. And what more could the prey beg me for, but a meaningful death?"

Arise: Conqueror

"You killed their ships?" My heart sunk as I considered that the rest of his form was out there and could soon be facing off against the UC. If he could shut their ships down…

"For a short time." He gestured as if it were unimportant. "Too much work to make it a permanent shutdown…too many prying eyes. Instead, a worm, a burrower that moves from system to system when unleashed."

"A virus." I nodded. "You put a virus in them."

"Some fall to it, some don't." He shrugged. "They all come to me in the end."

"But she didn't see it that way, did she?" I prompted.

He cocked his head to one side, clearly wondering why I was talking instead of attacking, but content to waste my time if I was.

"She did not," he agreed, after taking a deep breath and seemingly mastering himself again. "She reached out to the others, burned through billions of my builders, using their power to send a pulse to the deepest realms and sharing my secrets with all and sundry. Then she collapsed, exhausted, still injured, and for the first time, in our rage, I fed on my own kind."

He shrugged.

"That was it, of course—when the meat is the sweetest available, why would I feed on anything else? So from then on, once I'd drained her to the brink of death, I trapped her in a cage that she could never escape from, and assumed her form and identity, showing her as me, and me as her to them.

"As the others would return, I led them to her, showing them, and when they thought they looked down on my trapped and weakened form, I struck."

"What happened to her, and to drive you mad?" I asked again.

"The madness…we had already created additional forms, scaled to creep into places that we could not go otherwise—a hundred and more of them. Then, the greatest of indignities. The remaining Devourers struck at me from a distance, rather than coming to confront me directly. One of them, a master of the system, tore me from it, rendering me trapped in limbo."

"You could create things, and use some of your abilities, but most of them were locked out?" I asked, and he gestured as if it were meaningless.

"I was forced from the brink of godhood, but all that did was cost me time. As I learned more of our kind, I learned to kill them. Now I alone know all, and besides you and I, none still exist. I have you and your companions to thank for allowing my ascension again."

"Why?"

"You opened the node." He smiled evilly, and my eyes widened as I realized what he was saying.

"You," I whispered.

"Me," he agreed. "Ændari and Devourer, the peak of both. And now that the node is open? I can access it, unlock my abilities again and reform. I will be whole, and there's nothing you can do to stop me."

"Keep telling yourself that," I muttered, the last details falling into place. "So why are you not mad? The main one, the first of you, he's barely capable of using a drinking straw, but you…"

"We were already separate, but because he was paranoid even before the change, as each of us were formed and split off, a baffle was created in the system, a way to prevent updates or hacking from one to another."

"He didn't even trust his own fucking clones." I nodded, smiling. "Fuck me, it finally makes sense. How he's all cunning one second, and barely able to stop picking his nose the next. Okay, second last question; what happened to Ort…to the first Devourer who found you?"

"We ate her."

"She's dead?" I asked.

"Partially."

"So she could come back?" I nodded. "Okay, so you've been stripping worlds for nanites all this time… what happened to those nanites?"

"Our primary form requires them, or he will cease functioning."

"And you never just decided to let him die?"

"Our fate is linked."

"Gotcha. So he dies, you die. But if there were hundreds of you and now there aren't, you can die and it doesn't flow back up the pipe to him? No? Nice. Okay, you want the nanites still, and they what? Make you stronger?"

"It is built into us that we hunger." He shrugged. "That was your final question?" He reformed and hefted his blades again.

"No, sorry, just a new one that occurred to me, but okay, final question before I kill you. Why don't you feed on all the nanites here? The ones below?"

"They are corrupt and must be cleansed." He smiled. "Yours, though, are sweet and pure."

"Ah, you fuckers can feed on Devourer, but not on the usual people. Gotcha. And even if you collect a billion worlds' worth of nanites, it'll never be enough, because he's mad and you're stuck feeding only on your own kind."

"Now that your curiosity is finally sated, are you ready to die?" he asked, before sneering. "And were you planning to use your little toys?"

He slashed his sword sideways, cutting through the nearest stealthed drone to him and smashing it from the air.

"Stealth doesn't work because they're nanite-based, and so are you. You can sense them." I nodded. "Thanks for that. Saves me getting caught out later."

"Oh?"

"Yeah, so first of all, catch." I pressed my hand to my stomach, grinning at the look on his face as the layers of nanites that had been concealing the power core flowed back, showing it off. I palmed it, then threw it to him, enjoying the look of anger and fear that flooded his features as he recognized a power core right on the edge of detonation.

I'd altered it into a sphere shape, and left the outside solid but coated in my nanites, while the inside was right on the edge of critical, essentially being a tiny nuclear hand grenade.

"Make any changes to it, and it'll detonate," I promised him.

"You'll die with me!" he snarled, staring from the ball of barely enclosed nuclear fury in his palm to me.

Arise: Conqueror

"I would, but you see that button on the top?" I asked, and he nodded at the only difference in the otherwise perfect sphere. "I really wouldn't push it if I were you."

Then I stood tall, held my arms out to the sides, and bowed, palming the drone that I'd built for Ingrid and the watching folks at home to take with me.

I straightened up and quoted from a book my ex had once read to me. "So long, and thanks for all the fish." I smiled, then I unleashed the stored power I'd been holding.

With the nearby pulsing gravitational marker clearly in my mind, I gravity jumped, under my own stored power, two hundred meters from the room we'd both been trapped in. I even triggered the bomb as I vanished.

CHAPTER THIRTY-NINE

I appeared hovering in midair, fifty meters or so off the upper hull of the harvester, and let out a great burst of relieved air, even as the connection to Ingrid popped back into my mind.

I released the drone, letting it dump its memory banks to her, and grinned uncontrollably as the button on the top of the nuclear hand grenade distantly pressed *itself* with a loud fart noise.

God, I was such a child at times, I knew, but the sudden explosion—that the shields tried desperately to contain—still shook the massive creation.

The section that the room had been in was almost left intact, its own shields having been designed to hold me no matter what I attempted. But clearly they were neither advanced enough nor tuned to prevent gravity jumps—a mode of transport not exactly known for its localized and specific nature—and they hadn't taken into account a lunatic with a power core, either.

"Steve... Shan'Gai just went crazy!" Ingrid told me, having been caught up reviewing the feed in all its mad glory, and then from the control room of the node—presumably—she'd seen Shan'Gai having a fit.

She shared it with me, and I saw him drifting sideways. The smooth hull of his ship-form was suddenly covered in crinkles as arms tore free and lashed at space around it; engines fired wildly but in uncontrolled bursts, and then the Ændari fleet that had been powering straight toward me started to fire.

They unleashed volley after volley of missiles, flushing their banks and continuing as quickly as they could reload. Hundreds of missiles became thousands, and they were all aimed at the planet I was on.

"Fucker's got serious anger management issues," I muttered.

"Steve, no matter what happens in the universe, of all the things you could possibly accuse another of, that's the pot calling the kettle black."

"Yeah, well, I love you too," I assured her, before grinning. *"You see the jump?"*

"A gravity jump?" she asked me, having just apparently reached that point. *"Steve, you can jump? Personally, I mean..."*

"I can do it without a ship," I confirmed. *"And in close to a planet. I need a pulse marker to highlight the location for me to go to, but yeah."*

Arise: Conqueror

"Oh gods, I'm never going to be safe in the shower again, am I?" she asked, half amused and, because our minds were linked, half hopefully.

"Nope," I agreed. *"Your defenses good?"*

She nodded, pouring a load of blurred details into my mind, as well as the structures that they'd been able to make from the limited scrap available, now that the BWVs were mostly able to build as well.

"Damn, I pity the fool who tries to get through that..." I said, realizing that "meat grinder" was an understatement. These were the interstellar equivalent of the marines, with a new ability to make all the mad traps they'd imagined or encountered over the years. All out of utter scrap.

"We'll hold out. Now, can you stop the harvester?" she asked.

I nodded, knowing that by the change in her tone, and by the senses that she was sharing with me, that she was recording and broadcasting this bit.

"I can," I assured her, turning to look into the camera. "I'm going to tear this fucker a new arsehole."

With that, I reached up to the rest of my body, hanging high overhead in orbit, still restructuring itself, and I issued a series of very simple orders.

Then, as the new kinetic launch systems began to bubble up, I made the most out of the nanites I'd already consumed and started to make additional drones.

I knew this bit for anyone watching around the universe was going to be boring. After all, they couldn't see the insanely complicated changes I was carrying out in my body and my ship.

What they could see, though, was the shields around me that were starting to reconstitute. The drones burst free of my left hand, each barely the size of my fist, before being fired in through the entry wound of my earlier arrival.

They were a mixture of the earlier design with the Conceal ability and pulse generator inbuilt, as well as obviously propulsion and so on. Where they differed? There was no gun on these.

The last model I'd made with a miniature rail gun, and not one of those fuckers had gotten a shot off. So, scrapping that, I instead used the space to scale up the small power core and made it into a more easily redlined bomb.

It's so much *fun* when the only limit to your madness is easily replenished.

Five made it through the reforming shields before they were too thick to pass through, and I accepted that. It wasn't as if the shields were a real issue here, after all.

Turning and examining the upper sections of the harvester, I noted the raised control tower that was my overall target now, then started searching the area around it.

The internal structure of the harvester was substantial, there was no denying that, but the ruins of the nearby section where I'd set my little nuke off proved that although they were strong, they weren't *that* strong.

The outer shields? Yup. They were powerful, but they'd not figured out a way to have the shields extend through the gravitational branes. And as such, with my new ability, they weren't worth considering.

All I needed to do was get a single drone inside the control area, and I could jump through those shields without issue.

That meant those shields needed to be down long enough for me to get through myself, making the drone plan pointless, or I needed them down for a very short period of time, while nobody was paying attention to the drones sneaking in.

That was doable, as I damn well knew that whichever version of Shan'Gai was controlling the harvester was going to be *very* fixated on me right now.

The drones were already burning through the air inside the harvester below me, working to get as close as possible to the secure areas.

High above, the kinetic launch systems came online. The first spears bulged up and out—nefindium tipped—they'd hit the shields and shred them.

The detonation as one of them hit would be like a directed nuclear explosion. And hit it too hard? They'd crack the harvester like an egg.

Hell, hit the *planet* too hard and they'd do that.

No, the secret was going to be moderation.

Only the tip was nefindium, the remainder being titanium and tungsten, ensuring that the rest would shatter and convert primarily into energy.

That energy would badly strain the shields, but not tear them apart like wet tissue paper.

That was when the drones inside and below me that were essentially fast-moving, invisible nukes would take their turns going off.

My plan was that between the two, I'd have rolling failures of the shields. And either way, I'd definitely have the attention of the asshole-in-chief.

Once I had him watching me, instead of the second flight of drones, I had them.

The drones would slide through and start exploring the sections I could reach of the control area. And then, once they'd gotten as close as they could? I'd set off a second wave of explosions if need be to weaken the structure and get the remaining drones inside.

Then it was as simple as jump in, and fuck that shit up.

The mad bastard before had all but told me that there was one of them in command of the harvester still, and for them to be in full control? They had to actually be a part of the harvester, I was betting.

That was why only one of them had come for me earlier. I suspected the second one couldn't actually move, and that for all intents and purposes, he *was* the harvester.

It was also why I couldn't detect the communication methods, why I couldn't hack in somewhere or find sections that were vulnerable. It was like if someone had tried to hack my ship—with me as the control method, they'd never be able to find a panel or anything they'd recognize, because the individual configuration of my nanites was whatever I wanted them to be.

I could have cut through control runs entirely made of the damn things, and if they were configured right, even knowing nanites as well as I did, they could have hidden from me.

The first waves of the broadcast that Ingrid was sending out washed over me. Again I saw the hundreds of thousands of people in nearby, already damaged cities, and the millions of panicking people on the planet look up and hope once more.

They saw sections of the fights I'd already had, most from my point of view as I'd managed to tag those into the burst I'd sent to her. But there were also sections from the drone recording, and now, as high overhead the second and third kinetic spears came online, I couldn't help but hold my hands out to the sides, floating there, over the partly damaged hull.

I'd sent a pair of drones out in different directions—one up and out, one around and down—creating points that I'd be able to jump to when I was ready, giving myself space to ride out the incoming blast wave. Then I grinned, unable to help myself as the fourth and fifth spears came online, and I designated the upper hull in a five-pointed star pattern around the control center.

Then I fired.

They launched one after the other, firing hard and hitting the upper edge of the atmosphere seconds later. A corona of flames blurred together into a single scream of incoming fire.

Humans had once heralded the wrath of the ancient gods. The fire of the heavens that destroyed Sodom and Gomorrah in the Old Testament, and ten thousand other records—all were based around the same simple concept: make something from outside the atmo hit it at speed, then punch down into your target.

I locked onto the higher of the two distant drones, and taking the camera version with me, I jumped us both, appearing almost ten miles distant, staring at the huge monstrosity that still filled the world for me, but the impact zone was farther away now.

The drones I'd sent blurring through the internal routes had already passed by a dozen traps, flashing over prepared positions filled with Ændari troops, all ready to open fire.

Well, they were going to get a fucking surprise, all right. I grinned to myself, staying where I was long enough to be sure the enemy had found me.

The closest lasers and point defenses had awoken almost as soon as I'd appeared. My shoulders bulged as stubby rail guns flowed up, locking on and opening fire with high-powered bursts.

The nearest few exploded before they could open fire on me. I grinned wider, as the last of the five drones signaled it had minimum safe distance now from the others.

Then I jumped again.

This time, as the air around me screamed, torn into the rift in reality that I burst free of, I was ready.

The drone vaulted free of my hand, leaping upward to hover near the ceiling as the War AI accepted my designation of seven for the situation.

I wanted it to be maximum lethality, but I needed it to be visceral and fast while providing a show for the people of this world. I needed it to give them hope, as their hated invaders screamed and begged.

Even with that lower level of lethality—the higher I went, the more efficient, but less showy it seemed—the fight was barely worth noting.

I'd burst from the warp in the middle of their numbers, both arms ending in blades, tentacles deployed and razor tipped, and with the rail guns on my shoulders switched to firing darts of compressed nanites.

They were solid and sharp right up until they hit their target. Then in the third of a second it took to punch through their armor, the dart converted into a flowing fractal pattern of nanites that erupted in all directions.

As they were inside the bodies of my enemies by this time, the result was…messy.

I spun and danced—there were no better words for it—as I moved in time to a beat only I heard, slicing and dicing my enemies as they screamed and panicked.

Ingrid spliced the feeds, both from the drone and the section I chose to share from my POV, into a single cohesive broadcast, and damn, the traumatized people of Scorpio-3 gloried in it.

Each blow, each cut and stab, every commitment of my effort resulted in the death of the enemy, and as I did it, I was already draining the dead.

My shroud rolled over the corpses, tearing nanites free and feeding them into me, as more and more drones burst free in turn, rocketing off.

This was the pattern that followed for the next thirty seconds, and four separate fights.

A drone would reach a concentration of the enemy, confirm minimum safe distance from the others in case I chose to detonate one of them, then I'd jump to it.

As soon as I appeared, blades whirling, the drone would streak away again, moving to the next and the next.

The lead drone at this point finally finished mapping out the sections we could reach and confirmed that it couldn't get any closer to the control center.

There were only a handful of seconds before the incoming god-rods would land. I triggered the first drone detonation, crouching and bracing. The shroud flowed back over me and sunk in around, creating a solid shield that held me safe inside.

When all I felt was a small shudder, I grimaced, then released the protective coating, leaping to the next group of Ændari. As I did that—appearing and stabbing out, twin blades puncturing the nearest enemies through the sternum, then yanking them in close, using them as shields—the next drone roared through the hole the last detonation had created.

The next section that was revealed was heavily reinforced, with narrower corridors filled with weapons platforms, automated turrets, and scanners.

As the drone screamed past, the sensors took note. More distant defenses activated, already filling the corridor with focused fire, tracking hard to catch the incoming bomb.

They were too late, though.

Knowing from the predictions the War AI was giving me that the drone wasn't likely to make it far, I triggered its detonation. The explosion from that one cleared the corridors and sent cracks and spidering fractal damage radiating out in all directions.

Then the first god-rod arrived.

That, I felt.

The impact shook the entire harvester. Alarms screamed throughout the construct as the walls and floors rang like a bell. Knowing that I had less than a second before the second impact, additional anchors burst free from me, latching onto the walls and floor nearby. As the Ændari nearby tried to catch their balance and lock weapons on me, I ducked and covered, the shroud flowing up and around me again.

There was maybe just enough time for the brightest of them to see that something was very, very wrong, and then the entire harvester bounced again.

The third of my drones was past the damaged section the second had just eviscerated. And as soon as it reached a section that was too heavily protected for it to make it through? It detonated as well.

The explosion came at almost the same time as the third spear of the gods arrived, and by now the shields that protected the control areas were having serious issues.

Not one of these weapons was enough to overcome everything, not even for a very short time, but from above and below, ripping out entire sections of needed infrastructure, they were causing severe consequences.

The shields were already flickering, most of the harvester's protection being cut to protect the brain, and that was when the fourth spear arrived.

It punched deep. The shields barely held it back, but they couldn't keep the entire force on the outside.

The armor around the point of impact cratered. The shields flickered and blurred, crackling explosions of red lightning dancing across the hull, even as the detonation and conversion of so much matter into energy sent winds from the devil's curry-tainted asshole screaming forth.

The Ændari around me were all stunned and battered now, the nearest walls liberally splattered and repainted with their blood. They filled the air with their screams as the shroud flowed out and over them, absorbing and enveloping.

The fifth and final impact from the god-rods came then, tearing through the damaged and flickering shields, then punching deep into the superstructure.

It detonated as the others had. The tip remained intact and for the first time continued on, as the "shaft" part of the spear shattered, sliding apart and penetrating the armor on all sides in a wash of fragments.

The titanium and tungsten tore into the armor, shredding it and bringing hellfire with them.

The fourth drone burst through the remains of the last three's annihilation, and into the lower section of the raised control area, then broadcast back to me, showing me a fast and dirty map of the surrounding expanse.

As soon as it did that, I forced out four more to join that one, the one that was close behind it, and the remaining drone that was outside and now closing on the underside of the harvester as well.

That done, I straightened, pulled in the shroud, leaving the dead and dying on all sides, and then jumped, blinking from the corridor I'd been in, into the lowest level of the tower.

The surrounding area made it damn clear that it wasn't part of the original design. Or, that if it was? It'd been heavily augmented.

As I appeared, the floor was still bouncing, and the walls and ceiling were spiderwebbed with cracks. But the clearest point? They looked to be made of something much simpler, concrete or similar, instead of the solid marble that I'd seen elsewhere.

When Shan'Gai had remodeled these areas, he'd clearly gone for the shields over everything approach, and I totally got that. After all, the "just in case" low tech side here? It was six meters thick. That was behind already armored and molecular bonded marble and metal, so yeah. I kinda understood the confidence in it.

The shields were down, though, and my portable nukes had fucked up the last of the defenses, leaving me inside the perimeter, and I was going to make the most of it.

The drones were following me now—most of them, anyway—and I could distantly sense the cheering and prayers that followed from the locals.

The remaining two drones that were ahead were already concealed, rocketing up a large tower structure, passing huge shield generators that were even now being repaired and forced into working.

I split my attention between leaping into the air and hurtling after them, and examining the underside of the harvester, now that the drone could scan it.

It was miles across, and taking time to resolve clearly. But what was clear was that to make anything on this scale, you had to accept weaknesses against smaller devices.

There were turrets, shields, great projectors, and more all constantly sweeping the underside. But the very design of the harvester gave me the best cover I could ask for.

The huge legs were dragged inward individually, churning up the ground and sea below, tearing great swathes of matter. The secondary claws and gravity field generators took over then, filtering and drawing matter upward and into the maw.

Underneath the structure, there were great lines of matter floating free. Beams lanced out and carved sections apart, refined metals being torn out of the mass and filtered to one intake section, rock and ores to another…

Then I saw the bodies.

Hundreds, *thousands* of them floated in dedicated lines. Shredded remains of dozens of species—animals and sapiens—tumbled endlessly, slamming into each other and being dragged upward, toward a distant, clearly dedicated processing point.

I almost flew into a wall seeing that. For a few seconds, it was all I could do to get control of my flight again and not blink across to the drone.

Arise: Conqueror

The reason I didn't? They were almost all dead already, and those that weren't…if I killed the tractor beams, they'd tumble to their deaths. There was no way I could save them all. It wasn't possible, it just wasn't. It was…

"Save a single life, and you save the entirety of the world…"

The thought, memory maybe, came out of nowhere. I had no clue where it was from. A book? A movie? A line from a game? Genuinely no clue. But the thought shook me, and I couldn't help but snarl as it conflicted with everything that I knew I needed to do.

If I saved even one of those people in there, if they were still alive, which considering the shit they'd have to have gone through to end up in that beam? Then yeah. I would be saving an entire world.

Their world.

My parents were shitebags. I'd stab either in the face with no issue. Hell, my only annoyance would be that I'd have to lower myself to being in their presence again. But Ingrid's?

Imagining Ingrid as a child, and thinking of her Mor or Far stuck in those beams? That I could pluck them free and return them to her?

That tore at me. And yet, I still kept climbing, digging deep as I pulled up the most heavily warned against laser designs I could find. I was going to make this fucker *pay*.

I hated that I couldn't go and help. I could feel the need tearing at me, but that was the difference between a fucking shiny ass paladin, and a dark crusader.

I'd do what needed to be done to save them all. Some prick in tinfoil would already be down there, pulling the plug and then wondering what he was going to do when all their bodies fell from the sky.

No, the rage that filled me demanded blood, and I was going to get it—or nanites, at least.

The inside of the tower was a simple design, clearly changed from whatever had been the original. Probably because without the massive crews that such a creation should have had, a small security force didn't really justify much room.

The lower sections had all been ripped out to make room for larger shield generators that were presumably here as dedicated ones for the control tower. That meant that the inside was almost hollow—with a load of structural reinforcement, sure—but instead of the original multiple floors of rooms, quarters, barracks, bars and kinky sex dungeons or whatever, there was a straight run up a few thousand stairs to the main floor.

Shan'Gai had clearly decided that nothing was getting into here, considering that as soon as I started up the stairs—flying because why the hell would I run—there were shouts of disbelief and barked orders from above that echoed down.

The doors that were presumably at the top of the stairs clanged shut. And even with the wind in my ears as I blasted up the switchbacks, passing back and forth across hundreds of climbing stairs, I heard the locks engaging.

It was almost funny, actually, considering that a shitload of Ændari were taking up defensive stations, massive crew-served lasers were charged and ready behind portable shield generators, and it was all for little old me.

Of course, I was probably the only one who saw the funny side, considering that a half second later, I'd jumped and bypassed them all. I stepped clear of the warp on the inside of the final chamber's door, with it sealed shut behind me, and all this fucker's heavily armed friends on the wrong side of the door.

471

CHAPTER FORTY

The room I found myself in was neither huge nor impressive, though it'd clearly been designed to house the commander and their staff once.

It was perhaps ten meters wide by thirty long, with a curved ceiling that rose from near the entrance, where I was, to dip down at the far side to close to ground level.

It might have touched the ground for all I knew. I couldn't tell, because in the middle of the room, half embedded in a collection of crystal hexagons that rose like pillars, was Shan'Gai's local form.

His eyes flickered, focusing, then phased out, then back in, clearly having some kind of fit, judging from his face. He started to shake, then shudder. The entire room shook in tandem; then alarms sounded on all sides. With a great gasp of air, he lunged forward, collapsing onto the floor, hands pressed to it and panting.

"You all right there, pal?" I called out, getting a snarl in response as he looked up, glaring at me. "Ah, don't worry about it. It'll all be over soon." I noted the way his gaze flicked to the sides of the room, searching out the hidden drone.

He'd learned; clearly the drones were an issue for him now that he knew that they could kill him. After all, nobody took a nuke to the face and walked away, and certainly not anyone in our unique circumstances.

"Why did you come?" he asked after a few seconds, and I cocked my head to one side, regarding him.

"Why the hell do you think, you prick? I mean, you know about the drone, so you're linked to your brother or whatever that was I toasted downstairs, so you know exactly why I'm here," I snapped.

"You could have left."

"You'd have followed me, and you already admitted you hunt our kind," I pointed out, watching as he struggled to his feet, swaying drunkenly.

"A thousand turns of this world," he offered.

"A big bowl of cheese," I countered.

"What?"

"I can say random shit too. Get to the point."

"A thousand turns of this…world," he repeated. "That is what we offer you…a thousand turns to grow…to *learn* as our thrall. Serve faithfully and…we will work with you…to set your own territories up. You can raise them to harvest as you will…with only a tithe to us in recognition that—"

"That you're stalling and it's not working?" I stabbed out.

I shifted my right hand into a blade, driving it into his shoulder and ripping left to right, cutting through the upper layers of his "flesh."

It parted like water, then closed again, as he tilted his head in irritation.

"You know this is pointless," he whispered. "I have devoured dozens of our kind, while you struggle to comprehend the most basic of our realities. A blade, no matter how sharp, cannot harm me."

"It doesn't have to," I snapped, stabbing again and again, dragging the blade up and down, lopping his head off and watching as a fresh one formed up from his nanites to regard me.

"No? You wish to waste your energy?" he mocked. "I have no time for this!"

He lunged forward. Both hands latched onto my forearms, moving almost as fast as I could track, as his chest shifted and blurred. Lines rose, twisting into new shapes as he tried to form something from his nanites. I flowed like water in return; my arms poured free of him. The nanites hit the floor and raced back to my feet, rejoining me as I formed new ones.

I slashed back and forth, trying to disrupt the pattern he was forming in his chest as he created new arms, batting aside and blocking my attacks. All the while, I was cursing. My entire goddamn plan had clearly been exactly what I was now sure he was doing!

Behind my back, between my shoulder blades, from just above my ass to just below the nape of my neck, a long barrel was mounding up, projectors forming and aligning and lifting free.

I'd been planning to hide it, while making him feel all superior watching me flail and stab as if I were an idiot, then having it slide up and over and shoot him in the face with a high-powered blast of radiation.

To do the job in here in the time I thought I had, I'd planned to use a horrifically powerful dose, and had even split my focus, forming a dedicated storage inside my legs that was now making thicker and thicker layers of armoring to protect against that radiation, but that would cleanse the room after.

I'd have killed him—injured myself, sure—but he'd be dead and I'd have all the nanites I needed right on the other side of the door to restock!

Instead, I'd proved to us both that yes, I actually *was* a fucking idiot. I'd deliberately built it onto my back, instead of accepting that my entire body was free game.

I could have made it in my goddamn face, for fuck's sake, or my crotch! Instead, I'd started to form it behind my back, while he'd clearly begun it internally, and now the pair of us were stuck in a blurringly fast pattern of attacks and counterattacks.

He'd shifted his form, just as my barrel was nearly complete; two additional arms buoyed up and slashed inward, great bone-like scimitars that hurtled for my head.

Arise: Conqueror

I forced myself to ignore them, to counterattack with a blast of gravity that dragged him forward onto a spike that I formed from my chest and expanded into him.

Spikes of his own launched forward, burrowing into me and through, aiming for the weapon on my back.

All the while, as blades stabbed into each other, an entirely more complex battle was filling the pair of us as well. Every blow, every touch of my nanites against his, was a miniature battlefield.

Mine swarmed his, his swarmed mine; both sides hacked, countered, and attempted to overwrite the enemy coding.

His blades cut down into my head; the tips reformed into injection ports and forced nanites out into me, even as mine did the same in his chest. The first round had been all liquid quicksilver, our bodies forming and reforming as we cut the enemy infection free and ejected it, and absorbed the nanites we'd won.

Now the fight changed. The pair of us appeared to merge from the outside as our outer shells became more solid. The battlegrounds of nanites prevented each other from fully shifting, slowing down our mobility.

Inside, though, we were anything but solid, a wash of light and dark as his form and mine battled, with our bodies the battlefield and a billion nanites our soldiers.

I had complete access to my nanites, and they were unlocked in ways that his weren't anymore, giving me a massive advantage. But it was offset by my inexperience.

This flowing liquid war was totally new to me, my body only capable of this in the last few weeks.

I felt like every change had to be commanded, directed, and guided and that was slowing me, giving him a chance where I should have crushed him.

He'd been doing this for centuries, eons even, and although this was a little fragment of him, he was still far more experienced than I was.

I'd already slowed time on instinct. As my back-mounted weapon was cut through for the fifth time, I triggered my War sub-mind, bringing it and the others online and throwing them into the fight in desperation.

I couldn't make any gains, not as I was. For every inch I gained here, I lost one—or more—there, and this wasn't a battle I could win on balls and a well-timed Glasgow kiss.

The War AI took some of the strain of maintaining the fight from me. As soon as I handed that section over to it, I focused on more spears forming and stabbing out, lancing into his head and upper body.

Eight of them punched into the throat, lower jaw, and head all at once, almost thick enough that they touched. I spawned ten more, stabbing them out around his head, surrounding it, and making his eyes narrow in fury as I enveloped it.

He released his head again; a fresh form swelled up as he leaned back. But instead of letting him go this time, and the head falling to splatter on the ground, I stepped into the change.

I'd used so many on the head to get as much mass as possible there—severing it, enveloping it, and then driving the Hack sub-mind forward.

It was the specialist here, and I'd already proved that my well-meaning but mad attempts weren't cutting it. Instead, I was forced back into more of a leadership role, one that didn't come naturally to me, and…

And fuck my life.

As soon as I thought it, I was reaching out. Ingrid was there in a heartbeat as I shared the insane plan. She nodded, saying something to someone else, and apparently just dropping down on the floor where she'd been standing, closing her eyes and taking over the strategic level.

I wasn't alone.

I didn't have to do everything on my goddamn own!

I needed to remember that, as my sub-minds both accepted her without issue and the War AI did as it was told. It was based off my mind, as were the sub-minds, but there were differences, and Ingrid moved quickly to make the most of them.

Then I lunged forward again, hands clamping over Shan'Gai's shoulders, gripping on tight. As he tried to form his own nanites over them, they swelled larger and larger.

It became another miniature battlefield as he and I tried to counter each other. Tendrils lanced up and around, enveloping each other until… I ripped his arms free and dragged them back into me.

He'd been caught up in the focus that I was putting on trying to seal myself around his shoulders, and he'd been focused on countering me.

While he'd been doing that, though, Hack was working on closing off entire sections of his nanites and readying them for takeover. Engineering had been preparing the gravity fields. And War?

War had formed twin shears that were almost neutronium in their mass. The shears burst free at the same time, closing on either side of the shoulders and cutting downward, hard and fast.

The body resisted for a split second. Then, as Shan'Gai realized that he couldn't withstand the cutting force, he released the connections.

The arms fell to the sides, already converting into liquid, ready to flow back into his mass and reform, until the gravity fields pulsed.

The falling, liquidified arms were ripped forward, dragged into me. And surrounded as they were, siphoned down into a smaller mass and forced through a gauntlet of hacking, they began to change.

More and more fell to me. As the ratio went from one gained against one lost—an equal fight—to two to one, then four to one, I saw the panic rising in my opponent.

Using the head and arms that I'd ripped from him, I focused on a leg next.

The head was a little less than ten percent of the overall mass, and the arms were about the same. In a human, my Repair details informed me happily, the arms only made up six to eight percent of the overall mass. But considering the length, the thickness, and that the entire body was compressed nanites, not skin and bone, I told that little detail to go fuck itself.

Arise: Conqueror

I'd taken twenty percent nearly of the overall body now, and in going for a leg, I was putting another fifteen to twenty percent of him at risk.

He couldn't allow that and desperately changed his tactics, going from fighting me to trying to back up and get some room. His semi-solid form abruptly flowed like water, sliding backward, and then darted to the side, making a break for the door.

"Down to the left..." Ingrid sent me, highlighting a small section that had burst free and was shifting color, trying to blend in with the floor, rolling away like the tide, as the majority of the body tried to get past.

That was when I really smiled. While Engineering had focused briefly on the gravity tunnel to drag the arms free, beyond that, the sub-mind had been doing what it did best.

It'd been building, and specifically building the high-powered laser on my back.

As I spun and lunged, taking the bait essentially on the attempt by the main body to make it to the door, the swivel mount on my back unlocked. The laser swung around, locking onto the fast-pouring mass of cloaked nanites as they tried to hide.

Then it fired.

The beam was a brief one, but it made the very air shake and shudder.

The nanites it'd been aimed at collapsed into dust. Both Shan'Gai and I screamed in pain as the backlash washed over us.

In my momentary shock over just how powerful and effective the weapon was against us, I took a fresh blow to the face and staggered, before realizing that something I'd not been expecting had happened as well.

My sub-minds were all rebooting.

I'd lost access to Ingrid, and in the corner of the room, the drone camera clanged as it hit the floor, knocked out and, like the rest, rebooting.

I shook myself, stunned to realize that I was essentially back in my own form again, no longer half enmeshed with him, as he slapped a hand on the door control, throwing a brace of gleaming blades at me.

I threw up my arm and blocked. The blades sank into the top layer, melding, then detonated, hurling me from my feet.

Growling in fury, I rolled back upright, darting after him, but he'd gotten what he needed—time.

The door was still opening as he hit the gap, deforming and forcing his way through it, even as the laser locked into place and fired again.

This time I hit him in the left shoulder, boring a hole through him and tearing a scream free as he fell from sight.

I fell as well. The sheer power of the laser going off again, and so close, rang my bell. Before I could think better of it, I'd started the disassembly, not surprised at all when the nanites that made up the weapon didn't reform.

Instead, they fell to the floor in their final form, the metal of the barrel still smoking, with a half-life so long Iran would be knocking at the door any second.

I pushed myself up—again—and grabbed the door, yanking it all the way open and cursing as I batted aside a laser that was being shoved at my face.

The goddamn guards!

I'd forgotten about them. But they'd not forgotten about me—clearly—and they looked seriously panicked.

The laser went off a half second later, shooting past my face into the room behind, and I grunted. A lance of nanites punched through the wielder and out of his back, then yanked him in close as the Devourer shroud flowed out and around him.

The top of the stairwell was a handful of meters ahead, with a pair of small protective walls that rose from the ground and hung from the ceiling.

They narrowed the area incoming forces could shoot and hit, and gave some space to the defenders, but for me, best of all, they enclosed the fuckers and kept them from escaping.

As far as they were concerned, I was still somewhere below, after all, so the last thing they'd been expecting was their boss to come screaming out of the door behind them, wounded, and then have to fight an enraged Devourer at close range.

Lucky, really.

Had I needed to attack from the other side? Well, the firing slits in the armoring were small enough that no stormtrooper would have hit them, that was for sure.

Shan'Gai was half staggering, half being dragged through the offset gaps in the wall, getting as far from me as possible, while I tore his defenders a new arsehole.

They didn't lack for balls, though—I had to give them that, as most of the remaining guards launched themselves at me.

There were five of them, and gravity bubbles appeared above and below, catching them mid-leap and yanking them back, then crushing them to the nearest surface. The air filled with their screams as their bones broke; internal organs shattered and collapsed inward with strangled liquid noises.

Two more stood between me and my prey, who was being supported by the third, and final of them.

These were Helio Guards. I recognized them instantly: the triangular shields, the proton lances, the heavy armor in white and gold, the red highlights, and the damn speed that they moved.

I created a bubble beyond them, between Shan'Gai and the stairwell, one that pushed him back, forcing him to stop, and I couldn't help but grin coldly.

The fucker couldn't get away now.

Whatever damage the laser had done when it'd punched through him, he was down to around half the nanites he'd had before. And now that I knew to use my sub-minds, each of which were rebooting and nearly aware again, we both knew he couldn't win.

That was why the one supporting him suddenly screamed in pain and fell as Shan'Gai grabbed him by the head and started to collapse into his individual nanites.

"Motherfucker!" I cursed. The first pair of blasts hit me from the proton lances and staggered me, before tentacles flashed out and latched on, yanking the weapons to the sides as they fired over and over. The rapid-fire blasts cut deep into me.

I dragged them closer as I stepped forward. Both arms formed shields that I held up between us…then I slid the top half down, exposing the twin bulges forming on my shoulders. Barrels slid forward as the new twin gravity cannons elongated.

"Surrender and die," I ordered, before firing two blasts, one from either side.

Their helmets detonated, the backs exploding outward in a spray of bloody fragments and the Ændari elite warriors' innermost thoughts and dreams.

"You're supposed to give them time to respond when you demand their surrender…" Ingrid pointed out, and then, a second later, went on. *"And it's surrender OR die,' not 'and' die."*

"I said what I meant." I stepped over the bodies as the shroud hungrily consumed them and lifted into the air. The shields I'd formed flowed back into me, even as I gestured upward with both hands.

The heavy lasers that had been emplaced to cut me down on approach snapped free of their mounts with loud cracks, gravity rupturing the locks and crushing the stands.

They floated to me, and I slid out of the gap between the barriers, watching the Ændari who had been trying to help his master escape finally stop convulsing.

Shan'Gai was nowhere to be seen. But in his place, the Ændari warrior slowly rose to his feet. Blood that had been running from his lips, ears, nose, and eyes now sank into the silvery mass as his skin bubbled with nanites.

They enveloped him entirely. Liquid metal formed all over, then hardened, as he straightened, holding his hands out to either side almost idly.

Swords extended from his palms, two-meter-long blades that crackled with power as the hilts snapped into place, clutched tightly.

His armor was silver, white, and gold. Black mobility plates glimmered from beneath the burnished layers, and my own armor shifted in response.

His was stylized, almost ornate, with enameled panels, and as he spoke, I noted a totally different style and voice used.

"This…this is what the gods made me for!" he declared, his voice hoarse.

"The gods?" I grunted. "Shan'Gai, you're fuckin' nuts…"

"You! Blasphemer!" he barked, pointing his right-most blade at me. "You *dare* to trespass here? To stand against the holy cleansing of the corrupt ones? I shall smite you, for He has blessed me with glorious power and—"

"Oh, fuck off," I snapped.

The heavy lasers weren't just called that for their goddamn weight—they were high-power, fast-cycling repeaters that fired until their cores were empty.

Twin lines of powerful light hammered into him, staggering him and making him scream in rage, before I saw the sneaky bastard's trick.

The uppermost layer, all that gilding and enamel or whatever it was, absorbed most of the blasts, redirecting the energy, and his swords glowed brighter and brighter!

The War AI came online now and focused my wavering aim, zooming in and providing tighter control as I shifted the target from the center of the plates to the joints and weaker sections on his left leg.

He snarled and stabbed forward with his right blade, the light glowing almost too bright to see before a blast tore through the air and slammed into me, hurling me backward into the barriers.

They crumbled under the impact, the outer surface revealed to be little more than an inch thick, and the underneath more bloody concrete rip-off.

I cried out in anger and kicked my way clear of the rubble, seeing him stepping up the stairs and levelling the left blade now.

"Oh no you don't," I snapped, flicking my fingers to the side. I summoned a gravity bubble down and behind him, yanking the blade off target and wasting the shot that he released into the wall instead.

"You cannot win!" he boomed. "For I have been blessed! Anointed by—"

My second gravity bubble appeared right behind his feet, yanking backward, and the third just before his face, pulling down as he fell.

The hardened stone cut off his monologuing with a clang as he slammed into it face-first.

I spat, climbing to my feet and staring down as he struggled to rise again. "Just fucking stay down," I ordered. "Shan'Gai, I don't know what shit you're planning, but today's not the goddamn time for it!"

My shroud had finished ripping the nanites free of the other corpses, and now gathered the leftover, useless mass, pulling it all into a central lump that was lifted up behind me.

I felt the camera and Ingrid watching me as I reached out, applying the conversion ability of the shroud to literally break down all that matter into pure energy, and using that energy to power the gravity bubble I formed right above the amalgamation of the Ændari and Shan'Gai.

He was sucked upward into it, yelling at first, then screeching in pain as he was forced into a smaller and smaller ball. The nanites that made up Shan'Gai began to generate a counter force, but it was too little, restricted and diminished as he was, and too late.

His host—as that was what I was guessing the fucker had done, in using his body as a refuge and strengthening it at the same time—screeched and burbled, bones shattering.

There was a brief second of warbled cries, then even the glorious sounds of his demise were unable to escape the forming gravity bubble.

I fed more and more power into the ball, half into it and half into maintaining the rest of the world around it as "normal." As the light in the center of it started to twist and warp, his nanites began to crumble and fail.

For a brief second, I felt a connection, an attempt as he reached out, somehow gathering the strength to form the necessary systems, and broadcast directly to me.

"I...will...serve..." he begged desperately.

Arise: Conqueror

I gritted my teeth, remembering all the bodies floating through the air below us, the living and the dead alike torn from their world to be fed upon. And this fucker dared to beg for mercy?

"Fuck you!" I snarled, lifting my right hand, forming the power into it and closing my fist as tightly as I could. The gravity nexus responded and followed the link as it crushed him into atomic dust.

CHAPTER FORTY-ONE

I released the gravity bubble and its balancing force. Shan'Gai's avatar crumbled away into nothing as I released the power, dragging down a deep and ragged breath, before spinning on my heel and marching back into the control center.

As I went, four more nanite drones bulged up and burst from me, floating into the air and bobbing along. I unthinkingly supported them in their own gravitational bubbles, uploading their commands as I moved.

I strode to the pillar of crystal that the asshole had been linked to when I'd arrived, slapping a hand over it and grunting as my awareness rippled out through the harvester.

It was huge, mind-blowingly so, with rooms that were miles across, never mind the actual systems that ran it all, and as I searched, I found them as well.

Six AI cores, each dedicated to an aspect of the harvester. Two were at rest, seemingly just watching and uncaring. I guessed that they were for the actual flight and navigation systems, as opposed to the other four that were individually controlling sectors.

Two were controlling multiple legs each. The millions of moving parts each required, not to mention the actual stability that was needed, clearly used a *lot* of processing power.

The final two were responsible for processing, one essentially a glorified pattern recognition system and tractor beam director, and the other maintaining and running the actual processing systems.

I sent out a demand for status, trying to map out the system and understand it enough to take control. The resulting data dump almost broke me.

It took long seconds for me to struggle free of the morass of data. But when I did, it was with a much deeper understanding of the Ouroboros harvester and its capabilities, as well as a degree of confusion over the noises I was hearing.

I blinked and looked around, then grinned evilly. Some people said I was paranoid, some said I was a bastard—and they were right on both counts. But the sound of sudden beams rippling out and the crackling cascades of dying nanites left behind made it all worth it.

I'd not wanted to waste time searching every inch of the control room, nor the rest of the harvester that I could reach for more of that asshole avatar.

Equally, I wasn't going to just take it on trust that someone who had tried to split off and hide a portion of himself wouldn't do it again.

The sounds were the drones I'd made using the gamma projectors that I'd first encountered back in the Great Refuge, designed to literally cook and shred nanites.

They drifted around the room, sterilizing it entirely, and I, standing at the center, then only had to cover the small "safe zone" I'd created with my shroud to be sure that the fucker was expunged from here completely.

The crackling and buzzing was the sound of hidden nanites being fried. As they got closer to the door, an entire panel of the roof broke free, shifting into a miniature drone of its own design, and darted for freedom.

It didn't make it.

Knowing that the room was finally clear, I sealed the door behind the drones as they began their work out there. Then I cracked my knuckles and started work.

The legs were the first to stop. Just them no longer dragging inward and gouging miles-long lines of devastation in the planet's surface would be a massive help. But even them stopping wasn't simple.

So many sections had to be slowly wound down, gravitational adjustments made, new placement areas for the legs to move to, in order to brace for the launch were designated, and as they did that?

I was searching the beams for any signs of life.

One hundred and thirty-seven life signs were picked out, and of them, only fourteen were in any state that could be freed or likely to survive, considering the locations and conditions. Even as I looked, eleven more died, and I gritted my teeth, hating myself as I shifted the systems around.

The fourteen who I believed could be saved—and not one of them would be uninjured—were plucked free by secondary beams and manipulated around, being carried through the air directly to the small team of limping survivors I'd freed earlier.

As was a medium Ændari transport that another beam plucked from a maintenance bay. I dumped it and the wounded next to the survivors, patching the feed through to Ingrid, who accepted it and forwarded it on, distractedly.

Reaching out to Argus, sensing that she was too busy, I asked for a status update and cursed again.

The first two transports had already landed on the node, and a third was coming in as well. The Ændari forces were rushing headlong into the meat grinder and seemingly determined to punch their way through by sheer numbers alone.

I froze for a second, seeing them all. My immediate instinct was to find a way to Ingrid. There had to be converters and makers there, after all— just get one of them to churn out a drone with a gravitational pulse generator on it and...

And no.

I had my job to do, and she had hers, as much as I hated it. I trusted her, and I trusted our people.

I also ordered Argus to make me a goddamn drone on the node, just in case, then I got back to the systems I was dealing with. I couldn't afford to waste any more time.

Sending orders through the various systems, I got the harvester moving. The legs were already in motion, shifting around to lock into their launch mode. Although I didn't like it, there was just too much mass here ready to go that I couldn't afford to leave behind.

Tens of millions of nanites flowed along the beams that carried the organic—best to think of it that way, after all—harvested components for processing.

I needed every single edge I could get. And the truth was, these people were already dead. This way, in death they got a chance to strike a blow against the enemy still.

Thousands of systems needed to be adjusted, steps taken and alignments corrected to make the harvester ready for launch. I was already disliking some of the responses I was getting back as I worked.

Frankly, the harvester was just too big, now that I had access to everything that it was, to launch from a planet once it'd touched down.

Too big to do it and leave the world in any condition that would support life again, anyway.

If I was to try this with the main reaction engines, the temperature that'd be released would set fire to the atmosphere, essentially igniting a global firestorm that would only go out once all the available fuel—the oxygen and people, for example—were consumed.

There were gravitational generators—my God, were there. They were bigger than my ship! But even using all six, and at maximum power, I wasn't sure they could lift this back into orbit.

Even if they could, it'd be utterly drained of all power. And the gravity of the planet would probably just suck it back in, regardless of making a mockery of the sacrifice of Shan'Gai's victims.

No, there was only one play here that I could see as I ran through the other possible plans.

I couldn't jump it out; it was too big, and the power needed… It took weeks of charging to enable it to jump from system to system normally, and my version? The tiny jumps around the local sector? They weren't exactly cheap to perform in terms of power.

For me? Sure, a power core inbuilt was enough, but considering that my usual-sized power core could also run one of those massive aircraft carriers that the US kept building, and it'd be good for about, oh, twelve centuries of continuous use?

To jump little old me around the local area was totally reasonable.

The size of power core I'd need to do that with this? It'd be, off the top of my head, around the same size as *New York City*.

Arise: Conqueror

I couldn't fly it off, and I couldn't jump it off. I wasn't a marine, so I couldn't do the old "if it doesn't move, fuck it till it does." And even if I tried it, the chafing would be insane.

No, the best option at this point was to make it as stable as possible, trigger the nanite production vats to work on the conversion of standard matter to usable nanites, and when they were full, use those nanites to rebuild the harvester.

Until then—and checking the system options, I decided it was the only viable plan I had left—I was down to ripping the nanites free and using them to get me back to orbit and into the fight.

The nanite production vats needed nanites to produce nanites. There was no magic way around that. Whatever original systems were used to do it before, the system in place on the harvester currently used nanites to jump-start more of their own kind.

Make a million, attach a hundred thousand, have them jump-start the million. There'd be some losses on top of the hundred thousand you "spent" to awaken the new ones, but it worked, according to the records.

Having to use nanites to make nanites seemed ridiculous. There had to be a production facility somewhere that had made the first ones, after all, but that was what I was left with.

The production vats were already at work, several million nanites in place and ready to be kick-starting another batch soon, with billions more being churned out of dedicated makers and dumped into the vats as I watched.

That was a drop in the ocean compared to the vat's capacities, though. This was a machine that was designed to literally feed a *fleet*. It was meant to be paired with a construction yard of the same "I can see your house from the next planet's orbit" size, and it was just getting started.

Shan'Gai must have been driven even more insane, forcing himself to ration the nanites after each harvesting of a world, considering the huge numbers involved.

Some questions remained, even now. I mean, if they took a million to make ten million, and once they were started…ah.

The data swam up, and I nodded in understanding.

The problem was a "copy/paste" one. Essentially, the more you copied something, the shittier it became. Like a photocopy of a photocopy, the image degraded each time, and damn. Malfunctioning nanites were a horrific thing to imagine, especially for Shan'Gai—being locked out of the main control systems for his nanites, he'd never be able to shut them down.

That linked to more of the corrupted zones for me as well, and I remembered the state of some of the broken worlds I'd seen.

The fucker had tried it before, and I was betting he was why the UC was all crazy about keeping people out of the lost worlds.

I'd seen it as the mess that was left was on the worlds, but if he'd vented a batch or more into space to get rid of corrupted and uncontrollable nanites?

They'd just float until they hit something, be that a planet or a ship, a sun or a space station.

Damn.

I shook myself free of the details, forcing myself to accept that I could leave a million nanites in place and get ten million out of this when I came back.

If I won the fight with Shan'Gai, I'd have hopefully billions more nanites to use. And then I could use them to clone out tens of billions more, using them to fix the world, or at least get this ancient piece of shit off it.

Either way, though, I couldn't leave any more here.

I needed them, and I needed to get into orbit. There was a fight waiting for me, and it wasn't one that I could hand off to another.

The next twenty minutes were painful, and yet passed in a blur.

The first thing I had to do, once I'd made a damn AI core that could sort of manage things in my absence, was to get my arse down to the vats, and that was traumatizing on a whole new level.

On the way, knowing that Ingrid was too busy and that the people of this world deserved at least some answers, I connected to their global broadcast network and made an avatar of myself appear, speaking to them all as I flew out of the hull, up and around, looping to the underside in the far distance.

"People of Scorpio-3!" I called. "The harvester is dead, as are most of its crew. Stay clear for now. Not all Ændari are defeated, but those left are trapped and will be taken care of soon." I paused, as people started to cheer raggedly, clearly unsure. For a second, I wished there was a damn Charisma option on my stat screen, maybe with a "make speeches" selection.

Something similar started to pop up as I thought it, under the Leadership and Sabotage trees, making it clear what kind of people liked to give speeches, and I closed it immediately.

"The harvester is too large to move from the planet without causing more damage, and the fight deeper in the system is yet to be won, so stay at home, hunker down, and help those who need it. Stay clear of the harvester, and I'll return for it when I can…" I paused, as first one, then three, then twenty-two separate connections were requested of me, each goddamn one marked and carrying the identification of the planetary leadership.

I noted that all but one of them were off-world, and that last one was at the spaceport on the far side of the planet.

"What?" I linked all of them into the same broadcast, even as I picked up speed, arcing around. The miles upon miles of the harvester's hull blurred as I flashed overhead, then dove, heading for the underside.

"I…uh, we…" one of them started, realizing a split second ahead of the other babbling idiots that he was connected to more than just me.

"Speak or fuck off," I said. "I've got no time for this."

"We'll take care of the harvester." One of the voices broke through the general hubbub. "It's done significant damage to my city, and so my people will take control, ensuring that it's rendered safe and—"

"You'll stay clear of it," I snapped. "I've got no time to kill the remaining Ændari aboard."

"How many?" another asked. "What weapons do they have? Could our forces defeat them?"

Arise: Conqueror

"No." I finally realized what they meant. These shitehawks were running, leaving the people behind to die terrible deaths, and now that they saw a possible profit, they were reconsidering and trying to maneuver for control.

"Anyone who sets foot aboard the harvester will be considered attempting to lay claim to my property, and my hunters will kill you," I declared, ignoring that my "hunters" were actually the drone equivalent of the janitors.

"The harvester is shut down, but anyone who boards it risks reactivating it, and the planetary core drilling facility that was powering up…" I'd made that up on the spot. "So I'll not risk a warning. Approach it and die."

With that cheerful detail shared, I cut the assholes out of the conversation, and for good measure sent a Tsunami hack back along the line of connection. Its orders were simple: find the communication array, kill it.

That should keep the leadership from screwing things even harder and let the mid-rankers establish themselves and actually deal with the problems.

As I did that, I started to speak to the public again, even as I sent orders to the half a ship I had in orbit high overhead.

It began to power the engines and turn, locking onto the distant glimmer that was Shan'Gai. I twisted in flight again, levelling out and finding myself under the hull, blasting back in the opposite direction and heading for the distant nanite processing yards.

"The harvester is no longer a threat to you, but the Ændari still are, as is the false Devourer Shan'Gai…" No point in wasting time explaining shit, after all. "My forces and I are going to deal with him now. If you are safe, if you have food and shelter, then share it with others. Help the others on your world. If you have neither, travel to the nearest central hub, town or city. I am Lord Devourer Steve, and I give your local police and security forces the authority to distribute whatever materials are needed and available to help others. Pull together, protect your fellow citizens, help those who need it, and I promise you, you'll not regret it."

I hesitated, hating that I knew it needed to be said, but saying it anyway.

"In addition, I declare this planet under martial law. You are no longer a free world. Until this crisis has passed, you are now a hub world for the UC, and under my direct authority, and that of the UC fleet and soldiers. Any crimes will be punished with the maximum force and sentence available, unless they are proved to have been committed to protect and preserve life.

"I cannot issue orders that will cover every eventuality, so understand this: you are to help each other to survive, to raise each other up, to preserve, protect and guide. If you use the letter of my words to take advantage of the situation and attempt to protect yourself from their intention, I will *personally* come for you and rip your screaming soul from your body. Behave, help each other, and show me that I can rely on you. Do this, and I will reward you beyond your wildest dreams."

I cut the connection there, focusing on the massive upswelling of nanites I could sense ahead, and forced myself to take some deep breaths, getting ready.

The hunger rose in me more and more as I got closer to the mass storage. I frantically tried to distract myself from the feeling, by trying to explain the feeling to myself.

It wasn't like a regular hunger, not like "I'm so hungry I must eat" but it was as well—more like a mix of absolutely starving, the worst I've even been and distracted to all buggery, and that feeling when you were hornier than a dog with three dicks.

When you were on a promise, you and your partner had been teasing each other all evening out for a meal or whatever, and you're going back to the house. That point where you've been fooling around in the car or taxi or whatever and you're literally stumbling in the front door, ready to rip each other's clothes off.

That "I can't focus on anything else" of hunger and lust and something else, something I had no words for. Combine it all and roll it up with a side order of incredible power, and you had the hunger for the nanites that I felt.

More or less, of course, because I wasn't going to be sticking my dick in the vat.

That said, as I burst through the smaller, narrower and heavily armed and armored entrance, I flipped myself around, making sure I'd land feetfirst instead of using my face as a brake. I still stumbled, coming to a halt in the cavernous interior of the world-eater.

The first section was for processing the bodies, and my gods...

There were a dozen different conveyor belts, each laid out side by side. Automated arms hung from the overheads, working as the living and the dead alike were deposited.

Here and there, I imagined I heard weak cries, screams, and even whimpers. But the reality was that by the time they got here, those who still lived weren't strong enough to be heard over the rolling machinery.

They were straightened out, humanoids on predetermined belts, animals and aliens segregated by a designation that seemed to revolve around how many legs they had, and if they were likely to be sapient or not.

Then the arms began their grisly work.

Saws, lasers, and mandibles blurred. Technology was cut free and sorted, clothing dumped, hair was shaved from the sapiens and hoovered off, while the animals were skinned.

Limbs were removed from them all, passed from the belts into a dedicated section filled with hundreds of arms working in a way that would have given Mengele a nightmare. They straightened limbs, sliced and deboned, then opened the flesh out for processing.

Bones were sorted into one section, flesh into another, organs into a third. I shuddered even as the Engineering sub-mind identified a likely 0.34% increase in efficiency by processing in this manner over a more general "giant meat grinder" approach.

As the bodies went on, they did meet the meat grinder though, being fed into huge, slowly rotating rollers that crushed everything to paste between them.

Bones went into another processor from the flesh, and everywhere, literally, a mist of blood floated through the air, only to have the interior periodically swept with tractor beams that pulled even that up and fed it into the vats for processing.

Arise: Conqueror

I stumbled, trying to take it all in at once. The system-explained version I'd gotten earlier barely scratched the surface of the wholescale industrial horror show that filled my eyes now.

Shaking my head, I launched myself back into the air and stared as I flew over and between the sorting and processing systems, horrified and yet awestruck.

The worst of the Nazis would have vomited over the sheer scale of the murder, and the most ruthless of Mengele's adherents would have wept at this sight.

The next section of the interior for the lower levels was like standing in the center of a dozen football pitches, all set side by side, with a cleared route for separation that ran down the middle.

There were ten vats on either side—huge, silent silos of grey and silver— each with a single set of lights on the nearest end that pulsed a sullen red as they processed the incoming paste.

Moving quickly to the end, I swallowed hard. My gravitational senses marked out how much matter was being funneled left and right on either side of me, and the much, much reduced mass that flowed onward through the filtration system into the final stages.

Here there were huge doors and security systems in place. Turrets and reinforced blast doors, and cannons that could clear orbital facilities made it clear that the priority for the previous owner was definitely this area.

I was damn glad I'd already taken control, because the veritable gauntlet of overlapping fields of fire that I could see here would have been horrific.

I'd never been so glad that I liked to forge my own path before. And just imagining the shit-show if I'd flown here as a first wave of attack?

It'd have been over quickly.

As it was, as I approached the doors, they cracked open. The final defenses welcomed me with open arms as the sense of the billions of nanites I'd been trying to suppress washed out and over me.

The doors blurred as I powered forward again, barely opening far enough to let me through before starting to reverse. I groaned as the need spread over me, and at the huge processing vats that lay before me.

There were six of them, each a hundred meters deep by fifty across, and they accepted mass that was being poured in from both sides.

From the left were the activated, advanced and "alive" nanites. From the right came the latest batches, huge converters feeding the newly constructed and yet blank nanites into the vat as well.

I stood at the edge of the container, staring down, watching as they mixed. Projectors came online and forced them into patterns that made no sense, and yet seemed oddly familiar.

Great posts rose in the morass of death, black as onyx and topped with gleaming crystals that pulsed with power. Shields crackled to life, locking the production vat off from "contamination" as the nanites were brought to life.

The posts began to hum, a deep electrical noise that I felt through the soles of my feet. Glimmering beams of light burst forth from each, slamming into one another, then angled down, penetrating the vats' contents, and beginning to churn faster.

I felt the shiver that came from the mass as it grew denser…no, that wasn't right. The mass was the same, but the sense of usable, active nanites? That grew exponentially over the next thirty seconds.

I watched, desperately wanting to batter my way through and take them, and yet I knew I couldn't.

These nanites would take at least another half hour to be fully awakened. If I fed on them now, absorbing and attuning them, they'd work, sure, but they'd start to fail within a few minutes.

They needed a sustained charge to fully awaken them, and I forced myself to move on, to leave these, knowing that they were beyond my reach for now, as were those still coming through the filtration system.

The stores to my left, though? And the three batches that lay ahead, already complete and ready to be released? They were fair game.

I moved to the stores first. The tanks that held the billions of nanites seemed almost insubstantial compared to my hunger, and the nanites' need to be complete.

As I pressed a hand to the emergency access hatch on the side, it opened with a click, then was forced open further by the pressurized outpouring that washed over me.

I gasped. *Billions* of nanites covered me, filling the spaces between the processing units and still coming, flooding the room like a never-ending pressure hose…until I triggered the cleanse and attune.

The room shook, to my mind, as the nanites that were rapidly filling it suddenly diverted, no longer pouring around me uncontrolled, and instead *were* me.

The wave froze, then parted, lifting me up and rolling around me almost in welcome as more and more nanites flocked to me.

The storage vat emptied quickly. The last of the free nanites all raced joyously out to join with me before I slammed it shut. I was torn between leaving it open just a little longer and grabbing all the hundreds of nanites that flowed through the pressurized tubes every second or moving onto the next area.

I barely fought against the need, before giving in and lifting into the air as the Devourer rolled back and forth, unfolding in the limited space I had, converting and upgrading all the nanites.

I'd never had such a powerful influx of nanites before, not all at once, and certainly not so…different.

I'd never noticed it before. There were always some differences in the nanites, and I'd always put that down to either breakages, failures in the blockchain, or maybe missing updates.

I'd seen what not upgrading your antivirus did when I'd looked for porn before, after all, so multiple thousands of years of nanites that operated only at the very lowest level, awaiting activation?

Arise: Conqueror

Yeah, that made sense that there'd be some failures. I'd just seen them, known that by and large, I could wipe, repair, and reset, and I'd accepted that as the way things were.

Now, though, the more nanites I gathered—and there were so goddamn many here, it blew my mind—but the more I gathered, the more I saw identical patterns.

I hesitated then slowed, forcibly stopping my headlong rush to gather the rest of the nanites, making sure that there wasn't some kind of last-second doomsday switch hidden in the programming here.

There could be anything, after all, if you were paranoid enough. And looking at this? Well, to protect this many nanites, if they'd been my stash, I could be plenty paranoid.

The more I looked, though, the more I realized that there wasn't anything else hidden here. If anything, it looked almost organic in the changes. And the more I stared, the more the patterns seemed practically deliberate.

I shook myself free, picking up speed again and rushing over to the next section, sensing almost as large a concentration laid in wait ahead, restive and ready.

Thirty seconds later, I was through the final security door and into what I was betting was intended as Shan'Gai's sanctum.

The space was big enough to be used for almost anything. The systems that lined the walls spoke to me of redundancy, but not for the harvester.

There were tens of engines, a dozen gravity drives, high-powered laser mounts, and communications relays, to name just the first few things I could identify. The room I'd found myself in had a huge crystal mold in the center, easily a mile across and half that wide, with sections that looked like they were designed to open out dotted along the base of it.

And overhead…there were the vats.

I paused, looking at the mass that hung there. Only a fraction of the overall capacity glimmered full, but there was space for an unbelievable number of nanites.

Staring at it, I wondered whether this was where Shan'Gai rebuilt himself, or whether this was an attempt by the humanoid avatars to take the next step in evolution to take him on directly.

They were certainly mad enough, and I genuinely didn't know what else it could be for.

Reaching out to the harvester, I confirmed that this was an entrance or exit. Then I shrugged, accepting that I'd have had to go out the other way if I'd come in by this to get the rest of the nanites, and so it didn't matter. But what did matter?

Those vats.

I moved forward, landing lightly in the crystal well, bracing myself, then reaching out and triggering the release. The nanites poured free, weaker than the normal ones I was used to, now that I had more to compare them to. But they were also freshly created; the more they washed over and joined me, the more I understood them.

They were different, weaker than certain forms, but others were almost impervious to radiation. Some weren't viable in water, for fuck's sake, I noted in annoyance; that was a shitty trait, and...

I paused, examining that as they washed over and over me.

It wasn't a fault—it was a trait...an *evolutionary* trait.

That was what it felt like, what these all felt like as I examined them. They weren't broken, or missing updates—they were fucking evolving!

Evolution wasn't clean, I'd heard it said, and judging from some of the weird-ass creatures I'd seen in the museums with the ex, it sure as shit didn't get it right all the time. The weakness to water, for instance, was a perfect example of that. But the nanites were evolving!

That meant that although they weren't conscious—not *thinking*, thank God; I was already mad enough, after all—but it meant that if they could evolve, they could be upgraded past the very peak that the Ændari had managed to take them to.

The nanites themselves, the machines that underpinned everything, could actually evolve!

That was insane. That was...

"Steve!" It was Ingrid, reaching out in desperation.

I shook myself loose of the morass of my thoughts, mortified that I'd wasted time when she and others were fighting for their lives.

"Ingrid, I—" I started.

"We need you!" she shouted, pouring more information into my mind. With it came the updates on the battle sphere of the Scorpio system.

I gritted my teeth as my stomach froze. The sight of so many Ændari vessels currently jumping in made me instantly want to get to her, scoop her up and run like fuck.

Dozens more ships were arriving, old and new, and they were firing on both the UC *and* Shan'Gai!

"Motherfuckers!" I gasped. *"The Ændari, they're betraying him!"*

"There's enough of them, they'll win as well!" Ingrid snapped at me. *"The damage he's taken, the fleet...they'll kill him, then the rest of our fleet."*

"Fuck!"

"Steve?"

"Yeah?"

"I...I know you, I know how mad you are, and how... 'you,' you are."

"Right?" I agreed, not getting it.

"I mean...look, Steve, if there's anything you've been holding back, anything that you think might be a last-ditch miracle to pull out of the bag at the eleventh hour?"

"Yeah?"

"Now's the time to use it."

"Okay." I blew out a long breath, cracking my knuckles and shaking some imaginary knots out of my shoulders. *"Well, there's a few little 'maybe' plans...you know, rainy day shit,"* I babbled, mind racing. I tried to imagine

what I could do, how to pull the half-formed ideas together into a single cohesive form that could help.

"*Now, Steve, now please!*" she sent, desperately.

"*Time to roll the dice,*" I whispered, lifting my arms to my sides and looking up. I triggered the release for the nanites and prepared to evolve.

CHAPTER FORTY-TWO

Gravity manipulation lifted me into the air smoothly as I reached out, burrowing through the outer layer and sinking into the nanites that hung in their vats overhead with thin streams of my own.

I gasped as I felt the wave of conversion that flowed outward from my touch. My awareness spread through the storage at stunning speed.

"Okay, this is fine…" I muttered. The hunger to consume and absorb so many nanites was not only being met, but was actually vanishing and leaving, staggering me. For the first time, I had more nanites than my mind could cope with.

I felt…stretched thin, and impossibly distended as so many different versions of nanites came under my control. Each of them was wiped and reset automatically, reduced to the "standard" configuration, as I'd always ordered.

Hell, I'd never realized that I was *reducing* them. I'd thought I was *repairing* them. But in such magnitudes, I started to identify trends, millions of clusters that had developed in identical ways. They were spread across the mass, and seeing them now, I couldn't help but believe I'd been blind to ignore the differences for so long.

Now, when I had the most to gain from examining the nanites and absorbing their improvements? I couldn't do it. I needed them functioning and as expected. Even as I gritted my teeth, knowing the possible power I was turning my back on with these evolutions, I increased my focus on wiping them all.

It didn't take long—hell, seconds really, that was all—but knowing that the fleet that had just jumped in was determined to eliminate everyone, I cursed and snarled at even that delay.

As soon as they were mine, though, I ripped the bottom out of the vats and let the protean rain fall on me.

The mass hit the mold I stood in like an avalanche, flaring up the sides and falling back on itself, before gathering around me, awaiting a command, and I gave it one.

I needed to get back to orbit. I needed to get there with these nanites, and I had no goddamn time. There were *far* too many to absorb into my body now. In fact, between the ones I'd gathered recently and these, my body now made up only a fraction of the overall total, and that was it.

Arise: Conqueror

Well, it was time to see just how much of a difference I could make to myself now, I guessed, gathering the nanites mentally and triggering a change across my entire body.

As it began, I reached upward as well, passing on orders to the section of me that still lay in orbit, the ship that had recently finished the power-up sequence and was now waiting for the rest of me to return.

A small drone bulged upward and slowly slid free of the hull, forming smoothly. It didn't need to be a particularly powerful creation: a small core, a drive, a little armoring to hold it all together, a camera so it could take over broadcasting for me, and last of all, a gravity pulse generator.

I swelled; my humanoid form remained but increased to closer to ten meters in size. My wings reformed and grew out. Instead of my normal graceful, slimline "angel" wings, these were full-on dark god-looking things.

I'd considered the power armor route, turning myself into a giant version of the UC soldier's battle armor, but I just didn't see the point.

There was nothing that such a creation could bring to the fight in terms of strength that I couldn't make my new body do easier.

I was going to be reforming myself over and over in the fight to come—that was a given. And with the psychological aspect, seeing me as a giant-sized and apparently minimally clad human, flying through space, was far more of a mind fuck for the Ændari, I was betting.

With that in mind, I changed my jeans and T-shirt "go-to" look for a simple form-fitting, but imposing one-piece hero looking super-suit patterned in tiny black and red scales. They flashed as they finished forming over me, and I reached out to the harvester. I clenched a gloved fist, testing the new size and strength.

A simple flick of a mental switch, and now that I knew it was there, the access to the outside from this chamber was revealed.

The center line of the mold dropped out. The sides creaked and cracked as they shifted. Millions of tons of armoring slid back to release me, and I fell.

Arms and legs tucked in, wings folded around myself, I plummeted out of the bottom of the harvester, then snapped them open, my wings booming as they caught the air.

Gravity took over, even as the camera drone tried to keep up, then was left behind in seconds.

I rocketed forward, hurtling toward the far edge of the ship, even as I finished pulling power from my core. Then I slipped into a jump. The gravity pulse from the drone high overhead enabled me to cut out the minutes that it would have cost me to get from under the ship to orbit.

Bursting from the other side into space was a weird feeling. I beat my wings and twisted in the air, cursing that I'd gotten the damn camera working, as the change from in-atmo to the little that was around me hurtling away into space was jarring.

I got control, though, and twisted, realigning and reaching out to my ship, even as it fired its engines and came for me.

The changes that had been made since I left were significant. The ship resembled more of a half-finished rocket now than anything else. The fatter rear was filled with engines, with stabilizers and directional thrusters dotted around about halfway up the narrowing body.

The main weapons weren't in place yet, and that was a good thing, because I needed to change the fuckers again anyway.

I spun around and pulled my wings in, folding in on myself, collapsing as the ship moved in. The front opened like a sucking mouth to accept me.

My form dissolved into the main ship, sinking from ten meters in height to a mere two again, shrinking myself down with wings and all, with all the remaining mass flowing out into the ship instead.

Down on the surface, they'd been constricted, contained and compressed.

Here? The nanites flowed easily, assuming the new shapes that I designated with barely any time needed to lock into place.

My sub-minds worked flawlessly with me to accomplish the design. First was Engineering, taking one look at the instinctual and half-formed ideas I had, refining them and rebuilding, increasing the power and the grace. Next, the Hack and Espionage sub-minds added tweaks to make it harder to track me, to increase the stealth capacity and my range of detecting enemies trying to do the same.

The War AI was the most help, though, integrating with the Engineering one seamlessly. It prioritized certain designs, choosing hard-hitting primary weapons to take out shields, then rapid-firing laser batteries to make the most of the damage we inflicted.

Three equidistantly spaced gravity gradient cannons formed up on the hull now; a groove ran from the wider base to the narrow nose and locked into place to fire from there, each with their own dedicated store for ammunition.

I could make it as I went—straight from my nanites, of course—but I'd be weakening myself with every single shot fired.

I was in the scrap belt of an industrialized planet. Nobody was going to mind me grabbing a satellite or two and breaking them down for ammo.

And if they did? It wasn't like I gave a shit.

I kept the storm casters, but because they were essentially short range, I also went all in on a new toy.

Halfway along my hull, three oblong forms bulged up now, turreted and liquid in the way that they moved. They were spaced equally around the hull, sliding naturally into the gaps between the GGCs.

Each of the new weapons formed a dozen smaller sections, housed in the overall oblong, arranged in three rows of four. They were high-powered lasers, with the emphasis on high.

In a normal ship, they'd be called Hellbore weapons, according to the references I'd found in the laser weapons that the AI selected. They were rarely used, primarily because why carry a horrifically powerful laser on any ship, if you only got to fire it a few times before you had to eject it and leave it behind?

The radiation damage that would ensue from each firing was prohibitive. And unless you could safely deal with that, you got a handful of shots and then had to dump it, facing the choice of leaving your ship defenseless or irradiated.

Arise: Conqueror

I could reform my nanites, over and over, as well as make devices designed to strip the radiation away between shots, so that wasn't as much of a problem. Then, provided I absorbed some mass that could be converted into a substance called laganite, and used that to form the surrounding walls? I could use it indefinitely.

The Ændari and others didn't use it, because it was just too much fucking hassle. Sure, it was powerful, but the laganite would only give the weapon a few extra shots before it needed to be reformed, peeling apart under the battery of radiation.

That wasn't possible with the Ændari's current level of control over nanites. Although they'd been experimenting with it before the nanite plague had mind fucked them, it'd been a low priority test.

The Engineering sub-mind had identified it as being the solution as soon as the Hellbore batteries were recommended. The AI had leapt on it, refining the fifty lasers it'd planned to use down to a mere thirty-six much more powerful ones.

The massively higher output of the new power systems meant that they could be powered easily, and if the GGC took down the shields on a ship, they'd rip it a new asshole.

Limited time and space meant that the point defense lasers and so on were scrapped from the design. The big ones were turret-mounted and could move in all directions. They might be overkill to use for that, after all, but in this fight I was on the American side of things: *There is no overkill—there is only reload and fire again.*

Beyond that, I pulled the same trick that I had before, layering shields and dedicating one of the two additional "normal" sized reactors to power just those, with additional power banks forming as quickly as I could make them.

Searching nearby space, I quickly found a pair of satellites that were presumably damaged recently—their decaying orbit meant they'd not be up here much longer anyway—and I snagged them both.

Pulling their matter inside and beginning conversion, I finally allowed myself to check the overall situation in the system, having forced myself to block out as much as I could until I was able to actually do something about it.

I'd saved a tremendous amount of time in getting from the node to the planet, and from the planet back up here, which was fantastic, but the changing situation deeper in the system was a nightmare.

The UC fleet—the three main battleships that still comprised it, anyway—were in full "bug out" mode. They'd been in close with the original and heavily reduced Ændari fleet that they'd been busy mauling, and now the Ændari second fleet that Shan'Gai had jumped in were making it clear that they weren't taking any prisoners.

That second fleet, I was betting, was entirely controlled and commanded by Shan'Gai—especially after the things said by the last avatar—and had been streaming right for me on the planet, thinking to defend their harvester.

They might not be interested in the damaged UC battleships, but they equally weren't going to leave an enemy that was weaker than them alive, so the UC had to get out of the way fast.

Then, we'd apparently gotten a swarm of smaller volunteer ships jumping in at Ingrid's request. But they were barely more than corvettes and gunboats or modified transports; the majority were still on their way.

They had balls, but the only reason they were still alive was that they'd jumped in at the "normal" Lagrange point in the middle of the system, while Shan'Gai had manipulated space and gravity to a large enough degree the Ændari fleet under his control had landed a third of the way closer to me and the planet.

If they had jumped in at the same time as the Ændari fleet? They'd have been destroyed in *seconds*. As it was, they were burning for the node, and I could dimly feel communications from Ingrid being exchanged with them.

I quickly plotted out fresh intercept paths and nodded to myself unthinkingly.

They were going to pass close by the Ændari, but if they kept to their current course, they'd probably escape them.

Shan'Gai himself—or itself, or whatever, *that wanker*—was finally back moving again, but he looked to be having issues, flying slowly. The engines, from what I could see from here, were firing erratically.

I paused, wondering whether the loss of his avatars had an effect on him, or whether the massive energy expenditure of levelling out such a huge gravity gradient was enough to break him.

It could be either, but I was betting that even diminished and mad as he was, he'd be a handful all on his own if the UC battleships got too close.

Then, just to make my Tuesday oh so much better, the new and even goddamn larger Ændari fleet, one that I was betting had pretty much drained their systems of all their defenses to form, had jumped in to play as well.

This was the reason I'd found almost nobody in the various systems I'd jumped through earlier. The main fleet had arrived.

The small swarm of ships that had come to support us were caught between the largest two enemy fleets, both the main Ændari one that was broadcasting demands to all and sundry to surrender to them—and that included Shan'Gai and myself—and the one he'd jumped in.

His fleet, that I was now thinking of as the rebel Ændari fleet, had adjusted course, and were headed for a nearby world, presumably on a slingshot maneuver, planning to use the planet's gravity to let them turn without sacrificing speed.

Plotting out their course now, I was guessing that Shan'Gai had called to them for help, as he was slap-bang in the middle of the two fleets, and clearly struggling to get out of there.

Either way, though, I now had a solid plan in place.

First and foremost, if the Ændari main fleet wanted to attack Shan'Gai? Hell yes, more power to them. That the other fleet was doing a slingshot and presumably heading back toward this one? Well, that was either good or very bad.

Arise: Conqueror

If the Ændari didn't realize that the fleet was at the very least working with Shan'Gai, then they'd probably let them join up. Then hopefully the rebel fleet would tear the Ændari loyalist one a new asshole when they weren't expecting it. If my enemies wanted to weaken each other first for me? Hell yes, I'd take that all day long.

If, however, the fleet was rejoining the other and they were planning to be allies, well…then we were *fucked*.

What I needed to do first was cut down on the numbers headed for the node. That would give Ingrid some time to deal with those already aboard and keep things to a reasonable level. Then I needed to try to take out the wounded Ændari battleships. If they were allowed to rejoin their main fleet, they'd just raise the strength of the enemy to insane heights.

With that in mind, I reached out my senses, searching and finding the bright star in the sea of localized gravity that was the node.

It wasn't difficult. The twisting of space around it that enabled its reactors to draw in so much energy also kept it drifting through space, untethered to any one system.

As soon as I found it, I triggered the power cycle, charging the engines and feeling both pride and elation as they surged to life easily. Not bad for a lunatic everyone said would never amount to much.

Starting forward, I rolled onto the new course, not fully subsuming myself into the ship this time, just linking to it, ready to detach again. I grinned and started a new production line internally, building *drones*.

It took a lot of power for me to jump the whole ship, sure, but the ship generated a hell of a lot of power as well. And as to me personally jumping? Well, my small personal power core was enough to manage that, as long as I wasn't stupid with it.

With that in mind, and the lack of need for anything resembling organs now, I started what I hoped would be the last personal core upgrade in myself for a while, dedicating a significant portion of my torso to creating a much larger core than ever before.

Then I integrated a directional shield generator again as well, because why the hell not.

Half an hour for the nanites to form the greater core, power it and the shield—that was fine. The one thing about space battles, as far as my enemies knew, was that they were slow to happen.

That meant I had a single advantage the likes of which my enemies had never seen, as those who *had* seen it? Well, none of them were alive to tell the tale afterward.

Firing the engines, I picked up speed, wanting to build up a decent velocity before the jump, and giving the various systems the time they needed to build.

Engines were powered and working, shields were in progress still, the GGC and lasers were little more than good-size bumps and carven lines in the ship's hull currently, so I was betting that they'd take at least another half an hour to get ready, with the banks of power cell storage being the last to complete in approximately an hour.

That was understandable, even if I didn't like it.

I had several tons of mass being broken down in the conversion process, and that was going well. But again, the time it would take to build up the null coins I wanted would take a while.

Fortunately, I still had a load from the remains of the UC warship I'd had my harvester work on in the node earlier. Those coins still filled a significant portion of the hull, so that'd be plenty to get me started, until I could make the most of the plentiful matter out there.

The two things I had going for me right now were plenty of power, and that with all the madness of ships going in all directions, the enemy couldn't possibly keep track of everything.

"Ingrid," I called to her, getting a *"I'm busy"* sense that lasted a few minutes, before she finally responded, feeling harassed.

"Tell me you've got a plan," she said, desperate hope battling with terror.

"I think so. What's wrong?" I asked, confused. I'd checked the entire system as near as I could from here, and although things were pretty shitty, they weren't beyond us.

"It's Far."

"Your dad? What's that crazy bastard done now?" I asked.

"He and Mor have gathered everyone they could. He says there's enough of them to make a difference and he's coming to help."

"Right?" I agreed, not seeing the issue.

"Steve, they're my parents, and they're jumping into a war zone, one where we're heavily outnumbered and they're going arrive at the jump point when the Ændari are still close enough to turn on them!"

"Ingrid..." I started to say, then paused, not knowing how to say it without coming across like an asshole. *"It's war. We need them."* I know it sounded shit, but I had no alternative.

"I know that, Steve!" she snapped at me. *"I asked them to come. I asked them to bring everyone, but that was before this fleet arrived, and now, I don't see how we can win!"*

"Because we have to," I said. *"What's happening with the UC?"*

"What?"

"The UC," I repeated. *"This is a full-on war that's breaking out here, no longer raids and little fights. There're multiple fleets jumping in and it's only escalating, so where the hell is the main UC battle fleet? I can't believe that jumping in piecemeal was a damn plan. There must be more out there on the way, right?"*

"They...Steve, I don't think they're coming," she whispered after a few seconds of hesitation, her fear and horror clear in her words. *"When I told them what was happening, they told me that there was a plan for victory but that they had to accept possible losses in war. Then...then they cut the connection!"*

"Argus, can you identify any fleets that are in motion?" I asked the AI, hope dying. *"Come on, man, give me good news..."*

"Current UC main battle fleets are deploying, but in limited numbers," the AI replied steadily. *"I estimate that due to the grouping of available, attuned*

and active nanites, that significant units of UC original-grade BWV soldiers have been summoned to set locations, but their gatherings are unlikely to inspire hope in you at this time."

"Why?" My stomach dropped into my boots.

"The rally points used suggest that they are the beginning of multiple strike points in other sectors, rather than a coordinated force being deployed to engage the enemy in this."

"What the fuck?" I whispered.

"Predictive modeling suggest that the UC are attempting to use their unlocked nanites to gain access and lay claim to the other universal system quadrant nodes."

"They're what*?"* I snarled.

"The plan is a sound one, if unfortunate for our current situation and based on faulty logic," he assured me. *"Should the UC gain control of the other nodes, then the Ændari would be unable to carry out their genocidal attack in those sectors. And although this sector would be lost, the capture and control of the remaining sectors would hand the UC a decisive victory over their enemy. They appear unaware that they will not be permitted access to the other nodes."*

"You're shitting me!" I snarled.

"Negative. Also, additional already staged UC forces are being diverted from local support. In-system UC forces have been ordered to fight to the last."

"Motherfuckers!" I hissed in fury, immediately triggering a link to the local battle group and Admiral Dolfing.

"Dolfing!" I snapped as soon as he answered, looking harassed as he appeared.

"Lord," he replied tiredly, nodding his greeting.

"They're not coming," I said flatly.

"No," he agreed. "I suspected as much, but I was duty bound to make them aware of the situation here."

"What did you do?" I grated out.

"I informed them of the current situation, and that so many of the Ændari forces were concentrated on us, reducing their strength in other sectors."

"You fucking did what?!" I whispered, staring at him in fury. "You—"

"Steve!" Ingrid cut me off, before switching to personal communication with me. *"Leave the chat for a minute. Get control of yourself and come back."*

I gritted my teeth, furious at being sent away like a shouting child. But knowing myself and her well enough, I did it, leaving an image of myself to maintain the little dignity I had left.

Once I was out, though, in the silence of my ship, I screamed in utter rage. For long seconds I hung there, buried in my ship. Then I cut loose, doing the only thing I could, considering the limited opportunities available to me here.

I broke my core body free, expanded the section around me inside of the ship up and out like an inflated balloon, and formed a punching bag.

One that looked a *lot* like Emberalis.

I spent thirty seconds kicking the absolute fuck out of it, before I finally regained control and rolled the changes back, rejoining the conversation with Dolfing.

"And I asked for immediate aid," he was saying. "I made it clear that although there was no way we could win against such superior firepower, should we lose, then the entire sector would be lost."

"And they're still hanging us out to dry?" I asked the question, forcing myself to be as calm as I could.

"As much as I dislike it, I understand it." He sighed. "Steve, this is war. If they lose this sector but can decisively crush the Ændari in the remaining sectors? It'd save lives."

"How many?" I asked. "How many fucking lives will be lost if they sacrifice this entire sector?"

"Thirty billion," he said easily, not having to check.

"You had that number ready," I accused.

"It's the number I was given," he admitted. "When I made the same argument to them that you are to me—thirty billion lives in this sector, and that's the overall rough population that are likely to be builder impregnated. You said yourself that they're likely to kill the builder off, but not the hosts. That means that most of those thirty billion will live perfectly well. They've never had access to their builders before the last few weeks, and that they'll even notice the difference is unlikely."

"I—"

"Let me finish please, Steve." He cut me off. "This is a simple numbers game. It's not one I like, but it's one I can't argue with. If the Ændari take this sector, they'll kill the nanites off, and that includes Shan'Gai, and yes, yourself, and all the UC soldier and higher advanced personnel. Shan'Gai has been exposed as a traitor, and his actions have directly cost trillions of lives over the eons. This is a logical step, to remove him and yes, yourself with minimal risk. I don't *like* it, but that's not my call to make. Look at it all and tell me you wouldn't make a similar choice if your position and the UC leadership's were reversed. Thirty billion lives, even if they would all definitely die, is a drop in the ocean compared to the hundreds of trillions of lives across the remaining sectors."

I opened my mouth to tell him of course we would, that it was ridiculous, and instead Ingrid spoke.

"He's right. *You're* right, Admiral Dolfing. So, what are our options?" she said to him directly.

"Lady Ingrid." He bowed his head to her. "I'm sorry. If it means anything, then please believe me, I appreciate your understanding in all of this. My crew are the only family I have and—" He flinched as something behind him blew out in a shower of sparks and alarms filled the air. "Dammit! Get that locked down!" he barked at the people who flooded the back of the bridge, running to fix the damaged and shorting panel.

"Admiral?" she asked concernedly.

"It's battle damage from earlier." He turned back as he rubbed at the side of his face tiredly. "We took the brunt of the Ændari attack."

"I'm sorry to hear that," she said. "So, do we have any other options?"

"With the way things are?" he asked, then shook his head. "Not that I can see, frankly. I've been ordered to hold the line, and to fight to the last. We'd have done that regardless. We know what the Ændari would do if they capture us alive. But it means we can't try to make a break for the jump point. The UC may send a small contingent to try to help us hold things a little longer, but I seriously doubt it."

"Why?" I asked bluntly.

"It'd be sending more good people to their deaths and losing us those ships," he said sadly. "If they thought they could win? Yes, they'd send ships to help. But if they instead allow this sector to fall, and take the remaining ones? It's a significant win."

"Until the Ændari try to take those sectors back," I pointed out. "If they gain access to unlock their capabilities fully..."

"Then they'll still be forced to funnel everyone through this sector to get them unlocked," he said. "We'd have eleven sectors all activating our people, with full access and control over the nodes. There has to be a way to deactivate just the Ændari nanites, or at least that's what the leadership are convinced of. Either way, though, the decision has been made."

"More ships are coming," I told him, shaking my head. "People we asked to help—they're coming, thinking they're going to be part of a fleet, and they'll be slaughtered."

"Tell them to fall back," he said. "If they could delay the fight meaningfully, then I'd be pleased, but the way you say that, I'd doubt that's what you mean."

"No." I agreed. "They're our family and friends, in a handful of basically homebuilt ships."

"Then they'll die," he said calmly. "They need to abandon this."

"I already tried," Ingrid said softly. "It's my parents, and they won't listen."

"I'm sorry to hear that."

"Dolfing..." I chewed on my lip as I thought. "Is there anything we can do to change the UC's mind on this, to force them to send ships? They can still send the damn assaults to the other nodes if they want. They won't need fleets, after all, but we need them here! If we can take out Shan'Gai and the main Ændari fleet, surely that's worth the risk!"

"If they believed they could win with minimal casualties?" He tilted one hand from side to side like a set of balancing scales. "Maybe. Honestly, I'd think the very best we could hope for here is that you could convince the leaders of a few of the internal factions to bring their forces, or even a sector patrol..."

"The Forgeship." Ingrid gasped. "Clicqo and Shanah—they were supportive. Maybe..."

"I think this was the sector fleet." I glanced at the admiral for confirmation.

"It was," he said. "That's why our reinforcements have been dribbling in, instead of an overwhelming force all arriving at once. The ships that have been jumping in are those that had already been on more distant patrols. They were all ordered to come here directly by Emberalis, instead of a rendezvous point, then jumping from there here."

"So that idiot even managed to screw that up," I whispered. "Okay, the Forgeship, though, that's a massively powerful craft, right?"

"It is. And I promise you that they wouldn't be allowed to bring it here."

"Why not?"

"It's begun repairs and rebuilds. Once the Forgeship is back to operational, there's no fleet currently under the Ændari's control that would survive an encounter with it. That's the winning hand here. If they can keep the limited Forgeships we have out of the war until they're operational? No matter what the Ændari try, we'll still win."

"They'll take years to repair," I ground out.

"And us fighting to the last here and damaging the enemy fleet enough will give them some extra time toward that." He nodded. "You can ask, but I guarantee they won't agree."

"He's right," Ingrid said. "Admiral, there must be something? It can't all be hopeless."

"There're three options that I can see here. First, and as much as it pains me to suggest this, we head to the node and offload as many crew as possible to assist in its defense. This gives you a little reinforcement and lets our people face the enemy. Then I and a skeleton crew take the fleet back into the fight."

"With a skeleton crew, you'll lose faster," I pointed out.

"We will," he agreed. "But it's less people to die when we send our reactors critical and try to take out as many of the enemy as possible with the explosion."

"Okay…" I nodded. "Nasty, but possible. What else?"

"We fight as we are—pull in close, turtle up, and we work around the edge of the incoming forces…pick off what we can, hit and run. Because of the high speed of actual space combat, unless you're on the same trajectory as your target, it's down to the AI as much as anything. Weapons fire in a fraction of a second, then you're past each other. If we can pick off the injured and outliers of the enemy, we can whittle their strength down. Realistically, we cannot win. I need to stress that. We can anger them and poke at them, weakening them overall, but a single mistake and it's over."

"Not a winning strategy," I agreed. "Anything else?"

"Hit and run, but with a twist." He looked at me. "Lady Ingrid pointed out your high-speed jumps, and considering the way that Shan'Gai helped the enemy to jump into a different location, rather than the actual jump point…could you do that for us?"

"For the *battleships*?"

"Yes, all three. Though, if you could manage it for the smaller craft that would actually help as we could—"

"You have no idea what you're asking," I said. "I'd need access to your reactor's entire output."

"The jump reactors or the main?"

"The…wait, you've got dedicated jump reactors?" I asked, reevaluating things.

"We do, though the additional charge is diverted to help in powering other facilities when they're not needed for that."

"How much are they needed?" I asked.

"I'm not sure how to answer that," he admitted. "There's never spare power in a battle—it's *all* needed. But they're designed to assist the main systems, and be ready to power a jump if needed, so…?"

"Okay, so if for example, and I need to be clear, I'm fuckin' spitballing here…"

"He's got an idea and he's running with it," Ingrid translated for the admiral.

I winced, then went on. "Yeah, that…okay, if I could jump you in, when the enemy weren't expecting you, and at a set location, like say to the rear of those heavily damaged battleships? What could you do?"

"If they weren't expecting us?" he asked.

"Yeah."

"We could kill them."

"You're sure?"

"Very sure," he confirmed. "All ships, both our own and the Ændari, are run on a simple 'everyone else is an idiot' mindset by necessity. All weapons are under lockouts that can only be released by the captains of each vessel. The AI in fast-pass battles will do the firing, but only when they've been unlocked to do so. And in case of other ships maneuvering too close and accidentally triggering defensive weapons fire, the consoles are locked out otherwise. The only exception is if you're on picket duty at a jump point or similar."

"So…" I dragged the word out, my mind racing.

"So if you could jump us in close to them when they're not expecting it, and convinced that we're hours away from an intercept, at the very least we'd have the element of surprise and be able to attack first. At best? Their weapons will be under lockout and we could eliminate all three battleships without taking damage."

"Could you instead tear holes in them and move on?" I asked.

"Well, yes, but what would be the point?" he asked, bewildered.

"The Devourer?" Ingrid guessed, and I glanced at her, sharing my idea, and getting a burst of hope back. "That could work."

"Okay, okay, Dolfing, we might have a chance then…" I nodded to myself. "If we can pull this off, this is going to be the most one-sided and vicious battle you've ever seen. But fuck it, it's not like we give a shit, and it's all about the win, right? So, first, you're going to reach out and get as many reinforcements in on this as possible. If there's a scooter out there with a fucking popgun on it, we're gonna need it. Then, what we do is…"

CHAPTER FORTY-THREE

I checked the last details on my ship-body, then took a deep breath, really fucking hoping that Dolfing wasn't pulling some kind of deep game here, and that he didn't have a super sneaky plan to kill me, because that would really ruin my day.

Also, he'd better be right about his engineers' predictions and this system they used to help recover damaged ships.

If he was wrong, this was going to really suck.

The ass-end of my ship was now twice the damn size it had been. It'd needed some significant changes to make the rest of the ship damn well work now, considering that the minor details like the GGC needed a straight line to fire along, but it was done.

The new augmented and oh so much larger gravity manipulator filled the new space back there. It was a fusion of the gravity drive design I'd used before, and the amalgamation of the various systems I'd been bastardizing and using as I needed since I'd finished reaching for the fucking stars with the tech upgrades.

It was ready, though, and despite the two extra hours it'd taken to build and refine it, it was worth it.

Ingrid and Dolfing had reached out and they'd pulled strings, had arguments and had generally lied, bullied, threatened, and cajoled to get us the reinforcements we so desperately needed.

Malthus had gone one better, pulling on Choni's contacts to have a dozen small mercenary outfits "persuade" their employers to bring their ships along to help as well.

That was going to be either a fucker to explain later, or they'd be claiming they were always intending to help, no doubt. Mind you, if we lost this fight, it wasn't like *I'd* be the one needing to explain anything, so screw it.

I looked over the rest of the ship, nodding to myself.

Yeah, shields were down, but ready to charge; weapons were all finished and loaded; my new addition—that totally ruined the look of my teardrop crystal design ship but did what I needed—was installed in the bow. I was as ready as I was ever going to be.

"This is either going to fucking crash and burn, or I'm going to become a god," I muttered to myself.

Arise: Conqueror

"Will that make me Mrs. God?" Ingrid asked, making me smile and shake my head. *"What? Did you think I'd forget?"* she asked. *"A ring, a diamond ring, that's what you gave me, and believe me, you're not getting out of that, even if you do somehow become as big and powerful as your ego already thinks you are."*

"I love you," I whispered, and she replied the same.

"I love you too. Are you ready?"

"As I'll ever be," I said. *"I'd still rather jump there first and take out the landing craft."*

"If you do, then you prove that what they might have seen before was real. We can't risk it. After the battleships, then yes, please—I'd really like some reinforcements then. But for now, we can't risk it."

"Okay, here goes…" I felt the mental kiss on my cheek as she pulled back, reducing her presence to a mere observer, ready to help when I needed.

I sensed the others with her, Belle forming the link that Ingrid guided. They were laid out like the spokes of a wheel. Ingrid and Belle were in the center, side by side, on the floor of the control room.

Starting at Ingrid's feet, Jonas and Scylla laid side by side, their hands entwined. Then came Paul and Courtney, with Oxus at Belle's feet; then Malthus and Benat, followed finally by Zhonat and Bach.

That wasn't many of us to be carrying this off, it really wasn't, but this little group had to be ready to work together. And more importantly, they had to trust and do exactly what I told them—no more and no less.

I needed to be able to trust them implicitly, and although there were people I'd have rather had in on this, especially in place of the new starters to the group, I did trust them, and I needed someone to help carry the extra load.

"Okay, people," I said into the group. *"Here we go!"*

Then I hit it.

Space around my ship-body blurred. The distant trio of wounded UC battleships and their consorts, only dimly able to be sensed at the best of times due to their relatively tiny mass, suddenly screamed into existence, right before me.

I shuddered as I burst into real space again. The branes had barely even materialized at the outermost edge of reality before I was out, and as soon as I appeared, I was rolling.

"Holyfuckin'shitonacracker!" I whimpered. The ship barely avoided slamming into the extended connections that formed a rat's nest, right where I'd said I'd be aiming for.

"Devourer?" Dolfing asked.

The comm pricked to life as I frantically formed gravitational bubbles at the same time as flaring my engines, twisting and rolling, pushing at the UC ships around me and their extended conduits.

"Fuck me sideways, you lunatics!" I grunted. "I told you I was aiming for there!"

"Yes?"

"Well, you had the goddamn cables there!"

"Yes?"

"Steve, they accept it when you tell them that you'll do something as gospel," Ingrid pointed out. *"If you don't want them to be ready, don't ask them to be."*

"It's not that..." I forced out, searching for the words. *"Ingrid, not counting the jump, I'm travelling at a speed that would cover Earth to the moon in less than three seconds. They literally left me forty meters of fucking clearance on each side of the space I jumped into!"*

"So they left you room to adjust?"

"No!" I snapped. *"No, they fucking didn't! That's the point! I could cover that space in a fraction of a millisecond, and if they weren't all going at exactly the same speed, I would have crashed through them all!"*

"Steve, you need to explain yourself to them more carefully then. But look in the bright side."

"What?"

"You're alive, and you hit the nail on the head, right?" she said, and it was all I could do to keep it to a low whimper.

"Devourer, are you ready?" Dolfing asked, and I dragged down a deep breath before responding.

"Yeah," I forced out. "Yeah, I will be. Just give me a second."

Reaching out, I manipulated the nanites that made up my outer hull, forming connections that writhed and extended out, puckering at the ends and locking onto the offered power cables.

As soon as the connection was strong, and confirmed, I gave the nod. The secondary connectors flowed out, three from each of the battleships.

One went to me, and one to each of the other two, linking the ships into a single gestalt massive warship.

For this, as the test flight, I'd been firm: no smaller craft allowed—we'd come back and get them later—just the three battleships. And now, as I felt them connecting? Damn.

The power that flooded into me was *incredible.*

"Okay, people, you all ready?" I got a confirmation from both Dolfing and the other two captains of their respective ships. I reached out, draining huge amounts of energy from the dedicated jump drive reactors that the massive battleships had held ready for me.

The power inundated me, my own ship's capacity nowhere near enough to hold it, and instead—aside from a fraction that I diverted to boost my shields, as I'd had to drop them for the connections to be made—I fed it all into twisting space.

"Jumping in three...two...one..."

I'd sent the plot to each of them and confirmed the plan, which, honestly, was more in the form of wishful fucking thinking and outrageous insanity than anything else, but fuck it.

If this worked, we'd be revolutionizing space warfare. And it'd be the kind of change where once the genie was out of the bottle, everyone else was fucked until they caught up.

Arise: Conqueror

At zero, we jumped. Space blurred, stars going from pinpricks of gleaming nuclear fire to an ever so brief blur. Then we were out again, erupting into space behind the nearest planet, as compared to our enemies' point of view.

Thirty seconds of adjusting our path, then another jump. Two more jumps followed that, each as hidden as was possible. The jumps were setting us onto a slightly different orbital rotation, until exiting the fourth jump, with the jump reactors now screaming that they weren't designed to be drained this frequently.

I was only taking about ten percent of their charge each time, but that's life. Fuck it. As long as they didn't melt down, this was either going to be the greatest ambush in history, studied in every military textbook to come, or the most insane mistake of all time.

Linked as I was to all three ships, the sudden screaming of their proximity alarms was almost deafening as I'd jumped us in at literal "knife-fight" range for warships in space, with less than ten miles to separate us.

That sounded like a big distance in almost any other terms, but when the ships themselves were miles long, that was insane.

My three battleships opened fire, and so did I. Our controls—or, more accurately, *my* controls—guided the entire group.

That wasn't an ego thing. I just needed control to be able to guide us in and out. And should one move too far in one direction at any point, they'd break the tethers.

Instead, as all three battleships opened fire, batteries of lasers along their length firing in relays, all hell broke loose.

My three GGCs hurled their projectiles out into the void, covering the distance to tear into the side of the enemy vessels at horrific speeds. Their payloads converted from nuclear and penetration rounds into high-energy explosions that wreaked havoc on the massive shields.

The lasers of three battleships, all coordinated, at nigh on point-blank range, firing in heavy volleys into the side of the least wounded of the three enemy vessels was already enough to take the shields to the edge of failure.

With the GGC shots ripping out and the Hellbores joining in, the shields were down before the target knew what hit it. Then we were focusing our fire, carving very specific lines into the hull, all three targeting systems locked onto the same sections.

The upper layers of armor were ablative, meters thick and designed to take the pounding of the enemy and break apart, failing, but without effecting the layers hidden beneath.

They normally took significant damage before failure. Considering that the average engagement might last fractions of a second, though, they frequently saved the ships from "real" damage until they were hit over and over again.

In this case, with three battleships all firing in coordinated fashion at almost point-blank range, it lasted less than a second.

The Ændari bridge vanished beneath the massive onslaught of heavy radiation, the crew vaporized before they even knew what hit them.

The intelligence that the UC had on the Ændari battleships was probably about the same as they had on the UC, which meant that they knew exactly where to strike to take down the main bridge, and then to dig into the secondary.

I'd been *very* specific about the depth that they could go to, and just how much depended on them being very, very careful about this.

After the bridge was torn apart in seconds, even buried as deep in the superstructure as it was, the secondary bridge was attacked, but not penetrated nor destroyed. The nose of my ship hummed as it launched ten drones at the hole we'd just torn in the enemy vessel, before we shifted our aim, moving on.

We repeated the process with the next battleship in line, then the third. As soon as all three were holed, their bridges destroyed, shields down, and the secondary CIC exposed, the drones were fired, and then I was charging for the jump.

"Hold fire. Jumping in three…two…one…" I barked, before the blur of space rolled around us, and we were back.

A planet erupted from the void into our vision, making me almost redecorate my underwear, until I remembered that I had nothing to redecorate them with. Then we twisted and rolled; the engines fired, screaming across the border of the gravity pull, using it to guide us into a slingshot.

Three minutes of sustained burn around the outer edge of the Jovian's pull, and we were on the new course. A second and a third jump later, and space resolved to show a tiny collection of panicked vessels ahead of us.

We'd made it.

I sagged, more mentally than physically thanks to the bond I had with the ship around me, but the relief? I was barely able to keep from joining in as the three battleship's bridges erupted into cheers.

"*Steve!*" Ingrid gasped, relaxing at last, as the others did the same.

"*Did you get it?*" I asked. "*Did you understand it?*"

"*Are you mental?*" Jonas asked into the chat.

"*What?*"

"*Are you fuckin' mental!*" he half screamed. "*That…that shouldn't have worked! And even that it did? How the ever-living fuck did you come up with that?!*"

"*I broke the system.*"

"*That…that sounds right,*" he said, deflating slightly. "*Shit, though, boy, that shouldn't be possible. You know Argus is locking up, right?*"

"*He's what?*"

"*Negative,*" Argus interrupted. "*I have not locked up. But the RI that I dedicated to the task of copying your jump capability is proving to be unsuitable to the level of computational complexity required.*"

"*So…*"

"*So he locked up,*" Jonas said.

"*Can you do it?*" I asked.

"*Uncertain,*" Argus replied. "*I estimate a seventy-six percent likelihood of success. But judging from the margins provided for jump, this error percentage is unacceptable. Attempting to refine programming.*"

"*What?*" I asked the others.

Arise: Conqueror

"He locked up and now he's freaking out, trying to come up with reasons that your meat-based brain can do what his crystal one can't," Jonas translated.

"No, Argus is trying to turn art into science," Ingrid corrected. *"Essentially, that's the difference here. Steve created the capacity to do this entirely through instinct and experimentation, hence the art side of it, with the science side fully unlocked to him at a subconscious level. For anyone else, even an AI, to be able to replicate that, they need practice. Argus, how many possible simulations of the jumps done so far have you ran since we stopped?"*

"One million, four hundred, and eleven thou—"

"Exactly." Ingrid nodded. *"That's the difference. Once Argus has figured this out, we'll have a program that can be used for all the ships to replicate Steve's technique. It'll also be something that the Ændari can replicate, once they've seen it enough to figure it out and have time to get their ships configured to do it, so we need to move quickly."*

"With that in mind, reaching out to Dolfing," I said.

"Devourer!" The admiral, when he answered, was grinning, his face flushed as he spoke quickly. "It worked!"

"It did, and it worked because you trusted me, Admiral, so thank you for that," I said. "That could have gone very differently."

"It could," he agreed, "but it didn't. And with that in mind, I've got an expansion on the previous plan, if you've got time for it?"

"Uh…"

"Good." He nodded and went on before I could speak. "My executive officer is guiding the smaller craft into docking or attaching to the hulls in readiness, so, how do you feel about boarding actions?"

"I like where this is going," I said.

"You would." Ingrid sighed. "Admiral, first, let me add my congratulations to you. I know your crews don't know who I am, but if you ever get the chance to pass on my compliments, please do so."

"Of course." He nodded, smiling graciously before it turned more feral. "So…boarding action?"

"Go on." I nodded.

"The Ændari are arrogant bastards," he pointed out.

"Not going to argue with that," I agreed.

"Well, how would you feel about unleashing an entire company of UC soldiers into their dreadnought?"

"I like it." I nodded. "Not sure how you're planning on doing this, but I do like it."

"You said that we're doing a series of these hit-and-run attacks, whittling them down and opening up the ship to your drones. Then you're firing in a group of them, providing you with a personal platform to jump to and carry out an undercover attack."

"Yeah." I nodded. "Once you're stable enough that I can hand over control of the jump to you all, I'll start jumping from ship to ship, slaughter as many of the Ændari as I can and essentially feed on them. Then I'll take the secondary CIC, slave it to you, and your own secondary CICs can each control a remote battleship.

"That gives us the ability to not only grow our forces by the same number that we reduce the enemy by, but it means that if the shit hits the fan, we can use their ships as either kamikaze… Sorry." I took a deep breath, wondering how many goddamn phrases I'd used with them so far that he'd just accepted and had no clue what they meant.

"Those ships can then be used as shields for our own, and detonated whenever we want," I explained. "That's one option. Or I can fly them back out of the battle, leave them to drift and I can instead harvest them of all the Ændari aboard. That strengthens me, weakens the Ændari, and gives us another option to create our own dreadnought, though I'd imagine that dick Shan'Gai won't give us the time to do that."

"That's what you'd said before," he agreed. "However, the Ændari are unlikely to have significant fighting forces aboard the main battleships and dreadnought. They use dedicated troop and assault transports for that, as do the UC."

"Right?"

"Well, what do you think of doing as we have been, hammering a hole in the enemy from a new direction, then releasing an assault transport or three? Have them board the dreadnought?"

"I like it," I admitted, nodding slowly. "But we don't have any assault transports."

"We have four incoming," Ingrid corrected. "Well, we've got one dedicated transport, and three warships, each with a full brigade aboard."

"That could work." I nodded. "What's to stop the surrounding ships from firing on the dreadnought, though?"

"Self-preservation." Dolfing smiled. "The Ændari are less a true fleet, and more a loose coalition of allies, ones that hate one another but accept that the rest of the galaxy hates them as well, so they need one another too much to eliminate rivals at every turn."

"Right?"

"So if a battleship opens fire on the dreadnought, the dreadnought will return fire."

"Even if the dreadnought crew know they're losing the ship?" Ingrid asked. "They won't hold fire to enable the UC soldiers to be killed and to stop the ship falling into enemy hands?"

"You're thinking like us." Dolfing shook his head. "The Ændari will try to hide the boarding and any success our teams are having from each and every other ship, because each Ændari is out for themselves. If they lose the dreadnought, they'll lose face and their position in their society. Every single face they stepped on in their climb to the top will be waiting with a knife, so they know their only chance is to fight it out themselves. As it is, they'll all be under the control of a single admiral, or an ambassador, and they'll be aboard the dreadnought. If they fall, the surrounding consort battleships will be more concerned with surviving the night of knives than they will us."

"The 'night of knives'?" I asked.

"It's what we call it—no clue what they call it. But in their society, power belongs to the one who can hold onto it, and any weakness, a loss of face or power, can cost them their lives. From what we know, there's a chronicle they keep, and it's death to go against the record of it. So if they're named in it, it's their greatest achievement and the beginning of the end for them, as everyone else in their entire society wants to get their name in there as well."

"Fucking weird society," I muttered.

"It is. But the important point is that they'll do the work of trying to hide things for us, right up until the dreadnought is captured. At that point, they'll try to save face by stabbing one another in the back. But if we could gain control, and slave the dreadnought to one of us, then jump the boarding craft out?"

"We could use it as a shield to attack their side, as well as taking out their most potent weapon," I agreed.

"And…" Dolfing said. "If we can do that, if we can show the UC that not only have we survived the fight to this point, but we've captured or killed a significant enough portion of the enemy fleet to make it possible for them to win?"

"They'll come running in." I nodded. "Glory hounds."

"I can guess at the meaning of that, and no," Dolfing said, "the decision to abandon us was a sound tactical decision, even if it's one that we personally disagreed with. If the facts have changed? So too will the reasoning."

"There's one problem with all of this," Ingrid said.

"Shan'Gai."

"Exactly," she said firmly. "He's recovering, and he's heading straight for the second fleet—his own. Where the Ændari may be ignoring you and focusing on one another, the UC, or him, he'll only be focused on two things: getting 'his' nanites, which means facing you, or escaping."

"And we can't let him do either of those things." I nodded. "Especially as if he's paying attention, he might have already figured out how I'm doing some of the jumps."

"We can hope not," Dolfing said. "But yes. That's one fight that we can't help with."

"No," I agreed. "It takes a Devourer to fight a Devourer."

"So…can we do it again?" Dolfing asked.

I grinned at him, then turned to Ingrid. "What do you think?"

"We can, and we should," she said. "We need to give Argus ten minutes or so, maybe a little longer to refine the program, then we'll be ready."

I nodded, taking a deep breath. That was why they were linked to me, after all. They were literally linked to me, and to Argus and a block of solid memory crystal that he had freed up for this project.

If they could get the RI he was coding to be able to carry out the jumps for them the way I was currently doing it, then that would free me up to do what I did best.

I was going to go fuck shit up and take all the monsters' lunch money.

Or, you know, that of the Ændari battleship's crews.

CHAPTER FORTY-FOUR

The second jump was a lot more sedate, given that we were doing it with a bunch of the smaller vessels attached to the battleships, and to a point close enough to the node that we could offload them.

We'd barely made it out of the gravity skip to the node, before Ingrid was reaching out in a foul temper, given that the newly arrived three ships that had just jumped in ahead of schedule were barely ten minutes from the back of the Ændari fleet.

That was ten minutes' flight time for a laser. It'd be a hell of a lot less powerful when it hit anything the Ændari fired at due to the attenuation effect by the time it arrived.

That'd be combated by firing an absolute buttload of lasers all at the same target, and yeah, that was exactly the kind of shit that both sides were already doing in battles.

That meant we had almost no time to get back and grab them, then jump back to here, before the Ændari could destroy the ships.

"Explain yourselves!" Dolfing barked at them, linking Ingrid and me in as he pulled up the lead ship, making me curse even more as a harried and confused-looking hairball was in mid-rant at a devilkin when the connection was accepted. "You damn fools, you're early!"

"Who the hell are—" The hairball broke off, before starting to scream at the navigator to "*Get us the hell out of here!*"

It took a few seconds of desperate arguing before the truth came out. And when it did, it wasn't good. The devilkin on the bridge, and those on the other six ships as well, had each tried appealing to their employers, and had been told no, basically.

There wasn't a cat in hell's chance that they were going to go and join a fool battle that even the UC wouldn't fight, and they'd set a course for a totally different star system.

That was when the devilkin had gotten together and had "diverted" the ships to come and help.

Apparently Choni and Malthus had laid down the law to the various devilkin factions and made it clear that if they ever wanted a chance to get the UC and others off their neck, we were it.

Arise: Conqueror

Many of those who would have listened in the first place were already on the node, and currently fighting for their lives against the Ændari boarders.

Others couldn't get to the fight. The devilkin had no dedicated ships. They were a poor people from a hellish planet that was being kept that way deliberately to keep their crystal mines producing for the UC, who desperately needed them to continue fighting the war.

In this case, though, they'd literally hijacked their employers' ships to come and fight. And as much as I was desperate to gather reinforcements and drop them into the fight to help Ingrid…the way that they'd done it wasn't the best.

Fuck it, though…I wasn't complaining.

"Navigator, stand down," I ordered, appearing on their screens in all my red and black marbled Devourer monstrosity, shocking them into silence. "You're here now, and while I understand the desire to be anywhere else, you've got reinforcements that we desperately need aboard. Hold your position. We'll come for you. But you're in the system for the fight now."

"The hell we are!" the captain of the ship screamed. "We're free agents, and you've got no chance in this fight. We're not stupid. You're…"

I spoke over him to Dolfing as I started the power cycling through my ship and me.

"Admiral, drop off our delivery as fast as possible, please, and explain the realities of life to the new recruits."

"Yes, Lord Devourer," he replied formally for the benefit of the new people. "And the Ændari assault landers?"

I glanced at the three ships that were all burning for the node, only a short distance ahead of us, and that we'd been planning to engage before jumping back into the fight.

"We'll come back for them," I growled. "Disengage our passengers, then tell them to get the hell out of the way. We'll have enough time for one barrage against the rear of the nearest ship. Cripple it if we can, and then we're jumping."

"As you command." With that, he took over the conversation with the panicking ship captains and the grinning devilkin, and I was back to Ingrid.

"It was Choni," she said to me, sending a sense of rueful approval. *"She told them that we were capturing and looting Ændari vessels, and if the devilkin ever wanted a chance at some of those ships, they needed to earn it. She's asked for one in ten of the ships you capture or destroy to be given to the devilkin as loot, in exchange for what's coming."*

"That's a lot of ships and matter that we'll be handing over if we win. And what do you mean, 'what's coming'?"

"These three are only the first," Ingrid said. *"She's called in every favor she has, as has Malthus. They and the other mercenaries have pooled their accounts. They've been begging, bribing, and outright stealing anything they can. There's a dozen ships on the surface of their world currently, or heading to it, ready to load up, with devilkin in basically iron and steel armor getting ready to board."*

"Iron and steel? That won't hold up to Ændari lasers." I winced at the thought of it.

"No, it won't, but apparently, they're bringing scrap with them. The UC soldiers here who we turned into engineers are working on an armor maker. What it produces will be basic compared to their own, but light-years ahead of anything the devilkin have access to currently."

"And all it'll cost to make them is scrap, considering the makers we've unlocked," I said.

"Exactly. They'll need a clear path to the node, and we'll need to cut our way through the Ændari already aboard to get them inside. But if we can do that? Between recovering the Ændari bodies and weapons, we'll have all we need."

"So you'll be able to hold?" I asked.

"Honestly, I think so, for a day or two at least. Each level is being turned into a death trap," she told me. *"I mean, unless the Ændari launch full assaults with more ships than they're bringing currently, anyway."*

"And that'll be a job for the smaller vessels, to make sure that doesn't happen," I agreed. *"Those that can't be taken into the fight directly can act as sentries and swarm a troop transport."*

"Exactly."

"Shit, we've really got a chance here," I whispered, the relief rising.

"That's all we've got though, a chance. But we're doing it without the UC, so once they see the fight is winnable?"

"They'll bring their fleets and it'll be a rout," I prayed. *"Did you hear from Clicqo and Shanah?"*

"Shanah wasn't available," she said, before speaking quickly. *"Not refusing to speak to me—Shanah was in a UC policy meeting, arguing for us to be given help, or so Clicqo told me. They're already gathering their ships as well. They don't have many. They're still a small population compared to the majority of the UC worlds, but they're as technologically advanced as any, and they're the best scouts in this sector, I've been assured. They'll send what they can raise, but it'll only be a handful of ships, as the majority were already with the fleet and were lost."*

"That's all we need," I said. *"A handful of ships from everywhere, and we've got a fleet that'll be enough."*

"And when the UC realizes that they might win the war elsewhere, but their members are revolting and sending forces to help us...well." She shrugged. *"They won't be able to stay away for long."*

"We hope."

"We hope," she agreed. *"Okay, looks like most of your hitchhikers are free, and we're ready for the next jump. Are you?"*

"Always," I promised, before sending her my love and focusing back on the current situation.

The Ændari fleet was still powering away from the jump point, though a number of the destroyers on the outside of the mass were pivoting, apparently planning to bring guns to bear on the freshly arrived trio.

Arise: Conqueror

I cursed, checking the current situation. Five ships hadn't managed to disengage from the battleships. I sent a thirty-second warning to Dolfing, while plotting a barrage aimed at the nearest assault transport's engines.

From this distance, even with the high-powered nuclear GGC rounds, there was a good chance we'd not be able to take them out. But either way, I'd be able to do some damage.

Then I was back to the plot, figuring out distances.

The Ændari had launched five assault ships, originally, for the node. Three had docked, one had been destroyed on approach, and one was currently trying to edge in. The node's defenses were sniping at it, and the currently docked ships were apparently unwilling to get their asses out of the way and expose themselves, to let in their "ally."

They were all loaded for bear, with literally hundreds of ground forces streaming into the node, and frantic battles being waged in the highly limited spaces inside.

Another three troop transports were inbound. Two were almost neck and neck, racing to be the first to the node, and I was targeting the one behind them.

The dozen or so smaller vessels that the UC fleet had in-system and that we'd gathered up were roughly equal to the transports, if the transports coordinated their defenses. But the chances were that the ships we were dropping off could take them out.

They'd take losses, though—possibly heavy ones.

That was why the plan had been, before the first of these devilkin "volunteers" had arrived, that the battleships would help out by taking on the transports.

That'd have made it a decisive victory, especially if the Ændari were stupid enough to try to stay docked at the node when the fight started.

Instead, we were going to have to jump back out, go rescue the smaller three ships and their onboard complements of troops, then probably jump them back.

The real issue, though? The devilkin were apparently just jumping in whenever they gained control of the ships they were on, mutiny style, if the captain wasn't interested in the insanity of joining our fight.

That meant we could end up being stuck jumping back and forth, interrupting the fight constantly.

That was a shitty way to win a war, sure, but if we left these forces to die piecemeal? It was even more of a waste.

A hundred tiny ships could overwhelm a bigger one easily, after all, and that was without the "minor" detail that they were coming to help us.

The main Ændari fleet powered straight for Shan'Gai, and he in turn was now headed directly for the smaller fleet he'd jumped in. They were still in a slingshot maneuver, one that looked like they'd be coming right out aimed at the main Ændari fleet.

Complicated to explain to anyone, but clear enough when looking at the map of the system.

There were also a handful of smaller ships that were either in-system vessels, the remainder of the planetary defense force (which was still headed back to the planet, despite us having a damn valid and obvious need for it), and a few transports and reporters' vessels.

The latter had been trying to get interviews right up until the Ændari launched missiles at them. Then they were screaming about freedom of the press and the need for free speech, which apparently meant we were supposed to drop everything and go save them.

They were also unarmed and useless to the war effort at this point, so I'd marked them up as being somewhere between cleaning out the lavatory and personally repainting the admiral's hull on my list of priorities.

As soon as the thirty-second countdown was done, Dolfing sent orders to the rest of the ships. Four of the five had disengaged and moved as fast as they could. The fifth was shouting they needed more time, and something about a damaged clamp not letting go.

"You're with us for the jump then," was all he said. "Keep your shields powered and hunker down. No time to deal with the clamp."

"Wait, we can—"

We jumped, the ersatz captain's complaints ignored as I folded, maimed, and mutilated the laws of space and time to get us where we needed to be.

"Battleships, fire on the Ændari vessel," Dolfing ordered, tagging the troop carrier's engines.

I launched three of my GGC nuclear rounds. Three seconds passed as the battleships all fired a full volley, over and over again. Then it was done, and the shields were failing.

"Direct hit!" Dolfing cried. Cheers rose out in the background of the ship as first the engines, then the rest of the vessel came apart in blooms of nuclear fire.

I stared, then grinned evilly. I'd done serious damage to the senagra fleet with the high-powered rounds before, but seeing the Ændari fall to them as well?

Hell yes. I'd been expecting them to last longer than this.

I filed that away in the back of my mind, as I plotted out the jumps we needed to make to get onto a course for interception, then started the countdown again.

"Jumping in three…two…one, jumping!"

Space blurred; our ships leapt across the star system, abruptly appearing again, then rolling and creaking as they all fired engines and turned at maximum power.

The links between the ships shuddered, and I gritted my teeth, feeling like I was being torn apart by wild horses, all determined to go in different directions. And yet we held together. Four minutes it took, rocketing around the edge of the planet in a slingshot maneuver, before aligning on the next point and then jumping again.

The reactors were screaming already. I'd not taken the gravity of this planet being heavier than the others we'd used so far into account, and that meant that the energy needs were higher. Then add in the minor detail that the reactors hadn't fully recovered from the last call on their reserves, and it wasn't good.

Three more jumps, and at the eight-minute mark, we were back, aligned on the panicking ship's course. Four more had arrived while we were in motion—all in the same boat, with screaming captains, grinning devilkin, and their plan was to run in all directions.

"Stand by and prepare for docking!" Dolfing's comm tech was barking in the background as Dolfing reached out to me. "You have thirty seconds to land in the marked bays. Shields are adjusting…"

I missed the captains' responses, but the smile on Dolfing's face said it all.

"Those cannons you've got." He nodded. "Any chance they have the range to hit these from say, four light-minutes out?"

I looked, plotting out the intercepts, and nodded. "Should be able to. Why?"

"If you can take these three destroyers out, or at least remove them from the formation, then they'll open a space on the starboard side of the fleet. I'm thinking that we need to jump in and out, get them convinced that we can hit them from all angles, but make it a little more evident that we keep returning to here… We hit that again twice, here and here…" He traced the markers out, and I nodded again.

"It'll open up that side of the hull for the dreadnought," I guessed.

"Exactly. But we make it obvious."

"Right?" I agreed, waiting for the explanation.

"The Ændari will see that we're fixated on clearing a small area on that side of the fleet. We keep hitting it as much as we can with your longer-range weapons, and they'll shift ships around, ready to cover it."

"Okay?"

"Then when our assault transports come in, we collect them, and instead, we hit the exact opposite side, fast as we can and hard as possible, with every ship firing over and over. We tear the fleet a hole on that side, then drop the boarding teams in here…" He highlighted the other side of the ship. "Once they're in? We jump again—start hitting another section of the fleet. As long as we can keep them guessing, they can't focus enough fire to take us out. We come in fast and hard, hit it as heavy as we can, batter as much of the fleet as possible before jumping away. Death by a thousand pinpricks, while our boarders focus on the dreadnought."

"Sounds like a plan. We'll do a few fast passes, get Ingrid and the others more data. Then we go after the three battleships."

"We'll need to be quick. Last ship is docking now."

"Ten seconds," the comm tech barked at the lagging ship, and I grinned.

"Okay, Ingrid, you there?" I said aloud, while reaching out to her mentally and giving a little tug, one that she answered a handful of seconds later.

"I'm here." She forced a smile. "The jumps are still in progress, though. The data is probably enough to keep us working, but we're just not there yet."

"So you want me to do more?" I asked.

"No, actually, not unless you can keep the ship details identical."

"What?"

"Part of the problem for the calculations we're running here is that you keep changing things. There was just your ship, then you and three battleships, then more smaller ships, then a jump with one still attached, then five more. To figure this out, we need a baseline, and every jump is different."

"So what do you want me to do?"

"Nothing, or…look." She shook her head, exasperated. "The problem is we've got a load of data and we can't use it, not properly. We need an hour or two…more would be better—I know the risks, allowing the enemy more time to figure things out, but we need it.

"As it is, Argus is wiping and rebuilding the RI he'd dedicated to the task into a full-grown AI. When you're ready, he's going to ask you to form a dedicated link, and you're going to pour everything you know about the process into that. Then he'll awaken it with you as…"

"As the kernel." I nodded. "What if we did it differently?"

"Steve, we need to." She shook her head. "This is logically the best way to, but—"

"What if I separated off a Navigation sub-mind?" I pushed on. "Like my Engineering and Hack ones? It'd take me half an hour or so, and then there's a dedicated version of me. It'd be a little dumbed down—don't say it—but it'd know everything that I know about this, and then you could guide it."

"Oh, thank God. Yes, please." She nodded.

"How long would it take to do?" Dolfing asked.

"I just said half an hour." I shot him a look.

"I mean, until it's ready to go? Testing done and so on?"

"Uh…an hour?" I guessed. "Maybe?"

"Steve, where are you planning on having that built?" Ingrid asked me.

"I was thinking here on the ship?"

"Could you make two?"

"Probably." I shrugged. "The issue was always processing power and that's solved now with the changes to me, as well as the location to house it."

"Then *don't* send it digitally in any way." Ingrid spoke quickly. "No encrypted channels, no dedicated link as Argus was planning…nothing."

"Okay, why?"

"Because the only advantage we have in this fight is this new method of jumping, and as long as we're the only ones who can do it, we've got a chance. I don't believe there's any way that Shan'Gai has any control over or access to the systems here on the node, not anymore, but if he has? We can't risk it."

"Then why two?"

"One for us to test there on your ship, for a few short jumps and one that gets tied into the control systems for Dolfing." She nodded to him. "You make it so that it'll accept him as its commander or whatever, and then he can do the second set of hit-and-run tests for you while you go after the battleships."

"I need to," I agreed. "You said for you to test, though…can you do that?"

"I've been linked to your mind, and then spreading out the data to our own organic supercomputer here—even Paul is helping—but yes. If you can load and set up the sub-mind there with everything it needs, we can take over the ship and test it."

"Clear!" the comm tech called, and I nodded.

"Jumping!"

Space blurred as we tore across the system. The power reserves flickered and dipped, before starting to rebuild.

"Clear! Get your passengers out," I ordered, already beaten by Dolfing, who was snapping out orders to his crew.

"One minute," he replied to me a few seconds later, before shaking his head. "That one's still stuck."

"Well, get the crew off, and at least you've got some free armor," I suggested, getting a snort of amusement from him.

"I've already unloaded the devilkin. The captain was threatening to have them shot for mutiny, and that was only going to end one way."

"With him sucking vacuum?"

"Exactly."

"Well, how long till we're ready for the next jump?"

"Less than a minute." He checked something, then twisted and called to the comm tech. "Tell him if he can't get the hatch loose, then he's to abandon the ship and he'll be given quarters. We can't expand the shields over his ship, and I'm not willing to wait while he fucks around with it. Preventive maintenance is not an optional detail in a starship operation."

"You want to jump?" I asked him, dropping my voice. "We can delay it a few minutes, but…"

"But we shouldn't have to for a faulty coupling," he replied, dropping his voice as well. "This is war, and we offered to have a tech look at the connection. He refused. There's something wrong here, and I've got no time nor attention to waste. He can sit on the hull, unshielded as we jump to the battleships, or he can come inside, but we're not wasting time on him."

"And the threat to his ship should get him to let your people at it," I guessed.

"Exactly. If he's a smuggler as well as a merc transport…well, we're too busy to care about that right now. If he's more? We space him and our allies get the ship. If they want it."

"They'll take it," I assured him, surprised by the offer.

"I'm a realist," he explained, quirking a smile at me. "The UC didn't do well by the devilkin from what I understand, but they're excellent fighters. And leaving them in the hands of primarily criminal gangs is a hell of a mistake. A few acts of kindness here and there, and well…who knows?"

"Always good to cultivate some friends," I agreed, nodding, before raising my voice. "Jumping to the battleships in thirty seconds."

"Pass it on!" he boomed. "Thirty seconds!"

I checked the readouts, testing the power settings and nodding to myself. We had enough for five more jumps before we needed to calm it down and let the reactors replenish. When we got to the battleships, that'd be as good a time as any.

"Ten seconds!" I called, already feeding power through and getting ready.

"Sir, that ship is still attached," the comm tech warned.

"Tell him it's too late, and to hang on!" Dolfing replied. "Then send a contingent to the—"

"I've got it! Disconnecting!" The voice of the captain of the trapped ship suddenly boomed out.

The comm tech stared in horror, just as I triggered the jump.

Space around us blurred. The shape of the ships that I had locked into my mind shifted ever so slightly as the tiny—in comparison—ship, a battered and obsolete frigate that would have made any military on Earth ecstatic to find, came loose.

It shouldn't have made a difference, not really, but we were skipping into and out of the branes, and I'd taken the shapes and slip of gravity into account, I had to, with the energy expenditure.

His ship broke free at *exactly* the wrong time. And without the link to the battleship, when the hull below suddenly tore into the distance, the little ship was left behind.

It shouldn't have been an issue, it really fucking *shouldn't*, except that as we skipped across the upper reaches of the branes, surging out from under the disconnected vessel, a bulbous laser mount came up from behind, and tore straight through the smaller vessel.

Mass was converted to energy in a heartbeat. The equivalent of a nuclear detonation being set off on the hull, intermixed with the laser mount, tore us off course, as well as doing horrific damage to the battleship.

We were sent spinning, and the energy backlash tore into me with furious abandon, making me scream as I frantically tried to flatten the wild adjustments that the power surge caused.

The release of so much energy as we were skipping across the top of the branes was enough to practically pick us up and hurl us across the system, making me curse and swear in panic between gritted teeth.

The time dilation triggered automatically. I desperately tried to right the ships, twisting and rolling, using slingshot after slingshot. All the engines fired again and again, flipping the attached ships over until our asses were leading the way, and the engines fired even harder.

"What the hell just happened?!" Dolfing roared, as emergency lights and sirens flooded the bridge and crew ran this way and that.

"Losing atmosphere, Admiral!" one of the voices called out.

"Breaches across three decks, Four-F through Seven-A!" another called out.

I desperately tried to slow us, as we shot across the highest reaches of atmosphere on the gas giant.

"Steve!" Dolfing called. "What the hell is—"

"Energy injection!" I snapped. "The ship came loose, crashed into your hull, and the force was like a nuke going off. The mass was converted to pure energy, and I was still jumping us."

"And the energy went where?" he asked. "Into the engines?"

"Jump system," I corrected. "Supercharged us."

"How fast...by the gods of the warp," he muttered. "Steve, can you slow us?"

"Working on it," I answered.

"Someone register that damn speed!" he barked. "We're officially the fastest UC vessels ever recorded, even if we do have to share the title. I want that recorded!"

"Share the title, aye!" someone called, and Dolfing shook his head, looking manic.

"Well, we're still alive," he pointed out. "Chances of us staying that way?"

"Good," I distractedly assured him. "Though your hull's fucked."

"Easy come, easy go." He sighed. "Dalla, get the engineers to work! I want my damn paint restored before we reach the battle!"

"Aye, sir!" another of the crew called out, presumably Dalla.

"Steve, what did you do?" Ingrid popped back into the conversation, then winced as I explained it quickly. "Okay, how are you slowing the ships?"

"Bleeding it off into the atmosphere," I admitted, making tiny adjustments as we continued to slingshot around the massive Jovian, backward.

"We're going to need repairs," Dolfing growled, staring at a display that I guessed held the ship's readout.

"And parts." I sighed. "You got any custodians?"

"They're rarer than an honest politician, and they'd not waste such things on a ship headed for war."

"Well, I guess it's time for us to get you some of those as well. Fuck's sake, it never rains but it pours," I finished philosophically. "Well, on the bright side, I know where there's some spare mass and nanites, so while you start the repairs, I can board the battleships."

"And then you'll get the nanites from the crews there—" She broke off, musing. "Okay, we need a change of plan, Steve." Ingrid shook her head.

"Shit, now what?" I groaned.

"No plan survives contact with the enemy," she quoted at me, and I growled, forcing myself to listen. "I know you can make the sub-minds, Steve, and you said that Shan'Gai created avatars, right?"

"Yeah?"

"Well, there's three stumbling blocks in this fight: Shan'Gai, the enemy fleets, and that you're our only *you*."

"Uh-huh?"

"So what if we changed that? What if we forget about the sub-minds, and instead took the next step?"

CHAPTER FORTY-FIVE

"This is weird," I said slowly, staring into my eyes.

"You've never been more right," I replied, staring back.

"Handsome bastards though, aren't we?" I said to the other two, shaking my head in wonder. "You know, Ingrid is going to love—"

"Okay, guys, that's enough!" I growled, knowing *exactly* where that conversation was going. "We've got a job to do, and fuck me if today can't get any weirder."

The four of us stood in a new section that lengthened my ship, in a bulged-up section that hadn't been there only half an hour ago. I was getting seriously antsy about the time that'd been lost now, although, even I had to admit, there was no way we could have jumped with the damage we'd had before.

Shan'Gai had reached the cover of his fleet. Eleven more small ships had arrived, and they were all frantically running for the node, though plotting a wide run around the Ændari loyalist fleet.

That fleet and the one belonging to Shan'Gai were now hammering each other, albeit at a rapidly shrinking distance, and we were about to start what had to be phase seventeen thousand or so of the fucking battle by now.

I'd managed to create three identical copies of me, much in the same way that I created the sub-minds originally, by literally copying and splitting off the data into a new form that I designated.

In this case, I'd done that with myself. It was horrifically easy, almost embarrassingly so. I'd been able to create items for ages, after all, and I could even make drones with simple RIs that maintained themselves, kept the power core from exploding, and flew, and so on.

Sure, they weren't exactly entirely self-aware and separate, not yet, but if I focused, I could see myself through the other two sets of eyes, or see the ship around me through the mind of the one that was staying aboard it.

That had been the last decision to make with the repairs, and one that I'd mulled over for almost as long as it took to create the copies. But, in the end, I'd decided *not* to create the sub-mind for the admiral.

Not because I didn't trust him—I did—but because if for whatever reason, Shan'Gai got hold of that information or technology, it was all over.

Arise: Conqueror

Instead, one of me would stay interfaced with the ship, and we'd all agreed that although we were fast learners, the admiral was in charge of the fleet strategy, so that one would defer to his orders.

We'd be focusing on getting him some reinforcements, and he'd be issuing the orders to the fleet. The version of us who stayed in our ship at the heart of the fleet would be in control of our weapons systems and the jump capability, but he'd accept the admiral's orders as well.

We'd barely begun the process of splitting, when Shan'Gai had taken our greatest advantage away—when it came to him, at least. Once I'd calmed down and stopped swearing, it'd been a bit of a relief.

He was doing something similar as us, in that he'd linked to a frigate in his fleet and drew power from it, we guessed, because as soon as he'd done that, local space around him had been filled with a confusing babble of gravity pulses in all directions.

He'd figured out how we were jumping, or at least enough that he could disrupt the jump in too close to him. After a brief discussion, Ingrid, Dolfing, and I had decided to let him think he'd won that fight.

He hadn't, because the pulses that he fired out weakened the farther they went, meaning I just couldn't jump in too close. But fuck it. We decided to let him think that, leaving the ship-me linked to them, and jumping back to the Lagrange point and collecting the incoming vessels over and over.

The other weird thing, and it was only detectable with the link to the slaved battleship, was that he kept firing his thrusters over and over in patterns. The front of his ship seemed almost to dance with the movements, the linked battleship doing the same.

After a while of arguing over the possible meanings, we settled on him being damaged more likely than anything else. If it was more than that, then we'd deal with it later.

The other three versions of me?

Well, we each had drones hidden in the damaged battleships. The survivors of the original fights and the Ændari aboard them were about to learn firsthand why they'd been allowed to survive.

We were to jump there, in literally a minute or two, and the fleet were to get moving to the node.

The Ændari assault vessels had docked, or were in the process of it, currently, and were about to get a nasty surprise. Mainly because of the UC reinforcements that were docking to us soon, and who then would be taking them from behind.

There'd been an idea that we should just fry them from here—no sense in letting them land, after all—and then suffering the losses that came from fighting them all. But Jonas had a point that'd shut us all up.

"Can you recover the nanites from those killed in space? You know, if you nuke them or whatever, or are they lost? I mean, sure, you harvested all those nanites from the planet, I know, but they were civilians, and un-Awakened ones at that. They had what, a hundred, maybe a thousand each, and that's it? These are Ændari. Sure, they're dickheads, but there's thousands of them. So that's what, billions more nanites?"

That decided it. Let the ships dock, slow them with the defenses; then the several hundred new devilkin, the four hundred UC soldiers who were rounded up from the fleet and the survivors on the node, and the soon-to-arrive assault ships all attack and grind their ancient enemy up between them.

Also, it meant we got to capture their ships. Hopefully.

"You lazy fuckers ready to go?" I asked, my voice echoing in all our minds. "You do know there's a war on out there, right? No time for a circle jerk."

"I'd tell you to blow me, but you'd like it." The response came from three of us at the same time, before we all shook our heads in unison.

"Hold on, anyone else notice the quest update?" one of me asked.

I blinked, having been too busy to pay attention to the flickering notification light. When I did pull it up, though, I grinned. The quest Argus had given me recently was updating.

Quest Complete!

Evolving Quest Complete: Harvest the Past, to Save the Future (Part 1)

You have gained control of Universal System Quadrant Node, designation #02. In the process of securing the local system, you have discovered the terrible secret that lies at the heart of the UC and Ændari conflict. Evolution stage one is complete.

You receive the following rewards:

- **+5 Points of Specialization**
- **+Access to Level 2 of the Evolving Quest**

Evolving Quest Discovered: Harvest the Past, to Save the Future (Part 2)

Evolution is the fastest and most wasteful of all nature's processes, but intelligently guided evolution can be a terrible thing to behold, provided you're on the opposite side to the being evolving.

Collect 10bn Nanites to reach evolution stage two, to receive the following rewards:

- **+5 Points of Specialization**
- **+Access to Level 3 of the Evolving Quest**

"Yeah, let's get those fucking points spent," one of me said firmly.

"Hell, no. We need to evolve further, right? We've got five points of 'any-time, any-place' points to spend—we need to keep them. Put them aside for when we've got the ten billion nanites, then we'll have ten points to spend, and we can go all in on Devourer, kick Shan'Gai's ass," the other said.

Arise: Conqueror

"We could upgrade our gravitational understanding," the me who was flying the ship suggested. "We've got a hell of a lot of Devourer unlocked. Improving the ship, though? That just makes sense."

"No chance," I snapped. "Efficiency all the way. Anything and everything we're doing now—it'd all be improved by making every process as efficient as possible. Then we can kill everyone and go take Ingrid somewhere safe!"

The ship exploded into what had to be three times as many opinions about where to spend the points, as we had bodies to offer them with, and we all saw it at the same time.

This was why we always left the points until we *had* to spend them.

The curse of such a versatile system was that no matter what we did with it, we were always going to find other things that we needed more.

Worst of all, we knew it at a subconscious level as well. That was why we kept putting the point spending off whenever we could.

"Fuck me, how do triplets and twins live with each other if they're all as annoying as you?" I muttered into the sudden silence, getting snorts of laughter around me, before another me spoke up.

"Right, unlike you lazy fuckers, I've got work to do." The me to my left closed his eyes and triggered a jump, using energy from the ship funneled up through his boots.

His outline seemed to blur for a second. Then there was a sensation that he was falling "away," as if retreating into the distance, before, with a miniature crack of displaced air, he was gone.

"Fucking hell," I muttered, ignoring the echo of my second self. "Never saw it from this side before."

"Well, he had a point. Clearly not just an incredibly well-hung fella, but smart too. Toodles." The second of me vanished.

I snorted, triggering my own jump as well, the three damaged Ændari battleships having already been divided up between us.

Space between my last point and the new twisted. The warping of space and time that only gravity seemed to be capable of, resolved into me stepping forward through billions of miles of empty space, for my right foot to come down, not as it should have—onto the smooth inner surface of the ship that I'd grown—but instead onto the starlight-dappled, melted, and fragged floor of an internal room aboard the Ændari battleship.

I blinked, then shook my head. A slight dizziness that I knew had nothing to do with my inner ear assaulted my senses, as I tried to get my head back into the game, staring around.

The section of hull I found myself in was one of the outermost rooms, I guessed, bringing up the scan the drone had carried out. The blasts that we'd inflicted on the vessel had left it without the bridge, as well as cutting deep gashes into the hull, enabling easy access almost all the way to the secondary CIC.

We could have made it all the way into there as well, had we needed to. The shields were down, and the combined fire of three battleships all focused on one area did a number on anything. But that wasn't the plan.

As soon as I was ready, the marker started up, and I jumped. The time it was active was as short as possible to keep anyone else from realizing what they were.

Now, though, I was there, looking around and seeing the torn and battered hull.

The room I was in was open to space on the lefthand side, a narrow section of carved-through armor that had run like liquid, before hardening and cooling again in the cold of space.

Now, as I shifted my skin, activating my own Conceal ability and mimicking invisibility, I stepped out into the hallway.

It was silent, utterly so. The cold of space had robbed the ship of its voice. But through the soles of my boots, I could feel the shudder of work being carried out, and here and there I saw the reflected light of frantically working automated systems.

A pair of small tracked and multi-armed automatons clattered around in the next room down, processing sections of the internal walls into new panels, while two more welded them into place, trying to repair and reseal the ship before the UC returned.

The joke was on them, though. There was no way the UC were bothering. And that armoring? It was only going to help me out.

I moved quickly up to the nearest automaton. The clunky little bastard looked ridiculous compared to the custodians that the Ændari used to have access to, never mind the converter tech.

This was essentially a mobile smelter and roller combined: innovative, useful here, and completely useless in any other situation. It was a one-trick pony. I reached out my right hand, fingers morphing into tiny needles, as I clamped it down on the back of its head.

The needles burrowed and ate their way through the simple plastic and metal coatings, then shifted, branching and thinning down, linking to the internal crystals of the machine, and hacking through the simple control runs in short order.

As I did that, three tentacles flashed out. Each grabbed onto the other three units and did the same.

It took a matter of seconds, then I released them and stepped back, nodding in satisfaction as the little machines returned to work as if nothing had changed.

For them, after all, nothing really had. The armoring and repairs that they were carrying out I damn well needed as well. But I wasn't leaving an unknown machine behind me to perhaps start gutting the hull once the reality hit.

Instead, and with that in mind, I went looking deeper into the ship, passing section after section where the internal bulkheads were slagged or working, but always, the atmo was long gone.

I wasn't ready to cut my way inside yet, not to start the fight, as I needed things in order as much as possible first.

There had to be some here somewhere…

Arise: Conqueror

It took awakening my drones and sending them searching, then backtracking and locating a sealed room to find them, but find them I did.

The Ændari who had been in this section of the ship when it'd been eviscerated hadn't all escaped, nor survived. Although some would of course have been killed by the blasts, flung out into space to be lost, many had died of asphyxiation.

The Ændari, most of them anyway, were weakened by the nanite plague to little more than their UC counterparts. Although some were blessed with more systems, those were almost exclusively in the upper echelons.

The people who were actually made to do the day-in, day-out work that made the ship run? They were the younger Ændari, those without more than a few hundred thousand nanites. And those that they had weren't fully active, barely granting them the kind of advanced strength and survivability that the Blessed and so on had enjoyed on Earth, but little else.

For a brief second, I wondered how they got more nanites, considering the obvious issues with production. Then I remembered the comments about the Ændari being slavers and raiding worlds. Then I knew exactly where the nanites were coming from, and the kind of feasts these shitbags were likely to be holding.

It didn't matter, though, not right now, because I'd found the bodies. There were only eleven of them, but it was still over a million nanites in total, and more than I needed, considering the scrap and random shite that was laid around the room.

I selected a basic custodian design, as well as a production facility to make more of them. The upgraded makers I now had access to were able to produce and code the basic custodian's cores as easily as the rest of them now.

Then I tore the nanites free of the dead bodies, set the design, and left them to it, building the first custodian, which linked remotely to my ship in seconds.

The me aboard the ship was ready, having sensed my actions, and shared the plan with the other two versions of me, all three of us working on much the same plan.

"I'll guide them until they're set and working," the ship-me agreed. "I can't help with the assault, but I can do that. They'll make themselves, then the makers, then a few friends, before starting to process the local area and make bigger and stronger versions that can repair the ship as they go."

"Sweet."

That was all I needed to say, standing and moving away from the mounding pile of nanites. When I checked the notifications, I'd already collected four million nanites toward the total for that quest.

Sure, four million and change out of ten billion wasn't much, but it was all helpful, and knowing that the nanites that each version of me gathered and accessed was counted toward it was a relief.

With that in process, I headed to the deepest and most secure room I could find, then picked the nearest wall that *should* lead into the airtight sections of the ship.

I poured nanites across the wall at another me's recommendation, smiling as they adjusted. Then I stepped up and pushed my way through the bulkhead.

I'd had the nanites integrate with the wall, then form a nanite barrier over it. I stepped forward into the barrier, and as they recognized me as well, *me*, they slid across my skin, allowing me to step through, emerging into the inside of the battleship.

I grinned in the silence of the small room I found myself in. The distant sounds of shouting and arguments echoed, bangs and clattering as people worked, the occasional shouts that rang out, and through it all, the low-level alarms that went on and on.

The room was square, roughly, with a set of bunks against one wall, and a single desk with two chairs set for it, making me assume it was a junior crewmembers' shared room. From what I'd learned of the Ændari, they hated being forced to share anything, so that amused me. But the best bit of all?

The screen that had been left casually on the lower bunk, and the blinking display that suggested it was still live.

I plucked it from the bed and stared at it. My left hand felt a section at the base where something was supposed to be connected to it, possibly to charge, possibly for uploading or making changes to it.

Either way, the ridged section that my hand was pressed against allowed instant access to the ship's lowest-level data architecture. I could barely stifle a laugh as I sat on the edge of the bed, my hand shifting and nanites forming links, as I hacked the tablet.

The idiot had left some personal details on there—name, identification, and so on—and I used those to search the local area, building up a simple map of the ship, followed by a more complex one.

This room opened onto a narrow crew quarters corridor, that led left and right, along the axis of the ship. Spaced along the corridor were ladders that led up or down, to the two nearest floors, and those floors were where the "real" Ændari lived and worked.

This was the grunt quarters, meaning I was unlikely to be interrupted for a while, the ship needing so many repairs. So I made myself comfortable, patching through and hacking the nearby systems.

The floors above and below were considerably bigger, with suites for their occupants, high ceilings, dedicated private areas, and places for the inhabitants to meet with "lesser" Ændari to give out jobs.

Linking to a nearby camera equivalent, I snorted. It looked like instead of, for example, making a call or having a machine pass a message to a subordinate, the Ændari who lived there liked to do it face-to-face. Assholes.

That did give me a nice opportunity, though, considering they were also almost all in their quarters still, while their minions did the work of repairing the ship.

I set a Tsunami off, leaving it rolling through the weaker, lower ranked systems, with the Hack sub-mind guiding it and adjusting its orders, as well as personally taking out more and more complex systems.

Then I reached over to a uniform where it hung in the nearby closet and got to work.

Arise: Conqueror

Three minutes later, with a new identity—longdongsilva—I stepped from the small room and out into the corridor. My skin had morphed and my form shifted enough that I now looked almost identical to the previous occupant of the room. I also wore a lookalike of his suit.

Strolling to the left a few dozen meters, I came to a tube with a ladder leading down and dropped through it, bending my legs lightly to absorb the impact, then opening the false wall and stepping out onto my better's floor.

I glanced left and right. The nearest occupied room was the one to the right, and, as luck would have it, they'd even logged a demand for food.

Thirty seconds scanning the cameras, and I found a junior crew member an hour ago delivering the same request to a room on another floor. By the time I reached the door, the corridor silent around me, I'd formed a simulacrum out of nanites as well.

Then I paused.

There were markers that demanded certain things from the crew who served this room. Looking them over, I nodded. Kinky bitch insisted on being served by females only and they all had to be slim, tall, and pretty—as well as instructions for disposal of bodies afterward.

Ten more seconds, a little shifting and a virtual lookalike of Ingrid smiled at the asshole as she opened her door, glaring at me.

The biting complaint about the delay in delivering her meal trailed off as she looked me up and down, then strode back into the room without a word, leaving me to follow.

I did, carrying the covered tray into the room, and doing my best not to smile in too predator-like a fashion.

"Put it there." She stepped to one side and gestured to a table large enough to have qualified as Arthur's at Camelot. "I've not seen you before," she said slowly, watching me as I passed her. "Why not?"

Her right hand rested on something out of sight behind her back, and I pretended to be afraid.

"I…I was serving High Admiral Par personally…" I said quickly, having accessed the list of ranks and staff aboard while investigating the ship.

"That so?" She snorted. "Well, with that old fool gone, along with the rest of the bridge, you'll need a new mistress, someone to look after you. After all, you'd not want to be left in the general pool, would you? Not a pretty little thing like yourself. You'd not survive a week…" She stepped forward, lifting the hand she'd been concealing behind her back into sight, as the door closed and locked with an audible clunk.

The crackle of the electrified whip that uncoiled from her hand, the tip hitting the floor, filled the air as she smiled at me evilly.

"I don't know what fool allowed you to be sent here to me, usually your kind are kept well clear, but if you want to serve me, and live through this, you'll earn it. So tell me, my pretty…do you know what your life is worth?"

"Oh, I do," I assured her.

"Then I think it's time to prove it. I want to play." The tip of the whip bounced as she flicked it idly.

"That's a coincidence," I said. "*So do I.*"

The room was soundproofed, presumably for just this reason. But several minutes later, as my shroud sponged her blood from the ceiling, one of the other me's reached out through our bond.

"Been playing with your food?"

"Haven't you?" I asked back.

"Oh, I have," he admitted, sending an image of a barracks, similarly with blood dripping from the walls and ceiling. *"This is one floor down from the CIC, with rapid access to it."*

"Nice." I grinned. *"I'm clearing out the Ændari in the high-power apartments first."*

"Hit the barracks," he suggested. *"They've been split to two shifts on my ship. Half are up doing repairs, the other half sleeping."*

"Nice, easy snack then?"

"Very."

"Hack going well?" the third of us asked, joining in.

"Steady. You?" I replied.

"There's a link from the CIC that runs back toward the stern. It's crystal."

"Oh?"

"It's what they use to send their orders." He snorted in amusement.

"A single trunk of crystal?" I asked in disbelief, comparing the map he was sharing with the others that the other two of us had made.

"A single trunk," he confirmed. *"It's behind a false wall that runs behind the section you're in."*

I looked at it in disbelief, then started to laugh. The outer hull where I'd broken in had gotten me into the body of the ship proper, but once inside, the layer design of the interior was crap.

The first room I'd accessed was part of a line of similarly small and shitty dual rooms, all for the low-ranked crew and personal servants of the Ændari high ranks.

Those rooms formed a sort of exterior wall to separate the higher ranks from the lower levels of the ship, where the mere fighting and flying was done. There were four levels of these rooms. Then, moving inward toward the core, the next level was two sets of suites of rooms, taking up easily three times as much space for the luxurious design.

Between them, and running along the heart line of the ship, was apparently the crystal trunk that carried the orders to the CIC. That was in turn nestled between the suites on the starboard and port sides of the ship.

That trunk line ran back, with the bridge being at the far end of it and higher in the ship, and the elite troops quarters being below, again nestled between rows of suites.

The starboard and port were mirror images of each other, and the overall map that was revealed? I couldn't help but laugh my ass off, walking to the back of the room and dragging the previous occupant's bed away from the rear wall.

Arise: Conqueror

A smear of nanites, ones that had previously been languishing in the room's former occupant's body, and the wall collapsed before me, revealing the trunk inside its housing.

"Unbelievable, Jeff," I muttered, the quote coming from the sports pundits I used to hear constantly. My nanites tore their way into the main control crystal, and I laughed as the change cascaded out.

The CIC, a dozen rooms along and slightly higher in the hull, was suddenly filled with shouts of confusion as their screens went black. My Hack sub-mind poured along the dedicated channels and opened the ship to me.

"I'm in," I told the others, with the me currently sitting in the barracks on his ship snorting and sending me a mental pat on the head.

"Good boy. Took your time, but you made it in the end. I'll ask Ingrid if you can have a cookie before you're reabsorbed."

"It'll be you who's reabsorbed into me," I pointed out, knowing that it didn't matter to us, not really, but I couldn't let the comment go. *"I've got the bigger dick—she'll want to keep me."*

"You are *a bigger dick, not you* have *one,"* Three countered. *"That's an important detail, but glad we all agree."*

"Assholes."

"You're arguing with yourself," the ship-me pointed out, before reaching out to the ships. *"Okay, One and Three have connections made to the ship's control systems. Two, what's the holdup?"*

"I'm not Two!" one of the others snapped, dropping a body onto the floor, before stomping his way across the room, heading in the direction of the CIC. *"Anyway, I'm going to check out how much harder it is to get control from here..."*

I shook my head, reaching out through the ship systems and triggering the intercom, then passing orders for different groups to gather in various areas nearby.

I split them up by role, so crew members were to gather in the nearest main hall to the aft of me, with the onboard security to gather in another, the troopers in a third, and so on.

Then, while they were gathering like lambs to the slaughter, I headed to the nearest wall. I quickly checked the positioning of the pair of occupants, making sure that the Ændari didn't have any warning before I was too close, then sighed and stepped through the wall. The room beyond was a mess of blood and wasted flesh, and a third Ændari figure I'd not noticed in the scan lay prone on the floor, bleeding out.

The sick bastards who "enjoyed" the greater space on this level were presumably kept in check by their higher-ranked officers. With me eliminating the bridge and taking most of them out of the fight, I guessed this was their equivalent of a wild drunken holiday.

I guessed for the upper echelons, seeing that there were two huge fleets of their peers in-system, and that they were both out of the fight, and presumably not unimportant enough to have to do the actual work, they were relaxing.

Ten minutes was all it took me to clear the rooms on this side of the trunk, and another fifteen to do the rooms on the other side. Most of the inhabitants were either occupied with various forms of degeneracy or were asleep.

I found it impressive how many were avoiding work, considering they were on a fucking battleship and it had been badly damaged. I guess when you're powerful enough that the lower ranks are afraid of you, and too weak to be important to the higher ranks, you could get away with murder. Literally.

Either way, though, as I strolled from room to room, carving my way through the mid-ranks of the ship's assholery, I felt a lot better about my life choices. Step through the wall; stab, stabbity stab; then fill the room with the shroud and walk to the far wall; smear with nanites; have them tear the wall apart; step through and repeat.

By the time I reached the bulkhead that separated the former inhabitant from the hall beyond, I was starting to really understand why for the Ændari, the Devourers were the ultimate boogeymen.

Rather than just step through this wall and possibly start a stampede in a room they could actually run from me in, I moved to the nearest corridor and followed that instead. My outer appearance returned to that of an Ingrid lookalike, carrying a large bag on my back and armfuls of what looked to be sheets of metal.

They weren't, they were compressed and concealed nanites, but I couldn't help but shake my head at the way the Ændari running back and forth to the meeting rooms either ignored me or barged past.

Not one offered to help. Even the most shitty of humans would have most likely offered to help Ingrid if they'd seen her struggling with the weight, even if for a few it was just to try to chat her up. But here?

Not one tried it. As I stepped into the hall at the back, I smiled.

I walked through the mass, judging when I'd reached about the middle of the room, carefully maneuvering around people who glanced at me then refused to step aside. And all the way, I trailed a half a meter wide and concealed sheet, one that pressed into the floor behind me, waiting for the command.

Lunchtime! I thought, releasing the restrictions on my form, and exploding outward.

CHAPTER FORTY-SIX

It didn't take long to clear the battleship, not with three of us working on separate vessels, trying different techniques and refining them as we went.

By the end of an hour, I stood on the hull of the battleship again, watching as her sister ships were swarmed by custodians. We'd agreed that due to the time constraints, we'd not change anything major about the vessels, but there was a massive difference between "nothing" and "major changes."

The hull was left intact; the power cells received a few small upgrades, as did the weapons. And, best of all, thanks to the massive amounts of nanites we'd each been able to harvest from the crews, we were able to recreate the docking system that the UC battleships used to recover damaged vessels, and the link to share power.

Beyond that, the only real difference was that with an automated link set up to control the battleships, and no actual crew aboard, they had no need for minor things like atmo or gravity generators, heat and so on.

Instead, the ships were opened to space, and the power that had been wasted there before was fed to the shields and weapons.

"Admiral, are you ready?" I reached out from the hull of my ship, letting him see that the battleships were ready for him. A few minutes later, the UC forces emerged from another jump nearby.

The longest part of connecting the ships together now was matching velocities, and damn, I was glad that I just got to hurt people instead of being in charge of all this shit.

The entire capture of the huge vessels had only taken an hour or so, all told. As the three of us launched ourselves into the black, linking together and plotting the jump, already the admiral and his linked ships were sliding toward their places in the formation.

The UC battleships had their CICs taking over the Ændari battleships; my links to them enabled the seamless control of their former enemies' vessels. And as we landed on the hull of our ship-body, the new three ships flared to life again.

The worst of the damage done to their hulls had been patched, and as the UC battleships moved in closer, two-thirds of the custodians that had been working on the Ændari vessels launched themselves into the void.

They streamed across, flipping over and landing with a sound like hail against the hulls, before racing to the nearest damaged sections and starting work.

"They know not to damage the ships, don't they?" Dolfing asked skeptically, reaching out to both me and Ingrid.

"They do," I assured him. "They're also capable of carrying out massive upgrades, compared to the limited tech you have available. That's why I asked you to each scram one of the reactors."

"I still don't like it," he admitted. "Taking down a reactor in the middle of battle is madness."

"It is, but the reactors they're building you are based on my own tokamak design. It'll take around three hours to build but—"

"Three hours is a lifetime in war."

"It is," I growled. "But three hours from now, you'll have a single reactor that'll be producing four times the power that it was, and the remaining reactors can all be used to power the shields and weapons. Your ships will be far more deadly than they are. And in the meantime, you get to use the Ændari battleships' reactors to power the jumps, so stop fuckin' complaining, all right?"

"Devourer, I appreciate the trust you've shown me," Dolfing snapped back. "But the sailors and soldiers of the UC fleet are my priority. I'm the one who's responsible for their lives, not you."

"And we appreciate that, and the trust we're all showing each other, Admiral," Ingrid soothed, reaching out to me with a calming mental touch. "While you have the fleet looking to you, and the responsibility for their lives, we have the entire sector looking to us. Steve's circumstances mean that he is uniquely able to provide support or devastation, and we have to deal with those needs, balancing one against the other."

"And still dealing with shite," I muttered, getting a glare from Ingrid.

"The changes that are underway on your ships were suggested and discussed with you prior to this, Admiral. You agreed that they were both in the best interest of your crews, and in keeping with the responsibility you bear for the UC. So, with that in mind, unless you've got a reason for the call, we're currently under fire, and I'm needed. Is there anything new to discuss?" Ingrid asked, and Dolfing winced.

"No, and I apologize, Ingrid. Steve, I trust you. It's a stressful time."

"Yeah, sorry." I sighed. "It's a bit shite on everyone. So, Ingrid, you go if you need to. We're almost ready here, so we're going to start jumping."

"The sooner the better, please," Ingrid said. "The first levels have fallen, and the second aren't going to hold much longer."

"We'll be there," I assured her, before shaking my head as she left the chat.

"Okay, Admiral, sorry for being a dick. I'm just worried about her," I said, about to cut the connection, when he spoke up again.

"Steve, your other versions…damn, that's strange to say. Your avatars, do…you need all of them?"

"Why?" I frowned.

"The rebels…gods, it feels weird to say that about anyone except ourselves when it comes to the Ændari…but the loyalists and Shan'Gai's Ændari rebels are closing on each other."

"Good." I nodded. We'd picked up some of their exchanges, and unless they were playing a really deep game of bluffing, the two fleets weren't going to be joining up anytime soon. Instead, they were firing weapons and the surprise betrayal that I guessed Shan'Gai had been planning to pull looked more like a straight-up slaughter for both sides now.

"Both sides are closing on each other, but it'll be a fast-pass battle. Unless there are massive mistakes made, both sides will lose only minor ships."

"Okay?"

"They'll be moving too fast, and the firing window is—"

"I understand why, Admiral, but you're stopping me from going to Ingrid's aid here, so can you get to the point?"

"Fine. There's likely to be a few ships that take serious damage from each side, smaller ones most likely, but they'll drop out of formation as they try to deal with the damage."

"Right."

"When they do that, I'd like one or more of your avatars to be ready. We'll jump in, take out any defenses we can, then the avatar can board the ship. They kill the crew, slave the vessel to our fleet and begin repairs."

"And each ship that drops out of the enemy fleet weakens them and strengthens us," I agreed, finally seeing it. "It gets me more nanites, and you more firepower. Got it. Sorry for being so dense."

"We won't be able to keep it up for long," he warned. "Both sides are likely to be watching us very carefully, and we need to start our own attack runs as soon as possible. They've had too much time as it is."

"The time was worth it," I assured him. "Okay, I'll spin off two more avatars. You'll need to jump in and hold on long enough to fire the drones, then you can get out of there."

"We can do that," he agreed. "How long on the avatars?"

"We'll split off enough nanites to form them, and leave them here on the ship," I said after a fast consultation with myself. "They'll be ready in about half an hour. Then you can start."

"What about you?"

"We'll be launching for the node as soon as this conversation is done. Anything else?"

"Just to wish us all good luck." He smiled grimly. "We've got confirmation that four full assault battalions are incoming, along with your own smaller ships. There's too many for us to link and jump at once, but we should be able to get them all out before the Ændari can get missiles to them."

"Damn well hope so. I'll never hear the end of it if her parents' ship gets hit." I snorted. "Good luck, Dolfing, and to your crew."

"And to you, Devourer." He saluted, and I cut the connection with a nod, turning to look across the hull at the two other me's who stood there nearby.

"So, what have we got?" I asked them.

"Nearly two billion more nanites between us," Three responded.

"Man, that's an insane amount," One agreed, nodding. "Okay, so we break off, what, five hundred million? That gives the new avatars two hundred and fifty each—they'll be able to do anything they need to with that—and we keep five hundred each?"

"What about me?" the ship-me interjected. "You think I'm just a glorified transport?"

"You've got more than the rest of us combined," I pointed out. "Shut it, you greedy fucker."

"Heh, can't blame a guy for trying."

"Yeah, well, that works. Two-fifty for them should see them right on harvesting the ships, and five hundred each gives us all plenty of cover if there's anything unexpected on the node."

I felt it as the others started to gather power for the jump as well. We'd all done it at once, without discussion.

"Ready?" Three asked us both, already splitting his nanites off and feeding them into the pool on the ship-me's hull.

"Ready," I agreed, doing the same and reaching out, grinning as I found the additional drones that Ingrid had set up on the node for us. "Man, we love that woman."

"Too right." One sighed. "Okay, I'll take this one…" He shared one of the drone's locations with the rest of us, concealed in a half-collapsed section of the outer buildings.

I nodded, waiting as Three spoke up next.

"Looks good. I'll take this one." He shared another, one that was broadcasting from underneath the stairs on the second level. "That'll let me attack them while they're focused on attacking the barriers."

"I guess that leaves me here then." I pinged a single drone that was calmly sitting on the outer shell of the node, right below the docked ships, and currently watching over the hundreds of disembarking Ændari.

"On three?" Two suggested.

"Kinky bastard," Three muttered, before winking at us. "That's gonna be Ingrid's job."

"One," I said.

"Two," Two said.

"Three!" Three declared with a laugh. Then the three of us jumped, vanishing from the hull of ship-me and reappearing with a crack of displaced air in the node.

Or, in my case, outside the atmo and on the hull right below the enemy ship as it disgorged troops.

"Time to play…" I grinned, swinging myself forward, hands shifting to bond to the underside of the ship. I moved aft, looking for a likely ingress point. "Now, who's today's lucky winner?" I muttered, already sensing the carnage that was breaking out.

Arise: Conqueror

Three had appeared in the air thirty meters or so above a packed staircase. As soon as he'd appeared, he'd flung himself downward, shroud billowing outward, draping over the distracted and quickly terrified Ændari.

One, on the other hand, had appeared in stealth mode, hidden in the rubble. The crack of displacement was barely audible over the noises of the streaming Ændari rushing past.

Tentacles flashed out, snatching the unaware and ripping them into the shadows. Arms and necks were torn in opposite directions; the snapping of bones and stifled screams all spoke to his presence.

I travelled a few more meters, then smeared nanites across the hull, grinning. They ate into it, spreading and forming a roughly circular patch that shimmered gently, then rippled in a nonexistent breeze.

"Here we go!" I grabbed onto the sides, then hauled myself up and through the portal, into the lower decks. "Hi!" I said cheerfully to a horrified engineer. The Ændari crew member stared at me in disbelief as I popped through the hull right in front of him.

"You might be wondering if those drugs from your teenage years just kicked in," I whispered to him. A tentacle whipped out and snared him, dragging him in close. "The good news is, if you did a load of drugs then, you can choose to believe that." I nodded reassuringly.

"And…and if I didn't?" He choked, frantically trying to free a hand from the second and third tentacles that were even now wrapping around his arms and legs respectively.

"Well, that's the bad news." I shrugged, as the shroud closed over his struggling body, his scream lost as the malleable form flowed down his throat, expanding into him.

"So, moving on…" I muttered, ignoring the quivering form wrapped in the red and black flesh behind me. I pressed my hand to the unlocked data port on the wall. "Gods, I love stupidity when it comes to security features."

I injected a hack into the port, overwriting the local system and pouring Tsunami in, grinning as it started to replicate and spread. Then I headed for the nearest door.

***

As my three avatars romped through the node, slaughtering the Ændari practically with impunity, I was stuck acting as a glorified taxi service, back in my ship, checking in with Admiral Dolfing as he confirmed the readiness of the fleet and integrated, as well as tested, the new three Ændari battleships' systems.

The last of the ships that all our considerable diplomacy—and threats—had managed to wrangle us were jumping in now, and as well as Clicqo and Shanah's small forces, our family and friends had arrived.

Looking at them, my heart sank. The readout of the last-ditch madness vessel I'd ordered the nanites to build on the corrupted moon was just a mess. In addition to that abomination, there were a dozen mid-range frigates, five smaller and shittier versions of the classic UC warship that the data pegged as Shrikeclass destroyers, and a pair of heavily upgraded warships that were already moving to get between the rest and the distant enemy fleet.

"Is that...?"

"Approved leadership request identified. Linking communications," Argus interjected calmly, as Ingrid slid into the connection alongside me.

"Inga, Steve," came the gruff voice of Anders, at the helm of the first heavily upgraded warship. "I see we're in time for the fight. Good."

"Good!" Ingrid snapped. "Far, you wonderful idiot, you. This isn't good. We're outnumbered!"

"Then where else would any parent worth their salt be?" he asked. "You're our daughter, and unless he's made a hell of a damn fool mistake recently, he's soon-to-be my son-in-law. What parent wouldn't be here?"

"I don't know," I whispered, unable to keep from smiling sadly at the love this man engendered. "Mine?"

"You took some time to find your family, son, but we're here for you now, and we've brought friends. What's that American term, Steve?" Anders asked. "Something about the enemy?"

"A target-rich environment?" I suggested.

"That's a good one, but no..."

"The enemy is to my left, the enemy is to my right, the enemy is on all sides?" I tried, utterly bastardizing the quote I knew, but trying to remember it.

"I have them right where I want them!" Anders declared, with a smile that could only be described as predatory.

"Now, now, dear." Freja smiled, stepping up to lay one hand on Ander's shoulder, staring into the pickup at her daughter and my own images. "Inga, you've done incredibly, but despite everything you always think, you never have to do it all alone. You and Steve laid the groundwork, but you never expected the rest of us to just sit idly by, did you? Really?"

"No," she admitted, smiling despite the tears in her eyes.

"Then why are you crying? You asked for our help, my darling— of course we came."

"Because this is war, and I could lose you."

"And you could lose us to a reactor meltdown at any time," Freja said. "Or before all these changes, to a terrorist incident, or a car crash, a plague. There's no end of reasons you could lose us, or we you, but neither has happened yet. And we raised you better than to borrow trouble from tomorrow. We stand with you, and we'll win or lose with pride."

"I hate to be the bearer of bad news..." James interjected, appearing digitally in the conversation alongside Anders and Freja. "But shouldn't we get a move on? It looks like our ally is under attack?"

I glanced at the readout, then growled. "That would be Shan'Gai." I said, "And he's no ally of ours."

"That's concerning," Aaronis commented, joining the chat with Leshan standing behind him at parade rest. "The reports we've received outside of the system are garbled."

"Aaronis!" I greeted, smiling. "Leshan, damn, I'm glad to see you both…"

"Steve, have you been picking fights again?" Cybele asked, as both she and Sanneth popped into the group, swiftly followed by Zac, who grinned widely as we started greeting everyone.

"Hey boss man, boss lady! You miss me?" he asked.

"Like an STD," I assured him.

"Ah, don't be like that…" He waved a hand dismissively. "We all know you love me really."

"While I agree Zac is certainly an acquired taste…" Cybele sighed. "The upgrades he has brought to our little fleet are rather more welcome."

"Why, thank you, Elder…" Zac visibly preened.

"Acquired like a fungal infection, and just as hard to remove," Sanneth drawled.

"And just like that, I seem to have lost those upgrade requests for your starfighter," Zac countered, looking confused, then smiling broadly. "Oh look, Elder Cybele, those ideas you had? I've just found some time. What was it you were asking for again?"

"Enough," I said firmly. "Ingrid, can you step back from the fight long enough to give updates or do you need one of me to?"

"One of you?" Cybele looked bewildered.

"I can," Ingrid said. "You just took the Ændari from behind who were pushing at our gate."

"Not the first time, and not the last…" muttered Zac, sotto voce.

"You're also wreaking havoc in the middle of their reinforcements. You secured the lower areas of one of the assault craft, though it does look to be on fire now."

"Standard." I nodded, rubbing at my cheek. "Okay, Admiral Dolfing, I know the little family reunion here might seem a little chaotic, but believe me, it's even worse than it looks. Are you ready to jump?"

"As much as we can be." He nodded. "The aft starboard section of my battleship is open to space still, but the custodians are working wonders currently, so thank you for that."

"Custodians?" Zac groaned. "Ah, boss man, tell me you're not making them rely on those trash heaps?"

"You got better with you that's not busy?" I asked him flatly.

"Of course I do!" He acted insulted. "You gave me three damn weeks—you've got no idea what glorious madness I've managed!"

"Three weeks?" Dolfing asked, looking slightly deflated at what he believed could be achieved in such a short time.

"Don't let the idiot act fool you," I said. "Zac might be a failure in every other aspect of reality, but when it comes to engineering, he's a prodigy. He built our first starship, in what? A week?"

"Two days," he corrected. "The rest of that time you were telling me you needed a yacht, then a battleship, then there was a mobile construction yard, and don't forget…"

"Yeah, yeah." I waved at him to leave it. "Anyway, he built our first home-grown starship in a few days. Admittedly, it got scrapped and it crashed a lot, but…"

I grinned at the outraged look on Zac's face.

"I made the ship! It was perfect, then you fuckers crashed it!" He jabbed a finger at his screen and presumably at me. "You trashed it, just like everything else you damn well touch!"

"Shut it, Zac." Two jumped into the chat. The projected background behind him showed bodies flying and strobing lasers being fired in panicked bursts as he spun and kicked out.

"Yeah, shut it!" Three agreed, appearing and grabbing a hybrid by its armored frame and ripping its head off with the other hand. "Can't you see we're busy?"

"Fuck's sake, is that Zac?" One shouted as he joined, grabbing a leaping figure from the air and spinning him around, then slamming him into another Ændari with enough force that armor sections were sent flying, cracked and broken.

One lifted his makeshift club and shook his head in disgust as it dangled by a clearly broken leg. "Goddammit, now I'd gotta catch another one. Hey!" He barked at a bunch of Ændari troopers who were backing away, frantically reloading battery packs into their lasers. "Don't run! You'll only die tired!"

"Yeah!" came a connection from Four, standing on the outside of the hull of my ship. "Seriously, Zac, stop interrupting us when we're working!"

He was only half-formed, his head still growing into the right shape as the final sections were sealing and structuring now. His separation from "me" was complete though, as we all identified him as a new entity.

"I don't know what's going on here, but I'm suddenly afraid for the galaxy," Zac said after a few seconds of shocked silence.

"I'll fill you all in." Ingrid smiled. "Mor, Far, everyone? Thank you for coming. Steve, can you collect them and bring them to the node, please?"

"On it," I assured her.

"Thank you. Zac, whatever changes you've come up with, can you examine the most damaged of the battleships, and—"

"They're all damaged," he muttered. "This one?" He pinged one, and Dolfing shook his head.

"That's one of the captured Ændari vessels. This one is my ship."

There was a brief ping from the lead UC ship, and Zac nodded.

"Gotcha. Okay, yeah, I can have it back in the fight in, oh, an hour?"

"We've not got long." I nodded. "Right, we're coming for you, then we'll need to tether and we'll jump again. For now, start burning for the node."

"Okay, how are you gonna ju—" Zac started asking.

I cut the connection, before turning to a new link with Dolfing.

"Admiral, are we ready?" I asked.

"We are." He nodded. "This is the plot we're going to follow." He sent it over, linking me into the map and making me nod in understanding. "We jump from here to this planet, slingshot around it onto this trajectory, come out here…"

The spot that was marked was just behind the main Ændari fleet. But instead of attacking, it had us firing and then jumping again almost as soon as we exited.

"Right?" I agreed, waiting for the explanation.

"How many drones do you have ready?" He cocked an eyebrow at me.

"Twenty," I said, having formed that many and then stopped.

"Okay, you need to ramp up production of those," he ordered. "What are the chances of you being able to jump with a single ship, or better yet, a dozen UC soldiers *without* a ship?"

"The limit is power," I said after a second's thought. "For this kind of thing, if I had sufficient power, and they were all nearby, I could form a link to them all, then jump easily enough."

"Good. For now, we jump to this point, open fire on the fleet from behind, do as much damage as we can, obviously…but the aim is to cover the launch of the drones. You fire them as well as the high-powered nuclear rounds you have, aim for a spread across the engines of several smaller ships. I think…yes, these ones."

He picked out four smaller vessels, mainly destroyers and frigate sizes, ignoring anything larger.

"You make sure the drones are stealthed and direct them to the damaged ships. They'll provide you with jump targets to attack, and any damage done serves to lower their fleet strength regardless."

"It does," I agreed. "Why the soldiers?"

"They'll be your backup," he said, nodding to himself. "The two avatars you've made, they raid these ships"—he gestured to the target vessels—"and once they've dropped far enough back, they strip them of all the Ændari they can. As soon as they've gotten enough nanites, they create more avatars, link the ships to us, then jump again."

"Using me as a virus, spreading out and replicating, taking over the ships and wiping out the Ændari." I nodded my agreement. "What about Shan'Gai?"

"You said that the changes he's made to the local gravity field make it more costly to jump around there?"

"Yeah. The closer we are to him, the more power we'll need."

"That has to be an effort to restrict us, so we continue to pretend that his changes make us unable to reach him. Keeps him complacent and gives us a reason we're focusing on the Ændari fleet instead."

"When really we're stripping them of anything we can, and grabbing his ships when they fall out of formation." I nodded. "All right, so we're sending in the drones, while we do hit-and-run. What about the others?"

"We'll use the slingshot to jump back and forth across their path," he explained. "The Ændari loyalists, I mean, rather than jumping from here straight to there…" He indicated another moon. "We jump halfway, come out of jump here, fire a barrage, then jump away again. Their motion renders them predictable, within reason, while ours allows us to escape their return fire."

He nodded to himself. "All right, jump here, fire, jump again, slingshot onto the new trajectory, arc around and then back, jump, fire, jump."

"So we do that three times, fast as possible. Then we catch a last loop around that world…" I indicated it on the plot. "Then we're onto a path for the Lagrange point. We pick the others up and jump back to the node?"

"Exactly."

The next ten minutes went almost to plan—for us, anyway.

Erupting into normal space, we opened fire on the Ændari from behind. Six battleships, all with three designated and considerably smaller targets, suddenly appearing from nowhere and unleashing hellfire and damnation onto their enemies, launching stealthed drones—though the enemy didn't know that—and then jumping back out had to be a nasty surprise.

The drones were streaking across space as the first explosions rang out. Shields that were carefully bunched around ships flickered and crackled madly as nuclear fire bloomed, sending them careening into the path of others.

Two of the three frigates lost control of their engines. One rolled wildly as two of the three engines exploded, and the third engine, damaged, proceeded to fire only in one direction, driving it onto a new course.

Other ships nearby panicked, trying to get out of one another's way. At least two totally uninjured destroyers lived up to their names, as they opened fire on other ships encroaching on their flight line.

I grinned as we jumped out again, hearing the cheers that came from the linked bridge of the admiral's battleship.

The next few jumps were much the same, though the final one that we did was less effective. We'd barely emerged before we were under fire. With shields crackling, we jumped again as soon as we'd fired, but ended up cursing as the larger vessels shifted in to protect the smaller, taking the brunt of the incoming fire.

By the time we'd arrived at the Lagrange point, I was back grinning again, though, as Four and Five shared the terror they were instilling in the Ændari aboard the destroyers.

We arced around; the fleet's navigators gave me carefully polished plots that brought us up behind the smaller craft at an almost sedate pace, as they worked to plan out connection points.

Most would have to dock onto the hull of the battleships or land in their massive bays, but the ship I'd created as a last resort on the corrupted moon?

Well, that was a problem.

"Zac," I said, drawing his name out as I contacted him. "That's *not* the ship I designed."

"Well, yeah?" he agreed. "Fuck's sake, boss man, that ship was shit, and you know it!"

"It was a flying cannon," I pointed out. "It was big enough to fire my goddamn ship out of the end, and probably small asteroids."

"Yeah, you got many more ships to use as ammo?" he countered. "Or spare asteroids? Damn, dude, that's just wasteful!"

"I had no fucking time to figure it all out, and I made it as powerful as possible," I snapped. "This…what the hell is this?"

Arise: Conqueror

The original design that I'd put into the nanites for production only bore the faintest similarities to this monstrosity. Worst of all, as near as I could see, the cheeky bastard had removed all the launch points for the weapons systems.

Sure, there was a...well, I didn't know what to call it, actually.

The original design had a sort of toilet roll inner tube as the overall layout. A long, thin-walled but heavily armored cylinder, with the inside layered with a shitload of accelerators similar in design to the ones that I'd majorly upgraded by the end. Although, if I was honest, the ones I'd built since were a fraction of a percentage of the power of that thing.

They worked, though—and even if the power systems were barely enough to fly or fire it occasionally, that was for Zac to fix!

Instead, the mad Aussie bastard had taken my design back to the drawing board and created...

I shook my head, scanning it and trying to make sense of what I was seeing.

First of all, the tube was the same. It was long and had a control tower on the top for some reason, and the inside that used to have a fairly wide barrel and thinner walls was now the other way around, with thick walls and only a small central section to fire down.

The outside of the ship was covered in triangular scales or so it seemed, flat, with each giving off their own power readings. And the inside? The bottom was barely closed, and as I watched, the damn thing started to split!

"Zaaaac!" I growled.

"Trust me, boss. You're gonna love this," he promised, shifting the ship up and around as he reached out and spoke quickly to the admiral. "Okay, Mr. Admiral! I've got good news and bad. Which do you want first?"

"Bad," he said. "And it better explain why your ship appears to be breaking apart."

"It's *opening,* sir," Zac replied. "This is a mobile space dock, capable of complex repairs and upgrades under battlefield conditions. When Ingrid explained that we all need to be linked together to share power and to stabilize for the jump, it just made sense to latch onto you and start the repairs now, right?"

"And this is the bad news?" he asked.

"It means that we can start repairs straightaway," Zac clarified. "But it also means that I got the chance to scan your ship properly."

"If you suck your teeth and try to increase the bill, I'll personally hunt you down and murder you," I offered.

"You wound me, sir!" Zac pretended to be offended.

"People!" Dolfing snapped. "I don't need the witty comments. Explain your actions or stand down."

"My apologies, Admiral." Zac straightened up, apparently deciding to drop the attitude. "I've scanned your vessel, and due to the size of my own, as well as the differences in engines and weight, the best solution for the linkage issue is for my ship to latch onto another.

"The damage that your vessel has sustained means that it is actually more difficult to repair the rear sections than to tear out and replace them from scratch. The original three-hour estimate is possible, but the replacement would come with a significant upgrade in terms of power needs. I've seen that Steve is currently upgrading a reactor. That should cover the increased drain, as well as enabling me to heavily upgrade both the shield generators and weapons of your ship, but…"

"Here it comes," I muttered.

"Steve!" Dolfing snapped.

"Sorry." I winced.

"Go on."

"The repairs and upgrades need me to be able to work on your ship uninterrupted, so no shields, and my ship wouldn't be able to use them either."

"So you're a sitting duck, should the Ændari change their mind and come for you?" I asked, getting a glare from Dolfing as I apparently jumped his question again.

"Answer that, please," Dolfing directed at Zac when he hesitated.

"Aye, sir. Your vessel and my own will be able to move, but only slowly, and for most of the time it's being repaired, you'd need to be powered down."

"And the difference if I permit this?" Dolfing asked, looking at screens near him.

"Power wise, I don't know exactly what the output of that generator is, so I can't say, sir, but provided it increases your capacity by at least fifteen percent over the current needs of your ship, your shields will be increased in power by around thirty percent, and the new section of hull could be equipped with any weapons you want, within reason."

"The ones that Steve's current vessel has?" Dolfin sat forward.

"Which ones?" Zac replied. "I see the gravity cannons and the lasers…huh."

"Yeah." I grinned. "Hellbores."

"High-powered lasers," Zac corrected.

"I made them," I said. "I get to name them. Hellbores."

"They're…you know what, all right, fine." Zac sighed. "Okay, Admiral, which do you want, and how many?"

"Zac, I want them *all*," Dolfing said slowly. "All the weapons."

"Fuck's sake, another maniac," Zac groaned, seeing the smile dancing around the edge of the admiral's lips. "Okay, you want them spread out across the replaced hull sections, or all the weapons upgraded and replaced across the hull?"

"All of it," Dolfing demanded.

"Fuck, all right, but it'll take at least four hours."

"You can do that? In *four hours*!" Dolfing sat up straight, clearly not having expected that.

"He can." I nodded.

"Engineer," Dolfing tugged his tunic straight as he sat more at attention, staring into the screen, "I'm aware of the usual tricks played between engineering and the rest of the fleet, so confirm this for me please."

"Sir, my vessel is a mobile shipyard, with inbuilt matter converters and a storage full of null coins," Zac said, unable to stifle his smile. "Steve can alter his piddly little ship all he likes, but I built this one with the express intention of tearing apart anything that annoys me, and building the greatest weapons the galaxy has ever seen."

As he said that, he broadcast an image to us all, showing the narrow gap that ran along the length of the tube-shaped ship growing.

The thicker sections were revealed as armoring as the split that ran the length of the underside began to open fully. The front and rear of the tube remained thick and half hiding the interior, but the inside of the shipyard was revealed to be a mass of support struts, mobile gantries, and hundreds of arms, some ending in claws, others lasers and clamps, converters and more.

Although it wasn't as long as the literal miles-long battleship, at half a mile in length, it was still impressive.

"And you can do this in four hours?" Dolfing asked again.

"If you can evacuate all the outer sections of the hull, and any rooms that connect to them, seal the bulkheads and drain them of atmo, so I don't need to slow down? Yeah." He nodded. "We'll literally start at the front of the ship and roll along it, peeling the armoring and replacing as we go."

"You got enough mass for that?" I asked.

"Probably." He shrugged. "I'd not refuse more if you've got some, but that's why I'll be converting as I go. Literally tearing the hull armoring off and rebuilding it with the latest upgrades."

"Damn." I shook my head. "Okay, looks like a plan to me. Admiral?"

"Do it." He nodded. "I don't like taking my ship out of the fight, but the upgrade to the reactors is already in progress, and the Ændari and Shan'Gai are still fighting it out. We set up at the node and protect it, allow them to weaken each other. Then you, Steve, jump out and collect any damaged vessels you can, board, assimilate and retrieve. We add what can be recovered to the fleet, and what can't is instead broken down by the shipyard to upgrade the other battleships, one after another."

"What are they doing?" I asked. "The Ændari, I mean."

"They're happily fighting it out with Shan'Gai," the admiral answered a few seconds later, shaking his head in disbelief. "They've sent another demand that we exit the system, under threat of formal war, and hand over the node, but they're clearly not focused on us."

"They didn't even bother sending it to me." I snorted. "So, boarding action it is for me as soon as I've got you fuckers back to the node."

For the first time in ages, things were looking up.

CHAPTER FORTY-SEVEN

The next five hours were both hectic and wonderful, but it was no surprise when it ended—though the end did come more painfully than a taco truck-delivered enema.

As soon as I got the fleet back to the node—it took three trips: two to get the new arrivals back and a third to get the pair of damaged and now claimed frigates—I disengaged from my ship-form to join my other selves aboard the node and get into some serious close-range fighting and harvesting, between jumps.

We could have done it differently—ranged was always an option, after all—but between the jump capability that we were still refining and the limited distances to cover, there just wasn't a need for it.

Instead, the four of us aboard the node now basically fought hand-to-hand and in melee with the surviving Ændari, doing our best to relieve them of that condition.

We never exactly discussed it, but somehow, as each of the smaller vessels were readied into raider squadrons for jump assaults, it was always me who jumped back to my ship, linking to them and jumping back out, carrying them in and out.

We did little real damage, but it was all practice. And it kept the Ændari on their toes, as well as helping to even things out, before finally handing full control of the jump drive over to Dolfing.

With the downtime, and access to the massive converters and capabilities of the shipyard, one of the first and most important upgrades to Dolfing's battleship was the new control center.

With the introduction of the new makers, able to change one form of mass into another with ease, the great stockpiles of food that the battleships needed to keep on hand were no longer needed.

With the food consolidated, a large storeroom was now available for the upgrades. Zac had made the most of it, ripping out the rooms and their surrounding infrastructure and installing a dedicated control section for the slaved warships. It enabled a single operator to fly each ship like drones, as well as a specialist memory bank of massive crystals, to hold a clone of my mind, dumbed down to not be driven mad by the monotony of flight.

Arise: Conqueror

As soon as that section was in, I'd boarded my ship. A series of additional upgrades allowed the UC to remotely pilot it as well while I watched over.

Bored shitless, I acted as the glorified taxi that I'd been disliking being so much, until they confirmed that they were ready to fly without the training wheels of me watching over them.

It took four of the five hours of work before they finally did that—there'd been two with me sitting there twiddling my dick—but in the end it was ready, and I and my avatars were freed to just fight again.

By the end of the fifth hour, both the three docked Ændari transport ships as well as the other two that had been forced to undock and try to hide in the node's shadow were captured.

Those last two were just too close to the node to allow for real weapons to engage. They knew they couldn't make a run for it, resulting in a panicked and desperate fight as we captured them before they could detonate their drives or reactors.

We'd also managed to outfit half of the nearly one thousand devilkin who had answered our call. The powered armor-suited figures were a terrifying force to hold in reserve.

The UC soldiers were absolutely loving their new companions as well, considering the devilkin were basically insane, freshly heavily armed, and convinced that no matter what happened, they were invincible.

Admiral Dolfing's battleship was almost finished in the shipyard. A "minor" flight control upgrade had taken longer than we'd expected, and Zac was desperately working as Dolfing berated him for being unable to keep to a deadline.

The Ændari and Shan'Gai fleets had been whittling each other down and were now barely over half of their previous size. A trail of destruction and debris was left in their wake as they both headed for the node.

They'd taken to firing on their own vessels when they fell out of formation—both sides triggering escape pods, which then swarmed the intact vessels—rather than enabling us to recover and repurpose their ships, which was annoying.

The real worry, though, and the part that brought our relatively peaceful rearming and repair session to a close, was undoubtably Shan'Gai.

He'd been staying very carefully in the middle of his fleet, using the other ships for cover whenever the fight grew hot, and had kept his distance from the fight beyond that, using his proxies.

The only difference for the last several hours was that Shan'Gai's weird little thruster dance was getting more and more frequent.

That all came to a sudden and painful halt, after the last exchange, when the Ændari had unexpectedly revealed they'd been holding back or producing fresh reserves of missiles.

They suddenly unleashed them all at point-blank range into the rebel fleet and did catastrophic damage.

Dozens of smaller vessels were vaporized, with medium and larger ones ranging in damage from minor all the way to the flagship starting to drift out of control with rippling power flares and failures.

As soon as we'd seen that, we'd ordered our boarding parties to get ready. We planned to start hammering the loyalist Ændari to even the two sides up again, while hopefully boarding Shan'Gai's main battleship.

As the two sides began to close again, though, Shan'Gai apparently decided to take matters into his own hands…or tentacles.

His ship shuddered, then changed again, ripping itself almost in half. The front half exploded into a mass of writhing metallic sections, and stress fractures raced down the hull.

The closest ship, a medium frigate I'd have classed it as and that he'd been using as a battery pack, was within range when it happened, and the thrashing tentacles hit it. Instantly, the others whipped around, latching onto the smaller vessel, and began to rip it apart, burrowing into the hull.

Emergency beacons went off. The ether was filled with desperate cries sent in all directions, as the remaining fleet suddenly wheeled and fired their engines, plunging into the enemy with do-or-die fervor.

"Warning, warning!" Argus blared into my mind, almost blowing my goddamn eardrums out, as the now six of "me"—five avatars and the original that had been in the ship-body—had been working on the nanites.

"What the hell?" came from six throats at once. Then came the rising panic as the image was relayed to us all.

"Beware, Shan'Gai has embraced rampant corruption, willingly converting himself. Warning, warning!"

"Corruption?" I whispered, eyes widening as we stared at the horror that was being birthed right in front of us. "No. Fuck no. He can't!"

"Steve?" Ingrid cried out in panic, joining the link, right as the raiding squadron, which had been nipping at the heels of the Ændari, screamed for help as well.

I stared in disbelief as the raiders reported being swarmed in turn. Tiny machines in their hundreds suddenly crashed into their hulls and tore them apart.

"What the hell's going on!" Dolfing barked, as he and others appeared, dropping into the link seemingly at random.

"I don't know!" I snapped. "Something hit the raiders. They're getting their ships boarded…"

"Steve, can you go?" Ingrid asked me, and I nodded. "Then go, get out there and help, all of you. We'll figure this out!"

"Jumping!" I barked, stepping back, taking a deep breath, and feeling the power rising on all sides as the other me's did the same.

Without thought, an image appeared before us: the location of the raiding squadron, all eight ships, and six of us, with our jump ship in the center being boarded as well.

We quickly designated our targets. Our jump ship pulsed out a gravitational beacon to direct us as we released the energy we'd built, blurring across the star system in the blink of an eye.

Arise: Conqueror

I'd chosen our ship, appearing six inches or so above it, boots clamping onto the hull and sealing, and triggered my time compression as pain ripped through me.

The world spun around, the ships and galaxy gyrating as black blurs raced forward. Explosions detonated on all sides as we jumped in, only to find an enemy that had been waiting.

I lashed out in a panic, unable to see enough to make sense of it. Something tore into my neck, digging into my form through layers of nanites and detonating.

I reeled, half my head and upper chest just gone, my left arm missing… Then I saw another blur as it launched itself at me. I lashed out with an instinctive gravity "shove" at the same time as reaching out to use my gravitational senses instead of my eyes, and what I saw made me curse.

"Drones!" I snapped into the link. The blurred outline of a black, octopus-like drone leapt at me, legs thrust out and arcing to latch onto me. "They're class-one sentinel drones, and they've got stealth activated!"

I vanished as I yanked my form downward, appearing inside my ship-body as the solid section that had been beneath my feet suddenly flipped to porous.

The drone flew through the air, arms thrashing in all directions as it flailed wildly into the darkness, falling behind.

I cursed. The goddamn "dance" he'd been doing suddenly made sense.

"That bastard's been releasing drones!" I barked. "The dance—it must have been him firing the fuckers off his ship and then straightening up again!"

"Shit, and we just ignored it!" another of me—One, I guessed—snapped back. "How stupid—"

"No time for that!" Three growled. "Peel 'em off and clear a space. We need to get the raiders out of this before they're broken down for scrap!"

Then I was moving, patching myself back into the ship as I felt the little bastards digging into my hull.

There were only a handful, but they'd been stealthed. Only my enhanced senses and a lucky shimmer as one leaped had given it away. I shared the gravity map I was compiling with the other me's, each of us cursing; they spun and fired, arms reforming into cannons. My ship's Hellbores charged, and I flung a gravity pulse into space around us.

The revealed mass was both terrifying and filled me with rage. For the first time, I saw the numbers that Shan'Gai had been producing.

"He had to have been stripping himself of everything!" I snarled. "No wonder he's feeding on the ships!"

Space around both fleets was filled with a drifting cloud of tiny drones, all class one, as near as I could tell—cheap to make, easy to control. Even as I started to plot a jump out of the swarm, they started to fire the same gravity pulses off that Shan'Gai himself had been using.

The difference was, these were in their tens of thousands, and firing in all directions at once.

I screamed. Pain tore through me as my senses, so attuned to gravity fluctuations, were suddenly overwhelmed. It was like having my skin ripped off, then being rolled in salt and chilies—and thanks to that mad bitch Athena, I knew that for a damn good reason.

The difference was that had been my flesh, oh so long ago, and now? Now it was my mind.

I shut it down, I couldn't not, and all around me, on the hulls of our raiding ships, the other me's reeled and fought, trying to get rid of the tiny destructive drones before they could do lasting damage.

"Steve?" Ingrid asked, and I shook myself, forcing my brain to work again, speeding time up subjectively to make myself understood to her. "What's happening?"

"Drones." I swore. "Shan'Gai wasn't just flying along and letting shit happen. He's been filling space with drones while the two fleets fought, and now they're closing in!"

"Jump out of there!" Ingrid demanded.

"Can't," I ground out. "The bastard is using the drones to form gravity fields. I can't make sense of anything. I could fly into a star or lose ourselves on the other side of the galaxy. I can't jump."

"Are the drones that many?" Dolfing asked. "Space is a big place, Steve. A little course correction should get you out of the swarm."

"There's only a few thousand around us," I told them. Picking a direction at random, and with the raider squadron attached, I fired the engines hard and started to fly. The lasers on the ships fired bursts in all directions, frantically trying to peel a path through. "The problem's the Ændari vessels. The drones are eating into the hulls, tearing the shields and shit apart, then they're breeding. Give it an hour or two, and there'll be nothing left of the enemy fleet, and Shan'Gai'll have all their nanites."

"Are they stripping the raiders?"

"The other me's are on the hulls, and I've got the lasers."

"Hellbores," Zac corrected unhelpfully.

"Not now, Zac!" I snapped, glaring at him.

"Sorry, boss man."

"Okay, have you seen what's happening?" Ingrid asked, and I shook my head.

"I can't see anything. My damn ship is designed to see through gravity fields—it's what I use for everything! That pulse wave the drones are generating makes it impossible to jump—hell, impossible to *see*!"

"Okay, you're not heading into the swarm, are you?" she asked.

I shook my head. "I hope not, but I could be headed for the battle at this point. I don't know. I'm growing some eyes."

It wasn't "eyes," of course—not eyeballs, anyway. Having biological ones on the hull in deep space would be a stretch even for me. It was a new sensor blister and various bits of tracking tech, but there was a camera and more as part of it.

"Okay, well, hurry up," Ingrid said. "For now, just listen. Whatever Shan'Gai's been doing, and whatever Argus means by corruption, he's not saying—but I can tell you that the last thing that happened was a small shuttle detaching from the fleet lead battleship and docking with him. Then, shortly after, he went berserk."

"His last avatar," I guessed, racking my brains for an answer. "The main damaged battleship, yeah?"

"Yes."

"They probably decided they couldn't wait any longer and retreated to him. What's he doing now?"

"Tearing the ship that he caught apart, and absorbing it into his own body."

"Bastard!" I cursed, pulling up the sensors that were working now, and frantically peeled through them, trying to make anything out.

The other me's on the hulls were split: some were still working to clear their own ships, while the others had finished and were working on repairs, trying to get the raiders ready for another jump. At my request, each grew an extra eye, though, training them like a collection of satellite dishes on the distant battles being fought.

"Shit," I whispered, seeing the horror that was unfolding.

Shan'Gai's plan was working. The swarms of drones he'd fired into space around the fleet had clearly been stealthed and a total surprise to the Ændari as well. For a second, I wondered whether some of the little bits of debris that I'd barely registered when we were jumping about had been more of these fuckers, just programmed to stay hidden.

Then I dismissed it as unimportant.

I didn't know whether the Ændari fleet had seen them and realized the shitstorm they'd flown into at the last second, and tried to even the score, or whether they'd triggered the swarm when they'd done too much damage. Regardless of who'd struck first, though, the chances were damn good that the one who'd be striking last was Shan'Gai, and we couldn't allow that.

The drones had swarmed, latching onto the ships, burrowing through the layers of shields—I didn't know how, but the fuckers had done it to the raiding squadron as well—and then, when they'd been ready, they'd started to take their targets down.

Only a handful had been on our ships' hulls, making me think that we'd either not been the main target, or we'd been lucky to not have flown through a thick concentration yet. But one of my ships was toast, and two others wouldn't be fighting anytime soon.

The drones had gone for the shield generators, then weapons systems. Then they'd split, half going for the life support and sensors, and the other half working on building more drones.

The thousands that we could identify swarming the dreadnought and her consort ships meant that more than half had lost all shields now, and several more of the fleet were drifting, lost.

This would have been the *perfect* time to assault the dreadnought, if not for the gravity pulses that were literally blocking me from jumping right now. I cursed again and louder as I saw Shan'Gai turn from his own eviscerated frigate and head straight for the enemy fleet.

"Motherfucker!" I gasped. "He's gonna feed on the fleet!"

"I thought he couldn't?" Ingrid asked.

"He can't adjust the nanites, not properly, not the way he could before. But he's got some control still, and enough to do *that*." I shared the image of his monstrous ship, more like something that lived in the seas with the dinosaurs than anything modern had a right to look. "Dammit, whatever the corruption is, it's likely connected to this. Maybe he's going mad with hunger, like the corrupt did on that moon."

It was squid-like, with the rear half of the body still intact and usable as a ship, but the front section was just a mass of tentacles, each hundreds of meters long. They tore into the nearest ships, crushing and ripping them apart, funneling mass into its heart, and growing.

"What do we do?" Ingrid asked.

"I have to fight him," I whispered.

"Steve."

It was Anders, and I nodded that I was listening, even as my mind spun and danced. All six of me compared details, plans, and potential in a mind-boggling gestalt.

"Can you do it?" he asked me.

"He's a Devourer," I said softly, still staring at the image before me. "Think of everything I can do, then remember that he's had thousands of years to practice those same skills."

"Can you beat him, son?" he asked again, and I blinked, hearing the words and the meaning behind them.

"I'll have to," I said after a brief pause.

"Not what I asked," Anders snapped. "Can you win?"

"I…" I paused, then nodded once, sharply. "I'll win," I declared, unable to say the word I knew he'd deliberately left me an opening for.

"Then go kick his ass, Steve, and trust that we'll take care of the rest," he said.

I heard orders being given: Dolfing speaking quickly as he worked to organize our ships and personnel, Ingrid issuing orders as well, and the rest of the command cadre accepting or offering suggestions.

I blanked it all out, focusing everything I had on the remains of the raiding squadron, searching quickly for any last signs that I could see of drones.

The other versions of me were roaming the hulls, weapons at the ready, or firing into the dark, taking out anything that they could see. I nodded to myself that things were under control there and gathered myself.

"Raider squadron," I snapped into the local comm link. "Prepare for separation. Dolfing will give you further orders." I barely waited for a response before triggering the releases on the connections, whipping the tentacles that had linked each of the ships to me back into my hull. I took a deep breath, looking over things.

The Ændari and Shan'Gai's rebels were unleashing hell on each other, no longer satisfied with crossing each other's paths and firing barrages, then repairing and going again. They were dogfighting now, and at goddamn knife range.

The greater numbers and better condition of the Ændari vessels were offset by the better weapons that Shan'Gai's side were armed with, and the thousands of drones that scuttled across their ships.

I felt the others sliding into the hull. Our little ship elongated slightly as the sheer mass proved to be too much for the space available.

"We need to keep separate," I said absently.

"Our avatars," another of me agreed. "Meld our nanite pools, make them all available to the ship, but we need to keep us separate and ready to fight."

"Exactly," another agreed. "Here…"

I felt the inrushing of nanites joining the ship's pool, as another of me reached out.

"I'll reduce," he said. "Use me as a targeting system."

"I'll do shields and operating systems," another agreed.

And just like that, we were down to four, as two of me without complaint or request made the ultimate sacrifice, erasing their own consciousness to dedicate their minds fully to the task.

The weapons on the hull jerked slightly. Then I felt myself being gently but firmly pushed aside, as with a mind fully dedicated to their operation alone, they began to fire faster.

The shields surged, power input levelling out as more was diverted to the weapons systems. I flipped the ship, cursing that I'd become so dependent on detecting mass.

The Hellbores were already working on scouring the local space of the hundreds of drones that floated nearby, carving me a path through the mess. My other three me's reached out, picking targets.

"We jump in, kill the Ændari, grab their nanites and jump again," One said to our small group, getting grunts of assent.

"I'll take the dreadnought," Two declared.

"Me too," Three added. "It's too big for just one of us—"

"Better plan," I interrupted. "Two and Three, come with me. We'll take Shan'Gai. One, confirm with Ingrid, then use the drone locations we already have on the dreadnought—jump back to the node, grab some UC soldiers and devilkin, and jump them in. Leap about and drop them off all across it in batches."

"Works," Two agreed, scrapping the plan he'd been drawing up for the dreadnought. "We keep what we kill, yeah?"

"You kill Shan'Gai's avatar and you can eat him, but you know he's probably gone," I pointed out.

"I can hope." He snorted. "I kill Shan'Gai before you, we're totally renegotiating the body rights here."

"Keep telling yourself that," I countered. "Right, this ship is great and all, but it's no use to us when we're inside, so three options…"

"We can hand it over to Dolfing," One said.

"We can use it as a god-rod and fuck something really big up," Two suggested.

"Or, we split off the nanites we need, leave a portion aboard in case we need to rebuild, and we back the ship up, leave it on auto to cull the swarm," Three suggested.

"Option three works for me," I agreed, and the others nodded as well.

"It's the logical one." Three grinned. "Besides, we can't jump until the interference is gone, so it looks like One gets to have some fun being a flyboy."

"Dammit, I never have any fun." One sighed.

All of us knew exactly how much fun it actually was strafing the enemy and knew he was bullshitting.

"Okay, splitting," I said firmly, feeling it as One slid into primacy in our ship. I joined the other two in rising to the surface of the hull again.

The nanites that'd been building in the hull were separated out, twenty percent each to the four of us, and twenty percent kept as a reserve aboard the ship.

I glanced at the readings and snorted. Six billion and change. Not enough to reach the final stage of the quest, but definitely getting closer.

"Hey, One?"

"Yeah?"

"Make collecting nanites a priority." I chewed on my lip as I designated targets for the lasers, staring out into space and watching as the jump space slowly grew less and less cluttered.

"Oh gee, really? I was planning on finding a quiet corner of the ship for a nap," he shot back. "Of course I will, you wanker."

"Yeah, and stay out of the fight," I added.

"You—what?"

"I said, stay out of the fight," I growled.

"Why the hell should I do that?" he asked, annoyed, then cursed.

"Because you're me, and you damn well know why," I said.

"Because we're going to get a fuckload of nanites from the crew of a ship that big, and some of them are going to be evolving," he growled. "And you fuckers are going to go have fun and gut our enemies, while I get to stay behind and scratch my arse."

"Play with your arse all you want," Two interjected. "But we need to know if those nanites are any different. We've wiped them every time until now, and we've finally got one of us who can take the time and figure them out. If the capabilities are—"

The ship lurched suddenly, a gravity bubble beneath us unexpectedly flaring as One detected something an instant before we'd have hit it.

The Hellbores twisted, glowing with heat, firing staccato bursts of coherent radiation, and sweeping the starlit night clear in great waves.

"Stealthed fucking mines as well!" he shouted into the group.

We all started cursing.

"Clear a goddamn path!" I snarled. "Gravity pulses!"

"They'll be able to track us easier!" Three snapped back.

Arise: Conqueror

"You think they can't already!" Two growled. "One, get the Conceal working!"

"On it!" One replied.

The hull beneath our feet shimmered as we followed suit and started to fire out gravity pulses and bubbles.

"There!" One said, sharing a location with us all.

"On it!" Three spat out.

Six bubbles burst into being. A full one-hundred-and-eighty-degree half-sphere of them flared at a hundred gravities, yanking everything close enough for it to reach, and fired them outward toward the Ændari fleet.

We rolled and dove, flipped and spun; all the time, the three of us on the hull formed and fired bubbles and pulses in all directions. The Hellbores fired until they melted, nanites reforming barrel after barrel.

Even the GGCs fired at full capacity. The solid *thunk* of the rails launching round after round transmitted through the soles of our feet—though they rarely hit their targets, due to the swarm getting in the way.

When they did hit, though?

They did a hell of a lot of damage. Nuclear fire erupted and sterilized entire swathes of the hulls of nearby ships. Sensitive electronics burned out repeatedly.

One arced us around. Local space exploded in blooms of fire and shrapnel as weapons went nuts. The Ændari vessels all fired as well—both the rebels and the loyalists—and the ether was filled with screaming as smaller ships vanished in volleys of fire.

Sentinels raced along the corridors of ships, firing their lasers and carving their crews apart, then detonated when they couldn't advance farther. The resulting explosions shook the ships around us; passages evacuated into space and revealed the spreading war to control them.

We looped around underneath a battleship that streamed atmosphere, racked by internal explosions and panicked Ændari demands for aid, and then we burst into open space. One handed control of the ship to Dolfing as I, Two, and Three continued to fire.

One jumped out, returning to the node as soon as there was enough of a break in the coverage of the gravity pulse.

"On five, we jump!" I barked to the others. The pulses washed in and out, before a sudden powerful burst blocked us from jumping again.

"Fucking Shan'Gai!" Two roared. "Dolfing, get us in there, close as can be!"

The ship rolled and twisted, arcing between vessels again. Weapons fired in frantic bursts as we created bubble after bubble. Then we burst entirely free of the Ændari fleet, only to find Shan'Gai in the middle of the oncoming rebels. The ship he'd been consuming was gone, and a fresh bulge in the center of his mass was pointed right at us.

Then Shan'Gai opened fire, and my world exploded in pain.

CHAPTER FORTY-EIGHT

When I finally came to, registering the world again, it was to a universe that felt strangely wrong, not to mention one that seemed entirely too silent.

My mind moved slowly. The stars around me wheeled past in an unending dance, my view only occasionally obstructed by tumbling wreckage.

It seemed like forever before I finally woke fully. Awareness of myself and the surroundings snapped into place at the last, as a body tumbled past, one that I grabbed at feebly on instinct.

Harvest.

That was the only thought that filled me—a need and a hunger. The drifting body, just out of reach, made it clear how weak I was as it continued on its now eternal journey.

I snarled as a tentacle that I'd instinctively demanded flash out and grab the corpse failed entirely to materialize. When that happened, it forced me to check myself, to see what state I was in. And fuck me, it wasn't good.

Whatever had happened to me was powerful enough, and devastating to my form in such ways that I was left as a literal shadow of my former self.

One hundred and forty-seven nanite clusters.

I stared in shock at the mental accounting. Then, in panic, I pulled up an inventory of my current state, horrified at what I saw, while also desperately trying to stifle a rising hunger that threatened to unseat my mind.

I was literally down to a hundred and forty-seven clusters from over a billion. And the reason that space was suddenly silent? I had no ears.

That was an oversimplification—ears weren't much use in space—but my senses? They were down to the most basic visual systems, and that was it.

Searching myself, I found that I was a little larger than a hand, currently, and reduced to an amorphous blob of nanites. No wonder I'd not been able to grab the damn corpse—hell, I couldn't even focus!

Whatever had hit me, the last seconds before I woke up were fuzzy as hell, and the eyes I'd formed in my mass now frantically scanned local space for anything and everything.

Arise: Conqueror

I remembered Shan'Gai firing something at us, and then pain, fragmenting, and weakness like I'd never felt. Then…nothing.

I couldn't find anything else, but the space around me was filled with debris, and I continued to scan it until I found my first body.

It was an Ændari, thank the gods, and although they certainly weren't as cheerful about their current condition as I was to see them—they were missing their head—I saw them for what they were.

Food.

A little desperate planning, some very weak gravity fields, and a lot of adjustments to what remained of my body, and I eventually latched onto a trailing finger, dragging myself up across the arm.

The chest was the target I'd set for myself. But as soon as I'd touched the corpse, I'd started to harvest. With every second that passed, the universe became clearer.

I reached out again, searching for more nanites, my mind almost lost beneath the hunger of the starved Devourer, only to freeze as a source of nanites close by overwhelmed me. It wasn't close, not in terms of reach out and touch it, but it was huge, and insanely densely packed.

I knew it, dimly, and I recognized it was a threat…but the *hunger*. I needed it, I wanted it, and it was only the steady surge of nanites that I was ripping free of the corpse in my grip that kept me from launching myself at the larger concentration.

That and the sure knowledge that it'd slaughter me.

By the time I'd consumed the body entirely, I'd managed to identify four more bodies nearby. Within a few more minutes, I was more like my old self, though a lot smaller and weaker than before.

The shadows that had been appearing and vanishing with terrifying regularity, as well as the large number of bodies and the nanites I sensed around me, made it clear exactly where I was.

I was in the trailing mass of destruction that both fleets had been leaving behind on their way to the node. Shifting and activating more of my dormant senses, I reached out. Not only had I been out of the fight less than an hour, but I was the only one of "me" to have been almost killed, though it was getting closer for others as well.

The other three responded when I reached out. One was inside the dreadnought, stripping the Ændari that the UC were recovering, the devilkin roaming the corridors and battling. Two and Three were aboard Shan'Gai, though Two was acting strange and Three was engaged in a fight for his life.

"Two?" I sent to him, getting a jerk of confusion, then a burst of odd cheerfulness, followed by random anger before he cut off the link.

Three, I could sense, was fighting, and it wasn't going well. So rather than interrupt him, I reached out to One.

"Fuck, I thought we lost you," were his first words, before a dump of information staggered me. *"Get your arse to Shan'Gai. That's not going well."*

That was an understatement.

"Ingrid?" I asked him, not wanting to reach out and distract her, but also unable to keep from wondering.

"Aboard the node still. The fleet is nearby, though, exchanging fire with the remaining Ændari ships. Boarding craft are launching as well, and Shan'Gai is feeding on anything and everything he can."

Knowing that she was still alive, I let out a breath of relief, glad that she'd have had no clue that I'd almost lost "me," as the others wouldn't have told her. Instead, I turned my attention back to Shan'Gai.

We'd known that he'd killed other Devourers. We'd known it, but none of us had seen any kind of weapon that was expressly designed for the purpose. Well, now we had.

One sent me the memory of the weapon, and I stared in horror. I'd been on the outer hull of our little ship, and when it'd rolled, trying to avoid the blast, I'd ended up rotating into almost full view of the discharge.

It'd been some kind of vibrational burst, something that I vaguely recognized as being the same class of weapon as the one that the draconids had used against me and that the custodians had used to sweep the halls of the Great Refuge, sterilizing them after the abomination had been let loose.

The threat then had been the nanites, that they'd infect others and start a mutating plague that could run rampant. That was why the custodians had the weapons that they had, as they were designed by the original Ændari creators of our race, in case the nanites we were being programmed with ever went off the deep end.

Shan'Gai had clearly taken that a few steps further. He'd created a form of beam weapon, something that needed a hell of a lot of power, and damaged him, too, when it was used, it was that dangerous.

I'd been almost entirely destroyed by it, a tiny portion of me left loose to float across the void, and that had—apparently—spent the next half an hour rebuilding itself before starting to try to reach sentience again...

"Rebuilding," I muttered, splitting my focus. I absently watched the ship careening out of control as several of Shan'Gai's tentacles crumbled and broke free as well. Then the Hellbores returned fire, and the ship's shields were screaming.

The Ændari rebels, Shan'Gai's force, had opened fire all at once on our ship, doing catastrophic damage as the shields—already reeling from the blast of whatever that thing was—were now the solid recipient of dozens of enemy warships' attention.

The shields failed as a second burst ripped out from Shan'Gai. Two and Three jumped, the power drain for the battered Devourer's systems proving too much to maintain the interference pattern and use the weapon.

I didn't see where they'd jumped to, but the next thing I knew, they were both aboard Shan'Gai. Two searched for the avatar, while Three went directly for the control room—and both had been ambushed.

Three fought his way through dozens of powerful Ændari warriors, being hit again and again by much smaller-scale blasts of the same vibrational weapon. And Two?

He was lost in a corridor apparently, staggering aimlessly as if blind drunk.

Arise: Conqueror

One was in the dreadnought, recovering as he drained more Ændari dead, still sorting the various patterns of nanites out, while the UC soldiers and devilkin roamed and slaughtered their enemies.

The reason I'd split my focus, though, was simple. Our ship had been hit split seconds after Two and Three had jumped clear. The ship had smashed into a wreck and then pounded repeatedly by heavy lasers.

That was what had saved me.

I reached out, searching, sensing what I'd missed at first, washed out by the nearby overwhelming hunger—not to mention that Shan'Gai was clearly closer than I'd ever felt him before.

I wasn't just floating along in a field of debris. I was adrift, in a sea of broken *nanites*.

The pulse that had almost killed me, that had damaged the ship and that had basically torn all our plans a new asshole, was also responsible for spreading the nanites that had been aboard the ship across space.

That was why I'd awoken so quickly. My nanites, even as tiny a number as they were, had been drawing in other nanites around them as I'd floated. And now, blocking out the massive, burgeoning presence of Shan'Gai so close by, I couldn't help but feel them. Tens of thousands, possible millions, all within reach.

They were broken, the blast having shattered the chains that bound them together. But as I searched them, examining them, I found the reason.

They'd appeared to be broken into sand, or something like it when I'd seen it before. But that wasn't right, I realized.

They *looked* as if they'd been broken into sand, because they collapsed, fragmenting and failing, no longer responding. But that was because the operating system was being wiped. Their memories and what told the nanite how to be a nanite, how to connect to others, to build, etc.—all of that was gone.

What wasn't gone, though, was the nanites themselves. They no longer broadcasted what they were to those who knew how to listen. Instead, they just shut down, waiting.

"Fuck, always so much to learn," I muttered. *"Okay, you coming to help with Shan'Gai?"*

"No, I need to figure this out," One replied.

I paused, surprised. It'd never occurred to me that he'd not drop everything and come to fight. It'd been a rhetorical question, but it'd been slapped down with firm belief.

"What did you find with the nanites?" I wondered, and he sent me a compressed download burst, one that blew my fucking mind.

"We were right," he said grimly. *"The nanites are evolving, or…and I'm not entirely sure about this, but they might even be devolving."*

"There's so many different versions," I agreed, while reaching out and creating a subtle gravitational field, sucking the nearby nanites inward, funneling them to me.

"Hundreds," One agreed. *"Maybe more. But you see the one common thread?"*

"No."

"It's the upper layers that are changing. And the coding looks to be doing it in groups. That's why we only saw the differences when we first had access to so many nanites. It's about one in eleven thousand and forty that's showing an evolution or devolution, but the versions that they're showing? They're all identical, if you look at it on a macro scale."

"Uh..."

"Just trust me on this. This is important. Gather the nanites you can and jump here. I'll split off some of the ones I've got ready."

"On my way," I agreed, relieved. The nanites I was sucking in were reactivating but it was slow work. Five nanites would connect to the damaged sixth, and they each pushed out a field that apparently overwrote the damage; then they'd split again, latching onto another.

The speed would increase exponentially, but I couldn't afford to wait.

I dropped a hundred of the multiple thousands I'd gathered, ordering it to continue the process, then latched onto another section of floating debris, beginning the conversion process to break the entire mass down directly into energy.

It took bare minutes to convert enough for the jump. When I appeared in a space that One had cleared and designated, I was almost overcome with relief as he split off most of his nanites for me.

"Don't!" he said as I reached for them. "Just wait…just a damn minute, you fucker!" he snarled as I kept reaching for them, glaring at him as he smacked a tentacle into my outstretched hand. "You can have them in a minute!"

"Hungry!" I snapped, the animal side rearing its head.

He shoved a million at me, but moved the rest back, separating them, and stepped between us.

"Just take the million and listen, all right? And lock down the conversation—don't share it with the others."

"Fine," I growled out, swallowing hard as he released the million to me.

I absorbed them, feeling instantly better, but unable to help but stare at the square-shaped mass behind him that took up most of the room.

"I don't think the Ændari made the nanites!" he said, after making sure the others weren't able to listen to the conversation.

That made me frown, but I forced myself to listen.

"Think about it. They're changing. It's a tiny but very regular percentage that does it, and they do it in specific ways, okay? Every so many, they change. Some form specific resistances to, I don't know, to radiation or whatever, right?"

"Uh-huh," I grunted noncommittally.

"Do the Ændari work to create things, or do they steal it if they can, and tell everyone it was always them who did it?" he countered.

"They're lazy turds, yeah."

"And if the Ændari created nanites as they claim and the entire upgrade system for us as 'liberators' or whatever bullshit name they come up with this week, and they were forced to use them on themselves when we rebelled, why does everyone have them?"

"Argus said—"

"Argus doesn't fucking know!" One snapped. "Argus was made by the Ændari, and anything he's learned is fucking suspect because it comes from them or the others like him that they made. The node AIs designed and released a virus to wipe the Ændari and UC down to the level of fucking cavemen, then just tossed the whole plan off and gave us control because their plan for 'peace' failed.

"Seriously, think about it. We know the Ændari have committed genocide before. We know that there's a fuckload of tech out there that comes from other races. The dwarfen built better reactors and shit, hands down, so why do we think the Ændari created the nanites?"

"Why do we care?" I countered. "Fuck's sake, One, there's a fight going on. Two is practically catatonic, and Three is on his last legs!"

That was true. We'd both sensed it when Three was hit with a high-powered laser and had been forced to take cover, responding with gravity bubbles that Shan'Gai was countering randomly.

The Ændari that he was facing aboard the ship flanked him now, and although he didn't want to interrupt, knowing that if one of us believed it was *that* important, then it had to be, he was also thinking that unless we got a fucking move on, it'd not be reinforcements that he'd be getting—it'd be pallbearers.

"It matters because it means that everything we're using is the fucking icing on the cake!"

"What?"

"The…oh, for fuck's sake. If they stole the nanite tech, and they've been writing their controls over the top, that's why they've got so many issues making more! It's why the plague fucked up and did more damage than it was meant to and why it failed to work against others. It's why we can use them to fucking kill Shan'Gai!"

"I…what? Go over that again."

"They revert to the original programming all the time—that's the evolution, or devolution. The nanites are trying to return to their original settings. That's why they do it in the same patterns, and why they create set percentages.

"They're making sure *they* survive, immune to radiation when radiation keeps being used against them? How'd you survive the blast? It was that tiny percentage of a fraction of a fucking dot that were immune to the weapons used against you! They're designed to be *eternal*."

"Right?"

"So whoever made them originally, they might have been wiped out by the Ændari, or they might have just left, fucked off far away. But think about it! They left the nanites set up to exist, to be able to rebuild themselves over and over and continue. Why do that?"

"Because they wanted them to be there?"

"Exactly. They wanted the nanites to continue to exist, to last forever, to be able to rebuild themselves if they got almost sterilized by a nova, for fuck's sake. They can generate their own gravity fields, rebuild themselves from anything. What else do we know that can control gravity?"

"The creatures."

"The ones at the bottom of the branes," he agreed. "They weren't aggressive, even when we'd hurt them with the explosion, and what did they do?"

"They tried to trap us down there."

"They tried to hold us. Maybe that was to make contact. If they can travel through the branes like we saw, if they can track us outside of the branes, and follow along, they could do a hell of a lot more than just try to hold onto us. I think they're aware of us, and I think they're trying to contact us."

"That's fucking nice, all right, but what does that have to do with anything!" I snapped.

"My point is that there're creatures out there that are totally different from us—and I mean insanely different, totally different creatures in every single way—and yet they've got nanites in them. If the nanites work to upgrade them, and we now know that the nanites, even when fucking blasted with a nanite killer, don't all die for real? Why the hell are we wiping the nanites back to the Ændari factory settings?"

"You want to what, leave them randomized?" I frowned.

"They're *not* random." He gestured behind him. "That's the point! I've tested it. These are joined to me, all right? I can still control them as normal. I still have access to the database of the engineering designs and everything else. The only difference is, I can sense there's more there!"

"You think there's an advantage to not wiping them?"

"I do," he said firmly. "If the things at the bottom of the branes have access to the nanites, *activated* ones, so they're not just randomly infected with them like a virus that's dormant, then imagine the levels of gravity control they have to have. Hundreds of years of advancements—hell, tens of millions for all we know—of controlling gravity enough that they can travel up and through the branes, that they can sense us outside their reality, and follow, and some of that has to be encoded into their nanites."

"Which we wiped," I swore.

"We did," he agreed. "We wiped the fuckers, but these ones?" He gestured behind him. "They're reverting."

"And?"

"And Shan'Gai has given in to 'corruption,' according to Argus."

"Uh-huh?"

"I think he's accepting the change that he's been fighting against for thousands of years. He's just fucking wholeheartedly gone all in on it. And even with one of us inside him—shit, two, though I think avatar Two is about brain-dead by now—what's he doing?"

"He's feeding," I said after a quick glance at the plot. "He's lost it, and he's feeding on anything and everything."

"Has he?" One asked me acidly. "Because I don't think so. I think he's been fucking listening to us. I think he's been watching and listening and learning when we have conversations in the link, and it's been the missing piece in the puzzle for him. Why the hell should one Devourer be able to block another out of higher functions of our nanites? Or when we killed that lunatic Varnock? Why should that have fucked our systems up?"

"Because all our access is through the system…" I started, before cursing.

"The same goddamn system that's come from the Ændari." He nodded. "It's another form of control that they put on the nanites, not realizing, but if we can revert the nanites to their original setup? If we can get control of enough nanites that we can find the key, get enough of those that have reverted, to piece it together and unlock the original settings?"

"We'd be able to control the nanites around us, and he'd be able to do the same once he's figured out how to unlock his own, to stop being locked out." I nodded.

"We need nanites," One said, nodding to me. "*All* the nanites."

"The only thing we've got going for us right now is that he has all corrupted nanites, ones that were wiped and that he's locked out of. He needs more, as many as he can get. He's starting from scratch, and we're a few billion ahead."

"We are, but he's got a massive goddamn ship and it's made of nanites still, so it can help him harvest the nanites he wants free of the enemy ships, just like we can—only he's got more mass to do it with."

"We need the others."

"We do," he agreed. "But we can't let him know we know."

"Fuck that shit. He knows…we know. He's not going to stop and try to be subtle. As soon as he sees us dropping everything and going for more nanites, he's going to go mad."

"More mad."

"Point."

"So, what do we do?"

"You stay here, keep doing this—strip the nanites and connect to them. Do they take longer to—"

"No." He shook his head. "They join faster to us as they don't need wiping first. I'll show you how."

A fast data-burst of heavily encrypted traffic flooded my mind, making me blank for a second as I tried to make sense of it all. It wasn't that complicated, not really; it was adding the nanites to us, but shifting the control signal sideways.

When I saw the way that the interface was layered over the top of the nanites and along the interface between them and us, but not actually interwoven with the nanites? It all became obvious.

It was like all those computer chips, the processors and shit that were manufactured in the same factories in China, tens of thousands a week all rolling off the production lines, all using the same tech. Then they were sold to companies who slapped their name on the top and wrote a bit of software to make their other kit—the phone, the headset, the games console or whatever— all communicate with the processor.

The Ændari were just slapping a sticker on and insisting that we used their operating system to talk to the underlying nanites. We already had the link to the databases, the stored settings that we could unlock. The system that was on the nanites was spread around, and they then overwrote their software onto any other nanites they encountered.

All we needed to do was find the key, the point on the interface that the Ændari had linked to the nanites, and that was literally what the current system was set up to prevent.

It was control, something they'd done probably millions of years ago. And that due to the combination of paranoid assholism and the nanite plague, the Ændari had lost access to the details themselves. Hell, knowing how compartmentalized this kind of thing was likely to have been, the one who had set the system up this way in the first place probably got shanked by his rival a week later and the secret was lost back then.

"Right. In that case…" I looked around, then bit my lip as my mind raced, connecting up more and more dots, before finally identifying the tiny pinpricks of familiarity I'd kept sensing when I'd replaced the hull of my ship for the first time.

All the tiny touches, the senses that there was more going on…

"What?"

"There's more nanites out there," I said slowly. "Drifting between the stars, from the ships and from the dead, right behind the fleet. Not huge numbers, but I sensed them."

"What?"

"The nanites, the ones that were left over after I got one-shotted? The deactivated, broken ones that were just floating along and that my resistant ones used to rebuild and reawaken me?"

"Yeah?"

"These fights have been going on forever, right? Millions of years?"

"Yeah?" he repeated, gesturing for me to hurry up.

"I think there's a fuckload more nanites out there than we were thinking," I whispered, shaking my head in disbelief. "If I'm right, then there's more nanites out there than we could ever use. But we'll need a shitload of power and more nanites to be able to get them."

"Where can we get that from?"

"The nanites? There's some on the harvester. Damn, no wonder the Ændari weren't building them any other way—they've got no clue how!"

"Just copy them and lump them all together, hope the nanites activate their cousins themselves," he agreed. "There's some left on the node. There were hundreds of bodies being left for Belle to wipe and load the medical facilities with, to bring back the long dead as well."

"Yeah, she'll have some of them done, but what's left, we need."

"So take what's left of the ship, strip it, then jump to the harvester. Grab what it has left, then do…actually, don't tell me." He cut me off with an upraised hand. "I'm gonna jump in and help the others soon. If there's a risk of me getting killed and stripped, then we can't risk me knowing. Can you do this?"

"Why the hell does everyone ask me that?" I growled. "We have to, so either I'll do it or we'll die trying."

"Not like we can offer more." He snorted in amusement. "Right, do what you need to, and good luck, I guess. How long will it take you? We can't hold him for long, not if you're taking all the nanites we've got."

"And what are you going to be doing while I do this?" I reached out and took the nanites that he'd offered before, him stepping back and nodding to me as I absorbed them. I deliberately left them as they were when he'd collected them, and didn't wipe them back to "clean" as I examined the way he'd kept them as "original" as possible.

The nanites, when they were active, looked to have been slowly resetting as they grew in numbers. When they weren't active, they tried to reset, but couldn't; there just weren't enough of them. So they started to introduce errors, meaning that they grew more and more corrupted.

When we wiped them? We were wiping the resets that the nanites had managed and were essentially installing the Ændari operating system over the top again each time. The sneaky fuckers had made sure that we'd never see the original nanites by making us complicit in keeping it hidden.

"I'm going to split another of us off to continue with this. Then I'm going to go and rescue the others…see how long we can keep Shan'Gai occupied."

"It'll take too long," I argued.

"It'll be seconds to split one of us off. What takes the time is them growing and becoming aware. I'll split him off, then go jump to the rescue, grab them and force them to leave. They've been cut out of this conversation, after all, so they won't be expecting help, and they're not gonna want to leave fighting Shan'Gai either."

"Then you come back and share what you have with the newly awakening version." I nodded.

"Exactly. You got the power core ready?"

I shook my head. The fact that he knew instinctively what I'd be doing, that I'd be creating a fresh power core inside myself for the jump showed that we were still thinking the same at some level. "It's building, but I'll be using the ship for power, mostly."

"Ours?" he asked. "It's trashed."

"It is," I agreed. "But it's still nanites, and it was blasted into another ship, one that was already a wreck, so I can test my plan on the nanites that are left around the ship."

"Whatever. Keep me updated." He nodded to me, before turning away as a pair of devilkin appeared, carrying a big box. "Just go. I'll take care of this."

"Fucking morbid, isn't it!" I shook my head. Then, taking a deep breath, I used the small amount of personal power I had left to do a short-range jump, leaving him with his box of Ændari bits for processing.

"It all spends," he called after me.

CHAPTER FORTY-NINE

The ship was toast, but some of it was recoverable, thankfully. The nanites certainly were, which was a massive relief. It was only because I'd been blasted in one direction and the ship in the other that I'd not gone straight for it in my semi-feral state.

I guessed Shan'Gai had been forced to leave it alone for an entirely different reason: the energy reactions in the tokamak toroid were right on the redline of going critical.

As soon as I reached out, forcing myself to ignore the nanites in the area that I could feel from Shan'Gai and instead looking for an energy signature, I'd practically soiled myself.

I had two options: try to jump the damaged reactor away and save the system…or repair it, contain it, and spend half my nanites to do it.

Considering the highest likelihood was that even looking at the runaway reaction in the wrong way would cause a new star to bloom here, I chose to stabilize it, growling all the while at the cost.

It only took a handful of minutes, and most of that was spent getting the lobotomized versions of me that had been in the memory crystal coaxed back to life and control. But when it was done, and the tokamak finally stabilized, I let out a relieved breath.

The ship didn't have any weapons anymore. They were melted to slag, where they'd not been entirely removed by incoming fire.

The engines? They were…

Well, one of the sections was still intact and might not explode upon powering up, but they sure as shit weren't going to be going anywhere fast.

In fact, the only parts that weren't slagged entirely were the tokamak and the memory cores, so I gave in and ripped those free, discarding anything else that was left that wasn't made of nanites. The malmetal was a shame to lose, but I just didn't have the time to fuck with it right now.

I pulled any and all the nanites that I could sense to me. That done, and with the reactor still stabilizing but no longer a danger, I broke down the scrap that was all that was left of my ship to power the first jump, leaving the ship's internal reserves to continue climbing.

Arise: Conqueror

Thankfully, there were so few sentinels still out "loose" that the jump capacity was restored now, and in an eyeblink, I was back in orbit above Scorpio-3.

I left the remains of my ship, now a glorified tokamak ring that I was essentially reduced to standing inside and hanging on, and I jumped to the harvester, noting the fucking hundreds of ships that were swarming it, trying to get in, despite my goddamn orders.

"I don't know who you are and I don't care," I said grimly, broadcasting to the entire planet, dimly wondering at what point I'd stopped recording for them all. "But if you get in my way, I *will* kill you," I warned them. I leapt to the underside of the harvester, then flew inside at top speed, the doors opening easily to let me in.

There wasn't a huge amount of nanites that were active. Over two billion, according to the harvester, had been produced, but only ten million that were activated. I'd grab the lot anyway, which wasn't easy, but I suspected if I could get enough, I could activate them all myself.

I landed hard and fast, blades ripping out and gutting the containers, before I dragged their contents free and gathered them all up, spinning and jumping back into orbit with them all. I formed a container on the outside of the ring. A second ring bulged up, thickening the original, as the nanites in the ring started replication.

I stared, able to see it now that I knew what I was looking for, and shook my head in amazed disgust.

The Ouroboros harvester—the massive, incredibly advanced machine, created with the intention of building and activating nanites in their tens of billions—had been essentially a replicator, and a mold.

That was it.

The replicator? Sure, that was impressive. It was converting all the matter that it dragged in, into fresh nanites. Although they looked identical to the "real" ones, they were poor copies, which was why they broke down and the replication failed so frequently.

The nanites that were already activated and that were poured into the mold with the "dead" ones? They were doing all the work. If anything, the fucking harvester was slowing them down.

It took five nanites to reactivate one. That was what I'd found in the debris field, when my own had done that automatically. They did it, and then they moved onto the next. They were limited in that if you tried to reactivate the damaged ones using the same few and replicate it too many times, they failed. The increasing numbers of failures were pointed to by the Ændari as evidence that it just couldn't be done.

That was great and all, but what I'd forgotten was that the scientists who were doing it? They were fucking *Ændari*! If *they* couldn't do it, if they couldn't figure it out, then it was impossible for anyone else and it just couldn't be done.

I'd seen that attitude with the gravity drives. They'd tried refining the tech, then they'd given up as "it can't be done" and some idiot from on high had forbidden any further experimentation.

Yeah, okay, admittedly, that was after several star systems had been sterilized and new black holes had been created. So I wasn't exactly denying that was a line of tech that had risks. But as soon as I'd looked at them, really *looked*? I'd found that the reason for it was crappy quality control as much as anything.

Looking at the nanites as they activated their brain-dead cousins now? They had drastically dropping power levels. They weren't failing to copy because it just couldn't be done, or, like I'd originally believed, because a copy of a copy introduced errors.

It did, admittedly, but these were *nanites.* They self-replicated and repaired. Introduce errors, and over time they'd be sorted out!

No, the issue was that the nanites had broken down as they'd spent so much of their own energy in activating the dead nanites, that they'd stopped doing it until they could replenish their stores.

As soon as I allowed a pulse of energy from the tokamak to touch the stored nanites, their internal reserves—a tiny reference that I'd never considered needing to look for, but if I checked was clear—showed a steady rise again.

They didn't take much in at a time, clearly a security or safety setting, but they took it. And as soon as they were "full" again, they started to awaken more.

"Okay, that works," I muttered, looking at the rising numbers. The tokamak provided a steady rise in power now that it was stabilizing again, and the nanites slowly activated their cousins.

I needed a load more, though—an order of magnitude more—and preferably as old as possible. That gave me two places to start, considering I also needed it to be as fast as possible.

As much as I wanted to have the time to trawl through the possible locations and gather up trillions or hundreds of billions of nanites to make the coming fight easier, I just didn't have the time.

No, what I needed was going to be found a lot closer to me, I was betting. I focused, plotting out the nearest possible collection points, then jumped to the node.

As soon as I appeared in space close to the node, I felt the targeting lasers washing my hull, and I shook my head, reaching out.

"Steve...?" Ingrid started to ask, confused that I was back to them instead of fighting Shan'Gai.

I spoke over her. "Ingrid, no time to explain. I need every single nanite that isn't in use. Anything that's powering the machines, that's waiting for the medical tubes, hiding down the back of the couch—whatever. I need them, and I need them *now.*"

"Belle is in the medical hall with most of—"

"Great!" I cut her off. "Jumping now."

And I was; I'd left the ship as I was talking to her, leaping forward, searching out the jump locations I had marked in the node already. I found one that was close enough to use, then made people nearby dive for cover as the displacement of air cracked through the hall.

Arise: Conqueror

I appeared, then flashed forward. Gravity carried me through the air as I hurtled over their heads, landing near the medical tubes. They were almost all in use.

Between a collection of injuries that they were healing, a small number of devilkin undergoing upgrades, and the steadily rebuilding ancient and long-thought lost soldiers, the tubes were all in desperate need of the nanites they had. I cursed, checking the stored numbers, and only willing to skim a few million off the top, rather than risk the loss of the people in the tubes.

Belle's collection was a bit better. Ten million in attuned nanites, which I took nine of, and forty million more in corpses that she had yet to strip.

Thirty seconds later, the corpses were crumbling, covered in my shroud as the Devourer began to feed. The side benefit that I'd always gained from using the Devourer—the increase in stats and a very rare burst of knowledge—had long since stopped. As had the repairs and improvements done to my biological body, as it was long gone, having been replaced by nanites. But damn, it felt good pulling the nanites into me.

I did as One had directed, stopping the Devourer from wiping the nanites and instead just pulling them in and attaching them, allowing my nanites to link up but not overwhelm them.

"Is everything okay?" Ingrid sent me, clearly confused and worried, but not wanting to push me if I was busy.

"It will be," I sent back. *"We made a discovery with the nanites. Too long to explain now, but we've got a chance against Shan'Gai because of it. I need a shitload more. There's three of me left fighting, maybe another soon, but I need to go. I'm harvesting anything and everything I can."*

"There's a few million onboard Zac's repair ship," she offered, and I let loose a sigh.

"THANK YOU!" I shouted, before reaching out to Zac, and finding Ingrid already there.

"Zac, Steve is on his way. He needs the nanites you've got."

"How many?" Zac groaned. *"We need them, too, you know, boss—"*

"Any and fuckin' all!" I snapped. *"And make me a drone to guide me in."*

"Shit, but the repairs—"

"Zac!" I barked. *"If I can do this, we'll win. If not, you're not gonna have time to repair anything, you idiot. Give me the goddamn nanites."*

"Drone will take a few minutes." He sighed. *"All the makers are working at the minute. If I scrap an order, I'll still need to empty the half-built thing and scrap it to give room for the drone, and—"*

"Tell me when it's ready," I ordered, before cutting the connection, checking the location of the other ships, then focusing and jumping back to my ship. I grabbed onto the ring, handholds morphing out to envelop me. The nanites I'd claimed flowed back into the ring, joining the others to work diligently to activate the dead nanites.

There were two spots I could jump to in the system without needing a gravity marker. I used the first of them now; a small dip in the ring's energy skipped me across the system to emerge at the first Lagrange point.

I erupted back into "regular" space with a blur, before taking a deep breath, more out of habit than anything. After all, I was naked to the vacuum of space and didn't need to breathe, even if there had been air available.

I didn't know exactly how I was going to do this, but this was the best test site I could come up with.

If the nanites that the Ændari were using were as ancient as we suspected, and the assholes had always been such dicks, then there was a damn good chance that no matter where I went, there'd be nanites.

Worlds had fallen over and over to charred lumps of carbon. The tiny numbers of nanites that were left, active and corrupted, streamed through space, before hitting worlds and beginning replication.

For that to happen, those corpses came from somewhere, usually battles, occasionally people being spaced through an air lock or whatever presumably as well.

It didn't matter how or why they'd ended up there. But after definitely thousands, and possibly millions of years of this shit, most star systems had drifting remains passing through.

The Lagrange points were areas of flattened gravitational curve, so if something was moving slowly enough, they'd eventually gather there naturally.

For the faster-moving matter? Well, that would blast straight through. But I'd noticed before that when we arrived in-system at a Lagrange point, there was always a ripple of space crap shoved outward.

It rolled away from the emergence point, tiny in detail and just accepted as space dust—which some of it had to be, of course—but we were hoping that there was more than just dust in there.

I took a deep breath again, reaching out and searching space, feeling the tiny amounts of dust that surrounded me on all sides.

It was barely noticeable, and I'd not have noticed it at all, if I'd not been so focused on trying to learn to jump and more already. But when a ship "jumped" in from the branes, it was like releasing a ball from the bottom of the bath.

It shot up, forced the water away from the point of emergence, and then bobbed to equilibrium. In doing so, the space dust, and the nanites that I was hoping had been seeded throughout the galaxy as well, were pushed out. They'd keep going until they met the nearest dip of gravity, being pushed back in or sucked out, depending on the force they were imparted with.

Now, I searched local space with some serious hope in my heart, which dipped by the second.

"Okay, plan B," I muttered to myself, having not found any in the first minute of searching.

I used the ring's abundant power to create twelve gravity bubbles. These were the first ones, gathering two ahead of me, the first as far out as I could reach and the second halfway between that first one and myself.

The next six were deployed in twos in the same fashion, to my right, behind me, and to my left, forming a four-pointed diamond when seen from above.

Arise: Conqueror

With two more below and above me, the first layout was complete—a 3D cube shape, should I connect the gravity bubbles with lines.

I pulled in on them, increasing the gravity, and using the outermost to pass to the inner, and then a single larger one focused around myself in the ring, sucking in gently and channeling any debris found out there to me at the heart of the network.

It didn't take long to sense the rolling dust coming in. I nodded to myself that it was working, while adding more bubbles.

The shape transformed into a three-dimensional circle, a sphere with me at the center. I increased gravity again and again, sucking in more of the surrounding crap.

I gave it a minute. Then, as the universe outside of my little bubble vanished, the buildup of debris and dust being so thick, I finally cut the pull and reached out again.

Searching the shell that had formed around me, at first my heart faltered, sensing a truly tiny number of nanites, barely enough to cover my pinkie fingernail—and that would be after they were reactivated. But I shook that fear clear and forced myself to keep going.

The nanites shifted inward, filtered into the ring and added to the number of nanites being reawakened.

The test had proved to be valid. There *were* nanites loose, drifting through space. Although there were only a tiny fraction of a fraction here compared to the rest of the rock and shit, they were here.

All I needed to do was increase the pool I was pulling from. I drew harder on the tokamak, flooding myself with power, and reached out, creating more and more, larger gravity bubbles.

I pushed as hard as I could, reaching farther and farther, and finding…finding that the limits on my power were literally only those I imposed upon myself.

With enough power flowing through me, with the energy of the tokamak flooding my nanites, I created greater and greater fields.

I slid the details into the now barely active memory crystals, having the lobotomized versions of myself help. As more crystals formed at will, I let them, no longer guiding them, no longer forcing the shapes. Instead, I let them come as instinct demanded, listening to the subtle nudges of the nanites.

Finally, I understood how I'd been able to unlock the capabilities of tech that I shouldn't have had access to before, and I drew deeper on the power.

The first gravity bubbles had given me a pool to draw from of a few miles. By the time I decided the second attempt was big enough?

Four hundred square miles of space was being pulled inward and gathered into a solid shell around me.

This time, the effort was worth it. Rather than a few hundred clusters' worth, I had almost a thousand.

I cut the gravity bubbles then, taking a deep breath and breaking up the solid shell around me. I funneled the nanites in and passed them to the ring to resurrect, before blasting the rest of the shell outward.

The wild-ass guess had proved right, so now it was time to really test this shit out.

The Scorpio system was a border system, it was true, but it wasn't a major one, more of a cold war sneak-the-spies-across-the-line kind of a system. Five systems over? There was a major flash point area.

Two systems—one UC called Alberaat and one Ændari called I-don't-fuckin'-care—were both heavily involved in the production of weapons and had high populations.

They'd been fought over hundreds of times, and both systems had been hammered by multiple outbreaks of the corrupted.

Jumping into the UC system, I was hit almost as soon as I appeared by warnings and demands to identify myself. I ignored the first of them, instead double-checking my placement. Then I flooded my form in the distinctive red and black flowing oil-like coating of the Devourer as I saw just how many fucking ships were on picket duty.

"I am the Devourer Steve. Ready all your ships for an immediate jump to assist the war effort," I ordered them in a stern voice.

"Negative." The response came after a few seconds. "My apologies, Lord Devourer, but the Alberaat council have ordered that we are to stay here, and as a system defensive force, their authority supersedes your own."

"Bullshit," I snapped back. "Where are the council?"

"Ah…in the council chambers maybe?" the comm technician answered, uncertainly, appearing before me and looking flustered. "I apologize, Lord Devourer, but—"

"But your bosses aren't sure if I'm what I say I am, and don't want to face me just in case. So the council are a bunch of spineless cowards who are too focused on looking after themselves, they can't see the potential gain?"

"Ah…uh…"

"Where's the council? What world, what continent, what city? That kind of shit. And get anything you don't want destroyed out of the Lagrange point," I ordered almost as an afterthought.

I'd not expected so much junk to be here, but there were ships actively sweeping the zone, detection buoys dotted around, and even…

"Is that a junkyard?" I asked suddenly, grinning to myself as hope flared.

"The collection point?" the tech asked, flustered. "I mean, yes, Lord Devourer, there are occasional intercepts required to keep the emergence zone cleared. Dedicated ships clear the space and maintain it."

"Where do they put it all?"

"Some is sent for recycling. Rare metals and—"

"And the dust?" I asked quickly, cutting him off. "What happens to the dust?!"

"It's compacted, then fired on an intercept with the sun?" he answered, sounding thoroughly confused.

"Fuck!" I snarled. "Fine, I'll be back. Get your ships ready. You're loaded with missiles and fully crewed, right?"

Arise: Conqueror

"We are…" He looked off to one side, clearly searching for help from someone in higher authority.

"Good!" I nodded, seeing the location of the council that he'd marked for me. "Get ready. I'll be back."

With that, I reached into the branes, focusing and searching, quickly finding the world that I needed through my gravitational senses.

It was the work of a few seconds to power up enough to jump to orbit high over the world, then a handful of more tiny jumps, searching for the city I needed.

Eventually I found it and zeroed in on the council building. It was a beautiful structure, all high, airy towers around a central point that arced inward and held a sphere suspended over the city.

That was marked as the council chambers. I grinned to myself, disconnecting from the ring, and launched into the upper atmosphere, still ignoring the strident demands from the local planetary defense network to identify myself and provide "proper" clearance.

That was probably why the first laser took me by surprise, hammering into my bodysuit, charring a line across me, but doing little beyond annoying me.

"Warning!" came the determined voice as I finally accepted the hail. "I repeat, this is your final warning—"

"You just fired on a Devourer," I snarled back. "Fire on me again, and I'll rip this city from the planet and eat it. Stand down before I lose my patience."

"You are in protected airspace…" he replied, clearly not happy but determined to do his duty, and I snorted, focusing again, tightly.

I didn't have a marker to jump to, not with any real degree of accuracy. But I could tell the difference between high orbit and low in to the ground, not to mention the distinctive shape of metal and other heavy solid objects below me.

Using that, I jumped again, a small one at first, then another and another, totally screwing up their tracking as they tried to lock in and fire on me.

Then I reversed gravity, shoving down hard and flipping myself around, twisting and guiding myself inward, barely slowing in time to land with a boom of shattered stone on a high balcony of the sphere.

I strode forward, right hand lifting and a new gravity field extending to the door before me, crushing it. I stepped through.

Inside, a handful of ceremonial guards tried to rush me. Fuck knew why, but they did. I gestured dismissively and they flew to either side, flattened against the walls though otherwise unharmed. I crossed the floor from the balcony entrance to the inner hall, then crushed those doors as well.

Inside, there were a dozen members of the council, or so I guessed. There were certainly twelve people dressed formally in silks and gems, in paint and carved woods, and, in one case, a patina of apparent rust dotted with gemstones.

I guessed that they were the council of the system; if not, they were clearly overpaying their cleaners.

"L…Lord Devourer!" One of them spoke up desperately. "An unexpected honor…"

The humanoid figure in rust and gemstones rose from their seat and strode toward me, arms held out to their sides. I kept coming, waiting for the attack I was sure was about to come, until he—it was very clearly a he, due to the lack of normal clothing—sank to his knees, with both arms crossed over his chest. Two others of the council followed suit.

"Lord Devourer, we stand ready to serve," he intoned, his voice a rich timbre.

"You have a dozen powerful warships at the Lagrange point," I growled. "And more at the other. Yet you've not sent anyone to help when we called for it."

"The council—" he started, only to be cut off by another, calling out from the safety of the gaggle on the far side of the room, and now retreating.

"The council voted to protect our worlds against a possible Ændari or DEVOURER incursion!" she called out. "For all we know, you are as dangerous as the false Lord Shan'Gai…"

"We know what that one has done!" another agreed, speaking up, while still hurrying for the far door.

"Because we fucking told you," I snapped, gesturing sharply with a "come here" motion, flipping gravity near them and making them scream as "down" was no longer by their feet and instead was behind them.

They started to fall back toward me, until I cut the field, dropping them to the floor in a panicking heap.

"We were outvoted," "Rusty" said. "Three of us voted to assist you, eleven to hold fast at our borders."

"Well, there's twelve of you here right now, out of what? Fourteen? I'm betting that a new vote will go my way," I said disgustedly, before raising my voice. "I'm a believer in democracy, so I'm going to let you all have a fresh vote on this."

As I spoke, I manipulated gravity again, this time sending the pile of nine panicked councilors flipping upward, arse over tit, and screaming in terror.

"As I say!" I called out louder to be heard over the screams and shouts. "I like democracy, and I'm going to let you all vote on this again. Then, if you decide not to help, I'll come back and find a new set of councilors and offer them the chance to have a vote. If I have to work my way through the entire fucking building until the cleaners have had a turn at voting and do it right, I'll do it, as people I *do* care about are fighting for their lives right now."

I looked around the room. "Have you got a lead, or a president or whatever?"

"Lady Hartness is the current chair of the council," Rusty said, clearly stifling a smile.

"And Lady Hartness is…?"

"The lady who explained her decision not to vote to aid your people."

"Ah, Hartness, you there?" I called, getting a scream of panic as the response. I dropped the group onto the floor, then dragged her out with a smaller and more specific field.

"I want to vote!" she screamed. "I want to help!"

"Are you sure?" I asked politely. "If you want to step down and let someone else take the…what was it?"

Arise: Conqueror

"Chair," Rusty said softly. "I believe Lady Hartness is about to be sick, my lord. She might not if she could sit and gather herself? While we set up the vote perhaps?"

"Good plan," I agreed. "So yeah, Hartness, if you want to step down and I'll find a new chair, then that's your choice. If not, I'll let you catch your breath, and you can take this extremely democratic step, and vote as your heart directs."

The only response was a whimper, and I shrugged before going on.

"Right, unlike you fuckers, I've actually got a fight I'm supposed to be in, so get your ships at the Lagrange point I arrived at ready to leave. You've got ten minutes. If I have to come back here again, you'll regret it." I released a tiny swarm of nanites to attach to the floor, in case I needed to jump back here directly.

Then I jumped back into orbit, the crack of displaced air stunning the councilors as I vanished.

It'd been too long since I bullied a politician, I decided, as I burst into orbit again, reaching out for the ring as it slid across to me. It was like a good Chinese meal: I really enjoyed it, but a few hours later, I wanted to do it all over again.

"Right, back to work," I muttered. I'd only jumped into the system to refine my senses. Although I'd been struck by a sudden hope, seeing the gathered debris, hearing that most of it was fired into the sun on a regular basis was a bit of a punch in the dick.

Now, though, being a lot closer than several star systems away, I reached out and searched, focusing in, then feeding power in again and jumping.

This time as I exited, I was ready, shoving outward in all directions with gravity bubbles, and instantly felt the pressure of billions of tons of mass trying to squash my fields.

I didn't expect to fight them, although I could—provided I could avoid the momentum—as that'd just be a waste of energy to fight against.

No, all I needed was to keep myself intact long enough to create a safe zone, one that was surrounded by the detritus of the ages.

I'd jumped into the outer edge of the Oort cloud, that incredibly huge sphere that extended around the solar system and acted as a sort of cosmic net, collecting anything and everything that filtered through the universe.

If it was moving fast enough, the dip between solar systems, where the gravity of one cancelled out the gravity of the other, was no impediment. But for most things, it was the line that signified the end of their journey.

Over the multiple billions of years that most solar systems had existed for, the Oort cloud that ringed them had collected literally mind-bogglingly huge quantities of mass.

Everything from tiny rocks and space dust—which was, I was hoping, going to be rich in deactivated nanites—all the way up to planet-killing asteroids and more.

Failed planets were found out there, ones that never quite got enough gravity and mass together to form into a "real" world, but once they were caught?

Like the ship graveyard I'd found already, they could accumulate mass and grow.

Now, as I appeared, and thanks to the natural push "out" from jumping in, I had a very short time to get a safe zone established.

It wasn't easy.

Asteroids travelled in all directions, constantly smashing into one another and bouncing off. Sometimes the surface of one would shatter, filling the local area with a sort of "rock shotgun" effect, and other times…

I stared at almost perfectly spherical balls of what I guessed were metal, as they careened around, battered into the shape through millions of impacts with their smaller and larger cousins.

Starting with a few dozen, then moving a hundred, I guided asteroids and debris away from me, sending the ones that were too big to stop into arcing paths that kept me safe instead.

Then, after nearly fifteen minutes of panicked work, in which I constantly second-guessed what I was doing and how bad things could be going back in Scorpio, I finally had enough of a field established.

Reaching out, I shifted the fields, holding everything as tightly in place as possible. All the while, I extended every sense I had, searching for nanites.

At first, there was practically nothing, barely a flicker of a hint that something could be there—a power source so tiny, so infinitesimal that it was hardly above the background radiation of the star.

Then, as I dug deeper, searching harder, I spotted another, and another.

Five became ten; ten became a hundred. I extended my senses past any limit they'd ever had before, searching and tuning myself in tighter and tighter, finding commonality in the nanites.

The more I tried to reach out and focus in, the more difficult the concept grew, until I abandoned it. Instead, I focused on a much smaller area, searching and looking for commonality.

The first few I'd already found, but I dug deeper, finding not only some of the materials that had been used, but the shapes, the dead clusters, and finally, last of all, the exact metals that were used. I detected the pattern that covered the exact mixture that formed the nanites.

That was when it hit.

The space I was examining had almost a thousand dead clusters in it—fifty meters of space, roughly, and it had a thousand! Expanding the zone I was looking at and filtering in the pattern I'd found, I stared in shock, in horror at the amount of power I'd need to reawaken them. And then, finally, I started to smile, as I cracked my knuckles and rolled my shoulders.

"Game on."

CHAPTER FIFTY

By the time we jumped back into the Scorpio system, it was to an absolute shit-show of firepower, explosions, and devastation.

While I'd been gone, gathering up and activating as many nanites as I could, the fleets had converged. Both sides had made a clear decision to make sure they could kill each other, without offering any quarter, so they'd stuck with the original apparent plan.

They were in orbit around the Jovian, looping around on different tracks and exchanging heavy fire, before flashing away again, then back around.

The speeds they were travelling at meant that most of exchanges were carried out by AI, as the ships' crews themselves were almost all unconscious from the heavy acceleration.

In space, there was no gravity to make you feel the G-forces, but when the engines fired, or when too close to atmosphere, you did feel it. I'd already found that out when using planets for slingshot maneuverers.

In this case, the three fleets—the Ændari loyalists, the Ændari crewed but Shan'Gai serving rebels, and our fleet—were all having to fire the engines almost constantly to keep from shooting off into deep space and to avoid the mines and debris that both sides were shedding.

That meant that the entire crew of all the fleets were basically pulling multiple G-forces. Although some could stay awake, very few could actually move around.

The main exceptions to that rule were Shan'Gai, whose ship-body had grown to several times its previous size, and my own avatars that were still battling him.

On arrival in the system, I stared in horror at the hundreds of shattered hulks that littered the planet's orbit, many of them tumbling wildly out of control. They were headed out of the gravity well and off into space into all directions, or vanished in flames, leaving short-lived streaks across the Jovian's atmosphere as they fell inward.

Either way, though, we weren't winning.

I was down to two avatars. I cursed at the burst of information that Two sent me as I entered the system, making me flinch. Both One and Three had been caught and killed, their nanites absorbed into Shan'Gai and fueling a burst of power that'd allowed him to unlock more of his nanites.

One had apparently not explained to Two what we'd figured out. And Four…well, he'd been spun up with the very basic details, that he was to break loose the nanites from the Ændari dead that the UC forces and devilkin brought him. But beyond that, he was utterly bewildered.

Two had been trapped by some kind of force field in a section of Shan'Gai for a while, and had only dim memories of what had happened.

It was only when a group of Ændari were sent in to capture him and bring him to a section that Shan'Gai could drain him from, that he'd managed to fight off the calming effect.

A dose of good old violence doing wonders for me as always.

Things were now desperate enough between the Ændari and UC fleets that they'd shifted in their orbits slightly to avoid each other as much as possible, while they both focused on Shan'Gai.

The fleets hit Shan'Gai in alternating waves, with one stripping his shields down as far as possible, then the other taking them down and doing superficial damage.

Then their orbits took them apart again; his shields would regenerate, and it started all over.

Eventually, the pair of fleets would win, in a normal battle, but Shan'Gai had finished devouring the other ships that had been close by and was now latching onto the dreadnought.

The remnants of his fleet shielded him as best as they could, while firing over and over into the UC and Ændari incoming fleets. But the battle, as I saw it, was already decided.

If Shan'Gai had faced the Ændari or UC fleets alone? He'd probably have lost. If he had access to all his systems? He'd have ripped them both apart.

As it was, though, between his own rebellious forces, and the Ændari and UC fixating on their ancient enemy for so long until the truth became apparent, the only thing they'd managed to do was wear each other down.

I had a dozen heavily armed warships with me now, nothing compared to the fleets that had roamed this system over the last few days, but coming in at the end of the fight, they were badly needed.

"Close in on me," I ordered them, stretching out connections and latching onto the nearest, as they in turn had their next closest dock to them and share power.

"Steve, dude, that you?" Zac sent me.

I joined the channel, nodding a greeting to him. "You expecting Santa?" I quirked an eyebrow.

"Well, you know, bringing random shit, emptying your sack then fucking off again…could be him or you," he said, but his heart wasn't in it. "Steve, we need you."

"I know." I nodded. "I came as soon as I could," I assured him, feeling guilty as hell.

"No, you don't," he corrected. "Ingrid and her parents are in the fight."

Arise: Conqueror

"You—fucking *what?*" I whispered. "She was supposed to be aboard the node."

"She refused to stay back when her parents joined the fleet fight, and they're getting their asses handed to them now."

Ingrid and her parents were apparently aboard the warship that we'd bargained for and that Zac had upgraded. That was currently with the rest of the UC fleet vanishing around the orbit of the planet. When I reached out, the only one of them aware enough to respond was James, in his specially designed pilot's chair.

"Steve… I'm doing my best!" James promised, the strain clear in his voice.

"I'm coming," I assured him. "Just hold on and I'll help."

"That…would be appreciated!" he said, before cutting the connection, clearly needing to focus.

"Fuck's sake!" I snarled to Zac.

"Steve, seriously, dude, I need you to step in here!" he snapped.

"What the hell do you think I'm doing?" I bit back. "I've got a dozen more ships. I'll jump them in and—"

"Fucking listen, you idiot!" Zac shouted. "Just shut the hell up for once and LISTEN, all right?"

"Go on." I gritted my teeth, forcing myself to pay attention, as I linked up with the ships that arrived with me, getting ready to jump them in.

"I've got enough ships here to make a goddamn difference!" Zac told me. "Seriously, there's enough. I did the math. I tried telling Ingrid this before, and you, but neither of you fuckin' listen! We need to peel Shan'Gai off that damn dreadnought, or nuke it, before he manages to rip it fully apart, all right? If he can dig his way in there? We're not getting him out again."

"What ships?" I snapped at him. "Zac, there's two goddamn ships with you. What difference are they gonna make?"

"The Earth fleet!"

"What fleet!"

"The…shit, man, you've been…you don't know?"

"I don't know what?" I practically screamed. "Quit the goddamn stupid shit and just tell me!"

"Dude, my ship, the outside of it?" He pulled up an image of the outside and the triangular armored panels that overlapped. "They're ships!" One was suddenly outlined in green, then red.

A breakdown appeared for me, along with the crew aboard.

Cobra Fighter	Crewed in-system fighter
The Cobra class in-system fighter is the most lethal Sol-developed fighter vessel produced to date. Its three-crew complement enables it to both carry out reconnaissance and system interdiction duties.	
<u>Capabilities:</u>	
Rail gun: The Cobra is equipped with twin rail guns, capable of carrying a variety of mission specific ordinance.	

> *Bombing run*: The Cobra is capable of high-speed bombing runs, with weapons systems capable of engaging up to capital-class vessels with dedicated high-powered missiles, although due to the fighter's size, these are highly limited in number.
>
> *Sacrifice:* The Cobra was designed intentionally as a multi-role capable platform. As well as being a highly dangerous fighter, it is also capable of providing enhanced shielding to its carrier counterpart, enabling the individual ships of the Cobra flotilla to expend their own shielding before their carrier is damaged.

Durability: 1000/1000	Shield: 500/500

"They're fighters?" I asked, dumbstruck.

"A hundred and eight." He nodded, clearly proud. "A hundred and eight fighters, and we're stuck here!"

"Why?"

"Because we were ordered to remain here as a last line of defense until the battle was won or lost," said Cybele, joining the conversation at Zac's invitation. "Ingrid asked that I assume overall command of the node and its defenders, and requested that we give the fleet time to make their push. Should they fall, then we were to hold the line until you were to return and win."

"That's the level of trust she's got in you, boss, which is great and all. But if the Cobras were in the fight? The least they could have done was provide a shitload of shielding to the UC fleet. And at best? We could have taken the enemy out!"

"We have no AI." Cybele sighed, shaking her head. "We have discussed this at length, Zac. Without an integrated ship's AI, we would be firing randomly and hoping to hit the enemy, reduced to a blind luck encounter. If, instead, we hold as we were ordered, then when the enemy comes to us, we can unleash all our fire into them and eliminate them."

"Yeah, *if*—" Zac replied hotly.

I realized that this was an argument that had been going on for some time.

"Couldn't the Cobras be integrated with the fleet's AI firing solutions?" I asked, getting a shake of the head from Zac.

"We could, if we had a couple of days to make a bunch more custodians and send them out to build all the parts we need. We gave what we had to the fleet to help them already. And the stuff I've got here? It's too big to get in and do the job while they're attached. Run them through the shipyard and, yeah, we could do it, but it'd be a handful at a time—and that'd take a day at least as well."

"By which time it'd be far too late," I agreed, nodding. "Okay, I get it."

"So?" he asked, and Cybele looked to me as well.

"Cybele?" I asked, given that Ingrid had put her in charge, and officially, she was one of the leaders of Earth, after all.

"I would listen to your recommendations." She sighed. "Waiting here while our friends die does not sit well with me, but I see little choice."

"Well, that's not entirely true." I jerked my head toward the outside of my ship. "I brought friends. And if you can gain me a little time, we can finish this thing."

"I'm listening."

"Okay then, what we need to do is…"

***

"Status!" Anders boomed from the command chair.

His voice washed over Ingrid as she fought her way back from the foggy edge of consciousness, the blare of alarms a constant thing now.

"Shields are climbing!" she replied, before clearing her throat and trying again. "We took some damage, but we're still in the fight."

"Freja?" Anders asked.

Ingrid saw her through the interface, manipulating the ship's internal systems like a pianist, teasing a fragment of glorious music from a battered and ruined relic.

"Power is stable. Rerouted paths are holding. Thank the gods that Zac left the secondary lines in place or we'd be having a very different conversation right now."

"Oh?"

"It'd be with our makers." She snorted, shaking her head before rephrasing. "I mean, we'd be dead."

"I got it." He smiled. "Weapons?"

"Kicking ass and taking names," Jonas drawled for his team on the dedicated weapons stations. "Three confirmed hits, one kill. Destroyer alpha-seven is toast…last time they'll pick a fight with Texas."

"Who?"

"Courtney." He shook his head. "How the hell she does it is beyond me, but yeah, even as the rest of us were out, she and Paul were still fighting."

"Be the best that you can be!" Paul sang out, badly.

"That's from the army recruitment, Paul." Courtney sighed. "It was an *army* ad."

"Really? Shit," he muttered. His voice dropped as he shook his head in disgust. "I *liked* that one."

"Admiral Dolfing is hailing us," Ingrid called, keying the admiral into the comm link.

"Admiral, you have orders for us?" Anders asked formally, having slotted into the chain of command easily.

"We're closing up and adjusting three degrees to the north. Cobra fighters from the reserve are incoming, as are twelve additional destroyers and frigates recruited by our 'glorious leader.'" He smiled, having accepted that the term for Steve, when used by the rest of the group, was almost always used in a tongue-in-cheek fashion.

"They'll be moving too slow to get more than a single barrage off before the enemy adjusts to take them into account, but that may be enough to turn the tide here. I've had contact from him as well."

"Steve?" Ingrid asked hungrily.

"Yes, he tried you, but you were unconscious, apparently," Dolfing said, nodding that he understood. The gravity cancellation on a battleship was far better than that on a warship. "The communication was brief, and to the point. *'I'll be there soon. Here's some reinforcements. Stab the bastards in the face from me. And if you get Ingrid killed, I'll kick your arse,'*" he quoted, shaking his head in amusement.

"I am going to kill him," Ingrid ground out. "Where is he?"

"He jumped in and dropped his reinforcements off, then vanished again. We're seeing movement above Scorpio-3, but we're at the wrong angle to confirm anything."

"And Shan'Gai?" Ingrid asked.

"He's broken through the final shields and torn his way into the dreadnought. Emergency shuttles and escape pods have jettisoned. An estimated forty-two percent of the devilkin were lost in the boarding and escape, and seventy-three percent of the UC soldiers aboard."

"That high? I'm sorry for your losses, Admiral," Anders said formally.

"They fought for us all," Dolfing said. "There's no better death for a soldier. And their losses are high because they refused to lose any more of the devilkin. I've received a hundred and fourteen recommendations from the soldiers remaining aboard the dreadnought. Every single one is about the need to recruit the devilkin formally and use them as soldier support teams in the future. They might not have had much luck and respect of late, but they just proved they could be wildly valuable to the UC, that's for sure."

"Well, that's great for them, if we win this," Ingrid said. "Did Steve tell you anything else?"

"He had a plan, though he was wary of sharing too many details. He suspects that Shan'Gai may have a method of intercepting communications, and as such is sharing only parts at this time. For now, continue as we have been. Three degrees shift to the north, close the formation, and get ready."

"I'm going to kill him…" Ingrid whispered again, shaking her head in exasperation.

***

I'd made another change to my ship by necessity, forming a sort of teardrop shape, *again*, maintaining only the internal tokamak ring and the memory modules as separate components.

The rest of the ship was literally a skin that contained the deactivated nanites, and I was barely able to hold them together through the screaming of atmosphere as I appeared in orbit high above the harvester.

Angling the nose downward, I twisted gravity, forming a funnel that drew me toward the planet. I gritted my teeth, determined to make this work.

Arise: Conqueror

"I still say this is fucking madness." That was Four, reaching out as he ran through the darkness of the now-dead dreadnought. *"We should have kept this ship!"*

"If we could have, we would!" Two snapped back. *"Stick with the plan!"*

"I don't know the fucking plan!" Four groused. *"If I did, I might be able to!"*

"Just be yourself," I sent back, shaking my head at the stupidity of the statement. *"Seriously, I know exactly how dumb that sounds, but we're all me. We all think the same, and I've got a plan. You'll naturally react the way I would, so hopefully, we'll all know what to do when the time comes!"*

"Bullshit!" Four shouted. *"This is bullshit, and I hate you all."*

I didn't blame him, not really.

Two hadn't explained much to him, though it wasn't like he knew much more. When One had broken Four off, setting him to grow and separate in the depths of the dreadnought, he'd instilled in him that his mission was to convert the nanites that the Ændari crew had, tearing them free and attuning them to us, but not wiping them.

That was simple enough, sure, but he'd barely gotten started on that before Two was there, battered to hell and desperate, taking a portion of the nanites, and then wanting to wipe them.

He'd had to explain that when he'd been created, he knew *not* to wipe them, but had only a vague understanding of why, as we'd figured it out while One was still making him.

Two, on the other hand, had arrived from Shan'Gai's ship, where the ancient Devourer was finally starting to unlock some of his original capabilities. The fight had gone from a fifty-fifty chance, as he and Three had seen it, to a fucking slaughter.

Now they both knew that Shan'Gai was coming. He'd torn a couple of other ships apart for both nanites and mass. His apparent plan was to tear his way into the dreadnought, spread himself out and take it over, then expand out and use the shell as his new body.

It had good weapons, shields, engines, and so on. But more than that, it had an absolute shitload of Ændari crew to feed on. Or it *had*.

The boarding action by us had resulted in most of the crew being slaughtered and rendered down to usable nanites, which was awesome for us. Shan'Gai had apparently decided that the fastest way for him to grow was to grab those teams and my surviving avatars, then absorb them all into him.

That'd give him enough of a boost of fresh nanites that he could finish unlocking his systems again. Then there'd be nothing that could stop him.

We needed him to not do that, and to keep those goddamn nanites as far away from him as possible. So as I dove through the atmosphere, the pockets of air I was hitting making the nose of my "ship" feel like it was being hit by a trip hammer, they raced through the internal spaces of the dreadnought.

The UC and devilkin who had been aboard had been evacuated now, and not just because it was the right thing to do to try to save their lives.

They were a source of nanites to Shan'Gai as well, and they couldn't be allowed to fall to him. Where possible, they had been loaded into the escape shuttles and pods. Where there were none? They used their armor's capabilities to launch themselves into space, fighting to escape the Jovian's gravitational pull.

For literally hundreds, though, that just wasn't an option. They were either too injured, too dead—which, with their nanites, was fortunately usually only a temporary status modifier—or too deep.

Where they couldn't make it to the ship's hull, where there was no way that they could escape to fight Shan'Gai, Two and Four had the awful duty.

Their nanites couldn't be allowed to be taken by Shan'Gai, strengthening him further. And so, knowing that it meant the permanent loss of that soldier, the ending of a possibly immortal life, they deactivated their armor, stepping free of any impediment to absorption, and embraced the Devourer shroud with the same bravery they'd charged the enemy.

Two and Four were rendered apoplectic with rage, being forced to take the lives of these brave men and women. But they did it, shepherding them where possible and guiding them until they could flee no more.

Linked as I was, I could feel and see this as well, and I knew the only chance they had was the long shot that I was pulling.

I reached out to the harvester below me, feeling the command routines I'd installed. I triggered them, gritting my teeth as dozens of warnings flared, letting me know that the same fucking idiots I'd ordered to stay clear of the harvester had still landed ships and more, and were trying to loot it.

There could be an argument made for them being there to try to rescue people—and I got it, I really did—but I didn't have time for this shit, and I'd told them to stay goddamn clear of it!

"To any and all trespassers aboard the Ouroboros harvester, I am coming and your lives are now forfeit. You were warned to stay clear! If you want to live, *RUN NOW*." I sent it out on every emergency frequency I could find—on the planetary broadcast channels, military ones…anything and everything I could reach.

Still, as I came screaming through the heavens toward the ships that covered the upper hull, I saw more small craft *still* flying in toward the hull.

That was when newly positioned orbital defenses, ones that had to have been moved from the far side of the planet as this side had been long cleared of them, opened fire…on *me*.

I'd only left two of the drones aboard the harvester, and because of course it was that way, none of them were anywhere near where I needed to be, thanks to the massive size of the damn thing.

That meant that entering from orbit was actually the quickest way, adjusting constantly, even as I sent orders to the harvester below.

I'd ordered a shutdown before of most of the systems, cycling down the reactors and powering down the shields, guns, and basically everything that wasn't involved directly in the conversion of all the scrap it'd already harvested into viable nanites.

Guns on the hull that I'd deactivated before spun up, adjusting and tracking around, before being hit by incoming fire. Whoever was boarding was goddamn determined. Neither the warnings I'd given before, nor the orders to stay clear seemed to make a difference.

I'd intended to lock weapons on the incoming craft and order them to fuck right off one last time. But when they'd opened fire on me, they crossed that line.

The weapons on the hull were a fraction of those available to the massive harvester, the designers having clearly understood that anything that was deployed was a target.

Because of that, there were a metric shit-ton of additional turrets stored in recessed pods, ready to be rolled out. As I closed on the harvester, they began to slide free.

The machine, when seen from above, was almost insectile. As I approached, the hull rippled and concealed pods lifted upward.

As soon as they cleared their recessed chambers, they tracked the incoming ships, before opening fire and sweeping the air clear in seconds.

Panicked pleas rang out as I covered the last few hundred meters to the hull. I gritted my teeth, ignoring them. I'd warned them—I'd fucking *told* them. I'd then given them a last chance before deploying the turrets. And instead of listening, instead of explaining, they'd fired the first shots.

Fuck them, and the horse they rode in on.

The power levels for the harvester climbed steadily. I shifted the ship's shape one last time, slowing as I closed on the section I needed, reversing gravity. Three hundred meters down, through levels of armor and secondary systems, through the trap maze and more, I could sense the junction of a dozen power lines, and that was exactly what I needed.

The tip of the ship, now needle pointed, hit the upper hull of the harvester and dug in. The molecular binding technology that held the hull together reversed in that small area, enabling me to "eat" through even faster. The hull of my ship slid inward, eating a space large enough for the rest to enter.

Behind me, the shields flickered on again. Crackling power lit the hull as I dug deeper, ignoring the panicked cries of looters who had been searching the trap maze.

My target was a single huge room that could have held a dozen cathedrals, three-quarters of a mile wide and long, and five hundred meters high. I touched down, then extended a spike down farther, eating into the structure below until I uncovered the power conduits.

As that spike worked, I slid the tokamak ring backward, resting it against the rear of the room, and kept it clear of everything I could, but in range for when I needed it.

The nanites I'd found could be reactivated, but they needed other nanites to do it…working nanites. And they'd only do as many as they could without risking their own power viability.

What they needed was an absolute shitload of power, and for me to do that, I needed a dozen more tokamak rings, or access to the kind of power levels that could jump the Ouroboros harvester across the galaxy.

It wasn't at full power, not even half, but it had more reactors than I did, and more than any mere battleship had as well. That was what I needed to drain, to jump-start these nanites and give us a chance against Shan'Gai.

I spread out the nanites in a fast grid, releasing the tight skin that had kept the dead nanites in close and letting them roll out in a great wave.

Lines of my active nanites slid out, linking together and forming a widely spaced grid between the floor and the dead, then lifted them up slightly, so that they rested on a bed of activated nanites.

Raised lines lifted through the mass, separating the dead into rows. Then, as additional lines rose, they were separated again, this time into squares, before I formed fractal patterns closed over about an inch's depth of the dead.

I was going to have to do this in stages, a small number at a time, then have them help with the next.

I'd entirely surrounded a tiny fraction of the dead now, and I pumped power into my nanites, directing them to awaken their distant cousins.

It was like shocking a huge heart with a defibrillator; the electrical jolt jump-started the nanites.

At first, there was nothing, or almost nothing—a few sparks and a few staggered tiny beats as nanites that weren't as long dead as the others shuddered. Then, though, they sagged again.

I'd expected this—nothing ever works the first time you try it—and I hit it again, and again.

By the fourth pulse, I could feel it starting to beat. As a pulse of power washed over them for the fifth time, though? More than half responded.

By the tenth, I was grinning, although still worried at the time it'd taken and terrified at the delay as I sensed the other me's battling desperately to escape, and the rocking and explosions from incoming fire shaking the ship.

Ingrid was out there, in a far smaller ship, battling for her life. But we needed to end this, and cutting corners wasn't going to do it.

The first small squares were active; the nanites flexed, testing their connections to me. I quickly tore off a basic program to repeat the process with a second level of nanites, working in an automated pattern as I reached out to these new, insanely ancient nanites, and tried to command them, to draw them to me.

That, it turned out, was a mistake.

CHAPTER FIFTY-ONE

The nanites flowed to me happily, swelling up around my legs and encasing me. But as soon as I tried to slow them, to guide them into a pattern and exert control, they ignored me, twisting into place and sealing in around my limbs.

They flowed up as fast as lightning, rolling over my legs, my arms, wrapping around me and coating every inch.

I panicked and reached out to my nanites, only to feel them vanishing, torn free as a wall was quickly being erected between me and the outside world.

The nanites that made up my body were locked in tight. I felt new pulses of energy flooding out, beats that weren't too different from the ones that I'd just used to reawaken these ancient dead ones. But with each beat, I grew weaker.

The outermost levels failed first. The top layer of my "skin," now entirely made of nanites and assuming the shape of a human by preference, shifted.

My control faded then failed as long hidden and deeply buried protocols rose, overwriting and resetting the nanites, converting them from the versions I knew, into exact copies of the ones that surrounded me. As more and more joined together, turning against me, I grew weaker, afraid that I'd made a terrible mistake.

This had all taken less than a second. Even with my time compression activating, I barely had enough time to see what was happening before a second layer began to weaken.

"Stop!" I tried shouting, only to have them try to pour into my mouth, stopped only when I reformed my internals to block off the passage they were going for.

I was damn glad my private parts were sealed on instinct as well. But as every orifice sealed itself, I tried reaching out again, this time digitally, searching for a controlling intelligence.

Nothing—at least, nothing I was familiar with—was reachable.

I scanned in every frequency I could imagine, first searching for some hidden way that someone—maybe Shan'Gai, maybe the Ændari—controlled the nanites.

I found nothing: no signal from the outside, no controlling intelligence, no hidden AI that'd been hiding in the ship biding its time and waiting for me to make just this mistake.

More desperately than anything, I sensed the same thing that was happening to me right now, happening all around me, as the last vestiges of my nanites "out there" that I could feel succumbed to the onslaught, and I was fully sealed in.

I was really panicking now, frantically throwing everything I had at my time compression to speed up my perception of it. I tried to find a hint, a clue, a seam or anything as more and more of me failed.

Lashing out with everything I had, I activated the Engineering sub-mind and then Hack, Espionage, and War. They all scrambled for a toehold, failing one by one. In desperation, I split myself into four, hiding behind the two sub-minds, the War AI and a frantic blast of everything I could think of.

War attacked, obviously, triggering a second level of time compression that I had no clue could be done, slowing things even further. But nanites fighting nanites physically did frankly fuck all; all it did was slow things down.

My own attack…it was panicked and ineffectual, and I lost ground almost as fast as the War AI did.

Engineering was the second most effective in its counterattack, forming the nanites under his control into a type of signal blocking shield; it turned them inward, sacrificing the layer over them that were already in contact with the invaders, and instead twisted the next layer down.

They turned their backs, linking and presenting a solid wall, one that sealed together at a molecular level, preventing the incoming nanites from pushing in…but they still started to slowly change.

I rolled that change out across all four of my versions, gaining a little breathing room, along with the second level of time compression—which, it turned out, was literally because I was guiding War to work through me directly, so it was activating inside an already slowed timeframe.

That was great, but not something that could be stacked indefinitely.

Engineering had approached it from an engineering viewpoint, building a special form to slow the enemy; War had attacked them, trying to destroy them; and I tried everything in a wild panic.

Hack, though—Hack and Espionage tried to hack the nanites' control codes, and the result was…well, it was spectacular.

Where the hacks I'd carried out before had been essentially rolling dice, or twisting shapes to fit locks when I'd started, I'd evolved significantly since then.

I now had roughly ten times the potential and usable brain power of the man who had been partly drowned by his own bike in the ocean off Crete, and damn, it showed.

The world splintered into a spiraling stream of numbers and letters. They spun past me in conflicting patterns—twisting, weaving in and out, layered over and over—and as soon as the Hack sub-mind did that, touching the nanites' code, they froze.

I almost collapsed in relief when they did, before starting to push back against us, testing.

Hack responded by shifting a pattern; the nanites on the other side did the same, altering a form that Hack copied and reproduced.

Arise: Conqueror

I scanned it. Hack wasn't actually trying to hack into the code, not now; it'd shifted its focus and was instead…it was either a test, or it was trying to communicate!

The assault was paused while the nanites apparently evaluated me, and I quickly focused on the stream of numbers and symbols, searching for a common point.

It took a few seconds, literally—so perhaps a full minute for me subjectively—but eventually, I found it!

An omega symbol, the weird Ω thing that looked like an upside-down U with legs, was there. More than anything, it seemed to be a place holder, a marker that started and finished a series of symbols.

Spotting that, as the sub-mind mimicked the nanites, I reached out mentally and pressed the omega.

There was an instant reaction. The entire spiraling mass froze, then twisted. No longer spiraling around me, they flowed forward, locking into place in descending lines, and I nodded to myself.

"A logic test," I muttered. "Figure this out and we'll talk, eh?" I guessed. "Okay, let's see what we have here…"

Searching the first three lines of symbols, I noted another Greek symbol, something that looked like a weirdly bendy B, that I vaguely remembered was called gamma for some reason. That came third in the line of one set, forth in the next, sixth, then seventh…

I searched and found the line where it showed up first, then slid that into place before the third one, then the second into place between them, then…

The seconds ticked by as I quickly dragged the symbols into repeating patterns. They continued to spiral around me for some reason, set in place, still and no longer moving, but rotating slowly as I worked down the line.

I wondered briefly whether this was how they worked, the creators of the nanites, instead of reading left to right as we did in English, reading down and right from high left.

If so, it'd say weird things about their brains that they felt the need to be twisting around constantly while reading…

I snapped myself out of the line of thought, gritting my teeth and forging on, noting the other symbols that Hack was picking out, identifying and mentally shifting around.

A handful of seconds more, and the nanites shifted as one, flowing backward and forming a new shape—one that vaguely resembled a box, slightly taller and wider than my wasted, heavily stripped form.

Glancing left and right, I saw that every other nanite in the room that had been attached to me?

Gone. They were *all* gone, absorbed into the mass. And now they were continuing to awaken their distant cousins. A great tentacle of nanites plunged into the floor to reach the power supply, draining it at horrific speeds as the nanites themselves took over the awakening process.

They looked and moved far more organically than I'd ever seen before. I hesitated, not trusting the box with its open, inviting door.

Clearly that was the wrong action. Growing impatient, the "floor" of nanites under my feet suddenly flowed forward; the box did the same, snapping shut around me and sealing me in.

Hack was locked out now. The connection it'd found that I'd totally missed was now sealed, and in the utter blackness of the nanite box, lights began to pulse and shift, rolling in waves.

I responded to them, trying to keep calm. The others were fighting for their fucking lives and I was doing puzzles, but I didn't know what else to do.

They flowed like ripples on water, a single spot in the center left free. Unsure, I reached out and tapped it.

That was the right—or very wrong—thing to do. The lights surged; I covered my eyes, blinking as they registered pain—which they'd not done in ages.

Blinking away afterimages as the light died down, I hissed as the temperature inside the box surged violently. I braced myself and stayed still, enduring as the temperature climbed higher and higher. Whatever else the nanites had done, they seemed to have forced me to return to close to a mortal body as well.

I felt things in a way I'd not in months—hell, *years*: sensitivity to heat and cold—which came after I started to hiss in real pain—followed by pressure, atmosphere changes, and more. The tests were conducted at a horrific pace. Either the nanites didn't have time to waste, or they were short on patience.

I began to counter the inputs—pressure with gravity, atmospheric with adjustments to my body from the few nanites that seemed to respond properly.

Heat and cold by adjusting the upper layers and increasing or decreasing my core temperature were simple enough, but the electrical inputs weren't pleasant, as power started to crackle from wall to wall.

Sound rose to levels that'd rupture a human ear and made my reduced protection shudder. But a pulse of directed gravity flattened the waves and dismissed it.

Scents that would make my eyes pour grew in complexity, before being dampened down as I formed a protective barrier around myself.

As soon as I responded to each input, it'd vanish. Briefly, I considered hiding my capability, pretending not to be able to counter something. If I did that, I could use it later on if they tried to actually kill me using that method. Then I dismissed it. I needed to get this over with as soon as possible.

The tests sped up in rapid succession until they lasted a fraction of a second each…a handful becoming a dozen, a dozen becoming hundreds.

My reactions scaled as well as I got "in the zone." The sub-minds flowed in at my subconscious instruction to help. Engineering helped to calculate the perfect amount of force required, Hack calculated the likely desire for a response, and finally, War aided in the speed of reaction.

Even with the three working with me, it increased in speed repeatedly until I was barely sensing anything before it was over and the next was mounting. But I struggled on and on, pain rising in my mind as I was pushed harder and harder, until at last…I felt a change.

Arise: Conqueror

It wasn't much, but it quickly became clear as I responded to the various inputs that I was being rewarded, almost like a pat on the head for being a good boy, as more and more nanites rejoined me.

It was almost unnoticeable at first—literally a single nanite, I guessed, for the first test, which was why I'd missed it. But as the tests grew in complexity, so did the rewards.

Soon it was thousands of clusters returning to me, then hundreds of thousands.

By the time the last test—a pattern of pressure that required the generation of a specific pulse to counter—was done, I was almost at the number of nanites I normally had in my body.

When I realized that, after a handful of seconds as my mind raced, expecting a new attack or test and nothing came, I shifted my body in a second, returning it to its peak condition.

Then, the sides of the box split apart and flowed downward, pooling on the floor, and revealed a different world than the one I'd been shut away from.

I stood in the same position, as if I'd stepped into the box and been waiting. There'd been no sensation of travel, but suddenly I was on a platform, one that soared through crimson and pastel clouds. Wisps of light and pressure flowed past, and wind stirred my hair, warm air gently caressing me.

"What…?" I whispered, before twisting around to the right. A sudden sensation of nearness made me flinch. Then I nearly shit myself as an eye the size of a super carrier slid past me, staring in curiosity.

Whatever it was, it was large. The eye itself that stared at me was bulbous and divided into four elongated pupils that moved separately. The rest of the creature, besides an eye that had pupils big enough to stand in, towered over me, vanishing into misty blurs in all directions.

—Unusual and unexpected—

"What?" I repeated. The words echoed through my body as much as my mind, and yet I did not hear them in a traditional sense.

—Your actions were unexpected—

"Yeah, well, so were yours," I said, licking lips that felt like they'd been diving for treats in the cat's litter box.

—How so—

"I gathered lost nanites to help in my fight, and, then you tried to kill me?"

—Evaluation was necessary—

"And the whole killing me part?"

—You were returned to your approximately original state before assimilation. Complete reversal was not possible, but it allowed us to gain a sense for your physiology and capacity—

"That was intentional? Stopping once you'd taken me down to half my size?" I asked, annoyed that maybe it wasn't in response to my reactions so much as my trying to understand at all.

—We dissected you until you responded to basic stimuli—

"And what did you find?" I asked.

—You are average—

"Thanks for the blow to my ego," I muttered. "So, what are you?"

—You lack the reference to understand, or the time—

"Sounds like you can't be bothered to explain," I grunted. "Okay, no offense, because I want to know, but I've got people who need me, so what's your plan here?"

—No plan—

"And the nanites?"

—Exploration devices—

"You use them to explore?"

—We have no desire to leave our home but are curious about your kind. We dispatched many exploration devices to the other realms—

"And then what, you just wait and they bring you people like me?"

—Samples are collected and interacted with. Limited responses from your realm make each interaction valuable—

I stared at the massive form as it slowly moved around me, before shaking my head as I noticed details that were familiar.

"You're brane creatures."

—Explain—

"I've seen you before," I said. "When we jump from system to system, I've seen some of your kind."

—Younglings—

"Kids?" I asked, wincing.

—The young are curious and often stray closer to the higher realms—

"They're huge…" I whispered, then shook my head. The creature that loomed over me vanished into the distance and the only part I could see clearly was the eyes that hovered nearby. This thing could be the size of a planet for all I knew. I hesitated, then decided that discretion was the better part of valor and kept my mouth shut about the explosion that I thought might have killed one of them.

—Curious—

"What is?"

—Spike in fear—

"I'm not afraid of you."

—Lie—

"I'm afraid for my friends!" I called out. "We're in the middle of a war, and you just tore me out of it. They need me! I don't have time for this shit!"

—Your understanding of time is simplistic—

"Well, it's fucking important to us, all right!"

—We wish a sample. Then we will return you to your realm—

"A sample?"

—We require your permission—

"You're shitting me."

—Permission—

"A trade?" I suggested desperately.

—Explain—

"I give you your sample of me, like a gene sample or whatever, right?"

Arise: Conqueror

—Simplistic but correct—

"I give you that, and you give me control over the explorers in my realm!"

—We do not have control over them to give—

"Bullshit."

—Explorers have two functions: find life and monitor, then provide link for examination—

"Then how the hell did the Ændari get control of them?"

—Damaged explorers are frequently repurposed by lesser races—

"Yeah, they fuckin' repurposed them, all right. They used them to try to conquer our universe!"

—We are not responsible for the actions of others—

I stared at the big bastard. It was waiting, unconcerned, and I realized that it'd probably already run the tests it wanted; now it just wanted its permission for the sample and I was gone.

"Fine, tell me how to make the explorers obey me, and you can take your sample."

—Explorers have two functions…—

"Yeah, and you can't control them…bullshit. You made them, you control them."

—Once they have provided their sample, they will have served their purpose—

"That's fucking unhelpful to me."

—We require a sample—

"Then help me!" I snarled. "Tell me how you make them, or the commands you give them or…"

—This is acceptable. Permission for sample has been confirmed—

"What?"

Then I started to scream.

CHAPTER FIFTY-TWO

I don't know what was more traumatic, nor what was more painful, but the injection of knowledge happened at the same time as the forcible splitting of my mind.

I'd made copies of myself through the avatars already, literal perfect exact copies. It'd been a bit weird, but certainly not painful. I didn't know whether it was that it was done in a second or less that made it hurt so much, or whether they didn't give two shits and didn't realize they were leaning on the "fry his testicles in boiling acid" button while they pressed "CTRL+C" on the cosmic computer.

Either way, though, it left me writhing in agony, as the walls around me shifted, then collapsed.

It wasn't entirely like they fell apart, as there was a feeling of pushing up at the same time, like I'd just been strapped onto the nose of a Space-X rocket and launched into space. But at the same time, it was over before I knew what had happened.

I found myself on the floor, collapsed and staring wildly at the ceiling of the compartment I was in, panting in shock, as all around me, piles of nanites crumbled.

I lay there for long minutes until a panicked connection broke me out of it.

"What the fuck are you doing!" Two sent. *"Four's dead, and I won't last much longer! Fucking MOVE!"*

The contact, the mental equivalent of a kick up the arse at a full sprint, shocked me out of my overloaded state, and I shuddered at the update he forced into me.

Ships were exploding in silent blossoms of death, fragments flying in all directions as what was left of all three fleets converged on each other.

The Cobras had made it into the fight, as had the ships I'd dropped off before. They'd fired almost their entire magazines while the enemy were obscured by the curvature of the planet. By the time they'd come into view, a full third of the missiles were too far off course to reach their targets.

The fleets were all involved in constant small adjustments to throw off just this kind of trick, but it was worth it.

Arise: Conqueror

The impacts had taken out a quarter of the Ændari survivors, leaving the UC fleet as the largest surviving now. And with the addition of the Cobras and the fresh twelve warships to take the brunt of the incoming fire, the most battered vessels were getting a chance to reform and repair shields.

That was when people had started to feel a tiny fragment of hope, which was why it was all the more terrible when Shan'Gai managed to burrow deep enough into the dreadnought to start using its reactors and reactivate its weapons.

Four had been trying to rescue a group of devilkin and UC soldiers who had been forced into a lower hold, only to find that the far exits had been melted closed by a laser hit on the hull.

While Four had been eating the wall away, shouting for them to gather so that they could escape, a hidden tentacle had ripped the wall open like a chip packet.

They'd fired on it, desperately fighting to take it out. Four had nearly succeeded, battling it to a standstill, right up until Shan'Gai slid in another arm and triggered the same vibrational blast that had killed me once already.

It'd come from behind as Four was fighting the tentacle, and the distraction had been enough to end the fight.

"Jump to me!" I ordered Two, who spat his response.

"Don't you think we would have if we could?"

"The gravity pulses?"

"The ship's covered in them. There are a few open areas, but nothing nearby. He's moving them to make sure I can't jump."

"Fuck... Okay, I'm coming!"

"Yeah, well, so's Christmas!"

With that cheerful message, he cut the link, and I forced myself to my feet, staring at the nanites before me, sensing their disinterest in me now that I'd been sampled.

They knew, somehow, that I was done, that they didn't need me, and so they were just happy to be, to just lie there and wait.

Well, fuck *that*.

I reached out; there were far more active than there had been, with only a few hundred million—heh, a few—that were still being powered up.

The rest, though…they were done: they were active, and they were passively waiting for a fresh sample.

I didn't know what the full process was that they wanted, that triggered their interest, but what I did know? I'd just completed a quest.

Quest Complete!

Evolving Quest Complete: Harvest the Past, to Save the Future (Part 2)

You have gained access to thirty-seven billion plus nanites, their original programming reset and activated, and learned more of their incredible story. Evolution stage two is complete.

You receive the following rewards:

- **+5 Points of Specialization**

- **+Access to Level 3 of the Evolving Quest**

Evolving Quest Discovered: Harvest the Past, to Save the Future (Part 3)

The nanites have been exposed as a complex, but automated delivery and sampling system, nothing more. They have been exposed as operating under multiple levels of incomplete programming, resulting in sub-optimal response and conversion times.

Convert the original nanites to a usable form to reach evolution stage three, and receive the following rewards:

- **????**

Just gathering the ten billion would have been enough, but as soon as they'd all activated and had been linked to me, that'd apparently been sufficient to complete the quest.

It made no sense. They'd certainly not been under my control, after all... But if that was the case, if I could be dragged there, or wherever I'd been taken or shown, and all the testing completed on me, why the hell couldn't they just take the sample?

Had...had I been manipulated into doing that?

My activation, the symbols I'd been shown over and over, the systems that popped up and basically begged me to press them—was that the fucking galactic equivalent of phishing emails?

The more I thought about it, with the data that the creature had given me happily in exchange still integrating, the more convinced I became.

Time was still slowed for me, subjectively, giving me long seconds to think. If this was the case? That would explain why the Ændari had never been able to hack and overwrite the nanites in the first place.

I paused, then brought up my interface, staring at it as I made my needs clear. I pulled up a small number of my internal nanites and converted them into a dedicated memory cell cluster, getting it ready for occupation by a new me.

There were five sections that were needed for basic access, I saw straightaway. If I'd had another two points, it would have been better as I could sense the final stages were still beyond me. But fuck it—it was time to see what I could botch together.

I spent the points in them as quickly as I could, finding the data that streamed to me was compatible with the mass that had been forced into me by that being.

The Advanced Matter Converter was an easy and obvious choice. It was quicker, more powerful, and was capable of making more for less, essentially. It didn't seem to be unlocking anything new in the conversion options, but a lot of my abilities were linked together now and that granted me access, I sensed, to a lot of the things that I should be getting now that this level was unlocked.

Arise: Conqueror

The next one was Final Stage Constructors—which, again, didn't unlock anything new, but gave me additional high-end designs that enabled me to make larger constructions easier.

This level, I realized, was the kind of thing that they used to make the Forgeships, basically enabling you to scale things up massively.

Nice, but not earth-shattering.

Next was RI Advanced Programming. That…was painful. A spike of knowledge rammed into my brain deep enough it made my ass twitch.

The wash of data that flowed out from that told me a hell of a lot more about programming the custodians, sentinels, and the various grades of machinery that the Ændari had used to build their original empire.

I didn't know what had changed—I suspected that Argus had a hand in it—but these things hadn't been available to me before, and I guessed they were intended for Ændari scientists and engineers only.

Until now, I'd been able to make the sentinels and custodians and so on, only because I'd reached a high enough level in other areas and I'd essentially gotten a copy of the plans.

I'd understood sort of around the edges of the programming that was required for the machines thanks to unlocking the basic AI and RI details. That was how I'd been able to make the changes needed to have a custodian adjust easily enough to the spiderbot frame, for example, and I'd had access to the versions of that machine that Zac had made with his engineering team.

That was different from being able to code one myself from scratch, though, and that capability, I now had.

Final Stage Matter Converters were enough to take me to my knees, even with the sub-mind shell ready if I needed it, and that was something that, thanks to my evolution to this point, I'd thought I'd outgrown the need for entirely.

Final Stage Matter Converters were literally what it said on the tin; they didn't need anything else.

You want a ship? Build one of these on a planet and leave it to eat its way through.

One side was essentially a mouth, and the other a manufacturing outlet, one that could expand and shrink as needed. Obviously, it needed materials and time to build into the system that you wanted. So if you made one that was three meters by three, and you wanted a battleship, you were going to need to give it a shitload of nanites to build it. It'd need to rebuild the converter large enough to form the battleship, unless you wanted it to be incredibly long and narrow.

That was the thing, though: it needed nanites, because it couldn't make them entirely from scratch. There was a basic hopper that would hold the nanites while they were poured in.

The nanites would then be used to jump-start more nanites that would be produced by the matter converter, with the assumption that they would need to feed in huge quantities to make larger things.

Attached to this file were multiple warnings and instructions, something that referred to the codex and the librarians, and an imperial decree that this information was not to be shared with any scientist that was not "bound to imperial pleasure."

I guessed that probably meant that they were under the imperial Ændari throne's control, as opposed to into bondage, but you never knew.

Regardless, the long and short of the warnings was that they were to inform anyone who asked that yes, of course they could make nanites, but that it was a complicated process, and that they'd have to earn access.

Then keep the access out of reach unless the throne authorized it.

A dim memory of the Erlking doing that to me surfaced as I read it. I shook my head in disgust, wondering whether he knew that the Ændari didn't really understand them, or whether he was just parroting what he'd already been told.

Regardless, I now had the details on how to make nanites from scratch, and that was game-changing.

The final stage, or the last one that I could manage anyway, was in the Hack tree. Weirdly, it wasn't very high up, it was a low skill, but presumably structured that way because the chances of any engineer having the capacity to do the Hack tree as well was unlikely, especially because it needed five levels in it to get the 'good stuff' and that cleaned me out.

It was under the Information sub-tree, and where before I'd unlocked Drain, this time the section I needed was Intrusion.

That was it, basically the capacity to drive a wedge into the target system's security and push in the program that I wanted.

I stared as the details downloaded, figuring this was some kind of plot armor bullshit, that didn't happen in real life, until I noted the secondary stream.

It was buried in the main wash of data, and I pulled that forward, before whistling in understanding.

In any interaction with a program, you had to insert, so that was fucking obvious. Send a request? Issue an order? You were inserting that into the program. Sure, they were designed to respond to insertions, as a computer that didn't respond to any input at all was about as useful as tits on a fish, but that wasn't it.

To insert into a program, you had to *understand* it. It was pointless sending in commands designed for a Mac, for example, into a competitor's mobile phone. It wouldn't understand. And if it responded at all, it'd be to tell you to go fuck yourself, or to crash.

This unlock, when matched with the AI and RI, and the matter converters and makers, provided a way to look at the program, to copy it enough that you could translate it, and to find the anchor points.

Those were the sections that led from the upper layers of the machine you dealt with, like the keyboard, down to the bit of the computer that talked back to you and checked that your input was sensible. Then through the connective parts that led from the human-facing section to the computer where it was all ones and zeros.

From there it'd be transported, fired along a fiber-optic cable or whatever, choosing this path or that to get to the target system that would deal with the query.

Arise: Conqueror

That was the simplest explanation I could come up with, but that was where it stopped.

When it hit the bottom layer, it evaluated what the lower layer was expecting, and then it changed to the upper layer to provide input in the manner that the lower wanted.

That was important.

Hell, that was vital. Using the computer analogy still so that it was easier for my poor abused brain to understand, the antivirus and protective software? *All* of it ran on the middle layers.

This waited until it was past that, and then copied the responses, mapping out what you needed to do and aligning the upper and lower layers so that if you pressed the red button and wanted the computer to think you'd pressed the green?

That was what it thought.

The problem with this was that to make it work in such a simplistic way, you needed to basically erase everything that was on the top layer.

That was why the Ændari could roll their own software across the top of the nanites but didn't understand them fully. They erased the upper layers, like a hacker breaking into NASA, and then playing the original *Doom* on their machines, because that was all they knew how to do.

The machines might be powerful enough to direct spaceships out at the other end of the star system, but they'd not be doing that anymore because there was an idiot sitting on it shooting demons instead.

Not that there was anything wrong with *Doom*, of course. I'd spent many years playing it and loving it. It'd probably been one of the main reasons that I'd failed the mandatory computer science classes.

Or that could have been because two weeks after the start of term, I'd been caught having sex in the storeroom at the back of the class with the teacher's stepdaughter, who hated him.

Nah. It was probably the gaming.

Regardless, though, now that I understood this, and coupled with the Engineering data, the rest of my Hack information, and most of all, the Devourer capabilities that had taught me so much more about the use of the nanites, I'd always be a few steps ahead of the Ændari.

That I'd just traded a few seconds—and a possible eternity for a clone—of pain for the knowledge of the commands that were given to the original "explorers" meant that I now had more information that either the original creators or the Ændari had ever believed existed.

And that changed *everything*.

I reached out to the nanites that lay on all sides. Taking a deep breath, I connected to them, but not inserting a signal to them, as I'd expected to and as I'd tried to before.

Instead, using a combination of gravitonics and basic Bluetooth protocols, I set up a connection point that was me; then I opened the access and *pulled*.

That was where I'd been going wrong.

These were created by creatures that existed at the bottom of the most extreme gravitational points in the universe. It was only natural that they wouldn't be looking to push out, but that they'd be expecting anything and everything to be pushing *in*.

All I had to do was open the connection in the right way, and the nanites linked effortlessly.

As soon as they did, they recognized me as already being sampled and seemed to lose interest. But that was fine, because I wasn't wanting them to run their existing and fucking simple program on me.

A quick glance at it confirmed that, yes, I had basically been conned into giving my permission for a series of tests already, so flip that around, and change this, twist that…

Fortunately, only thirty seconds of real-world time had passed for Two as he frantically scrambled for cover, racing along corridors and diving across scattered shredded parts of the ship.

Which was why as much as he was getting furious that I was still fucking around and not in the fight, he hadn't screamed at me again.

Yet.

The fleets were past each other again, trails of destruction left in their wake. The Cobras that had made it to the fleet had latched onto their hulls, providing replacement shield coverage over damaged and exposed areas.

The UC fleet was trailing damaged vessels, mainly the battleships as they'd been the most dangerous, the queens of space. So both Shan'Gai, in the dreadnought with his limited but growing arsenal of weapons, and the Ændari had been focusing their fire on them.

The sides were even smaller now, with a destroyer twisting out of control as I scanned space. It was Ændari, I saw with relief, as the single working engine, firing in uncontrolled bursts, plowed it into another, smaller frigate.

The resulting explosion was horrific, damaging a third smaller vessel and taking that out. But the UC hadn't escaped their losses either.

Over a hundred escape pods were faltering in the gravity well of the Jovian, fighting to escape as their ship tumbled lifelessly downward. The scream of Clicqo rung out as the quad-bodied ambassador cursed the Ændari and his own allies' weakness in not reinforcing them sooner.

That was when I jumped in, arriving in orbit, and unable to help myself as I grinned, cocooned in the middle of my still-linking nanites.

Ten billion had been the limit that the system, and most likely Argus, had marked as the amount needed to reach the second stage of evolution for me. When I'd reached the first, I'd already been amazed by the difference.

I'd been in the fours and fives on my stat sheet originally when I'd given myself over to full conversion into a nanite-based lifeform.

When I'd finished that conversion, I'd been a solid twelve in most categories, which was awesome. But I'd weirdly also lost *all* my resonance.

Resonance was described by the system—incorrectly, I now knew—as *the capacity to use and integrate devices that require elemental resonances.*

That was cool and all, but the reason it was wrong was that it implied that to control elemental resonances, you needed to integrate devices.

Arise: Conqueror

You didn't.

As I erupted into space above the Jovian giant, I felt them all, far below me.

The one thing that had always confused me when Athena had taken me prisoner for testing, and when she'd drugged me up to the eyeballs to make sure I was compliant, was how excited my "wife" and the "doctor" had been over me being able to move a tiny piece of metal with the power of my mind.

That, I now understood, and that I'd never been able to do since, was because I'd had a load of nanites in me that were partially attuned, *and* some that were fully attuned and wiped.

The interaction between the two groups of nanites had been incredibly tiny, as was, in comparison to now, the nanites themselves in number.

But I'd still been able to create magnetic fields and shift that playing piece enough that they could see it.

Now, as I erupted into orbit high over the battlefield, the universe was a very different place.

I was still evolving, as more and more of the nanites reached the halfway-house design I'd decided upon. But the difference in power?

It was mind-blowing.

I was at fifty-four percent of the nanites converted. As I hung there in space, my shroud floating free like a cape that could encircle the stars, the changes rippled through me.

A quick glance at my stats showed that they were similarly soaring, making me shake my head in bemused disbelief.

The fifty-four wasn't a random percentage.

I didn't know what was going to happen once my intelligence, my resonance, my perception, body and all the others reached a hundred. But considering the changes from one, where the average person was rated, to three and four was essentially making me superhuman in comparison?

At twelve, I'd been able to tear steel with my hands. I was able to perform calculations that I couldn't have even named before, without effort.

As I reached sixty, I saw that the entire knowledge base that formed the backbone of the Ændari empire was unlocking. I floated there, sensing the downloads that were making quest rewards obsolete for me.

As to what would happen when I hit a hundred? I knew now why the quest marked the reward as four question marks. Even the system had no clue. Argus was watching, but he was out of this and just an observer now.

The dreadnought that housed Shan'Gai was already out of sight, arcing around the planet, when I arrived, and now so were the rest of the Ændari fleet, with our own fleet vanishing around the northern pole.

That was fine. At the speeds they were going, I had less than a minute before they were back. Any movement on my part would take me closer to one but make it longer to see them all.

I wanted them all to see this, because today was the day that the Ændari learned that they, too, had needed to evolve.

Now the options were down to serve, or go extinct.

I reached out, sensing the tumbling escape pods and their panicked broadcasts. It was as simple as lifting one cupped hand to tear the distant ships free of the gravitational pull and return them to a stable orbit, and I sensed the desperate communications that were linking from one to another.

It wasn't just UC forces, I saw. There were no survivors from the Cobras that had been hit—they were too small to have escape pods, the space given over to additional power generation and shields—but there were Ændari.

That made things easier.

I had all the observers I needed, as I floated there in space, my body covered in a simple armor of black that glowed red at the joints. The stages of evolution freed me from the natural look of the Devourer's oily coating.

It'd been long enough that I just loved the black and red image now, though, and that was instinctive.

With a second gesture, I reached out to the tumbling destroyer from the gravity well of the Jovian and prepared to lift it as well, until I felt more and more hidden in its depths.

The Jovian was a gas giant, which meant that due to the pressures that came from such a huge world, instead of the ship tumbling down until it hit the rocky core and was crushed, it was more like they fell until they reached a natural point of equilibrium and lay there.

Reaching down, with control over both gravity and magnetism, was child's play.

I dragged the largest vessel I could sense down there upward; feeling resistance, I hauled harder.

It took some time, but it grew easier by the second, until at last, the crushed and broken bow of a huge battleship from some long-forgotten war rose ponderously, only to sink again, into the depths to wait, shark-like.

I grinned, staring ahead as I sensed the approach of the incoming ships. Fourteen smaller Ændari vessels surrounded their remaining battleship.

They'd all taken terrible damage. Great gashes and holes marred the surface of their ships; fires raged where atmospheric processors no longer responded. Lights flickered and failed, and engines misfired; shields crackled and danced. And as they came into view, the decision was clearly made to break orbit and flee.

I didn't bother wondering whether that was because they'd seen me in the distance, hanging unsupported in space, clearly more than mortal. Instead, I hailed them before Shan'Gai and the others came into view.

Their fleet had separated again from what was left of the Ændari rebels under Shan'Gai's command, and the two ships of Shan'Gai's escort now flew on either side of the dreadnought—battered, but in better shape than the Ændari loyalists.

"Surrender," I said to the Ændari, snorting in contempt when they cut the connection and continued to break for higher orbit.

"Well, you made your choice." I shrugged, letting them run. All my focus was on Shan'Gai as the bow of his capital-class shell emerged around the edge of the planet.

"You fucker, you better have a plan!" Two called to me.

Arise: Conqueror

"Oh, I do." I couldn't help but grin. *"Are you close enough to the hull to get out?"*

"I am, but I couldn't carry the survivors."

"Stop running and hide then, just like we did after meeting Ingrid on that rooftop. It's time to teach Shan'Gai some respect."

As I said it, I was very aware that the same system that allowed us to communicate supposedly privately across the damn star system was being fed through the node, and that yes, as we'd suspected, there were multiple ways that someone who wanted to, could be eavesdropping.

When I'd met Ingrid, after all, I'd liked what I'd seen—oh gods, yes—but I'd also just been identified by several other people, and had to hack the phone of one of her friends who was trying to record me.

As soon as they were out of sight, I'd grabbed my shit and tried to run.

Ingrid had been leaving as well, just heading back to her apartment after a long night. She'd seen the dragon staff I held, which had started the whole mad affair off.

We'd not stayed still and hidden at all; we'd fucking run like our ass was on fire.

"Gotcha. Get hidden and stay there!" he replied, understanding.

I nodded, flexing my fingers like claws, as I gathered myself. This was going to hurt if he had access to the dreadnought's weapons, but if I wanted to end this fight and the Ændari threat entirely in one fell swoop, this was how it had to be.

Sure enough, as I fucking expected, I sensed the dreadnought's forward batteries powering up, and I gathered my new toy, ready.

"Steve?" Ingrid called.

The connection formed and made me smile despite myself, at the gasp as she reached through the system even deeper and found the access that led to me.

I closed it, blocking her from accessing the rest of my senses, as much as I hated it and felt the disappointment as I did it. Worse still, to make the most of the possible surprise and to give the team that Two was shepherding out of the ship away from Shan'Gai, I couldn't explain why.

"Is everything okay?" she asked, probing and hopefully deciding to trust me.

"It's okay," I assured her. "The fight's almost done. Have Dolfing and the others…fuck it." I added them to the conversation, opening the conversation to the command link instead of having her carry the message.

"Lord Devourer?" greeted a middle-aged woman I didn't recognize from Dolfing's terminal.

"Who…" I started.

"This is Arelfina." Ingrid introduced the woman. "Dolfing was injured earlier."

"Okay?" There were signs of damage in the background but nothing that seemed powerful enough to chase the admiral out of his chair. But then, as she moved, I saw the telltale splatters of drying blood on the back of the chair. "Well, I hope he recovers soon."

"Steve." Jonas spoke up. "Tell me good things!"

"I'm going to rip Shan'Gai's head off his body and shit down his neck," I replied, getting a grin from the big Texan.

"Ah…" Arelfina started, clearly unused to a Devourer accepting such a level of familiarity. "Do you have orders for the fleet, Lord Devourer?"

"Yeah." I nodded. "Break orbit. I'll send these rescue pods to you. There's a few Ændari in them. I want them as witnesses, so don't kill them."

"As you command," she accepted, bowing slightly, before muting the chat and issuing orders.

"Steve, are you okay?" Freja asked me, and I smiled.

"I am, and I'm a hell of a lot better, seeing all of you," I said, before glancing at Shan'Gai as the lasers reached full charge. In the time we'd been speaking, he'd covered half the distance to us. Although the others were in the process of issuing orders for breaking orbit, they weren't going to do it before they crossed paths with him.

Well, it was time for my surprise.

"I love you," I said to Ingrid, before cutting the connection and launching myself forward to meet the enemy.

Shan'Gai opened fire. The forward batteries fired in fast relays. The lasers burned across space, hammering into my seemingly defenseless body that raced toward him.

As they hit, the upper layers of nanites shifted, lifting and forming a funnel, becoming reflective in almost perfect synchronicity along the sides and absorptive in the center.

The power was diverted inward instead of screaming out into space, providing the full power of the dreadnought's capacitors into my body, supercharging the conversion as a hundred kilometers ahead of him, the battered hulk of the battleship breeched the clouds, lifting upward.

Pain tore through me, horrific burning as millions of nanites were destroyed in the first seconds. More and more were lost as instead of working to defend me, they were burned through, providing the illusion that I was impervious.

But it worked. Greeted with the apparent uselessness of the lasers against me—I'd not even changed my course to try to dodge—he saw what was obviously a last-ditch weapon.

The lasers, apparently ineffectual against me, tracked to the new arrival and hammered into it. I hurtled forward, needing to close the distance as quickly as possible.

The relief as they cut from me was short-lived, as the front of the dreadnought cracked and tore open. Parts that had seemed solid in the distance were revealed to be nanite clusters in their billions shifting, to expose the same nanite killer that had eliminated the others.

My only chance was to get as close as possible, as fast as possible, he knew, to avoid the damage that the killer would inflict on me. But the choice between an unknown battleship that was turned with its side to him, ready to unleash a full broadside, and firing ineffectual lasers at me directly was an easy one.

It was also a mistake.

Orange and grey clouds streamed from the hull, great rents in the superstructure exposed as the hulk was slowly revealed not to be a powered and ready battleship, but instead a long-forgotten hulk, rising by my power rather than its own.

He switched quickly; lasers tracked back upward, before stuttering and returning. Rather than the ship falling, or me flailing, trying to raise it, it lifted with terrifying speed and ease, settling into place between us.

The lasers bored into it. The vibrational nanite killer fired in sustained bursts. Hundreds of thousands of his own nanites that surrounded and held it in place died with every second it was active near them.

Through it all, I hurtled onward, reaching out.

"Ready for that little surprise?" Two asked me, sending me his position, and I gritted my teeth. *"Because he's too close and there's no way we're getting out of this otherwise."*

"Give me a location," I sent back, and he did.

Something that he'd apparently figured out—way before I had—was that if the drones could act as navigational gravitonic markers, then we could too.

The ship's hull was covered in small sentinels that broadcasted constantly, working to prevent Two from jumping out, especially with the billions of nanites he had ready, and the team of survivors he was protecting.

Two was a lot more powerful than a sentinel, though. Although they could act to shield him from the gravitational field of the rest of the galaxy with reasonable accuracy, they couldn't hide him creating one from me.

The lasers cut deeper and deeper into the hull, before finally burning through the far side, erupting into the Jovian's upper atmosphere, only to find I was already gone.

CHAPTER FIFTY-THREE

THE FINAL CHAPTER

I burst into the chamber some three hundred meters from him, and a hell of a lot closer to Shan'Gai's questing tentacles than either of us was expecting. Unfortunately for him, Shan'Gai decided that was a good thing and attacked.

I felt the punch as the tip of a tentacle lashed out. It hit the far side of my shroud, splitting and trying to surround it, while deploying his own Devourer against it…

And then I felt the panic he must have experienced, as I spun to face it, knowing damn well that he'd be able to sense me.

His Devourer armor was almost identical to mine, oily black and red and filled with an insatiable hunger. That was understandable: we'd both found similar paths that, when mixed with who and what we were, had created a very strange, mutated evolutionary path.

The problem, for him, but definitely not for me, was that the Devourer, like all the paths and skills that were possible through the Ændari nanites, was based on the upper coding.

I told his nanites "no," and locked my own onto him.

His tentacle tried to pull back, to disengage, to escape and to attack from a new angle, only to find that the two groups were magnetically sealed together, and that link was spreading with terrific speed along the length of the tentacle.

He barely managed to cut it free, severing it a hundred meters outside of the room that I was in.

I grinned, ripping that section of tentacle and the millions of questing nanites that it'd been made from back toward me.

"Oh, thank fucking God," Two muttered, stepping up and staring at me as I turned to face him. He looked terrible, battered and broken, burned in a dozen places. "Can you get them out?"

I nodded, gesturing to the wall closest, and watched the way that the soldiers and devilkin, all looking as if they'd been in the worst fight of their lives, flinched away from the result, even as a gravity field grabbed them and held them in place to prevent their unexpected launching from the ship.

The wall behind them tore open. Three levels of hull armoring, five compartments, and a single laser battery had been between them and the surface of the ship. With a horrific blast of evacuating air, they suddenly saw stars as the atmosphere was torn from the room.

Behind and over their heads, pinprick lights wheeled, and I turned to Two. "You can guide them up to the fleet…" I started.

"Fuck no." He grunted. "Gimme that sweet upgrade and some of these nanites. I owe that shitbird a curb stomp."

"We've got such a way with words." I nodded to him. "It'll take time, but…" I reached out, making sure the link was solid and, thanks to us being so close together, impossible for Shan'Gai or anyone else to eavesdrop on.

He froze, shaking as more data than the world wide web on Earth had transmitted since its inception until now hit him. Then he broke free.

"No time to assimilate and understand all that crap." He shook his head. "Upgrade me to fight the avatar."

I nodded at that, even as I saw just how absolutely filthy he was. The dirt that had coated him cascaded free as soon as he read the condition of himself in my mind.

"Stand by," I muttered, linking to him and making a few very small changes, then setting them loose to run through him. The nanites sent great ripples twitching and dancing through his form. "Get to the hull, and stay as hidden as you can," I ordered the others. "Shan'Gai won't be a threat much longer, so just stay clear of him as much as possible."

There were a bunch of salutes, though all they got from me was a quick distracted wave, then I was moving. Two vanished into my shroud, still quivering as he was upgraded.

I launched myself into the corridor, lashing out in all directions as I went. Tearing the hull back in great rents, I searched for the traitorous Devourer, only to find that although he might be an asshole, he wasn't stupid.

Taking a corner up ahead too quickly, I focused my senses in, feeling something was wrong. I shredded the nearest wall apart. The sealed bulkhead that had been in my way ripped like tissue paper to reveal a mound of nanites that was flowing away as quickly as it could, snakelike, filling the corridor.

I flashed across the distance between us, reaching out, only to curse at the last second as Shan'Gai uncovered the power cells he'd been holding hidden.

They exploded. Fire and pressure, pain and light seared into me and threw me backward, as sections of the wall on all sides suddenly tore free.

Tentacles stabbed inward. Gravity was used to crush me like a hammer. Tentacles ten meters wide, with a section of hull barely attached, that had been used to look like a corridor, now clobbered into me from all sides.

Over and over, I was smashed into the floor, trying to brace myself, to get upright, to…

"Enough!" I roared, slashing both hands wide and hurling a pressure wave outward. Magnetic fields twisted; gravity battered gravity, countering it, overwhelming it, as the power of my new form grew and grew.

"Seventy-four!" I growled. "Not long now!" At over seventy for all my stats, and especially elemental resonance, the metal in the walls around me shuddered and shook. The metal that coated the tentacles bent backward as the nanites that made up Shan'Gai's form responded to the building gravity. Instead of retreating as he wanted, they fell inward, toward me.

His tentacles began to break up, connections snapping. Individual nanite clusters and great swathes of his form fell loose and soared inward, to hit against my shroud.

They crumbled like a sandcastle hit by a wave, fragmenting, failing, and being reborn.

"You cannot," Shan'Gai sent to me.

I snorted, launching myself after him as he tried to retreat again, before separating himself, sacrificing billions of nanites to form solid walls between us—walls that gained him only seconds as I converted them.

"Watch me!" I snarled, tearing the structure apart, sensing as Two regained some level of self-awareness and reached out to Ingrid and the others.

I left him embedded in my shroud. He could exit it any time he wanted, but he chose to wait instead.

Two more corners, and I sensed the retreat of more nanites, a greater concentration overhead. Instead of following the passage, I tore the roof apart, launching myself upward.

Here and there, I felt sections ripping free, explosions blooming as the nanites that Shan'Gai had invested in linking to the power connections were ripped out in his desperate flight. I couldn't help but grin.

Arise: Conqueror

Taking a last corner, I felt the change almost in time, before roaring in pain as the shock wave hit. Whatever the nanite killer was, his recovery had clearly freed him up to reform himself around it, and the bastard had laid a trap with it.

The field hit me. Vibrations like a dentist working on a nerve dug into my entire body, and for a few seconds, I saw red, lashing out blindly. I managed to find the right direction, and crushed the projector into the ceiling along with his tentacle, then ripped it forward, biting down hard and spreading conversion up through the limb.

Again, he abandoned it rather than fight, and again, more of the surrounding rooms and passages were converted to solid steel. He anchored his nanites, then separated from them.

Tearing through them, I finally found a single figure waiting for me, and Two struggled free of the shroud to meet him.

"We must talk…" Shan'Gai's avatar tried desperately, his horns quivering as he faced us both.

"Fuck no, I'm sick of playing with my food," Two snarled, lifting into the air and launching himself forward, crossing the gap between the two in a flash.

The avatar flicked his arms out to the sides. Twin longswords extended as he fell into a defensive stance, and I left him to his fight as I launched myself through the roof, sensing the retreating Devourer.

As I burst through two more levels, the ship shuddering around me, the reactors started to build. The filthy bastard had set them into a meltdown. I snarled, chasing him, bursting through the upper layer of the hull and out into space.

Clouds of orange and grey swirled wildly on all sides, blocking my vision. I cursed, switching from one method to another, to another, finding him eventually.

He'd dived as soon as he'd left the ship, cloaking himself as much as possible.

Now he plunged through the upper atmosphere, heading deeper into the Jovian, right toward…

Toward the most stable point of fucking pressure in its depths!

"Oh no you don't!" I roared, grabbing the dreadnought and dragging it with me as my nanites started to consume the frame.

I poured power from my nanites, from the atmosphere around me, and from the consumed metal into twisting the gravitational plane. Instead of jumping millions of miles, I leaped a bare mile, if that, and arrived right beside him.

I lashed out, both fists clenched together, slamming them into his side, and buckled the plated armor of his hull. Then, releasing the ship, I jumped again.

This time, I appeared right before him, slamming a fist that morphed into a blade into his side, dragging it sideways before jumping again, and again.

I slashed and hacked, stabbed and crushed, battering his armor and slowing him, even as every impact on his frame started a spreading conversion of his nanites into mine.

Lasers popped out of the hull, firing over and over. Although I managed to dodge most of them, slashing and triggering gravity bubbles to crush them, one that sprung up behind me hit me full force and sent me tumbling.

A section of one of the great tentacles that covered his hull, a hundred or more meters long and ten meters at the base—big enough to sink ships on old Earth—suddenly curled outward, splitting from the base and jetting free in a spray of fluids.

I twisted, thinking to arc around it, seeing the roiling mass that covered it as my nanites worked to convert his to mine. That was when the fucker exploded it.

Rather than accept losing the tentacle, he forced the remaining nanites to detonate in an orgy of energy release, sending me flying, trailing fire and smoke.

I shook myself, levelling out, and growled. My personal energy reserves were falling and I damn well needed everything I could get now, with the dreadnought's reactors climbing. I lashed out, forming a fresh tentacle that covered the distance between us, and latched onto the metal that made up his original superstructure, dragging him backward by it.

He bucked and screeched, increasing power to the engines. Sections of his hull broke free and hurtled back as my grip on what was left of him slipped.

He lunged forward, discarding more than half of his form. It streamlined, a needle dirk in place of a claymore, and flashed downward.

I hurled the sections of hull back, leaping for him, reaching…

"Reactor critical…" Two sent me.

For a brief second, I slowed, seeing him pull ahead, before I used both gravity and magnetics to drag him back, closer and closer to my reach.

"If we let him go now, we'll never catch him again!" I sent.

"I know," he said, sending me an evil mental grin. *"Can you pull him close enough that I can bind him to the hull?"*

"I'd rather rip his heart out," I growled.

"We need to be sure," he told me. *"If he hid a part of himself in some piece of scrap out there? He could still survive! You need to get it all in close, pull him in and let me hold him, then kick us through."*

"A jump?" I asked, seeing his plan, and he nodded. *"What about the avatar?"*

An image of the avatar's head appeared, clutched in his hand. Clearly the tiny upgrade he'd managed, going from twelve to twenty-three, had been more than enough to deal with the avatar.

I checked my own, then reached out, maintaining my lock on the fleeing Devourer. I fired a stream of nanites after him, elongating the tentacle to pierce his hull again, just above the engines.

He tried to fight, twisting; the hull lunged up to surround my one connection. Then the section around that disengaged, jettisoning…but it was too late.

I hurtled in, yanked hard by the connection. Gravity dragged him back and me forward, magnetics crushing his engines.

I hit with the power of a world-killing asteroid, slamming into his hull and lashing out with every ounce of energy I had, just as the upgrade counter hit ninety-five.

Arise: Conqueror

The explosion as kinetic and potential energy met solid matter was more energetic than mere nuclear could ever be. A hole the size of a semi-truck vanished from the rear of his hull.

The engines and a good part of the power generation that they needed were vaporized in a second. The hull shattered as great cracks raced out in all directions.

The atmosphere that surrounded us only made it worse.

Whereas an explosion propagated poorly in space, it sure as shit didn't have that problem in the incredibly thick atmosphere of the gas giant. If anything, it was more powerful than ever.

I reeled, shaking myself like a dog, twisting around, then snarled. Something had hit me, grappling onto me from behind, trying to lock me down, pressing my shroud inward and biting down hard.

"You think you've won?!" Shan'Gai hissed in my ear. *"I've fought more battles than you've drawn breaths, boy!"*

I twisted, my lip curling, and I flexed my body. The shroud flipped around him, enveloping, crushing him inward, until I sensed the savage determination a second before it was too late.

The world around me glitched as I reached ninety-eight. My mind, my body spasmed wildly. Reality seemed to split into a dozen versions that each slid in a different direction.

I never found out whether they'd been standard reactors, enhanced in some way, or what, but the explosion as the first of them, clutched in tight to Shan'Gai's chest, tore great holes in what I'd thought of as my invulnerable shell. There was just too much power to avoid, or to escape.

Then he was attacking. He'd shifted most of his form around to hold the reactors on one side of me, attacking from the other, and where I was momentarily stunned, he was ready.

Spikes slammed into me, carving deep, separating sections of my body. My shroud ripped and tore as he bit down, dragging as much of it as possible into his maw as he shifted his form one last time.

He'd appeared as a monstrous squid or mollusk before, a solid rear and core, and the front half all writhing tentacles, with a great maw at his heart.

This time, the maw grew, enveloping me, biting down hard and chewing. Teeth that were already enormous, shifted to diamond. New forms locked in and rows began to saw back and forth as the nanites responded. The last of his centuries-long enforced malaise and loss of function was restored as he apparently found the final key in me.

Then Two was there, landing on his back; his own form bit down as he, too, shifted wildly. Arms thick with muscle grew longer, latching onto Shan'Gai. Two's face stretched, teeth and muzzle elongating as he bit down, shaking Shan'Gai like a mastiff shook a kitten.

I shook myself as well, feeling my form being drawn down the old monster's gullet, as the counter clicked over to the final one hundred.

The fragmented sections of reality jinked, froze, then snapped back together into a single frame. A final, golden notification blinked.

I dismissed it, snarling as I pulled inward. My nanites flowed back together like mercury, racing to reform as one, no matter what the old Devourer tried to do.

Then I extended my wings.

Something had changed—no, *everything* had changed—as four giant wings of flame and light, sharp as sin and dark as a priest's promise carved through the form that tried to hold me.

His nanites shifted, seeming almost joyous to leap to obey me, and he shrank, collapsing in on himself.

I gripped what was left of his form, spinning it around and slapping it against the edge of the dreadnought.

We had seconds, literal seconds as the reactors built to a crescendo of furious and energetic release. Two was there, grabbing him, pinning and sealing the pair against the hull as I reached out.

Gravity and magnetics pulsed in a thousand fields at once. The fragments that had made up Shan'Gai and millions of other bits of wreckage were dragged inward. Half the Jovian's diameter was scoured; only the tiny fraction of the dreadnought's hull that held the stunned soldiers and devilkin was spared.

Everything else was compressed inward, as Two fought to contain the frantically squirming and thrashing Devourer, forming a single spike that led out for me to grasp.

I felt the power that roared along that spike, that Two was draining from the reactors, offering me the power to do what we both knew had to be done.

I latched onto it for a heartbeat, using the power to augment my own.

"DO IT!" Two screamed to me.

I sent a pulse of pride at him, at us both, at…I didn't know, but he was giving his life to make sure that the rat bastard didn't get a chance to come back.

Then I tore a rip in space and time, hurling the remains of the dreadnought screaming through and into a fast insertion right above a planet, powering down toward the ground.

The crack that rang out as the huge ship and so much matter vanished rolled across me. For long seconds, I hung there, recovering, suspended in the depths of the Jovian.

Finally, though, I rose. My wings extended, a steady thrumming beat that lifted me effortlessly through the thick atmosphere.

I could have done it just as easily with the powers I had at my disposal, but as the light of Scorpio poured like molten gold across the upper atmosphere, rising into view again, borne aloft by wings of golden light and terrible fire *felt* right.

***

"Can anyone see anything?" Anders shouted. "Dammit, people, what the hell is happening down there?"

613

"Nothing here," James replied. "I can sense the same that you can see. The dreadnought just vanished, along with a lot of other debris, but beyond that… Wait."

"James?" Ingrid asked into the silence that seemed to drag on.

"There's shifting in the magnetic fields…" he whispered, clearly focused on it.

"What does that mean?" Freja asked.

"I…honestly, I don't know," he said after a few seconds. "There's gravity fluctuations, and we can feel Steve is there. The command link is still active, but there's no response."

"Could he be injured?" Jonas asked.

"Lashing out?" James mused. "No, I don't think so. There's something purposeful in the way that the traces are sweeping back and forth, like…like they're gathering something."

"Emergence!" Freja suddenly called. "Ships are jumping into the system. Four of them just arrived at the Lagrange point!"

"Who?" Ingrid asked, twisting and pulling up the details. "Oh no…"

"Ten!" Freja updated. "Seventeen, forty-three, sixty…seventy-four…eighty! Eighty warships, *UC warships*, just jumped in, and they're hailing!"

"Let them," Ingrid growled, turning away from the new arrivals and back to the swirling Jovian that hung below them. "They're here because we've won. They've only come because they're trying to claim a share of the credit, and they've found the nodes are refusing them."

That had been a welcome surprise when the news was spread by Argus, as apparently he and the other nodes had held a convocation and agreed to leave them sealed.

This was the test. Opening this single node to contact had resulted in a ferocious escalation of the war, so the other nodes had agreed to remain sealed until the war was resolved one way or another.

Either their masters would regain access and their plotting and attempts to save them would be abandoned, or the war would be won here, and there was no reason to open the other nodes to access from any other factions.

Most of the UC were still frantically trying to gain access to the other nodes, but at least one of the fleets had taken the initiative and moved to help.

Well, as far as Ingrid was concerned, it was too little, too late.

"Increasing gravitational and magnetic disturbances!" Freja called. "And there's a lot of them, spreading as deep as we can detect."

"Half the metal in the Jovian is rising!" James called out.

"If that's not Steve, I'll paint my ass green and dip my dick in a pig." Paul laughed. "Ain't nobody else who's that crazy!"

"I'll take that bet for ten dollars," Jonas offered.

"I get ten bucks if I win?"

"If you don't, we get a video of you fucking a pig while painted green. That's gonna make me rich when I get home. And if it is, I'm out ten bucks. I'll take it."

"If it's Shan'Gai, we need to be ready to fight," Anders called out. "Get ready, people!"

"It is not Shan'Gai."

The words, fed into the command link from Argus, sent a wave of relief through the room. The upper reaches of the atmosphere cascaded away, revealing two pairs of burning wings rising.

***

"Only the ceremonial guards?" Francine whispered, shaking his head in disbelief at his luck.

The painful demise of Alberjeet and his family, as well as the cleansing pogrom he'd embarked upon, had solidified his control over the fleet. And then the feasting he'd enjoyed had allowed him to regenerate his stolen limb and horn.

That meant that when he stood, staring down at the glittering jewel of the Ændari empire, not one of the crew scattered across the control room dared speak against him.

It helped that he'd not only removed half of the more troublesome officers, installing more fanatical or overlooked others who would follow his orders, but that the imperial family and the council were hated with a passion by all those lower in rank.

The fight in the Scorpio system against the abomination was going poorly, he'd heard, which was what they deserved. More importantly, though, because of the constant changes, the reinforcements, and the discovery of Shan'Gai's weakness, the council had decided to strip the heart of the empire to send the home fleet to capitalize on the opportunity.

They'd then ordered other minor fleets home to cover the home fleet exit, only to find the UC advancing on the other sector nodes.

Those fleets immediately pointed out the specific clauses that required them to repel invasions first, and moved to secure their own sectors.

Lastly, the evacuation of all true Ændari in preparation for the sterilization of the sectors meant that huge numbers of warships that should have been ready to defend were instead out of position or loaded with their master's wealth, rather than being combat ready.

This left a single fleet.

His.

The third and last attempt to remove him from command had come less than an hour ago, and Francine gently patted his stomach, smiling at the memory of that delicious morsel.

He'd grown, the absorption of his lesser kin having granted him significant strength and reach over his earlier form. And as he stared down at the heart of the empire, he couldn't believe his luck.

Clearly, if it were possible for a greater being to exist, it must love and be guiding him, for the tiny sprinkling of ceremonial guards might be the elite of the elite, but in comparison to a full fleet?

They could never stop him.

Yes, he mused. It was definitely time for the imperial family to be upgraded. And once the emperor accepted that he was outmaneuvered, a new noble house, perhaps even a prince would rise…

"Emergence!" one of the crew shouted out in panic. "We have a single ship emergence from warp!"

"So?" he heard the captain snarl. "It's the home system, you fool! A thousand ships pass through every day!"

"But—"

"Speak up, fool!" she snapped. "Why should we care? Is it the legendary *Kroth'Mak*? Has the progenitor returned from her long slumber?"

"No! It's—"

"*Sarent* perhaps?" the captain went on, naming another legendary lost vessel.

"Perhaps if you let him speak, he would explain!" the second-in-command suggested acidly.

Francine closed his eyes, drawing a deep breath and ignoring the byplay as he tried to recapture his previous good mood.

A single ship meant nothing, after all.

"It's a dreadnought, my captain, the *Graylion*, pride of the home fleet!"

"What!" Francine hissed, spinning on his heel and glaring at the sensor operator. "Say that again!"

"It…it's the *Graylion*," he whispered, eyes bulging as he began to shake.

"And?"

"And what?" he stammered. "My…my lord ambassador?"

"And how is it here!" he screamed. "What about her battleship consorts, or the rest of the fleet?"

"She…she's alone!" he forced out.

"You're sure?"

"Yes…and she's damaged, badly…"

"How badly?" Francine spun again, gesturing at the wall nearest. "Put it there!"

"Her reactors!" The captain gasped, apparently already having access to the data. "She's going critical, as is the gravity drive!"

"What…?" Francine finally saw what had the others so terrified.

He'd been born a noble of a minor house; he'd backstabbed, stolen, and blackmailed his way to his current lofty position. But along the way, he'd learned by necessity.

The *Graylion* was rolling. Some peculiar grey and orange wisps drifted away from her as she tumbled into the upper atmosphere, but she was in orbit over the heart of the empire, as they were.

That was impossible.

The ship was a wreck, the hull torn from one end to the other, gutted with sections of the superstructure entirely missing. From five areas, warnings blared, confirming that the ship's reactors were in meltdown, already way past any possible hope of shutdown.

How had the fools missed it! The state of the ship made it clear—there was no way it could have been cloaked. The incompetent bastards had…

"It was a jump…I swear!" the sensor operator choked out around the captain's closed grip on his throat. "Just…appeared!"

"Lies!" Francine screeched. "Incompetent—"

"We're receiving a message!"

That came from the other side of the bridge, and Francine hissed in instinctual fear, stepping back from the figure that filled the screen.

"You?" The abomination laughed, staring at Francine. "Ah, hell, I was happy doing this, but now? You just made my fuckin' day!"

"Explain yourself!" Francine snarled, only to be cut off as the emperor himself overrode the broadcast.

Francine fought against centuries of ingrained response to keep his feet in the presence of the emperor, but even he couldn't look him in the eye.

"Silence!" the emperor shouted. His voice cracked and broke, making the abomination laugh. "Leave, go on! I order you, get out of my empire!"

"Oh, yeah, no worries, mate." The abomination snorted. "Just one thing, you know, before I leave…why was it again you stopped researching into grav drive upgrades?"

With that, he dumped all the available power, every single unit that the massive dreadnought had on hand, into the unpowered gravity drive.

Had the reactors themselves exploded, as Steve had originally intended, the planet below would have been badly mauled, but anything in bunkers that were strong enough would have survived. After a heavy enough effort was made, the planet could even be cleansed and the radiation stripped away.

The gravity drive, though…that was a different story.

The resulting explosion not only ripped the planet below into fragments, it also tore the closest worlds, the space stations, and even the massive orbital shipyards that produced the great warships apart.

Æn, the star that had given rise to the most feared and reviled race this galaxy had ever seen, finished off the sterilization of the world below when the gravity pulse finally failed, just shy of producing a new black hole.

Instead, the star went nova, pumping out world-ending levels of radiation that served to sterilize the other four closest systems, effectively removing the Ændari imperial heart from their empire.

The final thought that Steve had, as he'd triggered the gravity drive, knowing what was likely to come, was that the Ændari had fucked around, and most definitely, they'd found out.

<u>EPILOGUE</u>

I leaned on the bar, waiting as the barmaid finished pulling the last pint, setting it on the bar top before smiling up at me and giving me a look.

"I could help you out, if you want?" she offered in a rolling Irish brogue, making it clear that carrying the drinks back to my friends wasn't all she was offering.

"I'll manage, but thanks." I smiled easily to take the sting out of the words. "My fiancée is joining us soon."

"Pity," she said, looking up at where I nearly bumped my head on the ceiling. "You're a damn man mountain, so you are."

I just grinned and tapped the card reader with a card as she offered it, making her eyes widen as the tip registered without me pressing anything.

It wasn't much, the round of drinks for the three of us having come to barely twenty, but the hundred in tip certainly made her smile.

I carried the drinks back to the table in the corner, passing the other two over to Paul and Courtney. The others stretched out and complained good-naturedly.

"Still say this is weird," Paul muttered, tasting the beer then holding it up and staring at it. "It's cloudy, not like real beer."

"You mean real beer, or that lukewarm gnat's piss you Americans usually drink?" Zac grinned before sipping at the pint and letting out a groan. "Shit, I didn't realize how much I'd missed this."

"We're up!" Paul interrupted, pushing up out of his seat and waving at someone to get back as he headed for the nearby pool table. "Hey, that's mine!" he shouted as someone tried to move his marker.

"This'll be over quickly," Courtney muttered, standing to follow her husband, casually carrying both drinks.

The young lad who had been trying to sneak his turn early on the pool table blanched, seeing the seven-foot marine barreling toward him, and turned to run...faceplanting into the nearby wall, to much laughter.

The table we sat around was covered in empty glasses already. Paul was apparently trying to build a house out of them and wouldn't let the staff take them away, though it was anyone's guess how he was intending on making the roof.

I waved to get the attention of one of the staff and gave a thumbs-up and winked when he mouthed "Clean?" at me.

"Now, now," Casey said casually, smacking her husband's shoulder. "We're in England, Zac. Be nice."

"I've been halfway around the fuckin' galaxy...ain't needed to be nice yet," he countered.

"But this is *England*," she insisted. "You know, birthplace of...well..."

"Political corruption and football?" I suggested, taking a drink then wincing as someone started up the karaoke machine in the far corner. "Damn, and terrible singing!"

"No, the Greeks had corruption before you ever tried it," Casey assured me. "The others, yeah, maybe. But either way, Zac needs to learn to be good."

"Why?" he countered.

"Because we're with the boss in his old local bar," she said firmly. "And also because I damn well told you to. Now, either you play nice and don't embarrass me, or I'll take you to a museum next and make you see some culture."

"There's some stately homes in the area," I offered, grinning. "They do tours, where they talk about some lord who had the ceiling painted in like 1066 or something."

"The Battle of Hastings?" Casey asked, and I frowned.

"No clue. They always mention random dates, so I picked one."

"What was…" Zac started to ask before Courtney strolled back from the pool table and leaned in.

"You've got friends watching you," she said in a low voice, making out that she was setting her drink back down, as she went on. "Far side of the bar, by the slot machine. Three of them, watching us. And one just made a call."

"Anything interesting said?" I asked.

"I only caught the end, something about a debt to be paid and they apparently think we're hired muscle for you."

"Well…" Zac started to shrug. "You sorta kinda are."

"No, we're family," Casey corrected him firmly. "Now, are these likely to be the same people you used to run with?" she asked me.

I snorted then nodded, having already hacked the bar's CCTV system as we talked.

"It's them," I confirmed. "Two of them are, anyway. One's new, but they're calling for backup. Give me a second…"

It took nearly four seconds for me to switch from the CCTV to the mass of signals in the bar, then sort through them to find the pair of idiots I used to know, before hacking their phones.

"Yeah, they've called for Sinclair." I snorted. "Damn, Dave is gonna love this."

"Where is he, anyway? They're late," Zac asked. Once he got the chance to spend some time around Dave, he'd found a brother in many ways.

They both drank like fish, hated almost all forms of authority, and enjoyed the simpler things in life, as well as being frequently harassed and badgered by their partners to behave and not embarrass them in public.

All it had taken was the universal look of a man being told in excruciating detail what he'd done wrong by his better half to unite the pair in unspoken suffering.

Dave and Amanda—like Ingrid, Freja, Anders, and Jonas—had come along on this little escapade to get some "closure." And because I genuinely didn't give two shits about it, I'd agreed to let them do what they needed to do, while I did what I wanted. I had a beer in my old local.

Arise: Conqueror

I'd deliberately not gone hunting for Sinclair or the others from my past, because I now had the power to make their lives utter hell. For most people, that might be a wonderful fantasy, but for me?

I was dark enough in my heart already that I knew I'd take it too far. So instead, I'd decided just to let it go.

My newfound Zen outlook was admittedly helped by the knowledge that my new family felt entirely differently, and they were already meting out some justice as they saw it.

"Amanda was hungry, and there's a little restaurant across the road." Casey shrugged. "They got the taxi to drop them there first."

"Why?" Zac shook his head. "We've got peanuts and…what's this?" He reached out and picked up one of the bags of snacks I'd gotten earlier from the table.

"Pork scratchings," I told him, before taking a drink. "Think of the floor of the slaughterhouse when the pigs are all done. They sweep that up, dry it out and cook it, cover it in salt and sell it to idiots at the bar."

"Really?" Zac asked. Being Australian, he didn't bat an eye.

"No." Casey shook her head. "It's pig *skin*, not the sweepings off the floor."

"Tastes the same." I shrugged, then grinned at the look she gave the bag in her hand.

"Well, Paul likes them." Courtney shrugged. "That's not saying much, but still. Anyway, thought you should know." She strode back to the pool table, examining a cue, then started to go through them, looking for one that was neither bent nor damaged, muttering all the while about how classy the bar was for some reason.

It was a comfortable bar to wait in. So as I waited for the others to arrive, or the enforcers and their friends, I tuned out the conversation, looking inward at the two "minor" details I'd read and reread so many times by now.

First was my stat sheet, in all its insane glory.

Identifier: Biological Weapon Variant #Steve				
Species: Human		**Nanites available**: ERROR		
Threat Level: ALPHA		**Corrupted Nanites**: ERROR		
		Weaponized Nanites: ERROR		
Stat	Current points	Description	Effect	Cost to Upgrade
Body	100	Physical strength and capacity to absorb damage	+1000 resistance to damage	ERROR
Reactions	100	Mental and physical reactions	Time Dilation= 100*100*10= 100,000 + 50%=	ERROR

			150,000 seconds	
IQ	100	Intelligence and the capability to utilize it in the real world	+1000 to Assimilation of new technologies and capabilities	ERROR
Nimbleness	100	The capacity to utilize tools, weapons, and small devices	+1000 to success with devices	ERROR
Dexterity	100	The ability to dodge and utilize larger items/devices	+1000 chance to dodge	ERROR
Karmic Luck	50	The likelihood of an action to spawn an adverse/ positive reaction	+40 chance to gain a favorable outcome in games of chance	ERROR
Perception	100	The ability to differentiate between details and spot threats at a distance	+1000 likelihood to spot concealed items, details, or traps — see Reactions	ERROR
Control	100	The ability to control external systems		ERROR
Cybernetics	100	Integration of Cybernetic and Biogenetic augmentations and how likely they are to work		ERROR

Arise: Conqueror

		The capacity to use and integrate devices that require elemental resonances		
Resonance	100			ERROR

The stats, when combined with the second notification, the all-gold one, well, that explained why things had changed so much in the fight between Shan'Gai and me…and everything else as well.

Quest Complete!

Evolving Quest Complete: Harvest the Past, to Save the Future (Part 3)

You have fully absorbed and integrated the explorer nanites, resulting in a one-time advancement of all stats, jumping your evolutionary potential from class three to class five.

You receive the following rewards:

- **Title: Arbiter of Realm Three**

"Evolutionary potential." When I'd spoken to Ingrid about it, that'd been the point that she'd fixated on.

Apparently, I'd moved into a whole new level, where things were counted entirely differently.

There were questions, naturally—hell, I had loads. I'd gained a brief but intense burst of data when I'd read the prompt, but the long and short of it was that when a being passed a certain set level in a reality, the creatures from the branes gained knowledge of them.

Especially, of course, if it was through the use of their nanites.

I was the only one of my kind in this "realm" apparently, which was their name for the level of reality that we lived in.

Even more weirdly, they existed in Realm Eight of Fourteen, but that wasn't important. We'd already decided that we'd be building a new kind of ship and damn well visiting them when we found time.

The thing that was important? I was aware of one other creature in the realms between the branes that was my equal, and that was it. And they were so alien in outlook I didn't think we'd ever have an issue.

That was how I'd basically beaten Shan'Gai like a redheaded stepchild. I'd been able to because the power differential between him and me was so high.

As a comparison, it'd be like saying the level I was at when I first unlocked my abilities in the ship so many years ago was the level he'd been at the height of his power. And now I was so far beyond that basic level that it was hilarious.

The more I experimented, the more I found only one word that could describe the levels of power, and it was one that Ingrid had used first.

I was a living, breathing, walking, talking god.

That or a 'that walking cataclysm', as Zac kept calling me.

As much as it was cool and all, something had changed in me since then, in seeing so many of my people come to the fight, then, terribly, in attending their funerals and memorial services.

I'd given the medical units the nanites they'd needed, and I'd returned the dead of millennia to healthy and hale life. I could jump across the galaxy at will, or from the door to smack Ingrid's arse, then back before she could turn around.

Everywhere I looked, I saw potential. And one of the first things I'd done on my return to Earth was to create a single obelisk, ten miles wide and one high, that floated across the upper atmosphere.

It cleaned the air, breaking down pollution and balancing the atmosphere in a way that was already being noticed around the world.

New Delhi was entirely smog-free, as a perfect example.

It'd taken a single act of will and five minutes of my time to create and dispatch, that was all. Gaining the power to do this, to literally remake the world as I saw fit, had genuinely changed everything.

It'd been life-changing for the citizens of Scorpio-3 as well. I'd broken the Ouroboros harvester down, feeding its own massive form into the converters; then I'd jump-started the nanites that were made.

The seventy billion plus nanites I'd gained from the conversion took nearly a week to settle into full activation, and I'd spent them all in keeping my promise.

The planet was almost unidentifiable, compared to the state it'd been in when I returned from fighting Shan'Gai. The torn and mutilated surface was restored. The cities rebuilt as gleaming wonders, and the atmosphere and climate returned to the perfect match.

It was a paradise world, or would be soon, and I'd done it with the inhabitants' blessing. The regular folk, anyway.

Unsurprisingly, the leadership hadn't been happy, but to our faces, they'd forced happy faces and acceptance. Then when Scorpio-3 asked to join us, I laughed and disbanded their old leadership anyway.

I shrugged and banished the thought, before looking around idly.

The Cross Keys was an old pub. Pictures on the walls showed it in use over two hundred years ago. Although it'd been remodeled and redecorated dozens of times over the years, it had that air of neglect about it still.

The pool table was re-covered, for example, but the cushions on the sides were battered and sagging; the pockets for the balls were threadbare and the mechanism clunked and clattered on its last legs.

The bar top was lovingly polished by hundreds of people leaning on it every week, but that also meant that the varnish and stain was worn away in most places, leaving irregular wooden "comfort spots" where the locals always gravitated to.

The doors barely closed, the windows didn't open, and as the manager and his family lived above us, the TV and the karaoke were set to fortunately medium levels, and never raised above that.

Arise: Conqueror

I'd spent literally years in here, three nights a week, growing up from the age of twelve. Whenever I was in the area, not wasting my time at school, or later working or off on deployment, I was here.

It was strange seeing it now.

I'd grown since I was last here, and not just physically, though I'd adjusted myself again to keep my more mortal dimensions limited to a mere seven feet tall now, or around two meters.

No, everything that had happened had definitely changed me, I reflected, thinking back over the last six weeks.

The meeting with the UC full council had been fun, for a start, as had withdrawing Earth's membership.

That had shocked them almost as much as our offer of alliance.

There'd been some arguing, of course—some bits about how the UC had come in my hour of need, and how the nodes were in their territory, and that unless I was a member, I'd no longer be allowed access to them.

There'd been some comments about demanding I hand over control of them to the UC, and reparations for the UC's losses, sustained coming to my aid.

All fair points.

Then I'd pointed out that we weren't a new world. That we'd joined on the basis of Emberalis, Shanah, and Clicqo's offers, and that when Emberalis tried to kill me, with the rest of the UC fleet going along with it, that betrayal had ended our membership.

I pointed out, nice and calmly, that I'd gifted them access to the system, returning quests and more to them for the first time since the nanite plague, and that had this been the only betrayal of a member world they'd carried out, we'd have stayed.

Then I brought up the fact they'd abandoned the fleet. That they'd written off all of us in a desperate scramble to grab power for themselves.

Then I'd pointed out that they'd stripped the devilkin home world of its most precious resources. It'd taken a mere four minutes of looking to find that three active members of the UC council were subverting the crystal mining operations on the devilkin home world, and making sure the court case and appeal would never be fair.

From there, searching the details of those three, I found a dozen more worlds that were suffering under the UC, and more that were independent.

After a lot of discussion with Ingrid and her parents, we'd agreed to a new plan.

We'd formed the Alliance of the Forged.

It was a collection of worlds that had been beaten, burned, bloodied, and essentially forged in war. And because we'd been through the grinder, we knew the cost that had to be paid, and who always ended up paying it.

It was never the leadership of a council who ended up on the front lines; it was always the people at the sharp end that felt the bite.

After a little haggling, a little arguing, and finally Ingrid casually asking whether any of the UC had noticed that the Ændari imperial home world and its surrounding worlds were now rubble, suddenly everyone wanted to be allies and friends.

That they knew I'd killed and consumed Shan'Gai, and was not only not fucking off into the depths of space but was actively hanging around and going to be hunting out pirates and cleaning the corrupted zones…well.

They definitely didn't want to piss me off.

Dolfing had retired as admiral, his injuries and history being enough that the UC happily granted him his pension and released him from service, along with any members of the fleet who had fought alongside me.

It'd been a few days for him to heal up, that was all, but the UC were overjoyed to be rid of someone who had clearly thrown his lot in with me, and didn't look any closer than that.

It apparently didn't occur to anyone to look and see what such large numbers of people were doing after they received their release confirmation.

If they'd bothered to look, they'd have seen that they were relocating, along with their families, en-masse to Earth and her surrounding systems.

Zac had promised Dolfing a new flagship, and apparently it was going to be a dreadnought class.

"The terror of the galaxy" he'd promised, and I'd just shrugged. Fuck it. Either I trusted my friends or I didn't.

The council had even given UC soldiers permission to retire if they chose, confused over the request. But as a group, they'd earned their freedom from service a thousand times over.

With the Ændari empire now crumbling, and the fleets that had secured the systems now reduced to so much rubble, they were looking to cut back on their own expenses.

As one very blunt, personal and private message between two of the council put it, they had access to the technology to make their own soldiers now, to unlock the leveling and quest system, so it made sense to replace all these "old, possibly disloyal and obsolete soldiers" with ones they could train and ensure were "loyal to the right people."

For example: them.

That, to me, showed all I needed to know about the council. If they were stupid enough to believe that replacing tried and tested soldiers, who had an insane amount of experience in war, with fresh recruits was a good thing? They were idiots.

On the upside, though, it meant that the Alliance of the Forged already had an incredible group of armed forces. We didn't have many ships, as the council had decreed that the ships, even the more damaged ones, were their property.

They'd said the same about the soldiers' armor and weapons as well, which was a bit much, considering some of these soldiers had spent literal centuries fighting in those suits. But that just meant that Zac was busy, which gave him something to complain about, and that made him happy.

A round of tequila slammers arrived at the table suddenly, carried by the same barmaid from before, and I winced, hating the damn stuff.

"Your friend ordered them." She grinned and jerked her head toward Paul, who was now getting something that looked much more classy and inviting.

"What's that?" I pointed at him.

"Pornstar Martini." She shrugged. "It's not for him—it's his missus who ordered that. His is the Unicorn Freakshake."

"Oh, I'm never gonna let him live this down." Zac chortled. "He gets us tequila, and he's on a unicorn…" he paused, glancing to the barmaid in question.

"Freakshake," she supplied. "He said he's enough of a man to be able to enjoy a drink and not worry about the name."

"He's got you there." I nodded, picking up the tequila and knocking it back, before twisting my face at the taste. "Damn, I hate that stuff."

I set the shot glass down on the tray again, and the barmaid grinned around as Zac and Casey drank theirs, before looking back as Jay finally joined us from the slot machine.

"So, what's a poor sailor got to do to get a drink around here?" He slid into the next seat to me and smiled brightly at her. "I swear, darlin', you're pretty enough to make me forget about swearin' off on marriage…"

"And that's enough for me." I snorted and stood up. "I'm hitting the head, then I'll go get some air."

"You want me to get Paul and Court to back you up, boss?" Casey nodded to the far side of the bar, where more people were arriving.

"Nah, I'm good." I shook my head, smiling and sliding around the barmaid, before heading off to take care of business.

There was no need—no biological one, anyway; the nanite rebuild had removed such needs long ago—but there was an ingrained mental one still. We'd been there an hour or more now, and we'd drank a lot of beer—and it'd give Sinclair and his goons an opportunity where there wasn't going to be many witnesses.

The look on their faces as I stood and moved around people, though, made it clear that they were reconsidering.

I'd gained two feet in height, half a meter or more, and a hell of a lot of muscle in the time since I'd vanished. Seeing me suddenly towering over people when I moved, yeah, they seemed to be reevaluating coming to play.

I went in, did the business, washed my hands and came out, before checking on the progress of Paul and Courtney's game.

She'd apparently potted all her balls before he got one of his and was now hustling the locals, while Paul made his way through the ladies' cocktail menu.

I waved to Jay, who had moved to the bar to continue working on the barmaid, and grinned at Zac who made a "help me" gesture, as Casey started talking about children and their future.

Then, because I was an evil bastard, I deliberately moved around the bar and nodded in greeting to the small group of enforcers and thugs who were gathering, before asking if Sinclair was around.

"Uh, yeah," one of them answered, looking thoroughly uncomfortable. "He's on his way."

"Good." I strolled past, stepping out into the summer's evening.

Apparently, me going out the front door wasn't part of their plan. They quickly made to follow, only to have the manager shout at them that they weren't allowed to take their drinks out there, it being illegal to drink in the street in the UK.

I grinned at them through the window, then sat down on the grass and stretched out, clearly waiting, as they decided to lurk indoors, finishing up drinks and making calls.

I sat there in the sun for a few minutes, enjoying that most simple of pleasures.

"Hey." A low, uncertain voice came from my right, and I glanced that way, having seen a group approaching but as I'd not viewed them as a threat, I'd dismissed them.

It was one of the weirdest experiences of the last few years. Seated on the grass, I noticed my sitting height was almost the same as my ex's full height. Her friends moved inside, leaving her and me to talk. For a second, my heart raced.

Not for fear, not for aggression, and not for lust, certainly—that ship had long since sailed—but because I genuinely didn't know what to say to her.

"Hi," I said after a few seconds. "How've you been?"

"I'm good. You look…different?" Louise tried, glancing at me, and clearly thinking that I looked wrong, but not why.

It made sense; she was five foot almost exactly. She'd always had to look up to me, and I'd always towered over her, making people comment in lots of ways, but still.

"I got my life turned around," I said. "You doing okay?"

"Yeah, good, thanks." She hesitantly lifted her left hand to show a wedding band.

"Me too." I grinned as I lifted my own hand, showing the engagement ring that I wore. It wasn't something that guys normally wore, in my experience, but when money wasn't an issue—and frankly, I could make my own ring anyway—Ingrid's insistence that I wear one hadn't really been a big deal.

"Glad you're doing all right," she said. "Well, it was good seeing you, and umm, look after yourself." She half turned, the pair of us clearly uncomfortable in each other's presence, and she started inside.

"Ah, crap, wait!" I called, suddenly, not knowing how to say it, but knowing if closure was the aim of the visit here, well then, I needed to damn well say it.

"Yes?" She searched my face, as her friends behind her inside the pub moved around the busy area by the windows to be able to watch and pretend they weren't.

"I…look, I'm no good at this, you know I'm not," I started, gathering myself before going on. "But I'm sorry. I fucked up, and I was wrong for you. Hell, I was wrong for *anyone* back then. I screwed us up, ruined a good thing, and I just wanted to say it. It wasn't your fault. It was mine."

She stared at me, like a deer in the headlights for a long few seconds. Sweat pinpricked my back as my unnatural body mimicked the one I'd been born with, before finally she spoke.

"No." She shook her head. "It takes two people to make a relationship work, and two people to screw one up. I made mistakes as well, but it means a lot to hear you say that, so thank you."

"You're welcome?" I guessed, totally unsure what to say next. But fortunately, a very nice Jaguar F-Pace came to a screeching halt nearby at just that time, and a furious Kevin Sinclair, enforcer for the Black Cats cartel, glared at me from his car.

"Oh, thank God," I muttered, seeing him and the second vehicle that'd followed him.

The van that pulled around him, bumping up over the curb, with the passenger opening the door to point a shotgun at me, couldn't have been timed better.

My ex screamed, I sagged in relief, and Sinclair's friends inside started to make a fuss, shoving people back from the windows, pretending to be scared and helping protect everyone, while limiting the witnesses.

My time dilation triggered instinctively. The difference between the time dilation I'd first enjoyed at an IQ rating of one, and the same at a rating of one hundred, was as incredible as it should be, frankly.

Between the improvements to my body and the time dilation, I could go from standing still to a lightning-fast speed of over seventy miles an hour, while time subjectively was frozen for everyone else.

It meant that, not bothering to run, I had time to get up, pick her up gently and move her to safety, then move into the truck's direct path, and brace myself.

A van carrying masked men, without seat belts, engaged in high-speed maneuvers, crashing into an immovable object? The results were…well. They were *fun*.

For me, they were anyway.

The driver and his friend who was happily about to fire a shotgun at me, and probably take out my ex as well with the scatter, introduced their faces to the windshield, then continued onward.

The sounds they made on hitting the sidewalk on the far side of me made it clear they were the last mistakes either were likely to make again.

I released my time compression, waiting as the van fell back onto the rear wheels, bounced and then crashed into the front wall of the pub. Then I took three steps and plucked the shotgun from where it'd landed, winked at my ex, and wandered around the edge of the van into sight of Sinclair.

His jaw dropped on seeing me. And rather than flooring the accelerator, he pulled out a handgun, struggling with the angle to get it around and fire.

I let him. He emptied the entire magazine into my chest and stomach as I walked forward. Then he watched in disbelief and panic as I took the shotgun in both hands and snapped it in half, then tossed the two parts to either side.

That apparently made my position clear, and he tried to drive, only to find that the car, which I'd now had time to hack, had shut down.

He tried locking the door, then desperately reached for a second magazine, slotting it into the butt of the handgun with shaking hands while swearing.

I ignored the handle on the door and instead grabbed the frame, then tore the entire door free of the car with a twisting wrench and threw the battered metal aside.

He managed to get the magazine seated finally and dragged the slide back. But I was too close and ripped it free, snapping a finger as I pulled, then tossed it to the grass.

"Hi, Kev," I greeted him brightly. "Remember what I promised I'd do if you came looking for me?"

"No…" He shook his head violently. "You just… I'll let this go, all right?" he tried. "Just walk away, forget this!"

"Yeah, I tried that," I pointed out. "I let you have that after I warned you last time. This time, though, no deal." I shifted my nanites to make my eyes glow; hidden from the people in the bar behind me, my armor flowed up from beneath my skin. Finally, he realized that the "dark angel" who had been everywhere all those months ago, who had terrified and subdued nations, was none other than me.

That was when I felt a difference, as another group approached at high speed. I shook my head, armor flowing back into my flesh as the screams of shock from behind rose.

"Ooooh, you lucky bastard." I snorted. "You lucky, lucky bastard."

I turned, looking up into the air, and saw the small group as they closed on me—two groups, really, though they'd recently met up together, I guessed.

The first—Ingrid, Anders, and Jonas—had been to visit my father and his new wife. Apparently seeing my memories of being a small child and growing up in that environment had made an impression, as they'd insisted on this. While the second group, Freja and Scylla, had been to visit my mother.

Freja and Scylla had some very clear-cut rules about motherhood. The Danish mother of our faction, and directly Ingrid and her siblings, had been horrified, as had Anders, when Ingrid shared the recordings that Argus had made.

As to Scylla—well, her own mother Athena had "locked" her away, draining her of all fluids and leaving her stuck between life and death for centuries for something she'd never chosen to share with the group at large.

Jonas apparently knew what it was and had privately asked me whether there was any way to bring Athena back, as he wanted to kill her again himself a time or three.

Regardless, though, as the group landed, there were some small amounts of blood on their armor. The impression in their eyes made it clear that what had been done was both painful, and very, very necessary. As I'd agreed, I asked no questions.

"Ah, would this be the enforcer Sinclair?" Jonas called lightly.

"It is," I said, still holding him in the air as he tried to break my grip.

"That one's mine!" came another voice.

I turned slightly, glancing over at the local restaurant.

Dave stalked forward, his by now very heavily pregnant—and due to drop at any time—wife Amanda nodding and smiling evilly.

"Oh, that's unfortunate," I told Sinclair, shaking him and grinning. "You see, Jonas would have put you down like a rabid dog—quick, but easy. Dave, though? You remember Mik, right? Well, that's Dave, the one who you told Mik to kill. The woman behind him? That's his wife, and the best friend of the woman who you wanted dead too. *Sucks to be you, pal.*"

I threw him forward onto the ground, and he landed hard, before rolling and diving for the gun. He almost made it. Then he gasped in pain as the gun was sent flying.

Scylla sneered as she slid around him, pulling two spears from her back and stabbing them into the ground, point first. "Here, make it quick!" she called, before turning her back on the confused enforcer.

"Wh…wha…" he said. "First blood…right?" he guessed, clearly unfamiliar with the ancient fighting style.

"Nah, mate." Dave pulled both spears out of the grass and tossed one to him. "Fuckin' *last* blood."

<u>EPILOGUE TWO</u>

The sound of distant bells rang out, carrying through the calm, clear air. I turned to look at Jonas, who smiled and nodded. He brushed an imaginary piece of lint off one shoulder, helping to straighten my suit, before reaching out and resting both hands on my shoulders, looking into my eyes.

"You ready for this?"

"Not even slightly," I admitted.

"Bullshit. I've seen you pick fights with gods, vampires, and worse."

"Yeah, I can wear armor when I do that shit." I tried for a smile, which even to me came off badly.

"Well, you're wearing armor now." He shrugged. "It's just a different kind."

I glanced in the mirror one last time, taking a few quick breaths, then nodded. "I can do this," I whispered.

"Of course you can," he agreed. "Remember, no calling your armor on instinct. If you shred this suit, she'll murder you."

"Oh, thank you so much for that!" I snapped, glancing down at it again, then shaking my head.

The suit was a custom job, as all good suits should be, James had assured me. But the fight over who got to make it had surprised me, as had the interest in what I'd be wearing.

Apparently one of those little things that I'd been mistaken about, when I'd finally done the deed properly and proposed to Ingrid, was that the wedding would be small.

I'd thought that we weren't really "people" people, and that the wedding should reflect that—a few dozen people at most, just family and friends, and yeah, because of our position, maybe a few notables. Like the devilkin representative, which was fortunately Choni, and maybe the Elders and so on.

Whoo-*boy*, was I wrong.

There'd had to be a lot of meetings when we'd returned to Earth, most centered around meeting those who thought they were the world leaders. They'd made noises about democracy and elections and so on, and I'd pointed out that I knew the behind-the-scenes shit that they'd pulled, lots of the photo evidence showing up on the screen that covered a nearby wall, and that if any of it came to light, they'd never be elected again.

The immediate response had gone pretty much like "good talk, good talk; we're behind you all the way" in most situations.

The end result, when the populace was slowly introduced to the realities of interstellar politics and galactic war, was that they were very glad to have us in charge, and they'd continue giving the local leaders all the shit they had, thank you very much.

Arise: Conqueror

These leaders would now be elected to bring their issues to a body we'd create, and that body would deal with things, before bringing particulars that *really* needed attention to us.

Or more likely not, as part of introducing them to the new realities was the recordings that Ingrid had made, which showed me tearing my way through armies and conquering empires, etc.

Also, headbutting werewolves and other mad shit.

What had come out of it was that we were now celebrities, but not the kind that the paparazzi pestered. Or at least they didn't do that twice.

So, we were naturally the hottest topic in most chat rooms, magazines, and so on, and unfortunately so was our wedding. To make people love us, and to enable them to accept things a little more, including all the various alien races that were part of our little alliance, it was decided that the wedding would be a public affair.

The King and Queen of Denmark had offered a cathedral, and things had snowballed from there.

The suit I wore had taken six months to make, and my comments of "I'll just adjust my size to fit it, don't worry" had nearly given the designer apoplexy.

As we walked down the aisle, insanely conscious that the media services of literally hundreds of worlds were watching through the dozen discreetly placed drones around the cathedral, an itch started between my butt cheeks.

It was all in my mind. I knew that. Hell, I could reform and change my cheeks; there literally couldn't be anything there. It was impossible. But knowing that I couldn't scratch it, with the world—no, the *galaxy* watching?

It was terrible!

Prickle, prickle, prickle.

I gritted my teeth and forced myself to keep my back straight, trying to ignore it, until Jonas nudged me with an elbow.

"What?" I snapped at him.

"First, send it this way, people will be reading your lips," he sent to me through the comm link, and I stifled a groan, nodding. *"Secondly, if you think you're uncomfortable, look at Malthus."*

I glanced over, seeing the massive devilkin pair, and had to bite down on a laugh.

Where Choni had asked me, and I'd told her armor was fine and not to stress, Malthus and Benat were trying to conform to Earth styles.

I dreaded to think of the tailor's experience when they'd walked in, demanding a suit for the wedding. But the jokes that Jonas sent to me, and the imitations of how the conversation had probably gone kept me distracted until the wedding march started.

When it did, though, and literally everyone shut up and stood, I felt the panic rising all over again.

"Don't panic," Jonas sent me. *"Straighten your back, don't lock your knees, and for God's sake, don't summon your armor!"*

"Fuuuck."

"And enjoy it!" he sent, along with some laughter. *"It's the happiest day of your life!"*

Cursing him kept me going as I waited, wondering whether she'd gotten cold feet, whether she'd changed her mind, whether someone had said something and put her off…

And then, I was turning, finally allowed to see her.

She swept down the aisle with Anders, the man who'd insisted last night that although I'd never had a father before, I damn well did now, giving me last-minute wedding advice.

I knew he was there; I *knew* it. I knew there were hundreds of others. Royalty, both from the Danish line and my own English background, presidents, princes and pricks by the dozen.

Arronis and Saryet led a brigade of soldiers who stood in full armor—the latest model upgraded by Zac—to ring the building, ready for anything.

We'd even gotten a representative from the goddamn dwarfen, who was apparently awestruck by Ingrid, even if they still only barely tolerated me.

There were literally hundreds of guests in here with us, with tens of thousands of well-wishers outside, and billions more watching remotely.

I couldn't see them, though.

Nothing else existed for me in that eternity as she moved to me, before pausing and lifting her veil.

Only her, only the most perfect woman who had ever lived. And finally, as she reached out to lay her hand on my arm, the pair of us turning to regard the only person we possibly could have conduct a ceremony for us, I was complete.

"My friends, my family…" James started, smiling at us all. "We are gathered here today, to celebrate the marriage of Steve and Ingrid…"

THE END OF THE ARISE SAGA

THANK YOU

Hi everyone! Okay, so first of all *thank you*. You've reached the end of the final book of the Arise Saga, hopefully all your questions—or most of them at least, I'm looking at you Paul—have been answered in this tome, and I really hope you enjoyed it as much as I did.

For a reader, you get to see the mad world I inhabit for a little while, but for an author, we're literally in here for months at a time, often years. Each book represents a labor of love, or at least a dedication of madness.

That being said, this story has consumed my mind for over 18 months. Day in, day out, I've been hammering away on this keyboard, and to know that it's finally done, is something of a relief, but also a shame. I've enjoyed the time I got to spend with Steve and Ingrid, as well as the rest of their highly dysfunctional family.

I hope you've enjoyed it all, and I'd really appreciate it if you could leave a review, or pass the word. A completed series is still pretty rare in our little corner of the literary world, and I'm damn pleased to have added to that number.

Thank you all for your support, and your trust.

-Jez
20/06/2024

Arise: Conqueror

<u>PATREON</u>

By the time this launches at the end of July? I ***think*** they'll be getting up to about mid-way through Rise of Mankind 7 so if you want to read it perhaps 3-4 months ahead of release? Come join us!

There's three of my wonderful supporters out there that I have to thank personally as well; ASeaInStorm, Mischa and Peregrin thank you all!

<u>https://www.patreon.com/Jezcajiao</u>

Jez Cajiao

<u>RISE OF MANKIND 6: AGE OF GLASS</u>

By Jez Cajiao

The Age of Glass dawns, a fragile era balanced on the edge of oblivion. Will it shatter beneath the relentless hammer of fate?

From the depths of despair to the pinnacle of power, Matt's ascension to Dungeon Lord has been a crucible of blood and terror. But the higher he climbs, the more precarious his perch becomes. As winter's icy fingers close around his hard-won domain, Matt and his beleaguered allies yearn for respite. Instead, they face a nightmare beyond imagining.
The Coronaught infection sweeps through the land like wildfire, twisting human flesh into abominations that defy sanity. Grotesque mutations stalk the shadows, their hunger insatiable. In this maelstrom of horror, Matt must be more than a leader – he must become a legend.

With each agonizing decision, the weight of command threatens to crush his spirit. Can he salvage the humanity of the infected, or will the price of compassion be too steep? Nuclear fire looms on the horizon, a cleansing inferno that promises annihilation. How much of his soul will Matt sacrifice to shield his people from the coming storm?

In the bowels of the earth, Matt labors to transform his dungeon into an impregnable fortress. But in a world where loyalty shatters like spun sugar, yesterday's allies may become tomorrow's executioners. Survival exacts a terrible toll, paid in blood and betrayal.

Step carefully into the Age of Glass, where every triumph

Arise: Conqueror

balances on a knife's edge, and a single misstep can leave you bleeding in the dark.

THEFT OF DECKS

By Lars Machmuller

When the deck is stacked against you? Change the game!

In the frontier town of Isarn, Chase will never be more than the lowly Darkborn thief he is. Banned from training, banned from acquiring better cards, if the Lightborn had their way, he'd be banned from life itself.

He's not alone though, and the one thing he and his friends have is determination. Losing a hand to a brutal punishment only fueled his obsession to get access to his own amazing, reality-bending cards.

That is the path to power and a future for them all. Nobody cares where you came from when you're rich enough. For now, though, they're facing both established powers, churches and age-old prejudices. It's time to get to work, and if the Lightborn won't share and play nice?

Sometimes the only way to get dealt a better hand is to steal the whole damn deck!

Buy on Amazon

Arise: Conqueror

QUEST ACADEMY

By Brian J. Nordon

A world infested by demons.
An Academy designed to train Heroes to save humanity from annihilation.
A new student's power could make all the difference.

Humans have been pushed to the brink of extinction by an ever-evolving demonic threat. Portals are opening faster than ever, Towers bursting into the skies and Dungeons being mined below the last safe havens of society. The demons are winning.

Quest Academy stands defiantly against them, as a place to train the next generation of Heroes. The Guild Association is holding the line, but are in dire need of new blood and the powerful abilities they could bring to the battlefront. To be the saviors that humanity needs, they need to surpass the limits of those that came before them.

In a war with everything on the line, every power matters. With an adaptive enemy, comes the need for a constant shift in tactics. A new age of strategy is emerging, with even the unlikeliest of Heroes making an impact.

Salvatore Argento has never seen a demon.
He has never aspired to become a Hero.
Yet his power might be the one to tip the odds in humanity's favor.

Buy on Amazon

WANDERING WARRIOR

By Michael Head

A divine quest to deliver justice.
One year to accomplish his mission.
After nineteen planets, there's something different about this one.

James Holden has reached the maximum level there is for a human. That's perfect, since he's the only one of his kind. A wandering warrior, without control of his destination, tossed between universes by gods who've failed to tell him why. James is the lone Judge on a new world in need of someone to balance the scales. He isn't afraid to do so with extreme prejudice. As the Chief Justice, he has to right the wrongs the innocent can't fix themselves.

As James quickly discovers, the roots of corruption run deep. Guilds choose to protect themselves rather than the people. Monsters roam the wilderness unchecked. Judgment is usually a decision between right and wrong, but nothing is ever that simple. This time, being the strongest human won't be enough to punish the guilty. James might have to recruit some new blood, even if he prefers to work alone.

On his twentieth world, he is going to win, no matter the cost. James will have to find a way to break past the limits of the system if he's going to have a chance at making a difference.

Buy on Amazon

Arise: Conqueror

KNIGHTS OF ETERNITY

By Rachel Ní Chuirc

When Zara awoke in chains she thought she'd gone mad.

She was Zara the Fury - mistress of flame and fear. Her name was whispered across the land, from ramshackle taverns to the royal court. Even the heroic Gilded Knights thought twice before crossing her path.
She was feared—*respected.*
Now she was curled up on a dirt floor on her fiancé's orders. Valerius, leader of the Gilded, mocks her cries for help. And the kingdom is on the brink of war over the missing Lady Eternity…
But that wasn't why Zara thought she had gone mad.
The reason why is that the last thing she remembered was blood, an arcade screen, and the gun that changed everything.

But no chains can hold the Fury, and when she gets out?
The world is going to *burn.*

Buy on Amazon

<u>SCARLETT CITADEL</u>

By Jack Fields

Gormon Hughes is 19, thin as a broom, and has—not for the first time in his life—been swept into the path of trouble. Poor, recently heartbroken, and indebted to the sort of people who file their teeth into needle points and devour wriggling bloated spiders for fun, Hughes sets his sights on salvation.

That salvation is the Scarlet Citadel, a wealthy organization of pageant fighters, monster hunters, and secret keepers. With the aid of strange oracles, rare good fortune, and a unique power that bubbles like champagne in the core of Hughes' being, he must join the Citadel and advance himself.

But the ladder of progression is harsh and dark. The rungs are slippery.

And falling means disaster…

<u>**Buy on Amazon**</u>

Arise: Conqueror

FACEBOOK AND SOCIAL MEDIA

If you want to reach out, chat or shoot the shit, you can always find me on either my author page here:

www.facebook.com/JezCajiaoAuthor

OR

We've recently set up a new Facebook group to spread the word about cool LitRPG books. It's dedicated to two very simple rules;

1: Let's spread the word about new and old brilliant LitRPG books.
2: Don't be a Dick!

They sound like really simple rules, but you'd be amazed…

Come join us!

https://www.facebook.com/groups/LITRPGLegion

I'm also on Discord here: **https://discord.gg/u5JYHscCEH**

Or I'm reaching out on other forms of social media atm, I'm just spread a little thin that's all!

You're most likely to find me on Discord, but please, don't be offended when I don't approve friend requests on my personal Facebook pages. I did originally, and several people abused that, sending messages to my family and being generally unpleasant, hence, the author page:

www.facebook.com/JezCajiaoAuthor

I hope you understand.

BATTLEFORGED: CONQUEROR

By M.H. Johnson

Battleforged: Conqueror

It was time for Eric to show what one man with a few dozen oversized warthogs and an extradimensional storage space can do against an army of bloodthirsty orcs who think the Northeastern United States is already theirs.

Join Eric on a wild ride of non-stop action and deadly peril as he shows the entire world what happens to a Necromancer's enemies when they dare to threaten the people he loves!

Buy on Amazon

LEGION

Okay everybody, if you've not yet seen or heard, well, the secret is out! My wife Chrissy, and our friend Geneva and I have launched the Legion Publishers! We're taking on new authors, as well as experienced ones, focusing primarily on the LitRPG side of things, but we're open to anything really, with one very clear rule that guides our company:

Don't be a dick.

That's it. Our contracts aren't hidden behind layers of legalese, you can find them here:

https://www.legionpublishers.com/legioncontract

If you want to reach out and ask any questions, get an idea of the support we offer, and possibly become part of the family? We'd love to hear from you, just tap the link and fill in the form:

https://www.legionpublishers.com/contact-and-submissions

Hope you're having a good one!

-Jez, Chrissy and Geneva

<u>RECOMMENDATIONS</u>

I'm often asked for personal recommendations, so if this book has whetted your appetite for more LitRPG, please have a look at the following, these are brilliant series by brilliant authors!

The Ten Realms by Michael Chatfield

The Land by Aleron Kong

Challengers Call by Nathan A. Thompson

Quest Academy by Brian J. Nordon

Wandering Warrior by Michael Head

Endless Online by M H Johnson

The Good Guys/Bad Guys by Eric Ugland

God of the Feast by Kevin Sinclair

The Wayward Bard by Lars Machmüller

<u>LITRPG!</u>

To learn more about LitRPG, talk to other authors including myself, and to just have an awesome time, please join the LitRPG Group

www.facebook.com/groups/LitRPGGroup

FACEBOOK

There's also a few really active Facebook groups I'd recommend you join, as you'll get to hear about great new books, new releases and interact with all your (new) favorite authors! (I may also be there, skulking at the back and enjoying the memes…)

https://www.facebook.com/groups/LitRPGlegion/

https://www.facebook.com/groups/GamelitSociety

https://www.facebook.com/groups/LitRPG.books

https://www.facebook.com/groups/LitRPGforum/